PENGUIN BOOKS

THREE NOVELS

A Dark-Adapted Eye
A Fatal Inversion
The House of Stairs

Barbara Vine is Ruth Rendell, the bestselling crime novelist. She has written many novels, including A Judgement in Stone, The Lake of Darkness, The Tree of Hands, Live Flesh and *The Bridesmaid.* As Barbara Vine she is also the author of *Gallowglass*, published by Penguin. *A Dark-Adapted Eye* received huge critical acclaim and won the Mystery Writers of America's Edgar Allan Poe Award, *A Fatal Inversion* was winner of the 1987 Crime Writers' Gold Dagger Award and *The House of Stairs* was winner of the Angel Award for Fiction. Ruth Rendell is a Fellow of the Royal Society of Literature.

THREE NOVELS

A Dark-Adapted Eye
A Fatal Inversion
The House of Stairs

BARBARA VINE

PENGUIN BOOKS

PENGUIN BOOKS

Published by the Penguin Group
Penguin Books Ltd, 27 Wrights Lane, London W8 5TZ, England
Viking Penguin, a division of Penguin Books USA Inc.
375 Hudson Street, New York, New York 10014, USA
Penguin Books Australia Ltd, Ringwood, Victoria, Australia
Penguin Books Canada Ltd, 2801 John Street, Markham, Ontario, Canada L3R 1B4
Penguin Books (NZ) Ltd, 182–190 Wairau Road, Auckland 10, New Zealand

Penguin Books Ltd, Registered Offices: Harmondsworth, Middlesex, England

Printed in England by Clays Ltd, St Ives plc
Filmset in Ehrhardt

Contents

A Dark-Adapted Eye

Dark adaptation: a condition of vision brought about progressively by remaining in complete darkness for a considerable period, and characterized by progressive increase in retinal sensitivity. A *dark-adapted eye* is an eye in which dark adaptation has taken place.

James Drever, *A Dictionary of Psychology*

On the morning Vera died I woke up very early. The birds had started, more of them and singing more loudly in our leafy suburb than in the country. They never sang like that outside Vera's windows in the Vale of Dedham. I lay there listening to something repeating itself monotonously. A thrush, it must have been, doing what Browning said it did and singing each song twice over. It was a Thursday in August, a hundred years ago. Not much more than a third of that, of course. It only feels so long.

In these circumstances alone one knows when someone is going to die. All other deaths can be predicted, conjectured, even anticipated with some certainty, but not to the hour, the minute, with no room for hope. Vera would die at eight o'clock and that was that. I began to feel sick. I lay there exaggeratedly still, listening for some sound from the next room. If I was awake my father would be. About my mother I was less sure. She had never made a secret of her dislike of both his sisters. It was one of the things which had made a rift between them, though there they were together in the next room, in the same bed still. People did not break a marriage, leave each other, so lightly in those days.

I thought of getting up but first I wanted to make sure where my father was. There was something terrible in the idea of encountering him in the passage, both of us dressing-gowned, thick-eyed with sleeplessness, each seeking the bathroom and each politely giving way to the other. Before I saw him I needed to be washed and brushed and dressed, my loins girded. I could hear nothing but that thrush uttering its idiot phrase five or six times over, not twice.

To work he would go as usual, I was sure of that. And Vera's name would not be mentioned. None of it had been spoken about at all in our house since the last time my father went to see Vera. There was one crumb of comfort for him. No one knew. A man may be very close to his sister, his twin, without anyone knowing of the relationship, and none of our neighbours knew he was Vera Hillyard's brother. None of the bank's clients knew. If today the head cashier remarked upon Vera's death, as he very likely might, as people would by reason of her sex among other things, I knew my father would present to him a bland, mildly interested face and utter some suitable platitude. He had, after all, to survive.

A floorboard creaked in the passage. I heard the bedroom door close and then the door of the bathroom, so I got up and looked at the day. A clean white still morning, with no sun and no blue in the sky, a morning that seemed to me to be waiting because I was. Six-thirty. There was an angle you could stand at looking out of this window where you could see no other house, so plentiful were the trees and shrubs, so thick their foliage. It was like looking into a clearing in a rather elaborate wood. Vera used to sneer at where my parents lived, saying it was neither town nor country.

My mother was up now. We were all stupidly early, as if we were going away on holiday. When I used to go to Sindon I was sometimes up as early as this, excited and looking forward to it. How could I have looked forward to the society of Vera, an unreasonable carping scold when on her own with me and, when Eden was there, the two of them closing ranks to exclude anyone who might try to penetrate their alliance? I hoped, I suppose. Each time I was older and because of this she might change. She never did – until almost the end. And by then she was too desperate for an ally to be choosy.

I went to the bathroom. It was always possible to tell if my father had finished in the bathroom. He used an old-fashioned cut-throat razor and wiped the blade after each stroke on a small square of newspaper. The newspaper and the jug of hot water he fetched himself but the remains were always left for my mother to clear away, the square of paper with its load of shaving soap full of stubble, the empty jug. I washed in cold water. In summer, we only lit the boiler once a week for baths. Vera and Eden bathed every day, and that was one of the things I *had* liked about Sindon, my daily bath, though Vera's attitude always was that I would have escaped it if I could.

The paper had come. It was tomorrow the announcement would be, of course, a few bald lines. Today there was nothing about Vera. She was stale, forgotten, until this morning when, in a brief flare-up, the whole country would talk of her, those who deplored and those who said it served her right. My father sat at the dining-table, reading the paper. It was the *Daily Telegraph*, than which no other daily paper was ever read in our family. The crossword puzzle he would save for the evening, just as Vera had done, once only in all the years phoning my father for the solution to a clue that was driving her crazy. When Eden had a home of her own and was rich, she often rang him up and got him to finish the puzzle for her over the phone. She had never been as good at it as they.

He looked up and nodded to me. He didn't smile. The table had yesterday's cloth on it, yellow check not to show the egg stains. Food was still rationed, meat being very scarce, and we ate eggs all the time, laid by my mother's chickens. Hence the crowing cockerels in our garden suburb, the fowl runs concealed behind hedges of lonicera and laurel. We had no eggs that morning, though. No cornflakes either. My mother would have considered cornflakes frivolous, in their white and orange packet. She had disliked Vera, had no patience with my father's intense family love, but she had a strong sense of occasion, of what was fitting. Without a word, she brought us toast that, while hot, had been thinly spread with margarine, a jar of marrow and ginger jam, a pot of tea.

I knew I shouldn't be able to eat. He ate. Business was to be as usual with him, I could tell that. It was over, wiped away, a monstrous effort made, if not to forget, at least to behave as if all was forgotten. The silence was broken by his voice, harsh and stagy, reading aloud. It was something about the war in Korea. He read on and on, columns of it, and it became embarrassing to listen because no one reads like that without introduction, explanation, excuse. It must have gone on for ten minutes. He read to the foot of the page, to where presumably you were told the story was continued inside. He didn't turn over. He broke off in mid-sentence. 'In the Far,' he said, never getting to 'East' but laying the paper down, aligning the pages, folding it once, twice, and once more, so that it was back in the shape it had been when the boy pushed it through the letterbox.

'In the Far' hung in the air, taking on a curious significance, quite different from what the writer had intended. He took another piece of toast but got no further towards eating it. My mother watched him. I think she had been tender with him once but he had had no time for it or room for it and so her tenderness had withered for want of encouragement. I did not expect her to go to him and take his hand or put her arms round him. Would I have done so myself if she had not been there? Perhaps. That family's mutual love had not usually found its expression in outward show. In other words, there had not been embraces. The twins, for instance, did not kiss each other, though the women pecked the air around each other's faces.

It was a quarter to eight now. I kept repeating over and over to myself (like the thrush, now silent), 'In the far, in the far'. When first it happened, when he was told, he went into paroxysms of rage, of disbelief, of impotent protest.

'Murdered, murdered!' he kept shouting, like someone in an Elizabethan tragedy, like someone who bursts into a castle hall with dreadful news. And then, 'My sister!' and 'My poor sister!' and 'My little sister!'

But silence and concealment fell like a shutter. It was lifted briefly, after Vera was dead, when, sitting in a closed room after dark, like conspirators, he and I heard from Josie what happened that April day. He never spoke of it again. His twin was erased from his mind and he even made himself – incredibly – into an only child. Once I heard him tell someone that he had never regretted having no brothers or sisters.

It was only when he was ill and not far from death himself that he resurrected memories of his sisters. And the stroke he had had, as if by some physiological action stripping away layers of reserve and inhibition, making him laugh sometimes and just as often cry, released an unrestrained gabbling about how he had felt that summer. His former love for Vera the repressive years had turned to repulsion and fear, his illusions broken as much by the tug-of-war and Eden's immorality – his word, not mine – as by the murder itself. My mother might have said, though she did not, that at last he was seeing his sisters as they really were.

He left the table, his tea half-drunk, his second piece of toast lying squarely in the middle of his plate, the *Telegraph* folded and lying with its edges compulsively lined up to the table corner. No word was spoken to my mother and me. He went upstairs, he came down, the front door closed behind him. He would walk the leafy roads, I thought, making detours, turning the half mile to the station into two miles, hiding from the time in places where there were no clocks. It was then that I noticed he had left his watch on the table. I picked up the paper and there was the watch underneath.

'We should have gone away somewhere,' I said.

My mother said fiercely, 'Why should we? She hardly ever came here. Why should we let her drive us away?'

'Well, we haven't,' I said.

I wondered which was right, the clock on the wall that said five to eight or my father's watch that said three minutes to. My own watch was upstairs. Time passes so slowly over such points in it. There still seemed an aeon to wait. My mother loaded the tray and took it into the kitchen, making a noise about it, banging cups, a way of showing that it was no fault of hers. Innocent herself, she had been dragged into this family by marriage, all unknowing. It was another matter for me who was of their blood.

I went upstairs. My watch was on the bedside table. It was new, a present bestowed by my parents for getting my degree. That, because of what had happened, it was a less good degree than everyone had expected, no one had commented upon. The watch face was small, not much larger than the cluster of little diamonds in my engagement ring that lay beside it, and you had to get close up to it to read the hands. I thought, in a moment the heavens will fall, there will be a great bolt of thunder, nature could not simply ignore. There was nothing. Only the birds had become silent, which they would do anyway at this time, their territorial claims being made, their trees settled on, the business of their day begun. What would the business of my day be? One thing I thought I would do. I would phone Helen, I would talk to Helen. Symbolic of my attitude to my engagement, my future marriage, this was, that it was to Helen I meant to fly for comfort, not the man who had given me the ring with a diamond cluster as big as a watch face.

I walked over to the bedside table, stagily, self-consciously, like a bad actress in an amateur production. The director would have halted me and told me to do it again, to walk away and do it again. I nearly did walk away so as not to see the time. But I picked up the watch and looked and had a long, rolling, falling feeling through my body as I saw that I had missed the moment. It was all over now and she was dead. The hands of the watch stood at five past eight.

The only kind of death that can be accurately predicted to the minute had taken place, the death that takes its victim.

> . . . feet foremost through the floor,
> Into an empty space.

Three times in the past thirty-five years I had seen her name in print. Once was in a newspaper headline over one of the parts in a series on women hanged in England this century. I was sitting in a tube train and I looked sideways at the tabloid page the man next to me was reading. The letters in her name leapt out at me, bold, black, upright, making me jump. At the next stop I got out. I longed in one way to see that evening paper, the *Star* in those days, but in another I dreaded it and dread won. Before that she had been in *The Times* when the abolition of capital punishment was the big issue of the day. An MP mentioned her in debate and it got into the parliamentary report. But first I had seen her name in a library book.

Vera Hillyard was printed on the book's spine along with *Ruth Ellis*, *Edith Thompson* and two or three others. I took it cautiously from the shelf, looking about me to make sure no one was watching. I held it in my hands and felt the weight and shape of it, but to take it out of the library, to open it and read – that seemed too big a step. I would wait. I would prepare myself, I would get into a relaxed objective frame of mind. Two days later I went back and the book had been taken out. By the time I finally borrowed it, I had succeeded in putting aside fears and prohibitions and had worked myself into a state of excitement. I longed by then to know what some outside observer might have to say about my aunt.

It was a disappointment – more than that. The author had got it all wrong. He had mishandled the atmosphere, reproduced not at all the *flavour* of our family, and above all, he had missed the point. Indignant and annoyed, I was determined to write to him, for a whole day I was set on writing to him to point out that Vera wasn't a jealous virago, Eden a browbeaten innocent. But I no more wrote than I finished reading the book, for I understood that those chapters had served a purpose for me. A kind of catharsis had taken place, an exorcism, making me look things in the face and tell myself: she was only your aunt, it touches only at a remove, you can think of it without real pain. And I found that I could. I was not involved, blood and bone, love and hate, as were those others so much closer to her. I even thought of writing something myself, an insider's account of Vera and of what led up to it all.

But there was Jamie to think of. That was before I had met him and talked to him by Landor's grave. The author of the account I had read wrote of him as a pawn who could know neither love nor pain, a wooden figure rather than a child, a puppet who was unimportant because he had not actually witnessed the murder but been snatched away in the nick of time and carried from the room. I had scarcely thought of him during the years in which he must have been growing up – incredible that I had once wistfully hoped to be made his godmother. But after I had read the piece in the library book, the piece that was so inaccurate and false that it might have been some other family the writer described, after that I began to think of him. I understood that he had become an embarrassment to certain family members. He was the catalyst who had brought it all about. It must have seemed to them that it would have been better if he had not been born – better for him too, and that is a dreadful thought. The wisest course, from his point of view and that of others, was to tuck him away. I thought then vaguely, unclearly, that one day when I was in Italy I would try to see him.

It was he in part, his existence, the fact that he had been born and was a man now capable of continued suffering, which stopped me writing anything myself. Besides, I doubted my own abilities to reconstruct Vera's life. Memories I had and many of them, but what of the great gaps, the spaces in the past? There were those years when I scarcely went to Sindon, stretches of time all-important in the fatal convergence of things, the winter for instance when Vera was ill, and the following year when she and Jamie escaped and fled like refugees from an oppressor.

Chad could have done it. He was a journalist, he knew how it should be done, and God knows he had seen as much of unfolding and the fulfilled destinies as I had – more than I had, for he was always at Laurel Cottage, unable to keep away, fixated on a place, a house, as lovers are for whom bricks and mortar can soak up the essence of the beloved the way that nursery floor soaked up blood.

But did I, after all, particularly want a Vera-book to be written? I had succeeded quite well at the business of forgetting her. My children were almost grown-up before they knew Vera Hillyard was their great-aunt – no, let me put that differently, before they knew that a woman who was their mother's aunt had been hanged for murder. The name of Vera Hillyard they had never heard. And when they knew they weren't shocked, of course they weren't, only curious and rather excited. My husband and I never mentioned her. I don't think I heard my own mother, for the rest of her life, ever name her. Vera, in all that time, made herself known to me only in occasional dreams, when I would be a child again, and coming back from Anne's to Laurel Cottage on a warm summer evening, be reproached for my lateness or asked in Vera's peculiarly brisk querulous way, how I ever thought I would be fit to do my school work in the morning? Or I open a dream door into a dream room and Vera is sitting there, Madonna-like, tranquil and splendid, her breasts bare and the suckling Jamie in her arms. The baby never looks at me, he turns his face away or covers it with his arm. But he is Jamie and all roads always lead back to him.

We were staying in a hotel in the Via Cavour. Later on, Jamie told me it was the one in which Francis had stayed when first they met after twenty years apart. In Francis's room were two pictures, ugly abstracts in raucous colours, and pretentious too. He got two narrow strips of white adhesive paper, wrote on one in Italian *Section Through a Blackhead* and on the other *Contents of a Drain in the Borgo Pinti*, and carefully stuck each on to a picture. Jamie asked me to try and get into Room 36 and take a look if I could. I did and the stickers were still there, *Contenuti d'un Canale dal Borgo Pinti* and the other which I don't remember the Italian for. No chambermaid or bellboy had ever spotted them, and if guests had seen and marvelled, they had never mentioned their discovery to the management. How typical of Francis this was! Jamie took a gleeful delight in it, in this aspect of Francis, laughing in his shrill hiccuping way at the very thought of Francis's teases and practical jokes. They had become friends of a kind, those two, the last thing one would have expected.

It was more than twenty years since I had seen Jamie, nearer twenty-five. Of course I knew he lived in Italy, had felt a special affinity with Italy since spending his school holidays with the Contessa who had a house somewhere near Verona. After school came to an end he stayed for a while in London with another Pearmain relative and then Tony sent him to the University of Bologna. Always, you see, he had to be kept out of sight, for he was an embarrassment and a reminder. In all this time I don't think Tony saw him but communicated with him through solicitors, like people in Victorian

18

novels, turning him into a remittance man, but one who in this case had committed no offence. But this may not be so, or not quite so, or different in detail. Jamie's life has been, and still is, a mystery, his very existence a mystery.

Patricia it was who told me he was a journalist, a war correspondent who had been in Vietnam. Helen believed otherwise. In her version, Jamie worked at the Biblioteca Nazionale and had been one of those concerned in the salvaging of precious books when the Arno over-flowed into the great library in November 1966. Francis might have told us the truth but none of us, not even Helen regularly, kept in touch with Francis except Gerald, his father. And Gerald, Helen said, must have been 'going strange' even then, for he averred Francis had told him Jamie was a cook.

All these beliefs contained something of the truth, as such beliefs usually do. I went to Florence without any idea of looking Jamie up, for this was the third or fourth time I had been there and without doing more than reflect that for a few days we would be in the same city, he and I. But at Pisa where, having just missed the Florence train, we had time to kill, we bought a newspaper, *La Nazione*, and on an inside page I found Jamie's name: James Ricardo. His by-line (as journalists call it, as years and years ago Chad Hamner first taught me to call it) was under a heading which, translated, means 'delicious crust' and over an article on how to make *pâté sablée*. Jamie *was* a journalist, he *was* a cook, and later on I heard from his own lips that it was true he had helped in the book rescue.

When we got to Florence I looked him up in the phone book. There were a lot of Ricardos but only one James. I was nervous about phoning him. People can put the phone down but all they can do with a letter is not answer it. I wrote him a note. This was before he went to live in the gardens of the Orcellari – the Otello restaurant is on the corner at the top – and the address was a street off the Viale Gramsci, up near where the Porta a'Pinti once stood. Jamie wrote back by return. He had heard of me, Francis had mentioned the existence of a cousin and said we knew each other when he was a child, but of that he had no recollection. Perhaps we should meet. Would I meet him in the English Cemetery when it opened at three on the following afternoon?

'Why can't he ask you to his house or come here like a civilized person?' said my husband.

I said that since his life and his origins were so shrouded in the mysterious, perhaps he enjoyed keeping up the mystery. He must like the arcane.

'I'm not sure *I* like the idea of my wife having assignations in cemeteries with strange cookery columnists,' he said. 'At any rate, you'd better look out for yourself crossing the piazza, the way the traffic sweeps round.'

But he wouldn't come with me, fearing Jamie might have turned out like Francis. He went off to buy a pair of shoes.

The Cimitero Protestante di Porta a'Pinti, known as the 'English Cemetery', though there are Americans and Poles and plenty of Swiss buried there too, stands like a hilly green island in the middle of the Piazza Donatello. And the traffic, as my husband said, rushes round and past it as a millrace might sweep past just such an island. It was a beautiful day, clear and sunny, blue-skied, hot by our standards though not by those of the Florentines who by the end of September, having endured months of true heat, were already wearing their winter leather and wool. The iron gates were closed but the custodian, seeing me, came out and unlocked them and showed me the way through the archway in the gatehouse into the graveyard on the other side.

It was not silent in the cemetery – how could it be with that traffic not a hundred yards away? – but it had an *air* of silence, an air of endeavouring to be silent, brought about by the ranks of pale, bright grey stones and the thin cypress trees. At first I didn't see Jamie. The cemetery appeared to be empty. I walked slowly up the path towards the Emperor Frederick William's marble column, past Elizabeth Barrett's tomb, looking rather cautiously from side to side, feeling exposed now, feeling watched. But Jamie wasn't watching me or even watching for me. I found him when I turned back, seated on the grave of Walter Savage Landor and reading, perhaps not too surprisingly, Brillat-Savarin's celebrated work on gastronomy, *La Physiologie du Goût*.

I hadn't known Landor was in there. Chad had quoted him on Eden's wedding day, standing by the lake in the garden at Walbrooks: 'There are no voices that are not soon mute, however tuneful; there is no name, with whatever emphasis of passionate love repeated, of which the echo is not faint at last.' The echo of Eden's name was faint by then. I had forgotten what Chad's voice sounded like, though his face I remembered and Hadrian's ears. Jamie looked up at me and then he got up.

'Yes,' he said, 'you look like a Longley. I would have recognized you as a Longley – from photographs, of course.'

I held out my hand to him. We shook hands.

'I mostly come here in the afternoons,' he said. 'It's peaceful without being quiet if you know what I mean. People don't come much. People are frightened of cemeteries.' And for the first time I heard that curious neighing laugh of his. 'I suppose you would have preferred to be invited to my apartment?'

The American term sounded strange in Jamie's voice which is English public school with overtones of Italian, especially about the r's. They are a bit too liquid, his r's, pronounced too high up in the mouth. I said I didn't mind, it was nice to be able to sit outside. We couldn't do much of that in England.

'I haven't been back there for fourteen years,' he said. 'I don't suppose I shall ever go now. The thought of England fills me with horror.'

It is disconcerting the way he laughs after he has said something not at all laughable, in just the same way as he laughs when he has expressed pleasure or amusement. The laughter died and he stared at me. Suddenly he made a flicking movement with his right hand towards his left shoulder, caught me looking and drew his hand away, laughing again. He is a thick-set, going-to-seed, not very tall man who looks older than he is. He also looks Italian with his round, full-featured, sallow face, his red lips and his dark curly hair. And this is very much what one would expect, all things considered. Though fair-haired as a child he always had olive skin. His eyes, which in those days the grown-ups looked at curiously, surreptitiously, watching for the colour to stay or to change, are a dark velvety glowing brown, animal eyes but feral, not meek. That time in the English Cemetery he reminded me a little of Chad, which is absurd. There was no real physical resemblance and Jamie was too young to have creases on his ear lobes. Perhaps what they had in common was a look of desire unsatisfied, of lives spoiled and incomplete.

I sat down facing him and he asked me hesitatingly, as if curiosity was overcoming his better judgement, to tell him about our family – his family too, of course, as much as mine. So I talked, going carefully, for I had rehearsed this on my long walk along Cavour. It wouldn't do, I felt, to mention Goodney Hall or the name of his mother or the men who had made themselves his enemies through no fault of his but because of his very existence and because of jealousy and resentment and hurt pride. My mother was still alive then, so I spoke about my parents, and about Helen and her children and her granddaughter.

'I called myself Richardson because of Aunt Helen,' he said. 'Pearmain didn't care. He wouldn't have cared what I called myself.' He neighed with laughter and I shuddered at the way he called Tony 'Pearmain' with such disgusted vehemence. His right hand came up again, flicking from his shoulder invisible contamination. 'Zia Francesca used to tell me how much he loved children. It was her way of making me feel all right about staying with her instead of being with him. He was too busy for me but he really loved children. Did you know he was a big shot in the Save the Children fund? He loved all the children in the world but me. Tough on him, wasn't it?' Jamie paused, staring into the sunlight, the thin parallel black shadows the cypresses made, like the bars of a cage. 'Aunt Helen used to tell me what wonderful people her grandparents were. I hadn't known many wonderful people, you see, so when Pearmain said – very stiff and shy about it, Pearmain was – that now I was going to prep school I mustn't be called by my surname any more and how about James Smith? I said not Smith but Richardson and it was all one to him. So I called myself Richardson and later on I had it changed to Ricardo. Have you ever heard an Eye-tie pronounce Richardson?'

He is practically Italian himself yet he calls Italians Eye-ties in a grinning cockney way each time he mentions them. His charmlessness suddenly clarified itself before me. It seemed to underline the absurdity of our meeting in a cemetery. The noble stones, the cypresses, the blue sky, the terracotta roofed gatehouse, all these should have formed the backdrop for someone tall, handsome and Byronic, a gracious man of character. And that was the way, I thought, Jamie had promised to grow up when last I had seen him and he was five. But the terrible things that had happened were already waiting for him, crowding at the gate, had been gathering there even before he was born.

'I don't remember anything that happened before I was six,' he said. 'The first thing I can remember is the summer when I was six and always being with two women I didn't like.'

22

'Mrs King and your nanny,' I said.

'I suppose so. Pearmain used to come and look at me sometimes, the way you'd go and look at a dog you'd had put in quarantine.'

I wanted to speak Vera's name then but I was afraid. The picture of the little boy – such an articulate, lively, *good* little boy he had been – alone at Goodney Hall with his two paid guardians upset me disproportionately. After all, it was long ago, it was lost in the past. Afraid and distressed, I wanted to say something about missing his mother, about my own feelings of sympathy for that, but I couldn't, and not only because of the effects of emotion. As much as that, doubt prevented my speaking, a doubt of how to phrase this expression of pity and what terms to use. He came to my rescue.

'Would you like to go somewhere for a coffee?'

I shook my head. One of the few things I dislike about Italy is the coffee. *Cappuccino* is out for me because I don't drink milk. *Espresso* would be fine if you could have half a pint of it and not a teaspoonful.

Jamie said, 'Next time you come I'll cook for you.'

I realized I was honoured. In this country of *haute cuisine* he, an Englishman, had made a name for himself as a cook and adviser of cooks. In that moment Vera came into my mind and I remembered her excellence in that sole aspect of culinary skill Englishwomen are best at – baking. I saw her with the puff pastry buttered and turned on the veined grey marble slab, the wood-handled marble rolling-pin in her hands, and I seemed to taste again her lemon-curd tarts, her Victoria sponges and all the rest of the panoply laid out for tea.

Jamie shocked me. 'My mother was a good cook,' he said.

The feeling I had was like what we have when we are in the presence of someone known to be mentally disturbed but whose manner and way of speaking is so rational that we forget the psychosis, the schizophrenia, until we are sharply and suddenly reminded of it by a remark he makes on the other side of sanity, out there in the region only the mad inhabit. Not that Jamie was anything but sane, remarkably normal really. It was more that what he said opened a door into the incredible and one's reaction was first to be horribly startled, then to feel the pity one has for those who take comfort from delusion.

His eyes that are like the eyes of a bear came back to meet mine. He jumped up, gave his shoulder a brisk brushing with his hand.

'Come on,' he said. 'I'll show you the graves. I'll show you Isa Blagden and Mrs Holman-Hunt.'

After that he walked back with me quite a long way down the Borgo Pinti. It was then that he told me about Francis and the paintings and asked me to check if the titles Francis had given them were still there. We were shaking hands again, about to part, when he said to me, and for the first time he seemed embarrassed:

'If anyone ever wants to write about all that – you know what I mean – if they do and they approach you, I mean they're just as likely to approach you as anyone, if they do, I wouldn't mind. I don't know about Francis but I wouldn't mind. As a matter of fact I'd welcome it to put the record straight, I'd like to see the *truth*.'

'But you say you don't remember,' I said.

His laughter echoed in that narrow street and people turned round to look. He said goodbye to me and walked away.

I couldn't agree with Jamie that any potential biographer of Vera would be as likely to approach me as anyone. For one thing I wouldn't have expected such a biographer to find me, for I have twice changed my name since Vera died. And for another I was a mere niece while she has a son and a husband and a sister living. Helen has reached an age when life itself has become fragile, when each day must be an only half-expected gift, when she knows there can be no future to talk about. Her memory for contemporary things is gone but her memory of the distant past is bright and as for her mental grasp of things, I know no one sounder of any age. Yet when she told me to expect a letter and a request I hardly took her seriously. This writer, this man called Daniel Stewart, might well have a Vera-book in mind as a project, might have asked Helen for information, but me, I was sure, he would ignore. And Helen, moreover, swore my name had not been given him by her. By Jamie then?

Stewart is a common enough name. I must have met many Stewarts and Stuarts in those intervening years, yet when I see it at the end of this letter, I am reminded of Mary Stuart whose life we acted out, Anne and I, and that Goodncy Hall was designed by Steuart, a fact that Eden and Tony always made much of. The letter accompanies a book: *Peter Starr, the Misunderstood Murderer* by Daniel Stewart, published by Heinemann at nine pounds ninety-five.

24

It is a London address on the headed paper, not too far from us on the other side of the Cromwell Road.

'Dear Mrs Severn,' he begins. 'By now you may have heard from others of the project I have in mind, a biographical reappraisal of the Vera Hillyard case. Your name and address were given me by your cousin Dr Frank Loder Hills who does not, however, personally wish to contribute a memoir . . .'

Francis, of course. Purely to cause trouble, I suppose, and then, as my husband suggests, to sue me and Stewart if we defame him. Stewart goes on to say he feels Vera has been in some ways misjudged. Apparently, he has made a speciality of reassessing murder cases, looking at them afresh and from the viewpoint of what he calls the perpetrator.

'Mr James Ricardo, of the Via Orti Orcellari, Florence, has undertaken to write something for me about his early memories. Mr Anthony Pearmain is at present in the Far East but . . .'

In the Far, in the Far . . . This geographical commonplace in newspapers and on radio and television I have never been able to see or hear without remembering my father on the morning of Vera's execution reading aloud in the toneless senseless voice of a mynah bird. 'In the Far . . .' he said and stopped and folded up the paper and sat there silent.

'Mrs Helen Chatteriss has already contributed a memoir and Mr Chad Hamner has promised to jot down for me some of his own impressions. His own intention to write a biography of Vera Hillyard he has now abandoned due to ill health.

'If you would be kind enough to read my book on Peter Starr, and if you feel satisfied with my abilities at this kind of *reportage*, I would like to send you a copy of my draft first and second chapter, my first being an account of the murder itself. I realize that since you were not present at Goodney Hall at the time you will be unable to judge the accuracy of this. Of those who were present, only Mrs June Stoddard is still alive and her memory of events, as she herself admits, is confused.

'My second chapter, however, purports to give some family history, beginning at the time of your own great-grandfather, William Longley. Your confirmation of this account would be invaluable to me as would any corrections you may like to make. You will see that I have drawn heavily on correspondence in the possession of Mrs Chatteriss and the Hubbard family as well as, to some extent, on information given in the Vera Hillyard section in Mary Gough-Williams's book *Women and Capital Punishment*.'

His letter stops quite abruptly. It is as if he realizes he is beginning to write on the assumption that I shall approve. I shall want to contribute. But how very much I dislike having to read a book for some set purpose. The days when I had to do that are so many years behind me and then, at that time, the time of the murder at Goodney Hall, the books I had to read seemed to me worthwhile, they were literature, the best that had been written. What a judgement I am making on Stewart's work! And it is not a bad book, not bad at all, clear and simply written in plain language without contrived sensationalism. There was enough sensationalism in Starr's life without exaggerating it, as there was in Vera's. I shan't finish it, though, I don't need to, for I know already that I shall write back and tell him yes. I have read enough to tell – to hope – he will be sensitive, he will not be too harsh, he will understand the terrible pressures of love.

She has come back into my life after an absence that extends over more than a third of a century. Helen and Daniel Stewart have brought her to me and she is here in the house, the awkward guest she always was when she stayed in the homes of other people. I almost fancy that I can see her – not the Vera of the photographs in 'the box', young, fair, earnest-eyed, but my thin, nervous, pernickety, often absurd aunt, performing that strange, uniquely characteristic action of hers, as unconscious as a tic, as unconscious as Jamie's flick of the hand, of pressing her palms together and bearing down on her clasped hands as if in some inner anguish. Time and time again these past days she has driven me to our unused littlest bedroom where 'the box' is and made me lift the lid and turn over the contents, pausing to look at a picture or read a line from a letter, or simply staring in a daydream of nostalgia at the memorabilia of his sisters my father left behind him.

What would poor Vera make of the moral climate of the present day? I can imagine her look of mulish incredulity. A sexual revolution took place and the world was changed. What happened to her and Eden could not have happened today. The motive and the murder were of their time, rooted in their time, not only impossible in these days but beyond the comprehension of the young unless that moral code is carefully explained to them. Because Vera is with me, is in my house like the sort of ghost that is visible to only one person, the one with the interest, I have tried to tell my daughter something of it, I have tried to elucidate.

'But why didn't she . . .?' is the way her interjections begin. 'Why didn't she tell him? Why didn't she just live with him? Why did she want to marry him if he felt like that?' And, 'But what could anyone have done to her?'

All I can say, lamely, is, 'It was different then.'

It was different. Does Stewart, also young, know how different it was? And if he doesn't, will he take my word? Or will I find myself, as I begin to think most likely, giving him the bare facts, correcting his obvious howlers, reminiscing a little, but keeping the real book that is Vera's life recorded on a tape run only in my own consciousness?

— 3 —

The deed is done and they have pinioned Vera and taken the knife from her, the knife she wanted to turn on herself, and they have tied her hands. In the nick of time Jamie hás been carried from the room. Was he crying by then? Did he cry out or call to his mother? No one has ever spoken of that as if it had been a passive stunned little creature Mrs King snatched up in her arms – and perhaps it was. Stewart has got it right, all of it, even to the clothes Vera was wearing, clothes contrived from cot blankets and pre-war remnants, even to the nursery frieze, even to the flying blood that splashed on to the blue and white and the shining fire-guard.

As far as I know. As he says, I wasn't there.

The nucleus of this mystery I see he had handled in the conventional way, repeating the accepted version. Can he be left to these innocent assumptions of his? Or shall I tell him there is a huge question still left unanswered?

Jamie knows the answer. Or so he tells me in the letter I have had from him today. This belief of his I began to have some inkling of when we met in the English Cemetery, but since he must be the most injured and most vulnerable actor in this drama, he can hardly be deemed an impartial judge. That, of course, is the last thing he would want to be but what then of his claim that he remembers nothing before he was six? His conviction, surely, is based solely on an inclination of the heart, on nostalgia for an adored and adoring presence that he sees in dreams but of which he has no waking recollection.

In Stewart's second chapter, the history of our family, Jamie has no place. Perhaps Stewart shirked it because he did not quite know where to put him.

The Victorian villa (Stewart writes) in the village of Great Sindon in Essex had been lived in by Longleys for less than thirty years. It was in no sense a family home. Arthur Longley bought it with the money from a small inheritance which came to his wife coincidentally with his enforced retirement from the Prudential Insurance Company. Before that, if the Longleys had roots, they were in the busy town of Colchester. There, since the early part of the nineteenth century, they had been shoemakers in a cottage with a shopfront almost under the shadow of the Castle.

Colchester is England's oldest recorded town. The Romans called it Camulodunum and there Queen Boudicca fought them. To the Saxons it was Colneceaste, its river being the Colne to this day. The castle is Romanesque, its keep built in 1080, and if you stand and look at its towers and pantiled roofs on a sunny day you might fancy yourself in Tuscany. Today Colchester is approached by dual carriageways, ringed with 'experimental' double roundabouts, and has a bypass often more congested than the way through the town itself. It has multistorey car parks inside red brick façades designed, not altogether happily, to resemble medieval fortifications, a relentless one-way street system and, just inside the old Roman walls, a labyrinth of ancient houses that has become a precinct of walking streets.

There in very different days, in a more peaceful and tranquil atmosphere, William Longley made and mended shoes and later, as he grew more prosperous, employed three men to sit at work in the room behind the shop. William's shop is still there, in a cul-de-sac off Short Wyre Street, the offices now of a firm of accountants. The door between shop and workroom still remains and there too is the circular pane of glass, two inches in diameter, inserted in the oak for William to spy through and check his men plied their needles.

William had married in 1859 Amelia Jackman of Layer-de-la-Haye. Three daughters were born to them and later a son. The boy was baptized Arthur William, was given a considerably superior education to that his father had enjoyed, but nevertheless was destined to follow him in the family business. Young Arthur was a promising and popular pupil at the Grammar School Henry the Eighth had founded in 1539, and he had other ideas. The lure of middle-classdom, so tempting to the Victorian working man of that particular stamp, the leaning towards what we today call the 'upwardly mobile', had ensnared him, and his father put up no opposition. William Longley took his daughter Amelia's husband into the cobbler's shop and Arthur joined the Prudential as an insurance agent. He began humbly enough, working his district on a bicycle and living at home with his parents and his unmarried sisters.

In spite of his ambitions, Arthur never earned much money. His district was not a prosperous one, so his commissions were small. What affluence he later enjoyed came to him through his marriage. His first wife was the daughter and only child of a gentleman, a landowner of substantial means called Abel Richardson. Arthur met her in a traditionally romantic way. Maud was out riding and her horse threw her just as Arthur happened to be passing through the outskirts of Stoke-by-Nayland on his bicycle. She had sprained her ankle and Arthur, who was strong, young and ardent, carried her the half mile home to Walbrooks. In the weeks that followed, it was only natural for the young man to call and inquire after Maud and natural, too, for Maud to arrange it, via a sympathetic parlourmaid, that next time he came he might choose a time when papa was with the hounds (he was the local Master of Foxhounds) and mamma out paying calls.

There is evidence that Abel Richardson strenuously opposed his daughter's intention to marry a more or less penniless and socially unacceptable insurance agent. After a year, however, he yielded to Maud's entreaties. Yielded sufficiently, in fact, not to withhold the fortune of five thousand pounds which in the past, before the advent of Arthur Longley into their lives, he had promised he would give with his daughter.

Five thousand pounds was a considerable sum in 1890, equivalent to perhaps twenty times that today. Arthur and Maud took one of the villas that were being built out on the Layer Road and settled down to live there very comfortably. To live, indeed, rather above their income, though this was augmented by frequent monetary gifts from Arthur's father-in-law. Maud kept her own carriage. Their household consisted of a cook and housemaid, a nurse for the child, a charwoman who came in to 'do the rough' and a coachman-cum-gardener.

Maud's daughter, Mrs Helen Chatteriss, now an old lady approaching ninety, has written this account of the household:

I was only five when it all came to an end. My memories will therefore be hazy and incomplete. I remember being driven out with my mother in a very smart carriage drawn by a chestnut horse. My mother used to leave calling cards but I believe that many houses of the local gentry were closed to us on account of my father not being a gentleman.

The only housework my mother ever did was to arrange the flowers and wash the best china. She lay down to rest every afternoon with white cotton gloves on to preserve her hands. My nurse was called Beatie. She was sixteen, the daughter of one of my grandfather Richardson's tenant farmer's labourers, and she used to take me to see her parents who lived in a one-room cottage with a brick floor. My mother found out and dismissed her.

I was told that my father had an important position in business but I remember him as usually being at home. He had a study where he would shut himself up for the morning. Now, looking back, I think he spent his time there reading novels. When he went out collecting insurance business, he would ride the second horse we kept, a roan gelding. I don't remember parties, dinners, that sort of thing, only my Richardson grandparents calling quite often and my Longley grandparents and aunts less often. I think my mother may have been ashamed of them.

This lifestyle came to an abrupt end in 1901 when Helen's mother died in childbirth. The baby, a boy, also died. Maud Longley's fortune, or what remained of it, was settled on her daughter, a careful provision insisted upon prior to the marriage by Abel Richardson, and by his wife's death Arthur Longley was left a poor man. He gave up his house, carriage, horses, and moved into what was hardly more than a cottage on the western outskirts of the town, dismissing his staff and keeping only a maid of all work.

Also dismissed was his daughter. At any rate, she was parted from her father and sent to live with Abel and May Richardson in

Stoke-by-Nayland. It was a separation that still rankles with Mrs Chatteriss after more than eighty years, in spite of the happy childhood, sheltered, indulged and luxurious, she enjoyed with her grandparents at Walbrooks.

'I suppose he thought I should be too much of a responsibility,' she says, 'and it may be, too, that my grandfather and grandmother persuaded him. I would have minded more except that my grandmother was so marvellous and I came to love her more than I had my mother. I seldom saw my father after my mother died.'

In 1906 he married again. The first Mrs Chatteriss knew of this second marriage was as a result of an unexpected encounter in Colchester, near St Botolph's. It was there that she attended a private school, being driven from Stoke and back in a pony carriage. Two years were yet to go before Abel Richardson made himself a pioneer in the neighbourhood by buying a Rolls-Royce sedan, its hide upholstery buttoned in ebony and its dashboard of rosewood. One afternoon, after school, she found her father and a strange lady waiting for her at the gates. The lady was introduced to Helen as her 'new mother' but thereafter no attempts were made to reinforce the relationship. Her grandparents knew nothing of it for months and were angry when they found out, more from having been kept in the dark than from Arthur Longley's having remarried.

He was thirty-nine. In the twenty-two years he had worked for the Prudential he had received no promotion and, his fortunes having dwindled, he had returned to going about his meagre business on a bicycle. His parents were dead, the family business had passed to his brother-in-law, James Hubbard, and what very little money there was to his two unmarried sisters. Nor had his bride any money, though she was not without expectations. Ivy Naughton was twenty-eight when she married Arthur, having been governess in a family who were his clients. She had neither training nor qualification for this post, other than having attended school until the age of sixteen and being able to play the piano. But the people she worked for, known to the Richardsons, were seed merchants with pretensions, to whom the boast of having a governess for their three daughters satisfied them independently of what educational benefit the girls might derive from it ... For this service Miss Naughton received her board and lodging and fifty pounds a year.

She and Arthur set up house together. Nine months after the

wedding, in the spring of 1907, twin children were born to them. Ivy's aunt, Miss Priscilla Naughton, who had her own house and a small clientele as dressmaker, was one of the godparents and another was Arthur's daughter, Helen, who had been confirmed a month before. The twins, a boy and a girl, were christened John William and Vera Ivy. Like her husband, Ivy Longley was a great reader of novels – it was 'talking about books' which had brought them together – and by coincidence, the heroine in each case of their favourite novel had the same Christian name.

'My father used to read Ouida,' Helen Chatteriss writes, 'and *Moths* was his favourite of her books. The heroine's name is Vera as is the name of the heroine of Marion Crawford's novel, *A Cigarette Maker's Romance*. According to my father, this was my stepmother's favourite book. And that was how they came to name Vera.'

Vera Longley and her brother, being of opposite sexes, were not, of course, identical twins. They bore no more resemblance to each other than if they had been born at separate births, but both had the very fair hair and intensely blue eyes which were distinctive features of the second Longley family. Arthur, his mother, and two of his sisters were fair-haired, and his second wife was a blonde with extremely fair skin and light eyes. Ivy Longley's forebears were fisherfolk from the coast of Norfolk and it was said that one of her grandfathers, a seafaring man, had brought home a wife from the Faroe Islands. John was a handsome boy, Vera a plain child whose looks underwent a transformation as she grew older. A photograph shows her at fourteen as a pretty, sharp-featured girl with a mass of nearly white blonde hair, large eyes and a serious, rather severe, expression.

Four years before that picture was taken, her father had been pensioned off by the Prudential, a medical examination having shown him to have a weak heart. He was fifty and the Great War in its third year. That war was not to touch the immediate Longley family directly, although Amelia's son, William Hubbard, lost his life in it at Vimy Ridge. Soon after Arthur's enforced retirement, Priscilla Naughton died, leaving her house and £500 to her niece, Ivy. The Longleys moved out into the country and by the spring of 1919 were settled in Great Sindon, a village some ten miles from Colchester in the Vale of Dedham.

*

It was in no sense a 'gentleman's house', which is how Arthur's villa on the Layer Road – now vanished to make way for a block of flats – might have been categorized. The agents through whom Arthur bought it described it as a cottage. Today we should consider this to diminish its status. Paul and Rosemary Oliver who now own the house have changed its name from 'Laurel Cottage' to 'Finches' and undertaken structural alterations to the ground floor so that the dining-room and kitchen have been converted into one large living-room, the dairy has become the kitchen and the drawing-room the dining area. But in the Longleys' day, and subsequently in Vera's, there were four rooms on the ground floor with the staircase running up through the centre of the house. When Arthur and Ivy moved in with their two children, there were four bedrooms. The smallest of these Arthur had converted into a bathroom, leaving the principal bedroom for his wife and himself and a room each for the son and daughter.

Externally, Laurel Cottage was built of the iron-free brick, yellowish-grey in colour, that is known as 'white brick', with facings of cream-painted plaster, and roofed in slate. It is a symmetrical house, the front door in the centre, a sash window on each side and three above. Similarly, the front garden is accurately bisected by a path which runs straight to the front door, or doors, for there are two, an outer of panelled wood and an inner of glass. The garden at the rear is large, containing, by the gate in the rear fence, an outbuilding that was apparently once a disused cottage in which the Longley children played on wet days, now converted by the Olivers into a garage.

What kind of childhood did Vera Longley have in Colchester and later in Great Sindon? What, if anything, happened to traumatize her? Two days after her twelfth birthday we find her writing to her half-sister, Helen:

Dear Helen, Thank you very much for the postal order. I am going to put it towards buying a tennis racquet. Tomorrow I am going on holiday to Cromer in Norfolk. I hope it will be fine as it is by the sea. With love from Vera.

And in the summer of the same year, 1919:

Dear Helen, Daddy showed me your letter. I should very much like to be your bridesmaid. I hope you will be very happy married to Captain Chatteriss.

Thank you for asking me to be your bridesmaid. It will be nice to meet soon and I am looking forward to it. With love from Vera.

The marriage took place in the autumn. Helen had met Victor Chatteriss of the Indian Army, then aged twenty-eight, when he was home on leave. In Helen's wedding photographs, Vera stands half a head taller than the other girl attendants, gawky, thin, with big, serious eyes, wearing a calf-length dress of some glossy material with inset lace panels. She seems to have been a favourite with her father who wrote to his sister, Clara:

... My little Vera is turning out a fine-looking girl, prettier than one could have hoped. She puts me in mind of you at that age, she has that same true gold hair that shows no sign of darkening. I think her brain superior to her brother's which I can't help being sorry about in one way, though proud in another. Her school reports are really excellent. She came top of her class in English and history last term. I am giving in to her and letting her have tennis coaching, an added expense I should prefer not to have but she is doing so well I did not like to say no. It is a good social advantage too, don't you think? I believe in providing the best in that way for one's girl. But she will tell you all about it when she comes to you next week ...

Clara, five years Arthur's senior, had married late in life and gone with her husband to live in Cromer where Vera spent occasional holidays. In Cromer her childless aunt made much of her and we have Vera writing to Helen in India that 'Auntie Clo' bought her two dress-lengths which were being made up by Clara's own dressmaker and had taken her to a photographer to have a studio portrait done. As well as the tennis, Vera attended classes in ballroom dancing. She received a school prize for perfect attendance in 1921 and another, a calf-bound copy of Ruskin's *Sesame and Lilies*, for coming top in handwork three terms in succession. On the face of it, this was a happy and successful girlhood.

In 1922, when her son and daughter were fifteen and her husband fifty-five, Ivy Longley, aged forty-four, gave birth to another child. It was a girl, to be christened Edith, a name that was already old-fashioned. Ivy had written to her aunt Priscilla Naughton in 1908 when the twins were babies that she dreaded having more children. After their birth she had been ill for months. The birth itself had been difficult and protracted, leaving her with a partial prolapse of the womb, and she had been unable to nurse the twins herself. To Miss Naughton she had written:

I am still only thirty and could certainly have several more children – dreadful prospect! They say you forget the details of birth, pain, etc., but I have not. Also there are twins in the family, as you know, not only mine but my mother had twin sisters who died as babies. I wonder sometimes if at forty I shall have a whole unwelcome brood . . .

Ivy's second daughter came at a time when she may have believed the danger past. According to all evidence and precedent, the new baby should have been an encumbrance. Its father was an elderly man with a weak heart, its mother menopausal and avowedly 'not fond of children', its siblings adolescents with established niches in the family. John, like his father before him, a pupil at Colchester Grammar School, was at an age when boys feel deep embarrassment in the society of their fellows at any evidence of sexuality on the part of their parents. And what stronger evidence could there be than a new baby? Besides, his parents were so old, his father twenty years older than most of his contemporaries' fathers. As for Vera, on the face of it we should need to look no further for a cause of personality damage. Here was a new child and of the same sex as herself come to oust her from her place in her parents' affections.

But none of this seems to have been the case. From the first, Edith – soon to re-name herself Eden – was generally loved. Adored might not be too strong a word, at any rate by her father, her brother and her sister. Mrs Longley's attitude towards the child remains a mystery. She was an infrequent letter writer, and seems to have written to no one between the time of the death of her aunt and the removal of her elder daughter to India. No photographs survive of her with Eden, if any existed. In one snapshot only do they appear together, and Arthur Longley, John, Vera and Clara Dawson are also in the photograph. It was taken on the beach at Cromer and shows Vera with the three-year-old Eden on her lap, Ivy very much in the background, sitting in a deckchair, her face shaded by a broad-brimmed hat.

Vera wrote to Helen Chatteriss in 1924:

I wish you could see my dear little sister. She is the most beautiful child that ever was and her photos don't at all do her justice. I will tell you something. When I take her out, holding her hand and walking with her or

35

pushing her in her pushcart, I hope people will think she is my baby and I am her mother. Do you think that very silly and fanciful? Of course I am not really old enough to be her mother but people tell me I look eighteen. Last week someone Mother knows who had not met me before asked if I was twenty-four! Mother was not too pleased, as you may guess, for it made her seem even older than she is.

We call Edith Eden now because that is what she called herself before she could pronounce 'th'. It is rather a lovely name, I think. Edith sounds like someone's old aunt. I can't think why mother and Dad chose it. Her hair is the most brilliant pure gold. I do hope it won't darken. Mine has not, of course, but then mine was white when I was her age . . .

On leaving school, John Longley obtained a post with the Midland Bank. At the opportunity of working at a branch in the City of London he hesitated no more than a day before accepting and at the same time becoming a paying guest in the home of his mother's cousin and her husband. Elizabeth Whitestreet had been a Naughton before her marriage. She and her husband and their two children lived at Wanstead which is in Essex but on the eastern outskirts of London. While living in their house, John met a young half-Swiss girl, Vranni Breuer, who also lodged there and who, though untrained, had some kind of job in the local orphanage as a children's nurse. Vranni's father died in the influenza epidemic of 1918, her mother seven years later. She, too, had been a children's nurse, or rather nanny, employed by a family in Zurich which was where she met Johann Breuer. Vranni was two years older than John Longley, having been born in Zurich in 1905, and it was partly her seniority which led to his parents' disapproval of his choice when she and the twenty-one-year-old John were married in 1928. A greater cause of dismay to Arthur and Ivy was Vranni's provenance. In the nineteen-twenties, English people, notably English country people, still retained a deep distrust of foreigners. It would be no exaggeration to say that Ivy Longley, in 1928, felt much the same about her son's choice of a bride as today a woman of her background might feel about her son's marrying a black African. It if were true that Ivy had a Faroese grandmother whose genes were responsible for much of her own and her daughters' beauty, she had conveniently forgotten it now. According to Mrs Chatteriss, her refusal to attend the wedding – though Arthur Longley did so, accompanied by the six-year-old Eden – was the cause of a permanent estrangement between herself and her daughter-in-law, and when John went to visit his mother, whom he adored, he was obliged to do so alone.

What Vera thought of John's departure from tradition is not known. She also was not present at his wedding for by this time she was in India and had herself been married for two years. When she was eighteen, an invitation came to her from her half-sister asking Vera to come out to Rawalpindi. Helen Chatteriss offered to put up half the cost of the sea trip. Vera went to India in the late summer of 1925, arriving at Bombay just as the rainy season came to an end. As speedily as her twin brother was to settle himself, Vera, in the first week of her arrival at Captain (now Major) and Mrs Chatteriss's bungalow, had met and been attracted by a young subaltern in Victor Chatteriss's regiment, Gerald Loder Hillyard.

Socially – and these things were still of great importance in 1925 – Gerald Hillyard was a cut above Vera, several cuts above in fact, though by a quirk of fate (and the unpaternal attitude of Arthur Longley), belonging in the same class as Helen Chatteriss. He was the third and youngest son of a Somerset squire, a small landowner of good birth and very little money. There was a family tradition of younger sons entering the Indian Army and Gerald Hillyard had a forebear who had distinguished himself for gallantry in the First Afghan War of 1839–42 and a great-uncle who was with Sir Henry Havelock in the Mutiny when he broke through to relieve the residency at Lucknow. Gerald Hillyard was an old Harrovian and had been to Sandhurst. Physically he bore a strong resemblance to George Orwell, or that is the impression his photographs give. He was very tall, over six feet three, thin to emaciation though perfectly healthy, with brown hair and a square, dark moustache. His younger sister, Mrs Catherine Clarke, writes:

I did not meet Vera until about seven years after they were married. They came home on leave in 1930 and 1933 but I was away at school the first time. My father was dead by 1933. I think my mother felt that Gerald had married beneath him, and that he had been deceived into marrying beneath him partly by his own inexperience and partly the fact that Vera was staying with the Chatterisses as Mrs Chatteriss's sister. You could say that, because she was with them in that way, she partook of their social position but really this would be a false impression. Of course, it is all nonsense but it wasn't then. My mother only spoke to me about it once. I remember that she said that Vera was ladylike in the wrong way.

37

The marriage took place in Rawalpindi in March 1926 when Vera was nineteen years old and Gerald Hillyard twenty-two. In the following year, their son, Francis Loder, was born. When he was six years old, Vera and Gerald came home on leave to England, bringing the child with them, and leaving him behind at a prep school in Somerset not far from where his grandmother Hillyard was living. Two years afterward, Vera returned alone. Her father was dying but she arrived in time only for the funeral, not to see him alive. She had been his favourite child and very much attached to him. It is unfortunate that none of the several hundred letters she wrote him from India survive.

Arthur Longley was dead and Ivy, his wife, had only a few months to live. It was 1935 and Ivy was only fifty-seven but she was suffering from inoperable cancer of the uterus. Instead of returning to Gerald in India, Vera stayed with her mother and when Ivy died in the spring of 1936 remained to take charge of her fourteen-year-old sister, Eden.

Helen Chatteriss writes:

After the first year or two Vera had not much cared for India. She was very fair, you see, very fair-skinned and she found the sun unbearable. As far as I know there was nothing wrong with the marriage, this wasn't a separation because she and Gerald no longer got on. It was simply that she was happier and more comfortable in the English climate, and, of course, her son was in England. As I think I've told you, she was particularly fond of Eden and in fact it was the idea of separating herself from Eden that had made her hesitate about coming to India in the first place. I admit it, I invited Vera to come to us to find herself a good, suitable husband. And she did. It's hard to imagine now because things have changed so much but in the twenties girls did want husbands more than anything else and the main business of their lives was to get them. An awful lot of young men who might have been potential husbands for girls like Vera had been killed in the War. But there were a lot of eligible young men in India. I've never regretted inviting Vera and introducing her to Gerald; I don't think it was a mistake on my part. The marriage *was* happy, at least for years it was, and I still think it was the war, I mean the war of 1939–45, that spoiled things for them as it spoiled things for so many of us.

Catherine Clarke writes:

My brother came home with his regiment in 1939. Victor Chatteriss had retired the year before with the rank of Major-General and he and his wife and children were living in the house she had inherited from her grand-parents in Suffolk somewhere. What home life my brother had was spent in the house called Laurel Cottage at Great Sindon with Vera and her younger sister. The house didn't belong to them. It had been left between Vera, her brother and this sister, each owning a third. When the war came, the regiment was sent up north – Yorkshire, I believe it was.

So in the early years of the Second World War we have Vera Hillyard living very quietly alone with her sister Eden in the house where Eden had been born, in a sleepy village that boasted one shop, a school, a typically enormous East Anglian 'wool' church and an infrequent bus service to Colchester. It is a truism to say of a mother and daughter who are close that they they are like sisters. Vera Hillyard and Eden Longley, who *were* sisters, were perhaps more like mother and daughter. Vera in 1939 was thirty-two, Eden seventeen. In the school holidays they were joined by Vera's son, Francis. Occasionally there were visits from John and Vranni Longley and their daughter, Faith. And, of course, a few miles away in Stoke-by-Nayland, lived the Chatterisses, the General and his wife and their two teenage children, Patricia and Andrew. A Naughton cousin would sometimes come to tea. And there were village acquaintances, among them Thora Morrell, whose husband Richard was rector of the parish.

But the life led by the two sisters was a gentle and uneventful one, their recreations sewing, embroidery, baking, listening to the wireless. Yet already the drama that was to erupt in that house was slowly unfolding.

— 4 —

The day after Vera appeared in the magistrates' court to be charged with murder, my father went about the house collecting up and concealing everything that might connect her with him. Destroying too, I have no doubt. This may sound callous. My father was not unfeeling, far from it, but respectability was very important to him, that and his probity, his need to be beyond reproach. People must not know Vera Hillyard was his sister, the bank and its clients particularly must not know. He sorrowed in silence, letting concealment feed upon him inwardly. The outer man conducted himself as if Vera had never been.

It was my mother who told me what happened that evening. I wasn't there, I was in Cambridge, stunned by what I had read in a newspaper. My father came home from the bank. He ate nothing, he had eaten nothing for two days. He said to my mother, and it seems a curious question for a bank manager to put to his wife:

'Haven't we got a strongbox somewhere?'

She told him where it was. He took the box up to the spare bedroom, that room where Eden had once spent a night and enraged my mother by dusting the furniture, and there out of her sight – he would not carry out this solemn, almost ritualistic, task under her eyes – filled the box with his sisters' letters and with photographs of them. In the room where my mother was sitting, our living-room, were two framed photographs, a portrait of Vera and one of Eden in her wedding-dress. My father came in and removed these pictures from their frames. One was the kind where the back is in the form of a hinged door secured shut by slips but the other was backed by a sheet of gummed paper and this he ripped away in a single movement, so anxious was he to rid the room of Vera and her baby son. He cut his finger on the corner of the thin sheet of glass and the brown mark, circular and, unless one knows, unidentifiable, on the edge of the photograph, is his blood.

It was one of those that went into the box. After my parents were dead, I found the box in the back of their wardrobe. There was a picture hanging on the spare bedroom wall that I had never liked though the frame was pretty. The backing had been clumsily sealed with scotch tape and when I pulled it away I discovered between the Millais print and the sheet of cardboard two snapshots of Eden as a child. This gave me ideas and all over the house I began finding mementoes of my father's sisters. Not for him to follow Chesterton's precept that the best place to hide a leaf is in a tree. He knew that the best place to hide things is where no one will look, not in the family album – every photograph extracted from there, the blank spaces bearing witness – but between the pages of an annotated New Testament, among the end papers of *A Girl of the Limberlost*, slipped inside the embroidered cover someone (Vera? Eden?) had made for the album of Kensitas cigarettes silk flower cards, between the plywood base of a drawer and the red oilcloth that lined it.

I put everything into the strongbox along with those mementoes which had seemed most precious to my father, took the box home with me and hid it in the cupboard under the stairs. A friend who came to stay found the box when sent by my husband in search of rubber boots to wear on a walk. We lived in the country then. She spent the evening going through the photographs while I answered her questions with white lies and my husband sat silent, looking at me sometimes, saying not a word. But I, too, am a Longley with my share of their need to be private and withdrawn. My friend found the portrait of Vera Great-aunt Clara had had taken of her in Cromer and passed over it with the comment only that she was a pretty girl, but when she came to the Colchester photograph of 1945, the one that was in all the papers, some chord in her memory was struck and she paused a long time, staring at it, and telling me she was sure she had seen it somewhere before, years ago, in connection, she thought, with something terrible.

When we moved here, I put the box in our littlest bedroom and covered it with a brown blanket stamped with the letters M of D that someone had acquired (or stolen) during the war. If I asked why my father hadn't thrown away the contents of the box, I might equally ask why hadn't I? It is as well for Daniel Stewart that I haven't.

Alone in the house at three in the afternoon – it is not Helen's day nor our day for sitting alongside Gerald's wheelchair – I feel as though embarked upon some guilty exercise and anticipating the flurry I should be in if surprised, I open the box and take out the pictures and letters I had only glanced at when I gathered them up from the bookshelves and drawers in my parents' house. My inquisitive friend hadn't, of course, looked at the letters, though I had been on tenterhooks that she would. She had withdrawn them, or some of them, from the large brown envelope that held them all and pushed them back again with a quick explanation that these must be family letters. But perhaps if she had read them they would have given her no real clue to the identities of the writers.

I unfold them. They have a stale, very faintly sulphurous smell. Vera and Eden invariably wrote to my father alone, not to my father and mother. Here, for example, is Vera thanking him for a wedding present, though it was certainly my mother who had chosen and bought and packed the damask tablecloth and the dozen napkins initialled VH. But Vera disapproved of my mother because she was not English and therefore for a long while felt it legitimate to behave as if no such person as her brother's wife existed. Two more letters from India come next, then, of greater significance, the one that announces Vera's intention to remain in England to 'make a home for' Eden at Laurel Cottage. Yet it is a mystery why he decided to keep some and discard others until I recall a factor that seems absurd in its arbitrariness today. Vera wrote often, at least once a month, and these letters my father would invariably read aloud to us at the breakfast table, thereby causing my mother intense irritation. The current letter, replaced in its envelope, would be stuck on the mantelpiece for a week, after which, if it was winter, it would be thrown in the fire, if summer, stuffed into a drawer by my mother or crumpled up in my father's pocket. Therefore letters written between May and October tended to be kept and letters written between October and May burnt – it was as simple as that.

Here, then, is Vera writing in June:

Dear John, I am very glad you see things as I do and feel that instead of selling the house and dividing the proceeds we should keep it, at least for a while, as a home for Eden. While she is still at school it would be upsetting for her to remove her from Sindon. Of course it has been very hard for her to lose both parents so young. She is wonderfully sensible and old for her age – I am not talking about her school work, though this is quite good enough in my humble opinion – I mean her outlook on life and nice ways and manners. She is delighted that I am going to stay in England and that we shall both live in this house which has always been her home and where she was born . . .

The first letter of Eden's that I look at gives me a jolt. I had seen it before (though it had never been read aloud), forgotten it over the years, recalling how long it had stayed rankling in my mind. I had been remiss and I deserved a reprimand, but quite like this? 'Dear John', she wrote when she was seventeen and I eleven.

I have to write and tell you that I think you might teach your child better manners. I have not had a word of thanks from her for the postal order I sent her for her birthday. Surely by the time someone is ten she ought to know it is the right thing to write a thank-you letter. Mother dinned this into me from the time I could hold a pencil and she must have done the same with you. It is not fair on Faith, apart from the rudeness to people who give her presents, to allow her . . .

Why had he kept this one? Because at heart he approved of it? Because at heart, as my mother accused him, if he did not hold his sisters in greater affection than his wife and daughter, at any rate he admired them more? Or is it here in this collection only because it came in May when there was no fire burning?

As I pick up the envelope and put away the letters, Eden's beautiful face appears, arising from a neckline that stands up and curves outwards like an arum lily. She is in her wedding-dress, her huge billowing veil tumbling as if it were made of some less substantial stuff than gauze, like a cascade of foam. She is as she was that morning when Francis held her in his arms and led her to the altar and Chad devoured with his eyes. These are the pictures my father tore from their frames, Vera and Gerald newly married, outside a late Victorian Gothic church with Gilbert Scott steeple, a banyan tree and a dome in the background, Vera and the infant Francis, my father's blood on her hair. And here is the photograph Stewart will surely want for his frontispiece. Eden's bright hair falls in the way the film star Veronica Lake made famous but she has modified the look and her eye is not covered by the fall of hair. Here are shown to advantage the high cheekbones, the ever so slightly aquiline nose, the short upper lip, round chin, well-defined angled jaw, that Eden had in common with Francis so that the two of them looked more like brother and sister than aunt and nephew. She wears a light-coloured dress with a draped crossover neckline and in the vee a pearl necklace. The soulful, not-quite-of-this-world look that was so typically Eden's is in her rather too wide open eyes and the parted lips which the photographer has told her to lick and thus catch a highlight on the fashionable dark coating of lipstick.

But I hardly suppose it is for me to give permission for the use of this picture. The copyright may belong to Tony – or to the photographer who took it? On the back is the name of a studio in Londonderry and that fits the hairstyle, the probable date, even the remote, mysterious, secretive look in Eden's eyes.

At the bottom of the pile is a snapshot taken for no purpose one can imagine unless to record how on a certain hot day in a certain summer a crowd of relations gathered together in a particular garden. I am in this picture, my mousy pigtail hanging over one shoulder, wearing the voile dress that was someone's cast-off, standing between Francis and Patricia. Behind us are Eden in what the magazines called a 'tub frock', Vera with her hair newly permed, my father and Helen and a bunch of Hubbard cousins. The General must have taken it or Andrew. If he existed, Jamie would have been in the picture, so he was not yet born and the date must be before 1944. I had my hair cut short in 1943. Perhaps it is as early as 1940 and Andrew has not yet gone to fight the Battle of Britain or Eden joined the WRNS.

I replace the lid on the box and sit there looking at it. I find that I am crying. The tears are running down my face, a curious thing, for it was all so long ago and I had loved none of these people except my father and mother. Oh, and Chad of course, but that was something different.

When I was young, to be fair-haired was to be beautiful. This statement is a slight exaggeration but broadly it is true. Gentlemen – and ladies and everyone – preferred blondes. Eden was so fair, such a dazzling golden blonde, that she would have been accounted lovely even without the bonus of her features. The first time I went to Great Sindon on my own Vera met me on that station platform at Colchester and, having lightly stung my cheek with her lips, held me at arm's length and pronounced:

'What a pity your hair has got so dark!'

The tone was accusing, the implication that I had carelessly allowed this darkening process, if not actually helped it along. I said nothing because I could think of no answer, a frequent reaction to remarks of Vera's. I smiled. I tried to seem polite while with a corner of my handkerchief trying to rub off the lipstick I knew Vera's mouth must have deposited on my cheek. Make-up for women in those years was powder on the nose and lipstick on the mouth, bright red lipstick and loose powder from a Coty orange and gold box patterned all over with powder puffs. Vera wouldn't have put head outside her front door without lipstick on.

'I wouldn't have bothered to kiss you,' she now said, 'if I'd known you were going to make such a fuss about it.'

I had not been surreptitious enough. I put the handkerchief away and we walked to the bus stop. No one that I knew had a car – well, no one among my family and friends. The parents of one or two girls at school did and there was one father, said to own a company and to be rich, who not only had a car but a white car, a daring departure from convention. I had expected to go to Great Sindon by bus and by bus we went, Vera humping my suitcase along and complaining about its weight.

'I can carry it,' I said.

Vera's response was to hang on to the case all the tighter, transferring it from her right hand to her left so that it wasn't between us.

'I don't know why you wanted to bring so many things. You must have brought your entire wardrobe. You're lucky to have so many clothes. Do you know that when Eden goes away, she plans what she's going to need so carefully that she can get it all into a small attaché case.'

This conversation must have affected me quite deeply, it and other homilies on the subject of suitcases and packing and prudence and preparedness which were delivered in the weeks to come, for even to this day I feel guilty if I take too much luggage with me on holiday. But then, for the life of me, I couldn't see how a smaller or less full case would have done. I was to be here indefinitely, autumn was coming and I would need both summer and winter clothes. However, Vera must be right. She was a grown-up and my father's sister, often held up to me along with Eden as examples of what women should be. The size and weight of the suitcase troubled me while we were on the bus and I asked myself why I had brought this or that and what was there I could have left out. Vera's reproach had started me off on the wrong foot, making me feel both feckless and given over to a shameful frivolity.

It was September 1939. Everyone was afraid of bombs. A few years before I had listened to the wireless with my parents and heard of the bombing of Nanking. It frightened me so much I couldn't go on listening but went away and hid in the downstairs lavatory where that voice couldn't penetrate. But at the start of this war, it was my parents who were afraid, not I. Nothing happened, it was the same as if war had not been declared a fortnight before. There were no plans to evacuate my school which was fourteen miles outside the centre of London. Term had begun and things went on as usual. My father panicked and sent me to Vera. I was nearly eleven; I had taken the examination which would admit me to the Grammar School and passed it, so with that hurdle behind me he probably thought missing a term's schooling would do me no harm.

The weather was warm, summer still. Vera wore a cotton frock with a turned-down collar and cuffs on the short puff sleeves, a belt of the same white material patterned with mauve and yellow pansies, a fashion which returned without undergoing much change a few years ago. Her hair was the colour of newly cleaned brass, not in the least yellow and not 'brassy'. It was rather tightly permed and set into deep, narrow waves and small round curls. Down grew on her upper lip, pale as thistleseed and only visible at certain angles, and her arms and bare legs bore a somewhat coarser growth that showed as a fair, gleaming sheen. A complexion so pale that time and the Indian sun had reddened it, especially about the nose. Vera's eyes, like mine and my father's, Eden's and Francis's, were the intense, glowing blue of the Wedgwood Ivanhoe plates Grandmother Longley had collected and which now hung on the dining-room walls at Laurel Cottage.

The bus took us through that countryside that somehow should be dull, unmemorable, without mountains or hills or rushing streams, moorland or lake or particular vegetation yet is not dull at all but has its own quiet, deep beauty. The loveliest houses in England are there, churches big as cathedrals, meadows that Constable painted and which then had changed very little since that day, before they pulled the hedges up and made a prairie of the fields.

Daniel Stewart makes Laurel Cottage sound small and ugly. Perhaps it was. It is almost impossible to be objective about a house one knew when one was young. In our suburb, a long way from the centre of London, we inhabited a house that my father had had built to an architect's design, a 'suntrap' startlingly, daringly modern. It was art deco and might have been lifted out of the environs of Los Angeles, a cream-coloured box with a green stripe painted senselessly round it like a ribbon tying up a parcel, windows of curved glass, a flat roof and a front door whose inset panel was a setting sun with rays of orange, yellow and amber stained glass. My father was reacting against the villa on the road to Myland where he was born and the terrace on the 'wrong' side of Wanstead Flats where he and my mother lived when first they were married. I was reacting against the suntrap, whose roof leaked because it was not designed for a rainy country and down whose Hollywood walls the water had run in grey rivulets.

I loved an old house, in such a one I thought I should have liked to live. Laurel Cottage was not, of course, old enough for me. I asked Vera why she thought my grandparents hadn't bought one of the thatched cottages of which there were many. Her reply was no doubt prudent and accurate – the fire insurance was much higher on thatched cottages and the upkeep of ancient houses costly – but it seemed to me unromantic. Each time I had come to this house with my parents, or more often just my father, I had looked up at the earthenware plaque set between the upper bays and reading the date 1862 had wished it older, if only by fifty years.

Vera was a scrupulous housekeeper. Laurel Cottage had its own smell, a mingling I suppose of various soaps and polishes, the same smell in Vera's as in my grandmother's day. House smells must be passed on through the female line, for when Eden came to have a home of her own, hers smelt just the same, though ours never did. My mother was rather slapdash, pooh-poohing an excessive attention to cleaning as unintelligent. But I liked the clean, fresh scent of Vera's house, the windows whose panes were never spotted, the waxed floors, the shining, unmarked surfaces, and the flowered chintz curtains I remember as always fluttering faintly in the breeze.

Francis had gone back to school. Eden, who was still at her day school and in the sixth form, would be home at four-thirty. An enormous spread of tea had been prepared in my honour. There was as yet no shortage of food and I was never to see in that house a lack of the kind of constituents that go to make cakes and pies and biscuits. Vera had no refrigerator. Few people did in 1939. Her Victoria sponge and gingerbread, lemon-curd tarts, Banbury cakes, drop scones and almond slices were on the kitchen table covered with clean, ironed teacloths to keep off the flies. Vera stayed always thin as a rail, though eating her fair share of that rich, sweet stuff. As we carried the cakes in, arranging them on the dining-table, laying the plates on a cloth embroidered by Eden in lazy-daisy and stem stitch, Vera (having adjured me not to drop anything, she hoped I wasn't a 'butterfingers') apologized for the poor quality of the tea and the lack of variety.

'I expect your mother would have an iced cake as well. Grandma used to insist on two big cakes always and at least two kinds of biscuits.'

I assured her that my mother would have provided no such thing. Tea would probably have been sandwiches and digestives or custard creams.

'Shop-bought biscuits?' Vera said, both shocked and pleased.

In my innocence I told her I didn't know any other kind existed. The effect on her was electric. Vera, even then, used to become disproportionately excited over trivial things. The point was that to her they were not trivial.

'What, and you've had tea in this house a dozen times to my knowledge! You didn't know the biscuits were home-made? My goodness, but Grandma would turn in her grave! I can see we were wasting our time making biscuits for you. Might as well have gone down to the grocer's and bought any old packet of Maries. I wonder what Eden would say to that. I don't suppose she's tasted a shop-bought biscuit in all her life. Well, I hope our humble, home-made stuff will suit you, I'm sure I do. We're not up to these sophisticated London ways and I can't see us changing now.'

It was a way she had of stunning me. I was silenced by it and made to feel guilty while obscurely knowing the onslaught was unfair. The technique was to seize upon an innocent remark of mine, attribute to me certain sentiments which might derive from it (though I had not felt or uttered them) and then castigate me for the expressions she had put into my mouth. She would do the same, or attempt to do the same, with Francis, but he was having none of it and would give her back as good as or better than he got. But when I was a child, I knew no way of handling it but to accept and be silent. And Vera, of course, desired no reply. She expected and wanted no defence. She was simply giving vent to the strong feelings she had about many things and looking for a peg to hang her violent expressions and beliefs on. Deeply conservative, she harked back to the old ways and customs and no doubt she truly believed that to buy a packet of biscuits was to set foot on the slippery slope to decadence. Only Eden was immune from these attacks. But Eden was immune from every violent, unreasonable assault of Vera's. When she had made this one on me, repeating herself a good many times, and embroidering on her theme, she was satisfied. I said nothing but went on helping to lay the table. But I think I was scarcely there for her as a person at that point. That her victim's *feelings* might be hurt, that one might have a sense of injury or outrage at being told that one's mother was hardly doing one a kindness by encouraging such tastes, that one was wrong to inflict one's refined London palate on country cousins and that one's ideas had better undergo some sharp revisions, never occurred to her.

The table laid, the teacloths once more shrouding all the plates, Vera's manner changed again and became kindly and interested. I was congratulated on my scholarship results, complimented on the whiteness of my teeth, the colour of my eyes (the Longley blue which I could in no way have been accounted responsible for, any more than I could for my mother's purchase of biscuits), and the fact that I had no spots on my face. I must come to the window with her and watch out for Eden. Eden would get off the bus in the village street and we should see her when she turned the corner. Great Sindon is a pretty village, was prettier then before there were new buildings, traffic signs, cars parked all along the roads. It was sleepy and quiet. You could not believe there was a war on and, of course, there scarcely was yet. Someone came down the hill on horseback, strolling down if a horse can stroll. The swallows were gathering on the electric wires. I knelt on the window seat, Vera behind me craning her neck.

I was conscious of the tension that emanated from her body. It was as if her body could not contain so much, such compression, such screwing up, so that the stress overflowed into the air around her. Can I really remember that? Probably I am projecting what certainly later I knew and felt on to that time. But it is true that always with Vera there could be no relaxing, of herself or those with her because they were with her. Eden came round the corner suddenly – how would it be otherwise, how but suddenly? – and Vera cried out:

'There she is!'

My arm was not actually lifted by Vera to be waved but it would have been if I had been three or four years younger. I was merely told to wave at Eden and I obliged, though feeling that a smile alone would have come more naturally to me. I got down from the window seat and prepared to meet her.

Young girls change so much in adolescence. This is apparent not only to their seniors but to children like me. It was a year since I had seen Eden and if I had met her in the street I would not have known her. She was beautiful and she was grown-up. The Veronica Lake hairdo was not yet in fashion and she wore her hair in that style too awful ever to have been revived, the front rolled up and back into a sausage, the back hanging loose. Eden's beauty could not be spoiled by it. To me it seemed wonderfully chic. She had a gymslip on, a plain, round-neck pinafore, not one of the old box-pleated kind, a dark red blazer with her school crest on the pocket, and hanging from one shoulder, her satchel. She kissed me and called me her little niece in a very kindly way, asked me how my parents were – Vera had forgotten to mention my mother but Eden did not – and said she hoped the train journey had been pleasant. Then she went away to her room, emerging ten minutes afterwards with powder on her nose and lipstick on her lips, her school tunic changed for a skirt and blouse. She seemed even older. We sat down to Vera's enormous tea, working our way through sandwiches and cakes and buns, and tea was always to be the principal meal of the day, this first one being no festive exception. It seems strange to me now to think of those teas, the bread and butter and mountains of sweet food we ate, at least four rounds of bread each, at least one slice of cake, a series of small buns, slices, biscuits, cupcakes. None of us put on weight or came out in spots. And we ate like that every day as a matter of course at five o'clock, Vera encouraging Eden and now me to stuff ourselves, saying it was all good, wholesome and home-made food. She seemed to have the idea that everything bought in a shop was bad for you and everything made at home good for you, a widely held view responsible, no doubt, for many an untimely death.

Eden said she would teach me to make puff pastry.

'Will you?' I said but perhaps in a doubtful tone.

'Wouldn't you like to learn?'

I didn't know. It was a subject on which I had no opinion. I was not even clear about what puff pastry was and I believe I confused it with the choux from which éclairs are made. My mother wasn't much of a cook and both my parents disapproved of girls being taught domestic science at school, my father, however, at the same time believing such things would come naturally as, in his innocence, he thought they had to his sisters.

'What do you like to cook?' asked Eden.

When we are old, we know how to answer. We know how we should have answered when we were children. I should have said I'm a little girl, and I've never so much as tried to toast a bit of bread without having my mother say, leave that, I'll do that. We had registered for food rationing though it was not to start until the following January. I should have said that if predictions were right in a little while there wouldn't be anything to make puff pastry with. But that would have been rude, even ruder than not thanking her for her birthday present . . .

'I can't,' I said, taking another lemon-curd tart for support, 'actually cook anything.'

They both registered the kind of shock that is not altogether surprised. A barrage of questions began as to what I *could* do, and this did not mean theorems and French verbs. Having elicited from me that I could neither knit nor sew, crochet or embroider, Vera sighed as heavily and looked as despondent as if I had said I could not master the alphabet or control my bodily functions. She said, incredibly:

'Well, I'm sure I don't know what kind of a wife you'll make.'

But Eden, always apparently kinder, told me not to worry about it. No doubt I had never had the opportunity to learn but now I was at Laurel Cottage – a place she made sound like an institute of good housekeeping – there were all sorts of things she would teach me. After that they ceased to give me their undivided attention, indeed they gave me scarcely any more attention at all, and began a mysterious, diffused conversation about people who lived in the village whom I had never heard of. One of the difficult things about my Great Sindon relatives was their way of assuming you knew exactly whom they meant when they referred to someone or other and when people called that you would know who they were without being introduced. This would have been all very well if they explained when you confessed your ignorance but instead they became very scathing, at least Vera did, and told you that certainly you did know, of course you knew, but due to some carelessness or forgetfulness well within your control – simple indifference probably – the identity of so-and-so had been allowed to slip your mind. And this assumption that the rest of the world was completely *au fait* with their ways extended to custom and habits, so that without being told one was expected to know what time to get up, when to use the bathroom, where the back-door key hung, when the milkman came, who was Eden's best friend, what subjects she was taking for her Higher

School Certificate, the vicar's name and have by heart the timetable of the Colchester bus.

I had expected great things of my stay with Vera, a stay of necessarily indeterminate length and governed by whether or not bombs started falling on the north-eastern suburbs of London. Homesickness I had considered as a possibility, for I had never stayed away from my parents before, but I thought this would be compensated for by my enthusiastic reception into a kind of sisterhood with Vera and Eden, I making a welcome third in their lonely sorority. My Uncle Gerald, I knew, was away somewhere in the north of England with his regiment. Francis was at school. I was old for my age, people frequently said so, and I thought my aunts, one only a few years my senior, would treat me as another adult, another sister even. It was a vision or dream I was never entirely to abandon, in spite of constant disillusionment. Desperately I wanted to belong. They had the power, those two, of making their world – narrow, confined and bourgeois, as I now see it – an esoteric, intensely desirable place, rather like an exclusive club with unimaginably strict conditions for membership and with rules no outsider could live up to. Sitting at tea that first day, not knowing what a weary haul was ahead of me, what attempts to enter and qualify, what failures, I listened attentively, hoping, though hoping in vain, for some inquiry to be put to me, asking my opinion instead of the kind of question I finally got:

'Do you always eat with your right hand?'

I had never thought about it. I looked at Vera, holding aloft (in my right hand) the last of the drop scones.

'I don't know.'

'Left hand for eating, right hand for drinking,' said Vera, adjusting as she spoke the positions of my plate and my cup and saucer.

I helped her with the dishes. My mother had told me that while I was at Laurel Cottage I must try to be of some service to Vera, and at a loss to know what service, had suggested drying dishes. Conversation had come to a stop, for Eden had retreated to the living-room with a book to read for homework, and talking was always easier when she was present. I think it was at this point that I was conscious of the homesickness beginning.

We joined Eden. We had the wireless on. At ten to eight Vera suggested that in ten minutes' time I go to bed. It had not crossed my mind I should go to bed before they did. Nine-thirty was my bedtime at home and that only when I had to go to school in the morning. There would be no school here.

'I was always in bed before eight when I was your age,' Eden told me. Her voice was sweet and low-pitched. It may be my imagination that makes me say it often had a vague note as if the speaker were not much interested in what she was saying or in the person to whom she was saying it.

'Children always make a fuss about bedtime,' said Vera.

'You mean Francis. I'm sure I never did.'

'No, I don't think you ever did, Eden. But you were different from other children in so many ways. Come along now, Faith. It's starting to get dark.'

In two months' time it would start to get dark at five!

'Good-night, little niece,' said Eden. 'You'll find you'll fall asleep as soon as your head touches the pillow.'

Nothing could have made me feel more thoroughly excluded from the sisterhood.

I was to sleep in Francis's room, though on subsequent visits always in Eden's. There was nothing of his about as far as I could see, nothing to show me that this was the bedroom of a boy of my own age. Artifacts made by Vera which proliferated about the house were not lacking here – embroidered cushion covers, seat covers in petit point, pictures made out of silver paper, a cross-stitch bell-pull, a rag rug. Perhaps Francis's own things had been put away in my honour. What had not was a round metal clock that stood on the mantelpiece.

I was aware as soon as I was inside the bedroom with the door closed of the loud, metallic ticking this clock made. When Vera had brought me up here earlier with my suitcase I had not noticed it.

I unpacked and put my clothes away, rather intimidated by the hangers in the wardrobe, all of which had covers on them of ruched satin in various colours, and each a lavender sachet attached to its hook. I put on my dressing-gown and went to the bathroom, the sounds from downstairs making my homesickness return in a wave. Vera and Eden were chatting away in an animated fashion and every now and then Eden laughed. It was quite unlike the way they had behaved while I was with them, lively and relaxed and somehow *cosy*, and the conclusion was inescapable that I had been sent early to bed because they could hardly wait to be rid of me.

The problem of the clock, too, began to loom large. I thought I shouldn't be able to sleep with that clock in the room and I quickly discovered that, short of breaking it, there is no way of stopping a clock of that sort once it has been wound up.

The book I had with me distracted me for a while but then I became nervous lest Vera or Eden saw the light under my door. Somehow, young as I was, I already knew that, though they had sent me to bed because they were tired of my company, so could scarcely care whether I slept or sat up all night reading provided I were out of the way, nevertheless they would not admit this, they never, never would, but would insist that the bedtime they had ordained was for my own health and well-being. Therefore they had better not see my light still on at nearly 9.30. Once it was out, the ticking seemed to grow much louder. The room was not dark, for the moon had come up, a glowing, yellow harvest moon. It afforded enough light for my purposes . . . I got out of bed, set one of the cushions on the seat of the pale blue and gilt Lloyd Loom chair and stuck the clock on it, having first wrapped it up in my dressing-gown.

The ticking was muffled but still audible. The awful feeling came over me that I should never be able to sleep and that this would not be for one night only but many, many nights, a hundred perhaps. I would be trapped in here with this clock, unable to escape it, sleeplessly suffering its tick like someone subjected to the Chinese water torture. With Hans Andersen's tale of the princess and the pea I was familiar, and it seemed to me that if the princess's discomfort had stemmed from an auditory rather than a tactile source it would have made a better story. For a while I thought about this, turning over in my mind what sound might be as disturbing to a princess as a pea buried under the twenty mattresses she is lying on. But it was only a momentary distraction from the ticking of the clock which thumped away through the folds of my dressing-gown.

Vera and Eden came up to bed. On the landing outside my room they kept their voices down so as not to wake me.

'Good-night, darling.'

'Good-night, darling. Sleep well.'

The landing light went out. I picked up the rag rug off the floor and wrapped it round my dressing-gown, round the clock. The muted tick was rather worse. I had reached that desperate point – often to be experienced later in hotel bedrooms – when the only way to escape the noise seemed to be to leave the room. I was no more able to do this in Laurel Cottage than I was at the Plaza in New York when an all-night party was going on next door. At the Plaza I made frequent fruitless calls to reception who were polite, willing but unhelpful. Here reception was asleep and would not, I sensed, have in any case taken kindly to a complaint of this sort. I opened the window and looked out.

Moonlight flooded Vera's beautiful garden. It had never been much of a garden in my grandparents' time but Vera had re-made it, replacing the flowering currants and sumacs with viburnums of esoteric varieties, with a *Cornus alba* and a smoke bush and many herbs. Of course I was not to know that then but its beauty I could appreciate, the refinement that had come to it by the substitution of these rarer plants for the common ones. The moonlight bathed whitely the leaves, brilliant gold at this season by day, of a delicate, fluttering, man-high liquidambar. The window sill was a broad one, made of stone. I unwrapped the clock, placed it on the sill and pulled down the sash.

Some momentary qualms came to me while I was doing this that Vera might come into the room in the morning with, say, a cup of tea. Or for some other, unknown, reason. I felt she would be sure to notice the absence of the clock. But with luck, anyway, I should waken before this happened.

The peace was so beautiful that I tried to stay awake simply for the pleasure of listening to the silence. This, of course, had the effect of sending me to sleep. When I woke up in the morning at about seven-thirty, I remembered the clock and fetched it in, beaded all over with dew but still ticking. There was no reason, I thought, why I shouldn't do this every night. Rain might present problems but I would worry about that when the time came. I began to wish I knew the proper time to get up and if I went into the bathroom, would I be keeping Eden, who certainly had a prior claim, out of it? The house was silent. I debated what to do and after about ten minutes, having decided that Vera and Eden were still in bed, I got up and went into the bathroom to wash. Later on Vera was to ask me why I hadn't had a bath and to adjure me to take a daily bath and not be 'lackadaisical' about it. There was still no sound in the house.

The clock back on the mantelpiece, wiped dry on my handkerchief, I made my way downstairs. The house was very neat, all the cushions in the living-room plumped up. The dining-room was empty. I pushed open the kitchen door, hardly knowing why since I was scarcely capable of making a cup of tea, still less my own breakfast. They were both in there, silently eating shredded wheat out of Woods Ware rectangular bowls. I jumped, a start observed by Vera, who seldom missed anything of that sort.

'My goodness, aren't you nervous! You shouldn't be like that at your age.'

Eden said that I had nearly missed her. She had to leave at eight-fifteen. Her voice was full of reproach and the implication that to come down to breakfast at this hour was to show a lazy disposition. Vera, who had sprung up when I came in and was now tensely poised between larder and stove, asked me what I should like for breakfast. A variety of foods was reeled off at high speed: poached eggs, boiled eggs, fried eggs, bacon, cereal, toast. There was, however, no porridge. Porridge, she said, was too much trouble to make when neither she nor Eden was likely to eat it. I said I hated porridge.

'It's a pity to take that attitude about wholesome food,' Vera said.

'But you said . . .' I began.

'I said, I said. I hope you're not going to take me up on every little thing I say, Faith. I don't suppose I am as logical as you and your mother. I don't have the time, for one thing. Now then, have you decided what you'd like for your breakfast or shall I sit down and finish my cereal while you think about it?'

I said I would have a boiled egg. Vera began moving about with over-burdened resignation to get out a saucepan, an egg from the rack. Eden jumped up.

'Let me do it. I've finished. Sit down, darling, you're up and down like a Jack-in-the-box.'

Eden, in gymslip, her hair tied back with a black silk bow, bustled prettily about, buttering 'soldiers' for me.

'Three minutes all right?'

'Could I have five, please?'

'Well, of course you *could*. But that will be a hard-boiled egg. Are you sure you're going to want to eat a hard-boiled egg?'

It wouldn't be, but this time I didn't make the mistake of arguing. Instead I said I would watch the egg and take it out of the water myself. Eden possibly thought this a good moment to begin the cooking lessons but Vera demurred.

'She'll only drop it on the floor, Eden, and you know the mess an egg makes.' Before I had time for indignant denials, Vera turned to me and said in a voice both scathing and reproachful, 'I'm sorry you don't like Eden's little clock. Eden put that in your bedroom herself because she thought it would be just the thing for someone without a wristwatch.'

'Don't you like it, Faith?' said Eden.

I could say nothing. Paralysis seized me.

'Well, she can't do. I mean very obviously she can't do. If she liked it she wouldn't put it outside the window, would she? Yes, I know, my dear, it is most extraordinary, but I assure you that's what she did. Your little clock was most definitely not a success. When I went down the garden first thing this morning, what did I see but your clock on Francis's window sill outside the window. It was a mercy it didn't get rained on, that's all I can say.'

If only it had been all she could say! She began describing the clock minutely as if neither Eden nor I had seen it before, speculating about the cost of it, whether this had been five shillings and sixpence or as much as five shillings and elevenpence, whether Eden had bought it this year or last year and whether the purchase had been made in Colchester or Sudbury. Eden interrupted to ask why I had put the clock outside the window.

'Was it just because you didn't like it, Faith?'

Did they think me completely mad?

'I didn't like it ticking,' I said.

'You didn't like it ticking?' Eden spoke as if I had revealed an incomprehensible phobia. My egg was forgotten, boiling away audibly but screened from view by Eden leaning against the stove. 'But clocks always do tick, except electric ones.'

'I know they do.' Does it sound absurd when I say that by now I was near to tears? 'I don't like them ticking. I can't help it. I put the clock outside the window so I shouldn't hear it ticking.'

'I never heard of anything like it,' said Vera.

'Why didn't you come and tell us if you didn't like it ticking?'

'I didn't want to disturb you.'

'Surely it would have been better to disturb me,' said Eden very gently and reasonably, 'than to have ruined my clock.'

'I haven't ruined it. It's still going.'

'There's no need to cry about it,' Vera said. 'Crying won't help. Now what's happening to that egg? That egg's been boiling away for at least ten minutes.'

Eden fished it out and put it in my eggcup. 'I said you wouldn't like it hard-boiled. My goodness, I must fly. Look at the time!'

I was left alone with Vera. She continued to talk for some minutes about clocks, the price of them, the inevitability of their ticking, digressing from her main theme to say what a pity it was I was so nervy at my age. I had never heard of projection then but now I recognize this as projection. My egg would be uneatable. I must let her do me another. Incapable herself of taking offence, she expected me to be unaffected by the drubbing I had received. I dried the dishes for her. When I went up to my bedroom I found that the clock had gone. Where it had disappeared to I never discovered but I did not see it again during the rest of my stay.

My visit was not destined to be a long one. The phony war soon showed itself to be phony, people talked of it all being over by Christmas, and my father came to Great Sindon and fetched me home after a fortnight. It was five months later, in the following March, that Eden sent me a five-shilling postal order for my birthday. Vera had come up to London for the day round about that time and presented me with two half-crowns, so I had been able to thank her in person.

The reason I didn't write to thank Eden was not because I was lazy or badly brought up or disliked writing letters or didn't like getting five shillings. I didn't write because I didn't know what to say. I could think of absolutely nothing to say to Eden beyond the bare thanks. My paramount feeling at that time for her and Vera equally was trepidation. One way and another they had humiliated me and beside them I felt humble, hopeless, unable in any way to match up. If I wrote there would be something wrong with the letter. The grammar would be bad or the handwriting indecipherable or the mode of address wrong. Of course I had written to Eden before, always signing my letters 'love from'. But would that be changed now we had spent so much time in each other's company and I had received so many lessons, practical and metaphysical, in the conduct of life? Should it be 'much love' or 'lots of love' or, because of her evident disappointment in me about the clock among many other matters, a cooler 'yours affectionately'? I didn't know so I did nothing. Eden's blast came to my father a month later.

It made him rather sad. I think it gave him a bad day.

'I wish you'd written to Eden,' was all he said at first, but he said it several times, and then, 'You will write to Eden now, won't you?'

I never did write. The incident upset me. Of course I should never be able to face Eden again or speak to her and as for that inclusion in the sisterhood, it was out of the question. The letter distanced us and for a while seemed to double the six years that separated our ages. At that time I thought only that I must be at fault, I imperfect, seeing in the conduct of their lives only a standard almost unattainable by me.

I thought – yes, it's true I thought about them a lot. In my fantasy they remained eternally the same, following the same quiet daily routine in the sweet-smelling, spotless house, eating the huge teas, stitching and embroidering, kissing each other good-night, two fastidious women behaving as women should. One day, if I tried hard, I might catch up with them, be like them, be welcomed in.

– 5 –

Some of this I have written down for Daniel Stewart, a synopsis of it really, for I have to bear in mind that it is not my story he wants but Vera's. Which brings me to the family secret. Am I going to tell him about it or not?

Of course it isn't really a secret. It is known, it is recorded and documented somewhere. For instance there must be a police record of it. I have no doubt the police keep records of this kind of thing for the sixty years it has been and probably for longer. The little girl's family – or should I say her collateral descendants? – they know it, and so do those surviving members of my own family. Or do they? Francis must, for Francis always knew everything, almost before it had happened sometimes. Neither Vera nor Eden ever spoke of it to me. It was my mother, not my father, who told me. She was angry at something Vera had said or done and suddenly she said she had something to tell me that showed how absurd it was of my father to keep holding his sisters up as paragons of virtue. Poor man, he was to be disillusioned soon enough.

Obviously Stewart doesn't know of it. If he did, he would hardly have left it out of that biographical chapter of his. Re-reading this chapter, it seems to me that he has left out a lot of things I think important, things essential to a true examination of Vera's character. I suppose he doesn't know of them and I must tell him. An example would be her illness at the age of fifteen, a few months after Eden was born. For a while the doctors thought it was meningitis. Today they would be more likely to diagnose one of those viral infections that do such strange things to people. Vera lay in bed for weeks (my father once told me), at first with a high temperature and delirium, later with her temperature normal each day but rising steeply in the evenings. One of her lungs collapsed. She lost a stone in weight. And then, quite suddenly, she was well again, with no after-effects except perhaps that extreme thinness that never changed. My grandmother had nursed her devotedly, necessarily depriving the new baby of attention in order to do so, but once she was well Vera took care of Eden more and more, becoming a second mother to her. And that brings me back to the secret again. Is it possible that Vera's illness had nothing to do with a virus and if it was psychosomatic nothing to do with jealousy over the new baby but brought about instead by the Kathleen March business? By guilt or remorse, possibly, but more probably in my view by simple misery that she had been blamed and ostracized.

Nor does Stewart mention the storm. It was Eden who told me about it, for this was a story she was fond of repeating. The first time I heard it – it was to be told me again on her wedding day – we were in the garden at Walbrooks one summer in the middle of the war. Eden must have been home on leave. She was wearing a dress made out of two old ones which Vera had contrived for her. It had a pink and white floral skirt and a blue bodice with pink and white collar and cuffs. Her hair was rolled back from the forehead and pinned while the rest of it hung down in a page-boy bob. On her right hand she wore her mother's wedding-ring, Eden being the kind of girl who always does wear her dead mother's wedding-ring.

Helen and Vera had gone into the house. Eden and I sat on the terrace in deckchairs. It was a sultry day with thunder rumbling and no doubt it was the sound of this which brought the story to Eden's mind.

'You see that hummock down there at the bottom of the lawn?'

I had sometimes wondered what it was, a swelling under the turf as if rocks were pushing through the soil, though there were no rocks in that countryside of gently undulating hills.

'There used to be a tree there, an enormous horse chestnut – you know, a conker tree. Well, when I was a baby in my pram – has nobody really ever told you this, Faith?'

'I don't think so. I don't know what it is yet.'

'You would if they'd told you. Naturally Vera wouldn't but I should have thought your father – aren't people peculiar? Anyway, as I said, I was a baby in my pram and the pram was under that tree. Helen was in India, of course. This was her grandparents' house then. I expect you knew that, didn't you?'

I wasn't sure but thought it wiser not to admit this.

'Mother and Dad and Vera and your father and me had all come over on our annual visit. They used to walk – can you imagine? – all the way from Myland. It must be six miles. Mother put me under the chestnut tree. It started to thunder and suddenly Vera had a sort of premonition of disaster. They were all eating their tea in the kitchen – trust those Richardsons to make them eat in the kitchen, they always looked down on Dad – and it had a window you could see the lawn from. Well, Mother was keeping an eye on me through the window as you can imagine, more or less deciding to run out and get me if it started raining, and they all thought Vera had gone mad when she jumped up and dashed outside without a word. You know what perfect manners Vera has, so you can see it would have to be something exceptional to make her leave a table without asking her hostess's permission. She went tearing down the garden and snatched me out of my pram and started to come back again when there was the most enormous flash of lightning like a bomb falling in the garden. That's what Mother said, though she hadn't really seen any bombs; I mean, they didn't in the first war, not like we have. Well, the lightning struck that tree and shattered it into thousands of bits. It knocked Vera over with me in her arms, but she wasn't hurt and I wasn't, apart from a few bruises. There was nothing left of the pram and nothing of the conker tree except that stump you can see under

61

the grass and about two feet of trunk but they kept on picking bits of tree up out of the flowerbeds for years. Still do, I expect.'

'So Vera saved your life?'

'Oh yes, I owe her my life. I do wonder John didn't tell you, it's quite peculiar of him.'

So if that illness of Vera's was psychosomatic (as now for the first time occurs to me it might have been), a way of diverting her mother's attention from the new baby to herself, a disease real enough in its physiological symptoms but brought on by jealousy, she was over that resentment within a few months. By then she loved her sister enough to risk her own life to save the baby's. She even loved her enough to forget her table manners.

I shall tell Stewart about the storm and I shall tell it as Eden told it to me so that he can use direct speech, a much more effective way, I should think, of writing a book like his. And I may also tell him about Vera finding old Mrs Hislop dead, even though this may not be really relevant. Why were none of these stories ever told to Chad Hamner? Or were they told him but he didn't listen or quickly forgot what he had been told, his attention, as I later knew, being elsewhere?

Vera used to go about visiting old people, a kind of survival from the days of the gentry doing good works in the parish (though the Longleys could never have aspired to gentility) and forerunner of community service. One afternoon she went round to Mrs Hislop's and found her dead. It must have been a bad shock for the girl who had arrived with a bundle of cast-off clothing and the cakes she had just made. Vera told me about it one day when she was in a rare expansive mood.

We were out walking with Jamie in his pushchair, just she and I, Eden at this time being in London with old Lady Rogerson. I was doing the pushing and Jamie had fallen asleep, the way he always did the moment the pushchair started to move so that he inevitably missed all the things you wanted to point out to him – horses in a meadow, a cat on a wall, a fire-engine. I can see him now, his round, peach-like cheek and the thick, dark lashes lying on it, his hair the true Longley gold, as yet uncut because Vera couldn't bear the idea of cutting off his curls. We came back home a way I had never been before, though by then I had regularly been visiting Sindon every year for five or six years. This was a lane that led nowhere, that petered out after a hundred yards and became a footpath. Vera and I had been forced to take this path after finding the road we intended to use blocked by flood water. It wound along the edge of a dreary meadow, past disused gravel workings, but this wasn't why Vera had shunned it so long. The cottage came in sight and she laughed a little to hide her embarrassment or perhaps some more powerful emotion.

'I never come this way if I can help it. It's silly after so long but I can't seem to alter my feelings.'

Today Mrs Hislop's cottage has been smartened up, all the studwork exposed and the roof, which used to be tiled, thatched. A teacher at the University of Essex lives there with his wife and son. When I saw it that first time, just after the war, it was a tumbledown lump of lath and plaster, the windows patched with corrugated iron, the garden overgrown with nettles and an old black and green Morris Ten disintegrating among them. Vera said Mrs Hislop used to collect all sorts of fungi in the fields and cook them for herself and people warned her it would be the death of her, she would kill herself. And when Vera found her, tip-toeing fearfully into the silent cottage, calling out, knowing there was going to be something dreadful behind the bedroom door, the old woman's body was bloated and swollen up with what they used to call dropsy, though she had never shown signs of this in life.

Mrs Hislop hadn't vomited or shown any of the usual signs of fungal poisoning. There was an inquest and the verdict was death from natural causes, though the village all knew she had poisoned herself, Vera said, if they didn't know how or what with. She hurried me past the cottage, not looking back. I think this shows her as a sensitive person, someone to whom place and atmosphere were evocative of painful memory, so why was she apparently indifferent to the spot where the little girl's body was found? For years she kept clear of Loom Lane and Mrs Hislop's cottage yet never attempted to avoid Church Meadow or the churchyard itself and when she went to church entered the churchyard as often by the lychgate as by the drive between the avenue of yews. An explanation could be that she felt some degree of guilt over Mrs Hislop, for not calling on her the evening before as she had promised, for instance, or for failing to tell anyone what she, and perhaps she alone, very well knew, that Mrs Hislop's eyes were shrouded with cataracts by then and she was too blind to tell one fungus from another. Guilt might account for her revulsion from the cottage whereas she might feel no guilt over

Kathleen March, being entirely blameless in the matter. But how could she be entirely blameless when the child had been in her care?

Stewart will want pointers in the early life of Vera to what came later, to the long, slow course of poisoning she embarked on and, when that failed, the sharp, savage finality. His postulation, I suppose, will be that murderers don't murder out of the blue. There must be something to lead up to it, a tendency to violence, an indifference to the value of the lives of others. But both Vera and Eden have descendants who have a better right than I to decide whether the secret should or should not be told, a better right even though they may not know the story. Rather than speak Kathleen March's name to Stewart (who, with that to guide him, would begin his own research), I must find out how Jamie feels about it and perhaps how Elizabeth and Giles feel. Writing to their father will be useless as Francis has never been known to answer letters from anyone in the family.

The Battle of Britain, the few in conflict up there above the heads of the many (in which Andrew took part), was what sent me back to Sindon in August 1940. I wanted very much to go, though most people would find that hard to believe after what I have said about my previous visit. My reasons had nothing to do with Vera, or rather, Vera as drawback was to be weighed off against the obvious advantages, seeing Eden, sleeping in a bed in a bedroom – at home we had an air-raid shelter in the house which I slept in while my parents' bed was in our living-room – the countryside. It was this last which had reconciled me to staying on last time. The rapturous pleasure some children, especially girls I think, take in a beautiful countryside in summertime is passed over or forgotten altogether by adults. Of course it is what Wordsworth is talking about in the Immortality Ode. Growing up destroys it. Meadow, grove and stream, the earth and every common sight lost the dream's glory and freshness in adolescence and after that one is just fond of country life. At least, so it was with me. I took intense delight in the fields and woods of Sindon, the birds and butterflies, when I was eleven, the fruits borne on trees that many would say bear no fruit – sycamores and field maples and alders – the formation of leaves, the life cycles of small creatures, a spider trundling its great egg, a butterfly emerging from its chrysalis, a string of toad spawn, a cinnabar moth alighting on a ragwort flower. All gone now. I do not see these things, or if I do there is no joy in them; I have no time to stand and stare. But then I did. I found them, or some of them, in the open areas of our still half-built-up suburb where further development had been stopped by the war. Even then I was very good at the art of half-closing my eyes and thus not seeing what I did not want to see, in this case, houses, in others, disquieting manifestations of the emotions. But at Great Sindon there was no need to close one's eyes. Laurel Cottage was one of the last houses to have been built there. It was all unspoilt pastoral glory.

And I wanted to be with Eden once more. It seems an eleven-year-old must have a crush on someone. Separation nourished my hero-worship. I even began to see the letter as just. After all, it was a reproach to my father, not me. Perhaps he should have taught me manners, had me taught to cook and sew and be womanly. Vera had once or twice said she could not see what good all those Latin declensions would do me, and although I would have taken very little notice of that, coming from where it did, Eden had smilingly agreed, telling us with Vera's very obvious approval how she herself had been so hopeless at Latin that she had stopped it after two terms. She was beautiful, elegant, poised, self-confident. Although a young girl, only eighteen, she was the sister, not the niece, of grown-ups and treated by them with the respect due to a contemporary. She had left school and got a job. On her I would model myself. Travelling down to Colchester on the train, I wondered if her hair were still as gold and if it was, whether I could put peroxide on my own without anyone finding out.

Somewhere over Essex a dogfight was going on. A fighter with smoke streaming from it tumbled out of the sky, its motion like a leaf falling. The passengers crowded to the windows, peering out and up. There was no man floating down on a parachute. He was still inside, whoever he was, burning inside there. It was a Messerschmitt, the passengers said, not one of ours, not a Spitfire or Hurricane. The sky emptied and the sun went on shining. Vera was at the station to meet me, to kiss the air an inch away from my cheek, to pronounce on my increased height, to grumble afresh about the weight of my suitcase.

This time, though, I was to remain for many months. Air attacks on London began that September and three months later, in one single night, there were 1,725 fires in the city. My father came down and saw the headmistress and got me into the school Eden had been to. By then I had made a friend in the village, a girl who also went there, so I was happy to have Anne to travel back and forth with and happy, as people of that age are, to conform. Meanwhile it was holiday time and Eden was waiting at Laurel Cottage. 'Getting the tea,' Vera said. That morning, in my honour, she had made a sponge as only Eden could make it, beating the eggs for no less than ten minutes.

At Laurel Cottage, too, though I had forgotten about this, was Francis.

Until Jamie came along, he was my only cousin, my mother's sister and brother both being childless. As small children we had sometimes met, played together no doubt, perhaps got on, I don't remember. He was about a year older than I. Of his presence in the house Vera being Vera of course said nothing, no doubt expecting me to know he would be there, as perhaps I should have done. After all, it was school holidays for him as well as me and where else would he be but at home? A good many other places, I was later to learn, but that was later too.

It is not hard to remember but it is hard to re-feel the sensations I had when I walked into the house and there was Francis in the living-room with Eden. A sinking of the heart, something not far from panic, an idea that now all would be spoiled. Why? Why did I mind so much? Why was I so certain in those first few seconds that he and I would dislike each other and, worse than that, that he would somehow always make me feel awkward, inept and stupid? In those first seconds, too, I was afraid of him, in a defensive way, drawing all my soft parts in under my shell.

Vera's perfect manners did not extend to re-introducing us to each other. Nor did Eden's. And perhaps I was ridiculous to expect anything. We were cousins, we were family – what kind of paranoid little prig was I that I wanted to be told things about him and him to be told things about me, for something we might have in common to be found, and for Vera or Eden, by means of a sympathy for others they conspicuously lacked, start us communicating? Instead I stood there silently, wondering – of all absurd speculations – where I was going to sleep. I knew I wasn't going to be able to bring myself to ask.

He was a handsome boy. If you want to know what he looked like, then get hold of some numbers of the old *Boy's Own Paper* or a late-nineteenth-century novel for boys with illustrations. Francis looked like the prototype of the young hero, the clean-limbed young Englishman, captain of the first eleven, head prefect, later on rugger Blue, kind to fags and a stern putter-down of injustices, of blue blood but modest about it, in American parlance, the perfect WASP, a youthful Sir Henry Curtis. Nowadays we would say he most resembled the actor Anthony Andrews. He was blond, his features chiselled, the jawline cloven out of teak with a sharp knife, his eyes a piercing blue, the lips not narrow but generously full. Apart from all this, he looked a lot like Eden. In appearance they were nearer to twins than my father and Vera, for Francis at thirteen was already taller than Eden.

We all sat down to tea, Vera embarking at once on praise of the large circular cake, its top scattered all over with someone's whole week's sugar ration. Eden giggled. Though a year older, she seemed less grown-up, less dignified. I could see, too, that others were not inevitably excluded from the charmed circle of two composed of her and Vera. And yet – no, I am wrong there. Now it was Eden and Francis who were a pair and Eden and Vera, but they were never a trio. Francis's behaviour to his mother I will go into later, though even at that first meeting, in those initial hours it shocked and intrigued me. He and Eden together were strange. They mystified and in a way alarmed me. I didn't know why, I was too young. The glances they exchanged, Eden's way of giggling at what he said, the whispering that brought reproaches from Vera to him if not to her, the apparent intense pleasure they took in each other's company until Eden seemed to recollect herself and become once more Vera's partisan – all this was outside my understanding. It threatened me (as the psychotherapists say) in that corner of my being that yearned, and still yearns, to belong. It seemed to set before me a standard of grown-up conduct to which I could never, I was sure, aspire. Years were to pass before I could analyse and solve the mystery. It was that they behaved like secret lovers.

But that evening I was at sea, drifting in an open boat on the deepest and least charted Longley waters. Conversation at tea was devoted to Eden's new job but since everyone expected me to know what I knew nothing of, the nature of the job, the means by which she had got it, the name of her employer, her starting date and so on, I couldn't join in. Without much success I decided to listen and gather what I could. Eden, now school was behind her, wore heavy make-up, one of those tinted liquid foundations that had not long come on to the market – or under the counter to be begged and queued for – bright scarlet lipstick, gingery brown pencil on her plucked eyebrows and a daring streak of blue shadow on her eyelids. Her hairstyle was elaborate, a construction in which the metal grips were visible, which was no drawback to chic in 1940.

The question of whether I should still be sent to bed at eight o'clock was one that I had been anxious about. Francis's presence, though in so many ways upsetting, eased my mind a little. They could hardly send me to bed and let him stay up, and somehow the two of us being sent to bed in the same ignominious fashion would be preferable to my isolated banishment. But soon after tea Francis disappeared.

I dried dishes. Vera and Eden continued to talk about Eden's job which I had by then gathered was something in a solicitor's office, answering the telephone and telling clients where to wait, and she had got it through General Chatteriss, who had been at school with the senior partner. I was relieved to have learned so much without asking. It meant that when the subject came up I should not have to show my ignorance and be castigated for it.

Francis, of course, was not expected to wash or dry dishes, or make his bed or do anything around the house. We returned to the living-room and I expected him to be where we had left him, lying in an armchair reading *Gone with the Wind*. Vera reacted violently (today we should say over-reacted) to his absence. Her face grew red. She stopped in the doorway and said loudly to Eden:

'He's doing it again, you see!'

'Darling, it's only ten to seven.' Eden, I had noticed, was coming to call Vera 'darling' more and more often.

'He takes advantage of our being out of the way.'

This interchange mystified me. Francis was free, it was early. Why shouldn't he go out about the village somewhere if he wished? No one said any more about it for the time being. Vera and Eden were like Victorian ladies with their 'work'. Their leisure they spent facing each other across a table or sitting in armchairs on either side of the fireplace, sewing or crocheting or doing embroidery. To their tasks they now settled, Eden rather an incongruous sight with her elaborate hairstyle and bright make-up occupied at such a Goody Two-Shoes pursuit as drawn-thread work on a handkerchief hem. But to me then everything she did was admirable and worthy of being copied and when she found me a crochet hook and ball of wool and set me to 'making squares' to be sewn together for blankets, I happily complied. Vera was embroidering a design for a firescreen, a lady in bonnet and crinoline with a basket over her arm. Crinoline ladies had been a very popular subject for this kind of art in the thirties and in Laurel Cottage they were all over the place on cushions and teacosies and nightdress cases.

I should have preferred to be out in the garden and the fields. But I feared to go in the light of what had been said of Francis's disappearance. Besides there was delicious pleasure in being at one with the grown-ups, performing a similar task to theirs and being helped by kind Eden who from time to time adjusted my clumsy hands, checked a tendency on my part to make uneven stitches and finally, when a square was complete, remarked:

'That's really quite good for a beginner!'

Vera had laid her embroidery aside to write a letter. Sneaking a look, I saw it was to her husband for it began 'Dear Gerry'. Where he was stationed she didn't know – 'somewhere in England' was all she was told unless he could indicate the place by hints subtle enough to get past the censor. The time was coming up to eight and in defiance of it I began another square but I underrated Eden, who heard the church clock chimes begin one minute before the hands of the living-room clock reached eight. She tucked her needle into the linen, folded it, laid it on the arm of the chair, sharp scissors on top, perfectly aligned, stood up smiling at me.

'Well, little niece, you're going to share my room so I'd better show you where you're to sleep.'

I followed her to the door, disappointed, but with compensation for my disappointment in that I should be sleeping in her room. Vera, however, suddenly jumped up, pushed past us and ran up the stairs. I heard her running from room to room, banging doors. Eden hesitated. She didn't look at me. Then she opened the door and we stood at the foot of the stairs. Vera came running down them, her face flushed, that look about her eyes and mouth of anger boiling up.

'He's not in the house! I told you, he's doing it again.'

She threw open the front door, ran down to the gate which she hung over, calling 'Francis, Francis!' to the left, and then 'Francis, Francis!' to the right.

We started up towards Eden's room. Vera's voice could be heard, calling Francis's name, first in the front, then in the back. His bedroom door was shut and Eden opened it to look inside but of course he wasn't in there. I didn't ask and she didn't explain. Her own room was extremely neat and tidy with lace mats for her hairbrush and various pots and jars to stand on, the predominating colour pink, the pictures on the walls including a coloured photograph of the statue of Peter Pan in Kensington Gardens. The beds were not side by side but placed at angles to each other and as far apart as the size of the room allowed. There was, I saw to my great relief, no clock.

My suitcase was already there waiting for me to unpack it. I was to hang my things in a certain allotted area of the wardrobe, Eden explained, and I could have the second drawer down in the chest.

Vera's feet pounded up the stairs. She threw open the door. Children are embarrassed by signs of strong emotion in adults and Vera was showing strong emotion at that moment, her face bright red with tears lying on it, her mouth working, her body screwed up spring-like, her hands held up in clenched fists. Eden went up to her, laid a hand on her arm.

'Why get yourself in such a state, darling?'

'He does it on purpose!'

'Well, of course he does. You should take no notice.' Eden remembered me, waiting awkwardly, wondering what had happened, what could have happened to bring about such intense, furious, hysterical misery.

'Good-night, Faith dear. I won't disturb you when I come up. I'll get undressed in the dark.'

She closed the door, shutting me on one side of it, herself and Vera and Vera's mysterious agony on the other. I wondered, as I unpacked, if she thought Francis had run away or even been kidnapped. Would the police be called? Was I in on the first scene of some dreadful family tragedy? I went out to the bathroom and saw his door wide open, the bed turned down – Vera turned everyone's bed down after tea, taking off and folding the counterpanes – the room empty. On the mantelpiece the noisy clock was ticking away.

Downstairs Vera was crying. I lay in bed, bewildered by the mystery, certain that the house would soon be invaded by policemen, neighbours, searchers. Someone crept up the stairs and I was sure it was Eden coming so I feigned sleep. But Eden didn't come for another half-hour and when she did and Vera with her, the noise they made would have awakened me anyway.

'He's there! Look at him. And the door wide open. He must have crept in behind our backs. I should like to kill him.'

'Darling, you shouldn't distress yourself.'

'Why does he do it? Why? What does he get out of it?'

Curiosity got the better of me. I got out of bed and opened the door and stood there. Vera didn't see me for a moment. Francis's door was still wide open, the clock ticking away with a metallic reverberation enough to keep awake the soundest sleeper, but it hadn't kept Francis awake. He lay sleeping, half uncovered, his breathing heavy, regular and deep.

'I could kill him,' Vera said again.

'The more wrought up you get, the more he's going to do it.'

Vera saw me.

'Now what are you doing out of bed?'

I said I wanted a glass of water.

'You get it for her, will you, Eden?'

'I can get it myself.'

'Yes, and leave the tap running. I don't know where you get this business of wanting water at night from. Your father and I and Eden never had that as children. I don't know why you were allowed to get into the way of it.'

She was venting on me the anger his sleeping prevented her venting on Francis, though I did not, of course, know this. Nor did I then know, though I was soon to find out, that this behaviour of Francis's was a nightly occurrence, part of the cruel and calculated mother-tease he embarked on at the start of his holidays. This particular feature of it consisted in his disappearing each evening at seven – originally probably to avoid the ignominy of being sent to bed – hiding within earshot of the loud rage and misery Vera was unable to control or inhibit when he couldn't be found and then, once she had begun sobbing in Eden's arms, creeping up the stairs to bed and leaving his door open to display himself as if to say, 'Look, here I am. What's all the fuss about?' Vera never became accustomed to it, never took Eden's advice and ignored it. Each evening the same hysterical scene took place, terminating in the two of them standing on the threshold of Francis's room, looking in on him with wonder like courtiers at the couchée of some king of France.

Why did he do it? What made him enjoy so much the sight and sound of Vera's impotent anger? For this was only one of many provocations, among them his obeying of her dictum about eating with one's left hand and drinking with one's right to the extent of holding knife and fork both in his left hand. Then there were his red days and his yellow days, times when he would consent to eat only red food at the three meals or only yellow food, in the latter case subjecting items such as lemon-curd tarts, saffron cake, a hard-boiled egg, to the careful analysis needed to establish whether they were yellow enough. Far too subtle and original to resort to conventional practical jokes of the salt-in-the-sugar-basin or apple-pie-bed kind, he preferred the bizarre, knowing only too well how especially this affronted Vera. One hot August day, he turned all the blue flowers in the garden green by carefully bending their heads over and dipping them in a jar with half an inch of ammonia in the bottom of it. The *Daily Telegraph* would arrive in the morning with the crossword puzzle clues still there but the frame cut out. Vera complained to the paper shop and involved herself in exchanges of abuse with the paper boy for weeks on end before she found out Francis was responsible. Francis would go to incredible lengths to carry out his teases and thought nothing of getting up at six to catch the newspaper and cut out the puzzle the moment it slipped through the door.

Eden asked him why he did it. I was in the room with them but for a while I think they had forgotten my presence. Vera had just run upstairs, weeping. It was one of Francis's white days. Food shortages were making themselves felt by then and there was a general consensus of opinion that it was unpatriotic not to eat up everything on one's plate. Francis had been able to eat his cauliflower and the white meat of chicken but there had been brown gravy on the potatoes which he had insisted on washing off under the tap. Vera – incredibly – went along with him in this food colours stuff to ensure that he ate, presumably, for she thought him too thin, and quite gravely produced this insipid meal with rice pudding to follow. Her compliance was not what Francis wanted. After the first spoonful of rice, he clapped his hand to his forehead like someone who has remembered too late a certain important injunction.

'Is it Tuesday?'

'Of course it's Tuesday,' Vera said.

'Then it should have been a green day. What a fool I am! It may not be too late to undo the evil, it may be that no harm is done. Quick – have we a tin of gooseberries in the house? An apple, only it must be a green one. A cucumber, even?'

Vera threw down her napkin and rushed upstairs. Francis laughed. With a sideways glance at him, neutral, not willing to commit herself, Eden said:

'You are awful. Why are you so awful?'

I had never before seen anyone eat a cucumber like a banana. He peeled it like a banana, though necessarily using the knife.

'When we lived in India,' he said, 'I had a nurse, an ayah, called Mumtaz.'

'You've told me about her before.'

'OK, so I've told you about her before. You said she had a funny name. It was only the name of the woman they built the Taj Mahal for. But I suppose that doesn't mean anything to you.'

'Don't be horrible, Francis,' said Eden.

'I don't think I will tell you. She died, anyway. She got something awful, typhus, and she died.'

'You had your mother,' Eden said. 'Not like me. My mother died when I was thirteen.'

'And you had *my* mother. The point is, I didn't. And I wasn't thirteen, I was seven. She sent me to school the minute she could, she got rid of me the moment she could. Nice, wasn't it? I was to go to school because they were in India, but *she* wasn't in India for long, she was here. And you were here. So she chose you and sent me away to school.'

Eden suddenly became very grown-up and lofty. She gave me a bright smile. 'Faith will get a really awful impression from what you've been saying, you know. Of course you don't mean it. I hope you know he doesn't mean it, Faith.'

I was a silent child, at that time without social grace, given to nods and shakes of the head. I nodded, which was about as ambiguous as you could get.

'Your mother did what was best for you, Francis. Or what she

73

thought was best for you. Maybe *I* would have liked to go away to school but I didn't get the chance, did I?'

'Don't be such a bloody prig, Eden.'

Middle-class people did not say 'bloody' much in 1940. To me 'damn' was strong language enough and I was shocked.

'You've made Faith blush.' It was true, he had, but I would have preferred Eden not to have drawn attention to it. 'She's bound to tell her father, you know. Every word you've said will get back to her father and of course you won't get the backlash. Vera will be blamed for the way she's brought you up.'

'Good,' said Francis, taking Vera's box of drawing-pins down from the shelf. First he pinned the lengths of cucumber peel together at their ends, then made a pattern of pins like studwork so that the peel looked like a belt. He rolled it up, took the belt from the pocket of Vera's raincoat and substituted for it the cucumber and drawing pin one.

I thought he was mad. I still think I may have been right and he was. It was all revenge, this behaviour of his, in no way a means of drawing attention to himself and thereby hoping to recapture his mother's love. He hated her and it was hatred, not something masquerading as hate, but the real, vicious, luxuriating thing itself. Eden maintained a subtle neutrality, giggling with Francis and sometimes seeming with her giggles to approve – she knew he would never repeat to Vera anything she said, he was too proud – and with Vera, doing no more than sighing, shaking her head and telling Vera to ignore it, he would grow out of it. She couldn't trust Vera not to go rushing to Francis with a quote hot off her tongue: 'Eden says you're disgusting, she's never known anyone treat his mother like you treat me!'

No one expected me to take sides. I was never appealed to. By this time I had met Anne Cambus and we were spending all our days together, much of them in her home, and this was good for me, not just for the obvious social reasons but because it showed me a contrast; that not all the world was either like Vera and Eden's household or aspiring to be so. Some people were easy-going and warm and casual, much as my mother was, and it was Vera's home, not mine, that was the exception. So for much of the daylight hours I was with Anne, wandering the fields and woods, going cycling with her on an old bicycle that had been Eden's, playing an involved,

absorbing game we called Mary, Queen of Scots, in which was simply
enacted over and over the events as we had been taught them in
Mary's life, each of us taking it in turn to play the Queen, while the
other took all the other roles – Darnley, Rizzio, Bothwell, Elizabeth
the First. In wet weather, this took place in the tumbledown cottage
at the end of Vera's garden everyone called the 'hovel'. A lot of the
houses in Sindon and the surrounding villages at that time had a
small cottage or the ruins of one in their gardens. The place must
once have been a warren of wattle and daub shacks, patched with
brickwork, huddled together for convenience of building and for
warmth, honeycombs of dirt and disease and discomfort. Vestiges of
them remained, preserved as storeplaces or washhouses. Whether
anyone had ever done washing in the Laurel Cottage hovel I don't
know. Certainly it contained an old copper with a bleached wooden
lid and a space beneath it, a kind of cave, to light a fire in. The floor
was of bricks. As a child, Eden once told me, she had been allowed
to use the place as a kind of Wendy house, and that accounted for its
less than derelict appearance. The tattered remains of gingham
curtains still hung at the small window, there was a rug on the floor,
an old gate-leg table, a couple of canvas deckchairs. Vera, being
Vera, routinely gave it a clean-up from time to time. Anne and I
crowned Mary Stuart and married her, betrayed her and beheaded
her over and over again in the hovel that summer and autumn. One
night, five years into the future, I was to see enacted there a stranger
ritual, but that was distant, impossible for a child to foresee.

By night I shared Eden's room. True to her promise, she
undressed and got into bed in the dark but on moonlit nights it was
not so very dark and sometimes I was still awake when she came to
bed, though feigning sleep. Even with the light off, she undressed
with extreme modesty, first taking off her dress or blouse, next
pulling the nightgown over her head, then slipping quickly out of her
underclothes. All Eden's nightdresses were of fine pink or white
lawn, embroidered by her or Vera at the neck and wrists and
sometimes at the hem as well. Nylon had been invented by then but
it was to take a long time to reach us.

In the dark too, or in the half-light, Eden sat at the dressing-table
and 'cleansed' her face in the way the women's magazines then used
to (and for all I know, now) recommend to their readers, finally
massaging in the skinfood. Her hair was wound up and pinned in

sausage curls, this confection covered with a pink chiffon scarf. Eden, as Helen has told Stewart her own mother did, slept in white cotton gloves to keep her hands nice. Pretending to be asleep, even to the extent of maintaining a loud regular breathing, I watched the nightly procedure with admiration and, I'm afraid, with envy.

Sometimes, of course, as the autumn came on, it was too dark to see for both her and me and all this must have been performed in the bathroom. And later I was moved into Francis's room, for Francis had gone back to school, having ended his holidays with a mother-tease *coup*.

This was on the evening of the day he tried to put an end to that left-hand/right-hand business once and for all. He didn't succeed but I think what he said shook Vera, for though she continued to point to our hands across the tablecloth and push our plates to the left-hand side of us, I felt that her heart was no longer in it.

Francis asked her if she knew that Muslims always ate with their right hands because they used their left hands for performing personal hygiene after defecation. I have put that euphemistically which wasn't at all what Francis said. He told her that they used their left hands to 'wipe their bums after they'd shat' and that was why cutting off a Muslim's right hand by way of punishment for stealing, say, was an even more cruel mutilation than it seemed. The victim was likely to starve to death.

Vera screamed with shock. She shouted that he made her feel ill, he made her feel sick with disgust. Later she said that there were no Muslims here, thank God, so why did he think we would be interested in their revolting customs?

'It makes you see what bringing people up by these rigid rules can lead to,' Francis said, and he was right there, in more ways than one.

A gloom seemed to settle on him as the day went on. He grew abstracted and silent and though it was a yellow day – Vera, on his instructions, had truculently served him with pease pudding and an omelette for lunch – he forgot about eating only madeira cake and lemon curd for tea and absent-mindedly got through a slice of date bread before he remembered. He got up and left the table without a word. Vera, missing him as usual that evening, found a suicide note left by him on his pillow when she turned down his bed. She drew back the counterpane – hours earlier tucked by her under the pillow and then smoothed over it and under the bedhead – to find an envelope inserted there by fingers that had ever so slightly disturbed her handiwork, making a wrinkle in the folkweave that was the first thing she saw as she entered the room. 'Mother' was printed on it in Francis's presently favourite mauve ink. (How *colourful* Francis was, how I remember him in colours, his mauve ink, his yellow days, his transformation of blue flowers into green.) The note told her he was so miserable he had decided to end it all.

Vera believed it. I certainly did, of course I did, I was aghast and afraid. Eden seemed to believe it, at any rate it was she who said Vera should get the police. The village constable came on his bicycle, later more policemen in a car. Vera went to get the note to show them but it had gone, Francis, of course, who was hiding in the house, having abstracted and destroyed it. When the fuss was at its height, three policemen in the house, the rector's wife – who had called about something to do with the Mothers' Union – Vera crying, Eden pacing, Francis walked in quietly to ask what all the fuss was about. He denied writing any note, denied the existence of a note, and the result was that everyone started doubting Vera. I hadn't been shown it but Eden had and it was extraordinary how cagey she was about it, never affirming that she, too, had read it, never coming out quite on Vera's side, but rather adopting the pose of nurse, confidante and general calmer-down, telling the police and Mrs Morrell that she would take care of Vera, Vera would be fine in no time, she was overwrought, she would soon be better. You could see the police thought Vera was a hysteric and that they had been called out over nothing. But Francis got what he had aimed at and went off to bed well-satisfied with the success of his culminating tease.

That autumn, though, someone in Great Sindon really did commit suicide. I have often wondered how significant this death was in what came afterwards. In other words, how much it contributed to the events that led up to the murder.

– 6 –

The rector of the parish of Great Sindon was called the Reverend Richard Morrell. I had spoken of him as the vicar for which I was roundly reproved by Vera and told not to be so silly, but in my ignorance I thought all clergymen of the Church of England were vicars, I thought of it as a generic term like 'butcher'. Vera went to church most Sundays, usually to Evensong. For some reason never made clear to me, my father did not want me to be confirmed. I suppose he had lost his faith or had ceased to accept formalized religion. At the time I rather resented missing this surely indispensable part of my education. A large framed photograph, much admired by me, of Eden in her white confirmation dress with a veil over her hair stood on the piano in the living-room at Laurel Cottage. Though lacking this positive entrée to the elect, or even the promise of it, I sometimes went to church with Vera, especially on the evenings when Eden came too. To walk along the village street with my two aunts, each of us carrying a Prayer Book – for no reason that I can fathom since a copy was placed in front of every pew seat – helped me towards that 'belonging' for which I was ever striving. After the service, we all shook hands with Mr Morrell, big, heavy and unkempt-looking, with the reputation of keeping the communion bread unwrapped in the pocket of his surplice. He was first cousin to a very eminent man who had been the Master of Balliol. I called him 'a master at' Balliol because I thought I had misheard and if he was head of a college he would have been called a headmaster, an error for which I again got the rough side of Vera's tongue.

The Morrells had a maidservant called Elsie. People still had live-in maids then, though they were soon to disappear into munitions or the Women's Land Army. Great Sindon Rectory was an enormous house with eight bedrooms and very old-fashioned. Elsie, who was sixteen, the daughter of a farm labourer living in a village three miles away, did all the rough work of the house, leaving dusting and bed-making and ironing, and of course, the cooking to Mrs Morrell. I knew her by sight. Anne and I, coming home from school, used sometimes to meet her on her afternoon off walking home to visit her mother, but we never spoke. We were dreadful little snobs. Although we knew we were not gentry in the way that Mrs Deliss at the Priory was, we considered ourselves several cuts above the village people. Elsie, moreover, not only came from labouring stock but was a servant. Vera expected her to call me Miss and address her as Madam. She was a thick-set, florid girl, her skin always looking pink and weatherbeaten, with very bright reddish-gold hair that I am sure was naturally that colour. Mrs Morrell used sometimes to call at

Laurel Cottage and, in conversation with Vera, grumble about Elsie, calling her lazy and slatternly. I think they enjoyed talking about what they called 'the servant problem'.

'You are so lucky not having that to contend with,' I heard Mrs Morrell say. 'What wouldn't I give for a house this size.' She wouldn't have given much in fact. Secretly, she, who, Anne told me, had been an unqualified teacher in a private school in Ipswich, adored living in a Georgian mansion bigger than Great Sindon Priory.

Once or twice when I had been there with Vera, I came across Elsie, broom in hand or on hands and knees scrubbing a stone floor. Vera always spoke to her which meant that poor Elsie had to get up and look respectful.

'I hope Mother and Father are well, Elsie.'

'Yes, thank you, madam.'

As far as I know, Vera was totally unacquainted with Elsie's parents. Certainly none of us knew her surname until it came out at the inquest.

On one of her afternoons off, Elsie disappeared. When she didn't come back that night and hadn't appeared in the morning, Mrs Morrell sent to her parents to find out what had happened. By 'sent', I mean she got the boy who came in once a week to cut the grass or sweep up the leaves to go over on his bicycle. Elsie wasn't with them either and later that day a farmer found her drowned body in his well.

Real wells that people actually use don't exist any more as far as I know but a few still did then. Most of the cottages and some of the farmhouses had no mains water and no electricity. Piped gas had never been brought to Great Sindon and has not to this day. This well was fed by a spring of fresh water and had very clean-looking weed like streaming green hair growing in it. Some time afterwards, when the well had been emptied and cleansed, Anne and I went to look at it. It was no more than three feet in diameter but reputedly very deep – reputedly, no doubt, much deeper than it really was – with a coping round its edge of small old bricks. Every time Elsie walked that way she had to pass the farm where the well was and in November, when the hedge was bare, it was visible to the passer-by. It was Anne from whom I first learned what had happened.

'Something awful – Elsie at the Rectory committed suicide. She's drowned herself. Mummy told me. She said I wasn't to talk about it but you don't matter. I mean, she knows I'd tell you.'

I was shocked and somehow overawed. We stood waiting for the school bus. It was a cold morning, the air, the wind, everything, the world, full of floating, blowing, falling leaves. Never before had I been in a place where the falling of leaves was so apparent, for the village heart was planted on the green and in divergent lanes with huge chestnuts, planes, sycamores and beeches. All of them were shedding their foliage, helped by the driving wind, so that to this day when I see leaves falling in autumn I am reminded of Elsie and her death by water.

I asked Anne why. Why had she done it? Sixteen is not the contemporary of twelve but sixteen is young still, not like twenty-six, say, which we considered well over the hill. How could anyone of sixteen want to die?

'Mummy said she could guess. I heard her say to Dad, I can guess the reason for that, but when I asked her she wouldn't tell me.'

'Well, I can't guess, can you?'

'Unless she was very miserable working for old Mrs Morrell,' said Anne. 'But if she was, I don't see why she couldn't have left and gone into a factory.'

Nothing was said about Elsie's death at Laurel Cottage. I mean *nothing*. It was not even mentioned with Anne's mother's warning not to discuss it with anyone. Secretiveness was an important feature in Longley family culture, even when there was no real reason for it. Information was not given and news was not told. One was expected to know it already or not to wish to know it. Often Vera and Eden seemed to have secrets for the sake of having them, to delight in the lowered voice, the over-the-shoulder glance, the whispering behind hands. I fancy there was rather more whispering than usual about the time of Elsie's death, more entering of rooms and closing the door on me with a 'Just a moment, Faith.' Certainly they must have known about it, there was no possibility they could have failed to have heard either from Mrs Morrell or from reading the local paper. Besides, the village buzzed with it. The stray bomb, last of a stick dropped by a damaged Dornier, which fell on a field near Bures and killed a cow, had been entirely superseded as current gossip topic by the death of Elsie. Vera and Eden knew and knew, too, the result of the inquest at which the reason for Elsie's suicide came out. Again, it was Anne who told me, though she was unable to say whether her mother's guess had been correct. We spent a great deal of time that winter speculating about Elsie, the whys and wherefores, and Elsie's state of mind.

Meanwhile London was being destroyed by German bombs. And not only London – Coventry, Bristol, Birmingham. Terrible fires raged in the City and there was little defence against night attacks. The fear of invasion apparently was still strong. It is said of the novels of Jane Austen how remarkable it is that while giving an accurate picture of the social life of her day she chose so thoroughly to ignore the war in which Britain for a greater part of her life was engaged, to omit entirely mention of the Battles of Trafalgar and Waterloo. Anne and I could have understood. We were not involved. The war did not interest or affect us. It was a long way away, not audible, not even known about if one chose to be out of the room when the wireless was on. The torpedoing of Italian ships by British planes in Taranto harbour, the situation in East Africa, the German infiltration of Romania – all this was as nothing to us compared to our fascination with the plight and wretched end of Elsie.

It may seem strange today but then, when I was twelve, I had never actually *known* anyone not married to have a baby. To be married was the prerequisite of having a baby. Anne and I, though mystified by the emotions involved, could understand perfectly the disgrace of being a single girl and giving birth to a baby in England in 1940.

'She couldn't have had it, could she?' said Anne. 'You can see that.'

I could see that. What would she have done with it in practical terms? An unmarried Elsie pushing a pram along the village street was unimaginable. Mr Morrell would surely have refused to christen it or else have had to do so under cover of darkness.

'What did she do it for?' I said.

By 'do it' I meant engage in the sexual act that had led to her pregnancy. Anne couldn't tell me. The facts of sex were known to us more or less accurately but of the emotions we knew nothing, we scarcely knew emotion would be involved. Sex was something we thought of as being entered into for the experience alone, for the sake of knowing what it was like. The identity of one's partner seemed unimportant while we did not know of the existence of desire. Elsie's conduct was therefore baffling to us, for though we

81

understood how someone might wish to 'do it' – we had confided in each other that we would like to 'do it' at any rate once in the course of life – we were mystified by anyone's taking so serious a step without due preparation and the forethought necessary to prevent conception.

The well was never used again. I don't know where the farmer got his drinking water from, for I am sure it was impossible to have a system linked to the mains in 1941. Perhaps there was a pump near by. Anne and I squeezed through the hedge and trespassed on his land to peer down the deep green hole. I am sorry to say that for a while playing Elsie displaced our Mary Stuart game and we would enact Elsie's walking along the lane, seeing the well and jumping down it. These actions we performed in Anne's garden, a pit that had once been an ice cave doing duty as the well. We were only twelve and that must be our excuse.

At school, just as on wet mornings at assembly, if 'Summer suns are glowing' was due to be sung, a more suitable hymn would be substituted for it, so a round we had enjoyed singing was abruptly removed from our repertoire.

> 'London's burning, London's burning,
> Fetch the engines, fetch the engines.
> Fire, fire! Fire, fire!
> Pour on water . . .'

would have constituted a serious breach of taste in January 1941.

I had been home for Christmas only, returning to Laurel Cottage for the start of the new term. In our suburb, after the All Clear had sounded, the children went about the streets collecting up the pieces of shell from anti-aircraft fire. I had a fine collection of shrapnel to show Anne. My Uncle Gerald had been home on leave for Christmas, Francis had his fourteenth birthday and Eden, to everyone's astonishment, announced her intention of joining the WRNS.

Vera had more or less come to terms with it and rallied by the time I saw her again. Or else she was putting on a good front for my benefit.

'Of course it's very much the most superior of the women's services,' she said. 'The ATS are the lowest and then the WAAF and the Wrens at the top. That's a well-known fact. Eden won't be doing any manual labour, that's quite out of the question.'

But she wouldn't be able to live at Laurel Cottage, I thought.

'The uniform is very attractive. Just like a smart navy-blue costume really. And that saucy little hat.'

A tear ran down the side of Vera's nose and splashed on to the magazine she was holding, right on to the photograph in fact of a Wren in uniform. Her tears embarrassed me. I was stunned and a little unnerved when she clutched my hand. I murmured that everything would be all right, the war would soon be over, while vistas of grown-up grief opened in my mind's eye before me and I glimpsed for a moment how limitless and infinitely varied these might be. Vera released my hand, dried her eyes and told me fiercely not to say a word to my father that she had 'broken down', still less to Eden herself.

Before I went back to London in the summer my Uncle Gerald had been home on embarkation leave. Almost certainly his destination and that of his regiment was North Africa. It may be that Vera suffered as deeply over his departure as she had over Eden's, it may have been even worse for her, but if she did and if it was she had learned by then to keep her unhappiness totally concealed. It was a fine Saturday in June when he left quite early in the morning. After he had gone Vera took all the bedroom curtains down and washed them at the kitchen sink.

24a Llangollen Gdns
Notting Hill Gate,
London W11.

12 March.

Dear Faith,

It was good to hear from you though I wish it could have been about something else. There is no reason why you should know this but I was seventeen before anyone told me who my grandmother was and then it was a girl at school who told me. I think it has set up a sort of block about anything to do with her. I shy away from it, I absolutely hate even thinking about it, and although I know it is unhealthy to be so uptight, I can't help it, I have tried.

Daniel Stewart did write to me and I wrote back and said what is the absolute truth, that I don't know any more about Vera Hillyard than everybody knows. Less, probably, as I have never read any accounts of the trial, etc. He seemed to think I was called Hillyard and addressed the envelope like that. Some sort of sixth sense made me open it – that name always makes my hair stand on end – and for weeks afterwards I imagined that other people in this house must guess that Elizabeth Hills is Vera Hillyard's granddaughter. That was stupid, of course, because they don't, most of them are too young to have heard of her, but it will give you some idea of the state I get into about the whole thing.

I have never heard anything about this secret. The name Kathleen March doesn't mean anything to me and I'm sure you'll find it doesn't to Giles either. As far as I'm concerned, you can tell it to Stewart who is in the market for any sort of dirt as these people always are. I shouldn't dream of reading his book so it doesn't matter to me. The only interest I have in it is in seeing that he doesn't mention my name or give any indication of who I am or where I live.

Mother sends her regards and says do give her a ring sometime. She says she would love to see you again. Sorry if this letter seems negative but you must understand by now how I feel.

> Yours,
> Elizabeth.

> 6 Blythe Place,
> London W14.
>
> 18 March.

Dear Faith Severn,

I'm afraid I can't remember if you and I have ever met. Daniel Stewart wrote to me but I didn't reply. As far as I am concerned my mother and Elizabeth are the only family I have and I want to keep it that way. I just don't want to know my relations, living or dead, and that goes for my father. Sorry about this if it sounds rude.

> Yours,
> Giles Hills.

> Via Orti Orcellari 90,
> Firenze,
>
> 20 March.

Dear Faith,

As you see from above, I have moved. I went round to the old place and they had kept your letter for me. If you do come to Florence this spring,

84

remember we have a date and I am going to cook for you. I am feeling pleased with myself because my first book has just been published. It would be nothing to Francis who is quite a blasé author by now with half a dozen under his belt. Mine, too, is about putting things under one's belt, in other words, is a cook book, *Cucina Ben Riuscita* (Mondadori, L20,000).

No, I have never heard of any family secret. Remember, I was six when it happened. Pearmain wasn't likely to give me any revelations, he hardly ever spoke to me. Now I am wondering if I want to know what it is or if I don't. On the whole I think not. I should like to say it can't be worse than what I do know but that is a very challenging statement, asking for trouble. I suppose it is something involving my mother when she was young and I am inclined to say, don't tell Stewart. I know what journalists are and he will only make it out worse than it was.

You can tell all (the secret too if you must) when you come here. Till then.

All the best,
Jamie.

16 Queens Gate Mews,
London SW7.

31 March.

Dear Mrs Severn,

I am afraid I have been thick-skinned. It has taken me a long time to realize how repugnant to you is the idea of telling me the story of your aunt and Kathleen March. But you will see by my use of that name that I have pinpointed it and have in fact done much more than that.

The files of the newspaper chain for which Chad Hamner once worked provided me with most of the facts. I wasn't specifically looking for the 'secret', just for anything which might have happened in Myland and later Great Sindon during the time your grandparents and their young family lived in those places. Also Mrs Adele Bacon is still alive, though nearly ninety. Three of Kathleen's siblings, all younger than she, survive. I have talked to all these people and seen the records in the possession of the Essex police, both for 1921 when the incident occurred and 1979 when the child's skeleton was found.

Enclosed is my account of what happened. Albert March has looked at it and says it is accurate as far as he knows. May I trouble you to read it? You may at any rate have the satisfaction of knowing that the information did not reach me through you and yet be able to correct my errors or misapprehensions. The account will form part of chapter three of my book, a section in which I shall attempt some kind of character analysis of Vera Hillyard.

This is a copy so there is no need to return it to me unless you want to make any actual changes or additions to the text.

I am very grateful.

Yours sincerely,
Daniel Stewart.

In the spring of 1916, a young soldier called Albert March became engaged to be married to a girl who had been his sweetheart since childhood. Her name was Adele Jephson and she and he were eighteen. A week after the engagement was formed, Albert went out to the trenches and in July 1917, during the Allied advance on Ypres, was very severely wounded.

Albert was told that it was unlikely he would ever be able to lead a normal life. It would, for instance, be unwise for him to marry. In civilian life he had been a signalman with the Great Eastern Railway at Colchester and in the opinion of doctors at the hospital where he had received treatment for his wounds to head and chest, there was no chance of his returning to this occupation. Albert, however, was strong-minded and determined. He would always suffer from breathlessness and headaches that prostrated him but he was determined notwithstanding these drawbacks to marry Adele and continue with his career. He and Adele were married in August 1918 at Great Sindon parish church, the Jephson family being parishioners.

At the time a branch line of the GER ran north-westwards from the main London/Marks Tey/Sudbury line, branching off at a station called Sindon Road, a mile from the village of Great Sindon. Albert managed to get himself put in charge of the signalbox there and he and Adele moved into a cottage in Bell Lane just off the Great Sindon main street. The row in which their house formed the last unit was called Inkerman Terrace, named for an earlier battle in an earlier war. Today the four cottages in the terrace have been converted into the Ringdove Gallery, an arts and crafts shop, and is also the home of its owners, Philip and Joy Lees.

Mrs Adele Bacon, formerly March, says:

'People expect something more when they are starting out in life these days. We had two rooms up and two down; we lit the cottage with oil lamps and drew our water from the pump on the village green along with the people in the other cottages in the row. It was all we needed and we thought ourselves lucky to get it. Of course, at

Laurel Cottage next door, they had water laid on and electric light, but that wasn't really a cottage, it was quite a big house by my standards. There was a Mr and Mrs Price living at Laurel Cottage when my husband and I moved in next door. Mr Price died and she sold the house to the Longleys.

'Mr Longley was quite elderly. I was very young at the time and to me he was an old man. His wife was younger and they had twins who were about twelve, John and Vera. Vera was a pretty girl, very fair and with blue eyes. Later on, she got something the matter with her which made her get very thin but when the Longleys first came she was lovely. She gave me a photo of herself as a bridesmaid at her half-sister's wedding.

'My first child was born soon after they moved in. It was a girl and we called her Kathleen Mary. Mary was after Albert's mother but Kathleen was just because we liked the name. Vera Longley was crazy about the baby. I hardly knew her mother, she was a bit standoffish, thought herself a few cuts above us, I daresay, but Vera was always in and out of my house, wanting to hold the baby and bath her, that sort of thing. And the truth was, I was a bit flattered. Times have changed so much, it's like a different world, but in those days a man who'd worked in insurance and who lived in a detached house with electricity laid on was miles above us, there was no comparison. My father was a farm labourer – well, agricultural worker you'd call him now – and my husband was a signalman on the railway. I really thought Vera was condescending coming into my house and I used to bend over backwards to make her welcome and have things nice for her.'

In the meantime, less than a year after the birth of Kathleen, Mrs March was delivered of a second child, a son this time called Albert after his father but always known as Bertie. The birth was a difficult one and Adele was ill for several months following it. Vera's help was therefore even more welcome and a pattern became established. She got into the habit of wheeling Kathleen out every afternoon during the long summer holidays in the old-fashioned perambulator that had been Adele's own when she was a baby.

Mr Albert 'Bertie' March, who now lives in Clacton and has recently retired from his job with the Anglian Water Authority, told the present writer:

'I was too young to remember anything about that afternoon.

87

Kathleen was a bit over two and I was fifteen months old. My mother never spoke about it. She never said a word at any time, it was just as if I had never had an older sister, and of course I can't remember Kathleen. It's only since my stepfather died and mother came to live with my wife and me that she's opened up at all and once or twice has said things about Kathleen. Like how she was just starting to talk and how she had very curly hair, that kind of thing.

'It was my father who told me about it. I was fourteen and out at work. It was a couple of years before he died. He was only thirty-five but he'd been knocked about in the Great War and that messed him up. He used to have these blinding headaches that came from a head wound he'd got at Ypres. The afternoon we lost Kathleen, he'd had to come home early. He was blind with pain. They didn't like men knocking off with headaches back in 1921, I can tell you, it was a different thing from today. You'd lose your pay for one thing and there wouldn't be any car to send you home in and don't-come-in-again-till-you're-better-Albert sort of thing. Not likely. But my Dad had to knock off, he was a danger to the company in that state, a responsible job like he'd got, responsible for hundreds of lives. And of course he had to walk home, though it wasn't much above a mile and that was nothing in those days.

'His way home he took by the back lanes, not the main road. You had to cross the river at a sort of ford we called the "wash" but there was a wooden bridge for people going on foot. As my father was crossing the bridge, he saw Vera Longley and another girl sitting on the river bank, and a few yards away from them, under some trees, a pram. The girls had their backs to the pram which was on high, flat ground while they had evidently scrambled down the bank. The thing was that my father didn't connect the pram with his own child, it didn't occur to him that his own child might be in it. Probably he wasn't able to think about anything much but the pain in his head.

'He had been home about an hour, he was lying in a chair with a wet rag on his head, my mother was attending to me, when Mrs Longley came to the door. She was expecting a child herself by then, the one they called Eden. She told my mother Kathleen was gone, she had disappeared from her pram. What always angered my mother was how Vera didn't come herself, she had to send her mother . . .'

Kathleen March was never seen again. The police were sent for and the village people mounted a hunt. A local farmer had a famous tracker dog which was called in to help in the search. Arthur Longley and his son John were in the search party. It was a bright, moonlight night and the fifty or so men kept up the search until dawn.

What did Vera Longley tell the police? No record of any interrogation of or interview with Vera – if any was undertaken – survives. Here again we have to rely on the March family, or rather on Mrs Bacon, remembering that Albert March was less than two years old at the time.

'Vera didn't want to see me and her mother didn't want her to. She said it would do no good. But I insisted. It was my child that was lost, wasn't it, my daughter? If she wouldn't come to me, I would go to her, I said, and I did. I went to Laurel Cottage and I saw Vera. Mrs Longley said she was in a terrible state, sobbing and crying, but she wasn't crying when I saw her. She was just very white and sort of haunted looking.

'My husband had told me what he'd seen. Vera and her friend sitting talking on the river bank. Vera said yes, that was right, she had met her school friend, Mavis Vaughan, and they had gone to the wash together. Kathleen had fallen asleep. They left the pram up on a bit of high ground and climbed down the bank themselves to the water's edge. She never took her eyes off the pram for more than five minutes, Vera told me, but I knew that couldn't have been true. She said Mavis sat with her for half an hour and then went off home along the river, leaving Vera alone. She said she kept watching the pram, watching for a movement, you know. If she saw it rock, she'd know Kathleen had woken up. Of course it never did move because there was no one in it by then. Or so she said. When she went up to it, she said, it was empty. Someone had come up behind her and taken Kathleen away. That was what she said. I never knew whether to believe her, but what could I do?'

Mavis Vaughan, later to become Mrs Broughton, died in 1978, aged seventy-one, but her story of what happened that day is well-known to her daughter, Mrs Judith Jones, who lives in nearby Sissington.

'Everything that happened in connection with the missing March child made a deep impression on my mother. Even in the light of what happened later – the murder, I mean – she was convinced Vera Hillyard had nothing to do with it. Vera loved children. Well, I would have thought the circumstances of the murder showed that really.

She loved Kathleen March as much as she was later to love her own baby sister. My mother said that Edith Longley being born when she was saved Vera's sanity, she really believed that. As it was, Vera was ill for months after the new baby came.

'A lot of things were said about what Vera and my mother were doing when Kathleen was taken. People suggested they had gone there to meet a couple of boys – you can imagine the kind of insinuations. It was all nonsense. They sat and talked, that was all, and they were never out of earshot of the pram, they were no more than a dozen yards away from it. Mother had been on her way to the shop at Great Sindon for *her* mother – they lived right out in the middle of nowhere at Cole Fen – when she met Vera, and she had to get on and do her shopping. She said she'd wished a thousand times she'd gone past the pram up to the lane so she'd have known once and for all if Kathleen was in there then or not. But she didn't. She climbed up the bank and got on to the footbridge. And it was deliberate, too. It was done so as not to disturb Kathleen. Ironical, wasn't it?

'Later on, of course, after the murder, people who could remember the Kathleen March case said Vera had killed her. They said Kathleen had cried and Vera had lost her temper with her. Vera did have a very bad temper, it was well-known, even my mother said that. But she never would believe that of Vera, not even after she was hanged . . .'

In the autumn of 1979, Mr George Treves, who farms 600 acres of land between Assington and Cole Fen, hired a contractor called Peter Somers to uproot a hedge. His project was that of turning four small fields into one large one in which he intended to raise a barley crop. After three days of working at the destruction of the hedge with a mechanical digger, Mr Somers discovered, buried at a depth of six or eight feet, an oil drum measuring eighteen inches in height and nine inches in diameter, its open end being roughly sealed with a plug of the yellow clay that runs in strata through the otherwise light, gravelly soil of these parts.

At first Mr Somers and Mr Treves thought it possible the drum might contain valuable artifacts such as archaeologists had recently shown an interest in or even the jewellery stolen from Cole Hall ten years before in a burglary which had become something of a local legend. This included a £10,000 string of pearls among a collection of loot that has never yet come to light. However, what they found inside the drum was a jumble of brownish bones and shreds of cloth. They took their find to the police.

The bones were human. At the inquest conducted on these remains, it was concluded that they belonged to a female child of about two who had been dead at least fifty years. To have discovered this much is nothing short of a miracle of forensic science, and no more was forthcoming. The origins of the oil drum could not be traced. If there were marks of violence on the child's body, time and the decay of more than half a century had obliterated them. The shreds of material mingling with the bones were found to be woollen fibres and Kathleen March when she vanished was dressed in a woollen vest under her cotton dress and a woollen jacket over it.

Was this Kathleen? Certainly the hedge at Cole Fen was no more than half a mile from the wash where Kathleen was last seen in her pram. We remember that this is where Mavis Broughton, née Vaughan, lived, at a distance not too far from Great Sindon for her mother to send her to the larger village on an errand. On the other hand, police records show that during a twenty-year period from 1920 to 1940, no fewer than five female children under the age of three went missing in the Great Sindon/Cole Fen/Sissington area of Essex. And of these baby girls, the body of only the eldest, a three-year-old from Sissington, was ever discovered.

It is unlikely that we shall ever know. But if Vera Longley committed this crime, there seems no possible reason or motive for it. Jealousy of attention given to the child can hardly have entered into it since Vera had only to make an excuse to Adele March in order never to see Kathleen again. Rather than kill her neighbour's two-year-old daughter, she would surely have been more likely to make away with her own infant sister of whom there is reason to believe she *was* jealous. Reason and motive played so large a part in the later crime that our aim to understand Vera Hillyard's character is not served by attempts to show her as an unreasoning psychopath, for which definition there is no evidence whatsoever.

The March family moved from Great Sindon in the following year, the year of Edith Longley's birth, into the signalman's house which had just become vacant at Sindon Road.

7

I have written back to Jamie to say I shall be in Florence in May. His mention of his book has struck a chord of memory. When I was about twelve, my mother's aunt died and left me a cookery book. Of course she was no relation to Jamie, being on the other side of my family, the sister of my mother's English mother. She had been a cook years before in a great house called Lytton Lodge at Woodford Green – that is, she had been *the* cook, a personage of some importance with kitchenmaids under her, an artist creating banquets. I remember her as a handsome old lady, very religious, almost totally deaf, the peak experience of whose life had been when the Prince of Wales, he who became Edward the Eighth and then Duke of Windsor, came to dine.

She died in the little room she rented in Seven Kings, and all the stuff in the room, which was everything she possessed, came to my mother, her only surviving relative. There was a New Testament with passages marked in red, a pair of folding scissors that had hung from her belt with her keys, a lot of framed photographs of people my mother couldn't identify, some ugly jewellery in old-fashioned settings, bombazine dresses and white lawn aprons that would fetch a small fortune today if we had kept them, and the cookery book. So I suppose that strictly it wasn't left to me but given to me by my mother.

It was called *Mrs A. B. Marshall's Cookery Book* and it had been published in 1884. Unlike *Cucina Ben Riuscita*, which I suppose Jamie has written for ambitious housewives, Mrs Marshall, who had run a cookery school, had devised this book for cooks with dinners of a dozen courses to prepare for two dozen guests. I used to read it during the war when the worst food shortages were on. I used to read it while eating sandwiches of grey bread, margarine and reconstituted egg. At Sindon I sometimes sat reading it on the river bank down by the wash, though I did not yet know at that time that this was where Vera had been sitting when Kathleen March was lost.

Mrs Marshall gave a menu for a ball supper for '400 to 500 persons' which consisted of three hot dishes, a consommé, lamb cutlets and quails, and no less than thirty cold dishes that included more quails and something called Siamese Twins that were double choux puffs iced with green icing and filled with cream that had been coloured with carmine and flavoured with rum. There was also a menu for a '*déjeuner maigre*' that presumably means a light luncheon but which I translated as a thin dinner, and then there was what Mrs Marshall and my late great-aunt no doubt thought of as a normal dinner, six courses not counting the vanilla soufflé with pineapple, the gâteau Metternich and the Parmesan fondue.

Vera took umbrage. She saw my reading Mrs Marshall as a reflection on her own culinary efforts, as indeed it was, though through no fault of hers as I eagerly pointed out. Reading it in these circumstances was, of course, an odd thing to do, I knew that, and Vera did not like people, notably her own family, doing odd things. One was expected to conform, yet within that conforming to excel or at least do rather better than the standard set. She was a snob, professing to have had no idea that 'ancestors' of my mother's had been in service.

'I hope you won't say anything about where that book came from, Faith,' she said to me when its provenance had first been explained to her. 'I mean in front of people who come here. The Morrells, for instance.'

I already knew why not. Richard Morrell's cousin was the Master of Balliol. And somewhere in his background, related to him by a tortuous route among the by-paths of second-cousinry, removes and marriages, was an earl's daughter.

'What shall I say if they ask, then?'

'You can say you don't know, can't you? You can say you found it on the bookshelves at home.'

Francis said, 'You mean she's to lie about it?'

'No, of course not. You always twist my words. It's true anyway. It would have been on a bookshelf in her home before she brought it here.'

'They were very good psychologists, those old lawyers,' said Francis. 'They had people like you in mind when they formulated the oath, I swear to tell the truth, the *whole* truth, and nothing but the truth. They knew all about leaving bits out and putting bits in.'

I wonder if Vera remembered that conversation when she stood in the dock at the Central Criminal Court and took that oath. Probably not, she had other things to think about. I never did lie about the cookery book, for if anyone came while I was reading it, I quickly took it away to my room. This room was mine exclusively now Eden was gone – to Portsmouth, we all guessed, though we were not supposed officially to know.

I was at Sindon for the long summer holidays only for, blasé now about raids, my parents had had me back home for Easter and there I had stayed, reverting to old school and old friends. I was never again to 'live' at Laurel Cottage, only to go back for holidays, drawn by the prospect of time spent with Anne. Vera, too, had written to ask me. I was surprised by this and immensely gratified. Why is it that when people are never specially nice to us or warm, we long all the more for their affection so that the least little crumb they let fall is bounty? I didn't like Vera, I didn't admire her, and I'm sure she never liked me, and yet I was inordinately pleased at her inviting me. Why, soon she would be letting me stay up till ten and confiding in me the truth behind all those secrets!

'Now Eden has gone,' said my mother, 'Vera will want a young girl in the house to mould into a true Longley woman. Not so much *Kinder, Küche, Kirche* as *Kauf, Klatsch, Kettelnadel.*'

We were all in the habit in those days of quoting Hitler's more hackneyed sayings. But only my mother, being half Swiss and a German speaker – something she concealed outside her own home in those war years – could be witty about them. She laughed and my father looked cross. I looked up the words in the German dictionary and found they meant 'shopping, gossip, embroidery needle'.

Was that what Vera wanted me for? Certainly the crochet squares, uneven pieces of work and no longer very clean, were awaiting me. So was Eden's room, virginal as ever, Peter Pan in Kensington Gardens up on the wall, poised on that curious ant hill he stands on, still communing with the wild creatures. The white lace mats lay on the dressing-table but the hairbrush was gone and so was the cleanser, the toner and the skinfood. Eden's bed was not made up, not even apparently made up which is what one would have expected at Laurel Cottage, but counterpane and blankets and pillows in plain white slips lay on the mattress in a neat pile, to keep me out, presumably, in case I had had any ideas of getting in there instead of into my own. That evening, while Francis was off doing his disappearing trick, and Vera, incapable of learning from experience, was running round the garden calling his name, I succumbed to temptation and explored all the drawers in Eden's dressing-table. Of course it was wrong of me, it was spying and a betrayal of hospitality and I was quite old enough to know better. The truth was that I was bored stiff with crochet, not a bit tired at eight, and outside it was still broad daylight.

The drawers were full of aids to beauty. The objects in them represented not only a great deal of money but also the time Eden must have spent queueing for these things and the effort put into wheedling, cajoling and bribing shopkeepers to keep them 'under the counter' for her. Very little was what a young girl would have today. Nothing for the hair or the eyes and very little for the body. The scent that emanated from those drawers as I opened them and peered in and sniffed was a mingling of talc, rosewater, lemons and acetone. There were dozens of lipsticks, literally dozens, for I counted one evening and made it a hundred and twenty-one. They were of all possible reds and there was one that was orange and only went red when you put in on your mouth. I knew that because I tried it out. I tried out most of the things in those drawers during the following weeks – the toners, the skinfood, the gloriously scented stuff mysteriously called 'mercolized wax', the Creme Simon, the Evening in Paris rouge. The notion in the forties of woman's role, the ideas of what constituted women's lives, were reflected in the quantity of preparations for the hands and nails. Such a collection today would consist mainly of shampoos and conditioners, body lotions and deodorants. Daringly in advance of her time, Eden had one deodorant, a red liquid in a small bottle that you put on and allowed ten minutes for drying while you held your arms up above your head.

It did not occur to me then – nor perhaps would it have done to an adult – what all this would signify to the psychology-indoctrinated observer of today, that Eden was both terribly vain and terribly insecure. I thought only, if she had left all this behind, what had she taken with her? More, surely. The *crème de la crème* in every sense. Thinking of what was at Laurel Cottage as her rejects or at any rate as her spare set somewhat comforted me when guilt about my use of her Tangee lipstick and Arden's Orange Skinfood got too strong.

Eden had gone but before she went she had brought home a boyfriend. Not that Vera would have used this word (it wasn't in anything like the general use for lover it is today, signifying a sixty-year-old live-in common-law husband, for instance), or even have

95

implied there might be anything remotely sexual in Chad Hamner's interest in Eden or hers in him. Vera would probably have referred to Chad as Eden's 'friend' if she had mentioned him at all or introduced him. These, though, weren't her ways. I came home dutifully at seven-thirty from an afternoon and evening at the Cambuses' to find a strange man sitting in the living-room with Vera and – wonder of wonders at this hour! – Francis. They were all drinking sherry, something one never saw any more and had never seen at Laurel Cottage.

I was astonished. I stopped in the doorway in the attitude in which certain novelists of the thirties described as that of a startled fawn. I knew this because Francis said so.

'The startled fawn,' he said.

He was drinking sherry like the others and there was a high colour up on his cheekbones. I coloured, too; I could feel it burning my face. Vera always filled stark or awkward moments with bustle, for which one could sometimes be thankful.

'Well, I'm sure I hope you've had your tea. You never said if you'd be eating with those people. I haven't got anything here for you unless you feel like a sausage sandwich, that's all there is.'

'Give her a drink.'

This was the strange man. Vera rounded on him, but not at all in the way she would have done on Francis or me. There was something coy and sprightly in her manner when she scolded Chad.

'Don't you dare! I can't think what my brother would say. She's only thirteen, she's not so old as Francis, and goodness knows, she doesn't even look that!'

'I don't want any,' I said, a remark that inevitably sounds sour and indignant.

Chad got up, held out his hand to me and said, 'How do you do? My name is Chad Hamner and I'm a friend of Eden's.'

'Well, of us all, I hope, Chad,' said Vera.

'Of you all, of course.'

I shook hands with him. I remember what I was wearing at that first meeting, the voile dress of the group photograph, a dress that had been handed down to me by a neighbour's daughter who had grown out of it, the material a little tired and with pulled threads on the faded orange nasturtiums. My hair was in two thick, untidy, long pigtails. Vera had tried to make me wear ankle socks until ankle socks became impossible to buy and I won the right to go about barefoot in old Start-Rite sandals. He treated me from the first as if I were grown-up. There was no cult of youth then, no frightened deference to teenagers. You wanted desperately to be older than you were or at least taken for older. Chad spoke to me always as if I were the same age as he, that is, the late twenties. Nor did he seem to distinguish me as female, any more than he did Vera, something that later was a source of bitterness. But at any rate to him I was a person worthy of respect and this I loved.

Though Vera uttered a shriek, disclaiming all responsibility for results and my possible fate, he insisted on giving me sherry in a small tulip glass. The bottle of sherry had been given him by a man he had interviewed and done an article about in his newspaper, the new president of the Rotary Club or the Horticultural Society or something of that sort. Chad was a reporter with a chain of local papers called North Essex and Stour Valley Publications Limited. He was nothing much to look at, neither tall nor short, thickset nor thin, fair nor dark. In the street no woman would have given him a second glance. Like many such nondescript people, he was transformed by his smile, not a radiant, broad smile but one of mysterious irony that enlarged to total open charm. And he had a beautiful voice that I, in my later dreams about him, likened to that of Alvar Liddell, the radio announcer.

No jeans in those days. No zipper jackets. No plastic synthetics. Young men and old men dressed the same. Young men and boys dressed the same. That evening I was in my ageing orange voile, Vera in a dress made out of two dresses, brown sleeves set into brown and orange spotted bodice, surely in 1941 the prototype of such a fashion, Francis in grey flannels, grey pullover, grey school shirt, Chad in grey flannels, cream Aertex shirt, greyish-blue mixture tweed jacket. He asked if I had intentionally been given the same name as Vera.

'We haven't got the same name,' Vera said. 'She's called Faith.' This, of course, he might not have known since no one, not even I myself, had mentioned it. She seemed to remember. 'Didn't I say? Didn't I tell you she was my niece Faith?'

Extraordinary the thrill, the warming sensation, of hearing those words 'my niece' uttered calmly, indifferently, *acceptingly*, by Vera. Why did I care?

'That's what I said. You have the same name. Vera means faith.'

'Vera means true,' said Vera. She seemed a little displeased.

'Vera means faith,' said Chad. 'Russian for faith.'

Vera looked as if she were going to argue. She wore her mulish expression. With the awful scathing savagery he reserved for his mother – he was unpleasant to everyone except Eden and Helen but he was savage to Vera – Francis said:

'He knows, doesn't he? It's not probable you'd know better than him, is it? Well, is it? You're not going to set yourself up against him *philologically*, are you? He's been to Oxford, he's got a degree. Well, then. It's rather laughable when someone like you sets up against him.'

Although I didn't know it at the time, Vera *was* right and *vera* is the feminine form of the Latin 'true'. Perhaps it is Russian too and they were both correct or else Chad, in this as in other matters, was not the infallible authority Francis at that time claimed him to be.

Vera looked at Francis. 'My own son,' she said. She sounded almost proud. It was as if she were fascinated by the possibilities of how far Francis might go. 'If I had spoken to my mother like that my father would have killed me.'

'Fortunately my father is in North Africa.'

'You're not supposed to know that! You're not supposed to say!'

'Careless talk costs lives,' said Francis. 'Of course this room is full of people who can't wait to get out of here and tell the Germans Major Gerald Hillyard, the mainstay of British Intelligence, is currently at the gates of Tobruk, making history.' He turned to Chad. 'My parents have a code that's defied even the censors. Exclamation mark for Egypt, inverted commas for Tripoli, colon for Far East et cetera . . .'

'Francis,' said Vera, her voice shaking.

'The last communication was laden with dialogue. *Quod erat demonstrandum.* Heaven knows what they will do if our armed forces ever reach the point of actually *invading* Europe. They haven't arranged for that. It doesn't show . . .'

Vera jumped up, covered her face with her hands and ran out of the room.

'. . . much optimism, does it? Not what you'd call much faith or vera.'

Most grown-ups I knew would have reprimanded Francis for his behaviour to his mother. Chad did not. He merely shrugged. It was his way to give enormous shrugs, rather Gallic, though he was as English as they possibly come, as English as his name.

'I was conceived in Chadwell Heath,' was how he explained it – explained it in fact to me that evening under pressure from Francis. The truth was that it was a name which had been in his family since it was given to his grandfather at the time the Victorians revived medieval Christian names. Vera, I was later to learn, had considerable respect for Chad's family who were minor local gentry, Masters of Foxhounds and with plaques on the church walls at Sissington, commemorating sons fallen in the Great War. How he came to have his tin-pot job on the *Sissington and Upper Stour Speaker* is another story. For war service he was apparently unfit, having had rheumatic fever as a child. Eden he had first seen in the magistrates' court in Colchester where she had come with notes for her boss and he had been in the press box. Of course (this was all Vera's story), they had later been properly introduced by some suitable person, a Chatteriss probably.

Vera came back into the room pink-eyed and tight-lipped to find Chad having a look at Mrs Marshall which I had forgotten to put away and saying that what he particularly fancied at that moment was Little Salpicons of Salmon à la Chevalier. Francis timed his remark to his mother's arrival and said that I had got it from my grandmother who was a cook.

'Her great-aunt, not her grandmother,' said Vera as if the collateral relationship improved things.

Chad sounded interested only, not in the least repelled. 'You never told me you had an aunt in service round here. Who was she with?'

Vera nearly screamed, she was in such a state. 'She wasn't *my* aunt! She wasn't anything to do with us! She was Faith's mother's aunt or something like that, something on Faith's side.'

The devil entered into me and I told him how she had cooked dinner for Edward the Eighth.

'And Mrs Simpson?'

I said I didn't know.

'Why do we have to talk about cooks? It's ridiculous anyway reading a cookery book these days, it's enough to make you ill. Personally, I should think it's time that wretched book went the way of your great-aunt or whatever she was, Faith.'

Francis, who had been reading Saki, said, 'She was a good cook as good cooks go and as good cooks go she went.'

He was rewarded by congratulatory laughter from Chad and a glare from his mother. For a moment or two he sat in one of his mystifying silences, not exactly smiling but looking immensely pleased with himself without smiling, and then he got up and said he was going to bed. Vera was thus foiled and had to take her frustration out on me, asking me as a preliminary if I knew what time it was, and then proceeding as if twenty-five minutes to nine was the small hours. I went upstairs and consoled myself by daubing my face with Miner's Liquid Make-up and Tangee lipstick. Chad soon went home. I heard Vera go out into the kitchen to wash the glasses before settling down with the *Daily Telegraph* crossword.

Family connections Vera was proud of were the Chatterisses who had everything to recommend them as relatives. She always spoke of Helen as 'my sister', never 'my half-sister', and Helen's husband as 'my brother-in-law, the General'. They lived at Walbrooks where Helen had been brought up and which she inherited when her grandparents died. It was there, of course, in the days when the old Richardsons were still alive, that Vera had performed her spectacular rescue of Eden from under the tree in the storm.

I was told by Vera that I must call them Uncle Victor and Auntie Helen just as I called her Auntie Vera, though Eden was always just Eden. Vera was very anxious, before that first visit, that I should behave well. The following year I was adjured, on pain of 'never being taken anywhere again', not to breathe a word to Helen about the cookery book. That first time I minded my manners and did what Vera said, only to have Helen repudiate 'auntie'. She said it was vulgar, which made Vera sit up a bit.

'Not "auntie", darling, I beg.' Helen talked, and still talks, with all the panoply of twenties slang and terminology and Mitford girls expressions. 'It makes me feel like someone's old charwoman with *corns* and *false teeth* and *whalebone corsets*.'

This was so much an antithesis of what she was that I stared.

'You call me Helen and him Victor and if you can't bring yourself to do that, call him "General". I always do, it sounds so grand and Victorian.'

She did, too. 'General, darling', as often as not. Like some lacewinged creature caught in amber, she remained for ever trapped in the twenties – more than that, in a hill station in the twenties, her frocks waistless and diaphanous, a pith helmet planted on her crimped golden hair whenever the sun shone. She smoked black Russian cigarettes – heaven knows where she got them in 1941 – in a carved ivory cigarette holder. Her daughter was in the WAAF, her son a fighter pilot, and she and the General were alone in that big house where the Richardsons had created a library, a music room, and outside a ha-ha, a gazebo and a shrubbery of exotics that battled on through the East Anglian winters. Two old women, one from Stoke Tye and one from Thorington Street, daily cycled over to wait on them. I believe the General did the cooking while Helen, in memsahib gear, swanned about the garden picking flowers and making magnificent arrangements all over the house of dahlias and astilbe and silver-mauve hosta.

I liked her very much. It is a long time now since that liking became love. She was very unlike Vera, being easy-going, light-hearted, easily amused, generous. All those things she still is. For a long while, until his *détente* with Jamie, she was the only member of our family with whom Francis continued to keep in touch. With her he seems to have had a special affinity and it wasn't hard to see why. Of course Helen was nice and there was no humbug about her, but he and she had something else in common that specially endeared her to him. They had both been abandoned – 'discarded' was the word Francis used – by a parent when they were children, Francis's mother having sent him off to boarding-school in order to devote her time to her sister, Helen's father sending her off to her grandparents and not having her back again even when he had a new wife and home ... I am not sure what Daniel Stewart means when he says 'the separation still rankles' with Helen. The story of how Arthur Longley had brought his bride Ivy to the school gates to be shown to Helen was well-known in our family and Helen used to tell it with no apparent resentment.

'Grandpapa and Grandmamma were such perfect angels,' she said, 'that going to live with them was utter bliss. What sometimes terrified me was that my father would take me back and that I couldn't have borne. Do you know the first thing Grandmamma did when I first came to them, the very first evening? She brought me these two Siamese kittens in a basket and said their mamma had died too and they would be so unhappy if they couldn't sleep on my bed.'

The next time I called Vera 'auntie', she said in an embarrassed way that 'aunt' might sound better. Would I try to get into the way of calling her 'Aunt Vera' as 'auntie' was rather vulgar. My first successful effort was overheard by Francis and it filled him with glee. He proceeded to drop the 'ie' or similar sounding suffix off every word that ended like that, ultimately driving Vera into hysterics.

At breakfast: 'Thank you ver much. I don't want an more coff. No postal deliver today? How absolute craze', and so on.

She was rubbing her hands together. 'Why are you doing this? Why do you torment me?'

'Avoid vulgarit at an price.'

The result was that I stopped calling Vera anything at all.

On a visit to Stoke I overheard her telling Helen she would have liked another child. When I say 'overheard', I don't mean I was listening outside a door or behind a curtain – though I dare say I was capable of this – but that although they knew I was present, Vera probably thought me too stupid to understand and Helen didn't care. Or they believed me just out of earshot if they kept their voices low. It was rather what I suppose the attitude of a Victorian pair of lovers must have been to the duenna planted in the same large room with them.

This was before my mother had told me the story of the lost child, Kathleen March, and before I had heard of the adolescent Vera's devotion to her baby sister. It surprised me to hear that Vera was fond of children and liked babies. Was this why she had invited me, who was still a child? Did she love me really and was somehow incapable of showing it?

'You know how I love children,' she said to Helen.

If Helen was sceptical she was too kind to show it.

'Why don't you have another one, darling? You're young still, you're only a baby yourself. Why, you're *aeons* younger than poor old me, you might be my daughter.'

To me it seemed incredible. Vera was thirty-four, with faded hair and a stringy neck. She was middle-aged.

'There is the little matter of Gerry being goodness knows where.'

'The war won't go on for ever, darling.'

'Won't it?' Vera said bitterly.

'You're missing Eden, too, aren't you?'

Vera was silent for a moment. She had developed a strange nervous habit that I think was unconscious. I have never seen anyone else do it. Standing or sitting, she would clasp her hands tightly and lean forward bearing on those clasped hands as if in acute pain or as if trying to exert great pressure on something. The nearest I can get to it is to say it was like someone stuffing a swollen cork into a bottle with a narrow neck. It lasted a second or two and then she relaxed. She did this now while Helen watched her with sympathetic curiosity. Then she said:

'Eden will never come back.'

'Darling, of course she will! What can you mean?'

'Not *that*. Her life's hardly in danger being a wireless telegraphist in Portsmouth. I mean she'll never come home again to live with me. This is the breakaway, isn't it? When the war's over she won't want to come back to Sindon, she'll want to live on her own.'

'By the time the war's over,' said Helen, 'Eden will be married.'

'There you are then. It amounts to the same thing.'

But she was wrong, for Eden did come back and so did Uncle Gerald and before the end of the seemingly endless war.

In the meantime, though, life went on much the same at Laurel Cottage. Francis and I were reprimanded for eating with our right hands, hunted down at bedtime – I successfully as often as not, he nearly always escaping – admonished for falling below the standard of gentlefolk; daily the crossword was done, weekly a letter was written to Uncle Gerald and rather more often than that to Eden. Was Vera worried because weeks, months, had passed since she had last heard from her husband? Women knew they must expect these silences. A week before I was due to leave for home and go back to school a letter came.

Her relief at its arrival was plain to see. But she did not seem to want to read it. After breakfast, she took the letter upstairs and shut herself up in her bedroom with it. Francis liked shocking me and in those days he always succeeded. He said:

'I read in a book that couples fuck more in the first two years of marriage than in all the rest of their lives. What do you think?'

'I don't know,' I said, going red.

'You're blushing again. I wish I could do that. So innocent and charming. You will have to teach me sometime.'

For the last few days of my stay, Francis went off to visit friends. He had everything his own way, he did just as he liked, and when Vera asked him who these people were and where they lived, he refused to tell her. She threatened to withhold his train fare but Francis didn't care about that. He always had money. I don't know where it came from. Teenagers in those days didn't take on menial tasks to earn money, at least middle-class teenagers didn't, and Francis doing a paper round was in any case unimaginable. But he said he earned it, smiling enigmatically, and when asked by doing what, replied, 'Oh, this and that.' The day before he went, he carried out the most ambitious Vera-tease he had ever attempted.

In one of her letters, Eden had mentioned a naval officer, a Commander Michael Franklin. He was her boss or commanding officer or someone in authority over her, and had praised her. This, apparently, was in fact all it amounted to. But Eden, being Eden and a Longley, had also mentioned that Franklin was an Honourable, the son of Lord Somebody or other. Anyway, Vera had been very impressed, and had talked about Franklin to the Morrells and the Chatterisses and anyone else who would listen, managing to give the impression that Eden's connection with him was something more than that of clerk and boss, in fact was romantic. I think she persuaded herself it was. Chad Hamner wasn't spared this either, even though he seemed to be regarded – particularly by Francis – as Eden's accredited boyfriend.

One evening the phone rang. This was itself unusual. It was bound to be Helen, Vera said to me, going to answer it. We were alone, making a joint onslaught on the crossword, perhaps the only common ground we had, while the clock approached the witching hour of eight. I couldn't hear what Vera was saying. Triumphant at finding the answer to a clue before she had, I was writing in 'Manning' for 'Cardinal deployment of work force' when she came rushing back, all excitement.

'Who do you think that was?'

Vera was always asking this and being scathing if one guessed wrong.

Of course I said I didn't know.

'Commander the Honourable Michael Franklin, RN.'

'Really?' I said. 'That man Eden works for?'

This wasn't the way Vera would have chosen to put it.

'I don't think it's necessary to use those terms, is it? "Works for"? "Works with" might be more appropriate, or even "friend".' She became heavily sarcastic. 'Yes, I don't think we should be going too far if we said "friend", Faith. On our side of the family we may not quite aspire to relatives who *cooked* for the Duke of Windsor but we do know some nice people we can call our *friends*, some well-bred people with nice backgrounds. I think we can say we do.'

She was extremely excited, something which always let loose her aggression. She gripped her left hand in her right hand and bore down, contorting her face. I asked her what he wanted.

'To come here and see us. Well, to see me, if the truth is told. I don't suppose he aspires to see you or my son. It's me he wants to see as Eden's sister. Those were his words. He has to go to Ipswich on something very confidential and hush-hush and might he call and see Eden's sister?'

It would be at lunchtime on the following Wednesday. He didn't want lunch, didn't expect it in these hard times, rather not, he would have a sandwich somewhere, but nevertheless it would be at lunchtime he would call. Oh, Francis was very clever, very subtle – he knew his mother. She invited the Chatterisses, the Morrells and, oddly, Chad Hamner. Chad was Eden's boyfriend but just the same she invited him to meet the man she hoped would be his supplanter, and hoped it on no grounds but that Franklin was the son and heir to a viscount. (Vera had found this out at the public library.) And Chad a scion of a no longer very gentle or landed house. She was not a very nice woman and some might say she deserved all she got but she was pathetic – oh, she was pathetic in her aspirations and her downfall!

They all accepted. There was no meat around to speak of and all our combined rations would be too meagre to feed nine people. Vera got hold of two rabbits, not wild ones but the kind you keep in hutches. These were Old English, the white sort with brown blotches, and Anne and I had gathered sow thistles and chickweed to feed them. When I protested, Vera told me not to be a sentimental fool. She roasted the rabbits and did roast potatoes to go with them and carrots cooked in cider, and runner beans, with blackberry pie and summer pudding to follow. I picked the blackberries. The vegetables she had grown herself in the beds which had once been Grandmother Longley's rose garden.

Of course Franklin didn't come. By that time, as we later discovered, he was on the high seas protecting a north Russian convoy, his vessel destined to be among the thousands of tons of British shipping lost in the following year and he with it. General Chatteriss, drinking the sherry which Chad had again produced from somewhere, kept looking at his watch and remarking from one till ten past:

'Feller's late.'

And from ten past till the half-hour:

'Feller's not comin'.'

Chad knew it was Francis's doing. Not all the time, I think, but only from mid-way through this miserable drinking session in which the Dry Fly was soon exhausted and Vera was in a pitiable state wondering what to give Franklin when he did come.

Or perhaps he had known all along. It must have been someone's home, not a phone box, from which Francis made that call, disguising his voice or maybe not disguising it. Her son speaking warmly or pleasantly would have been disguise enough to deceive Vera. But I don't think Chad connived at it; I didn't then and I don't now. Basically he was kind. And if he was desperately in love, ill with love, so that all stratagems which seemed to further his love were permitted, he nevertheless stopped short at cruelty. For in his way I think he loved Vera too. Everyone associated with the object of his love came into its orbit and was lit by it.

Eventually we ate the roast rabbit. It was dried up and flaky by then and the carrots tasted as if arrested in a phase of wine-making. Many an agonized bearing down on clasped hands, many a twisting of facial muscles took place before that wretched meal came to an end. And afterwards everyone left rather quickly.

Francis made the truth known to Vera in the classic fashion of all such revelations, by uttering a sentence in the voice of the man he had impersonated:

'I wouldn't expect luncheon in these hard times, Mrs Hillyard, rather not . . .'

8

Madagascar is a name that affords children much amusement. It is splendid for charades, for instance, if you don't mind making the game into a five-act play. I don't suppose Vera and Gerald had allowed for it in their code of possible war zones, though, so there must have been months during 1942 when Vera had no idea where he was.

British forces went in there in May in an endeavour to wrest it from the Vichy French. There was idea around that the Japanese might do so if they didn't and the Japanese would have had Vichy collaboration. We heard all about it when my Uncle Gerald eventually came home on leave the following spring but at the time we thought he was still in North Africa. Eden had leave that summer and came to stay a night with us, only one night, she explained, or Vera's feelings would be hurt.

She looked wonderful in uniform. Wrens wore hats, not caps, and Eden's hat particularly suited that thirties film-star face. She had lost weight, or 'fined down' as my mother put it. Her face would be too beautiful for today's taste, too flawless, with those perfectly regular features, large soulful eyes and dreamy look. It was the first time I had ever seen her out of her natural environment of Laurel Cottage and at first she was a little stiff with us, a little reserved and wary, sitting on our sofa with her knees and ankles pressed closely together. It had been a problem deciding where to put her for the night. Should she have one of our unused bedrooms or share the shelter in the hall with me? Our proximity in the latter case would have been almost embarrassing, a far cry from the bedroom at Laurel Cottage, for the shelter, an affair of sandbags and corrugated iron, measured only seven feet by four. Eden was a member of the armed forces and if not exactly on active service, my mother pointed out, at least accustomed to bombings and gunfire. Of course, my father could only see her as his little sister still. At last it was decided Eden should sleep upstairs but under strict instructions to get up and come down to the shelter if the sirens went.

My mother and I took her up to her room as soon as she arrived. It was not in my mother's nature to make rooms 'nice' for guests, she would not have known how to do this or understood the need for it.

The sheets were clean, the carpet brushed and the surfaces dusted. What more was necessary? It was I who had put flowers in a vase, *Woman* magazine and *Rebecca* on the bedside table, and checked the bulb in the bedlamp. Eden said:

'Oh dear, fancy you putting me up here while you're all snug and safe downstairs. Look at that great big window. I can just imagine the flying glass.'

'It's weeks since we had a raid,' my mother said.

'Don't tempt Providence.'

Eden repeated her remark about my parents being safe downstairs while she and my father were settling down to the crossword. He said at once that in that case he and my mother would also sleep upstairs to give her confidence. The bed in their old room would be made up and aired and they would sleep in it.

'You'll make it up and air it then,' my mother said.

In fact she did do this herself, though with a bad grace. I think she genuinely wanted to make Eden's short stay pleasant but the adulation Eden got from my father and the deference she received annoyed her. Besides, she read into Eden's attitude to her over every small thing a subtle unspoken criticism, and sometimes her resentment was justified. The sausage left on Eden's plate, the strawberries she had queued for picked over and the slightest unripe bit cut out, the bread crumbled and left. If we wasted food, we would get from my father an admonition to think of the starving Romanians (or Greeks or Yugoslavians) but Eden was exempted from reproof.

Though Eden did not mention poor Michael Franklin, who was very likely dead by then anyway, she talked a lot about the people she had met in Portsmouth. Naval officers, of course, abounded and it was possible for any girl 'who didn't look positively like the back of a bus' to have a wonderful time. The Americans had entered the war by then – the attack on Pearl Harbor having been made the previous December – and Eden had been surprised to find the members of the US forces she had met so nice, so *civilized*.

'Officers, of course,' she said. 'I can't speak for the other ranks and ratings. I know two girls who are engaged to American officers and really you can't blame them, considering the sort of future that's offered them.'

It was a new idea to me – outside the pages of Victorian fiction, that is – that women would get married for money, security and position; I had thought it was always for love. Eden talked a lot about money and security and what some friend of hers, engaged to a Major Wayne D. Lansky, had told her was in store for her in Norfolk, Virginia, when the war was over: a car of her own, hired help, an ocean-front home. My mother had not been in the room while this was discussed, so it was not bitchiness but genuine interest which made her inquire after Chad Hamner and ask when Eden would be seeing him. I, of course, had told my parents about Chad, not supposing there was any need for secrecy even in Longley terms. In 1942, the result of being in love was that you got married. A boyfriend invited home meant marriage was in the air. Marriages might be made on other foundations (such as cars and hired help and ocean-front houses) but it was still on the whole unthinkable that love could be consummated in any other way.

Eden looked very put out. She passed it off with a quick 'Oh yes, I'm sure to see him. He will be bound to look in when he knows I'm home.' Later on she had it out with me. Incongruously, this scolding took place in our air-raid shelter, for the inconsistencies of life being what they are, the Germans chose to bomb London that night – or at least deceived us into thinking they would do so. I can't recall hearing gunfire or the distant thunder of bombs, but the alert sounded at one in the morning, and everyone came down and woke me up.

Very soon my father went back to bed. My mother was in the kitchen making us all a cup of tea. Eden and I sat facing each other, I on my bunk, she on an upturned orange box with a cushion on top. Her beautiful face, an amalgam of those now forgotten film star faces, Veronica Lake, Annabella, Alice Faye, glistened with a skin-food not consigned to the obscurity of a drawer in Laurel Cottage. A pale blue chiffon scarf turbaned her head and she wore a dressing-gown of blue flowered cotton. Her manner of telling me off took a curious form.

'I was very disappointed, Faith, to hear you'd been telling tales to your father.'

At that point I really didn't know what she meant and I said so.

'Now don't pretend. You've been gossiping a little, I think, and now you want to wriggle out of it. What can have made you think Chad Hamner was my fiancé?'

'I didn't say that.'

'Chad of all people! Poor me, I should like to think I could do a wee bit better for myself than that. I'm quite sure Vera didn't tell you I was engaged to him. I don't wear an engagement ring, do I? Well, then. Chad is just a friend of the family, not me in particular. Have you got that straight?'

'I'm sorry,' I said. 'He told me he was *your* friend.'

'Oh, Faith, dear, one day you'll learn that what a man says in those circumstances and what is actually the case are two very different things. I expect Chad would like to be engaged to me. Don't you think he would?'

Humbly I agreed. I would have thought anyone from Gary Cooper to Lord Louis Mountbatten to General Montgomery would have liked to be engaged to her. She became confidential and sweet once more.

'Frankly, I always knew I should have trouble in that quarter from Chad. We met at the Tregears', you know' – George Tregear was the solicitor she had worked for – 'at a cocktail party and he was making sheep's eyes across the room at me from the first. He *pursued* me with phone calls – Vera and I were in fits – and really I think I only went out with him to put a stop to that everlasting ringing.'

There was a good deal more of this in the same vein until my mother came in with the tea, crawled in, rather, through a gap in the sandbags. It had struck me from the beginning that Vera's story and Eden's of how she and Chad had first met did not match. Vera had said in court but according to Eden it was at a party. Probably it wasn't important. I was upset that Eden had reproved me, gratified that I had been received back into favour.

Next morning, Eden left, not to go straight back to Great Sindon, that would have to wait till late afternoon. First she would be having lunch in the West End with some American army officer. The way she talked about it at breakfast made it sound as if this were a business meeting, an important 'liaising' between representatives of the British and the US forces, and my father, forgetting Eden was a wireless telegraphist, seemed to swallow this. But Eden, to my surprise, while maintaining a serious expression, slightly touched my foot with her toe under the table as she mentioned the American's name for the second time.

After she had gone, my mother went into Eden's bedroom to take off the sheets. Being my mother and the way she was, she was very likely speculating as to whether, rather than go into the wash, they could be used on the bed shared by herself and my father. She saw things in that bedroom that made her very angry. It had been cleaned. You might think that a woman who does not keep her house spotless neglects to do so because she is oblivious of dirt but this isn't always so. Sometimes she simply can't be bothered. Moderate cleanliness is enough. Every spot of dust need not be scoured away even if it is more than visible to the naked eye. There had been a little fluffy dust round the legs of Eden's bed where they touched the floor. This had been cleaned off, apparently with a damp cloth. The lampshade on the central hanging lamp, a parchment affair, which my mother said she had been meaning to 'give a wipe to' for weeks, had been carefully washed with soap and water. And in the bathroom things were even worse. Unlike most guests, who leave a ring on the bath, Eden had not only cleaned off her own ring and dried basin and bath, but had removed from the half-hidden tangle of pipes behind basin and lavatory the accumulated cobwebby grey fur of years and left it in a neat little heap on one of my father's squares of shaving-soap newspaper.

It was this, not something Vera did – I remember now – which sparked off in my mother the telling of the Kathleen March story. Of course Eden was in no way involved, she wasn't even born, but I think my mother wanted only to make an attack on the Longley women generally, to illustrate their imperfections, their clay feet, if you like.

'No one is saying she did anything to that child,' I remember she said, 'but she must have just abandoned it. She can't have been looking after it, she was indifferent. They're like that, self, self, self, and making an impression. It's all outward show and surface. I suppose she was there by that river or wherever it was and this friend came along and started flattering her, telling her how wonderful she was or something, buttering her up, and she forgot the little baby in her care. She was too wrapped up in herself to see some madman come along and snatch it away.'

I was learning tact. I was beginning to understand the small satisfactions and the influx of trouble attendant upon 'stirring it'. So I said nothing about Vera's remarks to Helen on the subject of babies. But my mother, by some exercise of a sixth sense or by the telepathy which often operated between us, said she wouldn't be surprised if Vera had more children after the war was over.

'She'll want to add to her family, you'll see. Now Eden's gone, she'll want at least another one. A girl preferably. Too bad we can't choose these things.'

'Won't she be too old?' I said.

My mother was indignant. 'She's younger than me!'

The sheets were taken off and thrown into the wash, my mother's reason being that 'some of that muck she plasters her face with' had got on to the pillowcase. She and my father had a nice little thank-you note from Eden by the morning's post – she must have written it in the train. The next time I saw her was in Helen's garden where she told me how Vera had saved her life.

Yesterday Helen came to tea with me. A cup of tea and a biscuit each it was really, ten minutes' pause, and then on to the drinks. That is what Helen likes. She calls it 'staying for cocktails' and drinks sherry or likes me to make her just two dry martinis, stirred not shaken, with green olives not lemon, and the mild joke must always be repeated that the nearest the vermouth gets is to show the bottle to the gin. Jamie had a job in a bar in Half Moon Street between leaving school and going to Bologna – in the circumstances Oxford wouldn't quite have done they said – and the day after he started, an American came in and asked for a dry martini. Jamie hadn't the faintest idea how to make it but he knew Martini was vermouth so he did his best. In a little while, the American brought it back to him and asked if he had put any gin in it.

'Certainly not!' Jamie said, quite indignant.

The American laughed and showed him how to make a dry martini and when he left he gave Jamie ten shillings, which was an enormous tip in 1962.

When the General died, Helen gave up Walbrooks to her son who had married for the second time by then and had a little girl. It is a beautiful house and the grounds are lovely, and it amuses me to think how nearly it was mine. But about that I have no regrets. She came to London, to a flat in Bina Gardens, just off the Old Brompton Road. I think she expected London to be much the same as when she had last spent much time there. That had been in 1918 when she had a single London season under the wing of a cousin of old Mrs Richardson's. Helen found it different but behaved as if it were the same, dressing much as she had done in those days, going everywhere in taxis, furnishing her flat in a mixture of art deco and Anglo-Indian, lumpy white furniture and Benares brass, with a touch of the Syrie Maughams. Every day she has tea at five and makes herself a cocktail at six: every other evening she phones her daughter and the alternate ones she phones her son. They often come to Bina Gardens to see her and her grandchildren come. She takes them to Claridge's Brasserie for the cut-rate smorgasbord lunch. And she has me, living a stone's throw away in Vicarage Road.

Helen is my aunt, of course, my half-aunt. But that half-blood, which Vera was all too happy to forget and call Helen her sister, somehow in my eyes deprives Helen entirely of aunthood. I have never called her aunt (by her own wish) and when I introduce her to people I say only her name, occasionally, though rarely, prefixing this with 'my friend'. I have never thought of her as my aunt, still less by that other title I once had the right to use.

She is eighty-nine, thin still, willowy even, but the willow tree is rheumaticky with creaking joints. Chiffon and other clinging diaphanous materials are still favourites of hers and she still invariably wears a hat. But she has given up those twenties styles at last and now dresses very much like the Queen Mother, in pale blue and with big hats. The gilt hair is snow-white but still done like Gertrude Lawrence did hers for the first production of *Private Lives*.

I had considered also asking Daniel Stewart. Helen put a stop to this with a very adamant negative when I asked her what she thought. She calls him the 'bookmaker' though she knows very well what a bookmaker is and what it is not.

'I don't mind talking to the bookmaker tête-a-tête,' she said, sitting down but keeping her hat on as she always does. 'Well, I do mind, of course I'd prefer not to, it's no joke having to talk in that way about poor Vera, but what I mean is I can stand it when it's just the bookmaker and me but a third person present, even darling you, would make it so dreadfully *public*.'

Perhaps later on, I suggested. She could prepare herself for such a confrontation, come along armed with Valium, for instance. And when Stewart's book came out she needn't read it. She gave me that wry look of hers she offers her companions when they speak of the future, of next year even. It means that the chances are there will be no next year for her.

I made tea and we each had what was described on the packet as a muesli biscuit. Helen nibbled hers under the shadow of a blue silk brim laden with nylon delphiniums. It is rare for us to talk about family at these meetings of ours, either on the occasions when she comes for tea and a drink or when we go together to visit Gerald. One way and another family is a sore point with both of us and we feel we are friends in spite of our family, not because of it. But there seemed nothing else to talk about. Besides, it was Vera's birthday. Had she lived, she would have been seventy-eight.

As people grown old they lose their good looks. This is a commonplace, a cliché. Losing beauty though is only the beginning of a chain. The next link in the chain is the loss of sex. At a certain age, perhaps the late seventies, old women can only be distinguished from old men by their clothes, by skirts and style of hair. And then there comes a point, from which good Lord deliver us, when humanity itself is gone and old apes sit in human clothes . . .

It is true that Helen, with her flat chest and her gnarled hands, might have been an old man but there is plenty of humanity left there. The cracked voice is full of life. The blue eyes sparkle, unwearied. And she smells wonderful, of something called *Magie Noire*, the way no old man ever smells. I wanted to move on with Stewart to 1943, so I asked her about Gerald's return.

'He came on leave that spring, darling, but then he was at the War House for a bit.'

I wanted to know how he had got home and why. When I was fourteen or fifteen, no one had told me these things. All I knew was that he had been in North Africa, then in Madagascar (thus missing the Battle of El Alamein) and early in 1943 he had come home. To fill in the gap I had looked up the Madagascar incident and found that the British had gone in there in May 1942 and captured a naval base called Diego Suarez. The hope was that the Vichy French Governor would agree to a rapprochement and give up the remainder of the island but in fact he was only waiting until the rains would come in October. So the British attacked Antanarivo, the capital, and the pro-Vichy forces withdrew southwards. There was a further advance and further victories; in November hostilities ceased and the Governor was interned.

'I think we must have got out of there altogether in the January or February,' Helen said. 'We put a Frenchman in as governor, one of de Gaulle's people. Bill Platt was in command of our troops – such a nice man, he used to dine.' This, of course, is Helen's way of saying that General Sir William Platt used to come to dinner with her and her husband. 'He sent Gerry home, you see, in a bomber. He was to report on the military situation there to someone very high up. It may have been Churchill for all I know. Or whoever the Minister of War was. If only the darling General were alive he could tell you so much better than I can. That business with poor Vera was the death of him, you know. I mean it literally killed him.'

Perhaps this is true. Helen and the General stuck it out in Stoke after Vera's death but it was hard for them. They were ostracized. The half-blood was of no account then. Generous Helen had called Vera her sister to the world, and now Vera had committed the worst of crimes and met with the worst of ends, she was not going to deny the relationship. It would have been little use to try anyway. Everyone knew. Everyone always does know in villages. The ostracism was not entirely due to a drawing aside of skirts, a not wanting to be associated with such people. A lot of it stemmed from diffidence and embarrass-ment, from simply not knowing what to say to Helen or Victor if you met them. I saw a lot of them in the years that followed, naturally I did, and I was actually in the house when the General had his first stroke. After that he was never really well again. Five years after Vera's death, he too died. In Helen's arms, as she liked to say, though I doubt if anyone ever actually does die in another person's arms.

'Gerry was quite bright,' Helen said. 'The General always said he was. He was such a stick, you know, with not a word to say for himself. Imagine being married to a man who never made you laugh.' I wouldn't have thought Victor Chatteriss any sparkling comedian but of course I didn't give a sign of what I felt.

'A crashing bore, frankly, but the General always said there was more to Gerry than met the eye. I mean, there had to be, darling, when you think of what does meet the eye, that dreadful blank look and those sticky-out eyeballs like, what's it called, Bright's Disease. He was like one of those things they have in the West Indies. Well, they have in films. A bongo or a zobo or something.'

'A zombie,' I said.

'That's it, a zombie. A zobo is a cross between a yak and a cow, we used to see them in India, but Gerry wasn't in the least like one of those. Anyway, as I said, he was quite bright in his way and that must have been why Bill picked him to carry back this important info. That must have been in January 1943 because Vera and Eden and Francis had all been with us for Christmas and Vera hadn't a clue he was coming then. Eden only spent one wartime Christmas with us and it couldn't have been the next one, could it? And '41 we weren't at home, we went to the General's sister in beastly Gleneagles.

'Isn't it funny,' Helen said, 'how I can remember so perfectly what happened forty years ago but if you asked me what I did yesterday I couldn't begin to tell you. They say it's because of all those millions of brain cells being destroyed or falling out or whatever they do – like one's poor hair, you know – and uncovering the memory cells that have been obscured for years. It doesn't really matter, does it? One might just as well have old memories as new ones, better really. I'm sure I was having a nicer time then than yesterday. Well,' she said, remembering, 'up till you-know-what anyway.'

Helen always calls Vera's execution 'you-know-what'. The pain of it is not to be expressed without euphemism. She told me once that not a day had passed without her thinking of it and wondering what being hanged was like, what happened to the mind and the body just before.

'They came to see us in London,' I said. 'Not to stay though. They stayed in one of those hotels that used to make people laugh and look knowing – the Strand Palace or the Regent Palace. Gerry told my mother they were having a second honeymoon.'

'They were *mating*, my dear. That's what they were doing, or poor Vera was doing. She was using the poor chap to get another child, I fear.'

I got up and started mixing our dry martinis. Helen eyed the Cinzano Secco warily.

'Just show the bottle to the gin, I beg. That summer he went off to Sicily with the Eighth Army. Well, he'd been with the Eighth Army before Madagascar. The Americans were in on that too, their Seventh and our Eighth. I'm afraid I can't come up with the date, darling. I know it was before old Musso stepped down.'

'It was July the ninth,' I said. 'July the ninth, 1943. I looked it up. He didn't come home again till the war was over.'

My husband came in. He went up to Helen and kissed her and asked if there was enough dry martini for him to have a small one. I rejoice that he and she get on, that they are friends when, the situation being what it is, they might so easily not be.

'We are talking about Gerald,' I said.

'This isn't your day for visiting him, is it?'

I shook my head. Gerald lives, and has lived for years, in a home for retired officers at Baron's Court and Helen and I sometimes go to see him. He is stone deaf and though younger than Helen, seems older.

'We were talking about what he would have called "his" war,' I said.

'The General,' said Helen, 'used to say Gerry had had a good war, all things considered, and I said jolly good show because he never had a very good peace. And, my dear, I nearly forgot to tell you – who do you think I met at Lucy's the other day?'

Lucy is her granddaughter. She is married to a diplomat and gives large parties in one of those flats in Hyde Park Gardens that have roof terraces. I said I couldn't guess. My husband gave Helen the second of the two martinis to which she rationed herself.

'Lady Glennon! What do you think of that?'

Nothing. It meant nothing. 'We don't move in these exalted circles, Helen,' my husband said.

'Well, you remember Michael Franklin, I suppose? She's his sister-in-law. His brother inherited after he went down with his ship. You must remember that dreadful day and poor Vera's roast rabbits and our dawning conviction that absolutely no Honourable Michael was going to breeze in. He would have been Viscount Glennon but for a German torpedo and things would all have been different and maybe it would have been darling Eden I met as Lady Glennon at Lucy's.'

'She never knew him,' I said, 'except to say "I've got the message in triplicate for you, sir."'

'I do wonder if you're right. Vera seemed so sure. Sometimes I think I mix him up with that other naval officer of Eden's. You're not going to say he wasn't real, are you, darling?'

I said I didn't know. How would I know?

'That would have been in September 1943, somewhere off Ireland.'

'What a memory you have, Helen,' said my husband. 'You're an example to us all.'

'Ah, but you could tell me what you had for breakfast this morning, darling, which is more than I could. Apropos of which, Mrs

Anstruther in the flat below went on the wireless, on *Woman's Hour*, talking about some diary of her grandmother's that's been published. She's as old as me actually, Mrs Anstruther I mean, not the grandmother who would naturally be *aeons* older if she were alive which she's not. Before they started whatever they call it, recording, they said they'd test for sound and to say something into the microphone. Well, naturally, Mrs Anstruther didn't know what to say – you don't, do you, in a case like that? – so the interviewer said, "Just say what you had for breakfast this morning." But Mrs Anstruther couldn't. She couldn't remember. She said, "I can't remember what I had for breakfast" into the microphone, "I'm too old," and they all laughed, though of course she hadn't meant it to be funny.

'Eden was in Londonderry then,' Helen went on. 'They'd transferred her to Londonderry in the spring. The ship came in for a refit or some such thing, and then off she went to Goose or Gander or one of those bird places but she never got there. Londonderry was full of Americans that summer. I've still got a letter from Eden somewhere telling me all about the lovely Americans, so rich, you know, and dripping with presents. The General used to say "Beware of the Americans bearing gifts." He said it to Patricia when she brought a girl friend of hers to Walbrooks on leave. It came from Virgil, he said, which he'd done at Eton, but I always had my doubts on account of America not being invented in those Roman times, don't you feel?'

My husband put her into a taxi to drive her round the corner. Daniel Stewart would want that letter, I thought. I sat drinking my very dry martini, the last of it, and thinking about that summer, the only one in ten summers I did not go to Sindon for my holidays. I was due to go, I was packed ready to go, but my mother had an emergency hysterectomy, a very major operation in those days, and for weeks afterwards she was frail and unable to do much. I stayed at home to look after her. Vera and Francis must have been alone at Laurel Cottage for all that long holiday between the summer and the autumn school terms. Still, it was the last long holiday they were ever destined to spend together without additional company.

The letter Vera wrote to my father in the autumn of 1943 is lost. Perhaps it came too early in the year for us to have had a fire. That it once existed I know very well. I remember it or bits of it being read at breakfast. The date must have been some time in October. When I saw Vera's writing on the envelope I resigned myself to the reproaches directed at me I was sure it would contain. That August I hadn't been to Sindon and though my mother's illness was excuse enough and Vera knew it, I thought it likely she would mention my defection, asking, for example, why I couldn't have come during my mother's stay in hospital if not during her convalescence. 'Faith couldn't put herself out to come down here', and 'I don't suppose Faith could be bothered now Eden is away' were the sort of thing I feared and which my father would deal with by asking me to write Vera 'a nice letter'. But in fact there were no reproaches and I was mentioned only along with my mother as a recipient of her love. My father said:

'Vera is expecting a baby.'

This announcement had the effect of making me blush. I suppose it embarrassed me. Luckily, there was no Francis present to point it out.

'Well, goodness,' said my mother, 'she's left it a long time. Francis must be – what?'

'Francis was sixteen last January,' I said.

'Oh yes, she says so here. "Francis will be seventeen in January so I am afraid there will be a big gap when the new baby comes along in April. I should dearly love a little girl this time but shall be happy with whatever comes . . ."'

My father began worrying about Vera. Her husband was away – in Italy, their code told her – and he was on active service in considerable danger. Her son was at school and I think my father knew as well as I did that he could in any case have been of no help or comfort to her. Eden was now in Londonderry from which port the North Atlantic convoy escorts set out. Vera was alone, pregnant, and likely to be alone – unless the war miraculously ended – until the baby was born and beyond that. So he worried about her and fretted and finally made up his mind to go and see her. He would go and see her and invite her to come and make her home with us. A while back that would have been unthinkable but 1943 had been the quietest year of the war. Once more we were all sleeping upstairs. And it was suggested that those people who still spent the nights in the London tubes did so more for the company, 'the light and gaiety', than in the interests of safety. There were still a couple of months to go before the 'Little Blitz' of the spring of 1944. In our suburb, Vera, it seemed, would be in scarcely more danger than in Great Sindon and she would be a lot less lonely.

Of course the idea did not appeal to my mother. Presumably this baby was not an accident, she said, presumably it was planned. Vera knew what she was letting herself in for. What my father said to her in private I don't know. He said very little in front of me. He was not the sort of man to discuss the possibility of pregnancies being accidents or otherwise in front of his fifteen-year-old daughter. My mother eventually agreed, with a bad grace, that Vera should be asked. She wasn't going to Sindon with him, though, not she. He and I talked a little in the train.

'From the tone of her letter,' he said, 'I wouldn't say she was – well, how shall I put it? – blissfully happy.'

'I once heard her telling Helen she longed for another baby.'

'Did you now?' He seemed to cheer up at this. 'That's a comfort then. When you were going to be born, we were so thrilled, we were so excited.' He shook his head. 'We were very young, of course. So you think Vera's happy?'

What a question! Had I ever known her happy? What form would Vera-happiness take? I had seen her busy, bustling, hysterical, panic-stricken, jubilant, triumphant, frustrated, petulant, angry, but I had never seen her happy.

I said firmly: 'She loves children. She was longing for a baby. Of course she's happy. You can't tell from letters.'

That calmed him. He sighed. The train was late, the bus had gone, and we waited hours, it seemed, for the next. Vera was there, hanging over the gate, scanning the street, this way and that, the way she used to look for Francis when he wouldn't come in at bedtime.

'I'd given you up, I thought you were never coming. What held you up? I've got two pheasants, Richard Morrell shot them, but I expect they're spoilt by now, they'll be done to a crisp.'

Pregnancy had not changed her – that is, her character was unaltered. Physically, she looked ill. There was a greenish look about her and her hair was exactly the colour of barley in the fields a month before they harvest it. She was yellowish-pale. The pregnancy, which even then I had observed does not show itself in most women before five months, had already swollen out her waist. With clothes rationing in full swing, a topcoat costing eighteen points and a dress eleven out of a possible sixty-six for fifteen months, no one was going to squander coupons on maternity clothes. Still, Vera, once so clothes-conscious, could surely, I thought, have done better than she had. She wore an old georgette dress with a small red and white pattern on it, the belt necessarily removed but the tabs through which the belt had passed still there, the hem uneven, a green cardigan over it, bedroom slippers and no stockings though it was November and cold.

We were rushed to the table. The pheasants – the first I had ever eaten – were wonderful, not overdone at all. Vera remained an excellent cook, quite in Mrs Marshall's class. All through the meal she talked about Eden, her promotion – she had become a Leading Wren – her friends, all high-ranking officers, British and American, the beautiful photograph she had sent her. Hadn't we had one? Eden had promised to send one to my father. Still, she, Vera, had two. And that is how I happen to have had in 'the box' the portrait of Eden with the Veronica Lake hair that the Londonderry photographer took.

'We want you to think about coming to stay with us at least until the child is born,' my father said.

'I don't need to think about it. It's out of the question. I couldn't possibly. I wouldn't dream of it.' Vera's yellowed face was flushed with colour so adamant was she. She remembered her manners. She said, 'It's very sweet of you, John, I do appreciate it,' and added, 'I can't imagine Vranni would be too keen on *that* idea.'

'Oh yes, she would. Vranni feels just as I do. You shouldn't be alone here. Not in your condition.'

'I've got my friends. Eden will have some leave. Helen isn't far away.'

We tried to persuade her, or my father did. I backed him up rather half-heartedly. Now it had come to the crunch, as they didn't say in those days, I wasn't all that keen on having Vera a permanent guest. After lunch she settled down to an inevitable task – making baby clothes. To this end she was painstakingly unpicking an old white jumper of Eden's, carding the wool preparatory to washing it to get the kinks out. Yesterday's washed wool had to be wound into a ball. I held the skein for her while she wound away. Francis was coming home on half-term tomorrow. Why didn't I stay on to see him?

This invitation I managed to decline politely. I walked up the village street to see the Cambuses. Anne and I had one of those friendships that I believe are common among adolescents. My friends at home were my permanent companions, she was my occasional friend, but none the less needed for that, having a peculiar and special place in my affections as she was always to have and still has after forty years. Such friendships were even more usual then, in those days of the constant movement of children from refuge to refuge and back again, than they are today. We seemed always to pick up the reins where, six months or a year before, we had let them fall. Our absences gave us much to talk about. Anne told me a curious thing.

One morning in September she had been on her way to school, which necessitated passing Laurel Cottage, when she had seen Vera come rushing out, her face contorted, the tears streaming down her cheeks, and run across the road towards the Rectory. Anne knew the Morrells were not there. Richard Morrell's mother had died and they were both in Norwich for the funeral. Sure enough, Vera came stumbling back – Anne was waiting at the bus stop by now – and returned to the house, still crying, her hands up to her face.

'Francis,' I said. 'It would be something Francis had done.'

'I suppose so. He wasn't home much in the summer holidays. He was away nearly all the time.'

In Eden's bedroom that night I noticed signs of her recent occupancy. She had been home on leave. The contents of the dressing-table drawers had changed. One had been cleared of cosmetics and filled instead with fine silk underwear, slips and french knickers, mostly in apricot, oyster, powder blue, silk stockings in envelopes of thin paper. In another, along with the Tokalon Biocel Skinfood and the mercolized wax was a bottle of Chanel No.5 perfume. I had seen pictures of this perfume before but never the thing itself. I gazed at it, tried it out on my wrist, sniffed it – rather like some poor primitive, I suppose, in possession for the first time of an ichor of civilization.

That was the last time I ever looked into any private caches of Eden's. I was fifteen, after all, and my conscience now troubled me too insistently to be ignored. I closed the drawers and, lying in bed in the icy room – no one heated bedrooms in 1943 – contemplated the Madonna-like photograph of Eden that Vera had given us, wondering if I would ever attain to such beauty and hoping desperately it might be so.

We were to return home after lunch next day. Where was Francis? Vera said she didn't expect him till teatime. I thought it rather odd to come home for your half-term on a Sunday afternoon. Why not the Friday? Francis's disappearances were always mystifying.

My father seemed pleased when Chad Hamner turned up on Sunday morning. He was young still, my father, not yet thirty-eight, very young to be my father, but he was as old-fashioned in his ideas and ideals as a sixty-year-old. His life had been sheltered and narrow, he had been strictly and carefully brought up, and he had married at twenty-one. Nothing Eden had said on that visit to us had affected his belief – planted there originally by me – that Chad was Eden's accredited suitor. In his personal Utopia, women, especially his sisters and his daughter, would each have one lover all their lives, an adorer to whom they became at last engaged, then married, then lived with ever after, happily or not as the case might be, but he would take happiness in those prescribed circumstances for granted. Chad, in my father's eyes, was that suitor and Eden's haughty denial of that fact he took for modesty, a coyness he honoured. So when Chad arrived, he was gratified to meet him, seeming to find nothing odd in the man he regarded as Eden's lover dropping in while Eden herself was hundreds of miles away in Northern Ireland.

To this he alluded at once. After, that is, Vera had told Chad how pleased he ought to be to meet her brother at last.

'We're poor substitutes for my sister Eden, I'm afraid.'

'Oh, Chad saw Eden when she was home a fortnight ago,' Vera said. 'I expect he had more than enough of her.' It was the first time I had ever heard her refer with even the mildest disparagement to Eden and I was astonished. If the world didn't exactly turn over, it tilted for a moment to one side. 'Of course I don't mean that. It was lovely having her, only we have to carry on with our humdrum lives regardless of all this excitement from the outside world.'

It was a remark worthy of Vera at her most obscure. I recalled uneasily what Mrs Cambus had said to me the day before, what Mrs Cambus ought perhaps not to have said to a girl of fifteen. But she was a gossip and known for it in the village.

'Never tell my mother anything,' Anne used to say. 'Absolutely *not anything*.'

What Mrs Cambus had said to me was: 'That young newspaper reporter is always round at Laurel Cottage. People do remark on it.

Of course, it's hardly for you to say anything to your aunt but your father might drop a hint.'

I repeated this to no one. It was extremely distasteful to me, giving me a crawly sensation on my skin whenever I thought of it. My skin crawled then as I looked at Chad, sitting so easily, so very much at home here, taking it for granted he would be asked to stay for lunch – cold pheasant eked out with canned Prem come over on Lease-Lend – knowing where the cutlery was kept, laying the table, pouring us glasses of Vera's home-made elderflower wine. And Vera's eyes were on him a great deal, watching his movements as if he fascinated her. I expected him to go when we did, his accompanying us to the bus stop signifying to me that he also intended to catch the bus, but when it appeared on the horizon, visible from at least a mile away on the Sissington road, he shook hands with both of us, saying:

'Back to a quiet afternoon of Make Do and Mend.'

My father looked a little puzzled. I knew Chad meant he would be tête-à-tête with Vera, holding her skein of wool, reading the *Sunday Express* to her while she converted bits of three old dresses into a maternity smock, making a log fire and talking secrets with the door closed. Until Francis arrived and disrupted everything. Or would the two of them have been doing something quite other?

My parents had had the telephone since 1937 but they had never become used to it. It was a sacred instrument into whose mouthpiece you protruded your lips till your breath condensed on the Bakelite and enunciated each syllable carefully and at a louder pitch than in normal conversation. It was for making local calls or use in an emergency, not to be handled lightly or wantonly, and long-distance calls, even over the comparatively short distance of sixty-five miles which separated us from Great Sindon, unthinkable. My father and Vera communicated by letter as they always had. Eden hardly ever wrote except at Christmas and birthdays, yet, strangely enough, it was Eden who took over the communication of news to us about Vera's baby when Vera herself fell silent.

At first, Vera's idea had been to have the child at home, something that would have been by no means unusual at that time. It was mildly frowned on to have a first baby at home but in no way vehemently denounced and more or less prohibited as it is today. Besides, this would not be a first baby. Later on, however, she changed her mind and booked into a nursing home in Colchester. We knew all this through Eden who occasionally phoned from Northern Ireland – to my father an awesome act and none the less astounding because paid for by the Government. Vera's letters, none of which survive, were infrequent, pedestrian accounts of the weather, the winter illnesses of her neighbours, and of her own apparently steady good health. Uncle Gerald was sometimes mentioned, but not where he was or where she thought he was, only as a subject for speculation of an I-wonder-what-Gerry-would-think-of-it or Gerry-wouldn't-believe-it-possible kind. Gradually, the secrecy, so dear to Vera's heart, so much a part of her character, closed in. The letters stopped and it was left to Eden.

My father began to worry. As April lengthened and ended and May began, he would say most evenings:

'I think I ought to phone Sindon,' as a person today – though only a person of straitened means and lack of sophistication – might say, I think I ought to phone Australia.

My mother, of course, never supported any plan of his that seemed to indulge his sisters. She would remark on the cost of phone calls or say something quite unjustified but irrefutable, such as:

'Suit yourself, you'll get no thanks for it.'

Eden, we knew, was due for leave and my father was comforted by hearing her voice when at last he did phone, first making great mental preparations and ensuring total silence in the house, wireless off, windows closed, before asking the operator to get him the Laurel Cottage number. Vera was well, very well, but no, there was no sign yet of the baby. Yes, it was overdue, but babies were often later than one expected, weren't they?

'And how's that young man of yours?'

Eden must have said a perhaps irritable, 'I don't know what you're talking about, John', for my father laughed and said he had no doubt there would soon be wedding bells. Then he sobered, recollected things. Of course, they were waiting for the war to end, was that it?

He ended rather pathetically. She would keep in touch, wouldn't she? She would send him a 'wire' when the baby came?

My parents' marriage was not a particularly happy one. They had married very young, they came from very dissimilar backgrounds. The young people today, my own children, say triumphantly to me:

'It lasted, didn't it? They stayed together. Isn't that the test?'

But the answer is no, it isn't. People did stay together in those days, ordinary middle-class, not very well-off people. Other possibilities were not really open to them. They had not committed adultery or been cruel or deserted each other. They had their home they had made together, their child, they were used to each other. And if they were not compatible, not united in soul and body, not blissful together and wretched apart, was this ground for dissolving a marriage at great cost in scandal, astonishment, deceit and money? I doubt if they ever considered it. My father continued to rile my mother with his silly, starry-eyed worship of his sisters, his old-fashioned, courteous, empty and meaningless idealization of women, and my mother, in her carping jealousy, never missed a chance of belittling his family and sneering at its members, winding up with a general denunciation of the English bourgeoisie.

I overheard her say to him:

'Gerald was in those Sicily landings. That was on the ninth of July last year. The ninth of July. You can't deny it, it's history.'

He came out of the room, his face white and set. I, too, had been doing my sums. Who could resist it? This must have been, I thought, the longest pregnancy on record. Eden's telegram came on May 10th. VERA HAS SON. BOTH DOING WELL. LOVE, EDEN.

— 9 —

It has been said that we can remember only from the time when we first learned to speak. We think in words, so memory also operates in words, and we can remember nothing of those first two or three years before we could speak. On the other hand, there is the school of thought which would have it that recall is possible from our time in the womb. Jamie has told me he can remember nothing of what happened to him before he was six (except for something which never happened), the reason, he alleges, being that he was too unhappy. His psyche, defending itself from further pain, blocked off the memories. I remember his early years, or episodes in them, very well. He could not have been unhappy. What more could a baby, a small child, need than such unwavering devoted love from a mother as Jamie had from Vera?

Is it perhaps that knowing what happened and how he was used as a pawn in a game, he believes his early childhood must have been wretched? I think this is the truth of it for I know I have not falsified the past, so deeply did the change in Vera impress itself on me that summer. No trauma has distorted my memory, no bias or fear altered what I saw and heard. For me, of course, there was no involvement of the emotions unless to contemplate maternity and wonder how one will oneself approach it when the time comes, is involvement.

Jamie was christened in August. I was going to stay with Vera for two weeks, my father joining me for a day and a night to attend the christening. It was as well we were there, for no other members of the family were, not Eden, not Francis, not Helen. Already formed in my mind was an image of how Vera would be with a baby. Routine-driven, I thought, everything done by the clock, a fanatical emphasis on hygiene, cot sheets ironed as well as laundered and napkins, too, I wouldn't have been surprised. He could not disappear at bed-time and be hunted through the house and streets but it could be impressed upon his infant ears that six o'clock was the crucial hour, the point in time after which no well-conditioned baby should be out of his cot.

It was not like that. He was a beautiful child, a blond angel. Vera had written that his eyes were a deep, intense blue, and only in this respect did he fail to accord with her adoring description. His eyes, clear, large and full of intelligent regard, were a curious, changing agate as if the blue they had at first been were being washed out by amber-coloured water. His face, his cheeks, his limbs, his wrists and ankles, were rounded and satiny. He was three months old and he had begun to smile, all his smiles being directed at Vera.

For once she was not at the gate, not scanning the street, preparing to tell us how late we were, how she had given us up, how she thought we were never coming. She came to the door carrying Jamie in her arms and when we followed her into the living-room she laid him down on the floor on a blanket and let him roll and flex his limbs and kick. I won't say I would not have known Vera if I had met her in the street. Of course the contours of the face were familiar, the quick bodily movements, but this was rather the Vera of the early photographs, the pretty, thin, fair-haired girl, than the sharp shrew with tight mouth and wrinkled eyelids. She was transformed by a serenity that clung to her like the most becoming of dresses, its rosy colour reflected in her cheeks, her knowledge of its flattery shining in her eyes.

'You're looking very well,' my father said, unable to stop looking at her, looking at her in a way so filled with admiration that I could not help thinking with resentment that he never looked at my mother like that and how gratified she would have been for a fraction of that admiring regard.

'I haven't felt so well for years,' Vera said. 'But never mind me. What do you think of Jamie? Isn't he beautiful? Isn't he adorable? When you think how I wanted a girl! I wouldn't change him for the loveliest, best-behaved girl. Not that he's not well-behaved – he's perfect, he never gives a scrap of trouble, do you, my angel, my lamb?'

I could not agree that he was no trouble. To me he seemed a terrible handful, a source of endless labour, much of it exacerbated by Vera herself and her insistence on holding him constantly, spending an hour or more over his feeds, rocking him to sleep in her arms or against her shoulder. Gone was the sewing, the fine embroidery, the unpicked garments and cards of wool, gone the repeated references to Eden, the proud boasting about Eden's achievements, and gone, too, apparently, the vindictive jibes at absent Francis. In fact we had to ask in order to know.

'Oh, Francis won't be home. He's so jealous of Jamie, though he won't admit it. And as for coming to the christening, he says he hasn't believed in God since he was seven. What do you believe in, then, I said, and he just said Me, meaning himself. Charming, isn't it?'

'It's a pity Eden can't be here,' said my father.

'You wouldn't expect her to come all the way from Gourock for a christening, would you?'

'Gourock?' said my father. 'I thought she was in Northern Ireland.'

Another secret, evidently, another mystery . . . Vera slightly averted her eyes and a flush appeared on her cheeks. She wasn't upset, she wasn't displeased, though she had been caught out in a lie or at any rate a prevarication. 'Oh, what does it matter where she is? "Somewhere in England", as they say. We're not supposed to know anyway, are we?' And she used the catchphrase everyone employed, from shopkeepers who had received requests for unobtainable goods to mothers criticized for unappetizing meals: Don't you know there's a war on?'

Jamie never cried. He wasn't allowed to. Babies who are carried, cuddled, their every want attended to, don't cry. Vera dressed him in the robe of white nun's veiling, trimmed with lace made by Great-Aunt Priscilla Naughton, which she and Eden and my father and, no doubt, Francis too, had worn to be christened in. It was a warm sultry day, no wind, the sky overcast. For the first time since I had visited there, the garden had been neglected and weeds grew in the flowerbeds, willowherb and giant hogweed and the six-foot-tall great mullein, its grey leaves and yellow flower buds eaten into holes by caterpillars. We walked to the church, Jamie in Vera's arms rather than the high and shiny black pram which had once been Francis's. We walked in a little procession, for Chad had arrived and joined us, along the main street and down the lane to St Mary's. The cattle and sheep which had been in the meadows when first I came to Sindon had largely disappeared and the fields been ploughed up for the war effort, for the growing of grain and sugarbeet. Jamie's magnificent robe flowed over and half-covered the tired, shabby dress of Macclesfield silk Vera wore. She waved to people in their gardens as she passed, something I could never have imagined her doing.

My father was Jamie's godfather. There were no other sponsors. I should have loved to be his godmother but it had never been suggested and I was too diffident to ask. Anyway, this is the great non-relationship, the meaningless function, godparents mostly being selected for their ability to give generous birthday and Christmas presents. Being his godfather gave my father no guardianship rights over Jamie when the time came, made him no surrogate parent. Nor, I suppose, did he, when Jamie was fourteen and at boarding school and holidaying with the Contessa, remember it was his duty to bring him before the bishop for confirmation. He whimpered a little when my father held him and again when he felt Mr Morrell's wet fingers on his forehead.

When we left the church I thought Chad would go home but he didn't. He returned with us to Laurel Cottage and he was nervous and preoccupied as if he were waiting for something to happen or someone to come. My father talked to him about Eden, not going quite so far as to ask when they intended to become officially engaged but implying the question in almost everything he said. Not in the role of the heavy brother inquiring into a suitor's intentions, I don't mean that, but warmly and enthusiastically as if there could be nothing in his opinion Chad would want to talk of more. I could see that he had weighed Chad in the balance as a future brother-in-law and found him substantial enough. At last Chad said:

'John, I think I should tell you there's no prospect at all of Eden and me getting married. I don't want you to be under a misapprehension. I feel you are and it may be my fault. I'm flattered, of course, very much so, but it won't ever be.'

Vera, who had laid the sleeping Jamie into a nest of blankets and broderie anglaise pillows on the sofa, averted her eyes. She clasped her hands together and pressed down, exerting her strength. It was the first time I had seen her do this since we arrived. My father looked embarrassed and upset. He had become rather pale. But he tried pathetically to pass it off with humour.

'Turned you down, has she?'

'You can put it that way if you like.'

'Faint heart never won fair lady, you know.'

'Brave hearts don't always triumph either.' Chad said this, it seemed to me, with infinite sadness. 'There's a sort of prevailing belief,' he said, 'that if you want something enough, you can have it. Only try hard enough and you can have it. It just isn't true.' He was one of those few, rare people I have known, the first of those few I have known, who could talk freely and without embarrassment about the emotions.

My family, on an imaginary scale of openness, could have been placed on the other extreme end of it. My father could almost be seen to be curling himself back into his shell when Chad said this and Vera had begun to look angry, fierce in the old way I was used to. And then Chad smiled the smile that transformed him, making him look young and handsome.

'Well, I have a train to catch,' said my father.

Chad stayed and we had one of Vera's magnificent teas, changed but not spoiled by austerity, the cakes made with mashed potato and dried egg tasting no less good. He produced one of those bottles of sherry and we wetted Jamie's head with it, there no longer being any talk of sending me to bed. But I couldn't forget what Mrs Cambus had hinted at and I found myself watching Vera and Chad for signs of the relationship she had seemed to suggest. Exactly what this relationship would be I was not clear about. All I knew of love affairs, clandestine and otherwise, was drawn from films. I was an ardent cinema-and theatre-goer. Adultery was a popular and compelling theme in the 1940s. It was *the* theme, whether the drama was historical or a light comedy or a war tragedy. If there were truly 'anything between' (Vera's own phrase) Vera and Chad I thought I would detect it. I thought, for instance, I might come into the room where they were and find them locked in each other's arms, only to spring guiltily apart at the sight of me. One thing I was certain of, I was too sophisticated, I thought, to be deceived as my father was into thinking it was Eden Chad was attached to. This was a mere blind, a cloak for his constant visits.

Mrs Cambus's remark had given me a very unpleasant feeling. This had been blunted a bit but I still felt guilty and ashamed over my suspicions, though not enough to stop me watching and speculating. Vera, who had seemed to me ugly, old and worn-out when first I considered and dismissed this possibility, looked quite different now, years younger. To me, whose standards were high, formed by film-stars and Eden, she even seemed passably attractive, attractive at any rate *enough*. But if there were embraces, kisses, whispering together, I saw none of it. Nor was there any attempt to get rid of me and be alone.

Helen came next day. She and the General came to lunch. She was elated, all laughter, hysterical with relief and happiness. Their son, Andrew, missing for weeks, his aircraft shot down somewhere over the Rhineland, was a prisoner in German hands. They had heard only that morning. There had been no more sinister explanation than this for the failure of the Chatterisses to attend the christening. Helen held Vera in her arms.

'You were a brick, darling, not to mind. It is so splendid when the people one is close to *understand*. I just felt I couldn't go to the christening of someone else's boy when my own boy . . .' She burst into wild sobs. Vera gave her some of Chad's sherry. The General patted her thin, shivering shoulders. 'Oh, the relief! To know he's safe!' Helen, too, can speak freely of the emotions, but only of a certain kind in a certain way, and that way widely acceptable.

'Your Hun,' said the General, 'is widely reputed to be a gentleman.' He lowered his voice when he said this. Perhaps he thought it came in the 'Careless Talk Costs Lives' category. We were all mere women, though, we were safe.

Helen, for some reason, had brought with her albums of photographs of her children, albums and loose snapshots, as if she had grabbed up anything she could find in the five minutes before leaving the house. Patricia, always said to be the favourite Chatteriss child, was ignored now. Andrew was all, Andrew in his pram, on his mother's lap, on a beach, in school uniform, in the uniform of a Pilot Officer, smiling, young, appearing too young to have been one of the Few. I would like to be able to say that I felt in looking at these pictures some stirring of expectation, some excitement, even some prevision of what was to come, but it would not be true. If I had thoughts of that kind, they were for Chad. As the object of my infatuation, he was beginning to replace Eden, who was growing shadowy, a voiceless, motionless, monochrome photograph with a long, pale fall of hair.

But they talked of her, Vera and Helen, that afternoon, while the General fell asleep in an armchair and Jamie lay on a rug on the floor, waving his arms and kicking his legs. Vera's notions of what Eden's future life would be had changed since I last heard her speak in this way of her. Then she had said sadly she was sure Eden would never come back to live permanently in Sindon.

Now it was different. She could have her old job back if she wanted it, she had written to Vera. And if that happened, where better to live than at Laurel Cottage? Eden was somewhere in Scotland at present. She, Vera, knew this because of the code they used, similar to the one she and Gerry had formulated. While she was speaking, Francis walked in. He arrived without warning, almost without sound, to my surprise going straight up to Helen and kissing her. I had never before seen him kiss anyone. She reached out to him one long, red-nailed, heavily ringed, delicate hand and would, I think, have told him at once about Andrew had Vera not still been speaking, continuing as if Francis had not come in, her tale of Eden's present whereabouts and occupation. It was the point about the code he seized on, though not to mock in the same way as he had done once before.

'Let me tell you what happened to someone I know at school. His brother is a prisoner with the Japanese. This man, the prisoner, wrote to save the stamps off his letters for him when he got home, to steam them off. Well, they steamed this one off and underneath the man had written: "The Japs have cut out my tongue."'

Helen gave a cry of horror and flung her hands up to her throat. I, too, thought the story horrible. As you see, I have never forgotten it, preposterous though it was. I swear Vera gathered spittle in her mouth before she spoke to Francis.

'It may interest you to know that your cousin Andrew is now a prisoner of war. Perhaps it will teach you to think of others before you speak. Now apologize at once at Aunt Helen.'

Ironically, this was the only time I ever saw Francis obey his mother. Helen cried out:

'Darling, he didn't mean it, he couldn't know!'

'Helen, I am truly sorry,' Francis said. He no more called her aunt than I did. Making it worse, 'I could cut out my tongue. Oh, Christ,' he said, 'forgive me.'

'He's in a German prison camp,' Helen said.

We did not know about the camps yet, nor about the implications of our own bombing of Dresden. Hiroshima was yet to come. We were innocent. Francis, who identified with Helen, who saw his own plight as an image of hers, as an identical link in the Longley chain of indifference or unkindness to children, had grown pale with wretchedness. His colouring was extraordinary, more spectacular than Eden's, the skin a fine, milky white, the hair so yellow, the eyes a hard violet blue. There was sweat in pinprick beads on his short, curled, upper lip. His were the features of Michelangelo's David in strange colours.

He looked at the baby on the rug as if he would have liked to kick it. I felt a momentary real fear. Francis was so strange, so unlike other people. I could conceive of a situation in which he killed Jamie and then coolly informed Vera of what he had done. The General slept on, having in his sleep managed to smother his face with the *Sunday Express*. Jamie began to whimper and Vera immediately picked him up, holding him against her shoulder, his round cheek against her thin one. Helen said, the subject utterly changed though not much for the better:

'You know, darling, I do believe his eyes are going to be brown. If they are, he'll be the first Longley to have brown eyes.'

Francis, very still, watched her.

'I can't remember if Gerry has brown eyes,' Helen said. 'Isn't that

133

too awful of me? Not to know the colour of one's brother-in-law's eyes? That's what war does for you. I do believe they are hazel. Is that right?'

'My father's eyes are blue,' said Francis in a dead voice. The sentence sounded curiously like the opening line of a play, a lost, never-acted Chekhov perhaps.

Jamie, however, had closed his eyes and fallen asleep in Vera's arms.

She breast-fed him. What will Daniel Stewart make of *that*? Jamie himself has made too much of it, to some extent a secure world. It has allowed him to shirk (what he calls 'to face') the truth about his mother. Francis, of course, denied that it ever happened. He remembered the feeding bottles boiled up on the kitchen stove in the big double-handled pans Vera used for jam-making. So do I remember. It has never been suggested that she had enough milk to feed Jamie without supplements. He got the 'government' powdered milk in bottles as well. Eden was incredulous.

'Vera feed Jamie?' I remember her saying. 'Like that, do you mean?' And with the true vulgarity of the mealy-mouthed, she held up her hands, palms inwards, an inch from her own breasts. 'Oh, never, impossible! Why, she didn't even do that for Francis!'

I had never before seen a woman suckle a child. For one thing she would have had to be something of a Bohemian to have done so in the presence of anyone save her husband or her mother. There was no scooping up of tee-shirts in tube trains in the 1940s. It was a subject I have never really thought about, though breast-feeding was coming back into fashion. When I opened Vera's bedroom door in response to her 'Come in!' – I wanted to tell her I was going swimming with Anne – I was embarrassed by what I saw. It seemed to have a raw earthiness about it not associated with Longleys. I had noticed on my arrival a new plumpness about Vera's bosom. She had always been rather flat-chested. The round white breast Jamie sucked at would fill out the bodice of a dress becomingly alongside its fellow, this other not covered as one might have expected, knowing Vera's modest ways, but also bared and with a single drop of milk pendent from the nipple.

Vera sat in a chair I had never seen before, a wooden one with a high back, squat legs and a round seat, a traditional old nursing chair that had in fact been used by my grandmother and her mother to suckle their babies. She sat upright, her legs spread apart, her head bent as she contemplated the steadily sucking child. He lay in the crook of her arm. Her other hand was lightly closed round the back of his fair, downy head. The look on her face I had never seen before, it was so young, so tender, so infinitely sweet and adoring.

I wish now that we had spoken of what she was doing. It might have made things clearer, it might have helped. As it was, she said not a word, only seeming in a curious way to offer to my eyes the spectacle of this deeply physical, profoundly emotional act. I was shy, I looked away.

'Is it all right if I go swimming?' I said. 'Down to the weir?'

She looked up and smiled. She nodded. I got my swimming things and ran down the stairs. I think I ran most of the way to Anne's. It was not that I was so deeply embarrassed, certainly I was not shocked. My body seemed full of excited energy that had to be dispelled. It was the first time I had been to the river since my mother told me the story of Kathleen March. Because I couldn't imagine Vera with a baby, it had never seemed real to me. Now it did. My mother had not gone so far as to suggest that Vera herself had harmed the child, only that she had neglected to look after it. I asked Anne if she had ever heard the story, but in asking I left out mention of Vera, telling her only that a baby left in its pram on the bank here had been taken out of it and never seen again.

Anne said she had heard about a lost baby but no details. We walked along the river bank to the part where, for some reason to do with a pumping station, the banks had been shored up and lined with concrete, creating a deep pool. There was so much more wild life then than there is now, such a proliferation of wild flowers and butterflies and dragonflies. The cleaning up of the English country-side, the sterilization had not yet begun. The hedges were still there and the deep, moist, unploughed water meadows. We watched a kingfisher swoop and flaunt its colours over the pool.

'Vera is feeding Jamie herself,' I said suddenly, I didn't know why. 'With her own milk.' I would have been shy to say 'breast' in front of Anne.

'Yes, I know,' Anne said. 'She told Mummy. She tells everyone.'

I was surprised. I knew Vera disliked Mrs Cambus.

We took off our clothes. We had our swimming costumes on under them. Anne could dive, though she had been told not to dive into the pool. She surfaced and said:

'It's all babies, isn't it? There was Elsie's baby that never was and now there's your aunt's and there was the baby that disappeared. Have you done *Macbeth* at school?'

It had been a set book for School Certificate – for her, apparently as well as for me.

'*Macbeth* is full of babies and milk,' said Anne. 'You have a look. It's really strange that a play like that which is full of horrors should have all that babies and milk stuff, isn't it?'

I asked her if she had thought that up for herself or had her English mistress told her? The English mistress, she admitted. I promised to look just the same, for Vera's story was full of babies and milk, too.

The day after I went home I went to the theatre. That was my year for going to the theatre on most Saturdays. It sounds grand but in fact what I was doing was going in the gallery, queueing up for a stool first thing in the morning, securing my seat on what seems a pittance now, half a crown or three shillings, and often attending a matinée as well as an evening performance. Two or three of us, all school friends, would go.

I wish I could positively remember what I saw that Saturday night. I think it was at the Cambridge and I think it was a musical called *Song of Norway*. Daniel Stewart can check up on that if he thinks what I have to tell him about that night is relevant. I saw so many plays that year and the year before and the year or two afterwards: Richardson and Olivier at the New in the Shakespeare Historicals and *Oedipus Rex* and *The Critic*, *Blithe Spirit* at the Piccadilly and *Private Lives* at the Fortune. But I know it was a musical I saw that night and in a big theatre where the gallery was up in the sky and to look down over the rail gave you vertigo even if you had a head for heights. We were lucky. We were in the middle of the front row.

Someone said, quoting *Lear*, which we had recently seen:

> 'How fearful and dizzy 'tis
> To cast one's eyes so low . . .'

We were all, of course, casting our eyes down over the rail on to the tops of heads in the stalls far below us. The temptation was to drop things on to those heads, orange pips being traditional. None of us had seen an orange for years. I looked down on a golden head and as I did so, it turned to look upwards, though attempting nothing higher than the dress circle. The head was Eden's.

My reaction was rather strange. I immediately – with a jerk, I think – looked away and sat back in my seat. There was nothing to look at up there but the ceiling, the usual ornate baroque mingling of cherubs and flowers. I made myself look down again and the head was still there, still turned, with the chin lifted. There was no doubt it was Eden. The chignon had just come into fashion and her hair was done up in one, the crown of it a study in complexities, curls and swirls nestling in a deep wave, almost as if designed for an aerial viewing. Veronica Lake had given place to Alexis Smith. I could not see what she was wearing, only that it was white and of some soft, thin material. What it definitely was not was a WRNS uniform. The man sitting next to her was her escort. I knew that because I saw him touch her. Her head was turned towards him. She must have got something in her eye. Their faces came very close as his hand, holding a radiantly white handkerchief, a handkerchief that positively gleamed down there among the blacks and gold and dark colours, approached her eye and, no doubt dextrously, made to remove the lash or grain of dust. I was at once convinced, for no more reason than this, that he must be a doctor. He wore a dark suit. The top of his head had a small bald spot in the middle of brown curls.

The lights dimmed and went out and the curtain came up. I couldn't quite put them from my mind. The play couldn't dispel them. The extraordinary thing was that I was very certain I did not want Eden to see me. I sensed, you see, that she didn't want it known she was in London and would hate to have me see her. She was in Londonderry or else she was in Scotland. Had Vera not told me, less than two weeks ago, that she was in Scotland and having recently had leave could expect no more yet?

There were two intervals. I was relatively safe from being seen because of the segregation of the audience in the stalls, dress circle and upper circle from us poor galleryites who even had to use a different entrance door. Nevertheless, I dreaded running into Eden and her doctor friend. Somehow I knew that if this happened, Eden would take me aside and tell me lies. How I knew this I don't know but I did. She would ask me not to tell Vera or my father that I had seen her and then give me a totally fabricated reason why I was to say nothing, such as that she was in London on some secret matter to do with the war. This I was afraid of, perhaps because I still kept the remnants of my 'crush' and total disillusionment is something one never courts even if one desires it. In the second interval I stayed behind in the auditorium while the others went out.

Why had I forgotten that the greatest risk would be afterwards, outside in the street? I had. I felt that the danger was over when the curtain fell and we stood for the National Anthem, which in those days was always played.

It may have been the Strand outside or Shaftesbury Avenue or the Haymarket. But I think it was the Charing Cross Road where Shaftesbury Avenue comes into it at Cambridge Circus. The long tyranny of the blackout had almost come to an end by then and a dim-out was to be allowed in its place. At the end of August, though – and for weeks to come due to a shortage of manpower and light bulbs – the West End continued in darkness. There was a full moon that night, and the moon was not obscured then by smog and pollution. We walked along the pavement with the crowd. It seemed to part as if by some stage instruction or command from a director, and there on the edge of the pavement in front of me stood the two of them, waiting to cross, her arm in his. In these days they would have been waiting for a taxi; then, they were making for a tube station, probably Leicester Square.

No more than three yards separated us. My weak smile was already forming, the 'Hallo, Eden' shaping itself on my tongue as her eyes met mine, lingered there, staring and wide – and looked away. In that moment I lost whatever feeling I had ever had for her. I was astounded, for in my eyes she was a grown-up and I still half a child, and I was also ashamed for her and dismayed. There was no doubt she had seen me. I knew she had seen and recognized me. Nothing kills like contempt and contempt for her came upon me in a hot flood of blushes so that I put my hands to my face, cooling it with my fingers. Eden and her man crossed the road and lost themselves in the crowd but when I closed my eyes, there she was, I could still see her, on the black retina, her beautifully made, fine-boned face like Francis's, the lipstick red as a clown's, pillarbox paint against that white skin, the eyes as blue as marbles and the hair as gilded as a cherub's on a ceiling. Her dress had been white, cross-over and draped, her legs bare and her feet in white Bettty Grable shoes with heels made for a high stepping trot like a horse's.

If I had mentioned it to my father, he would have said I was mistaken. I thought about it a lot. I thought of how I should have had to describe her, had he asked, and how, when he heard of the Grecian dress and the golden topknot, he would have said:

'That doesn't sound like my little sister. You mistook someone else for her.'

Of course I had not. It had been Eden and she was in London when everyone believed her in Scotland. The mysteries and secrecies beloved of the Longleys had a new mystery and a new secret. I wondered if Eden was still a Wren even and if she were living in London or only staying there. I even wondered, so paranoid an effect can this kind of thing have on one, if it was only I that was excluded from this secret, if all along, my father and my mother, too, had known Eden's precise whereabouts and had kept the truth from me for reasons unfathomable; if Vera had known when she told my father one day that Eden was in Londonderry and the next in Gourock. And what of poor Chad who had spoken, so it seemed to me, so sorrowfully of his failure to achieve Eden's love, though not for the want of trying?

I find myself creating mysteries, too. It is not for nothing that I am a Longley. Of course, I am trying to arrange these recollections of mine in sequence, not remembering events and revelations, so to speak, out of order. It was a good while later, though, years, before I did discover the truth of this. This was at the time of the uncovering of many truths. Eden *had* left the WRNS. That August, it was three quarters of a year since she had been Leading Wren Longley, stationed at Londonderry, and in Scotland she had never been. In London she had a job as secretary-companion to an old woman in Belgrave Square called Lady Rogerson. The odd thing was that she got this job through one of those gentlefolk relatives of Chad's that she had met through him, though Chad was ignorant of it all. Eden simply used him in her progress towards the main chance as she used everyone useful. She lived in Belgrave Square and after a while (she once told us), Lady Rogerson looked on her almost as a daughter – well, a niece. The man with the brown, curly hair was a sort of cousin of Lady Rogerson's and he too had a title, though I can't remember what. It was not he, anyway, whom Eden finally caught as a result of living in Belgravia.

All this was well known to Vera all the time.

— 10 —

I was so used to thinking of Laurel Cottage as Vera's house that it came as a shock to hear my father tell my mother that he supposed it would be sold now and the proceeds divided between Vera, Eden and himself. That, of course, was the way my grandmother had left it. My father had waived his right because Vera needed somewhere in which to make a home for Eden, and then the war had come, disrupting everything. The sale of Laurel Cottage might with luck realize fifteen hundred pounds and my father talked a lot about how he would use his five hundred share – build on to the house perhaps, move house, buy a car, re-furnish the living-room, go to Switzerland and see my mother's relations – spending it in imagination several times over. For a bank manager, which he had just become, he was naïve about money.

Harder-headed and altogether more realistic, my mother never believed in that money from the start. She was a woman who had no compunction about saying, I told you so. 'See if I'm not right' was another phrase of hers and she usually was.

'When your mother died, I told you to sell the house. Gerald would have got a house for Vera and Eden could have lived with us. Things would have been very different if that had happened.'

They would, indeed.

'Eden wouldn't have been made too big for her boots for one thing,' said my mother. 'It doesn't do people any good to be idolized.'

My father said in an unpleasant tone that there was not much risk of that round here. It was interesting to speculate what it would have been like having Eden as a sort of big sister. I had no idea this had ever been proposed. Would it have interfered with what George Eliot calls 'the stealthy convergence of human lots', altering the course of things, so that Vera on her seventy-eighth birthday might have come along to tea with me with Helen last week. And might Eden have been there, too, a sprightly, blonded sixty-three? Might Francis have strolled in among us to throw a word of disaster in that way he always had, as Ate flung the golden apple among the party guests? And Jamie, his name unchanged and his own, not a self-appointed exile? Who knows? I think somehow that things would have been much the same, given the war and the personalities of the players in the drama.

Eden never wrote. Vera often did and continued to mention Eden as being in Scotland and still in the WRNS. My father never wavered in his custom of reading her letters aloud at the breakfast table, and as I heard details of Eden's life relayed, though I didn't doubt my own eyes, I began to think she had been guilty of no greater subterfuge than that of coming to London on leave without visiting us or seeing Vera. We were enduring V1 attacks which only came to an end when the Allies overran the V1 launching sites in the Pas de Calais. But Duncan Sandys was a bit premature when in September he said that 'the Battle of London was over except for a few shots'.

That same month, the V2s started, those first rockets, which travelled so fast that one could not hear them before they exploded. By that time one was either dead or not as the case may be. We called them 'flying gas mains', just as we called the V1s that droned more loudly before they cut out and exploded, doodlebugs or buzz bombs. One of the last of these V2s to reach England fell on Colchester, making a direct hit on the nursing home where Vera had had Jamie and causing hundreds of casualties, more than fifty of them fatal. My father flew into a panic about Vera and Jamie. Suppose this were a new phase of the war, a kind of swan song of aggression to be unleashed on East Anglia?

Five months later it was all over. If Eden were still in the WRNS at the time the war ended, she must have been one of the first of the five million service men and women to be demobilized. Ernest Bevin announced that releases would begin on 18 June and a week later Vera wrote to say Eden had been 'demobbed'. Even my father thought that strange. Gerald had to wait a good deal longer and was not to reach home till the autumn of 1945, by which time Francis had gone up to Oxford and Vera, for a change, been to us on holiday.

My mother consented to this, I think, because she enjoyed the company of small children, a rarer quality in women than one might think. Most people, whatever they may say, find the company of little children boring. My mother, though intelligent and quite quick and brusque with adults, had infinite patience with children. She used to say she liked the way they had not yet learnt the shifts and slyness and affectations of grown-ups.

Jamie was about fifteen months old by this time. He had curious colouring, very attractive but unusual, his skin being a light, clear olive while his hair was brightly fair. His eyes were brown; not light brown or hazel or speckly blue-gold, but an uncompromising rich, dark brown, as deep a shade as a Spaniard's or even an Indian's might be. And he didn't look like anyone in the family. You know the way babies have a definite 'look' of some uncle or aunt or forebear, so that the overall impression is of a copy of that person, but when you examine the face feature by feature the similarity breaks down. I used to pore over albums of old Longley and Naughton photographs and saw this again and again, how the infant Vera, for instance, seemed a reincarnation of Great-aunt Priscilla, how my father immediately brought to mind old William, the shoemaker. Eden and Francis, as I have said, might have been taken for twins. Jamie, though, was himself and only himself. He looked no more like the Longleys (except for his hair) than he did like Gerald who has a very long face and almost pointed head that Helen says he used to attribute, I don't know how accurately, to his mother's narrow pelvis and the fact that he took an unconscionably long time being born. I decided Jamie must look like some Hillyard forebear but no Hillyard family albums were available to me.

He was devoted to his mother. This was only to be expected since he had lived since his birth almost exclusively in Vera's sole company. I know my mother would have liked to play with him and talk to him and hold him on her lap but of this she had very little chance. Jamie didn't cry much. He simply didn't respond to others. He would sit silent or stand with his thumb in his mouth, neither accepting nor rejecting overtures, and if you took him on your knees, he suffered your caressing hand, your smiles and your encouragement in wary tenseness, his body growing stiff, at last slipping down and going to Vera with his arms held out. To do her justice, she did not particularly encourage this. I thought her nicer than she used to be. She was much pleasanter to my mother, for one thing, adjuring Jamie to 'go to Aunt Vranni'. (Since Helen's comments, Vera had never again advocated the use of 'auntie'.) She even agreed to going out with my parents one evening and leaving me to baby-sit. Jamie, she said

142

proudly, had been brought up to know six was his bedtime and because of this he never gave her bad nights.

People loved going out and about London that summer. Austerity was with us and there was nothing nice to eat and nothing nice to wear, no luxury or even comfort, not much petrol, but the living theatre had never been better, or the cinema. And there was a delicious intoxication about wandering lighted streets in freedom and safety, knowing there would be no darkness to fall from the air. Vera said, without self-pity or touting for sympathy, quite cheerfully even:

'This will be the first time I've been out in the evening for over three years.'

Jamie woke up ten minutes after they had gone out. I believe now that somehow all the events of that evening – not the waking of Jamie, of course – were engineered by Vera and Eden for the furtherance of their purposes, but things had gone wrong. They had got the wrong evening. Or one or other of them had. Eden, probably. These things are not easy if you communicate mostly by letter. Vera had been very keen to go out on the Friday night, not the Saturday, so I assume all this had been pre-arranged by them for the Saturday but Eden had made a mistake. I believe now that they wanted to give, in the presence of my father and mother, and secondarily in that of Tony Pearmain, a *demonstration*. They wanted to show those three people, those most important three people – I don't think I counted much, I was only seventeen – how they had made their lives and how they were to be accepted before proceeding to the next phase.

Jamie's waking like that put me into a minor panic. I knew very little about babies and had no idea how to handle them when they cried. My instinct was to shut the door on Jamie, go out of earshot of his cries or stuff cotton wool into my ears.

Of course I didn't do this. I opened the door stealthily and looked in. At sight of me, his crying changed to screams. He was in a cot that had once been mine, encaged, standing up, shaking the bars, and I remember thinking how odd it was that we put our small children in cages, that we didn't construct a cot that had some other confining arrangement instead of bars. That was the last coherent rational thought I had for a long time.

Jamie had worked himself into a panic and at first he wouldn't let me touch him. He flung his body backwards and forwards, pushing and punching me when I tried to get hold of him. I suppose I have

143

since then heard children make worse noises, my own children for instance, but the noise Jamie made that evening has stuck in my mind as being uniquely horrible, perhaps because it was an absolutely uninhibited expression of real distress, real pain and loss. I am sure Vera genuinely believed he wouldn't wake up because he hadn't done so for months and months, I am sure she wouldn't have gone out if she had thought he would wake. Never before had he wakened to find her not there – worse, to find her not there and someone else there instead. His misery and terror seemed boundless. At last I succeeded in picking him up and getting him downstairs. He was sodden all over, from tears, dribble, urine and sweat.

There was nothing I could do to stop him crying. Vera no longer breast-fed him but she had weaned him on to a cup, not a bottle. No Longley child had ever been allowed a dummy. I tried to stick his thumb in his mouth but he screamed all the more and I later learned that Vera had spent months getting him out of that one by putting aloes on his thumb. I couldn't stop him yelling so I let him yell while I inexpertly changed his napkin and his pyjama trousers and dried his face. By then I was in almost as much of a panic as he was. He had been screaming for half an hour and his face was purple, the veins standing out on the forehead. I had heard of babies having convulsions and I was afraid he might have one, might in fact have been having one at that moment, for I doubted my ability to recognize a convulsion if I saw it.

I shouted at him, 'I will never baby-sit for anyone else as long as I live,' a resolution I have very nearly kept to, and at that moment the doorbell rang.

We had lived through violent times, we had lived through a war, but somehow one had a far greater sense of safety in those days. Alone in the evening with a baby in a London suburban house now, I would hesitate before opening the front door, I would certainly call out to know who it was. Then, it wouldn't have crossed my mind. Holding the screaming Jamie under my arm in the way I had seen market-going farmers in picture-books carry squealing pigs, bellowing at him to shut up, I opened the door. Outside on the step stood Eden and a man.

'Goodness, darling, I never heard such a fearful noise in all my life! You can hear it all the way down the street.'

'Were you trying to kill it and we interrupted you?' the man said.

The way I was carrying poor Jamie must have inspired this. I hoisted him on to my shoulder where he hung, sobbing.

'Aren't you going to ask us in?' said Eden. Typical Longley. The quintessence of Longleyism was to ask petty, pointless, rhetorical questions when one was up to one's neck in trouble. I opened the door wider and stood back.

Bludgeoned as I was by Jamie's roaring, there was enough awareness left in me to notice their appearance and be astonished by it. Parked at the kerb was a red sports car. (Had Eden really heard Jamie down the street inside *that*?) The two of them looked as if they had been dressed up to advertise it in some glossy magazine published perhaps in South Africa or New Zealand, since we had nothing glossy here, neither magazines nor clothes nor people to wear them. But these two glowed like no one but film-stars. They even looked cleaner than the rest of us and what with fuel scarcities and soap scarcities, no doubt they were. Eden had on a blue linen suit covered with a pattern of white flowers, her companion a blazer with some sort of badge that indicated he had rowed for something or played cricket for something and a shirt that glowed with whiteness, crisp and frosty as Wall's ice cream. He looked young even to me, in his middle twenties, a fresh-faced, brown-haired man, a lot like Richard Burton whom no one had heard of then.

Eden, of course, wasn't going to introduce him. Oblivious apparently to the din, she stood looking round her at our shabby hallway from which the air-raid shelter had been removed, leaving scars on the oak parquet floor, and where the black-out curtains still hung dispiritedly at the window by the front door.

'I'm Tony Pearmain,' he said. 'How do you do?'

I said who I was but Eden had already told him, giving him a run-down in the car, I expect, on what he would find when he got here.

'They're all out,' I said, shouting above Jamie.

'All?'

How was it that I seemed to know, even then, that she was acting? Perhaps because she was no actress.

'Didn't you know Vera was here?'

'Vera? Here?'

It was surprising, of course. Or it would have been a surprise if she hadn't already known.

'Well, of course. This is Jamie. Don't you recognize him?'

'They change so quickly at that age. Can't you stop him making that ghastly noise?'

Tony Pearmain put out his arms and took Jamie from me. The result was magical. Did he smell wonderful, radiate self-confidence, communicate in some mysterious fashion beyond the five senses, through his pores or his nerve ends, that here was security, here was infinite warmth and kindness, here were the everlasting arms? Whatever it was, Jamie recognized it and shut up. He laid his once more wet, sticky, sweaty face against the sleek pile of Tony Pearmain's blazer and grew silent, only gulping occasionally as he got his breath back. Poor Tony had this gift with children. Because he loved them, they loved him, and all gravitated towards him, pins to a lodestone, and his presence made them quiet and good. The abiding tragedy of his life has been that he has never had children of his own and that the one child he might have loved and been loved by, circumstances made repugnant to him.

That evening was the occasion of Jamie's first meeting with Tony. I have told him how Tony held him and quieted him but he shied away from this, he hated being told, and insisted I must be mistaken. This must have been some other boyfriend of Eden's, not 'Pearmain' who was so cold and distant with him, who sent him away as soon as he could – thus, of course, carrying on the Longley family tradition which had begun with Helen and continued with Francis. But Tony it was, Tony who performed this miracle. I stood in the hall, engulfed in relief, savouring the glorious peace, hardly aware for a while that Eden was there behind me.

'Where have they gone?'

'Out somewhere. To the West End. Perhaps the pictures.'

'How awfully annoying!'

I took them into our living-room. Their sleek young presences, their smart new clothes, showed up the deficiencies of a house that hadn't seen a coat of paint, a change of furnishings, during six years of war. The springs of the chair Tony sat in, his arms full of Jamie, were broken and the seat descended to the floor. There was no alcohol of any kind in the house, no coffee and not very much tea. I sensed that at any minute Eden would ask me if I was going to offer them anything to drink. All I could produce was orange squash of a very ersatz kind. I was tempted to offer Jamie's 'government' orange juice but feared Vera's wrath if I did. We had no refrigerator, of course, and the orange juice was lukewarm.

It was only about eight o'clock and unlikely that my parents and Vera would be back before ten thirty. Jamie fell asleep and Tony carried him upstairs. Instead of coming down at once, he sat up there by the cot, waiting to make sure he was going to go on sleeping. Eden was wearing a very beautiful pair of white leather shoes with low-cut perforated tops and high heels. The rest of us were reduced to wooden-soled clogs. I still don't know where and how she got those shoes. Two, three and four years later we were still standing in long queues on the chance of obtaining a pair of Joyce sandals. But Eden always knew people who could get her things, who had fingers and feet in the black market, who brought things into the country in diplomatic bags and book bags, who sold clothes coupons and bypassed queues and kept things 'under the counter' specially for her. She sat in another, slightly less dilapidated chair, contemplating those shoes, lightly stroking the right leg that was crossed over the left, looking at the right shoe with her head a little on one side, a long lock of golden hair falling forward. Without looking up, she said to me:

'He is one of *the* Pearmains, you know.'

I didn't know. She made me very aware of my old white blouse and dirndl skirt.

'I suppose you go shopping sometimes, don't you?'

'Oh, *that* Pearmain,' I said. 'You mean Brewster and Pearmain?' Swan and Edgar, Debenham and Freebody, Marshall and Snelgrove, Brewster and Pearmain. I felt quite overcome. I felt shy of Tony whereas I hadn't before. I had been going to ask her about that evening at the theatre, why she had looked through me, but somehow this revelation about Tony Pearmain made it impossible. And Eden, capitalizing on it, so to speak, as if she sensed the awe she had inspired in me, added:

'I met him at a party at Lady Rogerson's.'

Should I have known about Lady Rogerson? Had Vera perhaps told me when she spoke of Eden's being 'demobbed'? All this brought home to me how little I belonged even by then.

'Lady Rogerson looks on me more or less as a daughter. Naturally I went with her when she stayed at Fontlands. We'll be going again for the twelfth.'

This was incomprehensible. I think it was a couple of years before I understood that Fontlands was the Pearmains' country house (with grouse moor) in Yorkshire, Lady Rogerson the old woman she was being a companion to and the twelfth the twelfth of August when grouse shooting begins. Eden asked me what time the others would be back and when she heard it would be a couple of hours said she didn't think they would stay. Tony came back and said the 'poor little chap' was fast asleep and had I listened to the wireless that day? I shook my head. What was there to listen to any more?

'We've dropped a new sort of bomb on the Japs,' Tony said.

'What sort of bomb?' I said, not very interested. 'A kind of V2?'

'Bigger than that, it seems,' he said. 'Place called Hiroshima, or however you pronounce it.' He pronounced it Hero-sheema. 'The war in the Far East will be over now, you'll see. I left the little chap's door open so you'll hear him if he cries again.'

Off they went in the red sports car. That remark of Tony's about was I trying to kill Jamie was the only, even faintly, witty thing I ever heard him say. His family owned a huge department store, his cousin had married into the Italian nobility. He was, is, as dull as ditchwater and as rich as a goldmine. He was also good-looking, a far cry from Chad who was poor and nothing much to look at and never opened his mouth without saying something interesting or amusing or provocative. Eden seemed pleased with herself when she left, the bad temper she had shown when she found Vera and my parents were out quite gone. But, of course, even in their absence she must have accomplished most of what she set out to do by that visit and if nothing at all had been done for Vera, if matters had been made a little worse – well, *tant pis*.

My father considered himself middle class. He was constantly saying so with a kind of shameful pride. What he never said was that the middle class don't commit adultery whatever the upper and lower may do, but it was a deeply felt aspect of his creed. It would not have crossed his mind that a sister of his could be unfaithful to her husband. He and my mother did not get on well, nor can I say that at the bottom they loved each other for I am sure they did not, but while she lived my father would never have had to do with another woman. It would have been the same for him as stealing or engaging

148

in some fraud at the bank. Therefore, when Gerald came home and he and Vera almost immediately parted, my father's course was not to wonder why and come to the conclusion most people did, that Vera had been having a love affair with Chad Hamner, but to put the blame on Gerald. At first, though, he would not admit that a separation had taken place.

Vera didn't tell him about it. That wasn't her way. There was no question, of course, of Gerald being demobilized. He was a regular soldier. We had all supposed he would come home on leave and then, wherever he might be sent, possibly to Germany with the army of occupation, she would go with him. Laurel Cottage could then be sold and the proceeds divided three ways. However, Vera's letters made no mention of her accompanying Gerald when in the autumn he went with his regiment to somewhere near Lübeck, nor did she give any explanation or reason for her staying behind.

Eden quite often came to see us that winter, usually alone but once bringing Tony Pearmain to meet my parents. She was silent in a mysterious way on the subject of Vera and Gerald. That is, she gave the impression of knowing everything but of being unwilling to betray. It was Helen who told us.

She and my father had never really got on. He had always disliked her. He came near to admitting that he resented her being better off and having a higher social position than the children of my grandfather's second family. And his feelings were unaltered by the fact that Helen only had these things because her own father had rejected her. She was impossibly affected, he used to say. But they had never been not on speaking terms; there had never been an open quarrel. Helen wrote to him to ask if he would have any objection to her giving Eden's wedding reception at her house, and in this letter she mentioned the Vera–Gerald split.

At least my father already knew Eden was going to marry Tony Pearmain. Only just, but he had been told. Eden rang him up with the news the night before it was in *The Times*. Of course she shied away from telling him because, although Tony was more than suitable, was a great catch in fact and all that he should be in the eyes of an older brother, he was not Chad Hamner. My father really did go on about this sort of thing, behaving as if human beings were biologically monogamous, imprinted with the image of a single partner as the grey goose is or the gibbon. In his view, changing the mate you had first selected was tantamount to a defiance of nature. He looked gloomy when he put the phone down and came across the room to us shaking his head. I could find it in my heart to feel sorry for Eden who had been bubbling over with excitement and had surely not expected her brother to be quite so aghast.

Apparently he had believed Tony was some sort of relative of her employer (we all knew about the Lady Rogerson set-up by then) and that Eden occasionally acted as his secretary. My father was able to convince himself of anything he really wanted to be the case, however improbable, if only he tried hard enough.

'I had no idea,' he said, passing his hand across his forehead in a bewildered way. 'I thought she was all fixed up with that nice chap we met at the christening. I don't understand all this chopping and changing. What didn't she like about that journalist chap, I wonder?'

'Hadn't got enough money,' said my mother.

'People don't always have to stick to the same people all their lives,' I said, foreseeing difficulties of my own in this area and not wanting, when the time came, to face too many inquests with my father. 'Not when they meet them when they're eighteen, not for sixty years, surely?' It seemed appalling. 'I don't think Eden was ever in love with Chad anyway or he with her. I don't think it was that kind of thing.'

'What was it, then?' said my father. 'He didn't come to the house to see my sister Vera, did he?'

This was said in the scathing tone of someone presenting a totally absurd proposition, unworthy of serious consideration. It is rather disquieting to hear, as in this case, sarcasm and innocence combined. He was innocent. In the same tone he would have suggested Chad might have been coming to the house in order to make an offer for it or because Vera's wireless had better reception than his own. I said nothing, watching knowledge dawn in my mother's eyes and a smile twitch the corners of her mouth.

Next day we read the announcement in *The Times*. '*The engagement is announced and the marriage will shortly take place between Anthony Fairfax Pearmain, only son of Mr and Mrs Oliver Pearmain, of Fontlands, Ripon, Yorkshire, and Edith Mary, youngest daughter of the late Mr and Mrs Arthur Longley, of Great Sindon, Essex.*'

Helen's letter came a few days later. This was not one of those my father read aloud at the breakfast table. He read it and walked out of the room, taking the letter with him. Presently he came back, looking very flustered and upset, and gave the letter to my mother, the first page first, then, reluctantly, the second.

'A very nice place to have a wedding,' he said, making an effort. 'That's a lovely house they've got there.' He seemed to remember, which restored his gloom, his resentment of Helen's possession of Walbrooks, though he could surely never have convinced himself any other member of the family had a right to it. He turned pettishly to my mother. 'You see what that silly, affected woman says.'

'About the wedding, do you mean?'

She knew very well he didn't mean about the wedding but she said that to provoke him.

'Of course not about the wedding. About my sister Vera. Pernicious trouble-maker, that woman is. Naturally my sister doesn't want to go off living in married quarters in Germany of all places.'

But the damage was done. Or the truth was told. My mother just looked at him in that way she had developed lately when he made out, as she put it, that his sisters were 'a double reincarnation of the Virgin Mary'. She put her head on one side, opened her eyes wide and raised her eyebrows as high as they would go.

What exactly had Helen suggested? I never saw that letter and it was lost long ago. Probably my father destroyed it that same day. I doubt though if Helen went so far as to put forward what was in my mother's mind, what she actually retorted to my father some months later when she was suffering during one of their quarrels from being unfavourably compared with his sister.

'Gerald knows very well Jamie isn't his child. He knows he can't be his child. He may be a fool but he's not such a fool he doesn't know a woman isn't pregnant ten months!'

I was embarrassed that I had overheard. I wanted no more of it and began to long for the autumn when I should go away to Girton and no longer hear them getting into each other's skin, under the scabs where the sores never quite healed. For a long time now I had come to my mother's conclusion, had done the requisite arithmetic and noted Vera's impossible gestation of something around 312 days. I had got used to the idea of Vera and Chad, too, and had almost persuaded myself that I had actually witnessed their embraces, their kisses. While I had been sleeping in Eden's room, I told myself, Chad had come quietly to Vera, creeping up the stairs. It did not seem like him to do this. The whole affair seemed incongruous, Vera his senior and looking so much older, their sense of humour not at all the same, their tastes so divergent. But I had already learnt by then what a mysterious area sex is and how the reason for sexual relationships defies analysis. Jamie, of course, was Chad's child and that was why he had come to the christening – why also so many other people had not. Jamie had Chad's dark brown eyes and pale olive skin. I supposed there would be a divorce and Chad would marry Vera and this vaguely disappointed and irritated me. At the back of my mind was always the feeling that if only he would have waited, he could have had me.

It soon became very clear that Vera was going to live indefinitely at Laurel Cottage. I think there was some correspondence and a few phone calls as well as one interview between my father and Eden on this matter. There was no hardship for Eden. She was marrying a man whose family owned, Helen told me, no less than five country houses. Tony and Eden would be able to take their pick of which one they wanted to live in.

'Goodbye new house, new car, holiday in Switzerland,' said my mother.

'We couldn't have had all those, anyway,' my father said.

'Just one of them would have been nice.'

I should have liked to say to them that quite soon, no doubt, Chad would provide a home for his child and the mother of his child but of course I didn't. To my father, Chad was the rather nice chap who still carried a torch for Eden. And my mother, who took an almost gleeful pleasure in the fact that Jamie could not be Gerald's child, never went so far as to provide an alternative father for him, speaking as though Vera had produced him by parthenogenesis and as if this in itself were a solecism that put her beyond the pale.

Eden was married to Tony Pearmain at St Mary's, Great Sindon, on a fine, sunny Saturday in the summer of 1946.

Will you believe that I was one of Eden's bridesmaids? My dress cost me not a single clothing coupon, for all the silk came to Eden from Hong Kong, brought in by someone she knew in BOAC. Part of the time I stayed at Helen's, part with Vera. It was during the week before the wedding, while I was at Laurel Cottage, that Vera and I and Jamie took that walk which led us past the cottage where Vera as a child had found old Mrs Hislop's body. She was more expansive that day than I had ever known her but not so open that she could speak of the disappearance of Kathleen March.

The strange thing is that I have reached this point in my private reminiscing, my chronological going over in my thoughts of all my memories of Vera and Eden, of Chad and Francis and Jamie, when Daniel Stewart writes to me with his remarkable discovery. I even dreamed of Kathleen March the night before his letter came, having cast myself in the role of invisible onlooker watching Vera and Mavis sitting on the river bank and the unguarded pram with the child in it standing among the willowherb and the meadowsweet. Kathleen's father passed me on the bridge, blinded by headache. What woke me was the horror that came out of the bright meadows, the blue sky, a black and scaly monster one can hardly believe a woman of my age would fantasize, a thing that stepped straight from the illustration to an Andrew Lang fairy story. It snatched the child and I woke up with one of those cries that are the dreamer's attempt at a scream. The evening before I had been reading M. R. James's story *The Mezzotint* in which a similar incident to this takes place.

The morning post brings from Daniel Stewart a new chapter. He has stumbled on these facts by chance. He was sure no one else had spotted the connection. What did I think?

In the annals of unsolved murders (I read) the Kirby Theiston case must be one of the most bizarre and also the most neglected by criminologists. Is this because it has so many features in common with the Constance Kent mystery? Or because, until very recently, the apparently most important characters in the drama were still alive?

Constance Kent, a young girl still in her teens, living in the village of Rode in Somerset, was tried for the murder of her infant half-brother and acquitted. May Durham, a girl of seventeen, living in the village of Kirby Theiston in Norfolk, was arrested for the murder of her two-year-old half-sister but released without being brought to trial. Constance, always suspected, always looked on askance, ended her life in a convent. More than half a century later, May Durham, equally ostracized, was exiled by her own family to Australia in the company of an aunt where five years later she died of tuberculosis. In neither case was the true perpetrator ever found.

Kirby Theiston is a village with a population of around five hundred lying to the west of Norwich. In 1922 the population was rather greater than this and the dual carriageway road which now bisects the village had not yet been built. The church is Saint Michael and All Angels and the principal house, Theiston Hall, once the seat of a branch of the Digby family of Holkham, was occupied as it had been for the previous twenty years by Charles Ethelred Durham and his family. A fine English country house is Theiston Hall, parts of it dating from the fifteenth century, but largely rebuilt at the end of the seventeenth by Henry Dill, a pupil of Archer, in the baroque style with a bowed south front, octagonal drawing-room and hall with ceiling paintings by Thornhill. Durham was the grandson of a wealthy Victorian manufacturer of cotton goods from Rochdale, but neither he nor his father had ever had any occupation beyond that of country gentlemen. No less a landscapist than Loudon had designed the gardens in the late nineteenth century but Durham, a dilettante with artistic aspirations, uprooted the herbaceous borders, the parterres and the rosebeds soon after he came to Theiston and set about creating gardens on the model of those he had seen while travelling in Italy, at Bagnaia, at Settignano and the gardens of the Villa d'Este at Tivoli. Large quantities of statuary were imported and as late as 1922 men were still at work on the steps, ornamental ponds, follies and temples necessary to the 'Italianization' of the garden.

Durham was forty-six years old and had been twice married. His first wife, Honoria Filby, died when she was only twenty-seven, leaving him with a son Charles, always called Charlie, and a daughter, Honoria Mary, known as May. Durham married again seven years later in 1917 the daughter of a doctor with a prosperous practice in Norwich. Her name was Irene McAllister and by 1920 she had borne him three children, Edward, Julius and Sonia. This last was something of a vogue name in the late teens and early twenties of the century, due not to Russian influence, the Russian Revolution having taken place in 1917, but to a novel by Stephen McKenna with a heroine and title of that name, published the same year. The little girl, however, was always called Sunny, partly due to her particularly sweet nature and partly to her brother Edward's having made this diminutive of Sonia.

The household, therefore, at the time of the murder was a large one, consisting of Mr and Mrs Durham, Charlie, May, Edward, Julius and Sunny, with their servants, a butler called Thomas Chapman, Mrs Deedes, the housekeeper, Mrs Brown, the cook, two housemaids, a parlourmaid, a kitchenmaid, Sarah Keringle, the children's nurse, and the under-nurse, Bessie Stonebridge. Three gardeners were also employed, John Williams, the head gardener, Thomas Pritchard and Arthur Bailey. The land adjoining Theiston Hall was extensive and included thirty acres of woodland. Pheasants and partridges were preserved and Durham employed a gamekeeper, Robert Jephson, who occupied a cottage on the property next door to that in which John Williams, the head gardener, lived. In the month of May of 1922, the only member of this household not at home was Charlie, he being up at Oxford in his second year at Worcester College. Everyone else was present and the usual number was, in fact, augmented by the presence of guests in Jephson's cottage, for his sister, her husband and their two children were staying with him and his wife as they usually did at this time of the year. This visit served the double purpose of providing them with a holiday and securing help to Jephson in the rather finicking and time-consuming task of collecting the fallen eggs of gamebirds and setting them under hens or already sitting pheasants. The pheasant was a sacrosanct bird in those parts, precious at every phase of its life cycle, and there had been an unpleasant incident some years before when Jephson's predecessor, an elderly man called Brimley, had shot May Durham's pet cat when he caught it taking and decapitating pheasant chicks. Charles Durham had not exactly dismissed the man but had retired him on a small pension, depriving him of the cottage he had lived in for forty years.

May Durham was an extremely good-looking girl of seventeen years and nine months, with fine dark eyes and black hair so long she could sit on it but which she was considering having bobbed in the current fashion. She had been educated at home, her governess having left the previous Christmas, and Charles Durham had intended sending her to finishing school in France but that spring May had met the young Norwich architect, Thierry Watkin. He had asked her to marry him but Durham refused to sanction an official engagement until they had known each other longer. May, therefore, was living at home with little to do but go calling with her stepmother, arrange flowers, play tennis. She seems to have had no hobbies or intellectual interests of any kind and although considered an accomplished pianist never lifted the lid of the piano after her governess left. Her relationship with her stepmother was an uneasy one, though she seemed to have got over the intense, fierce resentment she had shown when her father first re-married. Of her small half-brothers she was fond, playing with them, taking them out and lavishing a good deal of attention on them, so that family friends smiled their approval at the projected marriage with Watkin, seeing May as the maternal type.

Sunny, however, she is said to have disliked. It is hard to imagine a beautiful, healthy, comfortably situated girl of seventeen disliking her two-year-old half-sister, especially as the child was known for her easy disposition and 'sunny' temperament. On the other hand, two things about Sunny might, if we are to see May as paranoid, or a near-psychopath, have inspired a pathological dislike in her. She bore an extraordinarily close resemblance to her mother, Mrs Irene Durham, and she was adored by her father to the extent perhaps of displacing May in his affections. Georgina Hallam-Saul, the only writer to have dealt at any length with the Kirby Theiston case, put forward a curious postulation. This is that in the early part of the twentieth century, more specifically from 1910 till about 1940, there was a definite cult of aligning blondeness with beauty, so that a dark-haired woman was considered less well-favoured than a fair one, often irrespective of other claims to beauty such as feature, figure or eye colour. Now May Durham, as has been said, was dark-haired and with very dark colouring, olive skin, brown eyes. She favoured her mother. Charles Durham inclined to fairness, his second wife was a very fair, pale-skinned blonde and their daughter Sunny had golden hair and blue eyes. Miss Hallam-Saul suggests this as a cause of envy and resentment on May's part of her half-sister but Miss

Hallam-Saul, of course, is committed to her theory of May as perpetrator.

It seems clear that May seldom chose to be accompanied by the little girl when out in the garden or the grounds while the little boys were always acceptable company on a walk or a visit to the various pet animals the Durham family kept – a pony, the sheepdog who had his kennel out in the stable yard, the guinea fowls in their run, the Old English rabbits. However, on this particular Tuesday morning in May 1922, when May Durham set off with Edward and Julius to show them for the first time the kittens to which her cat (successor to the one shot by Brimley) had given birth a week before, she also took Sunny. This was the second brood of kittens the cat had produced and, like the first time, she had chosen to have them, not in the lying-in quarters prepared for her by May Durham in May's own bedroom, but in the hollowed-out trunk of an oak tree.

What happened during that visit no one knows. Now no one will ever know. May's account was simply that she lost Sunny. The cat, though gentle with its owner, scratched Edward when he touched it and for a few minutes all May's attention was given to him, comforting him and wiping away the blood with her handkerchief. The tree where the cat's litter was was on the edge of the woods, not too far from the house but separated from it by the stable block and paddock. According to May, she believed Sunny to be sitting on a log next to Julius, but when she turned round, Julius was still there and Sunny had disappeared.

Julius Durham, now sixty-six years old, remembers nothing of that day. He was only three. His brother, Edward, eighteen months his senior, recalls details of that morning, though he admits that much of what he 'remembers' may be derived from what he was later told.

'May's cat scratched me on the hand. I suppose it was the first real pain I had ever felt. I don't remember blood, only May hugging me and telling me to be brave. Of course I was bawling and screaming. May tied her handkerchief round my hand and then I think we all started looking for Sunny but, as you know, we couldn't find her.'

May seems not to have been too worried. She thought the child had gone back to the house on her own, rather a curious conclusion for her to have come to considering Sunny was only just two and seldom walked any distance without being carried. And when she got back to the house with the boys, she made no inquiries about Sunny.

The reason she gave the police for not doing so was that, in the distance, in the lane which linked the stable yard with that part of the grounds where the gardener's and gamekeeper's cottages were, she saw Bessie Stonebridge, the under-nurse, talking to a woman and with them was a small girl she took for Sunny. In fact, this child was not a girl but a boy, nephew of the gamekeeper, and the woman was his mother. May Durham was short-sighted and it was vanity that stopped her wearing glasses.

It was therefore more than an hour later that Sunny was missed. The Durhams were giving a tennis party that afternoon and the young people of the neighbourhood were invited to play and their parents to watch. Pritchard had freshly marked out the court and May was with him checking the height of the net (one tennis racquet's vertical height plus the measurement of the head held horizontally) when the nurse Sarah Keringle came to her to say it was time for Miss Sunny's luncheon. May, aghast, admitted she thought the child was with Bessie but Bessie, for the past half-hour, had been in the nursery with the two little boys.

A search for Sunny was mounted, the searchers initially being Charles Durham, John William and Arthur Bailey. They were later joined by Mrs Durham and May. The first guest to arrive for the party – no one at Theiston Hall except Edward and Julius had had any lunch – was Thierry Watkin, and he too joined in the search. Sunny, however, could not be found and Charles Durham phoned the local police. To Thierry Watkin fell the unenviable task of turning away the party guests as they came.

The police arrived promptly enough, a village constable and later a sergeant from Norwich. They set about interviewing everyone who might have seen Sunny, beginning with the indoor and outdoor servants at Theiston Hall and proceeding to Kirby Theiston village. No one admitted to having seen her since eleven that morning. The occupants of Theiston Hall were obliged to go to bed that night without news of Sunny's whereabouts.

Next morning the child's body was found by Jephson's dog no more than fifty yards from the log where she had been sitting next to her brother. The body was in a shallow grave made by scooping up the leaf mould, a task that could easily have been done with the bare hands. Her throat had been cut.

There was no doubt it was murder. The mode of death put

accident out of the question. Norfolk CID came and questioned May. Sarah Keringle had told them that when Miss May came for the children she had been wearing a blue print cotton frock but later, when checking the height of the tennis net, had changed it for a linen skirt and black and white jumper. Why, the police asked, had she changed her dress *before* checking the net, why not after luncheon and before the party? May said there had been blood on the blue dress from Edward's scratched hand. It was then that the police took May to Norwich to the police station.

She spent one night there and was released next day. Chief Inspector John Finch had satisfied himself by then that Edward had been scratched by May's cat and that Sunny's killer would not have got a few spots of blood on his or her clothes but would have been liberally splashed with it. He and his men next turned their attention to the village and the various men living there known to be less respectable than their neighbours – one, for instance, who had spent a night in jail on a drunk and disorderly charge; another who was a known poacher. Needless to say, there was no one in Kirby Theiston who had ever remotely been suspected of child molestation, let alone the brutal murder of a child.

It was at this late stage that they finally came to question those relatives of Jephson who were guests in his cottage. An extraordinary aspect of the Kirby Theiston murder was that although Finch was told on the day of the discovery of Sunny's body that Jephson had his sister, his brother-in-law and his two-and-a-half-year-old nephew staying with him, he showed no interest in them and made no attempt to talk to them until *five days after* Sunny disappeared. When he did come to question them their visit was over and they were about to return to their own home at Sindon Road in Essex.

Robert Jephson's sister was named Adele and her husband was Albert March.

Two years before, the Marches had also lost a child, also a girl, also two years old – their daughter, Kathleen. This fact, it seems, was unknown to Chief Inspector Finch and his questions did not elicit it. Miss Hallam-Saul, in her examination of the Kirby Theiston case, does not mention it. Her mention of the March family is confined to two paragraphs in the chapter on the characters and antecedents of the outdoor servants at Theiston Hall.

In his collection of murder case histories, *Murder in East Anglia*, James Moore-Whyte gives pride of place to the Kirby Theiston mystery but he does not refer to the Marches beyond this slight reference in the following paragraph:

Chief Inspector Finch asked permission of Mrs Jephson, the gamekeeper's wife, to search the cottage. The hunt was on for bloodstained clothing and the knife which was the murder weapon. Mrs Jephson told Finch he could search all he liked as she and her husband would not be there for an hour or two. They were going to Norwich with her brother and sister-in-law who had been staying with them, to see them off at the station.

What questions, then, did Finch ask Albert and Adele March? Only, apparently, if they had ever seen the child Sunny and if they had ever seen anyone suspicious hanging about the grounds. To both they replied in the negative, left the house and were never questioned again.

Sunny Durham's killer was never found. Irene Durham believed her stepdaughter responsible, citing May's uncontrollable jealousy as motive. Herself on the verge of a mental breakdown – she had been pregnant when Sunny was killed and miscarried a week later – Irene struck May in the face when the girl tried to offer her sympathy and told her husband she and May could no longer continue to live under the same roof. There had been no positive engagement with Thierry Watkin, though something more than an understanding, but Watkin did not renew his proposals. He called only once after the day of the tennis party and shortly afterwards left the neighbourhood. Gradually it became obvious that the village believed May had killed her half-sister and had never been brought to trial only through lack of proof. One day she was stoned by a group of boys in the village and had stitches inserted in her forehead.

Did her father think her guilty? Instead of a finishing school in France, May was sent to a sanatorium near Brunnen in Switzerland, her health, it was suggested, having given way under the strain. Prior to this there had been no hint of May being phthisic, but it was of tuberculosis she died five years later, having passed the previous four in Melbourne in the company of her father's sister, Miss Mary Durham. Or did the Durham family somehow manage to hush up the fact that May, in fact, committed suicide?

Charles Durham died in 1939, his second wife, Irene, in 1962, his son, Charlie, five years after his stepmother. The son Irene gave birth to in 1925, christened Colin Jonathan, was killed climbing in the Himalayas in 1964. Only Edward and Julius Durham survive of the Durham family of Theiston Hall. The house is now a conference centre. John Williams, the head gardener, died in 1932; Thomas Pritchard in 1942; Arthur Bailey in 1946, and Sarah Keringle in 1952. Bessie Stonebridge married, became the mother of four children of her own and now, as Mrs Dryburgh, aged eighty-one, lives with her married daughter in Aberdeen. Of the other indoor servants, only the kitchenmaid, Margaret Otter, survives. At eighty, a single woman, she still lives in the neighbourhood of Norwich. Robert and Kitty Jephson, a childless couple, died within months of each other in 1970. Adele March died at the age of ninety a month before this was written, having survived her first husband, Albert, by fifty-five years and her second husband, William Bacon, by sixteen.

Kathleen March was two when she disappeared. So was Sonia 'Sunny' Durham. Each was in the care of a young girl and each young girl thereafter carried a stigma through life, the stigma of a universal, whispered belief that she was a child-killer. But the common factor in these cases surely is Albert March, known to have crossed the bridge at Sindon Weir round about the time of his child's disappearance, known to have been at Theiston Hall at the time of the disappearance of Sunny Durham. In the ten years between 1920 and 1930 – from a year after March's marriage, that is, until the year of his death – no fewer than five female children between eighteen months and five years disappeared in the north-Essex/south-Suffolk area. March had received a head wound while in France in the war of 1914–18 and this had left him liable to crushing headaches of the migraine type. Had it also caused brain damage of another kind, so that while afflicted with this almost intolerable head pain he was driven to commit acts for which he was in no way personally responsible and which he forgot once the headache was past?

I laid down these sheets of manuscript as shocked and moved as Daniel Stewart would have had me but not for the reasons he would have expected. It is true that I took in the burden of what he was saying, that all the evidence now pointed to Albert March having been guilty of Kathleen's murder and that therefore Vera must be exonerated, but I took it in with indifference; I had never thought Vera capable of killing a child.

What touched my feelings with a cold finger, what made me lay down the pages and find myself staring unseeing into the past, was the name Jonathan Durham. A Jonathan Durham had been Tony Pearmain's best man and had later married one of my fellow bridesmaids the way best men are supposed to but seldom do. Was it the same Jonathan Durham? It must be. I remember he was a climber and that he came from somewhere in Norfolk. And he would have been the right age. Here indeed was the stealthy convergence of human lots. I remember him well as I remember everything about that day, Eden's wedding day.

Sweet-pea colours we bridesmaids wore and I was the one in pale purple. The sugar-pink one was called Evelyn Something and it was she who later married Jonathan. Eden had refused to wear slipper satin which was the fashion and had a billowing dress made (she told Vera and me) out of twenty yards of white tulle. She spent the night before the wedding at Laurel Cottage and Vera was the first to see her dressed in this amazing confection with its tight bodice and sleeves and huge skirt. A girl who worked for a local hairdresser (and who lived with her parents in Inkerman Terrace next door to the house that had been the Marches') came at nine in the morning to do her hair first and then Vera's. My hair, being very long and straight, didn't need doing. The night before, it had been quite like old times, Francis sleeping in the room on the other side of the landing, Eden and I sharing her room, the beds still as far removed from each other as possible. When she opened one of the drawers in the dressing-table to hunt about for a pair of eyebrow tweezers, guilt got hold of me and I wondered if she had ever noticed my incursions into her privacy, if I had left a long, brown hair behind or the marks of none-too-clean twelve-year-old fingers. But it was soon apparent that she had discarded every cosmetic and perfume that dressing-table had contained. She had gone up the scale now and nothing but top-rank French toiletries would do for her. But her sophistication did not extend to the appointments of the room. Before she got into bed, she unhooked the Peter Pan photograph from the wall.

'I mustn't forget to take that with me,' she said. 'That's absolutely my favourite statue, you know, Faith. It was wonderful being in London and seeing it every week.'

I couldn't help remembering how she had been in London and had seen me but for reasons of her own chosen to ignore me.

'I suppose this room is going to be Jamie's,' I said.

'Really, I haven't thought about it,' she said. 'You'll have to ask Vera.'

Eden did not like children. Or so it seemed to me, seeing her with Jamie. She took very little notice of him except to tell him not to do things, more specifically not to touch things when the things were hers. She sat up in bed and transferred her engagement ring, which she wore night and day, from her left hand to her right. It was a spectacular ring, not so much a cluster as a *dome* of diamonds on a thin platinum band. Eden told me next morning that she hadn't slept a wink all night and perhaps this was true. Since I *had* slept, I was in no position to judge.

Her face looked a bit drawn and her eyes puffy. I was getting my energy together to get up and go for my bath. We all had to have a bath and since I was the least important I was to have mine first, at 7.30, to allow time for the hot-water tank to heat up again.

Eden said, 'Wait a minute,' and astounded me by making me the recipient of the first confidence I had ever had from her. And what a confidence! I had begun to get over my awkward habit of blushing by then but I felt my cheeks burn and I looked away, not meeting her eyes.

The words burst from her, unchecked. 'Is he going to know I'm not a virgin?'

'I don't know,' I said. 'How should I know?'

The six years between us were nothing, the relationship of aunt and niece was everything. A deep embarrassment conquered almost every other feeling. It wasn't until later that I reflected how incongruous it was that the girl who asked me this question was the same one who had stormed at my father over my failure to write a thank-you letter, the same one that had ignored me in the street.

'Only I'm not,' she said. 'They say men know.'

'Only if they've slept with lots of girls, I should think,' I said, common sense asserting itself. 'Has he?'

She said she didn't know. She sat up, wrapping her arms round her knees. With her head tied up in a chiffon scarf, she looked like Hope sitting on the world in that picture. Grandmother Longley used to have a print of it in sepia which disappeared when Vera took over.

'Why ask me?' I said. 'Why not ask Vera? She's more likely to know.'

'I can't.' Crisp and desperate. 'It's out of the question.'

'I read somewhere,' I said – all my experience came from books – 'that you get the same results from riding. Horses, I mean. Did you use to ride?'

She shook her head. 'That's something else I've got to tell him, that I've never been on a horse. He thinks I have. He's never known anyone who can't ride.'

With difficulty I kept a straight face. 'Well, don't go and tell him, will you? Not about the riding, the other thing. Remember what happened to Tess of the d'Urbervilles.'

But Eden had never heard of Tess. While I was having my bath I wondered which of the men it was Eden had lost her virginity to. Chad? Surely not, if he was Vera's man and Jamie's father. I flinched at the whole idea. The naval officer, the Honourable, who got drowned? The man she had gone to the theatre with? Or perhaps they had all been lovers of hers. I was intrigued and a bit shocked. This was 1946. The idea of a woman having lovers outside marriage was no longer horrifying, unspeakable, or the daring prerogative of an upper class, but it was still shocking to older people, and to my generation and Eden's something to be discreet and reticent about. That, I thought, was why she didn't want to ask Vera's opinion. Vera was nearly forty and things had been different when she was young. I don't know how I managed to hold this view while at the same time believing that Vera had been unfaithful to Gerald and was having a love affair with Chad, but I did.

This must be the only instance I have ever known of a woman being given in marriage by her own nephew. My father had been hurt by Eden's failure to ask him to give her away. She gave him (on the phone) a typical Longley excuse – you couldn't call it a reason – for not asking him. He put the phone down and came back to my mother and me, putting a brave face on things.

'She says it wouldn't do, not when I've got a daughter of my own. She says it would be another thing if you were married and I'd already given you away.'

'I'm afraid Faith can't get married just to oblige her,' said my mother.

Francis was to do it. He came down to breakfast wearing the pinstriped trousers of his morning suit and the white shirt that went with it, though no tie. Vera fussed about, saying he would get egg on his clothes. Francis, of course, played up to this with a tease I had seen once before. He left the table, sat in an armchair and balanced on one of its arms a full cup of tea in a saucer. Now I had scarcely ever seen Francis do a maladroit thing, he was a very graceful, manually dextrous person, who never dropped or spilt things except on purpose. And if I knew this, Vera must know it much better. But she never learned. Francis played up to her anxieties, moving his elbow in such a way as to come within a quarter of an inch of the cup, shifting in the chair to make it rock, lifting the cup to his mouth and replacing if off-centre in the saucer. If the tea had spilt, it would have gone all over his trousers and shirt sleeves too probably or else on to Jamie, who had chosen that particular patch of carpet to sit on and play with a stack of old wooden bricks that had once been my father's.

Vera could move Jamie. She did and he set up a howling until he was allowed back again. With Francis she could do nothing but beg him to move the cup. She even gave him a small side table, first removing all the knick-knacks with which it was loaded. Francis responded by placing on it the newspaper, his cigarettes and an expensive-looking gold cigarette lighter. The tea he had hardly touched.

'It's got cold,' he said. 'I'd better have a fresh cup,' and he tipped the tea away, refilling the cup and putting it back on the arm of the chair.

Why is it that really beautiful women when *en déshabille* can look so much more awful than ordinary-looking ones? I have noticed this again and again. They think it unnecessary to bother, I suppose. Men have told them they would look beautiful in a sack and possibly they would, indeed they would, a sack might not be an unflattering garment; it is not sacks we are talking about, though, but grubby old blue flannel dressing gowns and tatty stained headscarves, dirty marabou mules and flaking nail varnish. Eden sat at the table exhibiting all these, eating nothing, her face greasy, a bit of cherry skin from last night's supper trapped between her front teeth. Jamie, who was beginning to lose his total dependence on Vera as the only person in his world, went up to Eden with a toy car in his hand. She turned to him a face of impatient despair and without exactly pushing him away made at him that sort of gesture one makes when someone else's cat or dog is importunate – a brisk dismissive sweep of the arm.

Vera would never reproach Eden. They seemed less close than they had been but this rule still held. She looked wretched.

'Come to Mummy, my darling,' she said and she held out her arms to him.

It was extraordinary what happened then. The tea in the teacup having served its purpose, Francis poured it away and, going to Eden, raised her up into a standing position, took her in his arms and hugged her closely.

'Bear up, my old love.'

She hid her face in his shoulder. They stood there embraced, swaying slightly. I sat there at the table alone while on one side of me Vera hugged Jamie and on the other Francis hugged Eden and at first I felt bored by them and then – the old feeling back again – left out.

Vera said in a dreary, neutral sort of voice, 'The hairdresser will be here in ten minutes.'

Eden gave a little scream and let go of Francis.

'I have to talk to you!'

'Do you, sweetheart?' he said. 'I expect that can be managed. My time is all yours. I'm giving you my day.'

I guessed she was going to ask him what she had asked me. And somehow I knew he would know the answer. He was the kind of person who always knows things like that.

'Go get your bath,' he said, 'and then we'll let our hair down and take our knickers off or whatever girls do when they talk.'

'Francis!' Vera shouted at him. She held Jamie tight against her as if someone were menacing him. I thought she was going to reproach Francis for that remark about knickers. 'Smut' she would call it. But she didn't. 'What do you mean, "talk"? What can you have to talk about? Eden's getting married at midday.'

It was curious. I had the feeling she was talking to Eden yet it was Francis she addressed in that hectoring tone she would never have used to Eden. Is it hindsight that makes me say she looked pale and frightened? I expect it is. Stupidly she said:

'I forbid you to upset Eden!'

He burst out laughing. The hairdresser rang the front doorbell and I went to let her in.

For some reason, perhaps because I saw him as Gerald's successor, I expected Chad to come to the house during the morning. But he didn't come and his name wasn't mentioned. My parents were staying at a hotel in Sudbury, the bridegroom and his family at a much grander one in Dedham. There were going to be two hundred people at this wedding. Eden had wanted to spend her last night as Miss Longley at the Chatterisses' house, Helen later told me, had almost taken it for granted she would, having in mind a grand dinner to impress her future in-laws. Helen would have been quite happy to produce the dinner but her heart bled (as she put it) for poor Vera.

'Think how unhappy she would be, darling,' she had said to Eden. 'Do stay that one night with her, I beg. You have so much and, really, when you come to think of it, she has so little.'

And Eden, giving in with a bad grace, had said incomprehensibly, 'I should have thought Vera had had quite enough of me.'

On my way to dress, I passed Vera's open bedroom door and saw her inside dressing Jamie in blue shorts and white silk shirt. The last time I had seen them in there together, Jamie had been at Vera's breast. Her expression now was no less radiant, committed, adoring. Chad had told me that the way to make a character in fiction lovable is to give him something to love. His old mother will do, his spaniel will do, at a pinch his budgerigar will do. I had always rather disliked Vera but you couldn't dislike a woman who loved a child so dearly as Vera loved Jamie. She was transformed, softened, altogether sweetened by him. The awful word for what he was doing for her is 'tenderizing', the process used on steak.

'We thought he could be Aunt Eden's page, didn't we, my lovely?' she said. 'But Aunt Eden didn't like the idea. She thought children might be troublesome. Which,' she added reasonably, 'is quite understandable.'

What has become of Eden's wedding photographs? I suppose Tony has them still or, more likely, has long ago thrown them away. He has never re-married and spends most of his time abroad. In the Far. There is one wedding picture of Eden in 'the box', posed alone, but perhaps no record now exists of how Eden and Francis looked together, glorious fair-haired twins that they seemed, a Hollywood bridal couple in the days when film-stars were beautiful people, films were sleek and polished and grooming was obligatory before attending any function. They were a little unreal too, waiting there in Vera's living-room, standing because sitting more than she had to would have crumpled Eden's tulle. Waxworks they might have been with their smooth faces and gleaming hair, the sheen on their clothes and the stiffness in their fingers, facsimiles of people someone had the forethought to make, knowing that one day Tussaud's might be glad to have them. But it is Vera only who stands in Tussaud's, her effigy plumper and glossier than the real woman ever was but, by some grotesque accident or design, dressed in the suit she wore for Eden's wedding, dark blue with a fall of blue and white spotted foulard at the neck.

When I walked up the aisle behind Eden, one of a bevy of whom Evelyn who married Jonathan Durham, Patricia Chatteriss and a Naughton cousin called Audrey were the others, I saw Chad in a front pew on the bride's side but a long way from Vera who with Jamie was correctly sandwiched between Helen and my mother. On the other side of Helen, between her and the General, sat their son Andrew who had been a Hurricane pilot in the Battle of Britain and then a prisoner of war, my cousin but not quite my cousin, for we had one not two grandparents in common. Darker than any of us Longleys, he had a cadaverous look about him then, his face all hollows, his cheeks wasted. In the camp he had got very thin and had never regained that lost weight. To me there was something intensely romantic about his appearance, something heroic. What must it have been like to have an aircraft disintegrate around you, to embark on the terrible fall amid the fireworks of anti-aircraft guns, to drift down through the night sky into the enemy's country where God knew what awaited you? I looked at him and, without smiling, he winked at me. Later on I was pretty sure that wink had been meant for his sister but at the time I thought it was for me.

Chad was staring in Eden's direction with a peculiar, suffering intensity. It made me wonder if he had turned to Vera when Eden rejected him. I turned my eyes away, fixing them on the back of Eden's veil, not wanting later to be accused by Vera of unbridesmaidenly behaviour. What can you say about a wedding? All weddings are the same, all brides are beautiful, all flower arrangements the loveliest one has ever seen, all music the best one has ever heard – till next time. Except in *Jane Eyre*, no one ever does get up and speak of impediments. And for all the curious circumstances surrounding Eden's wedding, the paranoid strangeness of her and Vera's behaviour, no one could justifiably have done so. What had happened did not constitute an impediment in the legal sense, though no doubt it would have done in Tony Pearmain's eyes.

Who had chosen the Wedding March from *The Marriage of Figaro* for the walk back down the aisle? Not Eden who, I am sure, had scarcely heard of Mozart. Tony, then, or his mother, or his best man. It was a brave attempt at being original which failed because that march was written for an orchestra and defies all arrangements for the organ. The organist – sister of Mrs Deliss at the Priory – did her best, and the instrument jerked and wheezed and pounded and none of us knew how to walk in time to it, finally adopting a kind of goose step. I could see people in the congregation wincing. Chad, who I thought would sympathize with Eden, winced too and then went through the lip-pursing, face-contorting motions of someone who can't repress his laughter. He put his handkerchief up to his face and pretended to blow his nose.

Jamie sat quiet throughout the ceremony and came quiet and awed to Helen's house. But there he fell in with the caterers' people, maids who carried him off to the kitchens, swathed him in dinner napkins and fed him with ice cream. Food was served in the dining-room which had french windows opening on to the lawn, and poor enough food it was in 1946, needy nothing trimmed in jollity, the Richardson silver and the flowers distracting the mind and palate too from chicken and Spam, rabbit vol-au-vents and mock cream. It was a marvellous, hot day, one of those rare English summer days which are clear as well as sunny and there is no haze to mask the sky. Somehow or other, without help, the Chatterisses had managed to keep the garden going throughout the war. Helen, who looked as if her hands had never done heavier work than fine sewing or the washing of porcelain, had spent part of every day gardening while Andrew was missing, the best method, she used to say, of bringing herself a measure of peace of mind. Knowing nothing about it, but modelling her herbaceous borders on those she had seen on a pre-war visit to Glyndebourne, she had gone about her neighbours' gardens helping herself to snippets and cuttings of their plants until those borders that in Richardson days had held nothing but roses and lavender bushes, now formed long, thick ribbons of colour, filled as they were with the crimson and ivory spires of astilbe, with agapanthus, the blue poppy, and echinops, the blue thistle, with nepeta in a blue mist, silvery artemisia and cineraria, with southern-wood that is called lad's love, and *Alchemilla mollis*, the maiden's breath. The lawns ran down to the shallow sheet of water, lily-covered, that Helen called a pond and Vera, when speaking of it to acquaintances, 'the lake'. Standing by the water's edge with a glass of something that was not quite champagne in my hand, feeling with my toes through my thin pumps (satin shoes of my mother's from the twenties dyed purple) the iron-hard, callus-like remains of the great tree stump under the turf, I asked Andrew if they had imported the swans specially for the wedding. They drifted, with a dignity that was indifferent to these human watchers, among the bronze-coloured, dish-shaped lily leaves and under the willows that trailed their hoar leaves in the glassy stream.

'They arrived yesterday,' he said. 'We're very pleased to see them. There've been no swans at Walbrooks since the pair were shot.'

'Someone shot swans?' I said.

'Don't you know the story?'

'I never know stories,' I said. 'I don't know how it is that everyone knows them but me but that's the way it always is. I didn't know about Vera saving Eden's life under the tree that used to be here until three years ago.'

'Oh, *that*.' It was Francis. No one could sneer so splendidly as Francis. He had come up behind me with Chad.

'Well, it happened,' I said.

'She always had the instincts of a Girl Guide.'

'Tell me about the swans,' I said to Andrew.

'My great-grandparents, my mother's grandparents who used to live here, had a little boy. His name was Frederick and if he were alive today he would be seventy-eight. But they lost both their children, their son when he was three and their daughter, my mother's mother, in her twenties. There was a pair of swans nesting on the pond here. Frederick had a nurse who was an ignorant, backward sort of girl, more or less retarded, I suppose. She took him to the pond and showed him the cygnets and the cob – that's the male swan – attacked him and – well, beat him to death with its wings.'

'That's horrible!' I said.

'Yes. They dismissed the nurse. My great-grandfather got his shotgun and came down here and shot the cob and the pen and all the cygnets. I suppose he was out of his mind with shock and misery. But now, after seventy-five years, the swans have come back.'

Francis drawled, 'Do you suppose these have a family in the reeds? Perhaps we should get one of the caterers' girls – the one who dropped the sherry bottle – to bring Jamie down here.'

There was a shocked silence. Then Chad said:

'Not really amusing, dear lad.'

'That depends on your taste,' said Francis. 'I find I have a particularly sophisticated idea of what constitutes entertainment. For instance, I have often thought how much I should have enjoyed the Roman games. I should have liked to do what Wilde said Domitian did and peer through a clear emerald at the red shambles of the Circus.'

Andrew said nothing but his face was very severe and condemnatory. Chad was laughing. He began telling us how his grandfather had refused to let his mother, at the time a woman of twenty-five, keep a copy of *Dorian Gray* in the house. But suddenly he fell silent and quoted, in quite a different sort of voice:

'There is no name, with whatever emphasis of passionate love repeated, of which the echo is not faint at last.' He seemed to be addressing the swans. 'And thank God for that,' he said.

He and Francis went off – to tease someone else, presumably.

'I thought it unfortunate,' Andrew said, 'their mentioning Oscar Wilde in quite that way and quoting him too in your presence.'

I was enchanted by his gentlemanlike, not to say courtly, behaviour. I was so overcome I forbore to point out that the quotation was from Landor, not Wilde.

'An extraordinary pair. I find it hard to think of Francis as my cousin.'

'Do you find it hard to think of *me* as your cousin?' I said, emboldened by the mock champagne.

'I don't think I do quite. Think of you as my cousin, I mean. Do you want me to?'

'Oh, no.'

He looked curiously at me. Patricia and Evelyn and Jonathan Durham were approaching us across the lawn.

171

'Francis is up at Cambridge, isn't he?'

'Oxford,' I said.

'I must say that's rather a relief. I'm going up to Cambridge in October.' I did not tell him that I was, too. Why tell him something it would be more interesting for him to discover from some other source? 'I shall be rather a mature undergraduate,' he said, and broke off to introduce Jonathan to me.

I wonder now if Andrew had delayed telling the story of the little Richardson boy and the swans until Jonathan had joined us, would Jonathan have spoken of his own sister, killed at the same age? And if he had, mentioning Jephson in the telling, would I have made the connection forty years before Daniel Stewart? But the swan story was past and Jonathan had not heard it and soon it was time for Eden and Tony to leave for their honeymoon in a borrowed house in Derbyshire. Why is it that the upper classes, or at any rate the rich, from the royal family down, are lent country houses by their relatives for honeymoons while the rest of us go to such more interesting and exciting places as Brighton or Paris or Capri?

Back we went to Laurel Cottage, Vera and I and Jamie. This was pure altruism on my part and I was proud of myself for it. My parents had gone back to London. Helen asked me to stay at Walbrooks 'with the rest of the young people' and I would have liked to, I would have liked to very much, and surely it would be more tactful to leave Vera alone with Chad for the evening and perhaps the night?

'Jamie and I will be all on our own, then,' she said a little peevishly.

I thought this unlikely. Francis would surely be there. He was in the room with Helen and Vera and me while we discussed this, standing apart and listening in that way he had, like a character in the Jacobean drama, Bosola, for instance, gathering crumbs for future malicious use, I thought. But I said I would go back with Vera. Perhaps I sensed that today she had finally lost Eden for ever. I was unprepared for her cheerful manner, a quite unforced contentment, on the way home in Mr Morrell's car and afterwards as she was getting Jamie ready for bed.

'Things went very well, didn't they?' she said, dipping him into the bath amid his flotilla of toys. 'The weather couldn't have been better and it was a lovely service. Didn't you think the music was lovely?'

'Well,' I said, 'I wasn't too keen on that march they went out to. It sounded as if something had got broken in the organ.'

'Blessed is he,' said Vera, 'who sitteth not in the seat of the scornful.'

This was a favourite Bible quote of hers and my father's, Eden's too for all I know. They got it from their own mother. Considering their attitude to life, this is as fine an example of projection as one might come across. I should have known better than to criticize anything connected with Eden. Vera soaped Jamie and gently splashed him and he shrieked with delight and splashed her back. When she said that about the seat of the scornful, her face had creased up and packed itself into a hard, fixed mask. She was already getting that vertical pleating on her upper lip most people don't devlop before fifty. But playing with Jamie she was transformed again, young again, with the untried, innocent face of the portrait in 'the box'.

She surprised me by talking of Eden in a way I had never thought possible. I suppose she was beginning to think of me as grown-up. Up till then she had referred to Eden only to praise something she had made or done or to boast of her friends and her social position.

'If I'm not much mistaken,' (another typical Longley phrase, this one), 'Eden will have a baby within the year. You can imagine *he*'ll want children – well, he'll want an heir and his father will.'

It sounded feudal to me and I didn't feel I had any comment to make on it.

'Yes, they'll want a son. Of course Eden loves children, she worships them.'

That was not how it had seemed to me when I saw her push Jamie away that morning or on the innumerable occasions I had seen her ignore him when he spoke to her.

'Eden will want six, you can be sure of that. And since money is no object, I see no reason why they shouldn't have a big family. If I'm not much mistaken, my dear, the next big function we go to will be Eden's son's christening. He'll be a very lucky little boy.' This was addressed to the now dry, powdered, pyjamaed, sleepy Jamie. 'Everything handed to him on a gold platter. But one thing's for sure, isn't it, my sweetheart, he won't have more love than my boy. That's something no amount of money can buy.'

Francis had not returned with us and now, two hours later, he had

173

not appeared. Vera, tucking Jamie up in bed, lifted her face from kissing him and said:

'They're so lovely when they're little and when they grow up they're just people. They're not like you, they haven't got your ways and they're more unpleasant to you than they are to their worst enemy.'

I listened, fascinated, amazed at this unexpected sensitivity, hoping for more, destined, of course, to be disappointed.

'He isn't going to be like that, though, are you, my sweetheart? Francis was too much with other people, you know, that was the trouble. His ayah first, then his school. He hardly knew me. Little children are best when they are just with their mothers. You can see that in pictures of primitive people, can't you, savages and aborigines and so on. Those people always have their babies on their backs. I am going to see to it Jamie and I are never apart.'

Chad didn't come either. The sun had gone in at about six – if I were an adherent of the Pathetic Fallacy I would say it went in when Eden left – and the long summer evening was dull and gloomy. There is something depressing, anyway, about the evening after a wedding. One feels excluded. The point is that one *is* excluded, everyone is except the two that it was all for, for what they are embarking on no one may share in. It is rather as if one went along to the opera and had tea in the tea tent, walked round the lake, drank the champagne and, just as the curtain went up, was sent home again. I could have said that to Anne Cambus, to Chad, perhaps to Andrew Chatteriss, but not to Vera. So we sat there more or less in silence, she knitting a jumper for Jamie in a complicated Fair Isle pattern, I reading until the light failed. Vera had long given up attempting to teach me to knit or sew or crochet and she seemed resigned to my reading, though I believe she thought it a wicked waste of time. That evening, though, she had the advantage of me for she had reached a plain section of the jumper and could do the stocking stitch without looking at her work. For reasons of economy, presumably, she was always loath to put lights on. She deferred it even longer than usual and when I suggested having the table lamp on just for me, she reacted like the old irritable Vera of my childhood.

'The room will be full of insects. All those moths will get in.' It was impossible to convince her that not all moths, indeed not the vast majority, are the kind that eat your clothes. And this was a misapprehension made all the more ironical by the fact that her son was destined to become a distinguished entomologist. 'We shall be riddled with moths,' she said. 'I should have thought it was so peaceful just to sit in the twilight for once.'

In the twilight we sat, Vera's fingers moving automatically, and the needles, wooden wartime needles, making a soft click-click-click. What did I think about? Eden's wedding night, I fear. Young people then were more given to prurient curiosity. Experience came later to them and less variously. Principally I wondered how she had overcome, if she had overcome it, Tony's finding out he wasn't the first. Vera's earlier remarks about Eden's fondness for children and the large family she would have interested me hardly at all at the time and I am surprised now that I remember them. Probably my memory is inaccurate, though I am sure the gist, the essential inner sense of those remarks, remains. I have often thought of them since.

Was she afraid even then? Were her Eumenides gathering, sitting like crows in the trees about the darkening lawn or fluttering against the window panes like the moths she so disliked? I think so. I think future events cast their shadows even then, like the real shadows which suddenly flared in long bands across the lawn as the sun appeared briefly again before its setting.

It may be fanciful of me but I expect she thought she had paid. She had rendered up a heavy price: her husband, her freedom, a financially comfortable future, whatever of Francis she might have salvaged, Eden's devotion. She had given this enormous ransom to the Furies and I expect she hoped that they would keep away. One small thing only the gods had to do for her and why shouldn't they do it? For most women they did it, too frequently sometimes, constituting a curse and not a blessing. So why not here, in this instance? You might also have said of Vera that she wanted only to be left alone. When she said she wanted to sit in peace in the twilight, she meant that in more than a literal sense. I hardly think that the news which came to her almost immediately Eden returned from her honeymoon could have pleased her, though at the time the rest of the family saw it as being particularly to her advantage. Did her heart sink? Did she feel trapped? No doubt she prayed that the next letter would bring her the news she longed for or that one evening the telephone would ring . . .

The dusk grew depressing. I said that I thought of going down to the Cambuses for a while. Vera uttered her automatic, 'At this hour?' but put up no more objections. I think this must have been just before she met the new Mrs Cambus, who was to become her dear friend and support (and principal witness for the defence at her trial), or at any rate before she got to know her well, for in saying goodbye to me she did not mention her but merely told me to be sure and bolt the back door after me when I came in. How far I had progressed in growing up since the eight o'clock bedtime days – or how far she had in tolerance! But Josie Cambus was not mentioned as she certainly would have been had this visit been paid two or three months later when all sorts of messages would have been given to me to deliver and Vera's love sent.

Anne's mother had died of cancer and within six months her father had married again. My husband says Donald Cambus and Josie had been lovers for a long time and I think Anne suspected this, therefore resenting her new stepmother more than she might otherwise have done. Josie, who had been a widow with two sons, she saw as longing for her lover's wife to die, jubilant at her death, impatient to step into her shoes, though in fact I don't think this was Josie's nature at all. I got to know her well, eventually very well indeed, and I came to understand that her principal trait was *motherliness*; she was one of those people whose mission in life is to look after other people, and in coming to Sindon, giving up her secretarial job, her house in a suburb of London, she was driven as much by a desire to retrieve Donald Cambus's household and care for his children as by the need to be with him always.

But that evening she and Donald were out and Anne and I spent an hour or two alone together, talking about the wedding of course, about Eden's anxious inquiry of the morning (which I am afraid I unhesitatingly repeated) and then Anne grew venomous about poor Josie and what she called her designing ways. For her part, she couldn't wait to get away to teacher training college from which, she said, she would never return to her father's house.

I went home to Laurel Cottage the back way, something I had rarely been in the habit of doing at night. The gate in the back fence of the Cambuses' garden led into a narrow lane or path that eventually, after crossing the edge of a field, cutting the corner of a

176

farmyard and running between high flint walls, passed the back fence of the Laurel Cottage garden. The reason I avoided it was the farmer's dog, a black Labrador with a nasty temper. But this dog I had seen from the Cambuses' living-room window, setting out on a walk, correctly leashed, with its owner, so I took to the path, having switched on my torch. It was a bit after half-past ten.

Very dark. A dense, humid, by now quite cold, moonless night. Nobody knows what darkness is until they have lived in an English country village where the inhabitants stoutly oppose the installation of street lamps. It was impossible to see anything that night except a sort of lightening of the blackness overhead and a deepening of the blackness where a hedge was or a wall or tree. It was easy enough to find my way with the torch. I came to the gate in the Laurel Cottage fence and there saw the first lights since I had left the Cambuses'. There was a light on in Vera's bedroom and the faintest gleam or glow of light from the hovel.

It was still standing, still threatening to collapse without going further towards doing so. The falling house that never falls. Eden's Wendy house it had been, where she had played with dolls, washing them and mending their clothes, no doubt, putting them to bed at six. Inside its crumbling wattle and daub Anne and I had acted out, over and over, the tragedy of Mary Stuart, blowing up Darnley and hiding Rizzio in vain behind her skirts. As I came towards it its broken window flared with light, with guttering bouncing light. How far this little candle throws his means! So shines a good deed in a naughty world.

They didn't see me. They were otherwise occupied and their eyes were not for seeing passers-by. Their light, a candle in a saucer on the gate-leg table, was to enable them just to see each other. Out of politeness, I turned off my torch. If this sounds blasé, if it sounds as if I wasn't shocked, horrified, aghast, overturned into a tumult, it is not so, for I was, I was all those things. But discretion did not quite leave me, that and a shrinking from their seeing that I had seen *them*.

I looked once and went on towards the house. Chad and Francis were making love, undoubted, uncompromising sodomy – for I saw all that in their forked radish nakedness – on the hovel floor.

Eden could have had her pick of Pearmain houses. Instead she chose to buy Goodney Hall. My father was delighted and so was Helen. She and Vera would hardly be separated now, they would be able to see each other two or three times a week, for Tony's wedding present to Eden had been a car.

People said it was sweet of Eden, it was considerate of her, to make her home near her sister's. Later on they said it was malicious. I don't believe kindness or malice came into it. Eden had been brought up by Vera to be a snob and she had outdistanced her mentor. All her life, I think, she had longed and longed to be rich and have the power wealth brings, and whereas Vera frankly and honestly basked in the reflected glory of Helen's prestige, enjoying it vicariously, proud just to be able to have Helen for her sister and drop her name in company, Eden had envied her and felt resentment in much the way my father did. Now she could turn the tables on Helen. Walbrooks, after all, was only a farmhouse, if a grand one. Goodney Hall, at Goodney Parva on the Stoke side of the Stour, was what my grandmother Longley called a 'gentleman's house', and it was rather better than that, for it had been designed in 1786 by Steuart who was the architect of Attingham Park in Shropshire and St Chad's Church in Shrewsbury. It had a portico with immensely long columns, a Chinese drawing-room and principal bedroom described as Etruscan, and altogether it reminded me of the Pavilion at Brighton. But it was exactly what Eden wanted, it brought her ascendancy over Helen and almost everyone else she knew. When my father next wrote to Vera, he told her how pleased he was, but in her reply Eden and her move were not mentioned. Nor did Eden herself reply to the letter he sent her, asking her, now she was so comfortably settled, to consider he and she making over their shares in Laurel Cottage to Vera. And this may have been just as well, for mention of the project made my mother furious, igniting fearful quarrels between my parents.

'If you do that, I swear I'll leave you,' she said to him, 'and then you won't be able to give houses away, you'll have to find a home for me.'

My father hoped, and constantly expressed this hope, that Gerald and Vera would patch up their differences and live together again. They were not divorced and in those days before divorce became so easy as it did in the early seventies, had no prospect of being so. Adultery was a possible ground, yet I now wondered, in the light of what I knew, if there had indeed been adultery. Ten months children were not unknown, if rare. Blue-eyed parents may have a brown-eyed child if there are brown eyes among their forebears. Perhaps Gerald had known all this, had known there was no adultery, and the separation had come about simply because he and Vera had ceased to love each other, had grown indifferent or preferred the single life the war had taught them both to live. One thing was certain. Chad Hamner was not her lover and never had been. Jamie was not his son.

So many things became clear as a result of what I saw that night, by candlelight, in the hovel at the end of Vera's garden. So much was changed. I was no Go-between, though, I was no traumatized witness of a primal scene. It is true that I slept very little that night; it had been a shock what I saw, but it was rather an *interesting*, a fascinating, shock than an unpleasant one. It explained so much, and some of it not unflattering, a relief really, to myself.

As a possible lover of my own, the first perhaps, Chad had been put out of the running by becoming (as I thought) Vera's. After I thought he was Vera's I was not such a fool as to want him or to hope for him any more. But I had still minded that he could have preferred Vera to me, I was disappointed about that. I believed that he had loved Eden but that this was an early rehearsal for coming to love me, I thought he should have waited for me, and that it was only impatience or weakness of character that made him turn instead to Vera. I was relieved to understand none of this was so. I looked back, intrigued out of the possibility of sleep or thinking of anything else, by the revelations, the clarifications of so many words and acts of the past years.

Those inexplicable visits to the house in Eden's absence, always the day before Francis was due home or when a phone call from Francis was expected, these were explained. Those declarations of the hopelessness of his love, his remark to my father that brave hearts and persistence will not always triumph, his gazing in church, not at Eden as I had believed, but at Francis who escorted her – all these I now understood. And I understood Francis's coquettish behaviour, his posing, his wit, in Chad's presence. Somehow I knew, too, that this was not a happy love, a relationship of mutual desire and affection, but one-sided, a case of there being one who kisses and one who lets himself be kissed. But that not often, perhaps less and less often and at a price, Francis occasionally yielding rarefied favours to strengthen his hold.

And I saw something else, though not that night, not until I was myself older and better versed in these things. Chad had met Francis through Eden. How else would they ever have met each other? Chad – who had moved away, who had succeeded in getting himself a job on the *Oxford Mail* to be in the city where Francis was – had worked on the local paper in Colchester then and Eden had been working for her solicitor. Whether they had met in court or at a cocktail party or in the solicitor's office hardly mattered. They had met and Eden had introduced him to Francis. That meant she must have known. That meant that at eighteen, when Francis was only thirteen, she had known, had connived at and certainly encouraged a love affair which in the 1940s was criminal and was regarded by most people as disgusting, monstrous and beyond words unnatural. In other words, she had brought home to her sister's house a man who loved boys and had presented to him her sister's child as his catamite. As her accredited lover he came, or rather her suitor, so that he might set about – though not very successfully, not very happily, Francis being what he was – seducing a pre-pubertal boy.

I was never outraged, knowing Francis as I did, but I was astounded. I would not have thought Eden had it in her. Why had she done it? What was in it for her? I have never known and I don't know now. I can only make guesses. Secrets, having them, creating them, keeping them and half-keeping them, were the breath of life to her, and here was a secret she could keep from Vera. Or it may have been more practical and less neurotic than that. It may have been that in those days before she went into the WRNS, when she presented to the world the image of untouched, beautiful, innocent girlhood, a girl within a budding grove, an almost Victorian concept of perfect girlhood, quiet, meek, pure, accomplished, she was in fact engaged in a love affair with someone totally unsuitable. I rather incline to this view, based on guesswork though it is. It is so entirely the kind of thing Eden would have done, secretly met her uncouth or merely married lover, someone anyway Vera and my father and Helen and all would utterly have disapproved of, while Vera believed her in the safe company of Chad. And Chad, for his own purposes, would willingly have connived at this, while Francis watched the game with amusement, occasionally playing a hand or two when the fancy took him. Poor Vera, I had been used to thinking of her as in control, a presiding authority. I began to see her as everyone's dupe. Neither of these descriptions, of course, was entirely true, for she had alternated between the two.

And now Eden was installed, chatelaine-like, at Goodney Hall, 'a stone's throw', as my father put it, from Great Sindon, though in fact it was ten minutes' drive away, on the Suffolk side of the Stour Valley where the Weeping Hills rise and dip and roll away towards the Vale of Dedham. It was a year before I saw the house, for I had gone up to Cambridge the autumn after the wedding, and the following year when I returned to these places, to this neighbourhood, in the long vacation, it was with the Chatterisses I stayed and not with Vera or Eden.

People had started going abroad again for their holidays. Tony had taken Eden to Switzerland, to Lucerne, and Helen had had a postcard with a picture on it of Mount Pilatus, the lake in the summit of which is one of the seven ancient entrances to hell and where Pontius Pilate forever sits, washing his hands. Vera's card was of a chair lift and she seemed disproportionately pleased with it, even bringing it with her when she and Jamie came over for lunch next day.

'I expect they are making the most of it,' she said. 'This will be their last chance to go anywhere like that for a long time.'

'Eden will have a nanny for the baby,' Helen said. 'It won't make that much difference to their lives.'

This was the first I had heard of Eden's baby. She was not yet quite two months pregnant. Vera could talk of nothing else. She was overjoyed. Eden had been married more than a year now. She, Vera, had begun to wonder if anything could be wrong, for she knew how passionately Eden longed for children, but now all was well. Vera speculated as to the child's sex, what name would be chosen, whom it would look like, precisely when it would be born and what kind of labour Eden would have. This went on all through lunch, kind Helen showing no impatience, listening and responding to Vera, but the

General and Andrew and I restless and bored and Patricia, who had come home for a week's stay, frankly asked once or twice (though in vain) if we couldn't change the subject.

'I was the first to be told,' Vera said. 'Do you know, Eden told me what she suspected even before she told Tony? She said, I think, I hope, I'm almost certain I'm going to have a baby and I want you to be its godmother. I was so happy I burst into tears.'

Jamie was three and a bit, articulate in speech now, a 'good', quiet boy who still had a sleep in the afternoons and went to bed by six-thirty. He seemed intelligent. He had rather a stilted way of talking which was naturally appealing in such a young child because it was 'quaint'. He would refer to 'adults' instead of 'grown-ups' for instance, and get all his past tenses right, never saying 'rided' for 'rode', or 'eated' for 'ate'. And he was a happy child, he was very happy then, I would vouch for that. I wonder if he remembered that visit, that day at Walbrooks, when he chose to call himself an Italian version of Richardson. After lunch, Helen showed us all the 'surprise' the General had given her for her birthday, a likeness by Augustus John of a sweet, plain-faced woman in a dark dress with a lace collar. It was her grandmother, taken in late middle age, and it had been sold when the old Richardsons had died in the twenties by the lawyer who managed the estate for Helen, the heir, and who had not known Helen would have wanted every memento in existence of Mary Richardson. But the portrait had come on to the market again and the perspicacious General had bought it and now it hung in Helen's drawing-room.

Helen hardly ever talked about the hard part of her childhood, her father's abandonment of her just when she had lost her mother, she never made a heavy thing of it as Francis did of his deprivations. But she could not speak of her grandmother without passionate feeling and now as she stood in front of the painting, looking particularly at the folded hands, the third finger on the left hand with its weight of thick gold wedding ring and engagement ring of rubies in a cumbersome Victorian setting, the tears came into her eyes.

'I like that lady,' Jamie said. 'If I saw her I would sit on her lap.'

This was to be favoured indeed, for Jamie never sat on anyone's lap but Vera's.

'Would you, darling?' Helen was delighted. 'Well, she was a sweet, kind lady and she would have called you her lamb.'

'I should like you to call me your lamb,' Jamie told Vera, and then, of course, she had to and Jamie took her up on it every time she forgot.

Those holidays, too, we all went to see Eden. It was an extraordinary, dramatic and upsetting occasion. We went in the General's car, a 1937 Mercedes Benz that had been holed up in one of the Walbrooks stables while the war was on because the General said the village people might throw bricks at a German make of car. And rightly so, he said. He had had no business to be buying a German car even then, even secondhand, he must have been off his rocker, it was just pouring marks into Hitler's war effort. On the way we called for Vera and Jamie, both of whom were wearing new clothes made by Vera. Vera cut up her old cot blankets to make a jacket for herself and coats and trousers for Jamie. In 1947, if you didn't want to wear Utility clothing you made your own. Vera had made Helen's dress from the skirt of an old crêpe de Chine ball gown. I was wearing the skirt part of an old cotton frock with a cotton jumper my mother had knitted. I mention all this because of what Eden was wearing and what she had brought back from Switzerland.

The house, Goodney Hall? Well, it was – and is, I expect – a fine, elegant, not very large, eighteenth-century country house of which I am blasé enough to say there are many in England. The gardens had parterres and herbaceous borders and a pleached walk and rhododendrons that were famous and a greenhouse full of showy flowers. There did not seem much character to the house, no imprinting upon it of the personalities of its new owners. I heard later that Tony had bought it with all its furniture, bought it lock, stock and barrel, as they say, and perhaps there wasn't much else he could have done. He and Eden knew nothing about antiques and one could hardly have put Utility furniture into Goodney Hall. I remember Eden's house as furnished entirely in pink and green, though of course it can't have been like that. Surely there was yellow in the Chinese drawing-room and red in the Etruscan bedroom, but if there was I don't recall it. What I remember are pea-green carpets and French furniture with pink silk seats and big pink Chinese vases with smudgy patterns, truly boring pictures, mostly mezzotints, of north European towns and ships on stormy seas, and green velvet curtains with heavy tassels of tarnished gilt.

But Eden, you could tell, was immensely proud of it. She was also enormously happy. And she looked quite different. I don't mean she looked well in the sense of being healthy. She didn't. She was thinner and paler and her face was less full. This, I thought, must be because she was pregnant. She looked different in the way rich women do. One might paraphrase that interchange between Hemingway and Scott Fitzgerald and say the rich *look* different, they have more scope. In this particular way, Eden looked different even from Helen – Vera and I didn't enter the competition – who, after all, was wearing a home-made dress and had washed her hair herself. Everything about Eden, you see, was of the best, the most expensive top-grade stuff. The best hairdresser in London had cut her hair, she was wearing the most prestigious range of make-up available. She had on her huge diamond engagement ring and an eternity ring Tony had given her two weeks before when she told him she was pregnant. The dress she wore was white broderie anglaise, one of half a dozen she had brought back from Switzerland and which she had spread out on the (presumably) Etruscan bed before we arrived. The Swiss were different, too. There was no austerity there and nothing Utility. The shops were full of clothes, Eden told us, dresses and suits and shoes and silk underwear and silk stockings and she had bought masses, as much as they could – I waited for her to say 'afford' – carry home.

Vera was disproportionately grateful for her present. This was a brooch made in the shape of an edelweiss, of bone or horn, I suppose, but it looked like some prototype of plastic. It was a nasty little brooch, not at all well-made. Eden seemed to have bought a great many things, gentian and edelweiss jewellery, all intended as presents for this friend and that, discriminating not at all between her loved sister who had been a mother to her and the woman who came up from the village to do the rough work. Then there descended on to the bed from a fine carved wood chest quite a dozen carved wooden animals, exquisitely carved in the way only the Swiss can work, so that the reclining St Bernard looked about to get up and stroll away and you would not have been surprised if the Siamese cat had stretched itself and begun washing its whiskers.

Jamie, of course, became very excited. At first he was simply filled with awe. He had never seen anything like this before. I wasn't very fond of children then, I was never one of those girls who adore young children and want to hug them and take them out and look after them, but just the same, the expression on Jamie's face as he looked up at Vera moved me. He was so entranced, so overcome with wonder, with delight, at these things which literally looked like real animals in little, that first he smiled, then burst into joyful laughter.

'The dog!' he said. 'The cat! Look, Mummy, that one's a bear. Look, Mummy!'

He was a gentle child and it was a gentle hand he put out to touch the back of the dog that looked for all the world as if covered with fur.

'No, please don't touch!' Eden said rather sharply.

There were no toys in the shops for children. There were children born at the beginning of the war or just before it who had never had a new toy worth calling a toy, who had inherited siblings' hand-downs, some of whom were lucky enough to have relatives who could sew and knit dolls or carve horses and carts. But Jamie wasn't one of these latter. If Francis had ever had toys – of course he must have, though you couldn't imagine it – they had long been lost or given away. Jamie had had to make do with that old set of bricks that had been my father's, Vera's own worn, bald fluffy teddy, and such things as kitchen utensils. He took no notice of Eden. He picked up the dog and held it in his hands, close up to his face.

'Put it down! It's not a toy.' Eden snatched the dog from him. She said to Vera, 'Why do you let him do that? I thought he was supposed to be obedient.'

I remembered from long ago the letter to my father: 'I think you might teach your child better manners . . .' My heart didn't often go out to Vera but it did then. She made no retort to Eden, no defence of the child to whom these things were a wonder and a delight. Love had tamed and humbled her. She said nothing. She took Jamie into her arms and he cried into her shoulder. The curious thing was that his crying wasn't the normal, unrestrained howling and sobbing of a child deprived of something he very much wants to have. It was quiet, sustained, more like an adult's grief. And yet you had the impression – Andrew told me afterwards that he did too – that Vera was a rock to Jamie, that even in his misery, it was almost a pleasure to him to have *those* arms, *that* shoulder, *those* gentle, whispered words. Vera, too, drew a kind of sustenance from his unhappiness because it was confided in her only, only she could comfort and support, she alone was humankind to him.

We had to make a tour of the house and a tour of the garden. Vera had recovered and praised everything extravagantly, flattering Eden absurdly, complimenting her as if she personally had planted out and pruned the roses, grown the raspberries, embroidered the *petit point* chair seats and painted the lotuses and dragons on the porcelain. She was like one of those sycophants who hung about the nobility in the eighteenth century, like Mr Collins with Lady Catherine de Bourgh. Eden accepted it all with gracious smiles, but she did not look well, she looked tired and there was something languid about the way she moved, though she brightened up and became enthusiastic again, as effervescent as she had been over the Swiss booty, when we came to the room that was to be the new baby's nursery.

It was on the end of the house, a corner room with windows facing west and windows facing south, and it had been a child's room before, though perhaps a long time ago, for the paper on the walls was all faded Arthur Rackham fairies and between a pair of windows stood a dappled grey rocking horse with worn saddle and harness. I have a very clear, sharp recollection of standing in that room, filled with bright, soft August sunshine as it was, the sunshine making spots and squares on the pink carpet that had a pattern all round its edge of white convolvulus intertwined with improbably pale green ivy. The wallpaper reminded me of Eden's picture, her favourite she had said it was, of the Peter Pan statue, and I wondered if she would hang it in this room. The west-facing windows looked out over the Weeping Hills, that gentle range of slopes and dips and wooded rises so unlike a Suffolk landscape, and the south-facing ones over the broad sweep of lawns ringed by stately trees. All along the terrace below stood at intervals stone urns ornamented like Keats's urn with youths and maidens and people going to festivals and mysterious priests and heifers lowing to the skies and bold lovers never kissing, and in the urns grew *Agapanthus africanus*, the blue lily, and white and purple allium, in rare and special varieties, as Vera the sycophant had taken care to tell us. Vera now leaned out of one of these windows, praising the view. Helen looked a little bored, or as bored as kind Helen could ever show herself to be. Jamie, of course, had climbed on to the horse and this time Eden didn't stop him. She was telling us all how the room was going to be decorated and furnished and how the nanny would have the communicating one. Besides, the horse was old and shabby, doubtless to be chucked out along with the little wooden chairs and table and the brass bedstead, so it didn't matter about Jamie playing with it, did it?

Andrew said, 'You ought to have peacocks, Eden. You ought to have a pair of peacocks out on your terrace.'

'Goodness knows where you'd get peacocks, darling,' said Helen, 'Old Mrs Williams couldn't even get a budgie when her Bobby died.'

Eden turned round. 'I wouldn't dream of having peacocks.' She was suddenly petulant. 'Hateful things. Have you heard the noise they make? Have you heard them scream?' Her lips trembled. I couldn't imagine what was the matter with her. 'I don't want to be wakened up by screaming at four in the morning.'

'Good thing you're having a nanny then.'

Eden ignored this quip of Andrew's. 'Shall we have a drink before lunch?'

Poor Jamie once more had to be parted from an entrancing toy. He didn't cry this time. He put his hand in Vera's and walked along beside her, down the long corridor, down the balustraded staircase. Tony now appeared. He only went to work in London three days a week and this wasn't one of those days but he had been out somewhere seeing a man about coppicing their wood. At once he busied himself with pouring our drinks, and being the sort of man he was – kind, well-meaning, sociable, dull and totally insensitive to mood or the differences between people or their tastes in contrast with his – treated us while he did so to an account of exactly where and how he had obtained this gin, that whisky, that sherry, and where he expected the next bottles would come from. They had a great many glasses of all shapes and sizes and it was of the first importance to Tony to use the correct glass for each kind of drink. He even insisted on a different shape of glass being suitable for dry sherry from that suitable for medium sherry, something I have never come across since.

'And now how about this young chap?'

Vera said Jamie could have squash or some of the 'government' orange juice she had brought with her but Tony wouldn't allow that.

'Oh, come on, we can do better than that. Personally, I believe in getting a boy used to wine from an early age. It was what my father did for me and I've never had cause to regret it.'

'Hardly at three, surely?' said Andrew.

'I wouldn't be too sure of that. I wasn't much past that. My governor was set on my knowing wine, you see, and he said it was never too soon to start.'

'I suppose he laid down a pipe of Montrachet for you?' Andrew said very seriously.

I didn't hear Tony's reply. I was conscious only of thinking he shouldn't tease Tony, it was as bad as teasing Jamie would be, and then, looking up, reaching out for my sherry, I happened to glance in Eden's direction and saw blood running down her leg.

It had the effect of freezing me. My fingers had just made contact with the glass and there they rested on the cool, hard, slippery, rounded surface, or rather clutched at it, while my gaze fixed on Eden's left leg. She was standing up. The woman who lived in and looked after them, her husband being gardener and handyman, had come into the room with two platefuls of canapés, bits and pieces of egg and cheese and pickles on rounds of toast. Eden had taken these from her and was in the act of offering them to Helen. As she leant forward the full skirt of her white dress had swung up a little so that the backs of her knees were visible. None of us was wearing stockings – you had to give coupons for them and it was hard to get them anyway – but Eden had on very pale, thin stockings, Swiss no doubt, and the blood in a thick, dark trickle was flowing down the inside of her leg, had reached the knee, the calf, was approaching the ankle and the thin ankle strap of her white sandal.

Oddly enough, I didn't think of what this must mean. I only thought of periods and when things like that had happened or nearly happened to me. Most of all I thought of Eden sitting down when the canapés had been distributed and the blood staining her beautiful, ice-white, eyelet-embroidered skirt. But still I didn't know how to handle it. Come to that, I am not sure I would know how today. If I had whispered to her, when she and the plate were in front of me, to come outside with me a minute, I had something to tell her, I am quite sure she would have looked up and laughed and demanded of the company what could *I* possibly have to tell her that everyone might not hear, what could I possibly want to keep private from the rest?

She was like that. She was Eden. So I shook my head at the canapés and let her go past me and at last had the presence of mind to catch Helen's eye and give her a look of such entreaty that Helen, so clever, so tactful, so insightful, immediately got up and said to

Eden that she must use the bathroom before lunch and she expected I would like to also.

Women didn't talk about their periods then. Or not much. Perhaps to contemporaries, and usually with euphemisms. As soon as we were outside the door, I told Helen briefly what I had seen. I called it the 'curse'. At least that was an improvement on Vera's 'a visitor in the house'.

Helen laid a hand on my arm. 'But, darling, it can't be. She's pregnant.'

'Oh, God,' I said. 'I forgot that.'

'I mean, dearest heart, if that's what you saw, she *isn't* pregnant any more.'

And she wasn't. But we didn't have to tell her. When we went back into the room, Steuart's Chinese drawing-room that I remember as pink and green though it must surely have been yellow, Eden was gone and Andrew was looking mystified and Tony who ought to have been looking mystified, not to say anxious, was still going on about instructing children in worldly know-how, having proceeded by this time to the smoking of cigars. We sat there. We waited. Jamie said he was hungry. He didn't like scrambled egg and gherkins on cold toast and I can't say I blamed him. Suddenly Vera said:

'Is Eden all right?'

'Oh, absolutely,' said Tony. 'She just popped off to powder her nose.' Everyone says 'absolutely' now but no one did then except Tony and he said it all the time.

Vera went upstairs. She had to take Jamie with her because he wouldn't be left, he wouldn't be parted from her. Mrs King, the housekeeper, came in to say lunch was ready and Tony said, all right, we'd be along in a minute. He went off, too, but not to find out what was wrong with Eden as I believed but to open some wine that had to be allowed to 'breathe'.

I said to Andrew, 'Eden's having a miscarriage.'

'Christ.'

There was a phone in the room. At that moment we heard it make a sort of tinkle, a sign that the extension upstairs was being used. Somehow we all knew this was Vera phoning the doctor.

'Don't you feel,' said Helen, 'that we should stand not upon the order of our going – or whatever that tiresome woman said – but go at once? I mean, maybe take Jamie and leave Vera here with Eden?'

'*Not* take Jamie,' said Andrew. 'Please not. Peacocks would be preferable. But by all means go.'

'I couldn't eat anyway,' I said.

It was amazingly difficult to put all this across to Tony. Of course, it fell to Helen to do it, to explain, but we were there, we heard it, and his obtuseness was unbelievable. He kept insisting it must be a joke, Eden was teasing him, trying to make him anxious – what must their marriage have been like? – and she and Vera were upstairs 'talking secrets', all girls together. Then Vera came down. She was white-faced and grim. Jamie was in her arms, half-hanging over her shoulder.

'I've sent for the doctor. Eden's having quite a severe haemorrhage. I imagine she's lost the baby.'

The only one of us to have any lunch was Jamie. Vera looked distraught, deeply wretched and concerned, but Jamie still came first with her. She took him out to the kitchen and got him something to eat, milk and a chicken sandwich. Helen and Andrew and I went back to Walbrooks and eventually, late that afternoon, I suppose, Tony drove Vera and Jamie home. The doctor had Eden taken straight into hospital.

What happened to her there? I have never really known. No doubt Tony knows – that is, if he can remember, and if he can, will he want to talk about it? Would he want to tell Daniel Stewart? I am sure not. Eden had miscarried and she had some sort of operation. I have since thought that perhaps it was an ectopic pregnancy that she had had, one in which the foetus implants itself in a Fallopian tube. As the embryo grows, the tube may rupture, in which case the tube itself must be removed by surgery or the woman will die. On the other hand, the foetus may detach itself and be expelled without damage to the tube. I know only that after this miscarriage it was rumoured through the family that Eden would not or should not have children. It would be dangerous for her to become pregnant again or – this was the alternative version – impossible for her to become pregnant. My mother said:

'I can't help wondering if it's the result of the life she led in the Wrens.'

I didn't know what she meant. My father didn't know what she meant. We both thought this was some half-formed, half-superstitious, minatory legacy of Victorian morality. But what she suggested was quite feasible, quite medically accurate in fact. She was inferring that Eden, sleeping around, had contracted gonorrhoea, one of the possible after-effects of which is to bring about a blockage of the Fallopians. This is said to have been responsible in the past for many one-child families. The bride would catch gonorrhoea from her husband at the same time as she conceived, so that one child would be safely born. But the disease by then had done its work and the tube or tubes had been blocked so no further conception could take place. If Eden had indeed caught gonorrhoea from a lover, the result could have been an ectopic pregnancy.

There was no real reason to believe this. One hears of the Fallopians being blocked after abdominal surgery. Eden had had her appendix out as a child. Or surely it could be simple, unaccountable misfortune. All that seemed certain was that Tony Pearmain had no heir and most probably never would have.

— 13 —

Fifteen years or so after all this happened, Chad Hamner told me the story of his life over tea in Brown's Hotel. I had met him by chance in Bond Street, having gone there to have my hair cut at Vidal Sassoon's. Tea at Brown's is a very civilized business. You sink into your armchair and they bring you a small, home-made toasted teacake which they drop on to your plate with a pair of tongs. The implication is that this is what you *must* eat, this is what all English gentlefolk eat as a matter of course for their tea. The cakes, which arrive on a three-tier silver stand, are optional but in any case for later. There they are, looking inviting, but the teacake must be eaten first – like at nursery tea.

In this milieu, Chad and I were perhaps out of place. We didn't look out of place, of course, we looked like everyone else, just as elegant and urbane, me with my hair cut, Chad grown thinner and his hair beginning to go grey. He was the first man I ever came across to abandon the sports jacket for a casual one with a zipper. It was on the pavement outside Asprey's that we met. He put out his arms and I went into them and we stood there embraced, though the strange thing was that we had never hugged each other before, never kissed or even touched hands as far as I can remember. But the bond between us was a strange one. There cannot be many people who are linked together by a hanged woman.

I don't know why we went to Brown's. Certainly not because Chad was staying there or had become rich or even habitually went there. As a journalist he was free-lancing, he had a flat in Fulham (which in 1963 was not fashionable or interesting or 'upwardly mobile') and I don't think he was doing very well for himself. For Francis he had ruined his life, he had destroyed all prospects of success. He told me this while we ate our teacakes. For a long time he had accounted the world well lost for love, but the trouble with that one is that love doesn't last and then one remembers that the world was once there for the losing.

He wouldn't have started on it if I, with an emotional rush of desire to confide and confess, had not come out with what I had seen that night after Eden's wedding. I had told no one till then – not even Andrew, not even Louis. Chad looked me straight in the eye, a cool, steady gaze, unexpected really after what I had just told him.

'I was sick with love,' he said. 'That's what the translation of the Song of Solomon ought to say, not sick *of* love. I only wish I could have got to be sick *of* love. I fell in love with Francis when he was thirteen. Rather classical, don't you think? The Emperor Hadrian and Antinous. An ugly old chap and a beautiful youth.'

'Hardly old at thirty,' I said.

Chad gave one of his enormous Gallic shrugs. 'Age is a state of mind. I felt old when I was with Francis and I felt ugly. What I did was something most people would think abominable even today, but I didn't do it much, he wouldn't let me. And I wasn't the first. Does that surprise you? He used to let me make love to him approximately three times a year. Nineteen forty-five was my bonanza year – he must have been celebrating the war being over – and he let me do it four times. No wonder I couldn't get him out of my system.'

'Francis makes nonsense of Freud, doesn't he?' I said. 'Poor Vera wasn't exactly a domineering, possessive mother to him.'

'Yes, but Francis wasn't really queer. Not like I am, not to the core. I've never had a woman. Francis was simply all things to all men and women as it suited his book. I used to ask myself why he bothered with me and I came up with two answers. I'm still sure they were true. The first is that it's wonderful to be adored – I mean I should think it is. I've never been adored – wonderful to have someone worship you and know that nothing you can do, no amount of indifference and neglect and downright unkindness that you can mete out is going to make an atom of difference.'

'What's the other one?' I said.

'Francis liked doing things he and others believed to be wrong. He liked to do them simply for the sake of wrongdoing. Actually, that's very rare, it's much rarer than you might think. Even the great sinners of this world – Hitler, say, Stalin, certain multi-murderers – believed that what they were doing was right or that the end they were attaining to was right. Hardly anyone sets out to do evil like Milton's Lucifer does, and he never convinces us, he always seems rather a pleasant chap. And it's not a case of "Evil be thou my Good." Francis wanted evil to stay evil, to be his evil, and for that reason to be desirable to him. But none of that made any difference to my loving him. I would have followed him to the ends of the earth.'

A chord was struck. I thought of what Anne and I had used the hovel for on rainy days and what Chad and Francis had used it for on misty nights.

'Like Mary Stuart,' I said, 'following Bothwell in her shift.'

'Underpants in my case,' said Chad, 'only he seldom let me get that far. I missed so many opportunities for him, you know. I was stringer for a national paper and they offered me a job on the staff but I turned it down. I only got to see Francis in the school holidays as it was but if I'd been in Fleet Street I wouldn't have seen him at all. The *Oxford Mail* job seemed heaven-sent. It was possible to *see* him every day if not to speak to him. And then I got fired. About six months after you saw us together that night I got fired. And that again was through Francis. I don't mean it was Francis's fault, it wasn't, it was mine, but it was through him it happened.

'I had a job one evening for the paper, covering the annual dinner of a tennis club at Headington. You don't go to things like that, you get a handout beforehand of the general programme and pick the rest up from the secretary or someone afterwards. I had no intention of going. I was taking Francis out to dinner, it was going to be the first time I'd been alone with him for a month. You know they say everyone has a peak experience in his or her life? A day or a few hours when one knows the perfect, the highest degree of happiness, of ecstasy if you like, of one's entire existence. Well, that evening was mine. I thought so at the time and I've had no reason since to change my opinion. Francis came back to my flat and we made love and he was kind to me and I was gloriously happy and it was my peak experience. It was also the last time I was happy for a very long while – I mean the last time I was even moderately content. I wrote my tennis club story from the handout without checking up on it, the paper came out, and the next thing was I was up in front of the editor being asked why I hadn't thought to mention that the guest speaker at the dinner, a local bigwig, had dropped dead while making his speech. So I got the sack and came back to darkest north Essex – where at least I was more likely to see Francis than anywhere else – and because someone had left, they gave me my old job back.'

He told me a lot more that afternoon, how he had followed Francis to London and because Fleet Street wouldn't have him then, had gone to work as a reporter on a local paper out in northwest London called the *Willesden Citizen*. And how Francis had got tired of him at last and one day had struck him, knocking him down three flights of the staircase that led up to his bedsit in Brondesbury Park. There were even more painful things: how Francis turned his fondness, a fondness he even then still retained, for playing practical and more subtle jokes, upon *him*; how his determination to be rid of Chad had led him to humiliate him in public far more cleverly and deviously than in his boyhood he had ever humiliated Vera. So by the time Francis was in his mid-twenties and Chad over forty, it came to an end and Chad was no longer very well, no longer strong enough to do a general reporter's job in a bleak northern suburb.

'I'm like Hadrian in more ways than one,' he said and he pointed out to me the diagonal crease that crossed each of his ear lobes. Apparently these occur in people with a predisposition to coronary heart disease; it is medical fact this, it is proven, not an old wives' tale. We know from busts of Hadrian and Hadrian's head on coins that he had those lines on his ear lobes and it was from coronary heart disease that Hadrian died.

But before he told me about that he mentioned how he had been back in Essex, back in his old job by the winter of 1948, the winter that Vera was ill. And he was a fairly frequent visitor to Laurel Cottage. That people suggested he was or had been Vera's lover had never occurred to him, women as sexual partners were too alien to him for him to have thought of it, and when I enlightened him, it was a revelation. No, he hadn't known, it hadn't crossed his mind. If he had liked Vera and been friends with her, it was because she was Francis's mother and the place she lived in was imbued with Francis's presence. He visited her to be in Francis's home and talk about Francis if he got the chance, just as Hadrian, for all I know, might have dropped in on Antinous's mother up there in Bithynia. To be a family friend, he felt then, would be a way of ensuring that he had Francis for ever. In small measure, perhaps, remotely, vicariously, not seeing him for years on end, yet tenuously possessing him still, a better portion, far better, he thought it was, to be sure of those crumbs of news, those casual mentions of a name, even with the inevitable pain, than the alternative with nothing.

'You wanted to keep a foot in the door,' I said.

'That was part of it, yes. Our relationship – what a word! I hate it but what am I to call it? – our whatever-it-was was so thin on the ground, so hazardous, so *brittle* – well, brittle to him, fragile to me. But this way I could at any rate still see myself twenty years from then growing old with Vera at Vera's fireside, confided in, told where he was and what he was doing, his promotions and his publications. If I couldn't have more than that, at least I could have that, I thought, and I couldn't see what could take it from me if I was determined enough to arrange it. I only had to keep on going to Vera's house. And then, still, there was a chance of Francis being there. In theory, he still lived at home. The time would soon come, he had told me, when he would leave for good, he would never go home again. I didn't altogether believe him and anyway that time hadn't yet come and I lived in the present. That's supposed to be a good thing, you know, an ideal, according to modern psychology. Odd, because the truth is one lives in the present when the past is too bad to remember and the future too dreadful to contemplate.'

One day that winter, a week after Christmas it was, he went round to Laurel Cottage because he expected Francis to be there. Francis wasn't there. He had gone off to stay with some people he knew in Scotland for the New Year and of course he hadn't bothered to tell Chad. Chad said it was such a horrible disappointment, such a bitter shock, to find him gone, to know that he would return to Oxford without coming home first and that he, Chad, would therefore not see him for four months, all this so knocked him sideways that for a while he didn't notice that Vera was ill. He didn't really notice it till Vera asked him to excuse her for not offering him tea for she felt too weak to get out of her chair. Then he saw how pale she was, how heavy-eyed, and when he laid his hand on her forehead, a surge of sweat broke through the skin.

This was the beginning of what Chad told me in Brown's Hotel, going on to say that sometimes he had wondered since how instrumental he had been in stimulating later events. Suppose he had done what Vera asked of him – in the circumstances what a request for the mother of a little son to make to *him*! – would that terrible converging of human lots never have taken place? Would all have been well? I don't think so. I think Eden would have found a way and Vera would still have lost out. I told him that, I told him not to let it trouble his conscience. For all his knowledge, I knew them better than he did, they were my people. We parted never to meet again, never to hear of each other again until Daniel Stewart entered our lives.

I asked him one more thing. Perhaps it was wrong of me. What business was it of mine?

'Is the echo faint at last, Chad?'

He pretended not to understand.

And now I have before me, literally lying on the table before me as it has come out of its envelope, Chad's own account of what happened when he called on Vera that New Year's Eve. He has written it for Stewart at Stewart's request because there is no one else alive who knows, who was there, who was a witness. Chad, though in his seventies now, though stigmatized with the earlobes of Hadrian, seems very much alive, very *compos mentis*, but that style of his, once so lucid, so graceful, so pleasing – what became of it? I suppose it was thrown away and sacrificed for love of my cousin Francis. Stewart wants me to look at this account, to confirm it. That I can't do. I wasn't there. I was in London and Cambridge and sometimes in Stoke-by-Nayland, and all I knew of Vera's illness was contained in one letter which came from her to my father. But I shall read what Chad says just the same. I am curious to know the rest of it, the part he didn't tell me in Brown's Hotel.

I shall try to give you a factual account (Chad writes) without allowing hindsight to intrude and affect my statements. I shall try to write

196

what seemed to me to be true at the time. In 1948, on the last day of 1948, I knew nothing of any mystery surrounding James Ricardo, then Hillyard, whom we called Jamie. As far as I knew he was Gerald Hillyard's son and it had never crossed my mind to question this. The separation that had taken place between Mr and Mrs Hillyard I supposed due to some quite other cause. I was equally in the dark as to any breach between Vera Hillyard and Eden Pearmain. For as long as I had known them, they had been devoted to each other beyond, so to speak, the call of sisterliness. I believed this to be unchanged, and up to a point, even then, it was.

The 31st of December 1948 was a Friday. I had an inquest to cover for my paper in the morning and once I had written it up would have had a free day ahead of me. Some half-formed plan had been made of spending New Year's Eve with the Hillyard family. To confirm this arrangement I drove home from Colchester by way of Great Sindon and called at Vera Hillyard's house, Laurel Cottage.

She never locked the front door by day. Those were safer times. I let myself in, calling her name. The little boy, Jamie, came running out but Vera herself I found sitting in an armchair and she didn't get up when I came in. However, it was a little while before I realized there was anything wrong. I put her despondency down to the fact that her other son, Francis, had changed his mind and wouldn't be with us for the New Year. Then she told me she thought she might have flu, her temperature which she had just taken was 102. I asked her about fetching the doctor and she said he would only tell her to go to bed and how could she do that with Jamie to look after?

I was in a dilemma. Vera looked ill to me and she seemed to be getting worse. I saw the sweat break out on her face and then she was shivering and asking me to fetch her a blanket. It seemed wrong to leave her but on the other hand I could do nothing for her and I had no wish to catch flu myself. There was one thing I could do to help. I said I would take Jamie out for a couple of hours so that she could rest. This she agreed to. So I took the child home with me and made him lunch along with my own and wrote up my story while he played with an old Mah Jong set, and at about four I took him home.

Vera was much worse. She was in bed, or rather, she was lying on the bed still with her clothes on and turning from one side to the other, holding her chest and having difficulty with her breathing. This time I didn't hesitate. I phoned her doctor and asked him to come as soon as he could. In those days you could phone doctors and get to speak to them, not a receptionist or, worse, an answering service. And they would come to see you without the heavens falling. I don't know what this doctor's name was, I can't remember, but he lived in Great Sindon and came within half an hour.

Vera's temperature might have been 102 when she took it but when the doctor did it was 104. She had flu and he thought she might be getting pleurisy. He told her to keep warm, and stay in bed, drink plenty and take aspirin, and he would come back in the morning. She was lucky to have me there to look after her, he said. I believe he thought I was her husband. I quickly disabused his mind but promised I would stay the night. What else could I have done?

When the doctor had gone I asked Vera if she would like me to phone Eden, but this she wouldn't have. I was on no account to trouble Eden, especially on New Year's Eve. What was bothering me, of course, was Jamie. I could look after Vera for a couple of days but not a child of whatever he was – three going on four? – as well. However, I did manage to put him to bed and when Vera herself was asleep I tried to phone Eden. The housekeeper, a Mrs King, answered and said they were both out. It was New Year's Eve, she reminded me. That night I slept in the room that was Francis Hillyard's, setting the alarm so that I could get up and look in on Vera at two and again at five.

'Delirium' is a strong word and I won't say Vera was delirious. But her temperature was very high and she was light-headed. The second time I went in she got hold of my hand and held it and began talking to me in a high rapid voice, a meaningless jumble most of it, as I thought then, and some rather more lucid stuff about life being pointless without children, and then suddenly she recited a verse.

I had never thought of Vera as in the least 'literary' but I suppose she remembered this from school where it had made a strong impression on her.

> For there is no friend like a sister
> In calm or stormy weather;
> To cheer one on the tedious way,
> To fetch one if one goes astray,
> To lift one if one totters down,
> To strengthen whilst one stands.

I went back to bed and Jamie awoke me about seven. He wanted to be with his mother but I was afraid to let him in case he caught the flu. The doctor came, said she could be left if we could find someone to come in and see her two or three times a day. But she was on no account to be left with the child. Again I tried to phone Eden and again she was out. The housekeeper said she would take a message for Mrs Pearmain to call me when she came back at lunchtime. She was bound to be back by twelve as guests were expected for lunch.

Vera was still breathing unevenly and her voice was strained. I sat on her bed and told her what the doctor had said. I told her that I would have to go but I had spoken to Josie Cambus and she had promised to come in at lunchtime and again in the evening. However, I said, I would stay at least until Eden phoned back because we should have to make arrangements for someone to look after Jamie.

That had an electrifying effect on her, ill as she was. She seized my hand in both hers. She sat up, clutching my hand. I must take Jamie, I must promise her I would take Jamie and look after him. I can remember her exact words.

'You take him, Chad, he knows you. He will be all right with you. I should be easy, I should sleep if I knew he was with you.'

She would soon be better, she said, it was unthinkable that she could be ill for more than a day or two. She could not remember a day's illness since that trouble she had in her teens when Eden was a baby, and that had been anaemia, she thought, which would have been cured if anyone had had the sense to give her iron. She rambled on like this, tossing from side to side, gripping my hand. I would promise her, wouldn't I, that I would keep Jamie just till Monday. By Monday she would be better, she would be right as rain. Jamie would be no trouble, he would eat just what I ate, he never woke in the night, all his clean clothes were in the chest of drawers in his room. She would pack them herself if I would bring her a suitcase.

It never occurred to me for a moment to say yes. I thought it a ridiculous request to make of me. I was a single man living in a flat that was little more than a bedsit with a kitchen. What did I know about the needs, the tastes and whims of little children? Next morning, though it would be Sunday, I had an interview booked with our local MP, the only time he could see me. On Monday morning I would be due at work by nine. So I didn't even consider doing what Vera asked. For one thing, I didn't think there was a chance of her being well by Monday. I told her one of the women would have him, Eden would have him.

She reared up in bed as if she had seen a ghost come in the door. She stared at me as if she could see something dreadful behind me, a spectre that had entered and was standing there with arms upheld. In a way she had, though at that time it was invisible to the rest of the world. Clutching my hand, she held on to me as if she wanted to keep me a prisoner.

'Please keep Jamie, Chad!'

She was imploring me, begging me, and I thought her high temperature had made her mad. That's all I thought it was.

'I can't,' I said, 'be reasonable. You know I can't.'

'It's the only thing I've ever asked you. I'll never ask you to do a thing for me again. Please, Chad.'

'It isn't possible, Vera,' I said.

'Then will you get Josie to have him. He doesn't know Josie like he knows you but she's a kind woman, she'll be kind to him. Promise me you'll get Josie.'

I said I would ask her. I would do my best. Downstairs the phone was ringing. I went down to answer it and of course it was Eden. The housekeeper had given her the message that Vera was ill and once she had had lunch she was coming straight over, she wouldn't wait for her guests to leave, Tony would be there, she would come straight over and fetch Vera and Jamie and take them back with her to Goodney Hall.

It was a great relief. I felt a load lifted from my mind and that our troubles were over. Josie arrived just as I put the phone down with lunch for Vera which of course she couldn't eat, and being the rare (for those days) possessor of a washing machine, took away a pile of Vera's and Jamie's washing to do. I told Vera Eden was coming and got a very curious reaction.

She looked at me with mad eyes, but she wasn't hysterical, she didn't even sound delirious. She uttered this mad request in a sane, calm, intense voice.

'Jamie has his sleep in the afternoon. Lock him in his room, Chad, and tell Eden Josie's got him.'

What could I say? What does one say to apparently insane demands of that kind? I humoured her. I said all right. May God forgive me.

*

That was all I read of Chad's statement for the time being. I was finding it curiously upsetting. Of course I knew it had been bad, all of it, I knew about Vera's despair, but I didn't know it had been as bad as that. As for verifying things for Daniel Stewart, I couldn't do that anyway. What I could do was find the letter Vera wrote to my father about a week after that Saturday. It is dated 6 January 1949 and is one of the rare winter letters he kept. The remarkable thing about this letter is not what it says but what it doesn't say.

Dear John,

I should have written before to thank you for the PO you and Vranni kindly sent Jamie for Christmas. Unfortunately I have been laid up with flu for the past week. I have had a really bad go of it with throat and chest complications but everyone has been wonderfully kind and helpful, Josie and Thora Morrell coming in to see to me each day and Helen has been an absolute brick, spending hours with me, reading to me and sending food from Walbrooks.

Jamie is with Eden. I was rather worried she might not be strong enough yet to look after him but she assured me she was feeling quite fit again. It is the best place for him really, to be in that lovely house, and I should be able to have him back with me next week. Eden came over to fetch him the minute she knew I was ill . . .

This was read aloud, of course, at our breakfast table, my mother listening with her customary expression of wry exasperation.

'I'm glad the boy is with his aunt,' said my father. 'That's a load off my mind. He couldn't be in better hands. Eden will be kindness itself, it'll be the next best thing to his own mother.'

'I don't suppose it makes much difference,' my mother said in her neutral voice. By this I took her to mean that in her opinion, Vera and Eden would be equally horrid to any child in their care. My father thought the same, for he threw the letter down and asked her what she meant. She answered him obliquely.

'You know how I feel. I told you at the time it was all for the best your sister having that miscarriage. She doesn't like children, she's got no patience, you've only got to look at her to see that.'

They argued about this for a while, my father insisting that the maternal instinct had found its fullest expression in both his sisters equally, they got it from his mother. My mother had never forgotten the incident of Eden dusting her bedroom when she stayed with us. She let fly about Eden's selfishness, lack of thought, eye to the main chance and so on. I was remembering Eden's wedding morning when she had flung out her arm to gesture Jamie away and would have struck him if he hadn't dodged her hand. I remembered how she never spoke to him if she could avoid it and in my mind's eye I saw Jamie holding the carved Swiss dog and Eden turning on him.

'Put it down! It's not a toy!'

My father got up to go off to work. 'I really think that's the best place for him,' he said as if none of this argument had taken place. 'He'll be best off with his aunt.'

'I would gladly have had him here if I'd known,' said my mother.

Nobody once suggested the obvious person to look after Jamie and minister to poor Vera. I suppose the fact was that we had all given up Francis as a potentially useful or helpful or ordinary social being years before. We had almost given him up as a member of the family. It seems from what Chad has written that Vera never suggested fetching him home from wherever he was in the Highlands for Hogmanay. My parents had forgotten his existence. And I who, if we had been talking about any other family group, would naturally have asked why the sick woman's son couldn't be called upon, never considered Francis in this role. I looked through Chad's statement again, looked in vain for a mention of Francis in this connection, noting only how Chad had passed two nights in Francis's room, in Francis's bed no doubt, and wondering how that had been for him, ecstatic or painful or perhaps both.

I did not lock Jamie in his bedroom (Chad continued). I simply put him in there on his bed with his toys and hoped he would fall asleep for a while. Eden arrived at about three. You want the facts, you want everything I can remember, so I may as well tell you that though she wasn't drunk, she had been drinking a lot. She smelt of wine. Mme de Pompadour said that the only wine a woman can drink and still look beautiful afterwards is champagne, so I suppose it was champagne, among other things, Eden had been drinking. She shouldn't really have been driving a car. She went straight to Jamie's room and packed a suitcase for him and then she went in to see Vera.

I heard nothing of what they said to each other. Eden's going into his room had awakened Jamie and he was whimpering. I gave him some orange squash and a biscuit. By that time I was desperate to get away. I heard Eden calling my name and I went upstairs and found Vera lying on the landing where she had collapsed and fallen over. She wasn't unconscious, only too weak to get up. I thought she had been trying to reach the bathroom, that was what I thought at the time, but later on I came to a different conclusion. Eden was also out on the landing, her gloves on, her handbag under her arm. I think Eden had said goodbye to Vera and come out of the bedroom, and Vera had got up and followed her, tried to run after her perhaps and there in her weakness, fallen over. I picked her up in my arms and carried her back to bed. She lay back against the pillows with her eyes closed. Downstairs Jamie had begun to cry.

Vera murmured, 'Jamie – please, Chad . . .' Tears began to fall down her cheeks. I thought they were tears of weakness, of fever.

'It's best to leave her and let her get some sleep,' Eden said. Her speech was the slightest bit slurred. You wouldn't have noticed if you didn't know what her normal voice was like.

We went down to Jamie. He was crying because he had spilt his drink over himself. I cleaned him up and gave him some more. Nothing was said by Eden about taking both Vera and Jamie away with her. Nor did I remind her of what she had said earlier. Vera wasn't fit to be moved. The doctor himself had said she should stay in her room in bed. We have seen what happened when she tried to walk. I was wondering whether I dared leave her when Josie Cambus came in, carrying her knitting and a library book, all prepared to stay for the rest of the day and all night if necessary.

And that was it. Eden put Jamie on the back seat of her car and the suitcase in the boot and drove off. I told Josie I would give Vera a ring on Monday to find out how she was and then I, too, left. By Monday, however, I had flu. I was off work ill for the whole of that week and part of the next and when I finally phoned Vera, Josie answered to say she was much better but asleep just now. I did not speak to Vera again for a long time and when I did things were very much changed. Eden Pearmain I never saw again. My last sight of her was as she got into the driving seat of her car, the last words I ever heard her speak, those in which she told Jamie to mind his fingers in the door.

Vera was ill for a long time. Her appearance shocked me when I saw her that February and I thought Helen was right when she said Vera wasn't yet fit to have Jamie back.

I was staying at Walbrooks for the weekend, having come down with Andrew on the Friday night. If my father had heard from either Vera or Eden during the past weeks no news had been passed on to me beyond the information that Vera's convalescence was a long one. I arrived at Stoke-by-Nayland, concerning myself about Vera only in so far as my conscience was mildly troubling me. For reasons that must have been obvious to everyone, including herself and Eden, I now stayed with Helen instead of her when I was in this part of the country. No doubt Vera understood but I had deserted her all the same.

'Oh, darling,' Helen said, 'she wouldn't have wanted you. I don't mean it like that, of course, but she's not at all well. She's never got over that flu. But we'll go over tomorrow and you shall see for yourself. She wants Jamie back, she wants us all to go to Eden's and fetch him back but I don't know. You'll see.'

She was so thin I had to stop myself staring at her, and she had that faded worn-out look some fair women get as they age, the look of a dead leaf. Her skin had crumpled and there was a lot of grey in her hair, the bones in her wrists and knees were knobs, and when she smiled her face became a skull. In spite of all this, in spite of her evident weakness, she had spent the past week painting Jamie's bedroom. We all had to go up and admire her work, Helen and the General and Andrew and I. This was the room where I had slept, where I had watched Eden cream her face and put her hair in curlers and had myself experimented with her make-up. It was transformed. Vera had painted the walls white and the woodwork pale blue, made Jamie a rag rug out of blue and white material scraps, cut illustrations out of Beatrix Potter books and framed them in passe-partout.

'It looks heavenly,' said Helen. 'Isn't he going to adore it? But, darling, are you sure you're fit enough to cope?'

Vera gave a skull smile. 'Of course I am. Could I have done all this if I wasn't? Anyway, I don't suppose Eden would keep Jamie any longer. It would be a bit much to ask. She leads a very busy social life, you know. I expect she's fed up with having him, she'll be only too glad to see the back of him.'

It was said so brightly, so confidently, so – desperately?

'I could have him for a while.' Helen sounded anything but enthusiastic. Yet I am sure none of us doubted that she meant it. She would have Jamie if Vera wanted her to. 'I happily will, darling, if you don't feel up to it and Eden wants a rest.'

Vera didn't say anything. It struck me then that she was frightened. Or does hindsight make me say that? Did I notice anything at the time except her thinness, her tiredness, the way she shook her head, at the same time giving Helen a grateful yet dismissive smile? We all got into the car and drove to Goodney Hall. The house was approached by a long avenue of lime trees and around their roots and in patches on the parkland lay drifts of snow. The sky looked full of snow. It was deep, bleak midwinter, the worst time of the year, much worse than December, and although the evenings were lengthening, it was dark soon after five.

Steuart's beautiful house rested aloof on its raft of terraces and balustrades and steps. There wasn't even a coniferous tree or an evergreen up near it to break the monochrome, the greys of that house and the sky behind. It was three o'clock and not a light on yet. A curious thing happened as we approached the gravel sweep in front of the terrace. Eden came round the side of the house alone, walking slowly, pausing at the corner where a stone urn stood on the angle of the balustrade, and placing her hands on its pedestal stared first across the park, then in our direction. She was wrapped in a fur coat with a thick, upturned fur collar that framed her face. I am sure she didn't expect to see us, didn't know we were coming and was unpleasantly surprised by the sight of us.

Nor could she quite disguise this. She had not been born to this style of life or nurtured in a tradition of social grace, the concealment of feeling, the putting on of an artificially welcoming face. She came down the steps looking cross, then resigned. Her hair was entirely covered by a turban of some sort of dark jersey material and this and the red fox collar discouraged kissing. No one kissed. Eden said:

'Well, my goodness, how nice to see you all. What a surprise!'

'I told you we'd come on Saturday,' said Vera.

'Two weeks ago you said something about probably coming this weekend.'

They were both giving the impression that if Vera had tried to make a firm date, Eden would have turned her down. We went into the house. Although there was a fuel shortage just as there were shortages of almost everything, I had expected Goodney Hall to be warm inside. Eden and Tony would have found ways, I thought. It was cold, colder than college or Walbrooks or my parents' house. A small electric fire was switched on in the drawing-room. We all kept our coats on and perhaps because of this didn't attempt to sit down. Eden said it was Mrs King's day off but it was a bit early for tea anyway, wasn't it? Tony, too, was out somewhere.

Vera's voice had become strangely timid. 'Is Jamie still having his sleep?'

'Jamie?' Eden spoke as if he were someone whose name she had once heard and now vaguely remembered from the distant past. 'Jamie? Yes, I suppose he is. I really don't know.'

No one said anything. Andrew said to me afterwards that for a moment he had the curious feeling that Eden hadn't been looking after Jamie, that he wasn't in the house, that it was all some sort of delusion on Vera's part. She only *thought* Eden had been looking after him while all the time he had really been with Josie or Mrs Morrell. But this, of course, was Andrew's misapprehension for Eden, taking off the red fox coat and dropping it over an armchair, now said, with equally devastating effect:

'Shall I ask Nanny to bring him down or shall we go up?'

A little colour came into Vera's face. She looked as if she had two insect bites on her wasted face, one on each cheekbone.

'Nanny?'

'Yes, that's what I said.' Eden spoke in a pleasant tone.

'You had a nanny to look after Jamie?'

'We thought the most sensible thing would be to engage a professional who would know what she was doing, yes.'

As if Jamie were autistic or retarded or delinquent, Andrew later said to me.

'Is he up in that beautiful nursery we saw, Eden?' said Helen, very sweet, very cheerful. 'I'd truly love to see it in use.'

Eden shrugged. 'Come along, then.'

The General declined. He belonged in that generation of men, perhaps the last, for whom men's and women's roles were utterly differentiated. Men did not set foot in nurseries, converse with nannies. Men, like sultans, had nothing to do with children, even boy children, until they attained the age of reason. He picked up the *Daily Telegraph* – in which, I noted, Eden had half done the crossword – and sat on the sofa with it. A man's role was to drive the car and when the car was ready to be driven, he would do it. Andrew came with us, though, and as we went up the staircase, I took his hand.

Eden, when the fox was off, was dressed for the part of lady of the manor. She wore a tweed skirt with box pleats, a pale blue twinset, several strings of pearls and the eternity ring. Her brilliant gold hair was cut short and permed in symmetrical sausage curls. She led us down the long corridor to the corner of the house where the nursery was. It was so cold in that passage that my teeth started to chatter. But inside the nursery it wasn't cold. I hadn't noticed the fireplace on my previous visit. I noticed it now. A fire burned in it, a fire generously fed with good Welsh nuts, not logs, and it sent out a fierce red heat, more than competing with the two-bar electric fire that stood between the windows. These were misted with condensation, the air outside being icy. Last time I had seen this room, the sun was shining and making patterns all over the pink carpet which had a border of ivy and convolvulus. This carpet had gone and been replaced by a fitted one of light beige and there were new curtains of beige rep, but the table and chairs were still there and the rocking horse. A girl a bit older than I, perhaps Eden's age, was laying this table with a teacup and saucer, plates, a rabbit mug. She wore a grey dress, not exactly a uniform yet drab enough to be one. Jamie was on the rocking horse and seemed to have been jerking it vigorously back and forth. When we came in, the jerking stopped though the horse naturally went on swinging. He looked in our direction, then turned his face sharply away.

Eden went up to the nanny and muttered something inaudible to her. The girl immediately, as if in response to a button pressed or a lever thrown, said:

'Say hello to Mother, Jamie.'

She had a thick Suffolk accent so that this command (which was disobeyed) came out something like: 'Sah-allo ter Mawther, Jarmie.'

Vera was sensible enough not to show her bitter disappointment. I hadn't realized until that moment that she and Jamie hadn't seen each other since January the first, now six weeks past, and six weeks is a long time in the life of a four-year-old. Jamie got down off the horse, went to his nanny and stood close by her.

'Come on now, don't be a baby,' she said.

Jamie's face crumpled and he began to cry. The girl picked him up and held him. Rather awkwardly, I thought. Eden had detached

207

herself from the little drama that was developing, gone to the fireplace and, slipping her carefully manicured and be-ringed right hand into a coal glove, started prodding at the fire with a small brass poker.

Unable to contain herself any longer, Vera ran to Jamie and put out her arms. As anyone but she could have foretold, this had the effect of making Jamie cling all the tighter to the brawny, grey-cotton-clad shoulders. He buried his face. Vera gave a piteous cry and the nanny responded by shoving Jamie at her. The ensuing scene was painful to see. Such scenes – and they usually happen when a mother and her child have been separated over a long period – always are painful. Jamie screamed and fought, struggled out of Vera's arms, threw himself at his nanny's lap, bellowed, embraced his nanny's knees. All the while Eden poked and prodded at the fire. Outside it had begun to snow. Fat, fluffy flakes of snow were drifting thickly past those dewed windows. The nanny sat down, cuddling Jamie, and Vera stood trembling with clenched fists. Helen said:

'He's bound to be a bit unsettled at first, darling. Don't be upset. Shouldn't we just wrap him up warm and collect his things and go? Wouldn't that be best?'

Eden came over. 'You weren't intending to take him with you?'

'Yes, of course, darling, I thought you knew that.'

'I certainly did not. Anyway, it's out of the question. Look at the snow. He's had a bad cold and it would be very unwise indeed to take him out in this weather, wouldn't it, Nanny?'

I think we were all struck by the unsuitability of this girl as an oracle, and it so happened that she made no answer to Eden's appeal. She merely looked bovine, humping Jamie on to her hip and jigging about with him from one foot to the other. We probably all felt, too, that if anyone were consulted on the question of Jamie's health it should be Vera. Jamie struggled down, sat on the hearthrug and began sucking his thumb. Vera said:

'You never mentioned a cold.'

'No, well, I haven't spoken to you for about ten days, have I? He's had it since then.'

'I rang and rang. You were never in. That woman, your house-keeper, always answered.'

'Vera,' said Eden patiently. 'I can't stop in all day on the chance you might ring.'

'When can I have Jamie, then?' said Vera like a little girl who, having been denied a treat, tries to extract a fresh promise from a parent. 'When can I have him?'

Andrew was starting to get angry and the effect of Vera's humble pleading tone was to make him angrier still. He might be an undergraduate like me but he was much older, older than Eden, nearly thirty, had been in the Battle of Britain, had been a prisoner of war and was long past the category of 'children' of the family, in which I still belonged.

'You can have him when you like, Vera. He's your child. We'll wrap him up and he'll be perfectly all right. We came over here to fetch him and that's what we'll do.' He addressed the nanny in a tone worthy of a descendant of the Richardsons, wealthy gentlefolk that they were. 'Get his things ready, will you?'

I admired his manner. Emancipated as I was, sticking up even then for women's rights, I still expected a man to be able to 'take charge'. Helen too looked pleased. I watched dismay come into her face at Eden's high-handedness. Astonishingly it was Vera who demurred. She seemed determined to placate Eden, though Eden was firm rather than angry.

'If you really think it would be bad for him, Eden . . .'

'I do. I've already said so.' Eden went to one of the windows and lifted the curtain away from it, though it was perfectly easy to see the blizzard without that. Andrew said what we were surely all thinking:

'If the car is brought up to the front door he'll only be outside for about ten seconds,' and added scathingly, 'it isn't as if he's got to walk two miles to the station.'

'Why don't we say next weekend and make a firm date?' said Vera. It seemed, even then, a very curious way of putting it. 'Suppose I said next Saturday, Eden?'

'You'd better make sure my father's free next Saturday,' Andrew said, not very warmly.

'Josie's got a car. She'll drive me. Shall we say next Saturday, Eden?'

Eden took her time about answering. The fire in front of which Jamie was sitting, still sucking his thumb (the bitter-aloes aversion therapy all forgotten now), had been unguarded. Eden slipped her hand into the coal glove, put a couple of pieces of coal on the fire and placed a wire mesh guard in front of it. When she had finished doing this she took the glove off and in an absent-minded sort of way put her hand out and lightly ruffled Jamie's hair. He reacted not at all.

'You can come next Saturday if you like,' she said.

'I'll come in the morning and fetch him then, shall I?'

'Yes, come in the morning.'

The nanny came back with tea for all of us on a tray. Eden looked annoyed. She shook her head when the nanny started pouring tea into her cup. Vera sat down in one of the wooden nursery chairs. She looked as if she might have fainted if she hadn't done that. Silence prevailed until Helen began talking about the snow, relating snow anecdotes of her childhood at Walbrooks. During this, something odd, and in the light of what was to come, dreadfully painful, happened. Jamie got up off the hearthrug and made his way over to Vera's side. He stood by her chair. Again Vera behaved quite sensibly, not showing the emotion I believe she was feeling. She put out her arms to him, or her hands rather, in that tendering gesture that offers a casual cuddle if the child wants it. Jamie evidently did want it. He climbed on to her lap. For the first time since our arrival, he spoke.

'Eden is going to buy me a dog,' he said to Vera.

'Is she, darling? That's kind.'

'A big dog. But it will be little first.'

'Oh dear,' Vera said. 'I hadn't really anticipated having a dog, but if you've promised, Eden.'

Jamie nodded. 'She's promised.' He put his arms round Vera's neck and hugged her.

'Don't let your tea get cold,' Eden said and in her accents, precisely imitated, I'm sure, I heard my grandmother Longley, whose voice I thought I had forgotten.

The snow forced us to leave. The blizzard let up but it was apparent more snow would fall and some of the lanes would then have become impassable. As Andrew said later, to be forced to spend a night at Goodney Hall would be a fate worse than death.

Vera seemed much happier since Jamie had come to her and shown her affection. I thought, and believe Helen and Andrew did too, that this was the only trouble. She had been upset by his indifference. You could see, too, that he did have a cold. His nose was running and occasionally he made croupy sounds. The nursery was very hot and no doubt it wouldn't have been wise to take him out into the cold for even ten seconds. I think we all felt much better about the arrangement by the time we went downstairs and collected the General. Jamie had kissed Vera goodbye, had seemed quite cheerful in the nanny's arms, waving to us from the nursery door. And Eden also kissed Vera. Indeed she kissed us all and, shivering at the snow, begged us to phone her the moment we got to Walbrooks just to let her know we had got there.

That was the only weekend I spent away from Cambridge that term. I wasn't sufficiently interested or concerned to inquire what happened on the following Saturday. If I thought about it at all, I assumed Jamie was back with Vera at Laurel Cottage. I remember I did wonder how Vera would get on with a 'big dog', no pet animal ever having been kept by any Longley within memory of the oldest of them.

It was April before I learned that Jamie had never been returned to Vera but was still living at Goodney Hall, apparently with her acquiescence.

— 14 —

Daniel Stewart is a man who looks very young at first. One's first impression is how young he is, a mere boy. This is because he is thin and straight-backed and wears his hair long and hasn't gone bald. Helen has a theory that for the best effect, women – and men, too, for all I know – should dress ten years younger than they are, neither more nor less. Stewart dresses twenty years younger than he is, and it is too much, it is verging on the absurd. After a time one becomes insistently conscious of the lines on his face, so painful when he smiles, and the grey in his hair that the colour rinse has not dyed so deeply as the rest of it – copper threads, in fact, among the brown.

But all this is by the way. He is pleasant, a little ingratiating, intelligent. He sits in my drawing-room with a whole heap of books on fungi spread around him and we wait for Helen to come. He, of course, has met her before. I am listening to him with half an ear and with the other half the diesel throb of the taxi that will bring her.

'I want to get this straight,' he says. 'Was the poison Vera Hillyard used the same as that which killed the old woman she found dead in the cottage?'

'Mrs Hislop,' I tell him. 'You're asking me? I didn't even know it was poison that killed her. I knew she used to cook fungi for herself – what I'd call toadstools.'

'The inquest verdict was "natural causes". The death certificate said myocardial infarction, which is a sort of heart attack. In other words, she died of heart failure, which is what we all die of. At the post-mortem, considerable kidney deterioration was found but no comment was made on this. Mrs Hislop was, after all, nearly eighty. In the cottage was a basket of uncooked fungi and in the saucepan a kind of stew of fungi. Both were analysed and found to be harmless.'

I ask him if the post-mortem found any poisonous fungi in Mrs Hislop's body. I thought I wasn't interested in this kind of thing – for instance, I never read detective stories – but as we talk about it, I find I am.

'There was nothing, hence the verdict. But there was a great deal of talk about poisonous fungi at the inquest, largely, I think, because Mrs Hislop was known for dabbling with them. Vera Hillyard gave evidence at that inquest, of course, but you knew that.'

'No, I didn't,' I say and I am very surprised. This is because I remember Vera telling me how she found Mrs Hislop but not telling me she was at the inquest. Yet this surely must have made a profound and lasting impression on her, sheltered fourteen-year-old that she was. The implications of her failure to tell me are not lost on me. At the inquest she would have heard all the talk about fungi. She would have stored it up to turn over later in her mind.

'In spite of that verdict,' he says, 'I am sure Mrs Hislop did die of fungal poisoning and that the poison she used was the same that Vera Hillyard used nearly thirty years later. Nobody really knows what it was and nobody ever will know now. It's possible only to take the symptoms and calculate from that, to use, in fact, what we do know and make an intelligent guess from that.'

'Like the Emperor Hadrian's ears,' I say.

He doesn't take me up on that one. 'I'm wondering if it was a poison called orellanin that's responsible. It's found in the cortinarius species of fungi. For a long time, cortinarius was considered harmless and it wasn't until 1962 that the properties of *Cortinarius orellanus* were discovered by a Pole called Gryzmala. It damages the kidneys. Death has been caused in children after several days, in adults after weeks or months. The kidneys go wrong.'

'Mrs Hislop was in the habit of regularly eating strange fungus,' I say. 'You say that the post-mortem found kidney damage. Vera told me that when she found her, she looked "all swollen up". It could have happened months after she'd eaten what-do-you-call-it, *orellanus*.' I pick up his field guide to mushrooms and other fungi, read the relevant section and immediately see objections.

'Yes, but look here, it says that *orellanus* is rare or absent in Great Britain. Vera didn't go to Poland collecting fungi. And the other one, *turmalis*, that's rare or absent here, too.'

'I know,' Stewart says, 'I haven't missed that. But what about the purple agaric that isn't even in this book? Here it is.' He hands me a thin, flat booklet published by the then Ministry of Agriculture and Fisheries, some ten years before Vera began on her poisoning course. '*Cortinarius purpurascens*,' he says. 'Apparently it's fairly common. It says it has been listed as edible but the word is merely used in the sense that it has been eaten without ill effects.'

This book, a copy of it I mean, I have seen before. Although I know Vera was a murderess, although I know that before she used the knife she tried poison, nevertheless I have that curious sensation we call the heart turning over. The book (called *Bulletin No. 23, Edible and Poisonous Fungi*) is flat and dark green with a picture on its cover of a golden chantarelle such as one sees for sale in French markets. The date of publication was 1940, the price half a crown. In the little text beside the watercolour drawing of the purple agaric, a note explains that the species is difficult of determination even by experts and warns that experiments are not advisable. Nothing about orellanin, though, and just as I am beginning to say this to Stewart, I remember what he has told me, that its properties weren't discovered until twenty-two years after *Bulletin No 23* was published.

'It belongs to the cortinarius species,' he tells me, 'and therefore very probably contains the kidney-damaging orellanus.'

I gaze at the picture and remember with perfect clarity seeing purple mushrooms in the woods at Sindon. It was always late summer that I was there, wasn't it? For a long time it was only the late summer or early autumn. Anne and I would wander through the woods together. It was near the wash where the river was forded and a wooden bridge passed over it, there where Vera once sat gossiping with her school friend and Kathleen March was snatched from her pram, there it was that I had seen cortinarius, growing in clusters

213

through the leaf mould, date-brown olivaceous (as the book puts it), glutinous and opaque, expanded and marked with a raised, violet fuscous zone, the stem fibrillose, pallid, the gills bluish, then cinnamon, violaceous when bruised, broad and crowded, the flesh azure blue.

At this point, Helen comes in and how glad of it I am! The nausea of old remembered ugly things is in my throat. She embraces me, shakes hands with Stewart.

'I have brought my Valium with me, Mr Stewart, so if you want to talk about you-know-what, could you give me warning, and I can take one in good time.'

Stewart asks her only to describe Goodney Hall to him. The people now living there won't permit him to see over it. That won't upset her, will it? She shakes her head. The wide-brimmed hat she is wearing is the rich brownish-violet of the purple agaric, incurved lilac fuscous, and I am glad when she takes it off and bares her small, white, fluffy head.

'I won't take my Valium but perhaps we could have our sherry a wee bit early, darling?'

In wilder moments I have sometimes thought I married in order to have Helen for my mother-in-law. Or was that not the cause but merely the one good effect? Surely I married as I did because I was afraid, young, ignorant and inexperienced as I was, that if I didn't marry within the family, no one outside the family would have me. No one outside would marry a hanged woman's niece.

Helen can remember thirty-five years back better than I can. I remembered Eden's drawing-room as pink and green, the whole house pink and green, but Helen remembers crimsons and yellows. She remembers the Arthur Rackham paper on the nursery walls changed for a plain deep blue that made the room look cold even in summer or even when a fire was burning in the grate. And she remembers Jamie's nanny's name: June Poole. I am amazed at myself for forgetting it, for was not Grace Poole the nurse and keeper of Mr Rochester's wife? The situations were very different of course. Jamie wasn't deranged or female or a secret, though for a while he was a prisoner, and there was no part in this drama for a Jane Eyre.

June Poole was a girl from the village, from Goodney Parva, and her qualification, not a bad one perhaps, for being Jamie's nanny was that she was the oldest of seven siblings. She had known no other life than that of minding children. Whether she *liked* it was another matter. Did she even like Jamie? Helen, though, doesn't speak of this. I know she finds speaking of Jamie at four and five intensely painful. I have given her her sherry and she is talking of the rhododendron garden at Goodney Hall, famous all over the county and opened by Eden to the public that spring, when my husband comes in.

I love the way they are so pleased to see each other, he and Helen, and kiss and are at ease as if it were the most natural thing in the world. Yet I have never quite got used to it. I don't think he likes Stewart and certainly he dislikes the idea of Stewart's book.

'I hope you're keeping the law of libel in the forefront of your mind, Mr Stewart,' he says, winking at me behind the old young man's back.

Illness governed events at this time. First Vera was ill, then Jamie, lastly Eden. What Jamie's illness really was I never knew. Croup perhaps, though he was old for that, bronchitis, pleurisy, I don't know. This illness, though, was the reason given for his not going home to Sindon. Vera's letter to my father, dated 30 March 1949, survives.

'. . . Eden has kindly invited me to stay with them at Goodney Hall for a couple of weeks. Tony is sending one of the cars for me tomorrow . . .'

Poor Vera! Even in the extremity of her dread, snobbery – in this case vicarious snobbery – was not forgotten.

'Jamie has been there for nearly three months now, unfit to be moved since the bad cold with complications he had in the middle of February. I miss him dreadfully as you can imagine but have had to accept what I know to be the best for him. Certainly there was no question of moving him, taking him out, etc., during the very cold weather. Eden has been kindness itself, though I know you will agree that any other behaviour from *her* would have surprised us. She has lavished every care on him and daily kept me up to the minute with regard to his progress. It will be nice to spend time under the same roof with him. We shall really have to get acquainted all over again! By the time the two weeks are at an end, he should be fit enough to accompany me back to Laurel Cottage . . .'

These lines are a masterpiece of their kind for concealing true

215

facts and real feelings. They are also perhaps a sop to Providence or a placating of the Furies. If I put a brave face on things, if I make believe all is well, all *will* be well. Yet I, Faith, know so little and there is no one alive who knows more. For instance, had Vera and Eden by this time discussed the question of Jamie's future? Or Jamie's past, come to that? Had Eden made to Vera any actual declaration of intent? Or was poor Vera – and this I think to be most likely – left for all those months in suspense, knowing no more of this aspect of things than she had expressed to us that snowy day in February, no more than she told my father in the letter, but terribly afraid of the worst?

I think, in the light of Chad Hamner's statement and my own memories, that she had been aware she had something to fear from Eden's wedding day onwards, perhaps from earlier than that, the announcement of her engagement. Her fears became concrete, real, not chimeras, when Eden miscarried.

Often, since then, I have wondered what the two sisters said to each other when they were alone together during those two weeks of April. Tony went to London, by train from Colchester, at least three times a week. No doubt Eden's friends came sometimes, Mrs King would have been in and out and June Poole too. When they walked or were in the garden and at meals, too, Jamie would have been with them. But what of the long hours when they were alone, just the two of them?

Did they thrash things out, trying to find a compromise, trying to create a sharing future, a communal life? Or was Eden adamant and Vera pleading? Was the identity of Jamie's father ever discussed? Knowing them, these two sisters, I tend to believe that they were never open about any of it. They never said what they felt or meant to do but always spoke in half-shades and half-truths, Eden still keeping up the pretence that Jamie was 'delicate', 'not strong', Vera terrified of antagonizing her.

Did they reminisce about the past? That surely would have been too painful. Not for them, at that time, to look back into the distant past when Vera had saved the infant Eden's life, had rejected her own son to be a mother to her, had wept bitterly when the war took Eden away, those days when they had loved each other dearly – in the Far.

*

That summer, for part of the Long Vacation, I went with Andrew to Walbrooks. Of course I married him. Not then, not for another year and more and our Finals were done with and he had taken his First and I my disappointing Lower Second. Then, we were not even engaged. For a few months I was in love with him, but being no Desdemona, I could not love him for the dangers he had passed. The dangers he had passed began to bore me to death and I dreaded ever hearing the words Battle of Britain again. If Vera had not been hanged for murder I would have dropped Helen's son as gracefully as I could and hoped we might have become no more than cousins again.

But this is Vera's story, not mine. What was I then, or at any time, but a figure in one of Vera's dreams? A potential ally against Eden? What was anyone to her but that?

She had passed the greater part of that summer staying at Goodney Hall, sometimes going home to Laurel Cottage for a week or a few days, but Jamie had never gone with her. Now he was five, he had become five in May, and the question had come up of his going to school. Naturally, it was taken for granted that he would go to Sindon village school and probably remain there till he was eleven. Vera would not do with Jamie what had been done with Francis. Her beloved Jamie wouldn't be separated from her and sent away to prep school. Nor, we all thought, would Gerald be likely to intervene. It would be Vera's decision and Vera's only. I don't think any of us any longer believed – though we never spoke of it among ourselves – that Gerald was Jamie's father. Jamie had to have had a father and it wasn't Chad, so Vera had to have had another lover. My own view at the time, which I never expressed even to Andrew, was that some former boyfriend of Vera's, someone she had known before she knew Gerald, had come home on leave and they had met by chance, and frustration and nostalgia and perhaps an under-the-counter bottle of wine had done the rest. It didn't sound like Vera but people's sex lives seldom do sound like the people who have them.

Vera asked Andrew and me to help her kidnap Jamie.

We had been to Bury St Edmunds in the old Mercedes, just the two of us, and driving back went over the Stour at Sudbury into Essex and took in Great Sindon on our way home. It may have been that day that going into Sindon Wood down by the wash to pick up pine-cones for Helen's drawing-room fireplace, I saw the purple agaric growing out of the leaf mould. Certainly, according to Daniel Stewart's book, *Cortinarius purpurascens* abounds in July and August and this was July. Or it may have been some other day years before when Anne Cambus and I roamed Sindon Wood, or even years after when I went back alone.

I don't like to think that if we had agreed to Vera's request murder might never have been done. It wouldn't be true anyway. Only if we had agreed and our efforts been successful could that particular disaster have been avoided. And we know from subsequent events that our efforts would not have been successful.

Vera wasn't expecting us. We called on her by chance. I was all for driving on, avoiding the lane where Laurel Cottage was, but Andrew said it wouldn't look well if someone in the village saw us and passed it on to Vera. He was always a great stickler for appearances.

Josie Cambus was with her. That may have been the day I first heard mention of Josie's son by her previous marriage, for when we arrived she had been talking of this son and how he was reading law. Vera was as thin as when we last saw her and as aged. But she seemed to have regained her wiry strength. All the time we were there she was on the fidget, her hands constantly picking at the piping on the arms of the chair, and once or twice doing that bearing down business, straining as if pressing on a drill, her face contorted.

About five minutes after we came in, Josie left.

Vera said, 'Did you come in a car?' as if it were possible to visit Sindon by any other means in the middle of the afternoon, the lunchtime bus having gone two hours before and the teatime one not due till five.

As if doubting our answer, she went to the window and contemplated the Mercedes, parked up against her fuchsia hedge. She nodded. She was a pathetic sight, was Vera at forty-two – emaciated, gaunt, looking ten years older. Her mouth, though empty, worked like a gum chewer's.

Suddenly she began to speak, apropos of nothing that had gone before, yet as if this were only the continuation of a conversation she had been carrying on for weeks. And in a way it was, for later on I learned she had made a similar appeal to Josie, to the Morrells, and even to Helen, though Helen had said nothing of it to us.

'If we went over there now,' Vera said. 'Tony wouldn't be at home. I know that for a fact. And it's June's afternoon off. I've stayed there so much I know all the workings of that household. There would only be Mrs King with Eden and Mrs King's not very strong, she must be sixty if she's a day. We could easily do it. *I* could do it if you'd keep Eden talking. It would be easy.'

People with an obsession have their minds so filled with it to the exclusion of all else that they assume others must know what they are talking about without introduction. It was like this with Vera. It seems strange to me now that I hadn't the least idea what she meant and that Andrew hadn't.

'Fetch Jamie of course,' Vera said. She was impatient. 'Bring him home. Take him away by force. It's the only way.'

We both thought, we found out afterwards, that Vera had gone mad. Andrew said:

'Doesn't he want to come home, Vera? Is that it?' He spoke gently and cautiously.

'Of course he wants to come. He's only five, isn't he? What does he know? It's Eden won't let him. Everybody knows that. Eden wants to keep him because she can't have children of her own.'

'Now look, Vera. Wait a minute.' Andrew sounded as appalled as I felt. 'That can't be true. You're a bit overwrought, aren't you? You don't look well. But you mustn't exaggerate. Has Eden been putting pressure on you to let her adopt Jamie? Is that it?'

'Pressure!' said Vera. She gave a dreadful throaty laugh and, sitting down on the extreme edge of her chair, began to wring her hands.

'Because all you have to do is refuse. They can't take him from you. The law won't let them. Surely you know that?'

She made an impatient, rather violent, gesture of shaking her head back and forth. 'You've got the car and there are two of you and you're young and strong. You could fight Eden. You could shut Mrs King up in her room and Faith could keep Eden talking while I got Jamie from the nursery and if Eden saw before we got away, you could keep hold of Eden while Faith and I got away.'

'I can't drive,' I said.

Andrew glared at me. I suppose it did sound as if I were taking her seriously.

'Look, Vera,' he said, 'I think you ought to see your doctor. Get something for your nerves.' People did talk about nerves then and not neuroses. 'Have a quiet lie down and think about it. Any time you want to bring Jamie home, we'll fetch him for you. OK? Any time – you only have to say the word.' I loved him for that. He was being strong, the way I believed he always was. 'Only we have to do it above-board,' he said. 'Let Eden know and be firm about it, but we have to be civilized, too, don't we?'

She gave him a look of ineffable scorn. 'Why will no one help me?'

'You don't *need* help, Vera. Or not in that way. You need a doctor's help, if you ask me.'

'I don't ask you. The only thing I ask you, you won't do.'

Neither of us felt we should leave her in that state, though I think we were both beginning to feel a tremendous distaste for the whole business. We thought we understood, you see, we thought we understood about the pressures and the resistances. We suggested she come back with us to Walbrooks and Helen and stay for a few days and maybe see Helen's doctor. She would have none of it. If she went anywhere it would be back to Eden's to be with Jamie.

'But does Eden really want to adopt him?' I asked Helen that night.

'It seems like it, darling. She can't have babies, she never will be able to. And apparently she's been persuading Vera very hard for the past three months to let her adopt him legally. She's told me so herself. Of course, as to keeping him from Vera by force, that's all nonsense.'

'Is it though? What exactly happens if Vera says she wants him now and she's going to take him? She hasn't got a car. I mean, would Eden physically hold on to him? Would she shut him in the nursery? Would Tony and June Poole help her?'

'I can tell Vera's been talking to you.'

'No, she hasn't.' I protested. 'At any rate she didn't tell me all this.'

'The fact is, I suppose, darling, Vera doesn't want trouble. She doesn't want an outright breach with Eden. And of course she doesn't – we've been such a united family.'

I couldn't see it that way myself and said so. Arthur Longley hadn't been united to Helen when she was little and he married again. Gerald and Vera hadn't remained united and Francis had never been united with anyone. Those two sisters had always disliked my mother and she them, and my father and Helen had not got on. So much for being united. Andrew said – to my surprise:

'Don't get me wrong but mightn't it in the long run be the best thing in the world for Jamie if Eden adopted him? Vera hasn't seemed entirely sane lately. She's alone. She's not well off. You have to ask yourself how ideal she actually is as a parent.'

'Why do you have to ask yourself?' I said. I hate phrases like that. 'How ideal is any parent? The point is, surely, that she *is* his parent and the only parent he's got as far as one knows.' Helen registered shock at that. When I say 'registered', I mean it showed in Helen's special way, making an oooh mouth and putting up her eyebrows. 'Vera *loves* him, you don't seem to realize that. She really loves him passionately, doesn't she, Helen? I don't believe you've ever seen them together or you wouldn't talk about ideal parents.'

'I was thinking of the child,' Andrew said. 'I was thinking of his chances. This way he'd have two parents, young parents, too. A beautiful home. Money for his education. The right background.'

That disgusted me. 'Eden hates him,' I said. 'She hates children.'

'No, she doesn't, darling,' said Helen. 'I've seen them together, I saw them last week, and she's as doting as Vera now.'

That night it was when we began to take sides. No one openly expressed this, no one came out with it and said Eden should have him or Vera must keep him, but silently we took sides. Curiously enough, Andrew, for all his initial protestations, came into the Vera camp. I think his sole grounds were that he didn't like Eden and wanted her to get her come-uppance. The General was on Vera's side because he had sentimental ideas about maternity. Helen astounded me by taking up the attitude Andrew had held. In adoption by Eden and Tony she saw unparalleled material advantages for Jamie. Besides, this way the family would be less likely to be split, she felt, for Vera would spend half her time at Goodney Hall to be near Jamie whereas if Vera won, Eden would never speak to her again. I remembered the profound sisterly love there had once been between them and marvelled.

'What a pity it was Vera ever had that flu,' said Helen, as if this had brought it all about. But that was what we all thought at the time.

I must not give the impression that the Vera–Eden–Jamie business occupied us to the exclusion of all else. We thought about it a lot, we talked about it, but we had other things, too. Andrew and I specially had other things. We were moving from a friendship, a cousinship, into a love affair. Patricia, too, was contemplating marriage, and she brought the man she was living with in London down to Walbrooks for a fortnight. Not that any of that older generation knew she was living with him, it was not something one openly admitted to in 1949, and when they came to Helen's they were given separate bedrooms as a matter of course. There was a good deal of secret padding about the passages of the Richardsons' old house those August nights.

About a week after that visit of ours to Laurel Cottage, Eden dropped in one morning. She came alone, having left Jamie at home with June Poole and Mrs King. She was on her way, she said, to pick up Vera who was returning to Goodney Hall with her until the end of the month. I think the question of Jamie must have been preying on Helen's mind otherwise she would hardly have burst out as she did in our presence and that of Patricia's boyfriend, Alan. It was as if she couldn't contain herself.

'Darling, it really isn't fair to poor Vera to go on like this! You simply must make up your mind what you want to do and do it. And the poor little boy – what must he be feeling?'

Eden was very calm and aloof. She was wearing a dress of fine Indian cotton in large shaded checks of navy blue and yellow with a wide collar and deep décolleté, the neckline being filled in with ruffled lace. The skirt was full and longish and such were the formal fashions of the time, even for driving about the countryside in the mornings, that she had on nylon stockings with pointed clocks and dark seams and very high-heeled, ankle-strap shoes of navy-blue glacé kid. Her mouth and fingernails were painted crimson. The perfume she was wearing was a very pungent one, Coty's *Emeraude*.

'My mind *is* made up, Helen,' she said. 'Tony and I know exactly what we want. We want Jamie. There's no difficulty on our side. It's Vera you should be talking to.'

'If Vera isn't in agreement with you, young lady,' said the General, 'you'll have to give it up. You know that, I suppose?'

I could see Eden hated him calling her young lady as I hated it when he did it to me. It was a term he used to Patricia and Eden and myself when he was less than pleased with us.

'I don't want to talk about private things in front of all and sundry,' she said.

'Oh, darling, all and sundry! How can you? We're all family here.'

Eden didn't think Alan family, though she hadn't quite the nerve to say so. 'Anyway, it's private between Vera and me.'

'Not if you're upsetting your sister, it isn't,' said the General. It wasn't clear if he meant Vera or his own wife by 'sister'. The devil entered into me, for I knew that of all people's interference, Eden would hate mine the worst. Well, she would have hated my mother's more.

'Why can't you just adopt any baby?' I said. 'Why can't you go to an adoption society? I should have thought you'd want a little baby. Jamie's five.'

'I'm well aware how old Jamie is, Faith. Thank you very much for putting your oar in. What business it is of yours I don't quite know.'

'Please don't quarrel, darlings,' Helen cried. 'I can see you'd want your own nephew, Eden. I can see that. He's a sweet little boy anyway, he's a darling and – you could send him to Eton!'

This was so absurd it made us laugh and went some way to clearing the air. Eden said, still smiling:

'I may as well tell you since you've brought the subject up, that it's all settled. I didn't want to announce it till all the odds and ends are tidied up. We *are* going to keep Jamie, he will be our son, it's only a matter of a few formalities. And of course Vera will spend just as much time with us as she wants until she gets used to the new arrangement.'

We were all a bit stunned. Whichever camp we were in, I don't think we had envisaged anything like this happening quite so fast. And I remembered Vera begging us to kidnap Jamie. It was only a week ago that she had appealed to Andrew and me to help her.

'But Vera loves him,' I said. 'He's everything to her.'

Eden was hating me. It was that which gave me courage. 'All the more reason why she'd want the best for him.'

'You know that one doesn't work. No one is that self-denying.'

'I'm not going to talk about it with you, Faith. You're not old enough to understand. As far as I'm concerned, you're still more or less at school.'

'I know love when I see it,' I said. 'Vera told Andrew and me last week to get Jamie away from you. She implied you were keeping him by force.'

'Oh, Faith,' said Helen.

Andrew let me down. He didn't say a word. His father asked him.

He said, was that true, and Andrew just shrugged his shoulders. But if he had supported me, if they had all been made to believe, what could we have done? Patricia left the room, taking Alan with her. She said, 'Come on, Alan, let's go outside.'

'Do you really think,' said Eden with infinite scorn, 'that Vera would be coming to stay with me, that I'd be fetching her now, if she was opposed to our adopting Jamie? Do you? Do you think she'd allow it if she was? Why wouldn't she just get hold of Jamie and walk out of the house with him? Or does Faith think I'm keeping him a prisoner?'

There were no answers to that. Eden soon went, parting coldly from all of us. The General was cross with me after she had gone, calling me a firebrand. I had a tremendous row with Andrew in which at last I forced him to admit Vera had asked us to kidnap Jamie. I also got him to tell this to his parents, though he toned down and qualified the truth a lot, making it look as if Vera was hysterical and needed mental treatment.

This upset Helen disproportionately. People didn't accept mental illness then like they do today. They always had to defend themselves by saying there had never been anything like that in their family. That was what Helen did say but at the same time as being horrified at the idea of Vera's mental disturbance, she seemed anxious to blame everything on to it. She said she would make a point of finding out for herself, though. She would go over to Goodney Hall in a day or two and speak to Vera alone.

I should have liked to go with her but she wouldn't let me. Although she didn't put it quite like that, she implied I should only antagonize Eden. The Chatterisses didn't have any notions about economizing by not using the phone so I phoned my father and spoke to him about Vera and Jamie. He was never much good with phones, having come to them too late in life, and he always tended to address the mouthpiece rather than simply talk to the person at the other end. He spoke on phones as if everything he said was being recorded by people unused to the sound of English. This, added to the facts that, like Eden, he believed me too young to involve myself in this matter and also too *presumptuous* as a mere niece, made our talk unsatisfactory. He kept saying he couldn't follow any of it but Vera and Eden must know what they were doing. The most important thing was that I shouldn't get on bad terms with my aunts.

Helen came back, looking quite cheerful. Vera was perfectly normal, she couldn't imagine what Andrew had meant. She and Jamie had been out together, out for a walk to Goodney Parva, when Helen got there. Surely that could put paid to any ideas of Jamie's imprisonment? Vera had brought him back and sent him off upstairs to June Poole and talked to Helen about Jamie starting school. He would be going to Goodney Parva village school, starting that September.

'I asked her if she'd be living there too and she said, no, she'd be back at Laurel Cottage by the end of August. Then I came out with it and asked her if it was true Eden and Tony were going to adopt Jamie legally. She said she didn't know about "adopt legally" but they were going to keep him, have him living with them. I asked her why. She didn't say anything, just made a face. She was embroidering one of those ridiculous cushion covers, you know the way she and Eden do, darling, like they needed what-d'you-call-it? – occupational therapy. She just went on sewing away, not looking at me.'

'Did you actually get to the crux?' said the General. 'Did you ask her if that was what she wanted?'

'Yes, I did, darling. Don't interrogate me. She said quite calmly that it was absolutely what she wanted and not to talk about it any more. I don't think she's a bit mental, Andrew, really I don't. More *lethargic*, if you know what I mean.'

My father wrote me a letter. He said he had the greatest confidence in his sisters doing the right thing and putting their duty before personal considerations. They had been properly brought up and that was something that would stand them in good stead. There was no history of mental illness in our family, none whatsoever, and he wanted me to believe that. The last thing he wanted was for me to worry about that sort of thing. However, he thought it probable that my mother's dislike of his sisters, which he attributed to jealousy, had affected me and prejudiced me against them. It would cause him bitter sorrow to think that anyone could have attempted to destroy the affection and admiration he knew I felt for Vera and Eden. And so on. Wouldn't I go and stay with them for a few days before I came home? After all, there was no need for me to prolong my stay with Helen who was only a half-aunt.

Nothing would have induced me to stay at Goodney Hall, always supposing I had been asked. Eden, of course, didn't ask me. Eden being Eden would no doubt have expected a written apology before she even asked me to tea. I stayed at Walbrooks for about three weeks and then I went home to my parents, having promised to return in September and go up to Cambridge with Andrew at the start of the Michaelmas Term. It was impossible to make my father understand why I hadn't gone to Eden and Vera. I was growing tired of explanations, more particularly because I had come to guess that there were things both Vera and Eden knew that none of the rest of us did, and to act without that knowledge was useless. To speculate was useless. A letter came from Vera but it does not survive. Why, I don't know, as we certainly had no coal fires in September. It told my father that she would be returning to Sindon at the end of the week (she had stayed on a fortnight more than arranged already) and that Gerald wanted a divorce. He had met a woman he wished to marry and would provide Vera with grounds. In those days a woman had to prove that there had been a matrimonial offence, adultery or desertion or cruelty, to divorce her husband – breakdown of the marriage was not enough.

'She'll be well rid of him, he's treated her monstrously,' my father said.

Eden became ill at an awkward time for the Goodney Hall household. June Poole was on a week's holiday. Tony's father had had a slight heart attack and Tony was staying in Yorkshire. These things could not have been arranged. They were coincidental. What Eden had the matter with her was not specified and therefore gave rise to a mystery. It wasn't a cold or flu. Might it, we speculated, be another miscarriage? By the time I was back at Walbrooks she had been taken into hospital.

Vera was left alone at Goodney Hall with Jamie, with Mrs King, the housekeeper, and a woman from the village who came in twice a week to clean. What happened she told me herself one rainy evening two days before I returned to college. I had half complied with my father's request and was spending two nights with her, not at Goodney Hall but at Laurel Cottage. Upstairs Jamie was asleep in his newly decorated bedroom. Some time during the night, Francis would return. To Vera's dismay and anger, he had taken advantage of her absence to have a honeymoon in her house with a girl she said was a barmaid he had picked up in Ipswich. The village shuddered with the scandal and disgrace of it. The girl had gone and next day

Francis too would depart but she expected him back that night – in the small hours, doubtless.

'The doctor said Eden must go into hospital or he wouldn't be responsible for what happened,' Vera said. She lowered her voice a little, glancing about her, as if the house were full of people who might hear her and be disgusted. 'She was unable to pass water. She simply could not pass urine. The doctor said whatever it was had affected her kidneys. It's my belief it was the result of whatever it was they did to her when she lost the baby. Anyway, we don't want to talk about that. It's not the kind of thing I ought to talk about in front of you.

'They had an ambulance come for her. I phoned Tony at his father's and he said he'd come home straightaway. Jamie was at school. He'd just started school two weeks before. I didn't say anything to Mrs King. I packed our cases, Jamie's and mine, we'd accumulated so much stuff, you wouldn't believe, and left them in the hall with a note for Mrs King asking her to send them on. I walked down to the village and fetched Jamie from school and we just escaped together, it was really funny, we did laugh. It was such a *lark*, like a childhood prank. I kept thinking how cross Eden would be. And it's so nearly impossible getting from Goodney to Sindon without a car. We had to get three buses and it was eight before we got home. And then of course I found Francis here and the place in the most outrageous mess. I was exhausted but I didn't care. I put Jamie to bed in my bed and I crawled in with him an hour later and we just slept like that all night, it was such bliss.'

Next day Tony came. He told Vera he couldn't understand why she hadn't just stayed on at Goodney Hall. Vera had laughed and told him she wasn't coming back and Jamie wasn't coming back and if he thought she was going to visit Eden in hospital, he could think again. She wasn't going out to give him the chance to come in and take Jamie from her. Tony must have been aghast, a conventional, rigid person like that. He didn't know what she meant, either, he really didn't then. Eden had told him nothing at the time except that she wanted to adopt Jamie. He had consented, to placate her, presumably.

Vera told me all this with glittering eyes, laughing sometimes at her own cleverness in outwitting Eden. I was unpleasantly convinced she was going mad. It was uncomfortable to be with her. But I had no idea then, no one had any idea, that she was herself responsible for making Eden ill. I thought I understood everything, that Eden had pressurized Vera into letting her adopt Jamie on the grounds that it would be in Jamie's own best interests, that Vera, though torn by her love for Jamie, had consented but later had had second thoughts and had seized her opportunity. What I never considered was the effect all this might have on the child. I was too young, I suppose.

Next day I encountered Francis. Most of the time he lived with his father and was about to do a postgraduate course at London University. The descent on Laurel Cottage had come about because Gerald would not have consented to his taking the girl home to sleep. Gerald's own relations with his new woman were circumspect and he would be fixing the evidence of his divorce with a girl he was hiring for the purpose. Francis I had not seen since Eden's wedding day when I came upon him with Chad in the candlelit dark and I felt embarrassment.

'She ought to be certified,' Francis said. 'She's doing the same to that kid as she did to me.'

'Hardly,' I said. 'She seems to have pushed you out. She's doing her best to pull Jamie back.'

'It's all symptomatic. She's a paranoid schizophrenic.'

Jamie had come into the room. He was very quiet. I had noticed how extraordinarily quiet and 'good' he had become. At night he slept from the time Vera put him to bed at six until quite late into the morning. This morning it had been after nine. He came in holding a small tractor with caterpillar rubber wheels and he proceeded to run this thing all the way round the room, over chair backs, bookshelves, window sills, trundling it slowly, keeping up an apparently fierce concentration on what he was doing.

'So what?' said Francis. 'I don't like the kid. Why shouldn't he suffer? That's not the point. She is sick in her mind, her mind is warped. I'd like to have the pleasure of putting her away. That would be a gothic thing to do, wouldn't it? Consigning one's own mother to a madhouse.'

He no longer intimidated me. I didn't care what he thought of me either. Mine was a kind of indifferent repulsion.

'Why bother?' I said. 'What's in it for you? You don't live here. It's not as if you cared about Jamie and his future.'

'I'll tell you what his future will be. Eden will get better and come here and take him back and *she* won't have a leg to stand on. You'll see.'

'I shan't. I shan't be here either. And you're wrong. Vera will never let him go back. She never lets him out of her sight for more than five minutes. She'll be in here in a minute keeping an eye on him.'

He smiled slowly shaking his head. He has hooded eyes, has my cousin Francis. The effect had become more pronounced as he entered his twenties, as if the eyeballs had protruded more and the eyelids stretched to cover them, taking on at the same time a purplish, bruised colour like eyeshadow. The hoods lowered and he smiled.

'I told you she hasn't a leg to stand on. Eden will come for him as soon as she gets out of hospital.' He looked at the child. He looked at him penetratingly and Jamie continued running that tractor along the window sill, up the architrave of the door. 'I'd take him over to Goodney myself only I wouldn't trust that fool Tony to hang on to him.'

'You'd do that?'

'You are so naïve,' he said.

We all were. I came to believe that the family favoured Eden's keeping Jamie because everyone openly or secretly thought Vera mentally unstable. This seemed unjust to me. She could not have been kinder to him, gentler, more caring. It wasn't till I was back at Cambridge and thinking about Vera and her problems one day, wondering what the outcome would be, that I realized Jamie had not been to school while I was staying at Laurel Cottage. True, I had been there only two days and two nights, but the village school's term had begun. Had he not been attending school at Goodney Parva for two weeks before Vera snatched him away? But perhaps it was only that Vera hadn't been able to get him into Sindon School.

While I was there I met Josie Cambus again. Anne was at teacher training college in London and we had seen each other for a while the week before. She told me she had come to like her stepmother. I had never known Vera to have such a close friend. She and Mrs Morrell, for instance, had always called each other Mrs Hillyard and Mrs Morrell, and as for Chad Hamner – he had extended his friendship with an axe to grind. But Josie and Vera saw each other almost every day. They confided in each other – though not absolutely, as I was later to learn. Josie was the only person Vera would entrust Jamie to. Intense in the few affections she had, Vera seemed to have transferred to Josie the love she once lavished on Eden. Of Josie and her achievements she was proud, at the same time denigrating poor Donald Cambus whom she castigated as undeserving, ungrateful, totally unworthy of his second wife. Josie was an excellent cook, a Cordon Bleu cook according to Vera, she sang in the church choir, was no mean watercolourist, taught a yoga class before anyone had ever heard of yoga. Vera bragged about her unremittingly. What she saw in Vera I never knew and though, later on, I had ample opportunity to ask, I never did. If I never came to love Josie as I loved Helen, I did like her very much. I got on with her. But with her I discussed Vera only the once and on that occasion my father was present. We had all – strange trio of drinking partners! – drunk too much by design so that we might without too much pain, too much shameful suffering, hear from the only witness what happened at the end.

Josie gave evidence at Vera's trial but I was not there, I read no newspapers at the time, and only now have seen the transcript.

She has been dead ten years. When I first knew her, she was about fifty, a tall, heavily built, dark woman whose hair only began to turn grey when she was in her seventies. Her voice was very beautiful – I mean her speaking voice for I never heard her sing – and she was one of those people who are very calming to be with, very easy, so that you can relax in their company and never feel they have expectations of you that you can't fulfil. These two qualities her younger son inherited as well as her handsome Spanish looks, though he, as his mother was, is English through and through.

Josie, having her own car, offered to drive me to Stoke-by-Nayland the evening before Andrew and I were due to return. Vera, though Helen had invited her, refused to come with us. The road to Stoke, she said, passed through Goodney.

'All right, we won't go that way,' Josie said. 'We'll go the long way round.'

The bypasses that have now made main roads out of lanes and left the villages in peace were not built by then. If you didn't go through Goodney you would have to go miles round through Langham and Higham.

Vera pointed this out. 'I should see the signpost,' she said, from

230

which we were supposed to infer that even the printed name 'Goodney Parva' would upset her. 'You stay and have a cup of tea with Helen, though. I should like Helen to see you.'

This was very Vera-ish. It was not that she wanted Josie to see Helen but Helen to see Josie, just as in the past she had wanted to show off Eden and, more recently, Jamie.

In the car, why didn't we talk about Jamie and his future? We didn't, though he must have been uppermost in our minds. Perhaps Josie thought me too young. Not too young to discuss this but too young to be interested. She asked me about my final year at college instead, about what I wanted to be. Only when we were at Walbrooks, in sight of Helen, who had come down the front steps to greet us when she heard the car, did Josie say:

'I would give a lot to hear that the Pearmains had decided to emigrate to South Africa after all.'

'I didn't know they'd thought of it,' I said.

'Oh yes, but not any more, I'm afraid,' and then she was saying how-do-you-do to Helen and shaking hands.

Just after Christmas my father had a letter from Vera asking his permission as owner of one third of it to sell Laurel Cottage and move away. This letter doesn't survive and I remember nothing of it except the gist. He and my mother had spent a weekend with Vera during the autumn and while there, had visited Eden in hospital. She was in hospital for weeks and weeks, months even, while they tried to work out what was wrong with her. I don't know what happened that weekend. Did Vera go with them on the hospital visit, for instance? Did they see Tony? Was anything discussed about Jamie's future? My mother wrote to me only that they had been, that they had stayed with Vera, that Eden would be in hospital at least another month and that it had rained the whole weekend. Vera's letter put the cat among the pigeons. For a while my mother must have declared a truce in order to stay with Vera and visit Eden, but it was war again now.

'If that house is to be sold, we're taking our share out of it and she can buy a place for herself with the rest.'

My father immediately demurred. 'What could poor Vera possibly buy with a thousand pounds?'

'Let Eden make it up then. She's rolling in money. Why should

231

you subsidize your sister when she's got a husband who is making good money in the army and a son who's old enough to support her and I haven't even got a refrigerator?'

My father, in his way, also objected to Vera's moving. In this, at any rate, they were united. She had lived in Sindon all her life, he said, forgetting the India years, all her friends were there. By 'all her friends' he meant Josie and I did rather wonder how she would feel about leaving Josie behind.

'Why does she want to move?' he kept saying.

I was dreadfully afraid the answer might be to take Jamie out of Eden's reach. Eden was still in hospital, though she was better and expected to come out very soon. They had never found out what went wrong with her kidneys. They were back to normal now, for Eden was basically very strong and healthy. Once she was out and home again, would she do as Francis said she would, come to Laurel Cottage, perhaps with a supporting retinue of Mrs King and June Poole, and snatch Jamie back? It seemed unreal, a lawless, antediluvian thing comparable to rustling a neighbour's cattle. But when I was staying in Essex, someone had told me of a cattle-rustling incident that had taken place on a nearby farm only just before the war. Why not a kidnapping?

'Why does she want to move?'

'Doesn't she say in the letter?' said my mother.

He had given up reading them aloud, finally conquered by her relentless sarcasm.

'She says she feels like a change.'

Eden would have to be consulted. Hers was the third share in Laurel Cottage. She had a private room in the hospital and he could have phoned her but of course he wouldn't. He wrote instead, asking for her views. It was Tony who phoned us. Eden was home, he had fetched her home that afternoon. She was sitting beside him now, doing the *Daily Telegraph* crossword . . . In February he was going to take her to Majorca to convalesce. It sounds commonplace today, the place where everyone goes to if they can't afford better, but in 1950 Majorca was still an unspoilt, virtually unknown Mediterranean island. I had just about heard of it. They were going to Formentor, retreat of French film-stars. Vera's house? Laurel Cottage, he should say? No, they hadn't heard a word about plans to sell it. Eden came on the line and started off by asking him for the answer to a clue.

She didn't think Vera ought to sell. At least let her think it over. She should tell her to think it over and when she, Eden, came back from Majorca they could discuss it again.

'Doesn't want to trouble her pretty little head with her sister's affairs now she's rich,' said my mother.

In a fury my father screwed up the letter and threw it into the fire, which is why it doesn't survive.

That phone call made me feel better about things. I mustn't give the impression I was constantly worried about Vera and Jamie, I wasn't that altruistic, but it used to nag at me sometimes. I didn't, among other things, want Francis to be right. And now it looked as if he wouldn't be. Eden wouldn't laze around at home, planning a holiday almost a month off, take that holiday, itself a good month long, if she meant to rcncw her demands to have Jamie. So I reasoned. I had forgotten the hunter who leaves the stopped earth to take his leisurely lunch, the cat who can safely abandon watching the mouse's hole while it is daylight.

— 15 —

Every few weeks Helen and I go together to see Gerald. He is seven years younger than Helen but he is a poor, broken old man, who slobbers and cannot hear in spite of his deaf aid and sits all day in a wheelchair while Helen darts into the room where he is, her movements still swift and graceful, her hearing still acute, only her eyes misted over so that she peers to identify you and last time we went talked for some moments to another old man, mistakenly taking him for her brother-in-law.

I hardly know why I go. I knew Gerald only remotely while he was married to my aunt. He never married the woman he wrote to her about asking for a divorce. The hanging presumably was too much for her, the marrying Vera Hillyard's widower too much to contemplate. It was too much for all of us, driving me into a panic marriage, scaring off Patricia's lover, killing (according to Helen) the General, destroying what remained of my parents' marriage so that they became strangers who seldom spoke. But Helen never lost touch with Gerald. She, of course, had known him while he was a subaltern, long before he met Vera. Both alone and, to some extent, exiled, they used occasionally to meet in London. When he handed over the house he had bought in Highgate to Francis and moved into the Baron's Home for Retired Officers, she began visiting him there once a week. He chose the Baron's Home because it was in Baron's Court and not too far from Helen's Kensington flat. She goes there less often today because of her great age and perhaps my reason for going with her is that I don't think it a good idea for someone of ninety to be travelling alone about London.

The house is Victorian, red brick with white facing, a noisy place in one of those one-way streets that support a stream of traffic going south to cross the river. The front is more thickly double-glazed than anywhere I have seen but at the back is a big walled garden with magnificent fig trees growing along the walls that seem to like the dirt and the fumes. They are mostly men, the inmates, though not exclusively, which always surprises me. Of course, I know that there were women officers in the armed forces in the Second World War but I still find it odd that two of them should have ended up here among the Western Desert veterans and heroes of the Normandy landings. All of them sit for most of the day in a big drawing-room with french windows on to the fig garden. The television is never switched off, though no one seems to watch it except very desultorily, but if you pass in front of it or attempt to alter a channel, there is a murmur of grumbling. Nothing in the room indicates that these people are old soldiers (old sailors, old airmen), not a map, picture, war book. No one wears a regimental tie, much less a medal. One of the old men has the VC but he is the smallest and shyest of them and once I saw him get up and creep away when 'A Bridge Too Far' came on the television.

Gerald is still thin but very shrunken now, his skin wrinkled like hide that has been under water for a long time. He is senile. He has forgotten everything, not merely recent things but long past happenings, too. It is probably just as well. According to the woman in charge of this place, he loves to see us, our visits are high spots in his life, but he gives us no indication that this is so. He never smiles. He keeps his eyes on the television all the time we are there. When we come in, when we are beside him and indeed standing over him, he turns his eyes once and says:

'Ah, Helen!'

Me he does not recognize. He never has. He takes me for a daughter of Helen's, not Patricia, one whose name he has forgotten. I used to try to talk to him but I have given that up. What he likes is for me to hold his hand. He lays his right hand palm uppermost in his lap, takes my hand in his other and places it in the palm, finally gripping it quite hard. We sit like this, hands clasped, for the whole of our stay. We do not talk at all, for talking to each other seems unfeeling. Gerald faces the television, often with his eyes closed. I stare out of the french windows at the tall, brown backs of houses behind, the narrow canyons between them through which, occasionally a red bus can be seen passing, the gardens where nothing grows but plants and trees ugly enough and tough enough to withstand lead and petrol fumes, dirt and dehydration. Half-way through our visit, tea comes for the residents and cups of tea for us, though, mysteriously, we are never offered a cake or a biscuit.

Yesterday, just as tea arrived and our cups had been handed to us, a wrapped sugar lump in each saucer, a man came into the room and stood looking about him, looking for Gerald as it turned out, and not immediately realizing he was the occupant of the wheelchair between two women. When he did, he came over, as unsmiling as his father. It was Francis. It is twenty-five years since last I saw him. On that occasion I met him by chance with his wife and children, Giles and Elizabeth, at the open-air theatre in Regent's Park. I saw them again, Liz and her children, but not Francis, for soon after the Regent's Park encounter he had left them and gone off to South Africa looking for bugs. Francis has published two popular science books about the ways of insects. I wrote to congratulate him on the success of one of these which I had enjoyed reading, which seemed to me to have nothing of Francis in it, but he didn't reply.

He looks like Vera now. The Anthony Andrews look has faded, the Sebastian Flyte ambience gone. He is thin to emaciation – how could he be otherwise with those parents? – and perhaps because he is an entomologist the comparison that suggested itself to me was with a praying mantis. There is a dried-up wizened worn-out look to Francis, a bleached-to-greyness look like one of those trees that have died and the wood been stripped of bark and abraded by weather. I think I only recognized him because this visitor could not have been anyone else.

Helen shifted herself into a vacant armchair in order to give him the chair next to his father. He kissed her, holding his face against hers for a little longer than is usual for a merely formal kiss. I remembered he had always liked her. Francis is the sort of person who can greet one woman with a kiss and the other whom he knows equally well with a glance of indifference. He was wearing a grey velvet suit, very old and shabby, with an extremely expensive new-looking shirt, Per Spook (I guessed) tie and shoes from Tricker's. He gives the impression of being prosperous, the suit a rich man's eccentricity. Helen told me afterwards that he has remarried, this time the widow of a millionaire MP assassinated in Ireland. Why hadn't she told me before? I asked. She had forgotten, she said, and the new wife's name and almost everything about her. Now, if I had asked for his first wife's name and where they had married and when . . .

I said, 'How are you, Francis?'

'I am well.' I don't know why this should be an affectation, not qualifying the 'well' with a 'very' or a 'quite', but it is. If he ever writes letters Francis probably begins them with a name and no 'dear'. He didn't ask me how I was. He sat down next to his father and, to my astonishment, took his other hand.

Does he always do this? Does Gerald always hold hands with whoever comes under the age of ninety? He never holds Helen's hand. Or is it that Francis, who seemed to me incapable of love and to Chad Hamner capable only of the love of evil, loves his father? People are a mystery, an enigma. Gerald never changed his name. Hillyard was *his* name, not hers, and he stuck to it, but Francis, who seemed to care for the opinion of no one, who snapped his fingers at the world, called himself Hills from the day of his mother's arrest, anticipating the worst, as he would; and lecturing at his university, writing his books, collecting his bugs, he is Professor Frank Loder Hills.

So we sat there, each of us holding hands with Gerald, with Gerald gripping our hands, for he does grip, closing his hand more and more tightly over the imprisoned fingers until increasing pain directs the time to get up and leave. Gerald did not slacken his grip on my hand when he also had Francis's hand to hold but held it harder, so that weak and feeble as he is, he nevertheless seemed to be bearing down on our hands preparatory to taking a flying leap out of the wheelchair. I thought of Vera and that curious gesture of hers, leaning forward, pressing, crushing, as if to keep the pain from pouring out. Does

Gerald ever think of her now? Does Francis, also fair and lined and dehydrated, not remind him of her, his eyes that same clear sky blue? Sometimes surely, even now, he must think of how she tried to palm off someone else's child, a child as dark-skinned as its Puerto Rican father. I had forgotten about the eyes, forgotten how, when in my teens, I had tried to remember or find out what colour Gerald's eyes were. But when Daniel Stewart started on his book I remembered and on my next visit to Gerald, yesterday's visit, looked. They are blue. They are darker than Francis's and are a deep cornflower blue.

We left the Baron's Home for Retired Officers together, all three of us, Helen and I to take a taxi home, Francis to head for the nearest NCP where he had parked his car. He talked to Helen, not about the family, not about his father, but, of all things, about a Russian science-fiction film currently showing at our local cinema, the Paris-Pullman. Apparently, it is his local cinema too now, he and his wife having bought a house in Cresswell Place.

Taking no part in this conversation, I was looking for a taxi. On the opposite side of the street I saw an old man standing in the doorway of a shop, the kind of shop that is not much frequented, this one displaying in its window ceramic tiles. He seemed to be looking intently at us, or rather, to be looking at Francis who had thrown back his head and was laughing at something Helen had said. He was a smallish man, grey-headed, wearing an over-long, unbelted raincoat, a man with an unremarkable face, eyes that seemed even at that distance full of sadness. I had a clutching sensation in my chest. The echo was not yet faint then, the voice not yet mute . . .

Francis said to me, 'You've been assisting Stewart with this book of his, I hear.'

'Yes.'

'That sort of thing is so vulgar and uncalled for.'

'Vulgar it may be but not uncalled for. His publishers asked him to do it.'

'If he uses my name, that is, if he identifies me, I shall sue him. You can tell him that.'

'*I* tell him?'

'That's what I said. It would bring me into hatred, ridicule and contempt, all three of the grounds for libel. That husband of yours is a lawyer, isn't he? You ask him.'

'That's two tasks you've set me in the past five minutes, Francis or

Frank or whatever you call yourself,' I said. 'Just as well we only meet once every twenty-five years.'

A taxi came. As Francis was helping Helen into it, I looked once more across the street and saw that the man in the doorway had been joined by a woman, that he was kissing her, that, arms linked now, they were moving off in the direction of Blythe Road. What yearning in me for romantic dramas, even of the tragic kind, had led me for one moment to believe that this was Chad Hamner? There was no resemblance, there was no possibility even that the ageing process could have made Chad look like that. I was positive if he had passed closely enough I would have seen earlobes as unlined as a child's.

And suddenly, though between the two realizations there was no connection, suddenly I knew for certain that the event which Francis was so wrathfully anticipating, which made his eyes dark with rage as he glared at me, would never take place.

'You needn't worry,' I said. 'Stewart won't write that book.'

'What makes you say that?'

'By the time,' I said, 'I've finished assisting him, as you put it, he won't want to.'

That time he brought the girl to Laurel Cottage in Vera's absence was the last visit he ever paid to Sindon. It seems strange to me that someone who became an entomologist should have shown not the faintest interest, as far as I ever saw, in insects while he was a child. He didn't even pull the wings off flies, which is what one might have expected of Francis. After he went off to London University to do his postgraduate work, he turned his back for ever on Sindon, leaving behind, I was later to hear, a great many possessions, some of which were quite valuable and included presents from Chad. And Chad himself, who (whatever innocence in this matter he might claim) had used Vera as cover and deceived a good many people into believing that they were having a love affair, never again went to Laurel Cottage once Francis was gone. That New Year visit when Vera was taken ill was almost the last time. Francis went to Queen Mary College and Chad followed him as soon as he could, covering Townswomen's Guilds and church bazaars in Willesden and living in that room at the top of a house from which Francis threw him downstairs.

Vera was alone. But she had Josie. She had Jamie. Quite often she also had Helen. After Eden had gone to Formentor, my father went to Sindon and stayed overnight, the purpose of his visit being to attempt to discourage Vera from moving. Without his consent and Eden's, of course, she couldn't move but my father wanted it to seem her choice. She told him rather sorrowfully that she had never really believed he and Eden would consent, indeed she knew Eden wouldn't. It was just a long shot, worth trying, she said.

This conversation was later repeated to my mother who repeated it to me at some time between Vera's arrest and her trial. My father had asked Vera why she wanted to move but she would say no more than that she was fed up with Sindon. He knew she was concealing her real motives.

'She thought she could run away from Eden,' my mother said. 'She thought she could escape with Jamie. The ends of the earth wouldn't have been far enough, not with Eden having money on her side.'

'And right, I suppose,' I said.

Having failed with him and Eden as she had guessed she would, Vera tried to get Gerald to buy them out, to buy their shares in the house for her. This was what she told my father she would do and presumably she did attempt it. If he wanted a divorce, he must pay for it, she said. No buying out, no divorce. I think my father was shocked to hear one of his sisters, pearls of virtue and rectitude that he thought them, talk like this. That, at any rate, is what my mother said. But she would, wouldn't she?

He told her that if Gerald offered to buy his share, he would sell it to him but he couldn't answer for Eden. 'You must make her, you must make her,' Vera cried, clutching his arm, but she turned away then, saying it would be too late, it was all too late. My mother said Vera said a mysterious thing to him that we thought later we understood, though he, of course, did not at the time.

'Why did I do it this way?' she said. 'I could have done it myself at any time.'

Eden and Tony stayed in Majorca much longer than anyone expected. They had planned on a month and stayed nearly three. I suppose the weather began to get warm and the island pretty just as they were due to leave so they stayed on and on. We had postcards and Helen had postcards but according to my mother – how could she know? – Vera had none. They came back in the middle of April

239

while I was staying at Walbrooks. It was a Saturday when they returned, exhausted no doubt, having flown from Palma to Barcelona and come by train from Barcelona to Paris, Paris to Calais, boat to Dover, train to Victoria, across London to Liverpool Street, train to Colchester. But on the Monday morning, Eden was in Sindon, at Laurel Cottage, prepared to take Jamie away.

No warning of her coming had been given to Vera. She knew Eden and Tony were home only because Helen (in my hearing) had phoned and told her so, herself very surprised that Vera was in ignorance. She had had a whole day in which to prepare herself – well, she had had months really. I have said Josie was the only person to whom she would entrust Jamie but the truth was she scarcely ever left him. Josie had probably baby-sat with him once in the past year and a half and that was when Vera went to a Naughton relative's wedding.

Vera lied to Josie. She asked her to have Jamie because her solicitor was coming to see her about the divorce. Did Josie really believe this? Her own son was in practice by that time and she must have known solicitors don't usually travel miles out into the country-side to visit unimportant clients at nine in the morning. For it was as early as that Vera expected Eden to come and by then she had already taken him to Josie. When I first heard this, I thought of Moses being hidden by his mother in the bulrushes and I looked up the story in Exodus and found it wasn't like that at all. She made him an ark *out of* bulrushes and hid it in the flags by the river's brink, flags presumably being irises. But Jamie's concealment wasn't much like any of this, he being five and not an infant. Though he was young for his age in his need for Vera. By midday he was crying and asking for her and Josie, harassed by it, took him home. If there really had been a solicitor and he had come at nine, he would surely be gone by twelve.

Vera had miscalculated. The reason profably was that Eden got up late as a matter of course. She can't have had much to occupy her. Instead of nine, she arrived at eleven. Even today I don't like to think of what Vera's state of mind must have been during those two hours. At least Jamie wasn't there. It isn't hard to imagine the kind of thing Vera would have said, not if you knew her as I did.

'I've hidden him where you'll never find him!'

And then Josie came. She found Vera and Eden there alone, sitting facing each other in the living-room, each of them with the air of sticking it out as if for a siege. Vera put out her arms to Jamie when she saw him and he ran into them. Eden gave a scornful sort of laugh. She said:

'I suppose you rehearsed this little bit of drama.'

I know all this because Josie phoned Helen almost immediately after Eden had left. She was very angry and very upset and she poured some of it out to me – I answered the phone – before I handed her over to Helen. Eden had left at last without Jamie but not without promising to come back.

Vera, on seeing Josie, appealed to her to support her in physically repelling Eden's attempts to take Jamie. She seems to have seen everything in physical terms at this time, as if action and the expense of energy would save things while argument and reason wouldn't. She had something there, I suppose.

'I'll hold Jamie while you make her go,' was what Josie told us Vera said.

This shocked Josie. She told Vera she wouldn't dream of being a party to what she suggested. There must be no question of Eden taking Jamie from his mother. She had never heard of such a thing, she said. I daresay she hadn't. She asked Eden – very sternly and sharply, I understand – whatever made her think she had a right to take Jamie forcibly away from his mother and his home?

'He's not being properly looked after here,' Eden said. 'He's got no friends of his own age. He's kept isolated like a hermit. He's nearly six and the only time he's been to school is for two weeks while he was with me. She neglects him – look at his shoes!'

The facts were that Vera was poor, she received a very meagre sum each week from Gerald and nothing else. What was amiss with Jamie's shoes I don't know but no more than that they were unsuitable for the time of year or had the wrong colour laces in them, I am sure. Neglected he never was, rather the reverse, for leaving him to himself more would have done him good. Anyway Josie took no notice of this. She said if Eden was going to adopt Jamie it would have to be decided by lawyers in courts, not fought over like this.

'Make her go,' said Vera, holding Jamie in her arms.

'You hear what she says,' Josie said. 'You'd better go.'

241

The hatred between them hung in the air like poison gas, she said to Helen. 'Vibes' was what we called this sort of thing later on. It was terrible to see sisters so at loggerheads, she said. How would she have felt if she had seen them as they used to be, like I had?

'I'll go now but I'll be back,' Eden said.

This was the first time Josie had met her. She was not in the least intimidated by her wealth and what Vera called her 'power'.

'If this happens again,' she said, 'I'll call the police.'

Helen reacted by getting Andrew to drive her to Laurel Cottage and bringing Vera and Jamie back with her to Walbrooks. Once there she did her best to get an explanation of all of it out of Vera. We were all there. Things had become too serious to bother about appearances or excluding people on grounds of age.

Vera was calm by now, almost cool. I think she felt safe at Walbrooks, which must have made what happened subsequently all the worse for her. It was a beautiful day, very warm for April, and we sat in the big drawing-room where Eden's wedding reception had been, with the french windows open on to the garden and the sun streaming in. The great lawn that reached to the lake was scattered all round its edges with drifts of daffodils and up near the house were blue scillas and those little scarlet species tulips that are more beautiful than orchids.

'If you tell Eden firmly she has to forget all ideas about adopting Jamie, she will have to give it up,' Helen said to Vera. 'Perhaps you had better write to her, darling. Why don't we compose a letter now, an absolutely uncompromising one, and you can send it off. Faith and Andrew will walk up to the village and post it for you, won't you, darlings? And that way Eden will get it in the morning.'

Vera didn't seem keen on this. It would 'do no good', she said. It would just be 'making matters worse'.

'But why would it, Vera?' Helen insisted. 'Did you make Eden some sort of promise when you were ill that she could have Jamie and you're afraid to revoke now? Is that it? Because you shouldn't let that count with you at all, you'll have to forget that.'

'Of course I didn't promise that,' Vera said. 'Would I promise that?'

The General hated Eden. He was all for going to law.

'If I got hold of my solicitor,' he said, 'I know what he'd do. He'd take the lot of us along to a judge in chambers and get an injunction.

He'd get an injunction to restrain that little harpy from ever coming within a mile of you and the boy again.'

'Now, General,' said Helen, 'she's my sister too, you know.'

'Only of the half-blood,' he said, forgetting no doubt that this also applied to Vera.

However, nothing else happened that day or the next. Eden had become ill again. Not in the same way this time, not with her kidneys. The prosecution at Vera's trial said that Vera had made a second attempt to murder her by giving her some noxious substance in a cup of coffee at Laurel Cottage on the Monday morning. The two objections to that seem to me that this time Eden had sickness and diarrhoea, which at any rate argues a different kind of poison, and secondly that one simply cannot imagine Eden taking anything to eat or drink in those circumstances.

We found out about Eden because Helen phoned up to 'have a straight talk with her'. She didn't have any sort of talk at all. Mrs King answered and said Eden was in bed and the doctor had been sent for. Vera laughed when Helen told her and she said in a mad kind of way that God was not mocked. She talked like this a lot or in disjointed non sequiturs rather like Ophelia does. She stayed on at Walbrooks, alternating her behaviour between an almost cataleptic calm and excited, frenetic bursts of energy. I was due to go home in a few days' time and Andrew was coming with me for the rest of our holiday. It was to be our last term and Finals were looming. Now I felt for the first time I couldn't wait to get away from Walbrooks to London. One of the things Vera did during one of her energy peaks was to offer to lengthen all the kitchen curtains for Helen. They had been badly washed and had shrunk. There are five windows in the kitchen at Walbrooks so it would be quite a task. Ever since then, the sight of a woman sewing on a large piece of work, the stuff spread tapestry-wise across her lap, her head bent and pursed fingers dipping back and forth, brings Vera back to me. Perhaps it is why I never sew, never dreamt of making curtains for my own homes.

On the Friday morning, Andrew and I went off to London in the fifth-hand car Andrew had bought, an old Morris Ten. Helen told us not to stay and wait for Vera. She and the General would take her home. She had a feeling, she said, that we had heard the last of Eden's claims on Jamie. It was all over, it had been a try-on. The

General had probably hit the nail on the head when he talked of promises made when Vera was ill and feeble.

So we went, relieved but with no reason to feel relief. I told my father nothing about it and Andrew said nothing either, though we had made no pre-arrangement to avoid the subject. I think now that what we both felt, what we onlookers all felt, was that there was so much more to this than met the eye, so many submerged secrets contributing to it, things deliberately kept from us, that we should be making fools of ourselves if we expressed opinions and advised courses. Andrew and I didn't even discuss it with each other during those few days but when we were in the train taking us back to Cambridge, alone in the carriage, he said to me suddenly, in the manner of a man making a confession:

'I haven't told you this, I didn't tell anyone, I didn't want to cause concern. It's been on my conscience, after all that talk of solicitors and injunctions. While we were at home, the day before we left, I saw June Poole at the top of our drift.'

'Drift' is what they call a lane in that part of the country. This one led from the road down to the house, passing Walbrooks' cottages on the way, passing a boarded-up house no one had lived in for twenty years, passing barns and the stables.

'She might have been to one of the cottages, you know. She could have a cousin or an aunt there. It always seems to me that everyone down there is related to everyone else.'

Andrew said, 'She had her back to me, she was walking away, but I had the feeling she had been standing just inside the hedge waiting. And then she saw me.'

I asked him how he could be absolutely sure it was she. How far away had she been?

He was glad to clutch at any straw. At least a hundred yards, maybe more. If it had been a matter of swearing to it – well, no, he couldn't have done that. He was never asked to as it turned out but he came closer to doing so than he could have dreamed of when he made that dramatic-seeming declaration. I didn't think he should tell his father, then?

'What good would that do?' I said.

It reminds me now, all this, of Sunny Durham and the Kirby Theiston murder, though I hardly know why. There are few similarities. At the time I thought of Kathleen March, spirited away while in

Vera's care and killed. Was it really June Poole that Andrew had seen and had she been waiting in the hope of snatching Jamie?

I never saw Vera again. That Friday morning, I dutifully kissed her goodbye, or rather, we laid our cheeks in juxtaposition and kissed the air.

'Give my love to your father,' she said. 'I might come up to London and surprise him one of these fine days.'

The last words she ever spoke to me apart from goodbye. Longleys never say 'bye-bye' – did I mention that? There is a prohibition on it, strict as the ban on eating with one's right hand.

'Goodbye,' said Vera, waving, standing beside Helen on the drift and waving. 'Goodbye!' Jamie waved, too, both hands up, pinching his fingers open and shut the way I once saw an American professor, while lecturing, demonstrate inverted commas. The last time I looked back, he and Vera were walking back to the house hand in hand.

The rest I know from Helen and Josie. The General drove Vera and Jamie home to Sindon in the afternoon, by now convinced that all was well and that a great deal of what had happened had been in Vera's, if not Josie's, imagination. He stayed half an hour and went off home. Helen rang Vera next day and found her cheerful and calm. She rang Eden. Eden was much better, was expecting six people to lunch, refused to discuss the future guardianship of Jamie. There was nothing to discuss, she said, it was all settled. Helen took this to mean Eden had given up and was being haughty in defeat.

Nothing happened on Sunday. I have sometimes tried to imagine a day in Vera's life and Jamie's together at this time. It is hard for me to do this for I have never lived such a life myself, alone in a remote country village, with few friends, without a car, in genteel poverty. Vera couldn't afford to ask six people to lunch even if she had wanted to. What did they do? Got up early, I have no doubt, Vera to do housework, the dusting and polishing that was done every day while I stayed there, Jamie to play with his toys. Then for Vera, the *Sunday Express*, a walk perhaps; lunch, always a piece of roast meat, a tiny minuscule piece, the whole week's ration in 1950, roast potatoes, Yorkshire pudding, a green vegetable, and jam tart or custard trifle to follow. Another walk afterwards? A sleep? The wireless? Sewing or knitting, of course. She would have read a story to him, perhaps several stories, talked to him and played with him. But still the imagination is defeated by the task of filling those long hours, especially when it was cold or wet or got dark early. Vera never read except for the children's books she read aloud. The bookcase in the living-room was stocked with a non-reader's collection, school set books and surely unwelcome presents.

If I close my eyes I can see that bookcase now. I can see Jamie running his toy tank along the lower shelf and up the spines of the books. Was *Bulletin No 23, Edible and Poisonous Fungi* there at the time? I don't think it was. I can see what was there: *Precious Bane, Anthony Adverse, Sesame and Lilies,* that had been a school prize, *Black Bartlemy's Treasure,* Frohawk's *Complete Book of British Butterflies* ... So was I wrong in saying Francis showed no interest in entomology when young? Was this Francis's book? Was it possible, then, that the fungi book was also his and at that period was upstairs in the bookshelf in his room? *Wuthering Heights, The History of Mr Polly, Lamb's Tales* ... and is this dark green spine next to it perhaps *Bulletin No 23*? It can't have been in two places at the same time. It may not even have been in the house at all then. But I know that once I saw it there, in that bookcase, in Vera's living-room, dark green with a gold chantarelle on its cover and the fascinating mycological lore within.

That particular Sunday – I don't remember whether it was wet or fine – I was in Cambridge. At that particular time I was 'growing out' of my family, and this by leaps and bounds, making decisions that as a soon-to-be-independent person I would in future have no more to do with my father's sisters, regretfully contemplating, too, a breach with Helen which would be inevitable if I gave Andrew up. Since I gave a good deal of thought to all this, I was probably thinking of it that Sunday in between re-reading Spenser's *Faerie Queene* and meeting Andrew. I don't suppose, though, that I thought of Vera as a suffering person, drawn into the worst kind of the converging of human lots. Like the rest of us, I believed she and Eden had settled their differences. And fancying myself in those days as a sprightly feminist intellectual, I am afraid I probably also thought their petty squabbles beneath me.

For that I was to be punished. Murder reaches out through a family, stamping transfers of the Mark of Cain on a dozen foreheads, and though those grow pale in proportion to the distance of the kinship, they are there and they burn into the brain. A question, a chance word, will discover them, as invisible writing appears shimmeringly when exposed to fire. Only time bleaches them away and makes it possible to reach back into the past in a kind of tranquillity.

Monday came. Vera contemplated running away. Later in the day she told Josie she had thought of running away. She had even begun to pack a bag, to gather together Jamie's clothes and certain of his books and toys. As a refugee she saw herself – in the past years, however ignorant we may have been before, we had come to know what refugees were – fleeing ahead of an invading army, uncaring of what she left behind, taking with her the only precious thing she had. But where could she go and how would she live? She had no money and no means of earning any and nothing to sell.

At ten o'clock, Eden arrived with June Poole and Mrs King. June was wearing the grey dress we had seen her in and a grey felt hat, requisite nanny's garb. Mrs King had a box of Black Magic chocolates. Sweets were still rationed in the spring of 1950 (and were to be for years longer) so these chocolates would have been accounted a rare prize, if a rather unsuitable choice as a bribe for a child of six. It was a sunny morning, quite warm, and they found Jamie playing in the back garden of Laurel Cottage in a sandpit Vera had made for him up near the house. In my childhood and Eden's, the sandpit had been down at the bottom of the garden near the hovel, now irrevocably associated in my mind with the loves of Chad and Francis – but this would have been too far away for Vera. She needed him within her sight.

She soon saw what was happening for she was in the kitchen doing the washing. It was Monday, so Vera was doing the washing. It was to be the most terrible day of her life, and I think she knew it would be, but it was also Monday and therefore washing day. From the window she saw what was happening. June Poole, in her grey uniform, was squatting down on the edge of the sandpit with her arm round Jamie and Mrs King was bending over him, showing him the chocolates. How had Eden enlisted them in her private army? By convincing them, no doubt, of the rightness of her cause.

Vera didn't immediately see Eden. She ran out of the house with dripping hands, literally to be caught by Eden who was standing on the path that went past the back door. Eden took her by the shoulders and said:

'Now, Vera, be sensible. You know you're going to have to give in, so why not do it now without a scene?'

Vera let out a scream, struggled and ducked under Eden's arms. She ran to Jamie but June had picked Jamie up and was carrying him back the way they had come.

'That's the way, June,' Eden said. 'Just get him into the car as fast as you can and we'll be off.'

It was at this point that Josie arrived, calling as she did most mornings to see if Vera wanted any shopping or merely a chat and a cup of coffee. At first she couldn't believe what she saw. That is the way it is when we witness sensational acts that seem unreal in the context of a humdrum life. Josie thought, someone is acting, it's a game. But these feelings lasted only seconds. She could see Vera hanging on to June, being dragged away by the combined efforts of Eden and Mrs King, hear Vera screaming and crying. She shouted at Eden:

'What on earth do you think you're doing?'

Eden said, 'Stay out of this, please, Mrs Cambus. This is a matter between my sister and me.'

'Don't let them take him, Josie!' Vera screamed. 'Don't let them!'

By now Jamie was in the car. He was also screaming. Two or three of Vera's neighbours came out, though she had no very near neighbours, it was not like it would have been in a London street. Josie's first thought was for Vera whom she tried to take in her arms, but Vera threw herself on to the car, beating her hands on the windows and shouting Jamie's name.

Eden jumped into the driving seat. Josie thought she was going to slam the door on Vera's hand. She just missed. She started the car with a roar, turned once to look at Josie. The awful thing, Josie said, was that tears were pouring down Eden's face. Mrs King and June sat in the back, keeping hold of the by now nearly demented Jamie who was thrashing about screaming, 'Mummy, Mummy!'

Eden drove away and Vera would have been sent flying except that Josie caught her. With one arm around her, Vera's head buried in her shoulder, Josie led her back into the house.

This morning's post has brought from Daniel Stewart part of the transcript of Vera's trial. Until now I have kept myself in ignorance of what went on at the Central Criminal Court during that week in the summer of 1950. My father, too, died in ignorance of it. What we had instead was a first-hand version of what took place that Monday at Goodney Hall from Josie herself. But an account of the evening Josie and my father and myself spent closeted in our living-room, a stiff whisky inside each of us and more to come, I shall postpone until a little later.

Stewart wants me 'to add your own comments, please, Mrs Severn'. What comments can I have? I wasn't there. I was in Cambridge and that term I never read the papers. My father, in London, cancelled the *Daily Telegraph* from the day of Vera's appearance in the magistrates' court until a week after her trial ended, and when he came back to it found the crossword too difficult after this lapse of time ever to complete again. I tried to banish Vera from my mind, to cut myself off from her, but for all that I took a less good degree than was expected of me. That one paragraph I had read before I banned newspapers from my sight haunted me, coming often between my eyes and other, more literary, printed pages.

Vera Ivy Hillyard, 43, of Bell Lane, Great Sindon, Essex, appeared today at Colchester Magistrates' Court charged with the murder of her sister, Edith Mary Pearmain . . .

Andrew and I married in a panic, to keep it in the family. So many people knew Vera and Eden were our aunts. I imagined them gossiping and their gossip putting out tentacles to reach out as far away as London, as Cambridge. My resolution to shake off my family, to leave it behind like the snake's worn-out, no longer useful, skin had to be given up. What they had done made that impossible. I was stuck with them, tumbled with the other siblings and cousins, niece and nephew, into a kind of ghetto. It seems to me now that I married Andrew to be saved in much the same manner as someone may marry for citizenship or to avoid being deported. Or perhaps it was as the blind marry the blind or the crippled the handicapped. Two years our marriage lasted before we parted by mutual consent.

Soon after our divorce he married someone else who quickly gave

Helen a granddaughter. Helen was a widow by then and Walbrooks sold and Tony gone God knew where in the Far, having with the approval of higher authority planted Jamie in boarding-school. Jamie had been made a ward of court, being like Melchizedek, the Priest King, without father, without mother and without descent.

More than anyone I ever heard of, in fact.

Next week I am going to see him. He is going to cook the promised meal for me and we shall sit in his garden in the warm Florentine dusk and – compare notes.

Meanwhile, am I going to read this transcript? Why give myself the scratch of pain, the inevitable wincing, it is bound to bring? If this were the nineteen forties and a fire burned in my grate, might I not do as my father did with the winter letters, and drop these sheets of paper in the fire? Ah, but, I remind myself, he always read them first and often read them, considering from whom they came, many times.

So here goes, then. At least it isn't all here, only the vital bits, says Stewart. Josie was principal witness for the defence and this was part of her evidence. Counsel had asked her to describe what happened after Eden and her henchwomen took Jamie away.

Josephine Cambus: I went back into the house with her. She was hysterical, screaming and crying. There was some brandy in the house and I gave her some in a glass with water. I said to her that I would phone the police but she told me that would be useless so I said I would speak to my son. He would know what to do.

Mr Justice Lambert: Is your son a policeman?

Mrs Cambus: No, my Lord, a solicitor.

Counsel: Did you speak to your son, Mrs Cambus?

Mrs Cambus: I tried to. I had asked the operator for his number. Vera, Mrs Hillyard, took the phone out of my hand. She said lawyers and policemen would be useless.

Counsel: Did you ask her why?

Mrs Cambus: She said only she and her sister knew the ins and outs of it. Those were her words. She said she would go to Goodney Hall and talk to her sister and her sister's husband. It was important, she said, to speak to her sister's husband, and she would wait there, on the doorstep if necessary, until he came home. She was quite calm by then. She seemed fatalistic. She seemed . . .

Mr Justice Lambert: Never mind what she seemed, Mrs Cambus. The jury will wish to know what you saw and heard, not what you surmised.

Counsel: Did Mrs Hillyard then go to Goodney Hall and did you go with her?

Counsel for the prosecution: My Lord, is not my learned friend leading the witness?

Mr Justice Lambert: I think perhaps he is.

Counsel: I apologize, my Lord. I will re-phrase the question. What did Mrs Hillyard then do, Mrs Cambus?

Mrs Cambus: She put on her coat and fetched her handbag and said she would catch the bus to Bures and wait there for the bus to Goodney, unless I would take her there by car. I did not much want to go, I didn't want to be involved, but I agreed to take her, having some idea that I wouldn't go inside but would leave her there and return home. I went home and fetched my car and drove her to Goodney Hall. When we got there she begged me to go to the door on the grounds that if she went they wouldn't let her in.

Counsel: Did you in fact do as she asked?

Mrs Cambus: I refused at first, I didn't want to, but at last I did. Mr Pearmain opened the door to me. He said . . .

Counsel: You must not tell us what Mr Pearmain said to you unless Mrs Hillyard was present. Was she present?

Mrs Cambus: No, she was in the car.

Counsel: Very well. As a result of what Mr Pearmain said to you, what did you do?

Mrs Cambus: I went back to the car and fetched Mrs Hillyard and we both went into the house with Mr Pearmain. There was no one else present at that time. We went into a room I think they call the drawing-room. Mrs Hillyard said she had something to say to Mr Pearmain in private, something she wanted him to know, and would I go outside for a moment? I said I would go home, I had no reason to stay, but she begged me to wait for her, just to go out of the room for a short time. Mr Pearmain said he thought he knew what she wished to say but he knew already, his wife had told him a few days before. At this point Mrs Pearmain came into the room and said to Mrs Hillyard, 'I have told him everything . . .'

I laid the transcript down. I had read this sort of thing before, having been shown such by my husband and in *Notable British Trials*. They are all much of a muchness, all have that air of unreality in which people converse as if programmed in language confined exclusively to these particular surroundings. Yet I am told transcripts are faithful verbatim accounts of what was said. Strange . . . From this point, anyway, Josie had begun her own tale to us in the quiet, intimate, rather breathless atmosphere of my parents' overheated living-room. There she began by repeating to us the actual words Eden had used on walking into the drawing-room that April morning.

'You can't get your own way like that, Vera. I've told Tony everything. I've told him Jamie is my son.'

We knew, of course. We knew by then. The bare facts had reached us even though we chose to take ostrich attitudes to the trial. It was the details we wanted from Josie, the subtleties that clothed the bare facts in kind, veiling disguises. Leaning forward in her chair, not looking at us, but looking into the fire, she said:

'Vera cried out. I've never been able to make up my mind whether or not it was a denial. Tony – I never knew him as that but that's what I'll call him – Tony looked grim. He looked miserable. He stood there nodding, with his eyes almost closed. Your sister – I mean Edith, Eden – she said, "He's my child. Vera only brought him up. She offered to do it, I admit that, it was generous of her, a wonderful thing to do, but there was never any question of her having him for keeps." "You liar!" Vera said. Tony was terribly embarrassed. I think he's the sort of man who would be embarrassed more than anything else in a tragic situation. He said, "Mrs Cambus doesn't want to hear all this. This is a private matter, let's keep it so." "Oh no, we can't," said Vera. "Everyone's going to have to know. I'm not having you hush it up. I'll shout it from the housetops what she's been to me, a snake in the grass, a cruel tormentor. I want to see my boy," she said. "Where's my boy?" "He's not your boy," Eden said. "He's mine. He'll be mine and Tony's. We're going to adopt him legally." "How can you adopt your own child?" Vera said, and that was the nearest she got to conceding anything to Eden. Though of course you *can* adopt your own child if he's illegitimate, I asked my son about that.

'Vera began to abuse Eden. I don't suppose you want to know what she said, the actual words, I mean?'

My father shook his head. 'The gist,' he said.

'Well, I suppose you'd call them aspersions on Eden's moral character. Eden hated it. Tony looked as if he were going to faint but Eden was utterly calm. She told us the whole thing, I mean me and Tony. I'm sure he hadn't heard any of the details before. He sat down and put his head in his hands.'

The story that came out was that Eden had found herself pregnant in the autumn of 1943. By whom she made no attempt to say. It was Vera who interjected that she had been with half a dozen men, including a GI, a private soldier who was a Puerto Rican out of Spanish Harlem, and who was the most beautiful thing in Londonderry at that time. Josie had the impression that this must have been told Vera when Eden made the first outpourings of confession. It was true that Jamie, though fair-haired, had eyes of a rich, southern brown and a pale olive skin the sun never burned. Eden herself had, it seemed, tried to make Vera believe (and Vera *had* believed at the time) she had been having a passionate love affair with an officer in the Royal Navy who died when the *Lagan* was torpedoed in the September of 1943. Who could forget another naval officer claimed as Eden's lover or would-be lover, he who was the subject of Francis's most spectacular tease, he who also went down with his ship? Vera and Eden, poor things, were snobs to the end.

She had told Francis before she told Vera, I am sure of that. It is exactly what she would have done, and Francis's cryptic utterances to me on the morning before the first kidnap attempt confirm it. Francis probably told her where she could get an abortion, it is the kind of thing he would have known. And he may have given her the money, or some of the money, to pay for it. Francis always had money. I think he prostituted himself. For some reason, then, she didn't have an abortion. Did she tell Vera and did Vera talk her out of it, Vera who wanted a child and had told Helen so but was herself unable to conceive? Eden must have left the WRNS months, years even, before any of the rest of us knew she had. She came to Laurel Cottage and hid herself there.

It is hard today for us to understand, even for people of my age, how terrible it still was in 1944 for a conventional, middle-class girl to have an illegitimate child. And Eden had set herself up so, presented herself and been presented by that arch PR woman, her sister, as such a paragon. She could not have written to her brother and confessed this to him, explained it to her half-sister and her half-sister's husband, have it known in Sindon where she had been the sweet, grave adolescent, orphaned young. But if her sister, that older sister who had been a mother to her, would seem to be pregnant, would seem to give birth, would appear with a baby . . .?

Not all of this is what Josie told us that winter's evening. Some of it I have pieced together with my own knowledge, with observations I made and could not then account for, from my imagination and from

253

my knowledge of those two women, my aunts, my dead aunts, one murdered by the other.

Vera may have made her offer out of love of Eden, from sheer altruism and a desire to protect her reputation. She may have made it because she wanted a baby. Having failed so lamentably with Francis, she wanted to try again. Or, and this is most likely, it was both. She saw it as being to everyone's advantage. Who knows now what was said between them? Did Vera truly promise only to keep the child till Eden herself wanted him? Or did she take him over unconditionally, to be absolutely her own son? Yes, said Eden to the first. Vera said nothing, Josie said. She sat there, transfixed, listening.

The child was born in a nursing home in Colchester, the one which was bombed in the following year and all its records destroyed. Eden went in as Mrs Hillyard, she said. She has been to a doctor for antenatal examinations as Mrs Hillyard. Vera went away while she was in the nursing home and stayed in a boarding-house at Felix-stowe. They arranged things this way: Eden left the nursing home in a taxi with the baby. Vera left Felixstowe and they met in Colchester in the lounge of the George Hotel, being driven home together, all three of them, in another hired car. Vera laughed derisively when Eden said this, as if no fiction could be more absurd.

'Eden went out of the room,' Josie said, 'and came back with a long envelope with something in it. It was a birth certificate, Jamie's birth certificate.'

'Did you see it?' I asked her.

'Oh yes, I saw it. It was for James Longley, mother Edith Mary Longley, father unknown. Vera snatched it from me. She said it was a forgery. Then she said Eden had made a false declaration to the registrar and that was a serious offence punishable by years in prison. It was ridiculous of course. There was the birth certificate with the facts on it plain to see. Vera herself had never seen it before. I think she was afraid to see it, ever to ask to see it. She knew only too well what was on it.'

'But surely,' I said, 'if they'd made this arrangement, they must also have arranged that a false declaration *should* be made. Why didn't Vera herself, who was well, who hadn't got up from just having had a baby, why didn't she go to the registrar?'

Josie couldn't tell us that but I thought I knew the answer. I could imagine the way it was. Not so much Eden hedging her bets, making contingency plans just in case one day she would want Jamie, as simple fear at making a false declaration. The warnings against so doing are very stern in registrars' offices. Did she get there determined to register Jamie as the son of Vera Hillyard and Gerald Hillyard, yet when she got there, lose her nerve? But that doesn't answer the question, why didn't Vera go herself? Most likely because Eden simply got there first, went out alone a couple of days after they were back in Sindon and returned to present Vera with a *fait accompli*.

'Vera had it in her hands,' said Josie, 'and she tried to tear it up. Those things are made of reinforced paper and they're hard to tear but she tore a bit of it before Tony took it away from her. Not that it would have done any good, destroying it. A copy of it would have been there in the records at Somerset House.'

So Vera took Jamie to be her own son and Eden went away to London to this job she had lined up as companion to old Lady Rogerson. How much easier things would have been for Vera if Jamie had been born just a month earlier! Gerald would never have accepted a ten-and-a-half-months child. If she had told him the truth, would he have refused to let her claim Jamie as her own? Perhaps. Perhaps, even, he would have told people Eden was Jamie's true mother. In a way, I think, once she had lost Gerald, Vera wasn't displeased at having people suspect Chad of being her lover and Jamie's father. It gave her identity, it gave her youth. And she had Jamie. She could never have foreseen how devotedly she would come to love him.

Eden hardly ever came near her. She didn't inquire after Jamie, she didn't want to know. There is a Jewish joke concerning the man who says of an enemy: Why does he hate me so? I never did him any good. Was that how Eden felt towards Vera now? Vera had done her too much good, had done her a supreme service. It was too much for her to handle, the guilt was too heavy, and she transposed it into dislike for Vera. And then she met Tony and became engaged to him. She would have more babies now, Vera must have thought. It was all right, safe, for she would never want a husband to know about Jamie. But when no babies came, when there was a miscarriage, the result of an ectopic pregnancy, and the chances of a safe pregnancy, a delivery at term, looked unlikely, what then? It was then that Vera began to be afraid. She might never have seen the birth certificate but she would guess its contents. If Eden made a claim on Jamie, she wouldn't, as Francis said to me, have a leg to stand on. Perhaps it was made worse for her by Eden's evident indifference to Jamie. That would not prevent her taking him for the sake of having a son, of having an heir for Tony and his shop empire.

'Vera jumped up quite suddenly,' Josie said, 'and ran out of the room. No one was expecting it, least of all Eden. Eden sat there victorious, you know, her marriage in ruins, her family alienated, but triumphant just the same, unassailable, if you know what I mean. That was the feeling I had, anyway. She got up quite slowly and said, "I suppose she's gone to find him. I don't precisely know where he is."

'We followed her. I have often wished I hadn't. What was it to me, anyway? I was just Vera's friend who had driven her to the house. I should have gone home and I don't know why I didn't. It wasn't unwholesome curiosity. I had had enough of revelations, soul-baring. I expect it was a feeling that I shouldn't desert Vera there in the house of her enemies – for they were all her enemies, weren't they? Down to June Poole, that minion of Eden's.'

I could not look at my father nor he at me . . . In a curious, unwise way, he had made his idealization of Longley womanhood, embodied in his mother, then his sisters, a cornerstone of his life. It was all founded on illusion as idealization mostly is and it was very foolish of him to have sacrificed his marriage to it, to have made himself ridiculous by investing his sisters with qualities they not only did not have but which were the antitheses of what they did have. But how dreadfully sorry one felt for him! He had little left now because his world was altered. He even had to re-think his conception of his wife and daughter because hitherto he had seen them through Longley spectacles, one lens being Vera, the other Eden. He had seen them only in the light of comparison and contrast. I will say for my mother, much to her credit, that from the time of the murder and Vera's arrest, she uttered no word of disparagement of either of his sisters, and when she did speak of them, it was always with pity. But, for all that, she became a silent woman.

Josie told us the rest of it. She went on to the end and finished. Jamie was upstairs in the nursery. He was old to be in a nursery, he was old to *have* a nursery, but those two between them, in their different ways, had kept him a baby. The room was beautiful, Josie remembered. Of course she had never been there before, had never seen it when it had the fairy wallpaper, the carpet with the ivy leaves. The new carpet was pale beige and the furniture was white. Yachts sailed in a frieze along the walls on pale blue wavelets and seagulls flew above the sails. There was a print of the Boyhood of Raleigh, another of Stubbs horses and one of the Fighting Temeraire.

It wasn't a cold day but it was still only April and there was a fire with a fireguard in front of it. June Poole was at the far end of the room, folding linen. Jamie stood on the blue and white rug in front of the fire and Vera knelt in front of him. Josie had the impression he had had no occupation, was doing nothing at all when Vera came in, had just been standing or sitting there bewildered by the recent violent events. They burst into the room – Eden, Tony, Josie and Mrs King, though why she had joined them and at what point no one seemed to know.

'Eden said, "If you won't get out of here I will have you put out," and she looked at Mrs King and June. Mrs King did nothing but June Poole put down the pillowcase she was holding and came towards us, it seemed to me in rather a menacing way. Tony said, "Eden, this has got to stop," and Eden said, "I quite agree with you. I'm stopping it now," and she put out her arms to pick Jamie up.'

I shall quote from the transcript now. It is the official version, after all, and what Josie said in court pre-dates by six months what Josie said to us.

Counsel: What happened then, Mrs Cambus?
Mrs Cambus: Mrs Hillyard had a knife in her hand.
Counsel: What do you mean, a knife in her hand? Did she pick the knife up from somewhere? Did she bring it with her?
Mrs Cambus: I suppose she must have done. She took it out of her handbag. It was a long kitchen knife.
[Mrs Cambus was shown a knife, Exhibit B.]
Counsel: Is this the knife?
Mrs Cambus: It was like that, yes.
Counsel: Had you ever seen it before?
Mrs Cambus: Must I answer that?
Mr Justice Lambert: Certainly you must answer Counsel.
Mrs Cambus: Well, yes, then, I had seen it.
Counsel: Where?
Mrs Cambus: In Mrs Hillyard's kitchen. She used it for cutting vegetables. I have seen her sharpen it with a stone.

Counsel: So Mrs Hillyard took a knife from her bag. What happened?

Mrs Cambus: Mrs Hillyard lunged at Mrs Pearmain with the knife. Someone picked the boy up, Mrs King I think it was, yes, it was Mrs King. She picked the boy up and took him out of the room. Mr Pearmain tried to get hold of Mrs Hillyard. She stabbed him in the arm, the right arm. Then she attacked Mrs Pearmain, wounding her in the neck and the chest. There was a lot of blood, blood everywhere. Mrs Pearmain screamed and fell over, she fell on to all fours, she was bleeding dreadfully.

The blood went over the blue walls and the yachts and the wavelets and the seagulls. Eden vomited blood and died. She rolled over dead on the rug in front of the fire. Vera would have turned the knife on herself, almost did, but June Poole took her by the arms and tied her with the belt of her own dress.

— 17 —

Instead of Vera's story, Daniel Stewart is to write an examination of the Kirby Theiston case, tying the murder of Sunny Durham in with the disappearance of Kathleen March. This will be a reappraisal in the light of the new evidence he found while researching my family. And he will be able to use a great deal of what I have told him when he writes of the part Vera played. I think he is happy about it, quite excited even, and relieved to be free of Longley and Hillyard complexities. So I was right – though not wholly confident at the time – when I told Francis his mother's story would never be written.

The trial transcript I have destroyed after reading it twice. Morbid temptation might draw me back to it on wet afternoons or evenings when I am alone and I don't care to be so directly reminded of poor Vera's pain or, indirectly, of my own failures, my sad first marriage, my poor degree, results of a dread that Vera's notoriety would dog me for life. At twenty-two I was as lacking in foresight as Francis's daughter Elizabeth lacks judgement, believing that in the nineteen eighties the name of Vera Hillyard would arouse more than indifference. Having no fires or furnaces, I have given the transcript to my husband and he has handed over this particularly exciting and exotic morsel of food to be devoured by the paper shredder in his office.

As the accused in a murder trial Vera was not obliged to give evidence and she did not. Perhaps defending counsel persuaded her not to, knowing that anything she would say could only damn her further, or else Vera herself had no defence to offer and no arguments to put forward. Josie had told us of Vera's total apathy, how when she visited her in prison she had gone into a kind of fugue, retreating into herself and in a deep silence. I am sure she wanted to die. The alternative would have been years of imprisonment and during those years she would have had the daily torment of knowing Jamie was outside and in someone else's less than loving care. Counsel, of course, put up a defence. She had intended only to frighten, then only to wound, her sister. But frenzy had taken hold of her and she had struck again and again . . .

There is something else which has led to his abandonment of his project, the doubt at the heart of things, for if it is true that an element of mystery as to what really happened may enhance a work of this kind, the unanswered question is always one of who did it or how was it done. In Vera's case there is no doubt about that. The uncertainty hinges upon something quite different, upon a bizarre point of genesis, the kind of doubt rarely encountered in any family in any walk of life, and one to which no amount of research can supply a solution.

Memory is an imperfect function. We are resigned to not remembering things. It is the knowledge, imparted to us by unshakeable outside authority, that an incident we remember never took place, which we find so hard to accept. Jamie told me, when we sat in his garden after dinner, that Eden's blood had flown at him that day, splashing on to his clothes. It was the only thing he could remember. But when he read the trial transcript he saw he had been mistaken. He remembered something that had never happened, for Mrs King had carried him away before Vera struck out with her knife, seconds before. So the mannerism he has kept, the flicking at blood, is founded upon illusion.

Jamie has moved into a little house behind a high wall in the Orti Orcellari. There is a gate in this wall, one of those gates of wrought iron backed with iron, and on the portico, flanked by two urns that are linked by a stone garland of bay, are engraved these lines of Dante:

> *Ahi, quanto nella mente mi commossi,*
> *quando mi volsi per veder Beatrice,*

per non poter vedere; ben ch'io fossi
presso di lei, e nel mondo felice!

Has Jamie, too, been overthrown, his mind in a turmoil, through being shown once more what haunts him? Through seeing and not seeing? Without subscribing to specious psychotherapeutic doctrines of the let-it-come-up-and-it-will-go-away school, he tells me he is glad he read the transcript. At least it has made him face it. Ceasing to be a bugbear, a chimera, a half-imagined thing, it has come out into the open, no worse than what he imagined and no better, but the thing itself, the real thing. To use the jargon of those doctrines, he has confronted it.

He was laughing as much as ever, flicking at his shoulder as much as ever – though now with an impatient shake of the head and a conscious staying of his hand in mid-air – and he cooked for me as he promised, wonderful dishes, *farfalle con asparaghi, manzo per un dio biondo* (beef with grapes, beef for a blond god, which puts one in mind of Francis), *crema d'arancia* and *amaretti.* The sauce for the *manzo* he makes at the last minute, essential apparently for perfection, and while he stands at the stove I tell him that the pictures Francis gave those absurd titles to have disappeared from the Hotel Cavour. For we are staying there again, Louis and I, and I have looked into that bedroom and seen their places taken by innocuous and even pleasing aquarelles of Venice. Francis's and his new books lie side by side on the kitchen table, each newly published, each fresh from the binders and in glossy, multi-coloured jackets: *Nymphs, Naiads and Mayflies* and *Cucina Ben Riuscita.* And I have a sensation of peacefulness, of all things ultimately coming together for good.

Jamie's garden contains no flowers. Of course it doesn't, it is an Italian garden. Between the stone flags grow oxalis and arenaria and these have their own tiny blossoms, yellow and white, but otherwise the garden is the dark moss colour of evergreens and the weathered grey of stone. In urns that remind me of the ones that stood on the terrace of Goodney Hall grow plants that may be aspidistras and also the spike-leaved succulents called mother-in-law's tongue that rise out of beds of trailing ivy. There is a little stagnant pool, full of lilies, free of fish, and up under the walls and behind the walls and in the stone and brick caverns are cats, the feral cats that are everywhere in the cities of Italy. We hear them sometimes, bodies slipping between a branch and a broken pillar, and as the dark comes, see their eyes. Jamie has put a lamp on the table to which the moths come, and I remember Vera asking me to let her sit in the dusk for a while in peace, not to put the lights on and let the moths in.

'Tell me about my mother,' he says to me, his manner calm, his voice steady.

It is a catch question, isn't it? I remember what he said to me in the English Cemetery, about his mother being a good cook. The proverb says that it's a wise child that knows its own father. I get my courage up and tell him it is less usual to be in doubt as to one's *maternity*.

'I'm not in doubt,' he says. 'Whatever the family may think, whatever the world may think, I know Vera Hillyard was my mother.'

How can I argue with him? In a way it would be presumptuous of me to argue. I am not even sure if I want to. In the dusk, the dark now, with the moths around the lamp, I tell him about Vera, the nice things, carefully editing my memories: how much she loved him, her doting care, her selfless love of Eden, her housewifely skills, her dutiful life. She emerges from my descriptions as a perfect woman, nobly planned. Gone is the sharp tongue, the snobbery, the prejudice, the preoccupation with trivia, the coldness. I don't mention such rules as eating with the left hand, drinking with the right. I say nothing of her fear and dislike of Francis. And perhaps those virtues of Vera's did outweigh her faults and when I tell Jamie she was more sinned against than sinning, I am not far wrong.

'I'm glad Stewart has given up the idea,' he says. 'His book would have been written from the other point of view, of course, or at least he would have devoted his last chapter to pros and cons that don't really exist. I may write a book about her myself one of these days. Would you help me if I did?'

'No, Jamie,' I say to him. 'No, I don't think I would.'

A fine golden moon is rising behind the dark trees in the gardens of the Orcellari. I tell Jamie it is time for me to go and we have a little argument, he insisting he will go with me to find a taxi on the rank up by Santa Maria Novella, I determined on walking back to the Via Cavour. This time we kiss goodbye and I have the sensation of a brown bear snuggling up to me. But the illusion vanishes fast as he steps back frenetically to sweep invisible blood from his shoulder. In the end, he does come with me as far as the top of the street. From there onwards, it is light and busy, crowds thronging the Piazza della Stazione, and I persuade him I shall be safe. It is the menu outside the Otello that distracts him. I look back once and see him still studying it, for all the world as if he were without cares and without a history.

My husband has said he will walk part of the way to meet me and there he is coming from the corner of the Via Nazionale. After all these years, the clutch at the heart which comes to me when we see each other and wave is good to feel. His evening has been passed with a businessman, English but resident in Florence, bent on suing a newspaper for libel. Louis specializes in litigation, or rather, as he puts it, stopping people engaging in litigation. It was to him I went to be made free of Andrew, having chosen Josie's son because he was the only solicitor I knew of. I went to escape from one trap and immediately fell, though this time with a conviction never proved wrong of future happiness, into another. Out of the frying-pan into the fire. How lucky I am that the fire still burns so brightly!

I take his arm. I tell him about Jamie and what Jamie has said.

'What do *you* think?' I ask him.

'As to whose child Jamie truly was? Edith Pearmain's, surely.'

'For years,' I say, 'I didn't believe that, and then for years I thought so.'

'The point,' says Louis as we come to the hotel, 'is that it wasn't really relevant to the case against your aunt Vera. Or shall I say that it was wise of neither side to have anything to do with it. It was more *just*.'

'How can you say that!'

'Remember Edith Thompson in the twenties. She was certainly innocent of the murder of her husband. Bywaters stabbed him and not at her instigation. But Bywaters was her lover, she was a married woman, and that was what executed her. Remember Ruth Ellis a few years after Vera Hillyard. The climate of feeling still hadn't changed. It has been said that Ruth Ellis was hanged not because she had shot her lover but because she *had* a lover. If the defence had insisted Jamie was in fact Vera's child – instead of allowing it to be assumed he was Edith's – it would also have had to be made clear he wasn't Gerald Hillyard's. Do you see now?'

'It made no difference in the end.'

'No. There's no penalty worse than hanging. But it might have done, there was a chance.' Louis looks at me, one eyebrow up. 'He was Edith's – Eden's – wasn't he?'

'I don't know. No one will ever know now.'

I don't know. And that is the heart of the mystery that has frustrated Daniel Stewart and let him down.

It is perhaps most likely that Eden was Jamie's mother, but there is a great deal against that, isn't there? Certainly she became pregnant sometime in the summer of 1943 and the first person she went to in her trouble was Francis. There had always been close, secret things between them, arcane things. But if Francis told her the name of an abortionist and gave her the money, or some of it, for an abortion, why didn't she have one? Because she was afraid, because Vera talked her out of it? A post-mortem, according to Stewart, was carried out on Eden's body but not in order to discover whether she had ever been pregnant – that is, carried a child to term and delivered it.

And there is a very good argument for her having, in fact, had that abortion. Eden miscarried in 1948 as the result of an ectopic pregnancy. One of the principal factors contributing to an ectopic pregnancy, or the implantation of the foetus in one of the Fallopian tubes rather than in the uterus, is a previous abortion badly carried out and causing infection and the subsequent blocking of a tube. Of course other possibilities here are gonorrhoea (as my mother scandalously hinted) and a previous, carelessly attended birth. Perhaps we can't quite dismiss the venereal disease but surely we can the carelessly handled delivery. The nursing home where Jamie was born, to whichever woman it was, was a reputable one. I never heard the staff there impugned for any sort of negligence.

So perhaps the baby whose father was some Londonderry GI Eden did have aborted – and later bitterly regretted her decision. For that autumn she heard that her sister, her much older sister, was expecting a child, and she almost envied her. It was not Gerald's, though, that much is evident. Did it happen as I had earlier believed? Did Vera encounter some old boyfriend home on leave and in her loneliness make love with him? Anne Cambus once told me (not apropos of any of this) that a Sindon family, the Warners, owed their dark colouring to the fact that the children's grandfather, an old seafaring man, still alive when I was a child, had married a wife he brought back with him from Agadir. Two of their sons were in the army during the war, both officers. Is this too far-fetched? Am I being absurd? Perhaps.

Vera suckled Jamie, she fed him at her own breast. I saw it. I can't be mistaken here. And since then I have read accounts in newspapers and magazines – a whole book has been written on the subject, I believe – of women who, adopting or taking over other people's babies, have induced lactation. By the intensity of their love and by their determination, holding the child to the dry breast, persevering, they have done it. So why not Vera? She was exactly the sort of woman to achieve it, intense, conscientious, prone to obsessions, driven by a self-formulated notion of duty. Taking over Eden's child, she might very likely have held him to her breast, let him suck, seen one day a drop of milk exuded from the nipple, and then persevered for a variety of reasons: to make him more her own, to do what was best for him, to allay doubts in others that he was not her child.

But it is more probable, isn't it, that Jamie was her natural child and that lactation happened as it normally does from the action of the emptying of the womb? Vera was a prudish finicking woman who would have pulled a face and said 'How disgusting!' if told of the book by the self-induced lactator. She had never breast-fed Francis, though she was very young when he was born and nursing a baby would have come more easily to her. She would never have attempted to breast-feed a child not her own, for the idea would never have occurred to her.

You will say that if Jamie was Vera's own son, why did she allow Eden to name herself his mother on his birth certificate? The answer may be that she didn't, that she knew nothing of it until it was too late. Or she may, of course, have approved this false declaration. In her own eyes, after all, she had done a terrible thing. She had had a child by a man not her husband. That was bad enough. Was she to compound her wrongdoing by telling her husband Jamie was his? She lacked the nerve to confess he was not. Just to be on the safe side, why not let Eden do as she had offered and register Jamie as her own son? Neither of them wanted him at that time, anyway, he was an encumbrance to both, but their mutual devotion was great. Eden would do this generous thing for her so that one day – when and if Gerald came back, if he doubted her, if the child looked very unlike him or very like someone else – she could show Gerald that birth certificate and explain she had adopted Jamie for Eden's sake.

At the time of his birth she could not have foreseen how much she would come to love him or that Eden would ever want him herself.

So Jamie was Vera's son, as he himself believes, and her fears of losing him arose simply from a false declaration on a birth certificate. Never once, in court or at the time of the murder or beforehand or to Helen or my father when they visited her in the prison, did she admit that Eden had been telling the truth and that Jamie was her son. Never once did Vera weaken over her claim to be Jamie's mother.

But all the same he must have been Eden's. Why, otherwise, would she have left the WRNS when she did, telling no one in the family she had done so, virtually disappearing from the autumn of 1943 until the summer of 1945? Would anyone in her right mind make a false declaration to a registrar, and that declaration a claim to be the unmarried mother of an illegitimate child, to save a sister from a possible future contretemps with her husband? She could not then have foreseen that she would one day want to adopt a child. And a husband, not then in sight, might be involved. She was afraid to take the risk of having an abortion, afraid not to have the child, afraid to lie to the registrar, while clinging to Vera as her lifeline, sister-mother-saviour Vera who had offered to take the baby and bring him up as her own. Jamie was Eden's. She would never have said he was if he wasn't, prudent, hard-headed husband-hunter that she was. Those were the days when men still wanted virgin brides, or the kind of men Eden fancied did. At any rate, they didn't want the mothers of illegitimate children.

So it goes on, round and round in perpetual motion without ever coming to rest on Eden's square or Vera's. During these long past years I have come to know other people's beliefs as to the truth of it. They are all conflicting. Helen is for Eden. Jamie was Eden's son, she says, and believes this as firmly as Jamie himself takes the opposing view. Vera would never have been so afraid of Eden, she asserts, if she were truly Jamie's mother and the doubt rested solely on an error in a birth certificate. Gerald, however, once confided in Helen of his own certainty that Jamie was Vera's, for if he were Eden's and Vera in caring for him was merely doing her sister a service, she would not even have waited to tell him this when he came home, she would have written it to him at once. I wouldn't have guessed him capable of such subtlety in character analysis, but yes, he told Helen, Vera being what she was, she would have been more likely to tell him Jamie was Eden's when he was in fact her own than claim him as her own when he wasn't for the sake of protecting Eden. What she did in fact tell him was – nothing. She refused to speak of Jamie's paternity and this, ultimately, was why he left her.

Francis told Chad (and Chad told Stewart) that he knows Jamie was Eden's child. She came to him in the autumn of 1943, saying she was pregnant and asking for the money for an abortion. He got her the money and gave it to her with the proviso that if she changed her mind he wanted it back. She had told him she knew she must have an abortion but she was terrified of it, she was afraid the abortionist would kill her or so damage her as to make it impossible for her to have children in the future. But he didn't see her again for more than a year and he never got the money back. Chad himself has never doubted Jamie was Vera's for, like me, he came upon her with the baby at her breast. Josie, my mother-in-law, always said Jamie was Vera's on the grounds that during the long hours they spent together when Vera poured out her terrors, she would have admitted he was Eden's and not hers. Yet Tony was convinced Jamie was his wife's child, knew she would never have dared risk losing husband and home by such a confession unless it were true. And Anne Cambus can remember passing Laurel Cottage in the spring of 1944 and seeing Eden emerge for a moment from the front door, that equinoctial wind blowing her dress taut across her swollen body before she fled indoors. But Anne is not quite positive about this memory, she would not swear it was Eden she saw and not Vera, and she and I have wondered if like Jamie she has innocently distorted the past.

We are back from Italy and the usual mountain of post awaits us, as much for me this time as for Louis, for Daniel Stewart has sent me back all the letters and photographs. I postpone opening the three padded bags until next day, until I am alone. But this time there are no tears, only a feeling of rueful nostalgia, of folly and of waste.

Here is Eden's letter of reproach, admonishing my father for my rudeness, and here is Vera telling him of her intention to live in Laurel Cottage and make a home there for Eden. Vera, photographed with Francis on her knee, has a brown dappling on her hair, spots of my father's blood from the finger he cut when wrenching that picture from its frame. Soulful Eden in the photographer's studio in London-derry lies between radiant Eden in her arum-lily wedding-dress and Vera and Gerald with the dome and the banyan tree.

I go upstairs and fetch the box and put them all back, laying in last of all, placing on the top of the pile, the picture of us all in Vera's garden in summertime, a united family, wearing our innocent smiles, not yet imagining those births and marriages and deaths to come.

A Fatal Inversion

For Caroline
and Richard Jefferiss-Jones
with love
from Barbara

The body lay on a small square of carpet in the middle of the gun-room floor. Alec Chipstead looked around for something to put over it. He unhooked a raincoat from one of the pegs and, covering the body, reflected too late that he would never wear that again.

He went outside to see the vet off.

'I'm glad that's all over.'

'Extraordinary how painful these things can be,' said the vet. 'You'll get another dog, I suppose?'

'I expect so. That's really up to Meg.'

The vet nodded. He got into his car, put his head out of the window and asked Alec if he was sure he didn't want the body taken away. Alec said, no, thanks, really, he'd see to all that. He watched the car move off, up the long, sloping lane that in those parts was called a drift, under the overhanging branches of the trees, and disappear round the bend where the pine wood began. The sky was a pale silvery-blue, the trees still green but touched here and there with yellow. September had been a wet month and the lawns that ran gently to meet the wood were green too. On the edge of the grass, where a strip of flower border separated it from the paved drive, lay a rubber ball dented with toothmarks. How long had that been there? Months, probably. It was a long time since Fred had been up to playing with a ball. Alec put it into his pocket. He walked round the house, up the stone steps onto the terrace and in by the french windows.

Meg was sitting in the drawing room, pretending to read *Country Life*.

'He didn't know a thing,' Alec said. 'He just went to sleep.'

'What fools we are.'

'I held him on my lap and he went to sleep and the vet gave him the injection and he – died.'

273

'We couldn't have kept him any longer. Not with that chorea. It was too painful to watch and it must have been hell for him.'

'I know. I suppose if we'd had a family, love – I mean, Fred was just a dog and people go through this with kids. Can you imagine?'

Meg, made sharp-tongued by distress, said, 'I've yet to hear of parents calling in the doctor to put their sick children down.'

Alec didn't say any more. He went back through the house, across the large, finely proportioned hall with its pretty, curved staircase, under the wide arch to the kitchen area and thence to the gun-room. The front kitchen and the back kitchen had been converted into one, lined with the latest in cupboards and gadgets. You wouldn't have imagined, while in there, that the house was two hundred years old. It was the estate agent who had called the place where the freezer lived and where they hung their coats the gun-room. No guns were kept there now. No doubt there had been in the Berelands' time and some old Bereland squire had sat in here in a Windsor chair at a deal table, cleaning them . . .

He twitched the corner of the raincoat and had a last look at the dead beagle. Meg had come up behind him and was standing there. Sentimentally he thought, though did not say aloud, that the white and tan forehead was still at last, would suffer no more brutal spasms.

'His was a good life.'

'Yes. Where are we going to bury him?'

'On the other side of the lake, I thought, in the Little Wood.'

Alec wrapped the body up in his raincoat, wrapped it like a parcel. The raincoat had seen better days but it had come originally from Aquascutum, an expensive shroud. Alec had an obscure feeling that he owed this last sacrifice to Fred, this final tribute.

'I've got a better idea,' Meg said, putting on her anorak. 'The Bereland graveyard. Why the Little Wood when we've already got an animal cemetery? Oh, do let's, Alec. It seems so *right*. It's been a traditional burying place for pets for so long. I'd like Fred to be there, I really would.'

'Why not?'

'I know I'm a fool. I'm a sentimental idiot but I'd sort of like to think of him with those others. With Alexander and Pinto and Blaze. I am a fool, aren't I?'

'That makes two of us,' said Alec.

He went across to the old stable block where they kept the tractor and the wood that was stacked for winter and came back with a wheelbarrow and a couple of spades.

'We'll mark the grave with a wooden plaque, I think. I could make one out of a sycamore log, that's a nice white wood, and you could do the lettering on it.'

'All right. But we'll do that later.' Meg bent to lift up the parcel but recoiled at the last moment, straightening up again and shaking her head. It was Alec who put the dog into the barrow. They set off up the drift.

There were two woods, three if you counted the one below the lake. The lawn in front of the house in which a great black cedar grew ended at the old wood, five or six acres of deciduous trees, and beyond that, as the ground rose, a green ride of turf separated it from the pine wood. This was a plantation, rows of cluster and knob-cone pines, set rather too close together and now forming a dense reafforestation. It was larger than the deciduous wood, nearly twice the size of it, and formed a windbreak between it and the Nunes Road across which, since the uprooting of hedges, gales swept unchecked from the prairie-like fields.

Impenetrable the pine wood seemed to be from the drift and the Nunes Road. But on the southern side an offshoot from the green ride led in between the ranked trees, led in to the centre where it broadened out into a rough circular shape. Here both the Chipsteads had penetrated on one previous occasion, on a Sunday of exploration not long after they bought the house and land. If you have twenty acres of land it takes you a little time to learn exactly what your possession consists of. They had been a little moved by what they saw, gently derisive too, to conceal their sentimentality even from the other.

'This could only be in England,' Meg had said.

This time they knew exactly where they were going and what they would find. They left the drift by the green ride that was rather like a tunnel between the two kinds of wood and which at its distant end showed a little vista of green meadows piled in lozenge shapes, scraps of darker copse, a church tower. Underfoot, where the grass ended, was a slippery floor of pine needles. The air smelt of resin.

Turf covered the circular place, but here it was raised into a dozen or so small hummocks, shallow hills, grassy knolls. The monuments were mostly of wood, oak of course, or it would not have lasted so long, but even some of these had fallen and rotted. The rest were greened with lichen. Among them was the rare stone: a block of slate, a slab of pink granite, a kerb of bright white Iceland spar. On this last was engraved the name Alexander and the dates: 1901–1909.

What writing there might have been on the wooden crosses had been obscured by time and weather. But the inscription on the pink granite remained sharp and clear. Blaze was printed there in roman capitals and under it:

> THEY DO NOT SWEAT AND WHINE ABOUT THEIR CONDITION,
> THEY DO NOT LIE AWAKE IN THE DARK AND WEEP FOR THEIR
> SINS . . .
> NOT ONE IS RESPECTABLE OR UNHAPPY OVER THE WHOLE
> EARTH.

Meg stooped down to look at brush strokes almost obliterated by yellow mould. '"By what eternal streams, Pinto . . ."' she read. '"Gone from us after three short years." Do you think Pinto was a water spaniel?'

'Or a pet otter.' Alec lifted out Fred's shrouded body and laid it on the grass. 'I can remember doing this sort of thing when I was a kid. Only it was a rabbit we were burying. My brother and I had a rabbit funeral.'

'I bet you didn't have a ready-made cemetery.'

'No. It had to be the back of a flower bed.'

'Where shall we put him?'

Alec picked up the spade. 'Over here, I should think. Next to Blaze. It seems the obvious place. I should think Blaze was the last to be buried here, the date's 1957. Presumably succeeding occupants didn't have pets.'

Meg walked round, eyeing the graves, trying to calculate the order in which the plots had been used. It was hard to tell because of the collapse of so many of the wooden monuments, but certainly it seemed as if Blaze had been the last animal laid here, there being two rows of seven hummocks each behind his grave and three hummocks to the left of it.

'Put him on the right side of Blaze,' she said.

Now Alec had begun to dig Meg would have liked to get it over as soon as possible. It was all folly, it was beneath their dignity as middle-aged, presumably intelligent people, it was what children did.

Alec's recounting his pet rabbit's funeral brought this home to her. Why, at one moment she had almost been going to suggest uttering a few farewell words as Fred was laid to rest. They must bury him, they must replace the turf over him, forget all that nonsense about a memorial. White sycamore indeed! Meg seized the other spade and began digging rapidly, turning up the soft, needle-filled leaf mould. Once the turf was penetrated the ground yielded to the spade as easily as the sand on a beach above the water line.

'Easy does it,' Alec said. 'It's Fred we're burying, not a coffin six feet under.'

These were unfortunate words that he was to remember in the days to come with a squeeze of the stomach, a wrinkling of the nose. His spade struck what he thought was a stone, a long flint. He dug round it and cleared the blade-shaped bone. There was an animal buried here already then . . . Something that had a very big ribcage, he thought. He wasn't going to say anything to Meg, but just cover up that ribcage and that collar-bone quickly and start afresh up where she was digging.

Alec was aware of a rook cawing somewhere. Down in the tall limes of the deciduous wood, probably. The thought came unpleasantly to him that rooks were carrion birds. He plunged the spade in once more, slicing into the firm, dry turf. As he did so he saw that Meg was holding out her spade to him. On it lay what looked like the bones, the fan splay of metatarsals, of a very small foot.

'A monkey?' Meg said in a faint, faltering voice.

'It must be.'

'Why hasn't it got a headstone?'

He didn't answer. He dug down, lifting out spade-loads of resin-scented earth. Meg was digging up bones, she had a pile of them.

'We'll put them in a box or something. We'll re-bury them.'

'No,' he said. 'No, we can't do that. Meg . . .?'

'What is it? What's the matter?'

'Look,' he said and he lifted it up to show her. 'That's not a dog's skull, is it? That's not a monkey's?'

The things that had happened at Ecalpemos, Adam resisted thinking about. He dreamed of them, he could not expel them from his unconscious mind, and they also came back to him by association, but he never allowed himself to dwell on them, to operate any random access techniques, or eye for long the mental screen where options appeared. When the process began, when association started an entering procedure – at, for instance, the sound of a Greek or Spanish place-name, the taste of raspberries, the sight of candles out of doors – he had taught himself to touch an escape key, rather like that on the computers he sold.

There had never been, over the years, more than an associative reminder. He had been lucky. On that last day they had all agreed not only never to meet again, that went without saying, but also if a chance encounter should occur, not to seem to notice the other, to pass without recognition. It was a long time since Adam had ceased to speculate as to what had become of them, where their lives had led them. He had made no attempt to follow careers and had had no recourse to the phone book. If asked by an inner inquisitor and required to be honest, he might have said he would have felt most comfortable if he knew they were all dead.

His dreams were another story, a different area. They visited him there. The setting of the dream would always be Ecalpemos where, alone at night or on some hot, still afternoon, entering the walled garden or turning the corner to the back stairs where Zosie had seen the ghosts of Hilbert and of Blaze, he would meet one of them coming towards him. Vivien in her bright-blue dress, it had once been, and at another time Rufus, white-coated and with blood on his hands. After that particular one he had been afraid to go to sleep at night. He had lain awake purposely, for fear of having another dream like that. Soon after that the baby had been born and this had been an excuse for him to have restless, disturbed nights, to resist sleep until he was too tired to dream. It was his misfortune, really, that Abigail was such a good baby and slept seven and eight hours at a stretch.

This not only prevented him from putting forward the excuse of having to stay awake to nurse her but also had its own power to frighten. She slept so peacefully, she was so quiet and still. He had got into the habit of getting up five or six times a night and going into her room to see if she was all right. An anxiety so acute was not natural, Anne said, and he ought to see a psychiatrist if he was going to go on like that. She, the mother, slept dreamlessly, thankfully. Adam did see a psychiatrist and received some therapy which was not much use since it was impossible for him to be open and tell the truth about the past. When he told the therapist he was afraid of going into the room and finding his child dead, he was offered tranquillizers.

Abigail was now six months old and still very much alive, a placid child, large and bland-looking, who at lunchtime on a Thursday in late September took an incurious look at the check-in queue in which she found herself, laid her head back on the pushchair pillow and closed her eyes. A Spanish woman, going home, who had been watching her gave a sentimental sigh, while an American with a backpack, irked by the slowness of the service, opined that Abigail had the right idea. Adam and Anne and Abigail – if they ever had a son they intended to call him Aaron – were on their way to Tenerife with Iberian Airlines, a ten-day holiday carefully planned for when Abigail was too old to be at risk from climatic and environmental changes and young enough still to be dependent on her mother's milk.

Heathrow was densely crowded – when was it not, thought sophisticated Adam, a frequent traveller for his firm – a milling mass of strangely dressed people. You could always tell the seasoned ones, by their jeans and shirts, invulnerable garb, sweaters to roll up and stuff in the overhead locker, from the tyros in smart linen suits and Italian glitter and skin, boots that might have to be sliced open to release swollen feet at the other end.

'I'd prefer window to aisle,' said Adam, handing over their tickets. 'Oh, and non-smoking.'

'Smoking,' said Anne. 'Unless you're going to sit by yourself.'

'All right. Smoking.'

It so happened that there was no room left in smoking, and only aisle seats. Adam put their two big cases, one stuffed with disposable napkins in case these were not easily obtainable in the Canary Islands, onto the weighing machine. He kept his eye on them as they passed through to see that the correct label went on the handles.

Twice last year, going to Stockholm and Frankfurt, his baggage had been mislaid.

'I'd better change Abigail,' Anne said. 'And then we could go straight through and have a coffee in the departure place.'

'I'll have to find a bank first.'

Giggling, Anne pointed to the international sign indicating the mothers' room. 'Why a feeding bottle? Why not a breast?'

Adam nodded, absently acknowledging this. 'You have a coffee and I'll join you.' He had once had a sense of humour but it was all gone now. The dreams and the sub-text of anxiety that underwrote his actions and speech had eroded it. 'And don't have more than one Danish pastry,' he said. 'Having a baby doesn't just make you eat more, you know. It alters the metabolism. You need a whole lot less food to put on weight.' Whether or not this was true he wasn't sure but he had got back at her for wanting to sit in smoking.

Abigail opened her eyes and smiled at him. When she looked at him like that it made him think, with infinite pain and terror, of what losing her would be like, how he would instantly and without a thought kill anyone who harmed her, how gladly and easily he would die for her. But how much harder it is, thought Adam, to live with people than to die for them. The associative process brought another father to mind. Had he felt like that about his child, his baby? And had he recovered by now, did you ever recover? Adam touched the cancelling switch, experienced very briefly a frightening blackness, made his way with an empty mind across the check-in area towards the escalator.

Empty minds are abhorred by thought as vacuums are by nature and Adam's was quickly filled again by the small speculations and stresses which attached to banks and exchange rates. The crowd upstairs was even greater than that below, augmented by two plane-loads, one from Paris and one from Salzburg, which had taken their baggage from adjoining carousels and surged simultaneously through Customs. In the far distance Adam could see the illuminated turquoise-blue sign for Barclays Bank. It was a colour he deeply disliked, had almost an antipathy for, but some interior warning voice always stopped him enquiring of himself why this should be. Only reason, or reasonableness, had stopped him changing his bank on this account. He began battling towards this band of blue light, past ticket desks, apologized perfunctorily for sticking his elbow into the ribs of a woman in Tyrolese hat and *trachtenkleid* – and through a turbulent sea of faces looked into the face of the man he always thought of as the Indian.

His first name was Shiva, for the second god of the Hindu trinity. What his surname was Adam could not remember, though he supposed he must have known it once. The ten years that had gone by had not done much to Shiva's face, unless it was a little more set, carrying within it now the foreshadowing of a gauntness to come, an inborn racial sorrow. The skin was darkly polished, the colour of a horse-chestnut fruit, a conker, the eyes a bluish dark brown, as if the pupils floated in ink-stained water. It was a handsome face, more intensely Caucasian than any Englishman's, the features more Aryan than any Nazi ideal or prototype, sharply cut and over-chiselled except for the mouth, which was full and curved and delicately voluptuous, and was now shyly, hesitantly, parting in the beginnings of a smile.

The eyes of each of them held the other's for no more than a matter of seconds, an instant of time in which Adam felt his own features screw into a scowl, prohibiting, repelling, brought on by terror, while the smile on Shiva's face shrank and cooled and died away. Adam turned his head sharply. He pushed through the crowd, gained a freer space, hastened, almost running. There were too many people for running to be possible. He gained the bank where there was a queue and stood there breathing fast, momentarily closing his eyes, wondering what he would do, what he could possibly do or say, if Shiva were to pursue him, declare himself, *touch* him even. Adam thought he might actually faint or be sick if Shiva were to touch him.

He had come to the bank because it had occurred to him, while bound for Heathrow in a taxi, that though in possession of travellers' cheques and credit cards, he had no actual pesetas in cash. In Tenerife there would be another taxi-driver to pay and at the hotel a porter to tip. Adam turned over to the bank cashier half of what he had in his wallet, two ten-pound notes, and asked, in a voice so cracked that he had to clear his throat and cough to make it audible, for these to be converted into Spanish currency. When his money had been given to him he had to turn round to give way to the next person in the queue, there was no help for it. With a considerable effort of will he forced himself to lift his head and look ahead, down the long length of the arrivals area, at the milling host of travellers. He began to walk back. The crowd had cleared a little, to swell again no doubt in a minute or two when the plane-load arriving from Rome came through. He could make out several dark-skinned people, men and women of African, West Indian and Indian origin. Adam had not always been a racialist but he was one now. He thought how remarkable it was that these people could *afford* to travel about Europe.

'Europe, mark you,' as he had said to Anne when first they got there, and in answer to his scathing comment she had suggested that the black people might have been going home or arriving from lands of their own or ancestral origin. 'This is Terminal Two,' he said. 'You don't go to Jamaica or Calcutta from here.'

'I suppose we should be pleased,' she said. 'It says something for their living standards.'

'Hah,' said Adam.

He started looking for Shiva. His eye lighted on an Indian man who was evidently an airport employee, for he wore overalls and carried some kind of cleaning equipment. Could it have been this man he had previously seen? Or even the sleekly dressed business-man, passing him now, on whose luggage label was the name D. K. Patel? One Indian, Adam thought, looks very much like another. No doubt, to them, one white man looked very like another, but this was an aspect of things Adam felt to be far less significant. The important thing was that it might not have been Shiva he had glimpsed so briefly among the faces of the crowd. It might be that his mind, in general so prudently policed, had been allowed to get a little out of hand, to run amok as a result of the previous night's dreams, of his anxiety over Abigail, of the sight of that baggage label, and had thus become receptive to fears and fancies. Recognition there had seemed to be on the Indian's part but could he, Adam, not have been mistaken there? These people were often ingratiating and a scowl evoked in them a smile of hope, of defensiveness . . .

Shiva would not have smiled at him, Adam now thought, for he would surely have been as anxious to avoid a meeting as he was. They had done different things at Ecalpemos, he and Shiva – indeed all five of them had had different roles to play – but the actions they had taken, the dreadful and irrevocable steps, would have lived equally in the memory of each. Ten years afterwards they were not of a sort to raise a smile. And in some ways it might have been said that Shiva had been closer to the heart and core of it, though only in some ways.

'If I were he,' Adam found himself saying, not quite aloud, though his lips moved, 'I would have gone back to India. Give me half a chance.' He bit his lips to still them. Had Shiva been born here or in Delhi? He could not remember. I won't think of him or any of them, he said inwardly, silently. I will switch off.

How could he hope to enjoy his holiday with something like that on his mind? And he intended to enjoy his holiday. Not least among the blessings it would confer was sharing their bedroom with Abigail, whose cot would be (he would see to that) on his side of their bed so that he could keep his eye on her asleep through the long watches of the night. Now he could see Anne standing waiting for him outside the entrance to the departure halls. She had obeyed him and avoided food but, strangely, this made him feel more irritable towards her. She had taken Abigail out of the pushchair and was holding her in that fashion which is possible to women because they have well-defined hips, the sight of which angered Adam. Abigail sat on Anne's right hip with legs astride, her body snuggled into Anne's arm.

'You were so long,' Anne said, 'we thought you had been kidnapped.'

'Don't put your words into her mouth.'

He hated that. 'We thought,' 'Abigail thinks' – how did *she* know? Of course he had never told Anne anything about Ecalpemos, only that a legacy from a great-uncle had helped set him up in business, put him where he was today. In the days when he was 'in love' with Anne instead of just loving her (as he told himself one inevitably feels towards a wife of three years' standing) he had been tempted to pour it all out. There had been a time, a few weeks, perhaps two months in all, when they had been very close. They seemed to think each other's thoughts and to be shedding into each other's keeping all their secrets.

'What wouldn't you forgive?' she had asked him. They were in bed, in a cottage they had rented in Cornwall for a spring holiday.

'I don't know that it's for me to *forgive* anything, is it? I mean, I wouldn't think things you'd done my business.'

'Heine is supposed to have said on his deathbed, *"Dieu me pardonnera. C'est son métier."'*

283

She had to translate because his French was so bad. 'OK then, let's leave it to God, it's his job. And, Anne, let's not talk about it. Right?'

'There's nothing I wouldn't forgive you,' she said.

He took a deep breath, turned over, looked at the ceiling on which the irregular plaster between the dark, stained beams showed strange patterns and silhouettes, a naked woman with arms upraised, the head of a dog, an island shaped like Crete, long and beaky, a skeleton wing.

'Not – molesting kids?' he said. 'Not kidnap? Not murder?'

She laughed. 'We're talking about things you're *likely* to have done, aren't we?'

A distance yawned between them now so great as to make their relationship a mockery of what it had been during those days, during that time in Cornwall and a bit before and a bit after. If I had told her, he sometimes thought, when opportunity came and held open that door, if I had told her then we would either have parted for good or else moved towards a real marriage. But it was a long time since he had thought like this, since thinking like this was always handled by the escape key. Irritable shades of it crossed his consciousness now. He would have liked to carry Abigail through passport control but she was on Anne's passport and it was in Anne's arms that she sat as the official looked at her and at her name written there, and back again at her and smiled.

If it was Shiva, he thought, at least it was in *arrivals* that he had seen him, not *departures*. That meant Shiva was going home – wherever that might be, some ghetto in the north or east, some white no-go -place – while he was going away. There was therefore no possibility of his encountering Shiva again. And what harm, after all, could come of this chance sighting, if sighting it had been, if Shiva it had been? It was not as if he had seriously believed Shiva to be dead, any more than the rest of them were dead. Nor was it likely that he could hope to pass through life without ever seeing any of them again. Until now there had not been so much as a mention in a newspaper or word-of-mouth news. He had been lucky. He *was* lucky, for sighting Shiva had made no difference to things, had made them neither better than they had been before nor worse. Life would go on as it had been going on with Anne and Abigail, the business on a gradual ascent, their existence steadily upwardly mobile, exchanging their house next year perhaps for a rather better one, conceiving and bringing into being Aaron their son, the associative procedure retrieving Ecalpemos from among the stored files and the escape key banishing it.

Life would go on more or less in tranquillity and time, a day or two in Tenerife, would dim the memory of that brown and shining face glimpsed between pale, anxious, stressful faces. Most probably it had not even been Shiva. In the neighbourhood where Adam lived it happened to him seldom to see any but white people, so naturally he confused one dark-skinned person with another. Wasn't it natural too that whenever he saw an Indian face he should retrieve Shiva from his memory? It had happened before in shops, in post offices. And it hardly mattered anyway, for Shiva was gone now, gone for another ten years . . .

He humped their hand-cases off the baggage scrutiny, passed Anne her handbag, and had recourse to a therapy he sometimes employed for turning away the rage he felt towards her. This was with a false niceness.

'Come on,' he said, 'we've time to get you some perfume in the duty-free.'

— 3 —

Evil was a stupid word. It had the same sort of sense, largely meaningless, amorphous, diffuse, woolly, as applied to 'love'. Everyone had a vague idea of what it meant but none could precisely have defined it. It seemed, in a way, to imply something supernatural. These thoughts had been inspired in her husband's mind by a sentence from a review on the cover of a paperback novel Lili Manjusri had bought at Salzburg airport. 'A brooding cloud of evil,' the commentator had written, 'hovers over this dark and magnificent saga from the first page to the astonishing denouement.' Lili had bought it because it was the only work in English she could find at the bookstall.

Whenever Shiva considered the word he saw in his mind's eye a grinning Mephistopheles with small, curly ram's horns, capering in frock coat. Events in his own past he never thought of as evil but rather as mistaken, immensely regrettable, brought about by fear and greed. Shiva thought most of the folly of the world was brought about by fear and greed and to call this evil, as if it were the result of purposeful calculation and deliberate wrongdoing, was to show ignorance of human psychology. It was in this way that he was thinking when, with Lili by his side and their suitcases on a trolley he would abandon at the tube-station entrance, he looked up and met the eyes of Adam Verne-Smith.

Shiva had no doubt it was Adam he saw. To him Europeans did not specially all look alike. Adam and Rufus Fletcher, for instance, though both white, Caucasian and of more or less Anglo-Saxon-Celtic-Norse-Norman ancestry, were very dissimilar in appearance, Adam being slight and white-skinned with a lot of bushy (now receding) dark hair, while Rufus was burly and fair with curiously sharp, pointed features for so fleshy a man. Shiva had seen Rufus some years before, though he was absolutely certain Rufus had either not seen or not recognized him, while he was equally sure Adam knew perfectly well who he was. He began to smile from exactly the motive Adam had attributed to him, a desire to ingratiate and to defend himself, to turn away wrath. He had been born in England, had never seen India, spoke English as his cradle tongue and had forgotten all the Hindi he had ever learned but he had all the immigrant's protective reactions and all his self-consciousness. Indeed, he had *more*, he thought, since the events at Ecalpemos. Things had got worse since then. There had been a gradual slow decline in his fortunes, his fate, his happiness and his prosperity, or prospect of prosperity.

Adam glared back at him and looked away. Of course he would not want to know me, Shiva thought.

Lili asked him what he was looking at.

'A chap I used to know years ago.' Shiva used words like 'chap' now, and 'kiddy', words used by Indians wanting to sound like true Brits, though he would not have done this once.

'Do you want to go and say hallo to him?'

'Alas and alack, he doesn't want to know me. I am a poor Indian. He is not the kind of bloke who wishes to know his coloured brethren.'

'Don't talk like that,' said Lili.

Shiva smiled sadly and asked why not but he knew he was being unfair to Adam as well as to himself. Had they not all agreed when they left Ecalpemos and went their separate ways that it was to be as if they had never met, known each other, lived together, that in future they must be strangers and more than strangers? Adam, no doubt, adhered to this. So, probably, did Rufus and the girl. There was something, some quality, more fatalistic, more resigned, in Shiva. He might deceive others but he was incapable of deceiving himself, of pretending, of denying thoughts. It would not have occurred to him to attempt forgetfulness by inhibiting memories of Ecalpemos. He remembered it every day.

'It was at that place I told you about that I knew him,' he said to Lili. 'He was one of the group of us there. Well, he was *the* one, it was his place.'

'All the better not to know him then,' said Lili.

She bought their tickets. Adam had been right, and it was in an east London near-ghetto that Shiva lived. Lili tucked the two slips of green cardboard into a fold of her sari. She was only half Indian, her mother being a Viennese woman who had come to England as an au pair and married a doctor from Darjeeling, a surgical registrar in a Bradford hospital. When Lili grew up and the doctor died her mother went home and settled in Salzburg, selling *Glockenturm* beer mugs in a souvenir shop. It was there that they went each summer, in Shiva's holidays, their fares paid by Sabine Schnitzler who, having reverted to her maiden name and largely to her native tongue, sometimes wore a surprised, even bewildered, look at being surrounded, as she put it, by 'all those Indians'. For Lili, whose skin was nearly as white as Adam Verne-Smith's, was more Indian than true Indians, wore the sari, grew her curly brown Austrian hair down to her waist and took language lessons from a Bengali neighbour of theirs. In her voice were hints of the sing-song tone, Welsh in its rhythms, so characteristic of the Indian speaking English. Shiva thought he should be grateful for all this, though he was not. How would he have felt, he sometimes asked himself, if he had married a woman who set herself against his ethnic origins?

He had told Lili about Ecalpemos before they married. It would not have been in his nature, nor would he have been inclined, to do otherwise ... But he had not gone into details, giving only the bare outline, the facts, and Lili had asked few questions. He bore in mind that the time might come when he would have to tell her everything.

'It wasn't your fault,' she had finally said.

'It's true that they never consulted me. If I had given my advice it would have been ignored.'

'Well, then.'

He began haltingly to explain, but stopped himself. He could tell the truth but not all the truth. Openness did not demand that he tell her he had suggested it.

'You should try to forget,' she said.

'I suppose I feel that would be wrong. I ought never to forget about the kiddy.'

And it was perhaps inevitable that he should see the death of his own child, his and Lili's, as retribution, as a just punishment. Yet he was not a Christian, to look at things in this light. He was not really a Hindu either. His parents had neglected this aspect of his upbringing, having largely abandoned their religion but for a few outer forms before he was born. Some lingering race memory remained though, some pervading conviction common to all Orientals, that this life was but one of many on the great wheel of existence and that reincarnation as someone better endowed or worse (in his case surely worse) awaited him. He saw himself returning as a beggar with limbs deliberately deformed, whining for alms on the sea-front at Bombay. The incongruity was that at the same time he was convinced of retribution in this world. He saw the death of his son, a *placenta previa* child who died during Lili's labour, as direct vengeance, though he could not have said who was exacting it.

Crossing the hospital courtyard which divided the maternity wing from the general wards and administration building, hearing over and over in his head the words they had gently but coldly told him, the announcement of his son's death, leaving Lili asleep, carefully sedated, he had lifted his eyes and seen Rufus Fletcher. Rufus was wearing a white coat and had a stethoscope hanging round his neck. He was walking very rapidly, far faster than Shiva was going in the opposite direction, from a building with long windows and white-uniformed men and girls behind them that looked like a lab, towards the main block. He turned his head to look at Shiva, cast on him an indifferent glance, and turned away. Rufus had simply not known who he was, Shiva was sure of that, had not recognized him as one of the other two male members of the little community in which they had all lived in such contiguity for something like two months. Shiva was astonished to find that Rufus had in fact finished his studies and become a doctor. Of course he had known Rufus had this in mind, was three years through his time at medical school, had already considerable knowledge and *nous* – who could forget *that*? – but somehow he had imagined that the same fate would have overtaken the others as had overtaken him, a deathly stultifying, an inhibition on all that was ambitious and of ascendant character, a remorseful withdrawing into the shade. Only if they did not show their faces, only if they kept their heads low and lived in obscure corners, could they hope to pass at least in physical safety through life. So he had thought. But the others evidently had not, or Rufus had not, walking jauntily and with swinging stride across the tarmac, his stethoscope bobbing up and down, letting himself into the main hospital block, Shiva later saw, by a door marked 'Private', which he slammed behind him with a fine disregard for the notices exhorting all to silence.

Lili had had no more babies. Perhaps they would have another child one day. Lili was still under thirty and there was no reason, the hospital staff had said, why such an unfortunate thing as a *placenta previa* should occur again, or if it did, they would be ready for it. Shiva was not too keen. The area in which they lived was over-crowded and insalubrious and if there was rather less unemployment than in the north of England, that was about all that could be said for it.

The name of their street was Fifth Avenue. It is not the custom in English cities to name streets by numbers but it has happened. There are, for instance, no less than fourteen First Avenues in the London area, twelve Second Avenues, nine Third Avenues and three Fourth Avenues. The only other Fifth Avenues are in West Kilburn and Manor Park, both of which also possess a Sixth, while the latter possesses a Seventh. Shiva's Fifth Avenue was a long, curving, treeless street that dipped steeply down and switchbacked up again, though the neighbourhood was not in general a particularly hilly place. At the end nearest the tube station was a block of shops containing a small supermarket run by Pakistanis, a Greek restaurant run by Cypriots, a triple-fronted emporium given over to the sale of motor-cycle spare parts and equipment and a paper shop run by people who when asked where they came from ingenuously replied that they were Cape Coloureds. In the middle of Fifth Avenue, where Pevsner Road crossed it, was another small grocer's and a pub called the Boxer, and at the far end, opposite each other, a unisex hairdresser's and a betting shop. These were linked by belts of houses in infrequently broken blocks, composed of bricks in a dull purplish red or khaki yellow, and all now between ninety-seven and ninety-nine years old. A double line of parked cars ran parallel to the pavements from the paper shop to the pub and the grocer's to the hairdresser's. If you half-closed your eyes and looked at it you might have likened it to a string of coloured beads.

Shiva went into the paper shop. There were two Jamaican boys in there and they made a point of crowding the counter, holding their elbows akimbo, so that Shiva was unable to pick up his paper from the pile in front of them. Quietly he asked for the *Standard* and handed across his money between the jutting arms, he didn't want any trouble. It was the Indians they hated down here, not the whites. Well, there were few whites left except for very old people who couldn't have moved if they had wanted to.

Lili was waiting outside, standing between their cases. She was very brave, he thought, to wear the sari and shop in the Indian shops and have her Bengali lessons when all these things drew attention to her. It would have been easy for her to pass for a white girl. Only her eyes, distinctive dark bluish-brown, with somewhat protuberant, bluish whites, betrayed her. But people were not that perceptive and for God's sake this was London, not Johannesburg in the fifties. She could have got away with it and he had more than once suggested she should, begged her almost. But it was her identity, she said, it was all she had, and she went on putting a caste mark which she had no right to on her forehead and wearing all her gold bracelets and cooking *sag ghosht* and *dal* instead of the defrosted hamburgers and chips which was what most people ate around there. He picked up the cases and she took their hand-cases and they walked home, passing three separate black people who looked at them with silent hostility and two elderly white women who did not look at them at all.

Lili would start unpacking at once. She would put all the light clothes into one bag and all the dark into another and take them to the launderette in Pevsner Road. He knew it would be useless to try and hinder this, she would be fidgety and fretful if there were dirty clothes about. So long as she wasn't out after dark, he supposed it would be all right. Nothing much could happen to her on a sunny

September afternoon between here and the launderette, and Mrs Barakhda who ran it was a friend of hers, or the nearest Lili had to a friend.

He made her a cup of tea while she sorted the washing, closed up the cases and pushed them into the cupboard under the stairs. At least they had a whole house, with three bedrooms. Most of the houses down here were divided into two flats, two front doors squeezed in under the tiny porch. He offered to carry the bags for her but she wouldn't hear of it. In her reactionary way – for Lili had been brought up by an independent feminist mother – she thought it all right for men to carry suitcases but not bags of washing.

With his second cup of tea in front of him, he sat down to look at the newspaper.

There was a big picture of the Princess of Wales visiting a home for handicapped children. The main story was about trouble in the Middle East and a subsidiary one about racial trouble in West London, street fighting mainly and breaking shop windows. Shiva's eye travelled down the page. At the foot of one of the left-hand columns he read a headline. For the amount of text underneath it, a mere paragraph, it was a disproportionately large headline. It even rather spoiled the symmetry of the page.

The headline said: *'Skeleton Found in Woodland Grave'*, and the story beneath it ran: 'While digging a grave for his pet dog a Suffolk landowner, with a home near Hadleigh, unearthed a human skeleton. The remains appear to be those of a young woman. Police declined to comment further at this stage and Mr Alec Chipstead, a chartered surveyor, was not available for questioning.'

Shiva read it twice. It was rather strangely put, he thought. He felt this about most accounts and articles in newspapers. They didn't know much but they told you what they did know in the most cryptic way possible to whet your appetite and make you speculate. For instance, they didn't tell you if the landowner and Mr Alec Chipstead were one and the same person, though you could tell that was what they meant.

He could feel sweat standing on his face, on his upper lip and forehead. Wiping it away with his handkerchief, he closed his eyes, opened them and looked round the room, then back at the newsprint in front of him, as if he might have been dreaming or have imagined it. The paragraph, of course, was still there.

There was no reason, Shiva thought after the first shock had subsided, to suppose any connection between this find and Ecalpemos. Suffolk was the only link and he could remember quite distinctly, on first going to Nunes, how there had been some dispute as to whether it was in Suffolk or Essex. The blurring of boundaries, which took place at about that time, had created such anomalies as a householder having an Essex postal address while paying his rates to Suffolk County Council. This, surely, was what had actually happened to Adam Verne-Smith.

It was not quite true that this was the only connecting link. The other, of course, was the body, the young woman's body. Shiva thought, I must wait for more news, I must bear it and wait.

His patient was getting on for fifty, a handsome, tall woman, very well-dressed. Her expensive clothes – Jasper Conran, he guessed – she had put on again and, while behind the screen, a little more lipstick. He had just done a smear test on her.

'You have a very nice inside,' he told her, smiling.

The nurse smiled too. She could afford to, being twenty years younger and with her gynaecological problems, if any, taken care of by Dr Fletcher for free.

Mrs Strawson said she was very glad to hear it. She looked happy and relaxed. Rufus gave her a cigarette. One of the many aspects of his personality which endeared him to his patients – the others being good looks, charm, youth, boyishness and treating them like equals – was his inability to give up smoking.

'I am that monstrous sinner,' he would say to them, 'the doctor that smokes. Each one of us is said to be worth fifty thousand pounds of advertising per year to the tobacco companies.'

And the patient, especially if she didn't smoke, would feel empathy for him and maternal towards him. Poor boy, with all that stress, he works so hard, it's only natural he needs something to keep him going. Mrs Strawson inhaled gratefully. This was her first visit to Rufus Fletcher in Wimpole Street and she was already delighted to have taken up her friend's recommendation.

'Now how about contraception? Do you mind telling me what method you're using?'

After that implication that she was still in the prime of her fertile years, Mrs Strawson wouldn't have minded telling him anything. An account of an ancient intra-uterine device, implanted twenty years before and never since then disturbed, made them all laugh once more. Rufus, however, suggested he should take a look, just to be on the safe side.

The Jasper Conran dress removed once more, Mrs Strawson got back on the couch. Rufus had a probe around. It was impossible to tell whether the thing she had surprisingly described as being shaped like a Greek alpha was still there or not. His thoughts wandered to the *Standard* which he had folded up and stuffed into the top drawer of his desk when Mrs Strawson was announced. It could not refer to the events of ten years past, of course it couldn't. If it had been *the* house and *the* body it would surely have referred not to digging a woodland grave but to digging in an animal cemetery. They would not have got that wrong. Rufus had forgotten how often he castigated the press for inaccuracy, how he constantly said to Marigold that you couldn't believe a word you read. He told – or, rather, politely asked – Mrs Strawson to get dressed again.

'If we attempted to remove it,' he said to her, 'it would have to be done under anaesthetic. I don't suppose you want that, do you? It's not harming you. Rather the reverse, I should say. It seems to have done you proud. Why not let it continue with the good work?'

He sometimes thought how astonished, how appalled indeed, many of these women would be if they knew that these intra-uterine devices were not in fact contraceptives but abortifacients. Before the IUD could do its work conception must already have taken place, egg and sperm having fused in a fallopian, and the multiplying cells travelled down to the womb to seek a place of anchorage, a home which the alpha-shaped loop by its very presence denied them, causing the minute beginnings of an embryo to swim in vain and ultimately be shed. Rufus did not in the least care about the moral issue, but the subject itself interested him. He had long ago decided never to say a word about it to any of his patients. Marigold, his wife, he would not of course have permitted to give womb-room to such a foreign body or to take the pill or consider any so-called reversible tube-tyings. In his own bed in Mill Hill Rufus used a sheath or practised *coitus interruptus*, which he prided himself on being rather good at.

He said that was all, thank you, to Mrs Strawson, he would let her know the result of the smear, and he walked all the way back to the reception desk with her where her £40 fee was taken from her. They shook hands and Rufus wished her a pleasant journey home to Sevenoaks, she would just be in time to avoid the rush. He was aware of the accusation frequently levelled at doctors of his sort, that they are charming to their private patients who pay them, while treating like so many malfunctioning machines their National Health patients who merely pay the state. He was aware of this and in principle disliked it, attempting when he first set up in private practice, to resist it, but he had not been able to. In this land of two nations he was not big enough to be one of the just. At the hospital with its crowd of out-patients and wards full of in-patients he was so busy, so plagued and hassled and rushed off his feet, and the women so submissive and ignorant or merely sullen, that he forgot about principles. Nor did they speak nicely or carry handbags from Étienne Aigner in which reposed American Express Gold Cards. These two sorts of women seemed to belong to different species, being sisters only under their knickers, whether these came from Janet Reger or the British Home Stores. The treatment Rufus meted out to them was after all, the same. Special care he reserved for his own wife and not for the Mrs Strawsons of this world.

She was his last patient of the day. At this particular time he liked to begin the unwinding process. Whatever shamefaced and boyish confessions he might make to his patients, he controlled his smoking, rationing himself to between ten and fifteen a day. But in the afternoons he always smoked two after the last patient had gone. He sat smoking his cigarettes and reading the evening paper for the half-hour it took to accomplish these combined exercises, before leaving and getting into the tube at Bond Street.

Today this usually pleasurable half-hour was spoilt by the paragraph he had read prior to the arrival of Mrs Strawson. His nurse had brought the paper back from her lunch break and left it lying on the low coffee table during his appointments with his two previous patients. It was because Mrs Strawson was five minutes late — behaviour he made no demur at, though he would have refused to see a National Health patient who failed to turn up on time — that he had picked up the *Standard* and seen that paragraph.

The half-hour was spoilt but Rufus, just the same, was a disciplined man. He had not got where he was at the age of thirty-three by giving way to pointless speculation and neurotic inner enquiry. To have recovered as he had done, so successfully, so brilliantly, after such a traumatic experience, had been a considerable feat. He had subjected himself to his own personal therapy, requiring himself to sit alone in a hospital room and speak of those happenings aloud. He had been therapist and client both, had asked the questions and supplied the answers, aiming at total frankness, keeping nothing back, expressing to those bare walls, that metal table and black-leather swivel chair, that window with its half-drawn, dark-blue blind, the crawling distastes and shames, the self-disgust, the shrinking from light and the fear which seemed sometimes to beat with frenzied wings against bars in his brain.

It had worked – up to a point. This stuff (as he put it to himself) often does work up to a point. The point, though, is on a rather low threshold. Getting it all out and so getting rid of it – well, yes. Nobody tells you how it comes back again. With Rufus it did to some extent come back again and all he could do was grind it down and soldier on. Time, the best of all doctors, though he kills you in the end, had done more than therapy could and now days would pass, weeks, without Rufus thinking of Ecalpemos at all. For quite long periods of time it went away and he forgot it. The associative process did not work with Rufus in quite the same way as it did with his erstwhile friend, Adam Verne-Smith, for Adam was an 'arts' person and he a scientist, so that Greek or Spanish names, for instance, evoked none of it. Ecalpemos, after all, was not Greek and did not even sound so to Rufus who, unlike Adam, had not received a classical education. Nor was he neurotically sensitive about babies. It would hardly have done him much good in his professional life, where women were always wanting to know if they were having them or how to stop them or conceive them, if he had been. He had long ago got the whole business of Ecalpemos under tight control and lived in high hopes of never having to refer to it again in word or thought – and then there had appeared this paragraph.

If the house they referred to, thought Rufus, had been Wyvis Hall, why had they not said so? Or said 'near Nunes' rather than 'near Hadleigh'? The place had certainly been nearer Nunes than

Hadleigh, three miles nearer, though of course Hadleigh was a town and Nunes merely a small village. There were a great many houses in the vicinity of Hadleigh of the same sort of size as Wyvis Hall and a newspaper would be likely to describe anyone who possessed a few acres as a 'landowner'. For all he knew it might not be unusual to unearth human bones in grounds such as these. Possibly they were ancient bones . . .

The only really hard piece of information the *Standard* gave was the name of the present owner of the house: Alec Chipstead. A chartered surveyor, it said. Rufus stubbed out his second cigarette, put the paper into his briefcase and slung over his shoulders the marvellous black leather coat from Beltrami he had bought in Florence, which would have made him look like a gangster if he had not been so fair and ruddy-faced and with such blue, English eyes.

He said good-night to his nurse and to the receptionist and walked off down the street, across Wigmore Street towards Henrietta Place. It occurred to him that he could go into any public library where they kept phone directories for the whole country and look up Alec Chipstead and see if his address was Wyvis Hall. There might well be a public library very near where he was now walking. Rufus told himself now was no time to go hunting for libraries, he would go home first. He would go home and think what to do. He had an idea it was a rule with libraries to stay open late on Thursday evenings.

Deliberately, he switched his thoughts. Library or no library, he would take Marigold out to dinner. Hampstead somewhere, he thought, and then he might take the opportunity to slip into the big library at Swiss Cottage . . . No more of that. Over dinner they would talk about moving house. Rufus thought he was growing out of Mill Hill and it was time to consider a move to Hampstead. Marigold would have preferred Highgate, he knew, but in spite of the therapy and the control he shied away from Highgate. These places were all villages really, you got to know the neighbours, met people at parties and, given that you were a middle-class professional person, there was a limited number of like people it was possible to meet. Suppose he were to encounter the Ryemarks or even Robin Tatian? No, it was unthinkable.

A house in Hampstead would mean taking on an astronomical mortgage, but so what? Take what you want, have what you like, he had read somewhere, and drag your income along behind you. He was doing well, anyway, getting more patients each month, would soon have more than he could comfortably cope with.

The means he used for getting home was the Central Line to Tottenham Court Road and then the Northern Line to Colindale, where he had left his car. Rufus made it into the train before the rush began. Something happened which always pleased him: his wife opened the front door to him just as he was about to put his key in the lock.

Marigold's name suited her. She was tall and generously built and fair, with a high colour and a red mouth and white teeth. In other words, she looked a lot like him. If not twins, they might have been taken for brother and sister. Rufus was one of those people who admire their own kind of looks better than any other sort and whose partners are chosen because they belong in the same type as themselves. Soon after he met Marigold he had taken her to the opera to see *Die Walküre* and afterwards had said without forethought:

'The Brünnhilde was all wrong. She should have looked like you.'

She had made some preparations for their dinner but she didn't object to going out. She never did. It wasn't yet five-thirty, but not too early, in Rufus's opinion, for a drink. He looked forward to this drink, the first of the day, with a sensuous desire. Any white spirit would do for him, he wasn't fussy, and he poured himself a stiff vodka, some of that Polish stuff they had brought back from their Black Sea summer holiday. It flooded his head, charged it with recklessness and brought – he could feel it happening – a warm flush to his face.

'We'll go out and drink a lot and get pissed,' he said.

He gave her his golden ferocious grin. She knew that grin, it meant something had happened, but she wasn't going to ask what. Let him tell her if he liked. There was a lot of underlying violence in Rufus, and not all that underlying either, a lion-like aggression in times of stress that took the form of a whooping, destructive merriment. She didn't mind that, though sometimes she had a prevision that one day, when he was a rheumy old lion and she a worn-out, weary lioness, she might mind it very much.

'Go and put on something beautiful,' he said at seven, after he had had two overt vodkas, and poured, as was his habit, a single, large, secret one, and had taken her to bed.

297

Marigold disappeared into the bathroom. Rufus, sleek with love and ardent spirits, thought with wonder about how he had actually imagined for all of ten minutes that the house they talked about in the *Standard* might be Wyvis Hall. It amused him for a moment to speculate about the others, if they too had seen the paragraph and whether they had been astonished and afraid. The five of them, he repeated their names silently: Adam, himself, Shiva, Vivien and – Zosie.

They would be more discomposed than he. Discomposed, he thought, a word entirely different in meaning (as Adam himself might have pointed out) from its near-homophone, *de*composed. There was no point in dwelling on that. He and Adam had been at the same school, though he was a bit older. From the day they had all parted, diverging from Ecalpermos out into the world, he had never seen Adam again, but he knew all about him, knew for instance that he had become a partner in a company selling computers that called itself Verne-Smith-Duchini. And old man Verne-Smith and his wife, he knew, lived no more than a mile away, but them he avoided out of simple antipathy. What had the Indian's surname been? He had heard it, but not often, it was a strange one and it escaped him. Manresa? No, that was a town in Spain and a street in Chelsea. Malgudi? A place in the novels of R. K. Narayan that Marigold read. Anyway, it was something of that sort. Vivien had been called Goldman, not particularly euphonious or attractive, that. And Zosie? What was Zosie's name?

He got out of bed and put his clothes on, the same clothes but a clean shirt. Marigold was running a bath, stepping into the water. She always made a great splashing. Secrecy was a necessary ingredient of Rufus's life. Even if the things he kept from his wife – had once kept from parents, brother, girlfriends – were very minor, he had to have them, had, if need be, to create them. The photograph was one of these. All these years he had had it and kept it for safety and secrecy's sake inside a boring medical book. Not one of those books on healthy vaginas and wombs which Marigold might easily have looked into but a work on the nasty bacilli which may infest the human reproductive organs after a bungled or septic abortion. Rufus had not looked at the picture for years.

It was still there, though, and looking at it gave him a shock. If it was possible to be surprised by a shock Rufus was surprised. He had thought he could look at a picture of Wyvis Hall, a photograph he had taken himself with a cheap camera Zosie had stolen, with equanimity and even a rueful amusement, but it appeared he could not. It make him feel chilled and sober, as if the love and vodka had never been.

'I will get pissed tonight, by God,' he said aloud. 'And why not?'

The house stood remote, in the middle of nowhere, on the side of a river valley, embowered in trees of many kinds. Woodland, Rufus thought, a woodland grave. It had been built in the late eighteenth century, two storeys high, shallow slate roof, red brick, seven windows set in ashlar along the upper floor, six below and the front door set centrally under a portico and pillared porch. A chimney at each end. Outbuildings, the stable block. In front a broad sweep of gravel, and this side of it, just in the picture, a rolling lawn with a cedar set in it, a huge, black, ungainly tree that lurched like a galleon at sea when the wind blew. To take the photograph he must have stood on the edge of the wood, under the beech hedge which bounded it perhaps. The sun looked very bright, but when had it not been bright that summer?

Rufus found his heart was beating fast. He even considered fetching his sphygmomanometer and taking his blood pressure, simply out of curiosity. Instead he turned the photograph face-downwards. He then picked it up delicately between thumb and forefinger, as if he held something highly vulnerable in tweezers. He opened the medical book, placed the photograph inside the chapter on *Clostridium welchii*, a rod-shaped bacterium which decays the body while it is still alive, and went into his living room. On a window sill, hidden by the curtain hem, was his secret vodka, still half a glass left.

But he was already affected by a euphoria which induced courage and recklessness. His heart had steadied. He wondered why he had considered having recourse to a public library when he had a much simpler means to hand of identifying the house in the newspaper paragraph.

Now that his consciousness was changed, how could he possibly have allowed himself to speculate about its identity, postpone the means of putting his mind at rest and then, ostrich-like, avoid the issue altogether? This was no way to conduct one's life, as he had always maintained. You do not shirk things, was a first principle, you face up to them. One of the reasons why he drank a lot was because it made this possible.

He took a mouthful of the secret vodka, savouring it, carried it to the door, listened. The water was running out. She would be ten minutes. Rufus picked up the phone and dialled 192. Directory enquiries were better about answering these days than they had used to be. Something must have given them a shake-up.

It was a man's voice that said,

'What town?'

It was odd that he hadn't thought about that but immediately it came back to him, the name of the exchange, though Hilbert's phone had been disconnected.

'Colchester,' he said.

Rufus finished his vodka, slid a cigarette out of the packet on the shelf in front of him.

'Chipstead,' he enunicated carefully, and then he spelt it. 'C Charlie, H Harry, I Ivan, P Peter, S Sugar, T Tommy, E Edward, A Adam, D David.'

'A apple,' the voice corrected him.

'OK, A apple,' said Rufus, conscious of his Freudian slip. 'Wyvis Hall, Nunes, Colchester.'

He waited, anticipating the usually annoying rejoinder that they had no subscriber of that name on record. In this case it would possibly be that they had the name of the subscriber but . . .

The operator interrupted this thought.

'The number is six-two-six-two-oh-one-three.'

Rufus put the receiver back, feeling a clutch at his stomach as if a hard hand had made a grab at the muscles.

— 4 —

The picture, very like the one Rufus Fletcher had taken in the summer of 1976, occupied the screen for about fifteen seconds. The whole item was allowed no more than four times that in the BBC's Sunday evening news broadcast at 6.30. The other forty-five seconds were taken up by a policeman talking to a reporter about having nothing to say except that there would be an inquest. But Shiva and

Lili Manjusri saw the picture and so did Rufus Fletcher. Adam Verne-Smith, unwinding in Puerto de la Cruz, did not of course see it. He did not even see an English newspaper. They were expensive to buy and came a day late. He did not want to be reminded of home and the only paper he even glanced at was the *International Herald Tribune*, a copy of which Anne found on the beach.

His father, at home in Edgware, said to his wife:

'Good God, Wyvis Hall, as I live and breathe.'

Beryl Verne-Smith peered, but the picture immediately vanished.

'Yes, I suppose it was.'

The policeman talked, the reporter trying to jog him into revelations and failing. In the background, autumnal trees could be seen and a church on the summit of a low hill. Lewis Verne-Smith sat shaking his head, less as a gesture of denial than of a generalized despair at the state of the world. It was not that unpleasant memories were evoked, for these were always with him, his existence was inseparable from that old bitterness, but that a sight of the house, even the glimpse of a photograph, revived the precise feelings he had had – why, it must be getting on for eleven years ago.

'Ten and a half,' said his wife.

'I shall have to get in touch with the police. No two ways about it, I shall have to get in touch with them.'

'Not this evening, surely?' said Beryl, who wanted to watch *Mastermind*.

Lewis said nothing. The room in which they were sitting underwent the curious shrinking process to which it was subject whenever he was reminded of Wyvis Hall or his Uncle Hilbert or even if the county of Suffolk were mentioned. Suddenly it grew small and poky. The brick side-wall of his neighbour's house seemed to have moved itself four or five feet further towards the dividing fence, so that it loomed offensively. Lewis got up and pulled the curtains across with a pettish jerk of his hands.

'Shouldn't you wait until Adam gets back?' Beryl said.

'Why? What would that be in aid of?'

Beryl meant that Adam had been among the previous owners of Wyvis Hall while her husband had not, but she knew better than to point this out.

'There is no one living knows that lovely place better than I.'

'That's true.'

'I shan't wait till Adam returns,' Lewis said in that manner that had once led his daughter to call him the Frog Footman, 'but I shall wait until tomorrow.'

Men and women do not usually put their baser feelings and intentions into words, not even in the deep recesses of their own minds. So Lewis did not say, even to himself, when he was privately considering trying to get hold of his son in Tenerife, that he disliked Adam and would have been pleased to spoil his holiday. Instead, he rationalized his thoughts and justified himself. Adam probably – indeed, almost certainly – knew nothing about the find in the pine wood, but Adam had once owned the house and had thus taken on a responsibility. He could not shed that responsibility just because he had sold the place. Lewis would have agreed with Oscar Wilde that our past is what we are. We cannot rid ourselves of it. Therefore it was Adam's duty to come home and face the music, even though this might be no more than a short blast on a tin whistle.

But he had no precise idea where Adam was and he did not think Adam's travel agent (a personal friend of the young Verne-Smiths) would tell him. Some excuse would be made for not telling him. Lewis's bark, anyway, was always worse than his bite. He had virtually no bite, as he had once overheard Adam say to Bridget, and heard it with helpless chagrin.

'A bloody good thing or our childhood would have been a misery instead of just a bore.'

Lewis walked into his local police station in Edgware on Monday morning. They seemed surprised to see him but not astonished. The Suffolk police had begun hunting up previous owners of Wyvis Hall and they had been alerted that a Verne-Smith lived in their area. There were, after all, only two in the London phone directory.

This might be a bonus. He was asked to wait and then shown into a room where a detective sergeant prepared to take a statement from him. With busy pomposity Lewis dictated it to a typist and would have gone on and on had he not been diplomatically restrained.

'Wyvis Hall, Nunes, Suffolk, and the twenty acres of land surrounding it were the property, through his marriage, of my uncle, Hilbert Verne-Smith. They came into the possession of my son Hilbert John Adam Verne-Smith under my uncle's will, bypassing myself, though my son was no more than nineteen at the time of my uncle's death. Being an undergraduate at the time, my son naturally never considered actually residing in the house. He was in agreement with my suggestion that the property be sold and before he returned to college in the autumn of 1976, he took my advice and placed house and lands in the hands of an estate agent.

'Country properties were not selling well at the time. £45,000 was the asking price and I was not surprised that the sale, so to speak, hung fire. However, in the spring of 1977 an offer was made, which my son accepted. This sale later fell through and it was not until the following August that Wyvis Hall was finally sold to a Mr and Mrs Langan for the much improved figure of £51,995.

'As far as I know, my son's personal acquaintance with Wyvis Hall was confined to my uncle's lifetime when I, my wife and son and daughter frequently stayed with him. After my uncle's death in April 1976 he visited Wyvis Hall on perhaps two, or at the most three, separate occasions simply for the purpose of looking it over and reaching a decision about the disposal of furniture and effects.

'I suppose it is possible that squatters or other vagrants took possession of the house between the time of my uncle's death and the sale of the property. Certainly my son never let it or allowed anyone to occupy it on either a temporary or permanent basis.

'My son is at present on holiday in Tenerife with his wife and daughter. I cannot say precisely when I expect him to return, though I should suppose in about a week from now.'

It was all very small and quiet and low-key. The snippet in Rufus's Monday morning newspaper measured just an inch in depth. It answered the question he had asked himself and told him that the bones of a very young child had been found as well as those of a young woman. This was not a shock. How could it be otherwise, since this was Wyvis Hall and the pine wood and the animal cemetery?

To photograph the house for the news last night the cameraman must have stood just where he had stood himself, on the edge of the lawn with his back to the cedar tree. A popular mass-produced camera he had used, but quite a good one. One thing about Zosie's pilfering, she never stole rubbish. He had taken a picture of her after that and one of the animal cemetery.

'Why is the grass always so short up here?' Adam had asked.

'Rabbits, I expect.'

'Why can't bloody rabbits come and eat my lawns?'

Adam always referred to 'my lawns', 'my house', 'my furniture'. It had got up Rufus's nose a bit, though Adam had a perfect right to do this. It was his, all of it, and it went to his head rather. Nineteen-year-olds seldom inherit country mansions, after all.

It must have been some time in August when I took those pictures, Rufus thought, and a couple of weeks later it was all over. Coincidentally, as the community and their lives together broke up, so did the weather. It was raining intermittently all the time they were in the cemetery, the pines bowing and shivering in the wind. Sometimes they had had to stop and take shelter under the closely planted trees.

If the weather had held and still been hot and dry would they have dug deeper? Probably not. In spite of the rain, the earth was still as hard as iron. A sheet of rain had come down then, a hard, gusty shower, while they were laying the squares of turf back in place, and Adam had said something about the rain making the grass grow quickly, the rain being on their side.

'We should all go our separate ways as soon as we can,' Rufus had said. 'We should pack up now and go.'

The spade and the fork they had hung up among the other tools in the stables. They had packed and Adam had locked up the house. At some point Rufus himself had taken the things out of the fridge and left the door open to defrost it. Adam closed the front door and stood there for a moment as if he could not wrench himself away.

So much of its beauty had been stripped from it by the whipping winds. And by the neglect of the long hot summer. A sudden gust of rain dashed against the red bricks that were already stained in patches by water. The house that when he first saw it had seemed to float on a raft of golden mist, now lay in a wilderness, amidst ragged grass and straggling bushes and trees dead from the heat. Dirty grey clouds tumbled across the sky above the slate roof, now the only thing that shone, glazed with rain.

But Rufus admitted to himself that the beauties of nature and architecture had never meant much to him. It was the heat and sunshine and privacy he liked. And now he longed only to get away. They all got into Goblander and he drove away up the drift, Adam next to him, the others in the back. The drift had become a tunnel of overgrowth that dripped water onto the roof of the van. None of them allowed their eyes to turn towards the pine wood. At the top they came out into uncompromising, bright grey light, the bleak, hedgeless lane, the flat meadows where here and there stunted trees squatted like old men in cloaks. Adam's simile, not his, thought Rufus with a grimace.

No one asked where he was taking them. No one spoke. Adam had Hilbert's old golf-bag stuck between his legs and Rufus guessed the gun was inside it. They must have gone a good two miles before they met another car. Rufus overtook a bus going to Colchester and dropped the two in the back so that they could catch it. He took Adam on to Sudbury for him to catch a train there and at that point they parted. Adam got down from Goblander and said,

'For ever and for ever, farewell, Rufus.'

Which was probably a quotation from something, though Rufus did not know what and thought fastidiously that it was in bad taste, histrionic, though just like Adam.

'Take care,' said Rufus, and not looking back any more than he had done when they returned from the cemetery, drove off round the town he had got to know so well, over the Stour bridge, into Essex, heading for Halstead and Dunmow and Ongar and London.

He never had seen any of them again. There had been no need to pretend, to turn aside. Briefly, starting his fifth year in medical school something over thirteen months later, he had wondered if Shiva Manjusri would be one of the incoming freshmen. But no, his intuition had been accurate. At any rate Shiva's face was not among the several brown faces. As for the others, avoiding them had presented no problems.

Would they get in touch with him now?

No contingency plans had been made for this eventuality. So long as there was no hunt for a missing girl they had felt themselves reasonably safe. Their minds had not reached out to the terror of what had in fact happened. None of them had been the kind of people who could have imagined devotion to a pet animal or according to it funerary rites. It was Shiva who had proposed the site. They had congratulated him on his ingenuity.

Ten years . . .

An ovarian cyst, nothing to get upset about, Rufus told Ms Beauchamp. She was thirty-two, an editor with a distinguished publishing house, married to an investigative journalist. As yet they had no children, but she wanted four, she told Rufus.

'No reason why you shouldn't.' He had another glance at her notes. 'In fact, a peculiarity about this condition is that it seldom if ever occurs in a woman who's had a baby.'

'My God,' she said, putting her coat on, 'and there was I, making my husband's life a misery, sure I'd got the dreaded C.'

They all thought they'd got the dreaded C, poor things. You couldn't blame them. Rufus took her £40 off her by the reception desk, having set in train the arrangements by which she would be admitted to a fashionable West End clinic, with Rufus, her surgery and her hospitalization ultimately paid for by some provident association to which she and her husband subscribed. Rufus shook hands. He walked back to his consulting room, dying for a cigarette.

This was unlike him. He could usually get through quite easily until after lunch. He thought, I know what my idea of heaven would be, if by heaven we mean a place of bliss in which to pass eternity: a sanctuary where one might chain-smoke without impairment of breathing, destruction of the lungs or damage to the heart, light each fresh cigarette from the glowing butt of its predecessor, and drink ice-free but hundred-proof chilled vodka laced with two drops of angostura and a gill of newly opened Perrier endlessly, with increasing euphoria until a peak of joy and ease was reached but without any subsequent nausea or pain or dehydration or oblivion . . .

Sitting alone, he lit his cigarette, the first of the day, and there came that faint swimming in the head, a tautening of the gut. He closed his eyes. If it comes to light that I was in that house with Adam and the others, he thought with cold clarity, if someone tells the papers, or the police and thence the papers, that I was there during the summer of 1976, living there, it will be all up with me. I will lose my practice and my reputation and everything that I have and can look forward to, if not my liberty. And without the rest I shan't care about my liberty. It would be bad enough if I were a GP or an expert in some other branch of medicine, an orthopaedic surgeon, for instance, or an ear, nose and throat man, but I am a *gynaecologist*, and it is the bones of a young woman and a baby that have been found there . . . What worried woman would come to me? What Mrs Strawson or Ms Beauchamp? What GP would send her to me?

If I were innocent, thought Rufus, I know very well what I would do. I would pick up the phone and phone my solicitor and ask to come and see him and get his advice. He might advise me to make a statement to the police which I should of course do under his guidance. But I shall not do this because I am not innocent. I shall sit here and wait and sweat it out and look the facts in the face, trying to anticipate the worst that can happen.

– 5 –

When he said he did not know the date of Adam's return, Lewis Verne-Smith had not lied to the police. It would have been very unusual for him to have known a fact like that about his son's life and movements. If not exactly estranged, they were not close. Lewis was inclined to say he had 'no time for' Adam. He believed his son disliked him and this he thought outrageous. Sometimes he thought about Adam when he was a child and what a dear little boy he had been, affectionate and not troublesome.

'They undergo a complete change when they grow up,' he said to Beryl. 'Adam, for instance, he might not be the same person.'

He had decided to find out when Adam was coming back and drive to Heathrow and meet the plane. Adam lived as far away from the parental home as was possible while still living in north London. Without saying anything to his wife Lewis drove to Muswell Hill and checked that Adam's car was in its garage. It was. This meant they must have had a hired car to take them to the airport or have gone by tube. Adam's own car was bigger and newer than Lewis's and very clean and well-polished, all of which Lewis disliked.

An obscure feeling that he ought to have a key to this house made him resentful. It was something he found hard to understand, though of course it must be accepted, this escape of children from the parental bonds so that they could have secrets from you and hiding places you couldn't penetrate, that they were adults and possessed houses and cars which you had no hand in choosing or buying, that they could lock up those houses as they locked up their thoughts.

He made his way round the side of the house, peering in at the windows, noting that some dishes, though washed, had been left on the draining board. There were dead flowers in a vase half-full of green water. Lewis held simultaneously two opposing views of his son, one that he was a feckless, idle, good-for-nothing layabout and the other that he was a hard, ruthless, astute and already well-off businessman. When the former view of Adam predominated Lewis felt easier, happier, more justified.

On the way it had occurred to him that he might find the police at Adam's. It would not have surprised him as he walked clockwise round the house to have met a policeman proceeding widdershins. However, there was no one about, not even the neighbours. Lewis stood on the front lawn, looking up at the bedroom windows.

It was a very nice house, bigger than Lewis's own and in a more attractive neighbourhood, a neo-Georgian, double-fronted, detached house, altogether superior to the kind of thing most married men of twenty-nine could afford to live in. Adam could afford it because of the money he got from the sale of Wyvis Hall and later from the sale of the London house he bought with the money from the sale of Wyvis Hall. If things had happened differently he, Lewis, would be living in a house like this or in a flat in central London with a cottage in the country as well. And Adam would have what was proper for someone of his age and standing in the world, a terraced cottage in North Finchley or maybe Crouch End, the first rung on the slow ladder of upward mobility. Lewis thought bitterly that as it was, the only possible next step up for Adam would be Highgate village . . .

He drove home and this time he felt able to phone the travel-agent friend of Adam's without fear of a rebuff. And the man was very pleasant, reminding him that they had met at Adam's wedding. He had no objection to telling him when Adam and Anne were returning: next Tuesday on the Iberian Airlines flight from Tenerife that got in at 1.30 p.m.

After he had rung off Lewis considered informing the police, he thought this might be his duty, but on the other hand he did not want the police actually to be there when Adam arrived. He told his wife (and himself) that he was going to meet Adam in order to break the news gently to him that these awful discoveries had been made at Wyvis Hall and that foul play might have taken place while he, Adam, was actually its owner.

'Aren't you getting things out of proportion?' said Beryl.

'How so?'

'There hasn't been anything said about foul play yet.'

But even as she said this, as Lewis, rather dramatically, told her, the *Standard* was on the streets announcing that the police were treating the case as murder. It was only a few lines, it was tucked away, all very low key, but the word murder was there to be seen and read.

As he set off for the airport Lewis remembered that he had told Adam from the first that only trouble could come from a person of his youth and inexperience inheriting a big house and land of the dimensions of Wyvis Hall. And he was right, for trouble had come, if rather tardily. Ten years it had taken, more than ten years. In some ways it seemed longer than that to Lewis and in others only yesterday. On the other hand, he could not remember a time when it had not been taken for granted the Hall would one day be his own.

The Verne-Smiths were minor gentry. Lewis's grandfather had been a parson in a Suffolk village, with nothing but his stipend to live on, the father of seven children. Two of them had died young, one of Lewis's aunts had married and gone to America, the other two had remained spinsters, living as many unmarried women in the country used to do, in tiny cottages in the middle of a village, busy in a mouse-like way about parochial matters, having no youth, earning nothing, buried alive. The remaining brothers, his father and his Uncle Hilbert, were much younger. His father also took holy orders while Hilbert, practising as a solicitor in Ipswich, took care of himself by marrying a rich woman.

The Berelands were wealthy landowners. If a son or daughter married and no suitable home was in the offing, a house would be made available. Lilian Bereland brought Wyvis Hall with her, not as a grace and favour dwelling to revert to her family on her or her husband's death but hers to do with absolutely as she liked. Of course, in her father's estimation, it was not much of a house, a warren of smallish rooms was how he saw it, and set in a damp situation on the side of a river valley. There was not much sale for that kind of thing at the time of Hilbert's marriage.

The parson and his wife and children used to go there for their holidays. Lewis's father's parish was on the outskirts of Manchester and the vicarage was Victorian-Byzantine-Gothic, soot-blackened yellow bricks with the pseudo-Romanesque windows picked out in red bricks. Black-leaved ilexes grew in the churchyard and a brassy laburnum had flowers on it for one week out of the year. Wyvis Hall was the most beautiful place the seven-year-old Lewis had ever seen and the countryside was glorious. In those days the fields were still small and surrounded by hedges and the lanes ran deep between lush banks. Wild orchids grew in the fens and monk's-hood and hemp agrimony on the borders of the little streams where there were caddis-flies and water-boatmen and dragon-flies in gold velvet or silver armour. Clouded Yellow butterflies abounded and Small Coppers and Blues and once the little boy saw a Purple Emperor. A pair of spotted woodpeckers nested in what was known as the Little Wood below the lake and when the nuts were ripe on the copper cob trees a nuthatch came up quite close to the house.

That house! How differently did it appear to him from the Berelands' assessment! To him it was grand and spacious. In the drawing room a pair of pink marble pillars supported the embrasure of the windows. The staircase curved up prettily to a gallery. There was a library that Uncle Hilbert used as his study and, even more awe-inspiring, a gun-room with stuffed animals and shot-guns on the walls. But the interior meant less – though it was not always to be so – than the grounds, the lake, the woods. The place took on a magical quality for Lewis, who had towards it something of that feeling of the Grand Meaulnes for his lost domain. He used to long for his holidays and grow deeply depressed when they drew to an end. It was a glorious victory when he managed to persuade the grown-ups to let him stay on after his parents had gone back to Manchester.

Aunt Lilian had never had any children, and she died in 1960 when she was only fifty-five. Uncle Hilbert took the loss of his wife very hard and the only company he seemed to want was Lewis's. It was about this time that he started telling Lewis Wyvis Hall would be his one day.

He also informed Lewis's parents, who got into the habit of saying things like, 'when all this is yours', and 'when you come into your property'. Uncle Hilbert, however, was only just sixty, very hale and hearty, still very much in practice as a solicitor, and Lewis could not imagine stepping into his shoes, nor did he in those days think it very nice to anticipate such things. But he went down to Suffolk very often, much more often perhaps than he would have done had Wyvis

Hall been destined to pass back to the Berelands or on to one of those cousins in the United States.

His feeling for the place underwent many changes. In the nature of things meadow, grove and stream no longer appeared to him apparelled in celestial light, the glory and the freshness of a dream. He was growing up. He began to see the grounds as a *possession*, the gardens as something to impress others, the orchard and walled fruit-garden as places that would produce delicious food. Although he intended to live in the house, for at least part of the time, he saw it too as saleable and the value or price of it (however you liked to put it) going up every year. The pines in the wood, where Uncle Hilbert's hunt-terrier Blaze was the last creature laid to rest, he saw as a useful and lucrative crop. He noticed the pieces with which Wyvis Hall was furnished, taking books out of the public library on antiques and porcelain and measuring the remembered articles against illus-trations, catching his breath sometimes at mounting values. Another thing he did was picture himself and his wife in the drawing room receiving dinner guests. The address on his writing paper would simply be: Wyvis Hall, Nunes-by-Ipswich, Suffolk. It was one of Lewis's ambitions to have an address in which the name of the street might be left out without causing inconvenience to the post office. The house and grounds were marked on the Ordnance Survey map for that part of Suffolk and Lewis, when he was feeling low, would get it out and look at it to cheer himself up.

By the 1960s he was married and had two children, a son and a daughter. When his son was born he thought it would be nice, a nice gesture, to name him after Hilbert.

'An old family name,' he told his wife, though this was not true at all, his uncle's being thus christened having been an isolated instance of the use of Hilbert. There had been a fashion in the late nineteenth century for Germanic names and his uncle, born in 1902, had caught the tail end of it.

'I don't like that at all,' his wife had said. 'People will think it's really Gilbert or Albert. I don't want him teased, poor baby.'

'He will be called by his surname at his public school,' said Lewis, who though poor had grand ideas, as befitted the future owner of Wyvis Hall and its acres. So he won, or appeared to win, that battle and the child was christened Hilbert John Adam.

Lewis had written to Uncle Hilbert and told him of his intention to name his son after him, inviting him to be the child's godfather. Declining on the grounds that he no longer had any religious faith, Uncle Hilbert sent a silver christening mug, large enough to hold a pint of beer. But the note that accompanied it made no mention of the choice of name and it was rather a cold note. Later on, when Lewis and his wife and the baby went to stay at Wyvis Hall, Hilbert's only comment on his great-nephew's name was:

'Poor little devil.'

By then, anyway, the baby was always called Adam by everyone.

Lewis, who was no fool, soon saw that in some incomprehensible way he had put his uncle's back up. He set about rectifying matters, attempting to redress the balance. His uncle's birthday was noted, he must always have a Christmas present bought and sent in good time. He was invited to London and all sorts of treats were held out to him as to how he would be entertained on such a visit, trips to the theatre and concerts, a specially organized tour of 'Swinging London', Carnaby Street, the King's Road and so on. Lewis knew very well he should not do this, that he was sucking up to someone for the sake of inheriting his property. But he could not help himself, he could not do otherwise.

Of course he continued to take his family to Wyvis Hall regularly for their summer holidays. He had a daughter as well now whom he had been tempted to call Lilian but had seen the unwisdom of this in time and named her Bridget. His wife would have liked to go to Cornwall sometimes or even to Majorca but Lewis said it was out of the question, they couldn't afford it. Perhaps what he really meant was that they couldn't afford not to go to Nunes. By 1970 you couldn't buy a derelict cottage in the Nunes neighbourhood for less than £4,000 and Wyvis Hall would fetch five times that.

One day, soon after he had retired from his legal practice, Hilbert told Lewis he had made a will that was 'very much to your advantage'. He smiled in a benevolent sort of way when he said this. They were sitting out on the terrace on the low wall of which stood, in pairs, stone figures from classical mythology of a rather embarrassing kind. Under the drawing-room window *Agapanthus africanus*, the blue lily, was in full flower. Hilbert and Lewis and Beryl sat in old-fashioned deck chairs with striped canvas seats. Hilbert leant towards Lewis when he told him about the will and gave him a pat on the knee. Lewis said something about being very grateful.

312

'I finally made up my mind when you named the boy after me,' said Hilbert.

Lewis said more grateful things and about naming his son Hilbert being only proper and suitable under the circumstances.

'*In* the circumstances,' said Hilbert.

He was in the habit of correcting minor errors of grammar or usage. Adam must have got it from him, Lewis sometimes thought, or perhaps (he much later and very bitterly thought) a similar pedantry in Adam was among the things Hilbert liked about him.

Lewis did not like being corrected but he had to take it, and with a smile. It wouldn't go on for ever. The Verne-Smiths were not long livers. Lewis's father had died at sixty and his grandfather at sixty-two. His three aunts were all dead at under seventy. Hilbert would be seventy the following year and Lewis said to his wife that his uncle was beginning to look very frail. He began 'running down' to Suffolk at weekends on his own, and that Christmas he had his wife accompany him for four days, taking all the Christmas food with them. The woman who came in to clean and the old boy who saw to the garden had been instructed to call him 'Mr' Lewis and he felt very much the heir. His uncle hadn't much money, he supposed, but there would be a little, enough to put central heating in, say, and have the place redecorated. Lewis hadn't made up his mind whether to sell Wyvis Hall after he had smartened it up a bit and with the proceeds buy a bigger and better London house and a country cottage or to keep the Hall and sell of some of the land for agriculture. According to his estimate, the result of perusing estate agents' windows in Ipswich and Sudbury, Wyvis Hall by the end of 1972 was worth about £23,000.

It was a continual source of irritation to Lewis that Adam did not show more respect and deference to Hilbert. The boy was offhand and always trying to be clever. He called his great-uncle by his christian name with no prefix and did not jump to his feet when the old man entered the room. Lewis pressed Adam to accompany him on those solicitous weekend visits but Adam nearly always said he was too busy or would be bored. There had in fact only been one occasion during those last years that Lewis could remember and he was sure Adam had only gone because there had been a promise of some shooting. The visit had been far from successful, for Adam had sulked when offered the four-ten, the so-called 'lady's gun'.

Sometimes, since then, Lewis had wondered what would have happened if Adam had obeyed him and been kind and polite to the perverse old man. Would Hilbert have left his property to Bridget perhaps, or even to the Law Society?

It was to be three more years before his uncle died, thus becoming the longest-lived Verne-Smith that anyone had heard of. The daily woman found him dead one morning in the April of 1976. He was lying on the floor outside his bedroom at the top of the back stairs. The cause of death was a cerebral haemorrhage. Adam was nineteen and in his first year at university, though at that time at home for the Easter break. After the cremation, while the few mourners were looking gloomily at the flowers, his uncle's solicitor, a partner in the Ipswich practice, spoke to Lewis simply to say that he believed he already knew the contents of the will. Secure as he thought in possession, Lewis brushed this aside as being an unsuitable subject for discussion at such a time. The solicitor nodded and went on his way.

A week later Adam got a letter saying he was the sole beneficiary under the will of his late great-uncle. There was no money, Hilbert having used all he possessed to purchase himself an annuity, but Wyvis Hall and its contents were Adam's absolutely.

There were traffic jams all along the North Circular Road, a particularly long one at Stonebridge Park and another at Hanger Lane. Lewis, sensibly, had allowed himself a lot of time. Adam would be very surprised to see him. He would probably think something had happened to his mother and that Lewis was there as the bearer of bad news. Of course in a way he was, though not of that kind. For a moment or two, as he waited in the queue behind a container-truck full of German furniture and a self-drive hire removal-van, Lewis returned to speculating as to how and why those bones had got into the animal cemetery. Frankly, he did not suppose Adam had had anything directly to do with this at all. What seemed likely to him was that Adam had allowed some undesirable person or persons access to the place and it was these vagrants or hippies – there had been a lot of hippies still about then – who were responsible.

Adam himself had never shown any interest in Wyvis Hall, as far as he had noticed. That was part of the unfairness of it. He had seen this unlooked-for inheritance simply as a source of lucre.

When the letter came Lewis had nearly opened it himself. The postmark and the old-fashioned and precise direction (Esquire and the name of the house as well as the street number) told him it was from Hilbert's old firm. And he thought he knew what had happened. They had made a mistake, that was all, and sent it to his son. Or else it might be that Hilbert had left Adam some small memento or keepsake . . .

Adam was lying late in bed. Lewis would never forget that if he forgot all the rest. And he, for his part, was feeling so euphoric that instead of shouting to his son to get up and stir his stumps, he had actually gone in there and put the envelope on Adam's bedside table. The awful thing was that all this time Lewis had never any doubts he was himself the new owner of Wyvis Hall.

It must have been a Saturday or else Lewis for some reason or other was on holiday from work. Anyway he was at home that day, home for lunch, and he and Beryl were actually sitting at the table, talking as it happened about going down soon to take a look at the Hall, when Adam came in. He had very long hair at the time and a beard, Lewis remembered, and looked as they all did like some kind of weird prophet. To this day Lewis had a picture in his mind of how his son had looked walking into the dining room (or dining area of the living room really) wearing jeans of course, jeans with ragged hems, and a collarless tunic garment, tie-dyed with coloured inks. Afterwards Lewis wished he had said something scathing, alluding perhaps to the lateness of the hour or Adam's appearance. Well, he had alluded to Adam's appearance but in a genial way. He had been feeling cheerful, God help him!

'Just in time for the locusts and honey!'

Adam said, 'Something rather fantastic; old Hilbert's left me his house.'

'Yes, very funny,' Lewis had said. 'What *has* he left you? His desk? You always said you liked that.'

'No kidding, he's left me his house. Whatsitsname Hall. Unbelievable, isn't it? It was quite a shock. You can see the letter if you like.'

Lewis snatched the letter. He had begun to tremble. There it was in black and white: '. . . the property known as Wyvis Hall at Nunes in the county of Suffolk, the lands pertaining thereto . . .' But it must be a mistake.

'They've mistaken you for me, my boy,' Lewis said grimly.

Adam smiled. 'I doubt that.'

'*You* doubt it? You know nothing about it. Of course Wyvis Hall is mine, it's always been a matter of fact it would be mine. This is a simple mix-up, a confusion of names, though I must say it amounts to criminal carelessness.'

'You could phone them,' said Beryl.

'I shall. I shall phone them immediately I've finished my lunch.'

But he was not able to finish his lunch. He couldn't eat another mouthful. Adam ate. He ate his way through bread and butter and ham and pickles and drank a half-pint of milk. Lewis went out into the hall and phoned Hilbert's solicitors. The one he wanted was still out at lunch. Adam got up from the table and said he thought he might go over to Rufus's.

'You're not going anywhere,' said Lewis. 'I forbid you to leave this house.'

'You what?' said Adam, looking at him and grinning.

Beryl said, 'Just wait a few minutes, Adam, till we've got this cleared up.'

'Why's he getting his knickers in a twist anyway if he's so sure it's a mistake?'

It was not then but ten minutes afterwards, when he had spoken to the solicitor and been assured there was no mistake, that Lewis began to dislike his son. Adam said:

'You can't expect me to be *sorry* he left the place to me and not to you. Obviously, I think he made the right decision.'

'Can't you see what an outrage it is?'

Adam was excited. He wanted to go and tell the Fletcher family his good fortune. Lewis was boiling with rage and misery and shock.

'Can I have the car?' said Adam.

'No, you can't! Now or at any other time, and that's final!'

Lewis soon formulated a plan whereby they could all share Wyvis Hall. It was not ideal, it was not what he had anticipated, far from it, but it was better than abandoning it to Adam. After all, Adam would be back at college in a week's time, the will would have to be proved, but by the middle of the summer why shouldn't he and his wife and Bridget use the Hall regularly at weekends? Adam could have it for his long vacation. He, Lewis, was quite prepared to get the place redecorated at his own expense. It was a family house after all, no doubt Hilbert had intended Adam to share it with the rest of the family. He and Beryl and Bridget could go there at the weekends and they could all be there together for Christmas. What did a boy still at university, with no prospects yet of any sort of career, what did someone like that want with a massive country house?

'I want to sell it,' Adam said. 'I want the money.'

'Sell the land,' said Lewis.

'I don't want to sell the land. It wouldn't fetch much anyway, agricultural land. And who's going to want to buy it?' It was plain that Adam had gone into this aspect of things. 'No, since you ask . . .' Clearly, Adam was only reluctantly willing to share his plans with his parents. 'Since you ask, I'm going to go down and take a look at it as soon as I can and then I'm going to put it on the market.'

Adam returned to college. That summer Lewis thought perhaps he was on the verge of a nervous breakdown. He made all sorts of wild plans. He would go down to Nunes and take over the house. If necessary he would break in and take possession. The village people would support his cause – didn't they call him Mr Lewis? Wasn't he the rightful heir? Adam would never try to regain the house by force. By this time his fantasies took on the air of medieval barons' wars. He actually dreamed of himself in a suit of armour opening the big, oak front door with a mace in his hand and Adam riding up on a black, colourfully caparisoned horse. More practically, he consulted solicitors of his own in an attempt to have the will disputed. They advised him against trying. He had another go at persuasion and wrote Adam long letters to his college begging for compromises. Adam phoned home and asked his mother to stop his father bothering him when he was in the middle of exams. Lewis's doctor put him on tranquillizers and advised him to go away on holiday.

In the middle of June he suddenly gave up. He washed his hands of Adam and Wyvis Hall and the memory of his Uncle Hilbert. The whole thing disgusted him, he told Beryl, it was beneath his notice, only he couldn't help feeling utterly disillusioned with human nature. He wouldn't go to Wyvis Hall now if Adam invited him, if he went down on his bended knees.

His exams over, Adam came home. He slept one night at home and then went down to Nunes, taking Rufus Fletcher with him. Or, rather, being taken by Rufus in whose van they went. Lewis refused to show any interest. He practically ignored Adam for whom he now felt a deep, distasteful antipathy. A few months before, if anyone had told him you could feel dislike for your own child, a real aversion from your own flesh and blood, he would not have believed them. But that was how he felt. He couldn't get Adam out of the house fast enough. Two days later he was back. So much for Wyvis Hall. That was how much Adam appreciated the beautiful old house he had had the unheard-of good fortune to inherit at the age of nineteen. He was going to Greece with Rufus Fletcher and Rufus Fletcher's girlfriend who was an Honourable, the daughter of some titled person.

'You would think someone with her background would know better,' said Lewis.

'Know better than what?' said Adam.

'Well, a single girl staying in places with a man like that.'

Adam laughed.

'How long will you be away?' said Beryl.

'I don't know.' They never did know or if they did they weren't saying. Beryl might have saved her breath. 'Term starts on October 17th.'

'You're never going to be in Greece for four months!'

'I don't know. I might be. Greece is quite big.'

'Staying in tents, I suppose. Sleeping on beaches.' Lewis had forgotten to be indifferent and aloof, he couldn't help it. 'And what about that beautiful old house you've been unaccountably made responsible for? What about that? Is that to be allowed to go to rack and ruin?'

'It's not in ruins,' said Adam, looking him in the eye. 'I don't know what rack means. I've got someone from the village coming in every day to check that no one tries making a nuisance of themselves. Squatters, I mean. There's a lot of squatting going on.'

Lewis had known what he meant. He knew who Adam thought the squatters might be. It was a terrible way to speak to your own father.

Up in the short-term car-park at Terminal Two, Lewis had to drive from floor to floor before he found a slot in which to put the car. He was back in the present now, having exhausted those resentful memories. Adam had gone to Greece the next day and not reappeared until September. Lewis and Beryl, of course, had never gone near Wyvis Hall, they would not have laid themselves open to such humiliation, to the possibility of their way being barred by some yokel, paid by Adam to keep an eye on the place. Where had Adam got the money to pay someone to look in at Wyvis Hall daily?

Lewis asked himself this question as he went down in the lift and crossed the arrivals hall of Terminal Two to await the exodus from Customs. The flight from Tenerife was due in fifteen minutes and he saw that there was a screen on the wall that would show when it landed. People stood about meeting planes, men who seemed to be the drivers of hired cars carrying placards with the names of people or companies printed on them, families waiting for a returning father, a strange old woman in a red cloak, chewing gum. Lewis wondered what visitor from Rome or Amsterdam or the Canaries was going to have the misfortune to stay with her.

Perhaps he should have told the police that there had been someone going into Wyvis Hall every day during those months of summer. Certainly it would not have been a respectable person, such as Hilbert's gardener or cleaner, but most likely some unemployed derelict Adam had met in a pub. This person might easily be the perpetrator of the crime that led to that appalling interment. And by association Adam would be involved in it too. There did not appear to be any police in the crowd. No policemen had been sent to intercept Adam, unless of course they were in plain clothes – those two that looked like businessmen, for instance. They were probably detectives. Who else would be waiting at the arrival barrier at Heathrow at this hour?

Lewis began to feel excited. Suppose Adam were to be arrested before he even reached his father? He imagined himself driving a tearful Anne and Abigail back to Beryl, then finding Adam a good lawyer. Adam would have to admit he had been in the wrong, had been extremely negligent, criminally careless really, in allowing any Tom, Dick and Harry access to Wyvis Hall. He might not wish to reveal names to the police but he would have to. Pressure would be put on him. Eventually, he would come to confess that if his father had inherited the Hall as he had rightfully expected to do, none of this would have happened.

The arrival of flight IB 640 from Tenerife came up on the screen. By this time Lewis was off into a fantasy in which a girl Adam had got pregnant had been abandoned by him with their child at Wyvis Hall where she had later been murdered by a sinister caretaker. The first arrivals were coming out of Customs now: two middle-aged couples, a crowd of kids who looked like students, a family with four children and grandma, a man who looked as if he had been drinking on the plane, his collar undone and his tie hanging. The detectives who were not detectives after all stepped forward to meet him, one of them shaking hands, the other slapping him on the back. A woman came out wheeling a big tartan case and behind her was Adam, pushing cases on a trolley. Anne beside him looking brown and tired, pushing the empty pushcair with Abigail asleep on her shoulder.

Adam's face, when he saw his father, was a study in some unpleasant emotion, not so much anxiety as exasperation.

$$- 6 -$$

The wonderful thing about the human mind, Adam thought, is the way it copes when the worst happens. Beyond that worst happening you think there can be nothing, the unimaginable has taken place, and on the other side is death, destruction, the end. But the worst happens and you reel from it, you stagger, the shock is enormous, and then you begin to recover. You rally, you stand up and face it. *You get used to it.* An hour maybe and you are making contingency plans. For what had happened was not the worst, you realized that. The worst was yet to come, was perhaps always yet to come, never would actually come, because if it did you would know it, that would be reality, and there would be nothing then but to kill yourself. Quickly.

Now that he was able to, he assembled what had happened and laid the facts before himself. They had dug up those bones at Wyvis Hall and had decided it was murder they were investigating. Bones, skeletons, bodies, do not bury themselves. Those were the facts, as far as he knew them up to this moment. He would know more, much more, in the days to come. What was certain was that he could no longer use the escape key. It was defunct. The passages it cancelled had, in any case, as in certain programs, not been lost but stored on some limbo disc from whence they must now be retrieved.

Adam sat in his parents' house, drinking tea. There must be a total retrieval now, the one good thing about which was that it might banish his dreams. He was aware of a slight feeling of sickness and of cold, an absence of hunger, though he had been feeling quite hungry when he got off the plane.

Anne sat next to him on his mother's cretonne-covered settee and Abigail lay on a plaid rug on the floor, kicking with her legs and punching with her arms. His mother kept poking toys which she did not want at her. A passage from a novel by John O'Hara came back to Adam. He had memorized it years ago in the Ecalpemos epoch: 'The safest way to live is first, inherit money, second, be born without taste for liquor, third, have a legitimate job that keeps you busy, fourth, marry a wife who will cooperate in your sexual peculiarities, fifth, join some big church, sixth, don't live too long.' Apart from the last one which he hadn't got to yet and the penultimate one which seemed to apply in America more than here (here he had joined the golf club) he had complied with all the rest. Or his nature and luck had complied for him. Nemesis had still come down like the wolf on the fold.

He had not wanted to come back here. But there had been no spirit in him, the shock of what his father told him had been too great.

'Something that will interest you, Adam, something to make you sit up. They've dug up a lot of human bones at my old uncle's house . . .'

By the time he had rallied and got himself together and was thinking of things to say to the police it was too late and they were heading north. Anne was furious. When Lewis said to come back with him and eat there Adam had got a kick on the ankle from Anne and another kick when he hadn't replied.

He had turned on her and said with cold savagery, 'For fuck's sake, stop kicking me, will you?'

He expected his father to rise and say something about that being no way to speak to one's wife or not in front of the child, he was capable of that. But he had said nothing, only looked subdued, and Adam realized why. His own terrible fear and anger had communicated itself to his father and shown him what the better part of valour was: keeping silent. Having put the cat among the pigeons, made mischief in his special way, he was lying low now and waiting. The old bastard. Adam only wished Uncle Hilbert *had* left him Wyvis Hall and then there would have been no Ecalpemos, no Zosie, and no deaths. And Adam couldn't see he would have been much worse off. He and Anne would be living in a house like this one, rather than that neo-Georgian palace. Children, after all, he thought, looking at Abigail, were happy wherever they were, so long as they were loved . . .

His parents had not asked him what sort of holiday he had had or how the flight had been. The conversation was exclusively on the subject of the discovery at Wyvis Hall. Adam did not know whether to be glad or sorry he had not obtained an English newspaper while away. If he had done the shock would have been less but on the other hand, his holiday would have been spoilt. He would have liked very much to be alone. Of course he knew there was no possibility of this, now or when he returned home, for when you were married you never could be alone. Presumably that was the point. What was he going to tell Anne? How much was he going to tell her? He didn't know. None of it, if he could help it.

They sat at the table in the dining area to eat an absurdly early high tea. Lewis asked him if he could remember the day when he heard he had inherited Wyvis Hall and had walked in here and astounded them with his news.

'He had a beard then, Anne.' Lewis's subdued air had changed to one of high good humour. 'You wouldn't have recognized him, he looked like John the Baptist.'

Adam could remember very well but he wasn't going to say so.

'What a funny thing,' said Lewis. 'We had ham salad that day too. What a coincidence! Oh, yes, I've been meaning to ask you, who was it looked after Wyvis Hall while you were in Greece?'

Adam could eat nothing. The other time, he remembered, it was his father who hadn't been able to eat. He didn't know what Lewis meant about someone looking after the house but no doubt he, Adam, had at the time concocted some tale to keep his father quiet, to keep him away even.

'Someone from the village, you said,' Lewis persisted.

'How can I remember that far back?'

'The police will want to know. It may be of vital importance.'

'Aren't you going to eat your meat, dear?' said Beryl.

Abigail, who had been put upstairs in one of the bedrooms to sleep, set up a wailing sound. Adam was on his feet at once.

'I think we should go.'

They had to wait until his father was ready. Adam would have preferred to phone for a hire car but Lewis wouldn't hear of it. Anne sat in the front in the passenger seat while Adam was in the back with Abigail. If his father could have found out what flight they were coming on, the police certainly could. It was possible they might be waiting for him. They would wish to interview every former owner or occupant of Wyvis Hall. He looked again at the newspaper account of the adjourned inquest that his father had saved for him. It would be owners and occupants of Wyvis Hall between nine and twelve years before that they would wish to interview, and those were Great-Uncle Hilbert, who was dead, himself and Ivan Langan to whom he had sold the house. As for other occupants, how would they know who else had lived there?

It was ironical that ten days before he had seen Shiva at Heathrow. The encounter he now saw as an omen, a shadow cast by a coming event. What would that event be? Adam did not want at this point to speculate, it made him feel sick. He turned the newspaper over so that he could not see that headline and those paragraphs. In high spirits, his father was talking about the immense advances made in forensic science in recent years.

As soon as they got home, Anne started getting Abigail to bed. Their cases humped upstairs and put into the bedroom, Adam looked Rufus Fletcher up in the phone book. He was in there twice, at a Wimpole Street number and again at an address in Mill Hill: Rufus H. Fletcher, MB, MRCP. All these years then, or for some of them, Rufus had been living three or four miles from him. He couldn't look Shiva up because he couldn't remember his surname. Women marry and change their names, he thought, there was no point in pursuing that one. Of course he could look up Robin Tatian but where, really, would that get him? He was reaching for the blue directory when Anne came back with Abigail in her arms, so Adam took her and carried her back to bed himself and tucked her in and kissed her. She was almost asleep. He wondered if Rufus had children and if so did he worry about them coming to terrible harm the way Adam worried? Was his whole life affected by what had happened at Ecalpemos? Adam might have escaped the file memories for years, suppressed them and jerked violently away from them, but he had never been able to pretend he was unscathed by those events. Sometimes he felt that he was the person he was because of them and acted the way he did because of their effects.

He sat by Abigail's cot, not wanting to remember, but knowing that now he must. There was nothing in his house to remind him of Ecalpemos. Everything that was left, everything he and Rufus hadn't sold, had gone to Ivan Langan with the house. For a song, too, because he had not been able to bear the thought of going back, meeting a valuer, walking about the house, picking things off shelves and out of cupboards. Only once had he returned after they all left and that had been bad enough, like a dream – no, like stepping into the set and scenario of some frightening film, a Hitchcock movie perhaps. He asked the taxi he had taken to put him down at the top of the drift and he had walked to the house. It was almost a year since he had been there and in that time nothing had been done, nothing had been touched. From the pine wood he simply averted his eyes – till later.

The drift was thickly overgrown, a dank tunnel out of whose bushy sides the tendrils of brambles and briar roses caught at his clothes. One of these whipped back at him and as he caught at it a thorn drove into the fleshy pad of his finger. That thorn had been there, festering, for months. A dull cool summer it had been, as different as could be from the year before. No golden light bathed the red brick of the house. It no longer looked mellow. Beautiful, yes, but severe somehow and, to Adam's heightened awareness, reproachful. He found himself encouraging, fostering, the scenario illusion. Only thus, only by pretending unreality, pretending this was a part he acted, could he go on, cross the wild, shaggy grass, go past the black-branched cedar tree, arrive at the porch set in its four Doric columns and insert his key in the lock.

In the film there would have been something terrible awaiting him. A dead thing hanging in a noose over the stairs. There was nothing of course, only a faint smell compounded of dust and dry mould. Ecalpemos. He no longer called it that. It was Wyvis Hall once more, his house, but bringing him no pleasure, no deep, excited, almost sick joy. He breathed deeply, walked through the rooms, went upstairs, being the actor in the film. In a few moments the other participant in the sequence they were shooting would come, the estate agent from Sudbury.

While they had been there the previous year there had been hardly any visitors. It was as if the magic house in the wood had had an invisible fence set around it or – what did they call it? – a shutting spell. The clear air, Constable's unique Suffolk light, had in fact been impenetrable, a barrier that held off intruders as a sheet of glass might have. This was all fantasy, of course, for one or two people had come, Evans or Owens from Hadleigh, the coypu man, a meter reader, the man who wanted to do the garden and whom he had turned away with a lie. But for the most part they had been undisturbed in their magic island or resort that was closed to others but which they could leave when they pleased. Coming and going – there had been too much of that. Things would have been very different if they had stayed put.

The doorbell rang. It made him jump – inevitably. But it was just a bell that rang, it did not buzz or chime. He let in the estate agent and took him over the house, into the drawing room and the dining room, upstairs to the Pincushion Room, the Centaur Room, the Room of Astonishment, the Deathbed Room, the Room Without a Name, and then back down the back stairs to that jumble of kitchens and scullery and washhouse and coal-store, most of it a nineteenth-century addition. What a lot of this sort of thing the Victorians had needed!

It was all quite tidy and clean, as Vivien had left it. But he could not say Vivien's name then, he could not even think it, only look about him fearfully, clenching his hands.

He opened the door to the gun-room and showed the estate agent the interior. There was a table in there and a Windsor chair. The floor was of black and red quarry tiles and there were racks on the walls for the guns but these, of course, had gone, Hilbert's two shot-guns had gone, one buried in the Little Wood, the other in his bedroom at home in Edgware, zipped up in an old golf-bag under the bed.

The estate agent suggested an asking price and took some measurements and then a photograph, standing on the edge of the lawn that had become a meadow, where Rufus had stood and taken photographs a year before. It was windy and the cedar, which he had likened to a galleon and Zosie to a witch, danced witch-like, its branches arms and leaping legs and flying skirts.

The car went off up the drift as many times Goblander had gone. Adam had given his only key to the estate agent. He closed the front door behind him and started to walk. He had forgotten all about arranging for a taxi to pick him up or looking up bus times or anything like that. Presumably, the estate agent would have given him a lift somewhere. It was too late now. Cold water drops fell on his head from the leafy roof of the tunnel. In the deciduous wood a pheasant uttered its rattling call. He emptied his mind, he walked like an automaton up onto the green ride, seeing at the end of it the cameo of stacked meadows, segments of wood, a church tower. He was holding his breath.

His head he was keeping averted, looking in the direction of the drift, at the wall of cluster pines with their black needles and their green cones. He knew the distance from the ride, thirty paces. When he turned his head he kept his eyes closed, let out his breath, opened his eyes, looked and heard himself give a little whimpering sigh. It was the sound a man might make when in physical pain but trying not to show it, suppressing complaint.

There was nothing to see, nothing to show. The place was as it had always been, a downland in miniature, a terrain of small green hills on which little dolmens had been raised, pink granite, white marble, a slab or two of grey stone. Wooden crosses. 'By what eternal streams, Pinto . . .' Each in their narrow cells for ever laid were Alexander, Sal, Monty, Ranger, Blaze. And to the right of Blaze the green turf lay undisturbed, very slightly irregular, as the whole area was, a reticulation of tiny-leaved plants, minuscule flowers, netted into the grass, a small pit here filled with pine needles, a shallow rut there with a sandy bottom. Rabbits had mown the lawn here more effectively than any piece of machinery. Their droppings lay about like scattered handfuls of raisins.

Adam found he was holding both hands clamped over his mouth. He turned and ran, along the ride, up the drift, not looking back.

Anne, waiting downstairs for him with coffee and sandwiches on a tray, wanted to talk about the find at Wyvis Hall. He found himself unexpectedly touched by her simple assumption, the way she absolutely took it for granted, that he was innocent. Adam didn't want anything to eat. He was thinking of Hilbert's shot-gun that he still had but which he should perhaps not keep much longer.

'You've never told me any of this,' Anne began. 'When you got the solicitor's letter saying you'd inherited the place it must have come as a terrific shock. I mean, didn't you have a clue?'

'I thought my father would come in for it. Everyone did.'

'Why do you think he left it to you like that?'

'Not because he liked me. He hardly took any notice of me. He didn't like children and when I got older I stopped going. I hadn't been near the place for four years. My parents went.'

'Then I just don't understand.'

'Look, he was an unpleasant old man.' Adam looked hard at her. 'My father is an unpleasant old man and I daresay I shall be. Verne-Smiths are.' She didn't say anything. 'I think it happened this way. He saw through the toadying, of course he did. My father was just a blatant sycophant. He thought to himself, right, you've called the boy Hilbert to please me, to make me like him, so I damn well will like him, I'll like him more than you and leave him the place over your head.'

'Do people really behave like that?'

'Some do.' Adam thought. 'Frankly, if it were me, I would. I might.'

'Do you want some more coffee? No? I suppose you whizzed straight down there and had a look at your property?'

'No, I didn't as a matter of fact. I hadn't time, I had to go back to university. Anyway, I was going to sell it, I wasn't all starry-eyed about my lovely house, you know.'

That was just what he had been. Once, that is, he had seen it again after a four-year absence. But he had not guessed he would be and had postponed his visit till term ended in June. All that term his father had been planning ways and means, trying to overturn the will, looking for compromises, plotting for all Adam knew a frontal assault. What he did not know he had got from his sister, his ally against their parents if in nothing else.

'You'd been there for your holidays as a little boy? Did you love it then?'

'I don't think so. I can't remember. I think I'd have preferred the seaside. Kids do.'

'And did they show you the animal cemetery when you were a child?' Anne persisted.

'I suppose so. I can't remember. Do we have to talk about it?'

In fact, he couldn't remember ever having heard of it until the day Shiva came in and told them what he had found. Vivien thought it was *children* buried there. Adam shivered as he remembered that. Well, with her bent towards Indian mysticism she wouldn't be able to understand the way they went on about animals. Adam had a sudden awful vision of the spade going through that green turf and coming up with a skull on it. Something like that, it must have been like that.

Was the shot still there, among the bones?

Later he lay in bed beside Anne, trying to think of a satisfactory yet thoroughly non-committal story to tell the police. Like most middle-class English people who have never had anything to do with them, Adam thought the police were fools. Anne had fallen asleep almost immediately. She had a habit, when she slept on her back, of making soft sounds in her throat. This was not snoring but a kind of clicking, irregular and sporadic – that was what made it irritating – and liable to start when least expected. Adam had only heard one other make these sounds and when he first heard Anne make them his memory escape failed and those two nights were startlingly evoked, so disturbingly in fact that he had the terrible delusion that Anne was doing it to mock him. Of course that was nonsense. She had never heard of Catherine Ryemark and never would if he had his way.

Several minutes might pass without a click and then one would come and another would come and another one fifteen seconds after that. It drove Adam mad. Once, in a fit of temper, he had told her she only started doing it after they were married. If he had heard her do that in their single days he would never have married her. But now, the soft clicks coming with typical irregularity, he listened to them painfully and let his mind slide back ten years to what he must remember, to the truth he must recall if he were going to be able to tell lies. He lay still with his eyes open, staring into the darkness that was only half-darkness because this was London and not Suffolk, where on moonless nights the small hours were black as velvet. Click, pause, click, a long silence. At last it had been cold enough to need a blanket and a quilt, to hold Zosie in his arms without the sweat pouring off them both. For a long time that night too he had not slept, had lain thinking, wondering what to do, listening to the delicate sounds like tiny bubbles breaking – and then hearing them no more.

Adam closed his eyes and turned his head away from Anne. A down-stuffed duvet in a printed-cotton cover lay over them. It had been a quilt at Ecalpemos, faded yellow satin, brought in by Vivien from the terrace when the rain began. Quilts were what you lay on to sunbathe that summer, not for warmth on beds, but slung for lounging comfort as it might be on some Damascus rooftop. Night after night they had lain out there in the soft, scented warmth, looking at the stars, or lighting candles stuck in Rufus's wine bottles, eating and drinking, talking, hoping and happy. That summer – there had never been another like it, before or since.

It was the hottest, driest summer any of them had ever known. The previous one, 1975, had been very good, especially the latter part, but that one, the summer of Hilbert's death and of Ecalpemos, had been glorious from April till September. If it had been grey and raining and chilly he might have taken one look at Wyvis Hall and turned tail and fled to Crete or Delos or somewhere. Certainly he would have gone down there alone to spy out the land and check on his property. Rufus wouldn't have wanted to go and he would have had to go down on his own by train.

There were so many ifs and conditions, so many other eventualities that easily might have happened. In the first place he had only approached Rufus because Rufus had a car. If his father hadn't been so bloody-minded and had let him use the family car, he would no doubt have gone down alone and come back next day, having called on some estate agent in Hadleigh or Sudbury and asked them to sell the house for him, the very one probably that he had gone to in the following year.

But things had not gone that way. It had been a glorious sunny day and he had wakened up in the morning rather early for him in those days. About nine. His father was on holiday, though he and his mother were not going away anywhere, in spite of what the doctor had advised, but staying at home and 'going out for days'. Or that was what they said. They hadn't been out for any days since Adam had been at home.

18 June it was, a Friday. The date was stamped indelibly on his memory calendar, more than just stamped, etched in. He thought he would get up and go to Suffolk and take a look at his house. His generation – perhaps all generations at that age – hated making plans, making arrangements ahead. Adam had viewed with near-incredulity his mother's preparations in the past for going on holiday, the way everything in the house seemed to get washed, the way she and his

father wore their worst clothes for days beforehand because the best ones were packed, the phone calls she made, the notes she left for tradesmen. He liked to do things spontaneously, be up and off on the spur of the moment.

His father wouldn't let him have the car. It might be needed if they went out for the day. Adam said all right, not to worry, he would manage without, but this didn't seem to please Lewis either. He would have liked, Adam knew, to have lived in a time when a father could forbid his son to do things and the son would obey. Or rather, to have the rules of that former period prevailing now. Adam didn't say where he planned to go, though he thought his father guessed, but got on his bicycle and cycled over to Rufus's.

He couldn't remember what he had done with his bike when he got to the Fletchers', left it there and collected it next day perhaps, but he could remember most of the rest of it. What he had worn, for instance. Jeans cut off thigh-high to make shorts and a T-shirt he had made out of an old man's vest he had bought for 20p in a sale under the arches at Charing Cross Station and dyed green and yellow. His hair was tied back with a piece of tinsel string he had found in the Christmas decorations box. Those were the days before people dyed their hair bright colours, the days of henna. Adam had put henna on his hair and that and the sun had turned it reddish-gold. His beard, though, was black and rather curly. He must have looked a sight but he didn't think so then. His legs were bare and he was wearing Indian leather sandals, the kind you had to soak in water before you first put them on. It showed what the weather was and how they had started taking daily sunshine for granted that he hadn't got any sort of jacket or sweater with him even though he expected to be away overnight.

The Fletchers had a swimming pool. It was supposed to be a teardrop shape or shaped like a comma. This summer was the first anyone had made much use of the pool. Rufus was sitting on the blue-tiled rim of it with his feet dangling in the water. He was three years older than Adam and though they had been at the same school, Highgate, they had not been friends then. It was Rufus's younger brother Julius who had been in the same form as Adam, a rather dull, pompous boy, a sort of phoney intellectual, and they had never had much to do with one another. Adam and Rufus had met as members of the same squash club.

That was what they seemed to have in common, that and Rufus's brother and Adam knowing each other already, but after a while Adam got to see things he admired in Rufus, his toughness, the way he'd got himself organized and in hand, the way he knew where he was going and yet still could be amusing and casual. Of course he had got to know him a good deal better at Ecalpemos . . .

Rufus was very laid-back and Adam liked that. He also liked Rufus's occasional sensitivity, which didn't seem to go with the other aspects of his personality. And Rufus was wild too, the way medical students had a reputation for being. Adam thought of himself and Rufus as being wild and laid-back at the same time, equally like that, young adventurers with all the world before them and all the time they wanted to do what they liked with.

Rufus said, Hi, and come for a swim, so Adam took off his shorts and went into the water in his black nylon underpants. They would have swum naked only Rufus's father had discovered them doing this and made a fuss out of all proportion to the offence, if offence it was.

'I reckoned I might go and take a look at my inheritance,' Adam said, checking that the key to Wyvis Hall was safe in the pocket of his shorts.

'Now, d'you mean?'

'Yes. I guess so. Why not?'

'Want me to drive you?'

Rufus had an old Morris Minor van that he had bought third- or fourth-hand, but it went all right. It got you from A to B in one piece, as Adam's father remarked sneeringly of it.

That had been well before the motorway, the M25, was built. You went to Suffolk by the A12 through Chelmsford or took the country route. This was what Lewis had always called the route that went by narrower, winding roads through Ongar and Dunmow, Braintree and Halstead to Sudbury, and that was the way he had driven them when they all went out to visit old Hilbert. Adam did for Rufus what Lewis would have called 'navigating'. It maddened Adam, his misuse of this word, which couldn't of course be applied to guiding anyone on land, coming as it did from the Latin *navigare* and thence from *navis*, feminine, a ship, and *agere*, to drive or guide. Adam loved words, was fascinated by them, their meanings and what you could do with them, with anagrams and palindromes and rhetorical terms and etymology. One of the subjects in the mixed BA course he was doing at university was linguistics ... 'Directing' Rufus was what he was doing, he told himself. They had talked about words during that drive, well, place-names really, with particular reference to the villages that were called Roding after the river: High Roding, Berners Roding, Margaret Roding, and Rufus told him they were pronounced Roothing from the old Danish, which Adam hadn't known before.

It was a beautiful drive and the countryside looked wonderful, a kind of sparkling shimmering green in the heat and sunshine. The sky was huge, a pale, bright, cloudless blue, and the white surface of the road ahead rippled in the heat mirages that made it look like little waves. The farmers were hay-making, cutting the tall feathery grass and its dense admixture of wild flowers. The windows of the van were wide open and they had the radio on, not playing rock, which they both hated, but Mozart, one of the better known of the piano concertos.

In spite of all the times he had been there Adam missed the turn-off that was the drift leading down to Wyvis Hall. It was somewhere along the lane between Nunes and Hadleigh but so much vegetation had grown up that spring that everything looked different. They drove about a mile further, right up to the group of buildings called the Mill in the Pytle, and Rufus, turning the van round, asked what a pytle was. Adam said he would look it up. He told Rufus to drive a bit more slowly and this time he spotted the six-foot-wide gap in the hedge with, on the right-hand side, almost hidden by cow parsley growing up and elderflowers hanging down, the wooden box on legs with its hinged lid into which Hilbert's mail and newspapers and milk had been delivered. As a little boy, Adam had sometimes been sent up here in the morning to fetch the letters and the paper, carrying with him a wicker bottle-basket for the milk. There was no other sign that this was Wyvis Hall.

'Why's it called a drift?' said Rufus, lighting another cigarette. He had chain-smoked all the way down and Adam had had one or two to keep him company, though he didn't really like putting something lighted in his mouth. That was the trouble for him with dope. He liked the effects of it but didn't like having to smoke it.

'I don't know,' he said. 'I don't know why it's called a drift.'

'You can look it up when you look up "pytle",' said Rufus.

On either side the drift was thick with cow parsley, its powdery white heads coming to an end of their long blooming. It had a sweetish scent, like icing sugar, like childhood birthday cakes, that mingled with the winey perfume of the elders. All the trees were in full leaf but the oaks and beeches had not long so been, so that their foliage was still a fresh, bright colour and the lime trees were hung with pale, yellow-green, dangling flowers. The pine wood looked just the same as ever, it always did, it was always dark and dense with very narrow passages through it that would surely allow nothing bigger than a fox to weave its way through. Imperceptibly the trees must have grown, yet they seemed to Adam no different from when he was a child coming up to fetch the milk and when, on sunless mornings, he had felt a kind of menace from the wood. Even then he had not liked to look into it too much but had kept his eyes on the ground or straight ahead of him because the wood was the kind of place you saw in story-book illustrations or even in your dreams and out of which things were liable to come creeping.

At the foot of the slope, through the thinning trees, a field maple, alders with their feet in the stream, a late-blooming chestnut, that dramatic lawn-adornment, the cedar, the house came into view. Things, buildings, stretches of land, are said to look smaller when we grow up. And this seems only natural, just what one would expect. After all, the top of the table that was once on a line with our chin now reaches only to our thighs. Wyvis Hall, logically, should have looked smaller to Adam but it did not, it looked much larger. This must have been because it was his now, he owned it. It was his and it seemed a palace.

On the stable block, in which nothing had ever been stabled in Adam's memory, was a little tower with a running fox weathervane on it and below the small pitched roof a blue clock with hands of gold. The hands had stopped at five to four. Between the block and the house you could just see the walls of the walled garden, flint-built, crossed and coped with brickwork. A mass of flowers covered the house, a pink climbing rose and a creamy clematis. Adam had not known these names, but later on Mary Gage had told him. Because the sun shone so brightly the slate roof blazed like a slab of silver.

Rufus pulled up in front of the porch. The whole area out here was paved and small stonecrops and sedums with white and yellow starry flowers grew up between the stones. In a couple of narrow-mouthed stone vessels grew a conifer and a bay tree. The rose which mantled the house must have put out a thousand flowers and these were at the peak of their blooming, not a petal yet shed, each blossom the pink of a shell within and the pink of coral on its outer side. Adam got out of the van and felt in the pocket of his shorts for the key. He was aware of a profoundly warm, placid, peaceful silence as if the house were a happy animal asleep in the sun.

'And this is all yours?' said Rufus.

'All mine.' Adam was equally cool.

'I should be so lucky in my avuncular arrangements.'

Adam unlocked the front door and they went inside. The windows had been closed for nearly three months and the place had a dusty smell that got into your throat and made your eyes smart. It was also very hot, for the drawing room faced due south and the hot sun beat on the glass. Adam went about opening windows. The furniture was all his too, those cabinets with bulging fronts and curved legs, chairs with buttoned backs, a velvet-covered love seat, a big oval table supported on a wooden base shaped like a vase, mirrors framed in gilt, pale mauve and green watercolours and dark portraits in oils. He could not remember noticing any of this before. It had been there but he had not seen it. Nor noticed the pillars of rosy marble that supported the window embrasure, nor the alcoves, glass-fronted, that were filled with china. Only the overall impression was familiar, not the individual pieces. He felt a little sick, engorged with possessions and the pride of ownership. In each room a chandelier hung from the ceiling, of tarnished brass in the dining room, a cascade of prisms in the drawing room, in hall and study Italianate glass tubes twisted snake-like amid false candles. And everywhere the sun streamed or lay in golden pools or rainbow spots or squares made by windows patterned with the shadows of leaves.

Rufus was among the bookcases in Hilbert's study. Adam took down Edward Moor's *Suffolk Words and Phrases*, couldn't find 'drift' but here was 'pytle' or 'pightle', *a small meadow*. He went back into the drawing room where he unbolted, unlocked and threw open the french windows.

The sun came to him in a warm gust or like a warm veil enveloping him. It whitened the terrace beyond with a clear, unbroken glare. All along the terrace, on the low wall that bounded it, stood the statuary his father had once told him had been placed there by whoever inhabited the place before Hilbert and Lilian came. They represented, in some kind of fine-grained grey stone, the loves of Zeus. He remembered them all right. As a child he had studied them with fascination, enquiring what the bull was doing to the lady, and receiving from his parents no very satisfying answer. Hilbert he had been too much in awe of to ask. They had come from Italy. Some cousin of Lilian's two or three times removed had found them in Florence while there on her honeymoon and had had them shipped home. There was Zeus as Amphitryon with Alcmene; Zeus coming to Danae in a shower of gold (difficult in stone, this one); snatching Europa; swan-shaped, wooing Leda; standing before the hapless Semele in all his destructive glory, and in half a dozen other metamorphoses.

Someone had been looking after the garden, you could see that. Flower beds had been weeded, dead heads removed, the borders of the willow-fringed lake shorn and trimmed, the lawns recently mown. As they walked along one of the stone-flagged paths and came to the gate in the flint wall they saw a neat pile of mowings waiting, apparently, to be composted.

The walled garden too had been carefully maintained. Inside the netted fruit cage Adam saw the bright, ripe, vermilion gleam of strawberries nestling among their triform leaves, raspberries yet green on the canes. All along the facing wall espaliered trees, their trunks dark and shiny and twisted and knobbed, bore among a rough, dull foliage fruit turning gold. Nectarines, Adam remembered, and peaches too. Weren't there greengages somewhere that scarcely ever fruited but when they did were splendid? Red and white currants here in rows, berries like glass beads, gooseberries with a ripeness the colour of rust on their green cheeks.

They each took a handful of strawberries. They walked to the lake where there were two pairs of ducks, mallards with feathers as if painted in iridescent green, and from which a heron rose on gaunt wings, its legs dangling. Adam looked back at the house, at the honeysuckle that curtained the back of it in yellow and pink, at the martins, sharp-pinioned, that wheeled in and out from the eaves. He was in a state of tremulous excitement. He seemed only to be able to breathe shallowly. It was curiously sexual this feeling, exactly the way he had once or twice felt with a girl he was mad to make love to and who he thought would let him but was not quite sure, not absolutely sure. The slightest thing would turn his fortune, snatch it, send him home frustrated, bitter, in a sick rage. He felt like that now. If only he could breathe properly! And here was the finest country air, transparent sparkling sun, the distant low hills and soft basking meadows half-hidden by the blue haze of noon.

'You're actually going to sell this place?'

Rufus lit a cigarette, offered him one. Adam shook his head.

'What else can I do?'

What choice did he have? He couldn't live there, he couldn't keep it up. Adam lay in bed beside Anne, his mind repeating what he had said to Rufus on that wonderful day in June.

'What else can I do?'

Of course he should have said I don't have a choice. Come on, I'm hungry, let's go get some lunch and then we'll find an estate agent. But they had bought food on their way coming through Halstead, the 1976 version of takeaway, a couple of meat pies, apples, Coke, and they had had lunch lying in the grass by the lake. The magical quality of the place crept on them there like a spell, the warmth and the sunshine and the scents of the garden and the tranquil silence. But it was more than that. There was an indefinable ingredient, a kind of excitement. It had something to do with history and the past, that excitement, and something to do with potential as well, with what Orwell or somebody had said, that every man really knew in his heart the finest place to be was the countryside on a summer's day. I was happy, Adam thought, that's what it was.

The Garden of Eden. Shiva had called it that, but in his mouth it had not been the hackneyed expression it would have been if an English person had so referred to it. He was drawing an interesting image from the mythology of another culture and it had seemed to him fresh and new. Adam had merely shrugged. The Garden of Eden was the way certain people would describe any charming landscape. Yet the phrase had remained with him, particularly in its darker aspect, the way it appears to most of those who are bound by the puritan ethic, not as a haven to live in and enjoy but as a paradise to be expelled from. It was almost as if a necessary condition of being in this paradise was the commission of some frightful sin or crime that must result in expulsion from it. On the day they had gone, when the summer was over and the skies grey and a wind blowing, he had thought of that image. Their departure had something in it of the bowed and wretched mien of Adam and Eve in the many 'expulsion' paintings he had later seen, and by then the Garden itself had a ruined look, paradise destroyed.

He got out of bed to have a pee. He and Anne had a bathroom opening out of their bedroom but Adam, when he got up in the night, usually went to the other one that was on the far side of the landing. This was because his reason for getting up at all was to see if Abigail was all right. But he had used their bathroom and was back in bed again before he realized that he had forgotten to look at his daughter. His anxiety for her had been displaced by a greater worry – was that possible?

Ever since her birth he had been ultra-anxious without expressing, even to himself alone, his reason for this. Of course he knew what those reasons were but he had never faced them. Now he did and they did not seem absurd, they seemed like good reasons. He got up again and padded across to Abigail's room. Suppose, after all, that he had not gone to look and in the morning they had found her stiff and cold in her cot, her eyes glazed and unfocused, her lips blue? He shivered, gooseflesh standing on his face and arms. Abigail lay on her side, well tucked in, the teddy bear she was too young for sitting in the corner by her feet. Adam stood watching her, listening to her silent sleep.

− 7 −

With the specialist's contempt for the layman's ignorance, Rufus read accounts of the inquest in two newspapers. More prominence was given to the evidence of Alec Chipstead than to that of the Home Office Pathologist, Dr Aubrey Helier. The stuff Rufus wanted to know would be beyond the average reader's comprehension. He should really have gone to that inquest. That could be remedied, he could acquire a transcript of the proceedings or simply a copy of the pathologist's findings, but he did not dare, he was not prepared to show his hand to that extent.

Instead he tried to guess what might have been said. He put himself into the pathologist's shoes and stood in the witness box. He spoke of how he had established the sex of the larger skeleton. A fragment of the uterus remaining perhaps? It was this soft part that often persisted longest.

'Having established that the larger skeleton was that of a female, I set about making an estimate of the subject's age at the time of her death. It should be explained that between the ages of twelve and thirty the union of the epiphyses of most of the long bones with the shafts takes place, and by the age of twenty-four most of the ephiphyses have united. In the case of the subject I shall henceforward designate as Subject A I found that the medial end of the clavicle had not yet fused, though fusion had taken place at the acromion and verical border scapula. The bones of the arm had for the most part fused but fusion had not yet taken place between the radius and ulna, which would be expected to have occurred by the age of twenty-one. The heads of the metatarsals were fused, which one would expect to be accomplished by nineteen years, but fusion had not taken place in the secondary pelvic centres. The sutures of the skull remained open on their inner aspects . . .'

Something like that it must have been. He would not have been able to put a precise age on the skeleton. Between seventeen and twenty-one, say. And the cause of death? Rufus had another look at the paper. The pathologist had said it was at this stage impossible to give an opinion but the report also said the police were treating the case as murder. There was nothing about how the pathologist had reached the conclusion that death had taken place some time between 1974 and 1977. Rufus guessed again.

'Certain highly technical factors, intelligible only to the expert and with which I will not take up the time of this inquest, have led me to conclude that Subject A had been dead for more than nine years and less than twelve. Suffice it to say that I reached this estimate on the basis of the preservation of a vestige of the uterus and as a result of obtaining a chemical reaction for blood from periosteum. I should not have expected to obtain such a reaction if more than twelve years had elapsed since death.'

It was only conjecture about that bit of uterus. Rufus wondered if he might have invented that part because he had so much to do with wombs in the course of his own daily life. He knew very little about tests done on blood from bones, only that they could be carried out. Identification of 'Subject A' would be a more difficult matter altogether. There was no mention of hair, though Rufus knew hair could persist intact for far more years than those bones had been in the grave, and there was nothing about clothing. Would ten years in the earth have destroyed that cotton shroud? He imagined a police-man with nothing more to go on than a tiny, once brightly embroid-ered label, a square inch of bloodstained, earth-stained, half-rotted cloth, hawking it round boutiques in Kilburn and West Hendon, narrowing the field, finally coming to an importer's warehouse . . .

But no, she hadn't been wearing that dress, of course she hadn't. He asked himself how accurate his memory in fact was, how much time and a desire to repudiate the past had blocked off. He ought to try to remember, he must. There were ways of bringing memories to the surface and he must use them to protect himself. It was imperative too to keep cool and not allow things to get out of proportion. Most likely they would proceed no further than they had with the identifi-cation of 'Subject A', especially since there was no one (apart from themselves) to miss her and she had never been missed. In the case of a person missing ten years before who had never been reported missing, what hope was there now of establishing identity?

It might be somewhat different with regard to the other occupant of the grave. Rufus became the pathologist again.

'Now to the remains of the infant I shall call Subject B. Examin-ation of the pelvis usually allows sex to be determined with great confidence in very young children and even in the foetus. I found in Subject B the greater sciatic notch to be wide and shallow and the ischial tuberosities to be everted, the ilia inclined to the vertical and the brim of the pelvis almost circular in outline. The sub-pubic angle was rounded and somewhat of the order of 90 degrees. I can therefore state with total confidence that Subject B was of the female sex.

'The age of Subject B I estimate to have been more than four weeks and less than twelve. The skeleton *in toto* measured 22.5 inches. The anterior fontanelle was open. There was no appearance of ossification in the humeral head, though the cuboid was ossified . . .'

Rufus was getting into unknown terrain here. He had very little idea of how the baby's age could have been estimated. By the fusion of joints, certainly, it need hardly matter to him which ones. How old had the baby been anyway? Very young, without teeth. 'A primary deciduous dentition had not yet commenced', was no doubt how the pathologist would have put it. But what of Subject A's teeth?

That was primarily how dead bodies were identified, by their teeth. On the other hand, if the particular person had never been missed or reported missing, their existence scarcely recorded in the great reference log of National Insurance and medical cards, passports and driving licences, if the chance of their even being named seemed thin, what obscure dentist was going to rise up suddenly producing the relevant chart?

A certain assumption might of course be made.

'There is considerable danger here of drawing the conclusion that because the two sets of bones were found in conjunction and on the same date, they must have met their deaths at the same time. Although this is probably so, I am able to offer no evidence in proof of it. Nor have I come upon any factor to prove the truth of another assumption which may be made: to wit, that Subject A was the mother of Subject B. Experience and probability point to this being so but that is all.

'I am unable to state with any certainty the length of time which has elapsed since the death of Subject B or offer any suggestion as to the cause of death.'

That was something which could never be established after this lapse of time. Unfortunate in a way, Rufus thought. It would be an ironical stroke if investigations into the affair resulted not in the discovery of those happenings in which they had been guilty but only in those where they had been blameless.

The inquest had been adjourned. No doubt they were still digging up the little graveyard. Rufus was not squeamish, he had not been one of those medical students who become nauseous at their first sight of surgery, but, curiously enough, he did not much like to think of all those little bones, so alien to him, so unidentifiable, being dug up and sorted out and sifted through in case there should be a human fibula among them or a vertebra. Rufus did not even know if animal bones shared the same names as those of humans. Did dogs have fibulas? He was surprised to find himself shuddering.

If there was no shot in or among the human remains, in the cavities of the skull for instance, would it be possible to find it in the soil, among the sand and gravel and pine needles? Bird shot it would have been or somewhat larger. Rufus had only seen it while eating partridge which had been winged instead of shot in the head and had nearly broken one of his teeth on the tiny ball of lead. He imagined gravel being sifted, all the particles, the minute stones, being picked over by some policeman whose job it was to do that, the tiny flints laid in one tray, the wood fragments in another, and then, in a third, the shot.

He could remember so much, he had clear pictures of whole days spent at Ecalpemos, whole conversations recorded that could be rerun in his head. Why was it then that he couldn't remember where she had been shot? In the heart or the head or the spine? His mind blanked over that and there was a complete loss of recall. When he tried and saw the sky covered with rushing clouds, the lawn that had become a hay-field, the cedar's wheeling branches, the gun levelled, there would come an explosion in his memory like the firing of that shot-gun, a redness in front of his eyes with splintered edges, then black-out.

The gun he could remember, both guns. And the gun-room and the first time he went in there with Adam. They had eaten their lunch down by the lake. Two pork pies and a can of Coke each but not the apples which were imported Granny Smiths and bruised, and anyway they had strawberries. They must have each eaten about a pound of strawberries, for they kept going back to the fruit cage for more. Some time during the afternoon they decided not to go back but to stay overnight. That meant there was no hurry, they could have lain out there in the sun till the pubs opened. But Adam had this idea of phoning his mother to tell her he wouldn't be back that night. Rufus wouldn't have bothered, he came and went as he pleased, and anyway didn't believe parents should be pandered to in this way. Of course it wasn't quite pandering with Adam. He didn't want to get on worse terms with his mother, from whom he hoped to get a loan for his holiday in Greece, nor did he want the kind of thing that might have happened, his mother phoning hospitals or getting the police because they could have had an accident in Goblander.

As it turned out he didn't make that phone call until the evening and they found a call-box outside a pub in one of the villages, for Great-Uncle Hilbert's phone had been disconnected. But once they were indoors again they resumed exploring, found a genuine butler's pantry with a lot of silver in it packed away in canteens and boxes and green baize, and opening the next door, came into the gun-room.

Adam, as a child, had been strictly forbidden ever to go in there. Anyway, the door was usually kept locked. Presumably, in pre-Hilbert days, during Bereland squirearchy, it had contained an armoury of weapons, for all four walls were hung with gun racks. However, only two types of firearms remained, both shot-guns. There was a row of hooks for hanging up jackets and waterproofs and one of these hung there still, Hilbert's old shooting-jacket, tweed, with leather pads on the elbows.

A glass case on the windowsill contained a fat stuffed trout, another, on the circular table, a turtle – this certainly not of English provenance. The front half of a fox, paws and all, its rear end replaced by a shield-shaped slab of polished wood, appeared to be leaping out of the wall just below the picture rail, in the manner of a circus dog emerging from a paper hoop.

'Those aren't the sort of things you shoot, though, are they?' Rufus had asked.

'You most definitely don't shoot foxes.'

Adam said this in such a snooty, lord-of-the-manor way that Rufus yelled with laughter. He took one of the guns, the twelve bore, from the wall and Adam had another go at him, this time for pointing it in his direction.

'It's not loaded, for God's sake.'

'Never mind. You don't point guns at people.' It appeared then that Adam had actually been out shooting the last time he was here. He had only been fifteen and had been given the four-ten, the so-called lady's gun, which Rufus gathered had rather gone against the grain.

Since then he had often recalled what Adam said next, had taken the gun from him and remarked that it was a pump-action shot-gun.

'What does that mean?'

'You don't have to keep reloading. It's got a repeating action. You don't have to put a cartridge in each time before you fire.'

And Rufus, who didn't mind appearing ingenuous in this area, said, 'I thought all firearms worked like that.'

One of the drawers in the pine cabinet was stocked with cartridges, red ones and blue ones which Adam said indicated the size of the shot they contained.

'That's amazing, me inheriting a couple of guns as well. We might even get some shooting.'

'Not in June, squire. Even I know that.'

Was that the first hint, no more than a joke really, that they might stay at Wyvis Hall, that they might *live* there? And Adam had said:

'I didn't mean now.'

'I thought you were going to sell the place.'

Adam didn't say any more. They went back down the garden and after that out to a couple of pubs where they drank a lot and Rufus had to drive back to Wyvis Hall with one eye closed on account of getting double vision. They slept it off, not getting up till around eleven next morning, Rufus in the principal guest room, Adam at the other end of the house in what he christened the Pincushion Room because it had a picture on the wall of St Sebastian stuck full of arrows. Rufus looked out of the window and saw a man trimming the grass round one of the rose beds with a pair of long-handled shears.

He was elderly, bald, very thin, wearing a striped shirt of the kind that have detachable collars. It was the sound of his clipping which had woken Rufus up. The sun was blazing down and there wasn't a spot of shade anywhere till you came to the wood below the lake. Rufus, who hadn't much appreciation of nature usually, nevertheless found himself gazing in something like wonderment at all the roses, yellow and pink and apricot and dark red, a hedge of white ones, a cascade of peach-red that covered a pergola. The man with the shears laid them down on the grass, took a handkerchief from his pocket, made a knot in each of its four corners and placed this improvised sun-hat on his head.

Rufus had never seen anyone do that before, though he had seen it in pictures on seaside postcards. He was entranced. He put on his shorts and his sandals and went down. By the time he got outside Adam was already there, telling the man in the handkerchief hat that he didn't want him to come any more, he was going to sell the house.

'This old garden'll go to rack and ruin then. I been coming down here watering most nights.'

'That's not my problem,' said Adam. 'The people who buy it will have to handle that.'

'It do seem a wicked shame.' The gardener opened his shears and wiped the grass clippings off the blades with his forefinger. 'But it's not my place to argue. Mr Verne-Smith paid me up till the end of

343

April, so that's seven weeks you owe me – let's say six and a half to be fair.'

Adam looked rather shattered. 'I didn't actually ask you to come.'

'True, but I come, didn't I? I done the work and I'll want paying. Fair's fair. Look at the place. You can't deny I done the work.'

Adam couldn't. He didn't try. In the cagey, suspicious way he sometimes spoke he said:

'How much in fact would it be?'

'I come twice a week at a pound a time, so that's thirteen, say, and then there's all the times I've come with me cans. Fifteen I reckon would cover it.'

It was ludicrously less than Rufus had expected. For all that labour it was ridiculous. But this was the country, this was horticulture, and they ordered things differently there. He and Adam went into the house where they managed to scrounge up fifteen quid between the two of them, leaving them with just enough to cover the petrol for Goblander to get home on. Adam paid the man and he went off on a bicycle, still wearing the knotted handkerchief on his head. It was only after he had gone that they realized they had never asked his name or where he lived.

'You could have kept him on for two quid a week. It's nothing.'

'I haven't got two quid a week. I'm skint.'

And it was lack of money that stopped them going away. He, Rufus, could have got just about enough together for the petrol *en route* and maybe his own food. If Adam had had an equal amount they would have managed. In another year, at almost any other time, Adam would have touched his father or more probably his mother for a loan, but in June 1976 his father was barely speaking to him, and his mother would have been scared to go against her husband. Of course if Adam had invited his parents to make themselves at home at Wyvis Hall, use it as a hotel, while he was away, they would have lent him any amount, but that was the last thing Adam would have done. He did ask his sister for money. Bridget had been one of those teenagers who work all through their school holidays in restaurants or in shops or cleaning houses and she always had cash. But she would not lend him any. She was saving up to go skiing the next January and she knew there wasn't much chance of Adam repaying a loan by then.

It was ironical that Adam, who was the owner of that big house and all that land and the contents of the house, nevertheless went down to Nunes the second time with less than a fiver in his pocket. And that was everything he had. Instead of Greece they went to Wyvis Hall because Adam was broke and Mary was close to broke because that first time it had been so beautiful and peaceful and *private* there that you could hardly see what advantages Greece would have had over it. They had intended to stay a week. Rufus had suggested to Adam that he sell something out of the house, a piece of china or some silver. There were almost more antique and second-hand shops in some of those villages than there were houses. He had counted six in the place where they had gone to the pub. They talked about it on the way down in Goblander.

It was funny how good Adam had been at naming things, the rooms in the house, the house itself even, or at naming the idea of it, the concept, Ecalpemos. Goblander was not just an anagram on old banger, it really expressed the way that decrepit old van had of gobbling up petrol as it chugged through the countryside making awful noises because it needed a new silencer.

'You'll never even get near Greece in this,' said Mary. 'It'll just collapse and give up the ghost somewhere in France. I'm warning you.'

Her father was a life peer who had held some sort of office under a Labour government. It must have been the boarding-school she had been to which determined her voice, affected, sharp, shrill. She found fault a lot. The car was wrong, Rufus's clothes were wrong or funny or somehow unsuitable, he smoked too much, he was too fond of wine and his whole lifestyle left much to be desired. She started on Adam for taking up that shameful suggestion about selling what she called the family silver. How dreadful! What a desecration! He ought to have a feeling of reverence for the beautiful things his great-uncle had entrusted to him.

'He's not coming back,' said Adam, 'to see how I've discharged my duties.'

'He'll turn in his grave.'

'No, there'll just be a small upheaval in his ashes.'

He told her Great-Uncle Hilbert's ashes were the contents of an urn-shaped Crown Derby sweets-jar that stood on the drawing-room mantelpiece. Maybe she believed him, for Rufus had once caught her lifting the lid and looking into the jar at the wood ash Adam had scraped up from the site of the handkerchief man's last bonfire. Mary was rather difficult but she was also just about the most beautiful girl Rufus had ever come across. It gratified him to be seen in her company. He had always been a bit that way had Rufus, manifestly to be seen to be doing all right for himself, successful, forging ahead, accompanied by the best-looking girl possible. Mary was spectacular to look at and her own knowledge that she was made her capricious and difficult, expecting the best of everything. All that was her due because she looked like the young Elizabeth Taylor, had dark brown curly hair nearly to her waist, large, dark blue eyes, creamy velvet skin and a wonderful figure.

It was 20 June when they went back, all Goblander's windows open, the weather being perfect the way you expected it to be that summer, as if it were southern Europe where you woke up each morning to sunshine and unclouded skies. By that time, as Adam said, you would actually have been shocked if the temperature had dropped or a shower of rain fallen.

'It makes you think there mightn't be an awful lot of point in going to Greece,' he said. 'I mean, this could be the best summer ever and we'd miss it. It's always like this in Greece.'

They'd brought food with them, quite a lot of food. Adam said the first thing would be to get old Hilbert's fridge going. Of course it was his own fridge but he was still in the habit of speaking as if, as Mary had inferred, his great-uncle might return.

It must have been a strange experience for him, Rufus had thought, knowing he owned all sorts of things but not knowing quite what or where they were. They were the sort of things too which the parent generation owned, those old people that Adam, until Rufus laughed at him, had inadvertently called the grown-ups: sheets and blankets and knives and forks and pots and pans and more complicated appurtenances of living that if one ever thought about at all one supposed one would have to get together for oneself eventually. Someone else had got it together for Adam and there it all was. They found some sheets in a walk-in cupboard, linen ones with LVS embroidered on them. The sheets felt a bit damp so Mary spread them out on the terrace in the sun to dry. They ate out there too and drank one of the bottles of wine they had brought.

It was an amazing amount of wine they got through down at Wyvis Hall, and not only wine. But that first day they had only been able to afford two bottles of Anjou rosé. Later on they went all over the house, assessing what they might be able to sell, finding out just what Adam's inheritance amounted to. Rufus had been astonished by the quantities of junk in that house, the ornaments and knick-knacks and stuff like vases and candlesticks and ashtrays and glass and brass that Hilbert Verne-Smith and his wife had accumulated over the years. Mary got stroppy about it and said it was wrong what they were doing, it was a desecration. But Adam had retorted quite reasonably that it was *his* now, didn't she understand that? It was as much his to do as he liked with as the sandals on his feet and the change from that fiver he had in his pocket after buying the rosé. And then Mary said she felt as if Hilbert were there with them as they rifled through chests and drawers and cupboards, she could feel his presence standing behind them, looking over her shoulder.

By then it was dark, it was night time. And at Wyvis Hall, below the woods and above the river, with the nearest road half a mile away and the nearest house twice as far as that, total silence prevailed. The sky was clear, the colour of a very dark blue jewel, and on the surface of the lake the stars were mirrored. The house was full of moths because they had left the doors and windows open after they put the lights on. Mary screamed when a bat flew close to her, she said bats got in your hair, a bat had got into the hair of some relative of hers and bitten her scalp. Mary's scream sounded particularly loud in that dark silence. There was a loud echo in the grounds of Wyvis Hall, Mary's scream ringing back from off the wood and walls and starry waters, and Rufus, a town dweller who had never spent much time in the countryside, expected alarmed or annoyed people to arrive or the disconnected phone to start shrilling with complaints. Of course nothing happened. They could all have screamed the place down, Mary could have been bitten to death by bats, and no one would have come.

That was part of the trouble, that was how it was that events were set in motion. If Wyvis Hall had been less isolated, less silent . . .

Rufus had come a long way since the Goblander days and the car he got into to drive himself to the hospital he attended two mornings a week was a Mercedes, not yet a year old. At the garage where he bought petrol they offered him a complimentary sherry glass because he had bought more than thirty litres. Rufus refused. He already had

347

two of the things clinking about on the back seat. But the sight of the glass took him back into the past again, the past which he believed he had exorcized but was now fetched back in fragments and longer scenarios by every possible association. He had sat in that locked room talking, therapist and patient both, had talked it over and over. To the site of his trauma he had returned and re-lived it. He might just as well not have bothered, for it was there still, it would be there for ever, unless one day they found how to cut memory out of the brain with a scalpel.

On the back seat the two sherry glasses clinked as Rufus took a left turn rather too sharply. What they had eventually decided to sell before they went to bed that night (or the following morning really) were Great-Uncle Hilbert's dozen Waterford sherry glasses. As Adam said, none of them drank sherry and he didn't know anyone under fifty who did. Having wandered about all over the house, they had ended up in the dining room where the cabinet full of glass was. In another cupboard they found half a bottle of whisky and a dribble of brandy in the bottom of a Courvoisier bottle. There had been something extraordinarily delightful and exhilarating about sitting at that big oval mahogany table drinking whisky at two o'clock in the morning. The moon had come up and laid a greenish iridescence on the surface of the lake. It was so bright it made the stars disappear. They had to close the window because of the insects. Then they turned out the lights, the great brass chandelier with its false candles, and the moon's lemony radiance lay as still as cloths draped over the shining wood. Adam set the twelve sherry glasses that were cut in a Greek key pattern round their rims in the middle of the moonlight and said he would put them in a box tomorrow and try to sell them in Sudbury to the man who had the antique shop in Gainsborough Street that they had passed.

There had been a kind of innocence about them at that stage, Rufus thought. On one level they were just marking time, spending a few days in the country at a friend's house. On another they felt (as Mary put it) like burglars, prowling about the house, discovering treasures, half-expecting the true owner to return and surprise them.

'Suppose old Hilbert's face were to appear at the window now,' Adam had said as they went up the back stairs to bed.

There was a window at the top, on the landing, but outside there was only the blue jewel night. They had all slept heavily, the sleep if not of the just, of the innocent and artless. None of them doubted that they would eventually get to Greece. In those early days, that last week of June, it was merely a matter of raising enough money. Not that this had been easy. The Sudbury man was not forthcoming, he had been suspicious, wanting all sorts of information about them and the glasses.

'He thinks you've nicked them, doesn't he?' said Mary, who hadn't come in but stayed outside in Goblander. 'And of course he *would*. I mean just look at you!'

Adam's cut-off jeans with the fringed hems, she meant, and his yellow and red headband that he insisted on calling a fillet as if it were a bit of fish. And their long hair and bare feet.

'You reckon I should put on one of Hilbert's suits, do you?' Adam said.

He never did that. Instead they drove into Hadleigh and found an antique shop man who offered to drive to Wyvis Hall and give Adam a valuation for some of the furniture, the chandeliers and the ornaments. Two days later he actually came, an oldish man, at least sixty, and valued two of the cabinets as worth £500 apiece. When Adam heard that, he didn't want to sell, he was sure they must therefore be worth far more. The man bought a brass lantern and two little tables with the surfaces carved with flowers and fruit and the sherry glasses, giving Adam £150 for the lot.

Rufus could not remember the man's name, only that he had been the second visitor to Wyvis Hall, the gardener being the first. Would he remember? If still alive, he would be in his seventies by now. He had a confused impression of coming into the dining room while the man was there and hearing him rather grudgingly assess the value of the glass cabinet. The man had said good morning and Rufus had said hallo and had returned to the task he and Mary were embarked on, covering the flagstones of the terrace with quilts from the bedrooms. The terrace faced south and got the full sun, so it was too hot to be out there by day, but in the evenings and at night it was wonderful. They fetched a lightly padded patchwork quilt from the Centaur Room, a pink candlewick from the Room Without a Name, two of white cotton from the Room of Astonishment and a counterpane of heavy yellow satin they found in a cupboard in the Pincushion Room. Mary arranged some pillows out there and cushions from the drawing room and by the time they were finished the antiques man had gone.

Leaving them with £150.

So that evening they went out to spend some of it. Had they been noticed and noted as they drove through the village of Nunes? Rufus had always heard that nothing can go on in a village without the gossips knowing. Perhaps this would apply if they had walked along that village street or sat on the green or drunk in the local, but they had not. For some reason they had not much liked the look of this pub, called the Fir Tree, and though he had slowed a bit as they came to it, they had not stopped. He had seldom been to the village and only once on foot but he could remember the layout of it with surprising clarity.

A church that stood upon a grassy hill and to which you mounted by a flight of steep stone stairs. An avenue of yew trees. Behind it one of those screens of elms, all dead even by then of Dutch elm disease. A village street of houses and cottages, a garage, a grocer, but not a single antique shop. The green an isosceles triangle without a tree to it, but trees around the pub, the same kind as in Adam's pine wood, Rufus supposed, or very like, which the licensee or the brewery had probably thought its name required.

There was the inevitable council estate, the houses painted pale green, blue, pink, as in some child's drawing, and then, round a bend in the lane where you might have expected open fields, half a dozen houses of 1950s or '60s provenance, lavishly appointed, glamorously gardened, with big garages and big cars outside them.

'Hampstead Garden Suburb comes to Suffolk,' Adam had said.

Later on they had seen the coypu man's van parked on the front driveway of one of those houses. And they had had a discussion about it, speculating as to whether he actually lived there or was there to kill something, rats, moles, any sort of infestation. Snobbish Rufus had not thought it possible for someone like that to live there, but why not, after all? There was money to be made out of the destruction of pests in a country place.

Rufus had an out-patients' clinic and then a ward round, in the afternoon a very frightened woman to see in Wimpole Street, a woman who needed his kind reassurance, his urbane ways, the proffered cigarette, the support. His first cigarette of the day he smoked while he waited, extinguishing it two minutes before she was shown in and he had to tell her that her cervical smear had shown pre-cancerous signs.

Who would reassure *him*? Comfort *him*? No one, he thought, and despised himself for what was to him an unnatural need. The police would not necessarily assume that the bones in the graveyard were of people who had lived at Wyvis Hall, nor that those who had brought about their deaths had lived there. But it was *likely*. It was most probable. The existence of the cemetery was not generally known and on the lane side of the pine wood the trees were separated from the grass verge by a close-boarded fence.

They would ask a lot of questions in the village. They would make enquiries at Pytle Farm and the house called the Mill in the Pytle. By some means they would discover all the people who were likely to have called at Wyvis Hall in the capacity of tradesmen or service operatives: dustmen, meter readers, gardeners, antique dealers, perhaps – why not? – the coypu man. Adam would be questioned, was possibly being questioned at this moment. Unless he had changed a lot he would not make a good impression.

Had the time come to forget the promise they had made each other, the guarantee they had given never to meet or speak? Rufus reached for the blue phone directory and turned to the Vs, to Verne-Smith-Duchini, and had actually begun to dial when his patient was announced.

He put the receiver back and created, forcing his lips to perform, a wide smile.

– 8 –

The lake water was clear and cool, not cold. Weeks of sunshine had taken off the chill. Soon after they got up – which was always late, which was lunchtime – he and Rufus went in swimming, keeping their feet off the gravelly or slimy bottom and their arms clear of the blanket weed which was like green hair. The lily leaves lay flat on the surface, their flowers waxen crimson and palest yellow, their stems tough, glutinous, slippery, a tangle of entrails.

'Reminds me of the duodenum,' said Rufus, yanking out a long slimy stem and lassoing Adam with it, catching his neck in a halter of living rope.

They grappled together, the way schoolboys do, but they weren't schoolboys and Adam was suddenly aware of Rufus's body under the water, his hard muscles and smooth skin, legs briefly intertwined with his. And when Rufus's arms grabbed him from behind, ostensibly of course just to duck him under the surface, he found himself resisting in a way that Rufus recognized as real resistance and let him go. And Rufus knew why, grinning a little as their eyes met. He swam away and Adam swam away and very soon after that they came out of the lake and went back to Mary on the terrace.

A disturbing experience it had been, exciting and confusing. Adam had not known he carried within his mind a directory of the forbidden. Selling what he still thought of – in spite of what he said to Mary – as Hilbert's things, appeared only on the perimeter of it, in an area of doubt. Money they had to have. For the rest of the time they were there money did not exactly overshadow them but the pressing need for it was always there, it was always in their minds. And Mary's condemnation was not enough to keep him from succumbing. He had let the dealer from Hadleigh come, a man called Evans or Owens, one of those Welsh names, and sold him a brass lantern and two little carved tables and the sherry glasses. The money he gave them they had meant to use for the Greek trip but it was more than they expected and they had gone on a shopping, then a drinking, spree with it. Also Goblander had needed a new exhaust system and they had had that done immediately, not in the local Nunes garage though but at a big, impersonal place in Colchester. Rufus had thought Goblander needed a thorough overhaul and the mechanic confirmed this, adding that it would cost him. The bill would be around £75 but, as Mary had said, the van wouldn't get as far as Calais in its present state. Next day they had collected the rejuvenated Goblander, catching one of the rare buses to Colchester and taking all day about it. The cost of the service was nearer £85 than £75 and they spent a further £50 on food and drink. Drink mostly.

Adam drank very little these days. It nauseated him and wakened him in the night with a palpitating heart. He had been better able to tolerate it ten years ago, but then he had drunk alcohol to be like other people and to impress, not because he liked it. Rufus was different. Rufus had a great capacity and could metabolize (as he put it) large quantities of spirits and larger amounts of wine. It was not unusual for him, unaided, to drink two bottles of wine in as many hours. But he was wrong when he said it had no effect on him. The effects were very apparent, though they were not the common ones of slurred speech and unsteadiness and loss of memory.

Rufus used to say that if left to themselves most men would live on meat and cake. They might eat fruit and vegetables and dairy products but that was for their health, not because they liked them. It was versions of meat and cake that the three of them bought to store in Hilbert's – no, his – fridge, and they bought crisps and chocolate bars and a crate full of wines and spirits. He was a sybarite or an Epicurean, Adam thought, relishing words, but Epicurean sounded better, less pejorative.

No one drank the spirits but Rufus, and Adam suspected that he drank more than he let on about, probably keeping a private bottle somewhere.

'I don't see any point in self-denial,' he used to say.

'My father says being denied things refines the character.'

Rufus grinned, for of course Adam had told him all about Hilbert's will. 'He should know,' he said.

Adam suspected that these days Rufus might be quite fastidious about wine, a wine snob even, the kind that savours bouquets and talks about nice little domestic burgundies and so forth, but in those days it was plonk he wanted. So they bought the cheapest obtainable in order to get more of it, Nicolas, and stuff called Hirondelle.

'I shall have to sell the Gainsborough next,' Adam said.

Of course it turned out not to be a Gainsborough, in spite of what Evans or Owens had said. Having secured the tables and the glasses, he had peered at the dark discoloured oil of an elderly cleric in a shovel hat and opined that this was the work of 'our local genius'. Asked to explain, he said he meant Gainsborough, who had been born in Sudbury. Hadn't they seen the statue of him in the Market Place where he stood with his palette, apparently painting the pub and King's the grocer's?

They took the painting to Sudbury to get an expert opinion and there the signature at the bottom of the canvas was pointed out to them, that of one C. Prebble. So they took it back to Wyvis Hall and hung it up again and then they lay out on the terrace in the sun, eating rump steak and potato crisps and drinking Hirondelle rosé.

They used Hilbert's wine glasses because none of them could tolerate drinking from plastic or cartons but they ate off paper plates of which they had bought a hundred. It must have been that day or the next, Adam thought, that he or one of them, surely he, had first suggested the commune idea. But not then, not yet. He had brought with him reading that was expected of him during this vacation, works on sociology and on linguistics and some where these two studies converged, but these were not the sort of books one much wanted to read under the hot sun and the influence of wine. Instead he read Hilbert's books, notably selections from a shelf of classic pornography, not in any way hidden, the books not concealed under plain covers, but there on display for anyone to find. Adam rather admired his great-uncle for this. There was Guillaume Apollinaire and Henry Miller, Pisanus Fraxi and *My Secret Life*, Frank Harris's *My Life and Loves* and a dozen others. That afternoon Adam, knowing it was not the wisest thing to be doing in his celibate situation, lay on the terrace reading *Fanny Hill*.

Rufus and Mary lay quite near him on a candlewick bedspread Rufus had found in one of the spare bedrooms. They had been for some ten minutes locked in a close embrace, the length of their bodies pressed together. Sweat was running down Rufus's back, between his rather sharp shoulder blades. In spite of being so fair, his skin had taken on quite a deep tan in the few days they had been there. Adam had tried not to look but now he could not help looking. What he had feared would happen was happening now, though the feeling he had was not of being in any way rejected, nor was it embarrassment. It was simply a breathless, increasing, pulse-hammering sexual longing.

The two of them slid a little apart, Rufus rolling on to his back so that his pronounced erection showed, like a great clenched fist under his black trunks. He kept his head turned towards Mary, though, as between parted lips they licked the tips of each other's tongues. Adam found Rufus's great endowment as disturbing as Mary's naked breasts which lay round and creamy, soft and passive yet with hard, pointed nipples, between the open sides of her blouse. He turned his head away, pressed forehead and eyes hard down into the covers of *Fanny Hill*. After a while he heard the others move, heard Rufus take a great slurp of wine before they padded barefoot into the house and up the stairs to the Centaur Room.

When Adam was about eight his father had told him masturbating gave you scurvy. Saying scurvy was caused by a lack of vitamin C was just a blind, put about by doctors and nutritionists who ought to know better. Most of the people you saw with false teeth had masturbated when young, it was a well-known fact, only there was a conspiracy between dentists and what Lewis called the vitamin-C lobby to keep it secret. It was in their interests to make work for the dental profession and sell vitamin C, not to let it get about that simply by keeping their hands where they ought to be young people could have healthy teeth and gums for life. Later on Adam wondered if his father had made all this up or if he really believed it himself. It was not a theory to be come across elsewhere. But the curious thing was that the idea had somehow and much against his will taken root in his consciousness. He did not believe it, he ridiculed it – to his sister, for instance – but it partially attained the effect Lewis aimed at. If Adam ever got as far as masturbating, and naturally he sometimes did, he always had the feeling afterwards that his teeth were loose. His jaw would ache and once, when he cleaned his teeth at night, he found blood on his toothbrush.

So he had no recourse to masturbation that afternoon but went back into the lake instead, which was cold enough to supply one of the well-known Victorian antidotes to sexual desire.

Wading out of the lake, his legs muddy up to the knees, Adam sat on the bank among the bulrushes and the great, pale, leathery hosta leaves and looked at the house with its canopy of roses and honeysuckle, the martins' nest under the eaves, the long terrace with Zeus in his various avatars and his loves disporting themselves along the flint wall. Some brightly coloured butterflies, orange and yellow and black and white – his father would have known their names – sunned themselves on the mellow rosy brickwork, spreading their wings flat in the heat. The sky above the glittering slate roofs was as blue as the curious lilies which had just begun to come out under the dining-room window, trumpet flowers set like the seed-head of a dandelion but as blue as – the sky.

There would be things just as beautiful in Greece and it would be as hot or hotter. But it would not be *his*. He would not be proprietor of all he surveyed there. It was a revelation to him how important this was, how much it meant. He had never previously thought of himself as acquisitive or even as particularly materialistic. The truth was though, that until now he had never possessed anything much, so how could he know? It gave him a good feeling, it was satisfying, just to think as he walked up the stairs, those floors are mine, this carved wood, these moulded ceilings. And when he came into the Pincushion Room and rested his elbows on the window-ledge, he would look out of the window at the garden bright with midsummer sun or bathed in moonlight and think, all this is mine, that garden, that fruit cage within the flint walls, that lake, the Little Wood, as far as I can see on either side of me and in front of the house and behind, all that is mine . . .

He was beginning to think he could not bear to sell it.

It was a long time since Adam had had a dream about Zosie. Rufus, yes, and Shiva sometimes and Shiva with Vivien, but it was a year since Zosie had come into his sleep and materialized before him.

Things happened as they must have happened, only in fact it was Rufus who had picked her up and brought her back to Wyvis Hall. Stopping on the way to exact his pound of flesh, of course. No, that was unfair. He would have done the same – in those days. In his dream it was he who was driving home to Nunes from Colchester, not Goblander though, but the car he had now, the Granada. She was waiting where in life she had waited, outside the station, near where the road forked, going in one direction to Bures, in the other to Sudbury. There had been a great Victorian pile of a hospital there then, maybe still was unless they had demolished it, its chimney concealed inside a mock campanile.

Small and delicate, fine-boned, pale brown skin, beige really, pale brown, wispy, very short hair, fey-faced with a small, tip-tilted nose and golden eyes like a cat. Someone had said she was like an Abyssinian cat and so she was. Very young, a child, only she was not that. Jeans and a T-shirt but you never noticed what Zosie wore. What was it they called that term in rhetoric? Zeugma or syllepsis? She stood there wearing a back-pack and a face of woe.

He drew up ahead of her. She came running up to the van and climbed in beside him. It was a hot night but she was shivering. He asked her where she wanted to go.

'Anywhere,' she said.

'Anywhere?'

'I don't know where I am, so how can I say where I want to go?'

'You came here on the train, didn't you?'

She started laughing and through her laughter her teeth chattered.

'I came out of there.' She turned round and pointed back at the Victorian building with the campanile chimney.

'What is it?' he said.

'Don't you know? It's a bin. A funny farm. It's what my gran calls a lunatic asylum.'

Adam woke up. He lay thinking of Zosie. Had she been a bit mad? Perhaps, but temporarily and for a well-attested reason. And of course there was no question of her having escaped from a mental hospital or of ever having been in one. He shook the dream off him. Rufus had called her a waif and Adam had immediately ridiculed this word, said it was a romantic novelist's word, so they had looked it up in Hilbert's Shorter Oxford Dictionary and found illuminating things. 'Something waving or flapping'. 'Something borne or driven by the wind'. 'A person who is without home or friends; one who lives uncared-for; an outcast; an unowned or neglected child'.

'That's the one I meant,' said Rufus.

And then Adam had read aloud the first definition:

'A piece of property which is found ownerless and which, if unclaimed within a fixed period after due notice given, falls to the lord of the manor.'

Well, eventually, it was true that Zosie had fallen to him. The waif who was ownerless and unclaimed had fallen to the lord of the manor. A father himself now, he thought of those parents of hers, her mother and stepfather, who had lost her and apparently had never searched, had never even declared their loss, been glad to be rid of her.

Adam wondered if Abigail sometimes woke up and looked for him in the dark, in the empty room, and fretted for a while before she began to cry. He could not bear the idea of it. It was deep night, three or four o'clock. Mark Twain had written somewhere: We are all mad at night. He got out of bed silently, in the dark. So many times he had padded across this bedroom to go to Abigail that he knew it perfectly in the dark, only requiring to hold his hands out before him and, like a blind man, feel the bevelled corner of the wardrobe, the lacquered wicker of a chair back, the top of the radiator, cold at this hour, the glass sphere of the door knob.

Outside on the landing he put a light on. Abigail's door was ajar and he went into the room, bringing a segment of light with him, a triangle that fell short a yard from her cot. Instead of bending over her, he knelt down and looked at her face through the bars. She opened her eyes, but, like Lady Macbeth's, their sense was shut. Awake, she never looked at him without smiling. She did not smile now but her eyelids with those amazing lashes slowly closed and Abigail gave a sigh, wriggled her body, moved her head and subsided back into deep sleep. Adam knelt beside her, thinking of Zosie and Zosie's mother and stepfather who had not bothered to go to the police when their daughter unaccountably vanished. They had apparently felt as if a burden had been lifted from them and why tempt fate by attempting to get her back? But Zosie had been only seventeen. Or so she said, Adam thought. But perhaps she was a year or two older than that or even more. She was such a liar.

You might be able to tell a person's age after they were dead but often not while they were still alive. For instance, the newspaper had said the skeleton in the cemetery at Wyvis Hall was of a young woman between 18 and 21 years old. Not that that was specially relevant . . .

He got up and went to the window, looking out into his garden. A narrow plot of mean suburban proportions compared to the place he had once possessed. Street lamps were on in the distance, greenish or blobs of orange light. There was no moon, only the perpetual chemical twilight that subsists in suburbs by night. Autumn had laid a misty chill over everything that grew. Plants had become sticks, leaves were rags of wet, black plastic, tree branches were bones with arthritic joints. We are all mad at three in the morning.

There had never been another summer like that one. 1984 had been good but not as good as that. The night had been warm too, not just the daytime, and even after sunset the temperature had not seemed to drop much. They had driven home arguing about which night was Midsummer night. Mary said it was 20 June because that was the night before the solstice, the longest day, and Rufus said it was the 24th and he, Adam, said it was the 23rd because that was the eve of the 24th which was Midsummer day. They were all rather drunk and, by analogy from the argument, Rufus had sung at the top of his voice:

> 'Where the bee fucks
> There fuck I . . .'

There was a rugger-player side to Rufus. Mary, often so censorious, was sweetened by drink. Everything Rufus said made her giggle and clutch at him. They shared a cigarette, passing it from mouth to mouth. Lying on the back seat, Adam recited 'Grantchester', which in those days he knew by heart:

> 'And green and deep
> The stream mysterious glides beneath,
> Green as a dream and deep as death . . .'

Back at home they lay out on the terrace on the spread quilts and Rufus said he would sleep there. Gnats came in swarms from the lake to torment them, so they lit incense sticks to keep them away, peppermint and aniseed and sandalwood. Mary had found some oil of citronella in an old-fashioned medicine chest in the Deathbed Room and they rubbed it on themselves for good measure. Or rubbed it on each other, rather. That was what started it.

All was silent. Sometimes you heard a soft splash as a fish jumped for one of the swarming insects. Or the whispering rattle of a bat's wing. And occasionally, from the depths of the wood, came less agreeable sounds.

'The noise made by something being murdered by something else,' Rufus had told an acquaintance in one of the pubs.

Rabbit victims of foxes or weasels, Adam supposed it was. The thin, pitiful cries were somehow unearthly when they waked him in the dark small hours. But no cries came to them there on the terrace, the darkness lit by the moon, the bright stars spread like a net across a sky that never lost its blueness, the scented tapers burning between the statuary of the amorous god. Rufus had a bottle of red wine but he was drinking the wine out of one of Hilbert's brandy glasses.

'We're not going to Greece, are we?' Adam said.

'I shouldn't think so for a moment,' said Rufus, whose speech grew more precise when he was drunk. 'Why should we do that?'

'If you remember, it was our intention.'

'I want to go to Greece,' said Mary, but smilingly and rather sleepily.

'No, you don't, my sweetheart. You want to stay here and rub some of that disgusting stuff all over Adam.'

Rufus was setting it up. Adam didn't immediately realize this, but after a while he did. Rufus was always a sensation seeker, wanting new experiences, new indulgences. He would have made a good bad Roman Emperor. Adam had put out his hand for the citronella but Rufus stopped him.

'No, let her do it.'

Adam had a shirt on, the kind that buttons up, not a T-shirt, but now he began to take it off, having an idea of what might be about to happen. The mixture of gin and wine he had drunk hammered in his head, distorting reality, opening limitless possibilities, showing him a fantasy world that rocked and shimmered. But all he could say was,

'We'll save Greece for another year. We won't go to Greece this time . . .'

Mary's fingers moved lightly across his back. Rufus had propped himself up on one elbow, watching. He leaned across Adam to light a cigarette from one of the incense sticks and he smiled, letting the smoke trickle out between his teeth. Mary told Adam to turn round and face her, she would do his chest. It was a bit like having someone rub you with suntan cream, yet it wasn't like that at all – how could it be in the dark? What it was like was being anointed by some slave girl. Rufus threw his cigarette away and from behind her laid his hand lightly on Mary's bare shoulder. She was wearing a halter top thing that tied round the back of her neck.

All the time, right up till then and a little beyond, Mary hadn't known what was going on. Rufus, of course, had always known, Rufus had instigated the whole thing, and then, at this point, Adam realized it. The realization resulted in a leap of desire that was brought about as much by Rufus, by the recollection of their slippery, buoyant contact beneath the water, as by the sight of Mary as Rufus untied the knot on her neck and slid the halter top down with his hands.

This movement, as Rufus had no doubt intended, sent Mary toppling forward into Adam's arms, her breasts lightly slapping into his chest in a way that would have been blissful if it had been allowed to continue but Mary, drunk as she was, had sprung aside, actually sprung to her feet, and rather late in the day hugged her arms across her chest.

'Now what's the bloody matter?' drawled Rufus.

'I'm not doing tribadism, that's what's the matter.'

'Troilism,' sighed Adam, 'not tribadism.' He might be drunk and bursting with frustration but words came first with him. An etymologist he was to the bitter end. 'The confusion arises from that "tri", which isn't Latin though but part of the derivation from the Greek verb "to rub". A tribade is a lesbian, whereas a troilist . . .'

'Jesus,' said Rufus, 'I don't believe it.'

He rolled about on the quilts, roaring with laughter.

'Pray continue,' he said, 'with your most interesting lecture on rubbing. If we can't do it at least we can hear about it.'

'You bastard,' said Mary. 'You perverted sod.'

'Please, it was only a game. A Midsummer night's game.'

'It's not bloody Midsummer night,' she roared at him. 'How many times do I have to tell you?'

She stalked off into the house. Rufus went on laughing, hiccuping with laughter. He lay on his back, pouring red wine down his throat.

'You're crazy, Verne-Smith, did you know that? I set you up a mini-orgy, a nice little threesome, and the minute it rocks a bit, nothing a mite of persuasion wouldn't put right, you start giving an address on the Greek verb "to rub". You slay me, you really do. I shall remember that to my dying day, I shall remember it all my life.'

'You won't, said Adam. 'I bet you don't.'

'Do you reckon she's really a closet tribade?'

After that he often called Mary the closet tribade. She was right when she said he could be a bastard, he really could.

'How about going for another swim?' said Rufus, and he turned, his mouth all dabbled with wine, to look into Adam's eyes. And Adam had looked into his, the wine singing in his head, the incense tapers smouldering, scenting the warm dark air.

'Why not?'

But Rufus had lain there, not touching Adam, just smiling. He had languidly stretched one arm out and in doing so knocked over the wine bottle. It had fallen too slowly to break but the wine had flowed out and made a dark stain like blood on the white candlewick. The tips of his outflung fingers just touched Adam's bare shoulder and Adam had lain still, aware of that warm, faintly tingling pressure, but happily, even serenely, aware, trying for some unknown reason to count the stars. The last thing he remembered Rufus say was uttered on a murmuring chuckle.

'The Greek verb "to rub"!'

And then Rufus was asleep, his head turned on to the muscle of his upper arm, the fingers that had been on Adam's shoulder retracting as they relaxed. Adam slept too, very soon afterwards, and awoke shivering with cold at dawn as one does after sleeping uncovered in the open air. He had, and was going to have, the worst hangover of his life, but even in the throes of it he was aware of a sense of relief that they were staying there, they were not going to Greece. The sky was a clear, pale dome, covered in the east by a flock of tiny clouds that were already turned to pink by the sun that was still concealed, that had not yet risen. The garden was no longer silent but noisy with birdsong, with twittering, cheeping, cooing sounds, and with the true, clear notes of the blackbird and thrush. Adam got to his feet and, throwing one of the quilts over Rufus, went into the house.

Two things happened the next day. Or one of those things happened. He wasn't sure of remembering the date of the other thing. It might have been on the Saturday. The coypu-control man must have come on a weekday, though, and it was with that hangover that Adam associated his coming.

Now when he and Anne had people to stay they ran around after their guests making sure they were comfortable. One or both of them got up early to make breakfast in good time. They made enquiries as to whether the beds were all right and the water hot. It was what their parents had done when they had guests. But a different system had prevailed at Wyvis Hall, or rather no system had prevailed at all. Everyone fended for themselves. That was the way Adam wanted it and had in fact been vociferous on the subject, vowing that neither now nor in the future would he ever give in to those bourgeois values and customs.

So he did nothing for Mary or Rufus that morning, did not even seek them out, scarcely knew whether Rufus was still asleep on the terrace or back in bed with Mary, and when he found further sleep impossible because of his shivering body and pounding head, he sat in the kitchen making instant coffee for himself but took none up to them. He had already taken two aspirins about half an hour before and now he took four more. The table he sat at was circular and made of pine or what Hilbert and Adam's father had called deal. Adam was thinking about this interesting word that used to be simply another term for pine but which originally meant a certain size of plank, from the Low German *dele*, when there came a loud knocking on the back door. It gave him a shock in his fragile state. He crept to the door and opened it, blinking at the bright light. Outside stood a man, middle-aged, with thinning dark hair and a black moustache, wearing jeans and a lightweight jacket in pale blue plastic. He said his name was Pearson, he was from coypu control and would it be all right for him to take a look round the lake?

'What control?' said Adam.

'New here, are you? I used to see a Mr Smith.'

Adam said he was dead. Was 'coypu' an acronym? The man looked at him as if he was mad.

'It's a sort of rat, isn't it?'

Adam gave up. 'Look all you want,' he said.

'Right, and I'll take a shufti round the wood while I'm about it. That field next to you's down to sugar beet this year. Your coypu is crazy for sugar beet.'

They aren't mine, Adam wanted to say but desisted. In Hilbert's dictionary he found coypu defined as a South American aquatic rodent, *Myopotamus coypus*, somewhat smaller than a beaver. He liked the Latin name so much that he made up a sort of rhyme about it and chanted this as he went upstairs:

'Flittermus, ottermus,
Myopotamus . . .'

From the window of the Pincushion Room he watched the man pottering about the edge of the lake. In one hand he held a sack, in the other what might have been metal traps, or not that at all but some kind of implement. How could coypu have got into a Suffolk pond? Must be an escape from a zoo, he thought, just as mink could be from fur farms. Going down again in search of more coffee, he met Mary coming up the stairs wearing Rufus's jeans and a dirty T-shirt with Louisiana State University printed on it. Mary looked the nearest to ugly he had ever seen her. She gave him a sullen glare and said in a very distant way did he know there was some awful peasant trespassing round the lake?

'He isn't trespassing.' Adam started singing 'Flittermus, ottermus' to the tune of the Austrian Hymn.

'You mean hippopotamus.'

Adam said he didn't, he meant myopotamus, which in turn meant

coypu that were presumably now in the process of being extermi-
nated, whereupon Mary burst into shouts of anger and distress,
calling him a cruel beast and an enemy of ecology.

'There can't be anything ecological about preserving South American rodents in Suffolk,' Adam protested, but by then Mary was
tearing off downstairs, bent on tackling the coypu controller herself.

Adam took a look out of the window of the bedroom that had been
Hilbert's. The van, which had Vermstroy Pest Control Ltd, Ipswich
and Nunes, painted on its side, was turning round on the open area
in front of the garage. As Mary came running out of the front door
it moved off up the drift towards the wood. It made him laugh to
see her standing there, shaking her fist at the departing van. He
had begun to feel better, the aspirins and coffee were doing their
work.

Rufus was still lying asleep on the terrace, though at some point
he must have awakened, for he was shaded from the sun by Hilbert's
old black umbrella which he had opened and propped there to shelter
his head and face. Adam sat down beside him, wondering if he would
have to pay the coypu man. 'I could sell those guns,' he said, when
Rufus woke up.

'Or more directly, dismiss the coypu man, keep the guns and shoot
the coypu yourself.'

That was all very well but there were going to be a lot of things to
pay. Rates, for instance. Adam found himself not at all sure what
rates were but he knew that people who owned houses did pay them.
And there would be bills for electricity and water. The guns could be
sold and more of the furniture. Unless ... Unless he could rent
rooms out to people, or better still, gather a group of people here
who all paid their way, start a commune in fact.

This was the first thought he had ever had of the commune, it was
at that moment it first came to him, out on the terrace sitting beside
Rufus under Hilbert's umbrella, while the Vermstroy man hunted his
quarry along the woodland streams and Mary pursued him with cries
of protest.

Adam, among his computers, reflected on the coypu man, whose
bill he had later paid, but whom he had never seen again. Would the
coypu man remember? And if he did would he be able to declare
categorically to the police that Adam and Rufus and Mary had
actually been living there? It must have been on or about 25 June,

364

before the others had come. From the lake the coypu man would have seen Rufus sleeping under the umbrella on the terrace and no doubt also seen Mary and probably spoken to her – have practically been assaulted by her.

He was about fifty or rather more. Very likely he was still alive. Vermstroy operated from Ipswich but it also operated from Nunes. The coypu man lived in Nunes. Later on, on a rare trip through the village in Goblander Adam had seen that van parked in the front garden in one of those big Hampstead Garden Suburb houses.

Of course it was possible the van was parked there only because the man was inside destroying coypu or moles or rats or woodworm, but somehow Adam didn't think so. He recalled the way it had been parked, its nose halfway inside the open garage.

The man had been in the wood and had perhaps seen the animal cemetery. Adam could not know if he had but it was quite possible. He would know that there were people living at Wyvis Hall. If nothing else, the appearance of the terrace, arranged like a huge bed, would have told him that. Evans or Owens, the furniture man, who had come twice to the house, had been at least sixty then. He was hardly a danger. The gardener who had worn a knotted handkerchief on his head, whoever he might have been, had had no means of knowing then or later that Adam intended to live there. The visitor whose footsteps he had heard circling the house that last dawn they had ever spent there, if indeed he had heard them and not, in his state of panic, imagined them – that man or woman would have had no evidence for thinking anyone lived there but for the presence of Goblander on the drive.

But the coypu man was different. The coypu man could not be dismissed or the danger of him glossed over. Hope lay only in the possibility, the fairly strong possibility, that he was one of those who do not push themselves forward into police investigations unless directly called upon.

The next day or the day after perhaps, when they had talked a lot about the commune project, Mary had come up with Bella's name. It had been more roundabout than that but that was basically it. She and Rufus and Adam himself had all been putting forward the names of people they knew who might want to be part of a commune, likely people of the right sort of age and the right sort of temperament.

Mary herself was quite keen, stipulating though that she would only stay if Rufus did not. Since his sly suggestions of Thursday midnight she had been unremittingly at war with him, though they still ostensibly shared a bed. In fact Rufus had taken mostly to sleeping outdoors. He had no intention, he said, of being part of a permanent commune, he had his medical degree to get, but he might think of coming there for his holidays. He upset Mary further by saying he thought Adam's sister Bridget very attractive and it would be an inducement to him if she became one of the members.

Adam didn't want his sister, they didn't get on all that well. He could think of two of his fellow students who might be suitable but they too had degree courses to finish and Adam was beginning to think very seriously of not returning to college. The peculiar mixed course he was doing he had always had doubts about. The linguistics part he knew already, the English he could pick up on his own and the sociology bored him. What was the good of a BA from that tinpot redbrick place anyway? He might as well be at a polytechnic. If he wanted a degree he could just as well get one at the technical college in Ipswich . . .

Rufus put up two or three names, one being of someone they had both been at school with. You wanted at least one person who had been in a commune before, Mary said, and perhaps you ought to advertise along those lines. In *Time Out*, say.

'Or *Gay News*,' said Rufus. '"Tribade seeks fellow travellers' help out of the closet."'

'I do just wonder,' Mary said, 'why you go on and on and on about it. Could it just be you've got a closet of your own, d'you think?'

Rufus started laughing at that and said all the doors in his life were strictly never kept closed. 'Open house and bring your friends.'

'It's a mystery to me you've got any.'

Adam hadn't liked the idea of advertising. Besides money was short. Before they got on to the subject of the commune they had been discussing which item of Hilbert's former property they should sell next. One of the big cabinets, Rufus said, and no nonsense about it, get Evans or Owens back, but Adam could see his house being stripped bare. If people came and put money into the commune . . .

'There's a girl I know of called Bella something,' said Mary. 'I don't know her. It's my friend Linda that knows her. She used to be one of that Rajneesh lot, she always lives in communes, and Linda told me she was looking for somewhere. I mean I could find out more about this Bella.'

It was through Bella, of course, that Vivien found them and with her the Indian, Shiva, whose other name Adam could not remember.

Mary was the only one of them, as far as he knew, who had ever walked to the village and walked about in the village when she got there. It would not matter what any inhabitant of Nunes told the police about Mary, for she had departed soon after that. And if people remembered her they would not have known where she came from. She had gone to the village – as Vivien had later gone – to use the public phone-box outside the Fir Tree. Probably she went into the Fir Tree or the village shop to get change for those calls. She had been phoning people who might go to Greece with her or drive her there or, failing that, pay her air-fare, and eventually she succeeded in getting a loan from an aunt and an offer of a place in a minibus from an old school-fellow and her boyfriend.

The day before she left he thought of a new name for his house. For some days he had been mulling this over, trying to come up with something more interesting than Wyvis Hall. Myopotamus Manor, which had occurred to him, was just a joke. He began anagramming, twisting letters round, keeping in mind where they *had* been going, where Mary was still going . . .

Ecalpemos.

He asked the others what they thought Ecalpemos was.

'A greek island,' said Mary.

'Not an island,' said Rufus. 'More like a mountain. A volcano.'

'Or a resort on the Costa Brava.'

'You just made it up,' said Rufus lazily. 'It does sound rather like a community. Oneida, Walden, Ecalpemos.'

'It doesn't sound in the least like Oneida or Walden. I know what it is, it's like Erewhon: that's "nowhere" backwards.'

Adam was surprised at Mary's perspicacity but annoyed that she was leaving. He didn't like her much but wanted her to stay. He was finding he resented people who did not care for Wyvis Hall as much as he did.

'You don't know the difference between an anagram and an inversion, do you?' he said. 'Bloody illiteracy always puts my back up. Why talk about it if you don't know?'

'Hey-hey,' said Rufus. 'I'm the one that quarrels with her, remember?'

'Erewhon is an anagram on "nowhere". Ecalpemos is "some place" inverted.'

'Well, well, very clever. Don't you find "some place" has too much of an American flavour?'

'I don't give a sod about that,' said Adam. 'It's not being called "some place" anyway, it's going to be Ecalpemos.'

Which thereafter it always was.

The next day was 30 June, a Wednesday. Mary wanted Rufus to drive her all the way back to London but he said Colchester was his limit and she could get a train from there. There was a certain *rapprochement* though, as Mary came down with her things in the back-pack Rufus had lent her and wearing jeans and a pair of sandals for the first time for days.

'I actually adored it,' she said to Adam, 'only I'd promised myself I'd go to Greece these holidays and I absolutely can't not go now.'

'That's OK. Ecalpemos will still be here next year.'

'I did wonder if you'd like me to send cards to your parents and Rufus's from Athens. I mean ones you'd write here and I'd take them with me.'

'By a quite exceptional oversight,' said Rufus, 'I don't just happen to have any picture postcards of the Acropolis about me at present.'

'It was just a thought,' Mary said sulkily. 'It didn't have to be cards, it could have been a letter.'

'If mine got a letter from me,' said Rufus, 'they'd think I was dying or in jail.'

It amounted to the same thing for him. And why bother to write anyway? What was there to say? Mary had some vague idea that Adam's parents might suspect he was down here and come to see him. But Adam couldn't see why they should. If only he had acceded to that suggestion of hers! The ironical thing was that all the time, in a stack in Hilbert's desk, secured by a rubber band, were fifty or so old postcards collected by Hilbert and Lilian presumably on early travels and among them were two of Greece, one of Mount Lycabettos and the other the very view Rufus had spoken of so scathingly.

But they hadn't known that then, and if they had could not have known how much one day such postcards would have supported the story Adam was beginning to think he would tell. Always supposing their parents had kept the postcards, which, considering their rarity value, they might well have done. Mary's offer had been rejected without their thinking twice about it and she and Adam had said goodbye in a cool, offhand sort of way and Rufus had driven her off to the station in Goblander.

From that day to this Adam had never set eyes on Mary Gage and had hardly ever thought of her. If she had come into his mind he had operated his cancelling switch as he did when any of the denizens of Ecalpemos strayed into his thoughts. Once, not long ago, an old film called *National Velvet* had been on television and when the young Elizabeth Taylor appeared on the screen he had at once been sharply reminded of Mary – and had exited, not with the escape key but with the switch on the set.

He and Rufus had talked about money later that day. What could they sell next? Even to Adam's ignorant eye the Victorian watercolours of moorland or mountain streams, mounted on gold paper and framed in gilt, were valueless. There was a strange picture in one of the bedrooms of a centaur-like creature, a horse with the torso and head of a man, presenting itself at a forge to be shod, where it was eyed with fearful fascination by the smith and a crowd of onlookers. When they cut away the paper at the back of the frame it proved to be a Böcklin, but a print cut from a magazine, the original being in Budapest. They called the room where it hung the Centaur Room. Another strange picture hung in Hilbert's room, one that Adam had never allowed himself to think about. Since the birth of Abigail it would have been torture. And, besides, the picture no longer existed, having been burnt by Adam himself, destroyed on that pyre with certain other things.

A large gloomy bedroom had been the setting of it, hung with draperies, not the kind of thing you would expect a child to sleep in, but it was a little child that lay on the bed, white and still, the elderly man, evidently a doctor, who had seemingly just lifted a looking glass from the parted lips, turning to the young father and imparting the news of death, while the mother in a transport of grief clung to her husband, her head buried in his shoulder. Adam confronted this remembered picture now with a kind of stoicism. He forced himself to see it and recall those things which were connected with it. How extraordinary it seemed that he and Rufus had stood in front of that picture and *laughed* at it! To remember this now brought him an actual physical pain in the deeps of his body, in his intestines. He and Rufus had stood there drinking wine. Rufus had the last bottle of wine in his left hand and a glassful in his right. They were walking round the house speculating as to what they should sell and had paused here in this far from gloomy room, this warm, sunny, charming room, and laughed at that gloomy picture, at its sentimental naïvety. In fact he had even made some appropriately sophisticated comment.

'Dead and never called me Mother,' it had probably been.

That was the reason they named it the Deathbed Room.

On into the Room Without a Name they had passed and through to the room it communicated with, the Room of Astonishment, so called because it had a cupboard in it with a little staircase inside that wound its way up into the loft. They considered the saleability of a washstand, a swinging mirror, a flowered pottery basin and jug, and then as they descended by the back stairs, the plates in dull red and dark blue and gold glaze that hung on the wall there and might, from the hieroglyphs on their backs, possibly be Chinese and perhaps valuable.

Next day they had taken the mirror and the pottery and the porcelain to Long Melford because there were more antique shops in Long Melford than anywhere else they had seen, but £20 was all they got for the lot. When people came to join the commune, Adam thought, they would have to pay, they would have to contribute. And how were any suitable people going to know about it when he had no phone, or no phone that worked, and Mary Gage had probably forgotten all about this Bella?

There, of course, he had been wrong. All the time he and Rufus were living it up, driving about the countryside in Goblander, driving to London once to buy marijuana from the dealer Rufus knew in Notting Hill, drinking and smoking (as he had put it) Hilbert's furniture away, all that time Vivien and her boyfriend Shiva were making arrangements to join Ecalpemos. And they were expecting, of course, a well-run settlement, a sort of East Anglian kibbutz, where the members had appointed duties, where vegetarianism prevailed and brown rice had an almost holy significance and discussions on mystical or occult or philosophic subjects went on long into the night.

But first Zosie had come.

Rufus, driving back from London with the hashish his dealer swore was genuine Indian *charas* and a package of best Colombian, picked her off the street – 'a piece of property that is found ownerless'. And she had slept with Rufus in the Centaur Room, it being taken for granted she would share his bed, though Adam did not think her wishes had been consulted. Rufus was a bit of a centaur himself, a big roan stallion, and she was a little cat-eyed – waif.

It must have been a day or two afterwards that she had seen the picture. Exploring the house on the following day or the day after that, she had ventured into the Deathbed Room. She had gone in and looked at that picture and come running down the stairs crying, with her hands up to her face and the tears pouring.

'Why did you let me go in there? Why didn't you tell me what was in there?'

Just for a moment, standing by the window, dropping the edge of the curtain he had lifted and turning back towards the cot, Adam saw the picture again, saw it with an awful clarity on the darkness before his eyes.

The painting was destroyed. He had burned it himself on the fire he had made against the fruit-garden wall and it might be that no copies of it existed, yet in his mind's eye it re-created itself, the child for ever stilled, its face a waxen mask, the old doctor haggard with sorrow and lack of sleep, the mirror no breath had misted held in his hand, the parents in each other's arms.

– 9 –

Because he was without a qualification Shiva was not permitted to dispense. Kishan, with his pharmacology degree, did that and Mira his wife helped out at particularly busy times. Shiva served in the shop and arranged the displays and kept a check on the stock and sometimes recommended remedies for coughs and spots. Kishan really needed a second assistant but he couldn't afford one if he was going to continue paying Shiva a decent wage with small annual increases. Although he didn't want to lose him he was an altruistic man and was always trying to persuade Shiva to go back to college and finish his course so that he could set up as a pharmacist himself, not just work for one. Shiva knew he would never go back now, it would all be too fraught with memories and bitterness. Besides, he did not dislike the shop, the warmth of it and the delicious scents, the feeling of doing positive good when he was able to persuade someone of the virtues of vitamin C, the brief pleasure he took in selling a pretty girl a pretty shade of lipstick. He accepted. He did not expect to be fulfilled or enjoy job satisfaction or be happy.

Once he had been all those things. At school in the far west of London he had got three good A Levels and gone on to study pharmacology. This brought his father an almost delirious joy. Shiva's father was an uneducated though not an illiterate man, who had brought his wife and his widowed mother to this country some twenty years before. For some time he had worked for a tailor and his wife had been a machinist but, having a business sense and some foresight, he had observed the beginnings of the trend towards Indian-made clothes. Even he could not have imagined how immensely popular dresses and skirts and tops of embroidered Indian cotton would become or how the humble import business he started would make him if not a rich, at least a very comfortably-off man. It was in this comparative affluence that Shiva and his brother and sisters grew up, their home a big, semi-detached house in Southall. Shiva's elder brother, though he had won a scholarship to the City of London School, had not lived up to his early promise and had embarked on a career in a High Street bank. It was on Shiva therefore that his father pinned his hopes and ambitions. Shiva had just completed his first year at a college of technology where he had done very well, so well in fact that two of the lecturers there had privately told him – well, not exactly that he was wasting his time, but that he was mentally equipped for higher things. Both believed that he would be better suited to read medicine.

Of course he told his father. What should he do? Should he apply to medical schools? Probably that meant he would have to wait a year, always supposing he were accepted. His father, overwhelmed at the prospect of having a doctor for a son, was certain he would be accepted. And why not have a year off if that were necessary? There was money enough to keep him. It was all very pleasant to contemplate and think of at his leisure. Not entirely at his leisure either, for it would not have occurred to Shiva to live at home and do nothing.

The business could always do with the temporary help of an extra pair of hands.

Another source of Shiva's happiness was his relationship with Vivien Goldman. Of her he said nothing at home; his parents were progressive and though his grandmother might wring her hands, predicting curses and disaster, they would not have considered arranging marriages for their children. Just the same, they took it for granted they would marry among their own people. They probably took it for granted, Shiva thought, that their children would not even get to know members of the opposite sex who were English.

Vivien was Jewish. To Shiva's way of thinking she was only half Jewish because her father had been gentile, but Vivien said it was having a Jewish mother that made you a Jew. Not that she had seen her mother for many years, having been brought up in children's homes until she was eighteen. Shiva had met her at a party given by a fellow-student who lived in a squat near the river at Hammersmith where Vivien was also living. He had not at first been specially attracted by her, indeed he had been somewhat daunted, but she had singled him out and talked to him. She had talked to him about Indian philosophy and Indian mysticism, subjects on which Shiva was not well-informed, and confided in him how she intended to go to India to learn from a certain guru and sit at his feet. After the party Shiva had gone home with Vivien, not to make love but to talk and sleep and talk again.

Vivien was the only person Shiva had ever met whose aim in life was to find out what she was doing in this world, what the meaning of life was and to learn how to be good. To this end she had lived for a while on a kibbutz and in a commune in California and been a disciple of Bhagwan and attended hundreds of lectures and read hundreds of books. Shiva (whose mother described him as 'education mad') asked her why she didn't go to university and read philosophy, but Vivien despised formal education. After she left school and at the same time the children's home, she lived for a while on Social Security but, coming to believe that this was wrong, went out cleaning flats and in between the kibbutz and Bhagwan had been a children's nanny.

She was a small, dark girl, with long hair she wore in braids or wound tightly round her head. Shiva had never known her to wear trousers or any garments of a masculine cast. Vivien wore robes rather than dresses and sometimes she hung round her neck the Star of David and sometimes the Christian cross. Alone in the world and without ties, she seemed to have a hundred friends but no close ones and Shiva, when at last they made love, was only her second lover.

He parted from her with no thought of seeing her again until he returned to college in September. If he returned there. They would write to each other. The Hammersmith squat had no phone and Shiva would not have liked Vivien to phone him at home. He could imagine the scenes his grandmother would make if she found out he had an English girlfriend, and what praying there would be, what threats of retribution, and not made in vain either, for his mother was not so progressive as to fail in her deference to her mother-in-law and the old lady's opinions carried great weight in the house in Southall. So Shiva wrote to Vivien and received her letters which he told his parents were from a friend of his at college, a boy whose family was from Benares.

Then the letter came with the suggestion that Shiva might like to join Vivien in a community at Ecalpemos, wherever that might be, just for a trial period to see what it was like. She understood he would have to go back to college in September. But she might remain. It all depended on whether a centre for meditation might be established there.

Would he have to go back to college, though? Shiva asked himself. Perhaps not, not if he changed his mind about the pharmacology course and decided to try for medical school instead. In that case he would not be able to start until October twelve-month and in the interim might have to re-sit a less than excellent A Level. But he could work at his maths just as easily at Ecalpemos as in Southall and perhaps more easily. A house with gardens and land in the country, in Suffolk, Vivien had written.

Shiva, though far more deferential to his parents than any European contemporary would be, holding them in far greater esteem, nevertheless had no compunction about lying to them. He reasoned this way. If he told them he was going to spend two months in a centre for meditation with an English girl who had no parents to speak of and was partly Jewish, they would be very unhappy indeed and would worry, whereas if he said what in fact he did say, that he would be attending a summer school designed as a preparatory course for those contemplating a medical career they would be happy and gratified. Really there was no choice about it. That such a summer school did not and could not exist need be no obstacle since his father was ignorant about these things and trusted Shiva's word and opinions. He even gave them the address: Ecalpemos, Nunes, Suffolk, for he knew that nothing short of the death of one of them would induce the others to get in touch with him.

Shiva's father told him to help himself to a selection from the best of the Indian cotton shirts so that he might look smart during his stay. Shiva knew he would have no need of new shirts so he took a dress instead. No Indian woman had ever worn dresses like these, with low square necks and big sleeves and high waists and floor-length skirts, or ever would, but this bright turquoise-blue one embroidered on the bodice in scarlet and gold might have been made for small, pretty Vivien. It would be the first present he had ever given her.

The squat was in a row of condemned houses in a street very close to the river off the Fulham Palace Road. It was all gone now, Shiva had heard, the derelict cottages replaced by hygienic local authority housing and a day centre for the handicapped. When Vivien had been living there the row had been awaiting demolition and scheduled unfit for human occupation, but squatters had come just the same and knocked out openings in the communicating walls so that entering at number one, you could walk all the way through to number nine without going out into the street. Shiva walked through, stepping over people asleep on mattresses on the floor. No one in that squat except Vivien ever got up before midday. It was shabby rather than dirty and it smelt of the river.

He found Vivien in her room, sitting cross-legged and meditating. She turned on him her bright-eyed gaze but gave no other sign of greeting and he did not interrupt her. He sat down among the mats and cushions that furnished the place in a vaguely oriental way that was quite unlike the solid three-piece suites and carved wood and etched brass of his own home. There was a rack of essential oils in tiny phials on the windowsill and the case in which Vivien kept her Bach flower remedies. A reflexology chart hung on one wall and the chart of Vivien's own horoscope underneath it. Her book collection he found daunting: the Bible, the Koran, the Gita, *The Imitation of Christ*, *The Tibetan Book of the Dead*. The *I Ching* lay open on a cushion, with what looked like slips of straw beside it, as if before he came she had cast to know what her fate would be at Ecalpemos . . .

Since then he had sometimes wondered what the *I Ching* had told her. Not, surely, anything like an accurate forecast or she would hardly have gone. It was impossibly cryptic, anyway, it could be made to mean anything. He sat and waited, not minding, not impatient, but beginning to feel soothed and at peace as one did in Vivien's presence. Twenty minutes went by and then she got up. Her bag was packed but she opened it again and put the flower remedies in and a big dark-red shawl in case it got cold in the evenings. The bag was a holdall made of carpet, with padded cloth handles, for Vivien wore no leather or any animal material, not even wool.

'What time is the train?' Shiva asked.

'I don't know. If we go along to the station a train will come. They always do.'

He thought it quite amusing that Vivien should have to teach *him* this serene fatalism. 'Are you in a great hurry, Shiva?' she said. 'Have you got some pressing business at Ecalpemos that will vanish or be lost if you aren't there by nightfall?'

It was just a tradition, an accepted way of life, that you made haste, you rushed busily, irrespective of what you had to do when the end was reached. His parents were as much afflicted by it as English people.

'We have time,' Vivien often said. 'We're young. It's when we're eighty and we haven't much time left, then we'll have to rush.'

He gave her the turquoise-blue dress and immediately she put it on, for she had no understanding of the concept of keeping something for best. What would 'best' be? All days were alike to her and all places for her to look at, not where others would look at her.

It was a grey and cream striped Moroccan-cotton robe she had been wearing. She folded it carefully and laid it beside the *I Ching*.

'I won't need that now. I've got another dress with me.'

Shiva found her amazing. What other woman would go off for perhaps months with only two dresses?

'You can always collect it,' he said, 'if you have to come back to London for an interview.'

She had applied for a job as a children's nanny before Bella told her about Ecalpemos. But Shiva could tell that, though calm and unhurried, she was excited by the prospect before her. The job might

376

be disregarded if Ecalpemos turned out to be what she was always seeking, a real community of dedicated people, all with ideas like hers, people that she might teach and who might teach her something. He watched her write a note to someone else in the squat, ending it: 'love and peace, Vivien'.

Travelling with her was a placid, restful experience. They missed the fast Inter-City train because Vivien refused to run for it and got into a slow train instead that took fifteen minutes longer to get there, stopping at half-a-dozen stations on the way. The blue dress was very conspicuous, the embroidery on the bodice and low-cut neckline glistening like real jewellery. Vivien looked beautiful and exotic but a little bizarre too. Outside Colchester station, off the grass verge, she had picked a yellow flower of a very common sort, though Shiva did not know what sort, and stuck it in her hair. Perhaps because of the way she looked – and the way he looked too, come to that, a lithe, small-boned, dark-skinned Oriental – it was a while before a motorist stopped to give them a lift. Vivien had given no thought to the proximity or otherwise of Nunes to Colchester but they learned at the station that it was twelve miles away. There were buses but these were infrequent and the last one had gone. The car driver who picked them up said he would go into the village of Nunes but no further.

Shiva had seldom been out into the English countryside and it was with wonder and a certain amount of curiosity that he looked at the wide fields of yellowing wheat and barley across which exaggeratedly long shadows lay. It was the driver who told him they were wheat and barley; they might have been sesame and sainfoin, for all he knew. There was no wind. There were no animals in the meadows, which surprised him, for he had expected herds of fat black and white cattle. They passed not a single walker or cyclist and met few other cars. The houses which he thought would be the dwellings of the poor, ramshackle and mean, were for the most part large and prosperous-looking, set in gardens full of flowers.

It had been mid-July. The sun was on the point of setting but the sky was still a dense blue and quite cloudless. Vivien had found out from Bella precisely where Ecalpemos was and when she saw the first of the landmarks she had been told about, Nunes church, flint-walled, with a square tower and narrow, pointed spire, set on a grassy mound, she said they would get out and continue on foot. They

377

walked along quite slowly, watching the sun go down and, as it vanished below the dark wooded horizon, saw the sky warm at once to gold and gradually flush rosy-pink.

It was about half a mile along that they found the path. Both of them, Shiva knew, were disconcerted because there was no sign saying Ecalpemos. He suspected Vivien had anticipated a hand-crafted wooden sign with the name lettered on it and perhaps a carved flower or pair of acorns. But it must be the place. There were no other houses to be seen in any direction, only huge prairie-like fields. A farmhouse called the Mill in the Pytle they had passed ten minutes before. To the left of them was a dense pine wood that looked quite black at that hour, with the sky above it reddening as if from a distant fire.

They turned down the path, wondering and hoping. It was like entering a tunnel after a while, for the trees met overhead, though through the black network of branches you could still see the brilliant sky. This tunnel descended gradually, winding a little, then running straight down. It was the quietest place Shiva had ever been in, silent in a velvety, tactile way so that you felt you might have been stricken with deafness. And there were insects, flies and slow-wheeling, transparent winged things with dangling legs, and moths. A dustiness in the air and a dustiness underfoot and a scent of something sweet and something rotten. Not like England, he had thought, not what he had expected a bit. Vivien had not spoken for some minutes and their footfalls on the sandy surface of the path, the dry turf, were soundless.

The trees parted. Briefly and absurdly, Shiva had the notion that the trees had stepped aside to reveal the house to him. It lay bathed in the afterglow of sunset, its windows turned to flat sheets of gold, a mansion it seemed to him, old and dignified and belonging to an unknown world. The breeze of dusk, the little wind that Shiva had come to learn always raised itself at about this time, fluttered through the bushes, the treetops, a clustering of feather-headed flowers, as if a living thing had passed and ruffled the leaves with its invisible paw.

It was a gentle Nemesis Shiva felt was in pursuit of him, its approach slow and light-footed, but as sure as that breeze. Whether it was Vivien who had taught him to wait and accept, or if this were an inheritance from fatalistic forebears, he did not know. But he did not specially want an awareness of the true state of things, of the progress the police were making. He would have liked Adam or Rufus to get in touch with him. Their indifference, their treating him as of no account, caused him a pain he thought he had long got over. In one respect only he felt glad, he felt relieved, and this was in that he had kept nothing from Lili. To his parents and his grandmother he might have lied when the expediency of lying appealed to him, but to his wife he had told only the truth. His father had died four years before but his grandmother lived on, she and his mother sharing the Southall house, two widows, though his mother had never adopted the white sari. Abandoning that ambition to read medicine had caused Dilip Manjusri an enduring bitterness and sorrow, so much so that he hardly seemed to notice when his son gave up the pharmacology course as well. Of course by then Shiva had been very ill, had suffered a true mental breakdown which included physical collapse. It was curious, he sometimes thought, how in stories and books someone who had brought about another person's death recovered from it immediately, was just the same afterwards as before, was affected if at all only by the fear of discovery. The reality was very different. Lili understood that and it was this as much as anything which bound him to her. This was what he called his love for her.

The pharmacy closed early on Wednesdays. Shiva's bus took him to the top of Fifth Avenue and he walked home along the pavement, beside the bead string of parked cars, past the pub that was called the Boxer and past the grocer's shop, both of which had their windows boarded up. There had been trouble down here the previous Saturday night, starting in the Boxer when the barman refused to serve a man who was already drunk. The man happened to be Jamaican and the resultant mini-riot ensued, Shiva had heard, when he and his friends accused the barman of race discrimination. A lot of windows had got broken and by the time the police arrived someone had got as far as overturning a car. From inside their own house, snug in front of the television, Lili and Shiva had heard that car go over and Lili had been afraid. But the sound of the police sirens seemed to put an end to all of it, which was far from always being the case.

How horrified his father would have been if he could have seen this! He had loved England with the innocent worship of the immigrant who *has* made good, who has found the mother country indeed to be the land of milk and honey so many of his compatriots had warned him it was not. In many ways it was fortunate he died when he did. There had been rioting before that, but he was too ill to realize. London had been a cleaner place then too, Shiva fancied, not all this litter lying about the streets, cans in the gutter waiting to be kicked about and make that characteristic night sound of a city street, a hollow, empty, meaningless clatter.

Was there more packaging than there had been ten years ago? Or more eating in the streets? More children about who were never told not to throw wrappers on the ground? Suddenly a memory came very sharply to him. He could almost hear that drawling upper-middle-class voice, Rufus Fletcher's:

'These days breaking into most people's houses is easier than opening a packet of biscuits.'

In the kitchen at Ecalpemos, Vivien in her peacock-blue dress with a great bowl of strawberries in her arms, Rufus naked but for ragged shorts, stabbing at the cellophane covering on a custard-creams pack with a pair of scissors. The tough, transparent stuff split open with quite a loud crack, with an explosion almost, and the biscuits tumbled out on to the table and the tiled floor, breaking and scattering crumbs.

And Zosie sitting on the edge of the table, picking one up and putting it whole into her mouth and someone saying – Adam? Rufus? He couldn't remember – but saying:

'Zosie is the same colour as those biscuits, matt, smooth and lightly baked.'

Dark Shiva was more conscious of the colour of his skin when he was at Ecalpemos than perhaps he had ever been before. Though not more than he had been since. He should have said,

'And I suppose I'm the colour of a ginger-nut.'

Lili worked all day on Wednesdays and she had just an hour off at lunchtime but she made a point of coming home specially to get his lunch for him and be a proper Indian wife. She wore the kamiz and salwar, her neck and shoulders covered by a dupatta in very much the same shade as the blue dress he had given Vivien. It dismayed him to see her dress like this, it embarrassed him. Her ancestors were not from the Punjab – why did she wear the costume of Punjabi women? To be not *an* Indian but all India, he knew that. Their notions about this were diametrically opposed. Assimilation was the only answer, in his view. Would all those European Jews have died if they had assimilated, if the Diaspora had not set itself apart and exclusive? If Shiva had a dream it would be that the world might become like the ideal in a popular song he remembered from his childhood in which it was advocated that all races be blended in a melting pot. Shiva did not care about what was lost thereby, the kamizes and saris, the festivals and phylacteries, the tongues and the traditions. They could all go if the gas chambers and the burning cars went with them.

'I'll be going straight to my Bengali lesson after work,' Lili said.

'I know. I'll walk over and meet you.'

'Oh, why? You needn't.'

'I'll walk over and meet you,' Shiva said.

Two stressful sounds met Adam as he let himself into his own house, as he pushed open the front door: Abigail's crying and the phone ringing. The crying came from the living room, the door to which, on the left, stood ajar, the ringing from the phone that was on a table at the foot of the staircase straight ahead of him. Adam, seemingly without thought, instinctively perhaps, went to the phone and picked up the receiver. Immediately, before he even said hallo, he thought with a pang that caught him in the chest, I went to the phone first, I put her second, I went to the phone first.

It was the police.

Anne came running downstairs and into the living room. A voice was saying to Adam that he was Detective Inspector Someone-or-other and could he come to see him to 'clear a few matters up'. Abigail's crying stopped quite abruptly.

'What matters?' Adam asked, because he knew an innocent person would ask that.

'I'll explain all that when we meet, Mr Verne-Smith.'

Adam asked when he wanted to come.

'I'm sure you'll agree there's no time like the present, so shall we say half an hour?'

'All right.'

Anne came out with Abigail in her arms and Adam kissed his child and took her from Anne. In the way babies can, Abigail looked as if she had never cried in her life, would not have known how to cry. She had a glorious, angelic smile and her cheek against Adam's own felt cool and fat and satiny like a new-picked plum.

'My God,' Adam said, 'I came into the house and heard the phone ringing and her crying and I went to the phone first. What sort of a father does that make me?'

Had Anne only known it he was confiding in her, was opening his heart to his wife, and this might have been the beginning of a greater confidence, an abandonment of his self into her keeping, but she did not know it, she saw his outburst simply as another symptom of neurotic self-absorption. It exasperated her.

'But there was nothing wrong with her. She was only frustrated because she had thrown her teddy out and couldn't reach it.'

Adam shrugged. He held Abigail pressed against him. Suppose they were to take him away and he were not to see her again for years, for ten years, say? Of course that was nonsense, it must be nonsense, he was getting hysterical with worry. The fact was that he was terribly tired. To break into an area of memory that has been deliberately buried and turfed over for a decade was an exhausting process. It was his own thoughts that had worn him out, this once-buried thing which now obsessed him. He wished he could drink, he wished drinking could do something for him.

'Would you get me a small whisky with water in it?'

Anne looked at him in surprise.

'A lot of water.' He apologized. 'I can't get it without putting her down.'

He sat in a chair with Abigail in his lap. Taking off his watch, he held it to her ear and then he remembered – for her face registered nothing – that it was his new watch, the one with the battery, and therefore did not tick. Instead he gave her an ornament from the mantelpiece, a small china cat. Abigail put its head in her mouth. Adam felt sick with love for her, he felt as if his love for her was being pulled out of him with tongs, and he knew beyond a doubt, it was laughable even to consider a doubt, that he had never loved anyone before. Not even Zosie.

His drink was brought. Anne took the china cat away from Abigail and gave her a rattle which had just been washed and which smelt of the stuff with which her bottle and other utensils were disinfected. Adam said:

'The police want to come and see me. Something about that house my great-uncle left me.'

'When?'

382

'What do you mean, when?'

'When do they want to come and see you?'

'Now.' He looked at the watch that did not tick. 'Well, in twenty minutes or so.'

'I see. What's it all about, Adam? I mean you're not going to get into some sort of trouble, are you?'

Sometimes he felt tremendously distanced from her. She was less than the intermediary that produced Abigail from his seed. Worse than that, he felt he didn't know her at all, she was just a woman who had called round for something. Collecting for a charity perhaps. Canvassing for a political party or a religious sect. He did not know her, she was a stranger, even her face was unfamiliar, not an attractive face or a loved one, not a face he could ever have kissed.

'I can't tell them very much,' he said. 'It isn't as if I ever lived there. Well, I stayed there for a couple of weeks, and then I went off to Greece.'

'But you had someone come in to look after it, didn't you?'

'Actually no. I told my father that at the time to stop him saying I was letting the place go to ruin. How could I have afforded to pay anyone to go in there? I was broke. I had to sell some of Hilbert's furniture in order to get to Greece.'

'It was the bones of a girl they found and a baby.'

'I know what they found,' said Adam, and holding Abigail's round, strong, plump body, he closed his eyes.

Those two girls, the barmaid and her friend, that he and Rufus had picked up and brought to Ecalpemos for the night, would they go to the police? Hardly. One of them had been married, her husband away on a selling trip. A discreditable drunken spree ending in messy sex was scarcely a memory she would want to revive. That must have been very late in June, the 29th or 30th, a Wednesday anyway. And a few days later, at the end of the week, Zosie had come and then Vivien and the Indian. Adam thought he would tell the police he had left Wyvis Hall for Greece the first weekend in July and then if by any remote chance those two girls had talked to them, or one of them – the barmaid – had, it would still appear all right.

The Indian wouldn't go to the police. Perhaps he wasn't even in this country any longer. Maybe when Adam saw him he had been off abroad somewhere, possibly even to take a job abroad and live there. Adam could still remember the slight feeling of dismay he had had when the Indian had come that night, had walked around the side of the house with Vivien a little way behind him, stood on the grass below the terrace wall (between Zeus with Danaë and Zeus with Europa) and looked up at him and Rufus and Zosie and the inevitable wine bottles on the terrace.

Adam had never before spoken to an Indian. Well, that wasn't quite right, for of course he had spoken to Indian post-office clerks and supermarket assistants and ticket collectors but he had never been on social terms with one. He had never had a conversation with an Indian, for the Indian students at his college, of whom there were in any case not many, kept to themselves. This one looked as if he might be – well, there was no word for it these days, but what old Hilbert might have called a killjoy or a wet blanket. Adam sensed at once a disapproval at the mess on the terrace, the air of indolence, the atmosphere perhaps of debauch. The girl on the other hand who announced herself as Vivien seemed only smiling and friendly. She climbed up the steps at once and accepted the glass of wine Rufus offered her.

Had they spoken much to the Indian that night? Already Adam had been drunk, tired and feeble the way drink always made him even then. And Rufus had been as he always was, alive and alert, unaffected one might think until one knew him well. His eyes had gone speculatively to Vivien, summing her up, the level of attractiveness she might have on the scale he kept in his mind, the precise relationship she might be having with Shiva. To Adam that relationship was obvious from the first and he had never even asked them if they would prefer to sleep apart, but took them up to Hilbert's room as a matter of course, to the room where the painting of the dead child and its parents and the doctor hung on the wall facing the bed.

Next day Shiva had asked if he called it the Deathbed Room because his great-uncle had died there. He was the sort of person who is very bound up with his family and relatives. Adam knew Hilbert had not died there but outside the door at the top of the back stairs, though perhaps his body had lain in the room to await the arrival of undertakers. Anyway, they all came to believe it, to accept that it was Hilbert's death-chamber, along with the other absurdities of Ecalpemos.

Zosie used sometimes to say she saw Hilbert's ghost up there and a ghostly little dog at his heels. The extraordinary thing was that she described Hilbert very much as he had been, a small, spare man with a round face and thin, grey hair and gold-rimmed bifocals. She must have looked into one of the photograph albums in the study. And Adam did not think she had ever mentioned the little dog until after Shiva had been up in the pine wood and found the animal cemetery and Blaze's grave ...

The smell of the whisky made him shiver a little. He took a sip of it and as he set the glass down heard a car draw up outside. The police had come. He shook his head at Anne and went himself to let them in, carrying Abigail in his arms, as if their hard hearts might be softened by the sight of a father with his child.

— IO —

One of Rufus's patients had a drug-addicted daughter. Mrs Harding came for her check-up and her smear and then she would tell him the latest on Marilyn. Last time it had been the Methadone overdose Marilyn had taken, believing thus to get herself off heroin the sooner. Now Marilyn, though experiencing a precarious cure, was afraid she might have become a carrier of AIDS through using infected needles. Rufus, smoking a companionable cigarette with Mrs Harding, urged her to make Marilyn have a test done.

While commiserating with her he found himself wondering what she would think if she knew of his own less than innocent past in this connection. It was of course long over. Rufus had not smoked cannabis or eaten hashish or swallowed 'acid' – with heroin he had never experimented – since the expulsion from Ecalpemos. An addictive personality he might have, did have, but he knew where to stop. Rufus stopped at the rationed cigarettes and the half-glass of vodka behind the curtain. He got up and opened the door for Mrs Harding and she said, thank you *so* much, you don't know how marvellous it is just to *talk* ...

The stuff he used, he thought, had all come from the same dealer, an American who had originally come to England to escape the Vietnam draft and who lived in Notting Hill. Rufus wanted supplies before all the money ran out, the money Adam got from selling plates and a mirror and then, at his instigation, a set of silver fruit knives and forks. Whoever ate fruit with a knife and fork? The shopkeeper seemed to feel the same which was why they hadn't got all that much for them. But what they did get Rufus took with him to Notting Hill, going up from Nunes in Goblander around lunch-time on – when would it have been – July the first or second?

He had got to Notting Hill late in the afternoon, waited for Chuck for what seemed like hours in a pub called the Sun in Splendour, and eventually gone to Chuck's flat which was the basement of a house in Arundel Gardens. Chuck was displeased to see him, had forgotten their arrangement, and kept saying it looked bad to have a stream of people arriving at his door at all hours. Rufus, naturally, couldn't have cared less. He got his Colombian and his *charas*, fifty sodium amytal capsules for good measure, paid for them, and set off back to Nunes.

If he had had any money left, any real money instead of just enough to buy petrol and ten cigarettes, Rufus would have stayed in London much later and found something interesting to do with his evening. He had occasionally thought of that since, how everything would have been changed, whole lives would have been changed including his own, if he had had £20 in his pocket instead of £2.50. For if he had left London at eleven, say, instead of seven-thirty Zosie would not have been waiting outside the station at Colchester to hitch a lift to Nunes.

'Some great brute of a truck driver would have picked you up,' he had said to her a couple of days later, 'and maybe raped and murdered you and left your body in a ditch.'

'Well, you raped me,' said Zosie.

'I *what*?'

'I only did it to get my lift and a bed for the night. I only did it for *sanctuary*, and that's rape really.'

It was never policy with Rufus to recall ego-defacing rejoinders of that sort. He allowed himself to remember instead how from the first she had known it was Nunes she wanted to go to. She had never been there but she knew it was where she was heading. Home is where you go to, someone had written, and they have to take you in.

She looked about twelve until you got up close to her. Then, even in the dark, in the greenish lamplight, you could see she was more than that. Her hair was like a little cap of fawn satin. He hadn't said that, Adam had, Adam the wordsmith. She had a face like all the drawings there had ever been of fairy girls on birthday cards and illustrated children's books. Adam had said that too. Rufus saw only a small, slender, finely-made girl in jeans and a T-shirt with a back-pack that looked as if it hadn't much in it. And a face of despair or desperation which expressed itself in a big-eyed stare.

He drew up a few yards ahead of her and she ran up to the van.

'Where do you want to go to?'

'Anywhere!'

'Come on, give me a better idea than that.'

She hesitated fractionally. 'Nunes.'

'Surprise, surprise. By an amazing coincidence I'm going there myself.'

Frankly, and he had been quite frank about it to himself at the time, he had picked her up because he thought there might be a chance of sex and he had had no sex since Mary went (the encounter with the barmaid's friend not having amounted to much, he being too drunk at the time). At first she had not seemed particularly attractive. Zosie was like that. Her attractions made themselves felt slowly and then they grabbed you by the throat. She looked impossibly young.

'Could I have a cigarette?'

'I've only got six.'

'You could buy some in that pub.'

'I could if I had any money. I just bought a gallon of petrol. It was either that or a long night's smoke in a lay-by. Have you any money?'

'Of course I haven't.'

She couldn't have sounded more astonished, more *sullenly* astonished, if he had asked her if she had a mink coat in her back-pack.

'What's your name?'

'Zosie.'

'Zoe?'

'Not Zoe and not Sophie. *Zosie*. What's yours?'

'Rufus.'

'Woof-woof,' said Zosie.

He gave her a cigarette and he had one. He pulled Goblander off the road onto a car track down one of the lanes leading to Boxted and they smoked their cigarettes and he remembered the packet of marijuana in the pocket of the door. So he took one of his four remaining cigarettes to pieces and rolled a joint and they smoked it, moving gradually closer and closer together, touching each other's faces and lips with fingertips and each other's bodies with hands, until it was time to climb into the back of the van . . .

It was the quickest sexual encounter of Rufus's life, with the least preamble, the least working up to. Almost as easy as when you are married, Rufus thought now. He did not ask himself if she had liked it, had wanted to do it. She had moved in the right way and made the right noises and the expression he saw briefly on her face, blank yet wild, was probably indicative of pleasure.

Back in the front, driving on, his left hand on her knee, moving in a vaguely affectionate way, he asked her where in Nunes she wanted to go to.

'Where are *you* going?'

'To my friend's place. Maybe you know it? Wyvis Hall, a rather handsome Georgian house with a lot of land.'

'I've never been to Nunes. This friend of yours – is it his parents' place?'

'No, it's his. He owns it. Just he and I live there.'

'Rufus,' she said, and her voice was very small, very young, 'can I go there with you? Just for a little while? Just for the night?'

'Why not?' said Rufus, and then he said, 'Where had you been meaning to go?'

She said nothing for a moment or two.

'OK, you don't have to tell me. That's your business.'

'I was just hoping something would turn up,' she said.

'Haven't you really got any money?'

She said fiercely, 'What d'you want me to do? Pay you for it?'

'OK, sorry. I just wondered how you expected to get very far without money.'

'I've got 50p.' She fished in her back-pack for some coins to show him. The pack was half empty. There was a grey knitted sweater in it, a black leather belt with studs, a copy of *Honey* magazine and a half-eaten chocolate bar. Zosie pulled the sweater round her shoulders and sat hugging herself. 'I'd have gone home,' she said.

He could tell she didn't like being questioned, so he hadn't asked where home was. By then they were going along the road from which the lane led up to Nunes and the church and the village green. She stared out of the window, into the white moonlight, the dark spaces. He noticed she was shaking, though it was warm.

388

'Are you feeling all right?'

'I'm tired,' she said. 'Christ, I'm tired.'

She sat back and closed her eyes. He drove past the Mill in the Pytle, not a light showing in the house, not a light anywhere, and turned down Adam's drift. When Goblander stopped she woke up, whimpering like a child.

'Here we are,' said Rufus.

She got up, stretching herself, pushing her fists into her eyes.

'I'll carry that,' said Rufus, taking the back-pack from her.

Yawning hugely, she looked up at Wyvis Hall, at the pillared porch, at the lemony glow of the dining-room window through which the chandelier could be seen, above the pool of light it made on the surface of the oval mahogany table.

'This friend of yours, it all belongs to him? I mean, just him?'

'That's right.'

'How old is he, then?'

'Nineteen.'

'That's amazing,' said Zosie.

She wanted to know if she could go straight to bed. By then they were in the house and Adam had come in from the terrace. Rufus couldn't be sure how Adam felt about Zosie's arrival. He was looking at her speculatively, seemed indeed unable to keep his eyes off her. It was different somehow, this picking up of Zosie, from when they had brought the two girls, the barmaid and her married friend, home with them from Sudbury. Adam said:

'I'll show you where you'll sleep.'

Rufus didn't object. He had decided to open a bottle of wine. Their footsteps could be heard overhead which meant Adam must be showing her into his, Rufus's room, the Centaur Room, and that was all he cared about. He stood on the terrace with the wine glass in his hand, looking at the waters of the lake in which the white reflection of the moon lay like a disc of marble. He and Zosie had smoked all the cigarettes and Rufus had never liked getting through the night without a cigarette in the house . . .

He screwed his eyes tightly shut, opened them again to look at the Player's packet on his desk. It was slipped into the top drawer as the receptionist announced his next patient.

*

When Adam approached home after they had expelled themselves from Ecalpemos he felt, for the first time in his life, the wish to die. Alternatively he had the feeling man attributes to sick animals, that of needing to find a hole far away from the herd to creep into and hide. And he had hoped, after Rufus had left him and he had uttered with ridiculous drama Cassius's farewell to Brutus, that he would at least be able to get into the house unobserved and go up to his bedroom and be alone. But this was not allowed him.

His father stood in the front garden with a pair of secateurs in his hand. When he saw Adam he did not greet him but spoke in what Adam thought was a very strange way for someone who had not seen his only son for nearly three months.

'An afternoon is all it takes me to get this place shipshape, the whole lot weeded and tidied up. It's not as if I had a decent-sized garden, a few acres, something you could call a garden.'

Adam said nothing but stood there feeling hopeless and helpless.

Lewis Verne-Smith said, 'That's my old uncle's golf-bag you've got there.' He seemed to recollect that the bag must now, however unfairly, however productive of resentment, belong to Adam. 'You can imagine how my uncle treasured that. He used to take care of his things. I don't suppose you can understand that. I expect it's just an old golf-bag to you, something to be thrown about any old how.'

'I'm not going to throw it anywhere,' Adam said.

He went round the side of the house to the kitchen door, aware that his father was following him. He was beginning to think his father was going a bit mad. The loss of Wyvis Hall and brooding on that loss had unhinged him.

'So you've been to Greece,' he said.

'Mm-hm.'

'Is that all you can say?'

'What do you want me to say?'

'If I had had the incredible good fortune at your age to be permitted to have ten weeks' holiday in Greece I should have had a good deal more than "Mm-hm" to say about it, I can tell you.'

By then they were in the kitchen. His mother and Bridget were nowhere about.

'I don't imagine you've been near your inheritance all these weeks. It might have been broken into, set fire to, razed to the ground for all you know.' His father had worked himself into one of his rages.

'You're totally irresponsible, do you know that? No one knew where you were, nobody could have got in touch with you. We might all have died, that glorious house you don't give a damn for might have been razed to the ground – and where were you? Swanning about the Aegean.'

Adam went upstairs, carrying his stuff with him, and entered his bedroom and locked the door. He was glad now that he had let his father believe he had on that day returned from Greece. Later on, he remembered, his father had commented on his tan with ancillary remarks about *dolce far niente* and lotus eaters. But all he had been able to think of at the time was that phrase of his father's, 'swanning about the Aegean', and before his eyes as he climbed the stairs, as he entered his room and sat down on the bed, he had had a sort of vision of a dark-blue sea dotted with little green islands, the sun shining and the sky blue, and a team of white swans with golden collars round their necks and golden harness pulling a magic boat, a boat that was shaped rather like a gondola, in which he sat like some hero of antiquity, robed in white and trailing one graceful hand in the water.

The vision was so beautiful and reality so awful that he had lain on the bed and to his horror and shame burst out crying. He stuffed bedclothes into his mouth to muffle the sounds in case his father were standing outside the door. He had not cried for long. After a while he had got up and made himself undo the golf-bag and remove the shot-gun, the twelve bore. He wrapped a dirty T-shirt round his left hand and held the gun with it and then he wiped the gun with a dirty sock. The golf-bag with the gun in it he put under his bed.

Hadn't he been afraid his father might come poking about and find it? Adam made it a rule to keep his bedroom door locked always but that is not the kind of rule which one keeps and he often forgot. Still, if his father had found the gun he had never said and Adam had never moved it. He left it there when he went back to university a month later and it remained there until a year later when he moved out and into a house of his own that he bought with the money he got from the sale of Ecalpemos.

The gun was no longer in the golf-bag but in a cupboard in the smaller spare bedroom upstairs. Adam did not have a licence for it. But although made nervous by the arrival of the policeman he was not in a panic, he was not in a state to believe that on this initial visit they would search his house. Their attitude to him was impersonal – that and incredulous. No, not quite incredulous, this was the wrong word, signifying as it did an astonished overt disbelief. They were not like that. They behaved rather as if as a matter of course they never believed protestations of innocence but would all too readily accept admissions of guilt. And yet none of it was as explicit as this. He also had the impression that what they were doing was mere routine, boring to them even, something to be got over. But instead of comforting him, this served rather to increase his anxiety because he felt that important questions were being saved up, were postponed until the time when certain evidence and certain remarks of his had been sifted and studied. Then the policemen would come back and the subsequent interview would be very different in kind.

The inspector's name was Winder, the DC's Stretton, the former a bit older than himself, the latter a bit younger. They looked like his neighbours, or the people he worked with. He offered them a drink but this they refused. What Adam found a bit upsetting was the way neither of them, though politely acknowledging Anne, took the slightest notice of Abigail. Of course Anne took Abigail away to bed almost immediately Winder and Stretton arrived but even so Adam thought it strange that neither of them said good-night to her as she was carried from the room or commented upon her after she had gone.

Winder started by asking him if he had ever lived at Wyvis Hall and Adam replied, well, not *lived*, stayed there for a few days just to check on the place. He had been short of money and while there he was afraid he had sold some of the contents of the house, ornaments rather than pieces of furniture.

'It was yours, wasn't it?' said Winder, in his full, neutral voice.

'Yes, it was mine. I had a right to sell it.'

'How long did you live there, Mr Verne-Smith?'

'Stay there? A week or two. I don't remember exactly.' Adam waited to be asked if he had stayed there alone but he was not asked. Neither man was writing any of this down and this gave Adam a small amount of confidence. He did not like the impersonal, breezy, almost automaton-like tone of Winder's voice but it might be natural to him, it might be that he always talked like this, even to his wife and children.

'And after you left at the end of the week or two, did you ever go back?'

'Not to live there,' said Adam.

'You never lived there in the first place, did you? Did you ever stay there again?'

'No.'

'You put Wyvis Hall on the market, is that correct? Your father has told us you put it on the market in the autumn of 1976 and then withdrew it from sale in the spring when you had had no acceptable offers. You offered it again in the autumn of 1977, finally selling to to Mr Langan.'

None of this was being written down but this time Adam told the strict truth.

'I didn't offer it for sale at all until the late summer of 1977.'

'So your father is mistaken?'

'He must be.' Anticipating a fairly obvious question, Adam said, 'I was in my last year at university. I had my finals coming up. I didn't want the bother of selling property. Besides, I was told that if I hung on to it it would go up in value and it did.'

This seemed to satisfy them. Stretton asked him what he had been dreading but knew must come, the first of a series of questions that would lead up to the matter of the animal cemetery and the contents of the grave.

'Did you know there was an area on your property where family pets had been buried?'

'I used to go there when I was a child, you know. I think I must have been shown it then.'

'You think, Mr Verne-Smith?'

'I don't remember,' Adam said. 'I knew there was an animal cemetery there somewhere but I don't remember when I first saw it.'

'You didn't, for instance, go up to look at it while you stayed at Wyvis Hall in June 1976 or again before you offered the property for sale in August 1977?'

'I don't think so. Not that I recall.'

'You are aware, of course, of what was found buried in the animal cemetery a couple of weeks ago?'

'I think so.'

'The skeletons of a young woman and a baby. Death occurred

393

between nine and twelve years ago – which really means most probably ten or eleven years ago? Would you agree?'

Adam wasn't at all sure if he would. That is, he would not in general agree to an assumption of that sort and he was quite sure a court would not. On the other hand, he knew very well when death had occurred – ten years and two months ago.

'The young woman met a violent death. The child too, possibly. Suicide is a possibility in the woman's case but she didn't kill herself and dig her own grave. She didn't bury herself.'

Adam nodded. A rueful smile would have been in order but he could not smile. Winder had said 'kill' and not 'shoot' which meant they did not know a gun had been used, they didn't know about the pump-action twelve bore. Nor, perhaps, had they found the lady's gun, buried in the Little Wood. He had thought that if you shot something – for up till then he had only shot birds and few of them – the victim staggered, fell and died. Like on the screen, like on television. He had not anticipated the flying blood, the fountains of blood, as the shot struck arteries, great and small blood vessels. So it had been. So it must have been for Sebastian up in the Pincushion Room, the arrows summoning forth spouts of blood instead of the flesh receiving them passively as it might so many acupuncture needles . . .

He had to exert himself not to drop his head into his hands.

'While you were down there in the summer of 1976 – when would that have been exactly?'

'From 18 June for about a week,' said Adam.

'You didn't happen to see a young woman about, I suppose? Pushing a baby in a pram, for example? A girl might have taken a child for a walk down the entrance drive.'

'It's a private road.'

'Well, yes, Mr Verne-Smith, but the village people do use it occasionally. That sort of rule is more honoured in the breach than the observance, don't you find?'

Adam shook his head. The idea of people having walked up and down the drift without his knowledge made him feel almost faint.

'You never saw a girl in the vicinity while you were there?' He waited for Adam's denial. 'You won't mind my asking, I'm sure. It was a long time ago. You never had a girl staying with you there?'

'Absolutely not.' Adam was astonished at the vehemence with which he could lie.

Vivien came into his mind – inevitably. He saw her in her bright blue dress, the bodice embroidered with crude birds and flowers in red and gold. She had been a squatter. London was full of squatters in the mid-seventies.

'I believe people might have used the house in my absence. When I went back in 1977 there were – well, signs that people had been in, sort of camped there.'

They were keen on that. They wanted to know more. Yet even as he invented, describing a broken window in the washhouse, the paper wrappings nibbled by mice, a few missing ornaments, he sensed their disbelief. He sensed that they were simply interested in hearing what he would come up with next, that they were patiently paying out the rope, yards and yards of it, with which he would ultimately hang himself.

But it was over. They were going. They had not asked him where else he had been that summer and he had not had to invent a Greek holiday or involve others in an alibi. As he slowly eased himself from his chair, getting up ponderously as if he were prematurely arthritic, as he was poised there, supporting himself by his forearms pressing the arms of the chair, Winder said:

'Is there anything else you would like to tell us?'

It was uttered with the utmost casualness, lightly thrown away. But Adam found the question deeply disconcerting. It sounded sinister and deliberate.

He said again, 'I don't think so,' reflecting what an absurd rejoinder this is, this squeamish, cautious substitute for 'no'.

He opened the front door for Winder and Stretton, and Winder thanked him for his help, adding as if this were an afterthought, a tiny, minor matter, something so unimportant that it had nearly gone out of his head, that perhaps in the next few days Adam would not mind going into his local police station and there make a statement to the effect of what he had just told them. They were Suffolk police, but 'liaising' of course with the Crime Squad, and if Adam were to ask for CID or better still for Sergeant Fuller . . .

Anne had come out into the hall and was listening to what they said. She looked disdainful but at the same time quite upset.

'Sergeant Fuller would take the statement from you,' Winder said. 'Any time will do, at your convenience, but let's say before the weekend, shall we?'

'It's a funny thing,' said Stretton, prolonging their departure. 'It's a funny thing how people – the public, that is – how they think that just because a crime was committed a long time ago, I mean, say, ten years ago, it's less important than if it had been committed – well, yesterday. But that's not so at all. I mean that's not the way the police look at it.'

'No,' said Winder in a preoccupied way. 'No, you're right, it's not. We'll say good-night, then. Good-night, Mrs Verne-Smith.'

After he closed the door Adam felt a little like he had that day when he came home with the gun in the golf-bag and found his father in the front garden. He longed to be alone but he should not have married if he felt like that. One of the objectives of marriage was to have an ally.

'Just what is all this?' Anne said.

'It's nothing to do with me. They think squatters got into Wyvis Hall and lived there without my knowing.'

'Why did that man want a statement from you then?'

Adam did not answer her. He looked up Rufus's phone number once more. If she comes up behind me and touches me, he thought, if she says any more, I'll kill her. And then he thought how that phrase which was the general routine threat of the harassed person, was banned to him for ever, because to those others it was fantasy while to him it was real.

Anne was sitting in the armchair reading, but she was watching him with half an eye. Adam learnt Rufus's number and repeated it over and over to himself. He put the phone book back and thought how much he longed to talk to someone who *knew*, to one of them. It seemed to him that he had soldiered on, bearing this alone through aeons of time. Ten years in fact, but most intensely for five days.

'I thought I heard Abigail,' he said.

'Did you? I didn't.'

'I'll just go up and look.'

Anne's face wore that peevish, exasperated expression which always signified he was being too concerned a parent. In the hall Adam looked at his watch and the digits told him 9:56. A bit late to make a phone call but perhaps not too late. Five to ten at Ecalpemos had been the start of the evening, the infancy of the young night. And he and Rufus, like sultans, had reclined on quilts and smoked hashish, the pungent trails of smoke rising into the dark air and mingling with the scents of the summer night. For ever, and for ever, farewell, Rufus. And whether we shall meet again, I know not. Therefore our everlasting farewell take . . .

In his bedroom he lifted the receiver and put his forefinger to the nine button on the phone. Rufus's exchange was nine-five-nine. Adam knew he was being hysterical, a bit mad, those policemen had sent him over the edge, but he did not just want to talk to Rufus, he *longed* for Rufus. He wanted, at that moment, to hold Rufus in his arms and possess Rufus's body with his body, and be lost in him as he had once wanted to lose himself in Zosie.

He was trembling. He dialled the number very quickly, before his nerve could fail. If a woman answered he would put the phone down. He was holding his breath. The phone was answered and Rufus gave the number. It was the same languid drawl, very cool, very Rufus.

'This is Adam Verne-Smith.'

'Ah,' said Rufus.

Now he had done it he did not know what to say.

'I rather expected to hear from you,' Rufus said. 'Some time or other.'

'I have to talk to you.'

'Not now.' The voice was stony, remote.

'No, all right. Not now. Tomorrow? Thursday? We could meet.' Adam would know the minute Anne picked up the receiver downstairs, he would hear the click and have the sense of a door opening somewhere along the line, yet knowing this perfectly well he was nevertheless afraid he might already have missed hearing and sensing it and all the time Anne had been listening, was even now attending to this rather sinister exchange between him and Rufus. 'Hold on,' he said and he went to the head of the stairs, looked down, of course could see nothing, and had to come right up to the living-room door and look in to make sure she was still reading. She looked up and stared back at him, unsmiling. Adam returned to the phone and Rufus. 'Some policemen have been here.'

'Christ.'

'I didn't mention you – or anyone. I said I'd never lived there.'

'Where do you work?' said Rufus. 'I mean where's your office or whatever?'

'Sort of Victoria, Pimlico.'

'Call me tomorrow in Wimpole Street. We might have a drink.'

'All right.'

Rufus replaced his receiver first. But Adam found he did not much mind, it wasn't a rejection and it didn't hurt. It was strange how Rufus's tone had changed while he, Adam, was downstairs checking up on Anne. In those thirty seconds he had become the old Rufus again, his best friend, once very nearly his lover, his partner in crime, his Cassius. Suppose this were to pass away, all of it, suppose by a miracle they were to escape, would it be possible to be friends with Rufus again?

He found he was trembling at the thought of it and he got up from where he had been sitting on the bed and went into Abigail's room. Standing by the cot, looking down into it, he thought how unlikely it was he would sleep that night, how he must anticipate lying wakeful for hour upon hour.

And then he really looked at the cot, looked into it in the light that came in here from the landing, and saw his daughter lying face-downwards, utterly still, her face buried in the small flat pillow. His breath caught and held, he stared. He lowered the side of the cot. There was no movement at all, she wasn't breathing, there was no delicate rise and fall of the frail shape. The sheet and blanket and down quilt lay motionless on her small, rigid body.

The room was silent, warm, expectant of the most appalling disaster. Adam cried out, a yell of terror, and snatched up Abigail in his arms. Very much alive, she burst into screams of fright. Anne came running upstairs. The light was put on, was painfully bright, making Abigail sob and cry the more, poking fists into her eyes.

'What the hell are you doing to her?'

Adam gasped, 'I thought she was dead.'

'You're mad. You're insane, you ought to see someone. Give her to me.'

Without a word he handed her over. Instead of his wife and child, he seemed for a moment to see Zosie standing there with the baby in her arms. He could have married Zosie, he thought. She had wanted to marry a rich man and in her eyes then he had been rich, the lord of Ecalpemos. Avoiding such thoughts, he had never considered it till now, but was it he she had had in mind when she talked of her career? And had he thrown her away through simply failing to recognize this?

Exiled from Abigail's room, he went downstairs again, aware of his aloneness, appreciating this rare solitude. Anne he had deeply offended, but he was indifferent to this. It meant, anyway, that she would not pursue him with questions. He indulged in fantasizing briefly, in a dream of her leaving him, walking out on him and Abigail. He would have to get a nanny, of course, but he could afford that. Someone like Vivien perhaps . . .

All roads led back to Ecalpemos. Whatever he thought of brought him back into the Ecalpemos file which undo and quit keys only briefly expelled from his mind's screen. Or he had lost the knack of escape.

He was dozing in the armchair but he was awake, he wasn't dreaming. Zosie was coming across the garden and his hands were red, but with raspberry juice, not blood.

— I I —

The garden was beginning to get a dried-up look, the grass not growing much but the sun bleaching the green out of it. And in the full heat of the day the flowers hung down their heads. Even the leaves on bushes and small trees drooped when the sun was at its hottest. But inside the walled garden the fruit swelled and ripened, maturing to un-English reds and golds. The strawberries were over but the raspberries were at their peak, the height of their season, fat, juicy crimson fruit the size of rosebuds and safe from birds on their canes inside the cage, currants growing alongside them, black, red and the ones they called white which were really golden, and gooseberries with purple-flushed hairy cheeks that had over-ripened and split open. All along the old weathered wall of agate-coloured flints the nectarines had turned from green to yellow to orange and on some a rosy blush was appearing. Distantly, beyond the screen of walnut trees and hazels – for Adam had left open the arched green door in the wall – could be seen a yellow field of barley, almost ready to cut.

He was inside the cage eating raspberries. It was around noon and very hot, the sky cloudless and the sun high. Adam looked up and saw Zosie appear in the doorway, look about her until she saw him, then pull the door to behind her. This was her second day at Ecalpemos. She wore her jeans which she had cut off a good six inches above the knees and frayed the hems, a white cotton vest he thought might have been Hilbert's and a pair of pink espadrilles through which her toes had made holes. Her exposed skin, of which there was a good deal, was a uniform pale biscuit colour and her hair was this colour too and her eyebrows and her lips. Her eyes themselves were a little darker, the colour, he thought, as she approached the cage, of milkless tea. A good tea, Earl Grey perhaps. She looked at him gravely and then she smiled, showing small, very white teeth. Adam thought he had never seen such a small girl with such long legs. There was a slight but attractive disproportion here, so that for a moment Zosie seemed less like a real girl than some artist's impression of an ideal, the legs longer, the neck more fragile and attenuated, the waist extravagantly narrower than could have been in nature.

She came into the cage, carefully attending to the various hookings and pinnings necessary for closing the wire door.

'Have some raspberries,' Adam said.

She nodded. 'Thanks,' but she didn't pick any fruit. 'Adam,' she said, 'would it be all right for me to stay on for a bit?'

He thought, well, you're Rufus's girlfriend, aren't you? If he says so I suppose you can stay. He didn't say this aloud though, he didn't know why. There was something mysterious about her, something odd. Last night, when they all went out to the pubs in Stoke-by-Nayland she had insisted on crouching on the floor of the van until they were beyond Nunes village. He was disturbingly attracted by her and very confused by this, partly because she was Rufus's and partly because he had an uneasy feeling she might be very young indeed, she might only be about fourteen. On the other hand, there were times like now, when she remained quite still – she had sat down cross-legged on the ground – and she had fixed on him unblinking eyes that her face became hard and she looked in her early twenties.

'I really meant,' he said, 'for people to sort of pay their way. I want to get a commune going with people contributing.'

'Well, I haven't got any money,' Zosie said.

'No.'

'I expect I could sign on.'

The expression was not familiar to Adam who had never worked for his living or really known anyone who had lost his job and drew unemployment benefit. He looked at Zosie and put his eyebrows up.

'I could sign on and get the dole and give you some.'

'Could you?' Perhaps he could do that too. If he didn't go back to college. It would be a way of living. If she stayed, he thought, she might still be here after Rufus went . . .

'There are other ways of getting money. I can always get money.'

He could see the outline of her small round breasts through the white cotton, and the nipples, soft and meek, not erect, but evident enough.

'I wouldn't want you doing that.'

She wrinkled up her nose, a gesture of puzzlement with her where another girl might have cocked her head on one side.

'Doing what? Oh, I see.' She laughed in the funny breathy way she had without smiling. 'I didn't mean *that*. I suppose I would do that though, it wouldn't bother me. I expect you'd call it that when I let Woof-woof fuck me to get a bed for the night.'

Adam came as near to being shocked as was possible with him. At the same time he was pleased, exhilarated almost.

'What did you mean then?'

'About getting money?' She looked away. She picked a raspberry and then another, put the fruit in her mouth, tasting it as if she had never tried such a thing before. And she said, 'I've never actually picked fruit and eaten it like this. It's sort of always been bought in shops.'

'What did you mean about getting money?'

'I don't think I want to say. You'll see.'

'Zosie,' he said, 'whcrc did you come from when Rufus picked you up? I mean did you come on the train from somewhere?' He disliked asking questions of this sort, it made him like his parents. They always wanted to know where one had been and where one was going and what time one would be home. But something impelled him to ask these things of Zosie. He wanted to know about her, he had to know. 'Had you just got off the London train?'

She shook her head. 'Suppose I said I came out of the booby hatch.'

'The *what*?'

'The laughing house, the bin.'

'*Did* you?'

'Suppose I said I escaped and they're out looking for me? Psychiatric nurses in white coats that drive about in white vans? Why d'you think I don't want anyone seeing me when we go out of here? Why d'you think I get down on the floor when we're in Woof-woof's van?'

'OK, you don't have to tell me.'

So they had picked a couple of pounds of raspberries and filled the bowl Adam had brought out with him and eaten them for lunch on the terrace with a bottle of wine. Zosie had also eaten an incredible amount of bread and cheese and chocolate cake and drunk about a pint of milk. Sometimes she would eat like that, enormously, ravenously, and at others she seemed indifferent to food. Wine did not seem to affect her, she could drink it as she drank milk.

Everything changed with the coming of Zosie. Simultaneously with her arrival, or perhaps because of her arrival, Ecalpemos itself underwent a change for Adam. Whereas before he had simply liked it very much and been proud to own it but nevertheless looked upon it as a source of plunder, a kind of lucrative treasure chest, he began now to *love* it, to learn the house and grounds, to value it and to want desperately at whatever cost to keep it for himself. An instance of this change took place the very next day when, to Rufus's mirth, he set about watering the garden, using cans filled from the lake and humped a hundred yards across the lawn that seemed to sizzle in the sun. Zosie helped him. But they must have done something wrong, watered while the sun was still hot probably, for all the plants in the flower beds had scarred and blistered leaves next day.

Out in the yellow meadow the farmer had begun cutting the barley with a combine. The great lumbering machine wheeled quite close by where the Ecalpemos land ended at the grove of walnuts. The terrace was visible from there and the heaped quilts on it and the people who lay there sunbathing. Had the farmer noticed? Would he remember? Ten years was a long time if you had no special reasons to remember. Adam had too many special reasons for forgetting to be possible.

It must have been the next week or the week after that Shiva and Vivien had come. No, it was St Swithin's Day, July 15th. St Swithin's

Day, if thou dost rain, for forty days it shall remain . . . Rufus said it always rained on July 15th, but in fact it didn't that day, there was nothing for the rain to come out of, not even a tiny cloud, not even those pale high strips of cirrus which had lain on the horizon for two or three days past. St Swithin's Day, if thou be fair, for forty days shall rain no more. And it had not. For six more weeks the fair weather had continued, the Mediterranean come to England, tropical Suffolk, perpetual sunshine, and on the forty-first day a storm and rain and winds blowing and the summer gone for ever . . .

She dressed herself in a pillowcase. All she had with her was what she stood up in and a grey sweater and a leather belt with studs on it, so when she washed her shorts and her T-shirt she had to find something else to put on. It was a white linen pillowcase with Aunt Lilian's monogram L V S in a circle of embroidered leaves. Zosie unpicked the stitches in the middle bit at the other end and a little way down each side and made herself a sort of tunic. Wearing the belt made it more like a dress. Zosie looked beautiful in it, she made it into a new fashion.

It was what she wore when they drove into Sudbury to sell the silver, fish knives and forks this time and a filigree sweet-basket and two sauce-boats. Rufus said no one would want to use those things, they were quite useless, they would just lie in the bottom of a drawer or stand in a cupboard and no one would look at them for a lifetime or if he put them out they would go black with tarnish. As it was, all the silver and brass that stood about was badly discoloured from lack of attention. Adam did not at all want to sell the silver but nor could he think of anything with which to refute Rufus's argument. That they were his and a part of Ecalpemos and the whole that it was, the perfect whole, must be made up of its parts, he did not feel able to say this to Rufus. They needed money, they had very nearly nothing.

'If we can't have booze and a few fags and go out on the razzle when we want,' said Rufus, 'there's no point in being here.'

Adam did not see it that way, though he admitted he liked those things, they were a kind of prerequisite to enjoyment.

Zosie had said no more about drawing Social Security. She still slept in the Centaur Room but mostly Rufus did not. He had taken to sleeping out on the terrace all night and usually, around midnight or later, Zosie would creep away on her own. As Goblander came up out of the drift into the lane and turned towards the Mill in the Pytle Zosie got down on the floor and crouched there in the yoga praying position. It was only when they were out on the Sudbury Road that she emerged.

She came with them to sell the silver. The place they chose was an antique shop in Friar Street where the man had been forthcoming twice before and had asked no questions, though Adam suspected that the prices he paid were absurdly low. The shopkeeper stared at Zosie's pillowcase, which left about eight or nine inches of thigh showing. The mini-skirt had been out of fashion four or five years by then and people had got out of the habit of seeing it. She walked about the shop examining everything. Adam and Rufus went into the back to carry out their transaction and got £65 for the silver, which made Adam feel sick because he thought just one of the sauce-boats must have been worth that alone. Zosie was sitting on a bentwood chair, her hands folded in her lap, waiting for them.

Rufus bought wine, the cheapest stuff, bin ends and from places one would never have thought of as producing wine, like Romania. Zosie had gone off somewhere, saying she would meet them back at the van which was parked in the Market Place under the shadow of Gainsborough. The girl in the wine shop gave them a box to put the bottles in and Rufus's pack of two hundred Rothman king size. Adam pulled the bundle of notes out of his pocket and paid the girl, controlling his face, not showing to Rufus his misgivings, his dismay, until they were outside.

'He gave me £65 for the silver, didn't he?'

'Sure. Why?'

'I only had £55 when I paid for that lot.'

'Come on. You must have miscounted.'

So they set down the box full of bottles and Adam counted again, subtracting £34.72 for the wine and cigarettes.

'£20.28,' said Adam, 'and there ought to be £30.28.'

'You dropped a tenner somewhere.'

'I didn't.'

At this point, as Adam was unnecessarily counting the money again, as they stood in the middle of the pavement outside the Town Hall, the missing ten-pound note appeared in front of them in the shape of a new pair of jeans on Zosie who came rather diffidently towards them from behind the Gainsborough statue. They did not have to say this to each other. They knew. But neither of them felt they could put an accusation into words. They looked at Zosie, at the jeans which were of the cheapest kind, the poorest quality, and better to be described perhaps as cotton loons, the red T-shirt of the less-than-a-pound reject shop kind, at this new ensemble which was nevertheless infinitely more respectable than Aunt Lilian's pillowcase.

It brought Adam a good deal of humiliation to understand that Zosie had picked his pocket without his having the least idea of it.

'I had to have some clothes. I felt funny in that pillow thing.'

With that manner of hers that was at once meek and apprehensive she held out to Adam her closed fist. She opened it above his hand and dropped into his palm three screwed-up notes, a twenty-pound note and two tens.

'Where did all this come from?'

She shook her head. 'Never mind. It's for us. You said everyone had to contribute.' Turning her head this way and that she darted alert glances across the Market Place. She reminded Adam of a hare he had seen sitting up on the edge of the barley field. 'Let's go home now, can we?'

As they passed through Nunes she got down on the floor and stayed there until they were outside the front door of Ecalpemos. He kept the money she gave him, he asked no questions, he had a pretty good idea anyway what had happened, what she had done, and he made a mental resolve not to go near the shop in Friar Street again.

That also was the day Zosie saw the picture in the Deathbed Room. Rufus had opened a bottle of thick, dark-red wine, bull's blood stuff that Adam knew would give him a headache. But he took a glass and so did Zosie and they were drinking it at the kitchen table when Zosie said it was all right now, wasn't it, she could stay on now? Adam said yes but he said it rather unwillingly because the afternoon's happenings had shaken him and he had a feeling Zosie might bring trouble down on them all. On the other hand, he was beginning to realize, to his own discomfort, that more than anything in the world he wanted her to stay. It was almost that if she left Ecalpemos would lose its point and he would no longer want to be there. The curious yearning, the breathless hungry feeling that was never to be fully satisfied even when he had made limitless love to her, that had begun. When she asked him if she could stay the request pierced him with real pain, it made him wince.

'Can I go and explore the house? Can I go and look at everything?'

He would have offered to go with her but he was afraid to trespass on Rufus's territory. He looked at Rufus after Zosie had gone upstairs and Rufus grinned, smoke curling out from between his teeth.

'It's all yours if you want it,' Rufus said.

'I rather thought . . .'

'A brief aberration. A two-night stand.' Rufus refilled his glass. He always drank twice as much as anyone else twice as fast. 'Zosie is a woman of mystery. You'll have noticed I've been sleeping on the terrace this past couple of nights. Why don't you take her into Pincushion and let me have Centaur back again?'

Before he could answer – what could he have answered though? That she was not his slave, his creature? – Zosie came back saying she had seen an old man at the top of the stairs, a little thin old man with gold-rimmed glasses and a bald head. Rufus had laughed and Adam hadn't taken any of it very seriously, for she had been in the study looking at photographs. It was different when, half an hour later, she rushed in with the tears fountaining from her eyes.

'Why did you let me go in there? Why did you let me see it?'

It took a while to elicit from her what she meant. Rufus pushed a glass of wine across the table to her.

'It's only a picture,' Adam said. 'It's not a photograph, it's just a sentimental Victorian painting.'

But Rufus only looked at her and looked away, nodding a little, as if he had received confirmation of something he suspected or almost knew for sure. Zosie dried her eyes and felt better after a while and Adam said she need never go in there again, there was no reason for her to go in there, and soon perhaps other people would come and use the room. He had not of course known how soon this was to happen.

Some of those who steal, steal love, the psychiatrists say. Those who have inside their lives an empty space need to fill it with love if they can and if they cannot, with things. And they need to please others in order that others may give them love. Those who need love with the hunger the rest of mankind keeps for food, for the necessaries of life, give their bodies simply and without reflection for a return of love, would give their soul if they knew how, are reduced to thievery of the basest kind and of the basest things because this is the easiest way. Adam knew none of that then but he did think Zosie might be a little mad. 'Disturbed' was the word he used to himself. He thought she might be 'schizoid' (the fashionable expression) for she seemed to have no idea at all of reality.

'Flittermus, ottermus,
Myopotamus,'

Adam said to Zosie, expecting her to correct the last word to 'hippopotamus', as Mary Gage had done. But she only nodded and pushed at the poor corpse with the toe of her sandal.

'It's a coypu.'

He was surprised she knew but he didn't want to tell her how the creature had probably died, he didn't want hysterics. Let her think it had met a natural death.

'Some of those things,' she said, 'they give them pellets with cyanide in and then you mustn't let the carrion crows get them. They give moles worms with cyanide. Isn't that hateful?'

Adam was pretty sure the coypu man hadn't had poison with him, only traps, yet how then had this large, coarse-pelted animal died? 'We ought to bury it.'

They had been in the fruit cage, gathering more raspberries, had walked back along the farther shore of the lake eating raspberries, the red juice staining their fingers. Rufus saw their red hands and said, 'You didn't touch the thing, did you? You could get leptospirosis.' A rat was a rat as far as he was concerned, irrespective of size or variety. They put on gardening gloves they found in the stable block and took down a spade from the wall where a primitive tool rack had been made by knocking long nails into the boards. There were two spades, Adam remembered, this one and a bigger one with a slightly rounded blade. It was this bigger one they had used later on when they dug the grave . . .

But on the evening of 15 July, a Thursday evening, Adam had used the smaller lightweight spade and dug a shallow pit in the Little Wood. He lifted the body of the coypu in and they put back the earth and trod it down hard. The grass and weeds would soon grow and cover it, he said to Zosie, but they had not. It was too dry and hot for that.

Side by side at the kitchen sink they washed their hands, hygiene-conscious Rufus standing over them. He wouldn't give them any wine until he was satisfied their hands were clean and pure once more. It was the bin-end hock and the Romanian Chianti they drank that night. Adam had made little hashish cakes with flour and sugar and an egg and the *charas*. Somehow he had expected Zosie to refuse to have anything to do with them but she had eaten two of them greedily, as if starving for a change of consciousness.

They were all on the terrace, stupid with hashish and wine, silent, lying on the quilts and watching the sky change from blue to gold and gold to rose as the sun set, when Shiva and Vivien came. A breeze ruffled the garden as always at this time, as if it were an invisible creature that passed over the grass and between the rose trees, swayed the leafy ropes that hung from the willows, blew the reeds and set them shivering. Adam lay on the white quilt and Zosie only a yard away from him on the yellow and they looked into each other's dazed faces, eye to eye, and Adam's hand moved to the edge of the white candlewick and Zosie's to the ruffled border of the yellow satin, but their fingers did not quite meet. Rufus lay sprawled on his back, an outflung hand grasping the almost empty fourth bottle of wine. And it was thus that they were found by Shiva and Vivien walking round the house in search of signs of life.

On the lawn below the Loves of Zeus they stood and Adam thought he saw disapproval in their faces. It was Chinese people who were called inscrutable but Adam wondered if perhaps this did not apply even more to Indians. The Indian's expression was curious and watchful. There were murmurs of Mary Gage's name and of Bella's, and the girl said she would have phoned first to ask if they could come, she had looked him up in the phone book, but all she got was an unobtainable signal.

The Indian said his name was Shiva and gave his surname which Adam had since forgotten, if indeed it had ever registered with him.

'And this is Vivien Goldman.'

The real trouble, at the time, was that he was in no fit condition to speak at all, still less talk about terms and conditions. Stupefied with wine and hashish, poisoned with these things really, he could hardly stand, hardly cope with the banging in his head. Rufus, of course, was indifferent. Having elevated himself on to his elbows and said hi, he had lain down again and lit a fresh cigarette. Zosie crouched on the yellow quilt, her hare look back again.

Adam took them into the house. He was unsure now what he could in fact recall of that night and what came later. Small dark Vivien with her long hair braided and coiled round her head – had he observed and absorbed that on this evening? She had been wearing the blue dress that one thought of as inseparable from her, as if she were an exotic bird, as if it were her natural plumage. From the first, from that evening, he had been aware of her disappointment. As they walked through the house and up the back stairs, she looked about her warily, ruefully, at the furniture, the pictures, the carpets, because she had expected rush matting and earthenware pots and earnest folk meditating or pounding up herbs.

Why hadn't he summoned up the strength to tell them this place was more a hotel than a commune? He wanted to be paid. They could camp out for tonight in one of the outbuildings but tomorrow they must go unless they could pay their way. In fact he was sure he had never mentioned money. Poisoned by drink, born without a taste or capacity for liquor, he staggered up the stairs ahead of them, showed them into the Deathbed Room, muttered in a thick slurred voice he was ashamed of even at that time, that they would find a kettle and tea and coffee in the kitchen, wine if they wanted it. After that his memory blanked. The last thing of that night he could recall was Vivien opening the big cylindrical carpet-bag she carried and his seeing for the first time all those Bach flower remedies and little bottles of homoeopathic pills and herbal stuff. Or was he manufacturing a memory out of what he knew had come later?

The Indian was so neat and clean. 'Dapper' was the word, thought word-loving Adam. Someone, a downtrodden mother or sister probably, had ironed creases down the front of his jeans. His crisp starched shirt was the colour of the blue lilies that grew outside the dining-room window.

'What a beautiful house this is,' he said very politely. 'It is quite a privilege to be here.'

Had that been next day or the day after? It was on the morning, Adam thought, when the postwoman appeared with the letter for him. He had just got up, for it was hardly morning, it was past noon, and was sitting in the kitchen, much hungover, feeling as if he were recovering from some long debilitating illness, when something red and shiny flashed past the window. It was the postwoman's bicycle, but he had not known this immediately. The letterbox on the front door made a double rap sound, something he had heard, every now and again, years before, when Hilbert was alive, but not since.

What she had brought was a demand for the half-year's rates. And at that hour it must have been the second post. Rufus had seen her, Rufus was outside and had seen her and she had seen him. No doubt she had also seen Goblander.

'Some young rustic beauty,' Rufus had said. 'A milkmaid on a bike.'

The box at the top of the lane was supposed to be for the post. Perhaps she hadn't known that, or perhaps she was sticking dutifully to the rules. Shiva had said in his sententious way:

'They are obliged by the law of the land to bring your mail up to the door.'

Eventually he had paid those rates. Deeply humiliated but with no other course before him, he had borrowed the money from his father who had required its return plus all the accumulated interest as soon as Adam had sold Wyvis Hall. That year Adam couldn't bear to think of, from the time when he had returned home with the gun in the golf-bag to the return to Ecalpemos and his meeting there with the estate agent. For months the hue and cry over Catherine Ryemark had gone on. Back at college, at any rate, he had not been obliged to see newspapers. But in the Christmas and Easter breaks, at home, each time the phone rang, each time the front doorbell rang, his stomach clenched and turned . . .

As it was clenching and turning now. Alone in his office in Pimlico, he dialled Rufus's Wimpole Street number. He didn't need to look it up, he had it by heart. Rufus, when he came to the phone, sounded distant and preoccupied. How he, Adam, had longed and longed to phone Rufus during that year, but had never dared, had never been prepared to risk the receiver being put down without a word spoken. Besides, he had always had that irrational fear that the Verne-Smith and Fletcher phones were bugged, that the police were waiting patiently for this very thing to happen, for them to get in touch.

Adam had no such notions now. Patient they might be, but they would never have waited ten years. He and Rufus arranged, without discussion, to meet at six. Adam went down the passage to the lavatory and threw up with violent painful spasms, leaning against the wall afterwards and gasping for breath.

On her skin was a fine tracery of bluish marks, like the downy feathers of a little bird a cat has plucked. They were all over the tops of her thighs and the iliac crest and faintly on the flat stomach. More than feathers they looked like silk where, through stretching, the weft has been compressed to expose the warp. One day they would fade and bleach white but that had not yet happened and they would never go away entirely.

Rufus had twice made love to Zosie before he saw the marks, once in the back of the van and once in the bed in the Centaur Room (erstwhile scene of placid slumbrous nights enjoyed by Lewis and Beryl Verne-Smith), but it was not until the third night that he actually looked at her naked body. She lay waiting for him like a sacrificial victim and though she was silent her whole attitude, supine, receptive, patient, uttered to him: I will do anything you want, I am yours – or not. I know I must pay for my board and lodging and for sanctuary and this is one way I know how to do that.

It was scarcely provocative. Rufus, however, did not much care about this, but about what the marks signified he did, and as he stood there he thought about what involvement might mean and about his future career and the risks he was taking – had indeed already taken – and instead of getting into bed with Zosie he took a pillow from the bed and one of the blankets he had long discarded and dumped on the floor, and departed for the terrace.

That was before she stole the silver bracelet, for that was what she had done a few days before Shiva and Vivien came. While they were in the back of the shop in Friar Street selling the fish knives and the sauce-boats Zosie had helped herself to the bracelet from a display table of jewellery. Because she looked somewhat disreputable in the pillowcase she had bought jeans and a T-shirt with the tenner she nicked out of Adam's pocket, taken the bracelet to a dealer in Gainsborough Street and sold it for £40.

Of course it was all of a piece, all understandable. Rufus had watched it, wondering what Zosie would do next. It had been a case history for him and he had even thought of writing it up. The pattern of the stealing had been so interesting, not meaningless kleptomania any of it, but calculated thieving of saleable goods or edible items.

The food had been produced so proudly to be stowed in the back of Goblander, as any henchman of Robin Hood might have robbed for the poor.

Until the incident of the little boy, of course. And that, or something very like it, might have been predicted. Well, something very like it had happened.

A woman of mystery, he had called her. Zosie as woman was an almost laughable concept. She was a child. And yet of course she was not, she was in some ways older than any of them. She had done and known more. Adam would have said – and did say – that she had suffered. They had tried to ask her about her life, who she was, where she came from, where she was going.

'Are you a student?' Vivien had wanted to know.

The other three were, so why not Zosie?

And she replied with absurd naïvety, with what sounded like disingenuousness but was not, was simply Zosie's way:

'I'm just a person.'

Vivien had persisted:

'Do you have a job?' She was wearing, as Adam put it, her 'social worker's hat'.

'I don't have a job and I'm not a student.' Zosie added after a pause for thought, 'I was at school.'

'We were all at school,' said Shiva. 'In this modern world you have to go to school. It's compulsory.' He smiled with pleasure because he had amused the others.

'What do you want to do then, Zosie?'

'Well,' she said and she sighed a little. 'Well, I don't *want* to do anything. I'd quite like to live here for ever, in this house, and just never do anything ever. But what I will do is marry a rich man and maybe he'll buy this house, Adam. Maybe he'll buy it off you for me. Would you like that?'

They wanted to know why she was called Zosie, what did it mean, what was it short for? It was for someone named Zosima in a Russian book, she said.

'Do you mean Dostoevsky?' said Adam. 'Father Zosima's a man.'

'My mother's very ignorant, she wouldn't know. She'd just have liked the sound.'

So Adam wanted to know where Zosie's mother and father lived but she wouldn't say, only that she hadn't a father. Her father had died and her mother remarried. And Zosie sat on the terrace with her knees drawn up to her chin and her arms clasping her knees and darted her eyes this way and that like a nervous animal and Rufus, who admitted to himself he was not usually sensitive or caring, suddenly felt they were all persecuting her and changed the subject to talk about where they should go that night.

A pub presumably it had been or perhaps that drinking club they found in Colchester. A place very different at any rate from where he was now heading to meet Adam who in other circumstances would have changed from the Victoria onto the Northern Line at Warren Street but had agreed to get off at Oxford Circus and meet him in a pub not far from Langham Place.

Rufus would not have recognized him. But there was simply no one else there that it could have been. The beard had gone – had long gone, Rufus suspected – but this depilation usually makes a man look younger and Adam looked older than he was. He looked careworn and irritable, sitting there with a drink in front of him that might have been gin and tonic but was probably Perrier. Rufus did not remember Adam having such a high domed forehead and then he understood, almost grinning at the realization, that it had not been so high ten years before but that in the meantime Adam's hair had receded.

He walked up to the table and stood there and they looked at each other. To Rufus's surprise Adam was blushing, his face darkened to a mottled purplish colour. Neither of them said hallo. Rufus finally said:

'Well, well, after all this time,' and then he said, 'I'm going to get myself a drink.'

Gin and tonic but not much tonic. This sort of thing inevitably gave one a shake-up. Rufus sat down. It was the only vacant chair in the place, which was smoky and hot and full of laughing, chattering people, semi-hysterical at being released from work for another fourteen hours.

'I'd like to dispense with all that how-are-you and what-have-you-been-doing-all-this-time stuff,' said Adam, 'if you don't mind, that is. It's a mere matter of form, we can't really want to know.'

Time hadn't improved him, Rufus thought. The basic rudeness was more than basic now. He shrugged but didn't say anything, tasting his gin and thinking how the whole of life and its pain and its irritations and its stress were worth that first taste that came just once a day.

'The others haven't contacted me. I rather expected they would.' Adam moved his glass about, making wet rings on the wood, and then more rings to link up the first ones. 'I thought they might be anxious about what I would tell the police. About them, I mean, mentioning their names.'

'And have you mentioned names to the police?'

'No,' said Adam. 'No, I haven't.'

'But they've been to you? They've questioned you?'

'Yes, but I haven't mentioned you or anyone.'

'I see.' Rufus did not really see. He felt, though, an overwhelming surge of relief, the kind of surprising relief we feel when we have not known how horribly anxious we have previously been. He found himself really looking at Adam for the first time since he came into the pub, at his tired, reddish, rough skin, and receding hairline and the dark marks under his eyes and the little pulse that jumped at the corner of his mouth. And he had a strange incongruous feeling of loss, of a ruined past and friendship destroyed and wasted, and rage welled up in him so that he would have liked to sweep the glasses from the table and overturn it and sweep the glasses from the next table and overturn that and make general mayhem. He controlled it as he usually did. 'Why not?' he said.

'I've told them I wasn't there. I mean, they asked me if I had ever lived there and I said no, only stayed there for a week or two.' Adam looked up at Rufus and away. 'At the beginning of the time we were actually there. They didn't ask if I was alone, so I didn't have to say. They asked if I had a girl with me and I just said no, certainly not.'

Rufus could not stop the start of a grin.

'It's not funny. Christ, it's not *funny*.'

'Everything is funny in a sort of way,' said Rufus.

'Do you want another drink?'

'Of course I want another drink. I haven't changed that much. It's gin with something in it. I don't care what they put in it, it doesn't matter.'

Adam came back with just one glass, Rufus's. He must be an uncomfortable sort of man to live with, Rufus thought.

'I suppose you're married?'

'Yes. And you?'

'Yes.' They had not been going to talk about this sort of thing, all this was among the private life history to be avoided, and Rufus was a little surprised when Adam said:

'I've got a daughter.'

'Have you? I can't imagine you with kids.'

'Thanks very much,' said Adam, looking displeased. Two frown lines appeared between his eyes and then his whole forehead corrugated. He seemed to be holding his breath. Exhaling, he said in a rush, 'I've more or less undertaken to go into my local police station some time before the weekend and make a statement and sign it. Well, not more or less. I've said I would.'

'If you've already answered their questions that's not such an ordeal, is it?'

Like a peevish schoolboy Adam said, 'It's all very well for you. You haven't got to perjure yourself, because that's what it amounts to. It's one thing talking to a couple of blokes in your own living room and another thing signing sworn statements. I've managed to keep you out of it – so far.'

Rufus didn't believe in altruism. 'It wouldn't help you to mention us, come on. If you stick to what you've already said they'll accept it. Why wouldn't they? They've only come to you because you're one of the past owners of the place. Whoever you sold the place to is coming in for the same.'

'I hope you're bloody right,' said Adam, but he looked a little less wretched. 'Do you think I ought to get in touch with Shiva Whatshisname?'

'What *was* his name? I've been trying to remember. You're afraid he might go to the police and make a voluntary statement? I don't think he would do that.'

An unasked question lay between them. Rufus was not fanciful, he liked to boast that he had no imagination, but he was aware, just for a moment, of something very strange happening. It was as if a third had come and sat down at the table, an invisible being on an invisible chair, bringing with her the scent of herself, dry and salty and young, and laying on his arm a finger like a moth alighting. He actually brushed at his sleeve. There was no one there, of course, there was no room for anything to be there. He looked at Adam.

'Women get married and change their names. That's the difficulty.'

415

'She isn't in the phone book,' said Adam and it was as if the words were being wrenched out of him on hooks. Someone laughed nearby and Rufus missed whatever else it was he said.

'Why don't you just go ahead and make that statement. You'll probably feel a good deal of relief once you've done that.'

'You reckon it will be cathartic, do you?'

'Why not?'

'I don't know if you've ever thought about this but there were a lot of people who knew we were living there or must have guessed we were.'

'Not a *lot*.'

'There was the gardener and there was the antiques man from Hadleigh.'

'Yes, what was his name?'

'Evans, Owens, one of those Welsh names. He was quite old though, and he may be dead by now. There was the pest control that we called the coypu man and there was the postgirl that came with the rates that time, and came – ' Adam hesitated, ' – on that last day too.'

'And the farmer, come to that. Presumably he lived or lives at Pytle Farm.'

'In detective stories,' said Adam, 'people in our sort of situation go round murdering possible witnesses.'

'I don't think I've ever read a detective story.'

'And there are Mary Gage and Bella. And didn't you come back in a taxi one day? There's the taxi-driver. He was young. He won't be dead. The postgirl looked about eighteen.'

'Mary Gage married someone and went to Brazil.' Rufus had meant to say something about their collective guilt and now he thought he would. 'I expect, in the eyes of the law, we'd all be guilty, you know. I mean we were all there. Not to be guilty one of us would have had to go rushing off to the police.'

'Like Vivien,' said Adam very quietly.

'Well, Vivien wasn't guilty of anything, that's for sure. When you've made that statement give me a ring and tell me, at Wimpole Street, would you, Adam?'

It was the first use of a christian name. Adam's face had a rigid look. He compounded the *détente*.

'Your wife knows nothing of all this, Rufus?'

Rufus shook his head. 'And yours?'

'No.'

Silence locked them within itself. Rufus experienced a great quiet, while aware that the hubbub around them was still there, was if anything more intense. Adam was looking at him. The memory came, quite unsought, of that evening at Ecalpemos, while Mary Gage was still there, after she had left the terrace to go to bed, and Rufus had meant to make love to Adam. He would have laughed in derision if anyone had suggested he might have homosexual or even bisexual feelings, but that night he had wanted Adam. Because he loved him. It had been as simple as that. An intensity of love for Adam had come to him like a release of heat breaking over the body and the only natural thing to do with it seemed to be to make love to its object, to turn to Adam and take him in his arms. Rufus had never done that with any man and he had not done it with Adam that night because he was drunk, and with his mind full of muzzy love and amused tenderness, he had fallen asleep.

He got up and pushed his chair back.

'Soldier on,' said Rufus with a faint smile.

It was likely enough he would never hear another word about it. Rufus realized, as he went to find his car, that he had said nothing about the shot-gun, the twelve bore. Adam would speak to him again once he had made that statement and there would be time enough to ask about it then. Who was it that had suggested those guns be sold? Shiva, he thought, or perhaps Vivien. No, not Vivien, she had reacted to the very existence of the guns as anyone else might to an instrument of torture in the house, a genuine medieval rack or wheel. Mary Gage's dismay at the presence of the coypu man had been nothing to Vivien's distress at the guns and the purpose for which they had been used. You might have expected therefore that she would be glad to see them sold but not a bit of it; she would not have dreamt of profiting from such a sale. Shiva it was who had taken the lady's gun down from the wall and said to Adam:

'I expect this is quite valuable. You could sell this and the other one instead of your beautiful family silver.'

'I don't want to sell them. I'm going to use them.'

'What, shoot birds?'

'Birds, hares – why not? Meat's expensive.'

'Please give me advance warning of when you're going to do that and I'll go out somewhere for the day,' said Vivien.

She was the kind of person Rufus found ridiculous, had done then and did now. With her to Ecalpemos she had brought a medicine chest full of remedies, mysterious and very nearly occult, for every known disease. Some of the plants and flowers that formed their ingredients had to be picked at certain stages of the moon for perfect efficacy. Rufus adjudged all that with incredulous contempt, with the disgust of the orthodox medical practitioner. Vivien also had among her baggage something called a 'rescue remedy' of which she urged people to accept a few drops if they ever received anything in the nature of a shock, if they got an insect bite, for instance, or a minor burn. She was a devotee too of many alternative therapies – charlatanism, Rufus called them – iridology and reflexology and aromatherapy. She meditated, she was a sort of Hindu of the kind, Rufus thought, that takes the short cut to enlightenment. On the whole she did not talk of it much, she did not inflict all this on the rest of them too overtly, he had to admit that, but it was so much a part of her, it *was* her, that she carried with her an ambience of it wherever she went and all the time.

If it had been left to him, he would not have let her stay. She and Shiva would have been asked to go if not the moment they arrived, certainly on the following day. Rufus liked people to be amusing and wild and rather 'way out', or he had done then, and Vivien was none of these things. Shiva was quite abysmally none of these things. But before Adam could have been brought round to this way of thinking, Vivien had consolidated her position, had done this the very next morning, by taking over the management of Ecalpemos. Rufus had not thought they needed a cook or a cleaner, a herb grower and home maker. When the sun shone and there was wine and marijuana, who needed all that? Adam, apparently, thought very differently. Subtly Adam was becoming a householder who wanted a clean, polished house and his money saved by the food being cooked at home. And then – although Rufus had not realized this before, had not dreamed of it, and viewed this revelation with wonder and an amount of distaste – Adam and Zosie, both it seemed, wanted a mother and found their mother in Vivien. Like brother and sister, albeit by then an incestuous pair, they came to Vivien's apron strings for comfort or giggled together in rebellion against her, while Shiva, an awkward elder brother, watched with anxious wistful smiles, rubbing his hands, longing himself to be accepted and not knowing how to go about attaining this.

'I am not in this world to live up to your expectations and you are not in this world to live up to mine. I am I and you are you. And if we find each other that's beautiful, if not it can't be helped'. Something like that, he might not have got it entirely right, there might have been more of it. It was called the Gestalt Prayer and Vivien pinned it up on the kitchen wall. Rufus had laughed and said how did anyone know, that might be why one was in this world, why not? But Zosie had liked it and said she longed for people to live that way and Shiva nodded sagely.

'Love is about allowing,' said Vivien. 'Love is about letting people be free. You leave the cage door open and if you're really loved the bird flies back to be with you. That's the only kind of love worth having.'

Rufus had seen something like that printed on a T-shirt, so he did not receive it with the awed gravity of the others – well, not Adam. He winked at Adam behind Vivien's back and Adam half-grinned back.

'You weren't very allowing about me shooting birds,' he said.

'That's different,' Vivien said, frowning. She was quite without a sense of humour. Her small earnest face was often puckered with worry about moral questions. She pondered on such matters as Jesuitical responses, half-truths, on doing good by stealth so that the mind may avoid a consciousness of virtue. 'I said I'd go out, anyway. I didn't say I'd stop you.'

She had wanted to organize them, to give them all appointed household tasks, like a big family or a kibbutz. There would be a rota pinned up on the wall beside the Gestalt Prayer. And the day was to begin with meditation, she would teach them to meditate, an appropriate mantra provided for each. Of course no one had agreed to any of this, even Shiva, usually meek and obliging, had rebelled. Picking all the fruit and selling it at the top of the drift, coppicing the wood to get timber for winter fires, learning to weave, keeping a goat, growing potatoes, all these ideas of Vivien's were met with incredulity, then with firm refusals. It was too hot, it would be too boring, it was much easier to sell Hilbert's silver.

No one changed their ways. They went on drinking and smoking and lying in the sun, swimming in the lake and going on pub sprees and then on selling and buying trips. It might have been expected that Vivien, finding that nobody was interested in truly communal living, in working to be self-supporting which was the idea, might herself have yielded and joined in. But she never had. Without support and without much in the way of thanks, she cooked for them and baked bread, cleaned the rooms and took the bed-linen to the launderette in Sudbury. She did not explain why until pressed.

'It's to earn my keep. I can't contribute any cash.'

No one else thought of it in those terms.

And yet Vivien had no intention of staying at Ecalpemos. Perhaps she might have done if the set-up had been different, if it had been more like her idea of a commune. But that would have meant forgoing the job she had already applied for. Shiva would not stay either, for whether he continued with his pharmacology course or gave it up for medicine, he would have to return eventually and present himself submissively to his father. For his part, Rufus intended to be back by the first week of October, if not sooner, to enter on his fourth year at University College Hospital. Adam only would remain – and Zosie. Adam and Zosie, orphans of the storm, the Babes in the Wood.

One afternoon, looking for his secret drink which he had hidden on some sill or shelf, behind a curtain or a row of ornaments, Rufus came upon them embraced. They were on the sofa, lying close, lost in each other, their faces joined at searching, sucking mouths. He looked at them for a moment or two, feeling ever so slightly a pang of envy, of the rejection such a sight induces in all but the continuously satiated. And then it was gone and he was grinning at them. But they were oblivious of him, they did not see him, fused together as they were, striving to make their separate bodies one. For a long while that day they disappeared together, returning to the company quite late at night, vague-faced and with smiling, glazed eyes. There were candles burning on the terrace, candles that were set in saucers between the statuary. Vivien sat cross-legged, Shiva had his own candle to read his maths book by, Rufus had just opened a fresh bottle of wine. Such pleasure, the withdrawing of the cork, the first pouring! The air was full of moths, soft-winged, dusky, feathery, floating on the candlelight as if made languid by the warmth.

The moon was rising, a huge red orb, ascending with mysterious aplomb out of the dark low hills crested with black woodland. Adam came out of the house and sat beside him and then he saw Zosie standing in the shimmer of the candlelight, her arms wound round one of the heads of Zeus, his curls of stone, his flowing beard, her head lifted to gaze at the red moon. In that shiny slippery light she looked herself like a statue, only one made of bronze, fey-faced, nymph-like, unreal.

'"O! she doth teach the torches to burn bright."'

Rufus looked at him. 'Bloody hell,' he said.

He didn't sleep on the terrace that night. He knew he would find the Centaur Room empty. And when he went to bed at last, the remains of the last bottle of wine with him, he found that Zosie's things had gone. He opened all the windows to get rid of the smell of her that was salty and flowery, like the smell of a child.

At home, his dinner eaten, Rufus went to the cabinet and fetched himself a second drink, identical to the first which he had left in the room called 'Marigold's studio', where the television was. She was watching *Bookmark* on television because there was a bit on it about a now quite famous poet that her mother had once lived next door to. This double measure, slightly diluted in a squat spirit glass, would be his evening's 'secret drink', to be tasted immediately and then concealed behind the hem of a curtain or among Marigold's prolif-erating houseplant pots and swigged from at intervals until bedtime. At times of stress Rufus indulged in this neurotic behaviour even when he was alone. Of course he knew it was neurotic but he did not particularly on this account wish to change it. At some point, when the level in the secret glass fell below the halfway mark, he would secretly recharge it, putting in another single measure of vodka. The legitimate or above-board drink was to be sipped from in front of Marigold and made to last the whole evening. The thing about all this that did cause Rufus some anxiety was the disproportionate excitement and actual happiness, a kind of exultant glee, having this hidden drink brought him.

He sat down on the settee next to Marigold. Poets did not interest him much because they were not, in his view, commercially successful or entertaining or possessed of obvious intellectual superiority. This one, small and bearded, stood at a lectern reading from his own works. Adam, as far as Rufus knew, had never written poetry but he used to recite it sometimes and Vivien had wanted them to devote an evening to each of them reading aloud their favourite poetry. Rufus had soon squashed that. They had lain out there in the garden long into the small hours, everyone unwilling to go to bed, until a lightening appeared in the sky, a pale glow that gradually suffused it, and Adam with his arm round Zosie, who had fallen asleep with her head on his chest, said in a vague remote voice:

'I suffer from eosophobia.'

'From *what*?'

'An irrational fear of the dawn.'

Rufus wondered what had made him remember that. Something the poet on the screen had said perhaps. That was the day, the next day rather, when Vivien had her interview with Robin Tatian. Of course they had all wanted to sleep on and on and Rufus would have stayed in bed until the afternoon but Vivien came in and woke him, had shaken him awake, then presented him with coffee and breakfast on a tray, reminding him he had promised to drive her to London.

Wasn't it rather strange that it had been he and Vivien and Zosie who had gone, leaving Adam and Shiva behind? Not that there had ever been any question of Shiva's going. Off on one of his exploratory walks, he had on that afternoon discovered the animal cemetery. Adam, Rufus seemed to remember, had balked at going to London, anyway to north London, on the grounds that he might encounter one or both of his parents who believed him to be in Greece.

Vivien, before she came to Ecalpemos, had applied for a job as nanny to the child of a man who lived in Highgate called Robin Tatian. Tatian was an architect and presumably a successful one and rich, to judge by the address in View Road. Rufus and Adam both knew the neighbourhood well, having been to Highgate School. It seemed strange to Rufus now that he had never seen Tatian, but knew what he looked like only from Vivien's description when she came back from the interview.

'He's tall and suntanned and he's got brown curly hair. About thirty-five.'

'Sounds yummy,' said Zosie.

'I didn't actually see him,' Vivien said. 'The woman showed me a photograph of him with the baby. She's his sister. She said she "handled all the staff for him".'

'A snooty bitch by the sound.'

Tatian had probably been at his office or studio or wherever architects worked. It was a Thursday, the third or fourth week of July, Rufus thought. And the hot weather went on and on. They had all Goblander's windows open and it wasn't too much, even when he was driving quite fast up the A12. The girls sat in the back because they hadn't been able to decide which one should sit in the front with him.

'I'm saving up to go to India,' Vivien said. 'If I save up all my salary for six months I'll get enough to go to India. If I don't spend anything and I needn't, I'll be living in.'

'What do you want to go to India *for*?'

'There's this mystic – well, a *sadhu*. I've read about him. People go to him and learn, lots of people.' Vivien became reticent and embarrassed but she went on explaining, her voice getting low. 'I would go and live there and it would be a *start* for me. I might stay there or I might come back here, I don't know, but if I never go I shall feel I've missed my chance, I'd regret it all my life.'

'Is there some sort of ashram there for you to stay in?' Rufus asked. 'I mean, will you wear yellow robes and ring a little brass bell?'

When he mocked her she reacted by treating his remarks as if they had been perfectly serious. It wasn't a bad technique either, he had to admit it. If it was a technique. If it wasn't, which was what he suspected, a simple lack of even a rudimentary sense of humour.

'I shall take a room in the village,' she said.

'You will make yourself ill,' said the doctor in Rufus, 'on unwholesome food and infected water and very likely get amoebic dysentery.'

'I don't think so. I shall be careful.'

'Well, at least you don't say what does the welfare of the body matter compared to the soul.'

'I'm not stupid,' said Vivien, and Zosie said,

'I wish I could go with you!'

Rufus couldn't see Vivien because she was in the back and he was driving but he imagined she must be holding out her arms in hieratic fashion and smiling with uplifted eyes as she uttered the single word:

'Come!'

The interview was to be at Tatian's house at three o'clock. Vivien was wearing the bright blue dress with the embroidered bodice and her hair was plaited and wound tightly round her head. She looked like a minor character in a Rossetti painting, one of the maidens holding up the canopy in *Dante's Dream* perhaps, not at all the prospective nanny. This picture was one of the few Rufus could actually recognize. A reproduction of it hung in his parents' house and, curiously enough, now in his. Marigold, the first time he took her home, expressed enthusiasm, fervour, for this painting. Afterwards she told him she was just being polite. But the result was that his mother gave it to Marigold as part of her wedding present and it now hung in a corner of the hall. As the poet faded from the screen Rufus got up and went out into the hall, pausing on the way for a nip from the secret drink.

Rufus could no longer see any resemblance. The girls in the painting were both red-headed, one wore a dress of a pale lettuce-green, the other's was a darker, bluer shade. And the pale delicate faces with their wistful expressions were more like Zosie's than Vivien's. Rufus closed his eyes. Vivien had just the two dresses, one of cream cheesecloth and that blue one, both with long skirts, square necks, full sleeves which, in those hot days, she wore rolled up to the upper arms, to the shoulders. He couldn't remember that he had ever seen her legs. But her feet he remembered and her thin bony ankles. As often as not she went barefoot. That day, though, she was wearing blue cotton espadrilles.

'Have you got any references?' Zosie said, a display of worldly knowledge that had rather surprised Rufus.

'I've looked after someone's baby before. She'd give me a reference, I think. I'm going to give her address if I'm asked.'

He hadn't been able to see Zosie any more than he had Vivien and it was hindsight that made him recall a stricken face, a faltering note as she asked:

'Do you like babies?'

'Yes, of course. I'm a woman.'

Rufus burst out laughing.

'It isn't funny. Women naturally like babies.'

Zosie always spoke with great simplicity. She was like a child, yet more straightforward, more naïve. 'Why doesn't his wife look after her baby?'

'I suppose she's too rich,' said Vivien. 'The baby's got a nanny now but she's leaving soon. There's another child, a bit older.'

Returning to Marigold, Rufus took a longer pull at the vodka behind the curtain, then decided it was in need of recharging. He took the glass to the bottle, not the bottle to the glass. This is the way of the secret drinkers who will thus not, or less probably, be caught with a bottle in their hands. The glass he restored to its niche behind the curtain hem.

It was then, as they came into the far eastern suburbs of London, Romford and Ilford and Newbury Park, that he had thought of drawing Zosie out, of eliciting from her the answers to a few questions. The time seemed ripe, the conversation tending in appropriate directions. And he had started in with:

'That wouldn't do for you, Zosie. You wouldn't have anything to do with babies, would you?'

The silence was long. The traffic was getting thick, three lanes of it, brakes groaning and squeaking as it pulled up at lights. As if she had been drowning, coming up with a gasp to clutch at a lifeline, in the voice of someone whose head has been under water, Zosie said:

'I would. I'd like six, I'd like twelve.'

That made him laugh. They were stopped on a red light. He turned round and looked at the two girls, at Vivien who had taken Zosie in her arms and was holding her. It was so hot he could see a wet patch on Zosie's back where the sweat had come through her T-shirt. Vivien's strong capable hands, large for someone so small, held her shoulders with maternal sureness, not patting in an embarrassed way which is what most people do when called to take part in a spontaneous hug.

They delivered her to View Road. The house was called Cranmer Lodge, white with a green-tiled roof and green iron balconies. Topiaried trees cut in tiers, cones of thick dark plates, stood on either side of the front door. The front gates were of wrought iron and there were stone pineapples on the gate pillars.

Zosie, who had been silent in the back except for an occasional muffled sound that might have been crying, said, 'I love that house. Isn't it lovely?'

It was big, Rufus had thought, you could say that for it, imposing and rather pretentious. He had been back there just once and that was to pick Vivien up an hour and a half later. But never again, never nearer than North Hill out of which View Road turned and on that occasion he had been taking one of the routes out of London up to the North Circular Road. The district had an unpleasant feel, as if –

and this was more a typical Adam reaction – it were full of eyes and memories. The school years were lost, the later days remembered. He wouldn't dream of considering moving to Highgate, which Marigold had suggested.

Sitting down next to her, he tried to think where they had gone, Zosie and he. They had gone somewhere to kill time while Vivien was in that house – some big store it had been, or group of big stores, some shopping precinct. It might have been Brent Cross or John Barnes which, at that time, had still been at Swiss Cottage.

'When did Brent Cross open?' he asked Marigold.

She turned to him, astonished. 'What made you ask that?'

'I don't know. When did it?'

'I was still at school,' she said. 'I was only about eleven, I think.'

So it might have been Brent Cross. He had a distinct memory of somewhere that was air-conditioned. You hardly ever needed air-conditioning in an English summer but you had that year. The van he had parked nearby, in a car-park he thought, which argued for its being Brent Cross, and now he recalled a central hall and escalators, and a feeling of excited anticipation, the stomach muscles tautening. Zosie would steal something and he wanted to see her do it. He found himself observing her as one might watch the behaviour of a laboratory animal in a drug trial. All desire he had ever had for her was dead. He would not even have cared to touch her.

In and out of shops they had wandered – or simply through the departments of stores? A food department he could remember and all those clothes and the crowds and the heat. So perhaps there had been no air-conditioning or only part air-conditioning. If Zosie took anything from a shelf or out of one of those bins filled with stockings, with tights, with underclothes, he didn't see her. He lit a cigarette and a man in a suit with a lapel badge came and asked him to put it out. Then the message came over the public address system. The exact words he had forgotten but the gist of it he remembered.

'Will the parent or person in charge of a small boy aged about three dressed in a white shirt, blue shorts and blue sandals, please come to . . .'

And there had followed directions to some manager's office where the child could be claimed. Rufus could remember perfectly where he had been when he heard the message, by some trick of memory – so arbitrarily selective, so lacking in respect for the recall one most needed – photographed forever and printed on some wall of the mind. On one side of a bank of shelves packed with cosmetics he had been and the black and silver Mary Quant packaging he could see now. Zosie was on the other side of it, hidden from him but no more than six feet away. He heard the message about the lost boy and immediately turned to find Zosie, but she was gone, she too was lost.

He looked for her. The place was very crowded. The curious thing was that though Zosie was beautiful she was not very memorable, she was not unusual to look at. Thousands of young girls looked like her – or superficially like her, they looked like her from a distance. They all wore jeans and T-shirts and sandals and no make-up and had hair that was very long or very short.

She knew where the van was as well as he did. She knew the time – or did she? Of course she didn't possess a watch. But he didn't care, he wasn't going to wait for her past ten past four. They were due to pick Vivien up at four-thirty. If Zosie got left behind in London she would find her way back. Home is where you go to when you have nowhere else to go. Home is the only port in a storm.

Rufus sat in the van smoking. He saw Zosie coming towards him along the aisle between parked cars, the metal glittering, the tarmac surface quivering with heat distortion, her shadow and that of the little boy, black, short, dancing. He was fair-haired, blue-eyed, bewildered. He had a white shirt on and blue shorts and blue sandals, and he was holding Zosie's hand.

'Open the door, Rufus, quick. He can come in the back with me. Let's get away quickly.'

Rufus wasn't often frightened. He prided himself on being easy, laid-back, cucumber-cool. But he was frightened then, fear hit him in the pit of the stomach, it was as physical as that. He jumped out, he slammed the van door.

'Are you mad?'

He knew she was. It wasn't a real question.

'Take him back. How did you get hold of him? No, never mind. I don't care. Just take him back. Put him inside the doors and leave him, anything.'

'I want him, Rufus. He's called Andrew. He said he was called Andrew. He was saying Andrew wants Mummy so I walked in and I said here's Mummy, Andrew, whatever happened to you? I said, and come on, let's go. They didn't stop me, they didn't ask anything, and he just came. Look, he likes me. We can take him back to Ecalpemos and he can live with us.'

From the first Rufus had been always aware of his future career, that he must keep his hands clean. That, at any rate, he must appear to have clean hands. It ruled him, that principle, it kept him from the worst excesses. Shiva had it too, but Shiva was a loser, Shiva, through not being ruthless enough, would go down. Rufus had nightmares about doing something or something happening to wreck his qualifying and prevent for ever what might come after qualifying. They were nightmares but he had them in the daytime when fully conscious.

'Take him back!'

The child, up till then stunned perhaps by events, began to cry. Rufus picked him up and held him up on his shoulders. His heart was in his mouth, he literally had that feeling, of choking, of imminent nausea and throwing up. But he ran across the tarmac with the child in his arms, the child who by then was screaming, ran under some sort of covered way and in through glass double doors and into the first shop he came to, a shoe shop, where he thrust the little boy into the arms of an assistant and shouted:

'He's the lost boy, he's called Andrew. There was a message . . .'

Between them they nearly dropped the boy. His screams shattered the air. Rufus turned and fled. He jumped into the van, aware that he was swearing aloud, muttering every obscenity he could think of, spitting out at Zosie that he would kill her, that she was criminally insane. She was crying, lying back on the seat with her head hanging back and weeping. He brought the van out as fast as he could, his heart knocking, his hands shaking. To think of it now even started his heart going. He brought the licit drink, the one on the table by him, up to his mouth. The vodka had warmed and sweetened. But then nothing compared to the first taste of it.

They had driven a long way in silence – silence but for the sound of Zosie's sobbing. He should have known then, he should have been warned. The marks on her body he had seen, the blue and therefore recent stretch marks. He had seen her look at the picture and now she had tried to steal a child. What had happened to her own baby? He did not ask, he did not speak at all. They were late collecting Vivien and, incredibly now, he was more concerned about the delay than about Zosie and what she had done or what she might do. Indeed he had not thought at all about what she might do.

The traffic was building up because it was close to rush hour time. He drove along Aylmer Road, down the Archway Road and into North Hill, with a whole lot of stopping at lights that gave him the chance to turn round and tell Zosie to shut up, to control herself. There was no one following them. Of course there wasn't. What had he expected? Police cars? Posses of policemen brandishing truncheons? The conclusion reached had probably been that he, Rufus, had found the child wandering after his second abandonment and carried him in to safety.

Zosie turned her face into Goblander's threadbare upholstery and drew her legs up into a foetal position. She had stopped crying. Rufus turned into View Road, seeing ahead of him Vivien waiting, seated on a garden wall, her bright-blue dress incongruous among all the greens and greys, the hard whiteness of the light and faded lawns.

She got in beside him, gave Zosie a glance and looked discreetly away.

'How did you get on?'

'It was his sister I saw, not his wife. His wife's dead. She died when the baby was born, she had an embolism or something.'

'Unusual,' said Rufus, 'but it still does happen.' He started driving back towards the North Circular Road.

Zosie put her head up. 'What's an embolism?'

'A bubble of air in a vein and if it touches the heart or the brain you die. Is that right, Rufus?'

'More or less,' he said. Already, even at that time, he disliked discussing these esoteric matters with lay people. 'Did you get the job or don't you know?'

'They're going to let me know. The sister was interviewing some more people before she goes back to America. She lives in America. They've got a nanny now for Nicola – that's the baby – and the other little girl, Naomi, but she's leaving, she's getting married.'

Zosie said, 'How old is the little baby?'

'She's nine months old.'

'What is she like? Is she lovely?'

'Yes, of course. Beautiful.' Vivien hesitated. She lightly touched Rufus's arm. 'Do you know, I think I've done something silly. She said she'd write to me and I told her my address was Ecalpemos, Nunes, Suffolk. It isn't really called that, is it?'

'It's Wyvis Hall,' said Rufus, laughing. 'You'll have to phone them and set them right.'

'Or just wait and phone in a couple of weeks' time. She said she'd let me know in about two weeks.'

Recalling this, Rufus thought that at least the presence of a Miss Vivien Goldman at Wyvis Hall in July 1976 could not be traced through the Post Office. No officious clerk with a superlative memory would be around to remember an envelope. Nor had that pretty postgirl ever brought a letter from Robin Tatian to the front door or left it in the box at the top of the drift. Such a letter had been written, addressed to Ecalpemos, and perhaps eventually returned to its sender, marked 'unknown'.

Only Adam had received letters while there: that rates demand, and on the last day, an electricity bill. Sometimes, though, Rufus had lifted the lid off the big wooden mailbox that was up near the road on the pine wood side, and looked inside. He had done so that day on their return from London and found lying there, a dead leaf on top of it, a copy of the Nunes parish magazine.

Halfway down the drift they met Adam and Shiva coming up, off to view the animal cemetery which Shiva must have just discovered. He parked Goblander and it was then that Zosie showed him what else she had stolen – a small, mass-produced camera. They all got out and followed the others up to the pine wood, Vivien scolding Zosie in a mild motherly way, reproaching her for being 'a little thief'. Rufus could remember Zosie's sulky face and the way she took dancing steps and fluttered her hands. He could remember the slanting rays of the sun penetrating the wood, and the muted tuneless twitter of birds going to roost.

'Do you want another drink?' said Marigold.

He shook his head. She turned off the television, picked up his empty glass, touched his shoulder in a vaguely caressing way as she went from the room. Rufus retrieved his secret drink, wondering if she knew about it, if she had known all the time, but tactfully did not say. Once or twice he had forgotten to remove and wash the secret drink glass but it had been gone next day.

The phone began to ring.

Rufus picked up the receiver, said hallo. A voice he would not have known, just a young woman's ordinary voice, said,

'Rufus, this is Mary Passant, Mary Gage that was.'

— 13 —

The Gestalt Prayer on the kitchen wall was a daily reminder to Shiva that Rufus and Adam were not in this world to live up to his expectations. They did nothing, they seldom got up before noon. They used drugs and Rufus drank excessively. Shiva had looked forward to discussions on the nature of existence, the future of the world, varieties of religious experience and other aspects of moral philosophy, but Rufus and Adam, though obviously mentally equipped to hold views on these subjects, talked only of trivia, of food and drink, of places they had been to and films they had seen, of people they knew, and they engaged in incomprehensible, presumably witty, repartee.

Shiva had difficulty in finding ways to pass the time. He worked at his maths. He helped Vivien in the kitchen, though feeling rather resentful that the other men never did, though they came from a less patriarchal culture than his own. He tried to engage Rufus in conversations about medicine and the medical profession, the various medical schools and his chances of getting into one of them, but Rufus was not very forthcoming. Though perfectly kind and pleasant, he seemed curiously indifferent to the subject, acting on the amazing assumption that anyone could get into medical school if he or she wanted to.

One of the ways in which he filled up his time was by exploring the place, though he seldom went out on the roads. He could have roads at home. He walked the fields where strictly he should not have been, but he did not know this. In these days of mechanized agriculture there was no one to warn him off. Sometimes he walked through the high yellowing barley and wheat but he was too lithe and light-footed to harm the growing crops. The names of plants and trees were quite unknown to him, he literally could not tell a dandelion from a dog-rose, but perhaps they were all the more wonderful to him for this reason, for their mysteriousness. He followed the course of the little river, looking at the hair-like green weed that streamed beneath the surface, and sometimes seeing dragon-flies skim the water. Once he saw a kingfisher that was the colour of Vivien's dress but more jewel-like, more glowing, as if a light burned inside the bird's bright blue feathers. Overhead the sky was always blue, occasionally covered by a reticulation of thin, fuzzy cirrus, but more often cloudless, and every day the sun renewed itself, hot, powerful, seemingly permanent.

It was after he and Vivien had been at Ecalpemos for about two weeks that he found the cemetery in the pine wood. Vivien and Zosie had gone to London with Rufus for Vivien to have her interview at the architect's house in Highgate. Adam was lying on the terrace reading a nineteenth-century dirty book which had been his great-uncle's. It was late afternoon or early evening, though the sun seemed as hot as at noon, and Shiva remembered he had promised Vivien to fetch in some kindling so that she could light the kitchen range and bake some bread.

Really it was too hot to consider heating up a stove that would make the place even hotter, but Shiva fetched from the stable block the shallow flat basket Vivien said was called a trug and set off. He walked up the long almost totally enclosed tunnel that the drift had become, remembering a fallen tree that lay on the northern border of the wood.

At first all the trees were of the deciduous kind, oaks and ashes and beeches and limes. All the coniferous ones were at the top near the road. The scent which grew stronger as he got to the top of the slope reminded him of a certain kind of bath essence. Putting two and two together but still with a sense of serendipity, Shiva concluded that the pine which was the bath essence perfume was the same as, or similar to, these trees, and he looked at them with new eyes. They were of a very dark green, nearly black, their needles borne in dense round clusters. Among the clusters grew long pointed cones of a pale, fresh green but the cones that lay on the ground, on a brown blanket of millions and millions of fallen needles, were also brown and with a shiny look as if each one of them had been hewn from a block of wood, carved in a pineapple design and polished. The pines grew thickly, close together and in symmetrical rows, so that the wood, to Shiva's fanciful imagination, looked like some ancient

432

pillared hall, overtopped by a roof of somewhat forbidding darkness.

It occurred to him that the cones might make better kindling than fallen wood and he began picking them up and putting them in his basket. But as he gathered them it seemed to him that there were always finer cones lying deeper in the wood and he gradually made his way further and further in, soon finding that he had to squeeze between the pine branches, so closely had the trees been planted. It was dry, silent and rather stuffy in there. It was very still. The wood was not very large – he knew this from having seen the whole of it spread out when returning one afternoon from Hadleigh in Rufus's van – so there was no possibility of his getting lost. What he had also seen from this hilltop if not quite aerial view was that a sandy ride bisected the wood, running from north to south, a provision supposedly for getting logs out. Very soon, Shiva thought, he must reach this ride, and after struggling on for another fifty yards or so, gathering cones as he went, he saw light gleaming ahead and a thinning of the trees. Above his head a bird's nest hung from a branch, a nest shaped like a little basket, but Shiva did not see the goldcrests, a pair of tiny twittering yellow birds, until he had reached the ride and come out into the open.

As soon as he emerged from the densely ranked pine trees he saw that the ride going southwards must lead uninterruptedly to the open area of grass that divided the pines from the deciduous wood. He would go out that way and avoid the awkwardness of groping through a maze of wooden columns and stiff sharp branches. He looked about him. On the opposite side of the ride, a little way to the right, the straight line of pines was broken, or rather indented, the trees there forming three sides of an open square. This square space was turfed as the verges of the ride were but instead of smooth, as were those verges, raised into a dozen or perhaps fifteen shallow tumuli. The effect was of a range of little green hills, a midget country viewed from a midget aircraft, or of molehills the grass had grown over. The whole place, however, was scattered with what seemed to be monuments. Carrying his basket of cones, Shiva came closer.

It was a graveyard that he was looking at. The monuments were mostly of wood, grey as stone or greened over with a patina of lichen, and some had fallen over and lay on their sides. Here and there was a headstone of marble, pink, mottled grey, white, and on this last Shiva read engraved the single name Alexander and the dates

1901–1909. On another monument was a verse he found incomprehensible but the simpler tributes touched him. He was moved by, 'Gone from us after three short years', and, 'By what eternal streams, Pinto . . .' The dead who lay here had known such short lives, the oldest being a certain Blaze who had died in 1957 at the age of fifteen. Shiva had little doubt he had come upon a children's graveyard. These were the dead offspring of the Verne-Smith family lying in their ancestral burying-place. The earliest date was 1867, the latest, excepting that of Blaze's death, 1912. Infant mortality during those years in England he knew to have been quite high and he felt his heart wrenched by the thought of these losses, by that of the little three-year-old, by Alexander who had died at the age of eight. But as he walked away along the ride it cheered him up to realize he now had something to tell the others, for the first time he would be able to impart to them a piece of interesting information. Adam, he was sure, knew nothing about it. Adam had told him he had never been into the pine wood.

Enjoying in anticipation, however, the element of surprise, Shiva told Adam only that he had something interesting to show him. He said the same to the others whom he and Adam met in Goblander as they were returning up the drift. Later he was greatly relieved that he had not announced his discovery of children's graves. It would have been hard to live that down.

Vivien didn't know either. He and she came from very different backgrounds but they were closer to each other than either was to Rufus or Adam. As for Zosie, she merely stood staring, holding one fist up against her mouth. The two Englishmen had behind them a long tradition, a mythology rather, which Shiva knew he would never understand, which his father would not have understood for all his vaunted love of England and admiration of English ways.

Adam laughed when Vivien reacted as Shiva had done – well, not as Shiva had done, far more impulsively than that, with a cry of pain for bereaved parents and bygone suffering.

'They are dogs and cats,' Adam said. 'I suppose there may be a goat or a parrot there as well but it's mostly dogs and cats.'

'How can you know?'

'I just know,' Adam said and Rufus nodded. He just knew too. 'People like the Berelands – they were my great-aunt's family – they were the sort to have animal cemeteries.'

434

Vivien said, 'And I was thinking what short lives those poor little dead ones had.'

'They were quite long-lived really, weren't they? Old Blaze lived to be 105 in dog years.'

Zosie's eyes were swollen as if she had been crying, Shiva had already noticed, and she looked as if she might begin crying again. She spoke in the childlike ingenuous voice she reverted to when distressed.

'Do you think anyone else will ever be buried there?'

'If by "anyone" you mean any more animals I shouldn't think so. I can't imagine I'd ever keep a pet.'

'Oh, Adam, wouldn't you? You don't mean you wouldn't let anyone else? Couldn't I have a dog if I wanted one or a kitten?'

Adam put his arm round her but he didn't make her any answer. Zosie was quite possibly mentally retarded, Shiva thought as they all walked back to the house. He had never known anyone to behave the way she did. Her conduct in coming to Ecalpemos as Rufus's girlfriend – he had gradually gathered all this – and then removing herself to Adam's bed profoundly shocked him. A kind of precociously vicious child-whore was how he thought of her. He had never really spoken to her and had they ever found themselves alone together he would not have known what to say.

'She had had a baby,' he said to Lili. 'This child had had a baby. It was born before she had her seventeenth birthday.'

'That was very sad, Shiva,' Lili was faintly reproving.

'Well, it was not sad for the baby. The baby was adopted. My goodness, it must be ten now. More than ten. She was a tremendous liar, you know. One day she told Vivien her stepfather was the baby's father and another time it was a boy at her school or a teacher at her school. Who knows what the truth was? She opened her heart to Vivien. Vivien was like a mother to her and Adam.'

'Do people open their hearts to their mothers? I never do to mine.'

'That was a manner of speaking, Lili. Anyway she didn't really open her heart if half of what she said was lies, did she? But it was clear she left school because she was going to have a baby and after it was born she went to live in this place where young girls who were not married lived with their babies until they were adopted. She didn't go back to live with her mother, though of course she meant

435

to later. She thought she *had* to later because there was no one else till Rufus found her by the roadside.'

'She was sick in her mind,' said Lili. 'You always said she was sick in her mind.'

'Some women get sick that way after they've had a baby, don't they?'

Lili looked away. 'There's something called post-partum depression.'

'It wasn't depression. Zosie wasn't depressed. She was unhappy, mad with unhappiness. She was broken-hearted. Rufus knew. He was halfway to being a doctor. He should have done something, got her to a doctor. But they encouraged her, Rufus and Adam, they encouraged her to steal. It amused them. It was love she was stealing, a psychiatrist would say.'

With a shrug Lili said, 'She had her parents – well, she had her mother. Didn't she love her?'

'Zosie told Vivien her mother was embarrassed when she got pregnant. Not angry or upset, mark you, but embarrassed. She was afraid of what the people she knew would say.'

'Why didn't Zosie have an abortion?'

'Vivien said she wouldn't face up to things. She pretended it wasn't happening. By the time she told her mother it was too late to do anything. The only thing her mother could think of was having the baby adopted. It was a piece of luck for her – the mother, I mean – that she and her husband were moving house just about the time Zosie was due to give birth, so that with luck the old neighbours wouldn't know and the new ones would never find out. That was why Zosie was supposed to go to this hostel place for single parents after the baby was born.'

'They used to call girls like that unmarried mothers. Did you know? I read it in a novel.'

'Some of them must have been too young to *be* married. Zosie almost was. She had the baby in a hospital in London and she was only there five days and then she came out and went to this place. A week after that she gave up the baby to the adoption people and it went to its new parents.'

'Was it a boy or a girl?'

'I don't know,' said Shiva. 'I didn't ask and Vivien didn't say.'

'It seems important.'

'Zosie couldn't stay on there without the baby. She couldn't go back to her school. Her mother and stepfather had moved but of course she had their new address. Her mother wasn't as bad as that. She probably expected Zosie to come home – that is, to the new place. And Zosie went because there was nothing else for it. She had nowhere else to go and no money.'

Shiva stopped and picked up the paper once more. It was a paragraph on an inside page which had started this conversation. This said that new evidence was leading police to believe a positive identification might soon be made of the remains of a young woman and a baby found in the animal cemetery at Wyvis Hall. That was all. Shiva re-read it carefully.

'You weren't to blame,' said Lili. 'It was nothing to do with you. It was only that you happened to be there.'

'No, it was more than that. I should have left anyway. When I saw the way things were going I should have left. Instead I actually persuaded Vivien to stay on. When she heard she had got the job with Robin Tatian she thought of going back to London, back to the squat. Things hadn't worked out at Ecalpemos the way she had expected them to. Nobody did anything but her, you see. They didn't pull their weight and they took what she did for granted – like you take what mother does for granted. You can stay on, Shiva, she said. It doesn't mean you have to go because I do. I knew then that whatever there had been between us was over. Do you mind me talking like this, Lili?'

She shook her head, looking at him with a fleeting smile.

'I didn't think you minded. You've no cause. It was never much of a love affair we had, more a friendship. We slept in the same bed at Ecalpemos but we never touched. I believe Vivien was coming to believe there wasn't room in her life for the distractions of sex, and in a funny sort of way there wasn't time. I used to wake up sometimes in the night and see her sitting in a corner of the room with a lamp on but shaded, reading the Gita. That made me feel strange, her doing that when I was the Indian and I hadn't even read it.

'I persuaded her to stay on. The others – well, the others were very distant from me. I'll be frank. I was in awe of them, I was even a bit afraid of them. Not Zosie, I don't mean Zosie, I mean the men. I've said Vivien was like a mother to Zosie and Adam but she was like my mother too, I'll confess it. I felt she was a protection, a sort of shield between me and them. I said to her, please, to stay just till she went to her job, not to desert me, and she said all right, she wouldn't. I don't think she wanted to but she was practising what she preached, you see, she was being good.

After she said that she thanked me for being Indian. We'd never even talked about Hinduism, I don't know anything about it anyway, but she said that for her purposes it was enough my just being Indian, it pointed the way for her. I've never really known what she meant.'

He fell silent. Lili waited, looking at him, and then she picked up the book she had been reading. She turned a page and stared at the text but he did not think she was really reading it. Shiva went out into the hall and looked up Adam's name in the blue phone directory and then Rufus's in the pink one. It was not so much that he was afraid to phone either or both of them as that he did not know what he would say. What was there to say? Don't mention my name, don't say I was ever there. They would either say or not say and nothing he begged of them would make a difference.

Closing the pink directory, he switched off the light. They were economical with electricity in Fifth Avenue. He looked out of the little window and across the half-lit street. The people opposite were moving out. They had been one of the last white families left in this particular section of Fifth Avenue, a young couple with two children. The For Sale board had stood there for months and months but at last the house had sold. For five thousand less than was asked, Lili had told him, and five thousand was a big percentage of the kind of prices they could ask down here. All day the removal van had stood outside but it was gone now. No one had moved in and the windows were without curtains. If the new occupants didn't move in fast, thought Shiva, squatters would come or else all those windows be broken.

The two lines of parked cars were strung up over the hill colourless in the sodium light, their roofs glittering, the pub lights orange, as if fires burned behind the leaded stained glass but not a soul to be seen. There was something sinister and menacing about urban emptiness. A street of houses should have people in it but it was a measure of the kind of society they lived in, Shiva thought, that he was glad when the street was empty of people, he was relieved, he was thankful for the safety that came with the absence of his fellow men.

Living beings are without number: I vow to row them to the other shore.
Defilements are without number: I vow to remove them from myself.
The teachings are immeasurable: I vow to study and practise them.
The way is very long. I vow to arrive at the end.

He did not know where it came from, some Hindu or Buddhist writings presumably. They were all like that, all posing for the devotee impossible goals. That passage Vivien had copied out and the sheet of paper it was written on lay on the table in their room underneath the painting of the dead child, its parents and the doctor. It was there all the time they were, the paper weighted down with Vivien's bottle of sandalwood oil. He remembered it now because for six weeks, the duration of their stay, he had seen and read it every day.

Vivien had been alone in the world, brought up in a children's home. Shiva could remember her saying that her mother had had so many children there had not been time or room for her. She was taken into care because her mother had been ill and could not cope with her large family. When she recovered and indeed settled down somewhat, marrying the man she had been living with, somehow Vivien and one of her brothers also in care were forgotten. Neither of them ever went home again and one day Vivien found out that she had been truly abandoned, for a whole year before her mother and the rest of the family had moved away to quite a distant part of the country.

This account Vivien had given in a not at all self-pitying way but speculating as to how many siblings she might actually by then have. Zosie had been there and had listened with a kind of staring intensity, her elbows on the table and her little pale face held in the cup of her hands.

'My mother's abandoned me too,' she said.

That was before she had told Vivien about the baby. She was still the mystery girl, come out of nowhere.

'My mother doesn't know where I am,' she said. 'She doesn't care, does she? She hasn't tried to find me, she hasn't looked for me, she hasn't told the police. I'm missing but she doesn't care.'

'How do you know?' Rufus said. 'It was you ran away from her not she from you. Or so one gathers. How do you know she's not going spare?'

'We've had the radio on every day and there's been nothing. I bought a paper while we were in London. I've looked at papers every time we've been in Sudbury and there's never been a word. She doesn't care, she's glad I've gone.'

'So what?' said reasonable Rufus. 'Isn't that what you want? I thought you said the last thing you wanted was to go home. You don't want your mother fussing around you, do you?'

Shiva thought he had understood. Vivien certainly had. Vivien said it was one thing a young girl running away from home and being glad to leave her parents but quite another for her to find out the parents were relieved she'd gone. And Zosie said:

'Don't you see how terrible it is? I'm missing from home and my mother isn't worried. I might have been murdered. For Christ's sake, I'm only seventeen.'

She began to cry, tearing sobs. Vivien sat down beside her and put an arm round her, then she turned her round and held her in her arms. It was later that day that Zosie had told Vivien everything – or almost everything. At any rate she had told her about the baby. And things about Adam. Adam had told her he was in love with her, he was mad for her, and by the way he looked at her, devouring her with his eyes, Shiva had no difficulty in believing this. How Zosie felt about this, whether or not she reciprocated, she had not told Vivien, or if she had Vivien had not repeated what she was told. One thing she had said to Vivien was perhaps significant.

'If I'd known before, I could have kept my baby.'

Vivien asked her what she meant.

'He wants me to stay here with him. He wants me to live here with him for ever. That's what he says. He's not going back to London, he's not going back to university. This is going to be my home for always, he says. I keep thinking, if only I'd known, if only I'd known before I gave up my baby. I could have had my baby here and we could have lived here, all three of us, like a family. And I can't bear to think of that, how it might have been if only I'd known.'

The few lines about the prospective identification of the bones at Wyvis Hall Adam happened to read while he was waiting to make his statement to the police. He was actually sitting in the police station waiting to be attended to and he took a look at the evening paper

440

which he had just bought. Immediately he imagined that all eyes were on him, that the policemen who stood behind a kind of counter, the two or three other members of the public who were also waiting, all knew exactly the position of that paragraph on the page, knew to what it referred and were measuring the degree of his guilty involvement. He folded up the paper, trying to do this nonchalantly. But his heart had begun to beat painfully as he registered the import of what he had read.

Five minutes afterwards he was in a small bleak office with the man called Sergeant Fuller. Adam, though nervous enough about this interview, had told himself over and over that after all he had already said everything he intended to say to Stretton and Winder. It was they who were *au fait* with the case. This Fuller would know nothing about it, he was a mere official whose rank or simply his availability placed him here as the recipient of this statement. He was therefore very taken aback when, having repeated what he had said to Winder and seen it taken down on a typewriter by a policewoman, Fuller said in an idle conversational sort of way:

'In point of fact, just for the record, where were you for the rest of those summer holidays? Vacation, you'd call it, wouldn't you? At home with your people, were you, or did you go off somewhere?'

'I went to Greece,' Adam said.

'On your own, were you?'

'I don't see what this has got to do with Wyvis Hall. I wasn't there and I should have thought that was all that mattered.'

'All that mattered?' said Sergeant Fuller. 'That would be a very tall order, don't you think? All that mattered – whatever that might be.'

Adam was afraid to say he had gone to Greece on his own in case his father had already told the police he had gone with Rufus. Why hadn't he checked with his father as to exactly what he had told them? He said:

'If you've finished with me I do happen to be rather busy . . .'

'You have to sign it, Mr Verne-Smith.'

Adam signed.

'You were going to tell me who you went to Greece with,' said Fuller.

'I went with a friend of mine called Rufus Fletcher. He's Doctor Fletcher now.'

'Perhaps you'd give me Dr Fletcher's address, Mr Verne-Smith.'

Adam regretted it as soon as he had said it. 'He's in the phone book.'

Fuller said nothing but he looked hard at Adam and Adam knew what he must be thinking. If this man is a friend of yours how do you know his name is in the phone book? You would surely either remember his phone number or have it written down in a personal directory. Or did you mean he *used to be* a friend of yours but is this no longer and you know he is in the phone book because you had to look up his number in order to phone him and warn him, or discuss this case with him or concoct an alibi? And if this is so, Mr Verne-Smith, it gives rise to all kinds of interesting possibilities . . .

He would have to warn Rufus. They would certainly want to confirm this with Rufus. Adam felt weary of it, he felt slightly stunned as if he had been struck but not hard enough to knock him out. Usually at this time, returning home, he began to feel an anticipatory joy at the prospect of seeing Abigail, but thinking of the child now only filled him with despair. As for Anne, he understood now, all humbug and self-deception past, that he remained with her solely because of Abigail. He had loved just two people in his life, Zosie and Abigail, and the Zosie he remembered came back to him as nearly as young and small and vulnerable as his daughter.

The bluish-white marks on her body he had at first taken for some peculiarity of her own, what Rufus would have called ideopathic. Zosie's skin was pastel brown, and the little white feather marks were not like scars but in themselves rather beautiful, piquant. Idly, one afternoon, he asked her what they were. She was lying on her side, resting on one elbow and cupping her chin in her hand, a character-istic gesture of hers. She was looking at the painting of St Sebastian facing an archery squad of Roman soldiers.

'I was shot full of arrows,' she said.

'Come on, Zosie, tell me.'

'My skin was stretched and stretched and when the stretching stopped it could never go back to what it used to be. Imagine doing it to a piece of silk. Go on.' She jumped off the bed and got hold of the hem of one of the old faded pink silk curtains. She held it in her fists and pulled. There was a splitting sound. 'Oh dear, it's too old, it's rotten. I'm young you see, so I didn't split.'

He said to her, 'Zosie, Zosie, what do you mean?'

'Shall I tell you? Shall I tell you now?'

He held out his arms to her and she came into them, nestling close and confidingly, whispering into his shoulder. The curious thing was that it had not meant much to him. To hear now of a girl of just seventeen having a baby and giving it up for adoption, running away from a hostel and sleeping first with one man, then another, while she was still post-parturitive, without any proper medical examination and using no contraceptives, would shock him and rouse his indignation. But then he had not seen it like that. About the contraception or lack of it he had not thought at all, it had not crossed his mind. He had not even known in those days that a woman should not be sexually active after childbirth until six weeks have elapsed and she has been given medical clearance. Apart from all that, he had not even given much consideration to the baby or what Zosie's feelings for it might have been. And he was ashamed now to recall his gross insensitivity. The truth was that at nineteen he had thought of a baby as an encumbrance any single girl would wish to be rid of, either at birth or preferably earlier by abortion. So when she told him that those blue-white feathers were the stretch marks of pregnancy he had given her the only sort of sympathy he thought she wanted.

'They don't spoil you, darling Zosie, they're not ugly. They're sweet, I think they're lovely.'

A shiver ran down the length of her. Her nipples were erect from the shiver, not from desire. He longed and longed for her to desire him as he desired her, for he suspected that she never did at all, but why this should be he could not understand, and thought it must only be necessary for him to be more expert and more inventive, to achieve a longer performance. It never occurred to him that she might be suffering from a post-childbirth frigidity, he did not know of such things. It had been a case of hopeless misunderstanding, Adam now thought. Not once, that July and August, had he ever attributed Zosie's unhappiness to her separation from her baby or supposed that her sometimes strange behaviour might be a form of post-natal psychosis. Because she slept with him and let him make love to her whenever he wanted to – which was at least once a day and often two or three times – he assumed that she wanted it. And she was not passive, she was not limp and dry, but she moved and moaned and writhed her limbs, and those hot nights the sweat lay on her in drops like glass beads and rolled off her pear-shaped breasts

443

and down her thighs over the feather scars. How was he to have known anyway? How was any man ever to know? It was a dark wood, that place of woman's response. How was any man to know what was real and what they pretended to for their own ends, though God knew what those ends might be.

Has any woman ever come with me? Adam thought. I don't know. I am married but even so I don't know. I only know what they have said. And Zosie did not even say. She wept sometimes and sometimes she laughed in a mad sort of way and sometimes she squeezed me in-out, in-out, and drew up her legs and bounced her buttocks – and I never knew it was all payment, it was all to make me let her stay. As if I could have sent her away! But I didn't know anything, I didn't understand anything. She said to me,

'If only I'd known you lived here and you'd want me to live here with you I needn't have given up my baby, I could have kept my baby. Why don't things happen in the right order, Adam?'

'What would we do with a baby here, Zosie?' he had said. 'It would be a terrible nuisance and we wouldn't be able to go out.'

When Abigail was born he had been present at the birth and he had felt as much her mother as Anne was. Abigail had come out in a rush and the midwife had lifted her up in triumph to gasping, smiling Anne and Adam who was weeping, down whose face the tears were coursing. Later on Anne had reproached him for that, saying she thought the Verne-Smiths (you bloody Verne-Smiths) didn't know the meaning of emotion, yet here he was crying because he'd seen a baby born. It was impossible to explain that he had wept for joy and for the delight of loving once again and for becoming a parent, which to him was a miracle. Later too, when he saw the child clean and dressed and in Anne's arms, nuzzling at the breast, he remembered Zosie and for the first time he bled for her.

Having a baby when you were very young and then having that baby taken away from you might drive you over the edge, might make you mad for a little while, a kleptomaniac and a visionary, might make you see ghosts. He had never been afraid *for* Zosie, he thought, only afraid *of* her, of what she might do. His fear that she might steal something in one of those shops had made him leave her in Goblander and thus left the way open for her to commit something far worse than simple theft . . .

It was nearly a month before that when she and Rufus and Vivien

444

went to London and she had stolen a camera. In the evening they had all gone up to the animal cemetery for the first time, Vivien admonishing her for being a thief, telling her the camera should go back, and Zosie sulky and giggling by turns. She must have stolen a film too or Rufus had bought a film, for he took pictures of the cemetery and then one of the house. He stood on the grass in front of the cedar trees as the breeze of dusk blew and swayed its branches and took a picture of the house. Then Zosie posed on the terrace like Juliet and he posed on the lawn below like Romeo and Rufus took more pictures. What had happened to those photographs? Rufus might have them still, but if there was danger Rufus would destroy them.

Was that the night the temperature dropped so low? Adam thought he could recall that happening on the last or nearly the last night of July. It was getting dark and Zosie was at the end of the passage, having come up by the back stairs, when she saw Hilbert ahead of her and the little dog Blaze with him, running round his legs and jumping up at him. Only it was an old man she saw and a puppy, which did not quite fit the facts. It was all made less believable by her mentioning the dog only after they had all seen its grave in the animal cemetery.

The night was cold and they were glad of the heat from the kitchen range. This was the end of the fine weather, they all thought that, but it came back next day, it came back for nearly all the month of August, as hot as ever. That cold night, enveloped in her grey sweater, Zosie asked him if she could have a kitten of her own and he had said yes, but later, when the others had gone and they were alone, a cat and a dog and a lamb and a pony too for all he cared.

'I wasn't allowed to have them at home. Anyway, I wouldn't have, I wouldn't have dared. Cliff kills animals.'

'Who's Cliff?' he said.

'My stepfather.' She sat close to him, hugging him as a child might. Her face was buried in his neck, her lips touching his skin. 'He kills little things, he has no mercy.'

'You mean he hunts and shoots?'

'He hunts them down, yes. He hasn't hunted me, though, has he? Perhaps he doesn't know where to begin, he doesn't have a scent.' And she laughed, nuzzling his neck, nuzzling like a child at the breast.

One of the few nights that had been when he could hold her close without the heat stifling them, without the sweat rolling off their locked bodies . . .

Entering the house rather later than usual, Adam went straight upstairs. He could hear the sounds of Abigail being bathed, the splashing and the shrieks. The bathroom door was ajar. He called out to Anne but did not put his head round the door lest the enchanting sight of Abigail with her floating dolphins and her duck and her inflatable fish seduce him from his task. He went into the spare bedroom where he kept the shot-gun, Hilbert's twelve bore. It seemed to him imprudent in the extreme to keep that gun in the house a moment longer. The arrival of the police with a search warrant would not in the least have surprised him.

The shot-gun was still in the golf-bag in which he had fetched it away from Ecalpemos. Would it still work? Or would it have to be cleaned and oiled first? Carrying it downstairs past that bathroom from which issued those sounds of innocent hilarity, he thought for the first time of using the gun on himself, of the peace that would ensue and an end to the torments of anxiety. 'Tir'd with all these, from these would I be gone, save that, to die, I leave my love alone.' There was Abigail to think of . . .

Several times these past few days there had come to him a thought that was deeply distressing. Zosie *could* have had her baby back, she could have fetched it and lived there with him, all of them could have lived on at Ecalpemos, the happy paradise that was some place spelled backwards, for it was by no means too late for her to have said no to the making of an adoption order, only she had not known it and he had not known it then.

Adam lifted up the lid of his car boot and put the gun inside, concealing it under the plastic sheet he kept there for covering the windscreen in icy weather.

— 14 —

Mary Gage was into her second marriage, she told Rufus, and although she did not quite say so, he gathered it was no more successful than the first. She had read the papers on her return to

446

London on a flying visit. Five days more and she would be gone again, back to Rio, but she had felt somehow, what with one thing and another, that she ought to phone him. Of course she did not really suppose that the discovery in the grave in the animal cemetery had any connection with Adam and him . . .

'I don't remember any animal cemetery,' she said.

Marigold came through the room, on her way to have her bath. She looked at her husband, her eyebrows up. Rufus covered the mouthpiece with his hand.

'Mary Passant,' he said.

Of course Marigold didn't know who that was but that he had spoken the name so openly would allay any possible suspicions on her part. And later he would explain. He would be the frank, honest husband who trusted and expected trust in his turn and who therefore could tell his wife this was a former girlfriend, calling him up because she happened to be home on holiday for ten days.

'Who were you talking to?' Mary Gage said.

'My wife.'

Marigold must have heard that reply too before she closed the door.

Mary gave a little sigh. 'So you don't know anything about it? Well, how could you?'

'How indeed? Adam and I didn't stay long after you left.'

'So that girl Bella never found anyone to make up a commune with you?'

'What a memory you have, Mary,' Rufus said in his light bantering way, though he had felt a brief sensation of coldness, almost a shiver. After ten years she had remembered Bella's name. It was a tremendous relief to hear her say:

'Oh, I only remember because someone told me yesterday that she had died. She died of some awful thing and she was only thirty.'

Rufus felt quite buoyant and euphoric suddenly. Bella was dead so Bella could never be found by the police, could never tell them how she had sent Shiva and Vivien to Ecalpemos on 15 July 1976.

'When exactly do you go back?' he said.

'In five days' time – well, four really. I mean Tuesday, and I'll be making an early start.'

The earlier the better, he thought. There was no reason to think she would speak to the police unless they sought her out, and how could they?

'Do you know, we haven't actually spoken since that day you drove me into Colchester and I got the train to London.'

'That's right,' said Rufus. He resigned himself to a chat. From upstairs he could hear Marigold's bath water beginning to run out down the plug hole. He reached for the secret drink and sipped it. It tasted stale, warm and sickly.

'Are you drinking?' she said. 'My God, it doesn't sound as if you've changed much.'

One minute more and they had run out of things to say. He wished her a good journey quite cordially and said goodbye. Really he should be happy she had phoned. It was good news she had brought – the best. Vivien's origins now remained lost in obscurity. Rufus lit a cigarette, his last of the day, and drew a deep lungful of smoke. If Adam could not remember Shiva's surname, all the better. What he could not remember he could not tell the police. He would not mention Zosie at all if he had any sense, poor little doomed, mouse-like Zosie. It was strange how when one thought of her it was often to compare her to some small pretty animal whose vulnerability is great and life expectancy short. As a hare one thought of her in her alert listening aspect, a mouse when her eyes grew round and large, or a little cat that sleeps yet never really relaxes. She had been so frightened and so desperate . . .

Rufus went up to bed, Mary Gage almost forgotten, his thoughts at Ecalpemos.

Because of Zosie's theft and subsequent sale of the silver bracelet they had felt unable to carry out any more of their dealings in silver and ornaments in any of the Sudbury shops. Adam believed, and perhaps accurately, that the two relevant shopkeepers had risen up in their wrath and alerted all the others so that now the whole antique and secondhand dealers' fraternity of the town was lying in wait to trap them when next they appeared with goods to dispose of. And if this were so, would their description and reputation for dishonesty not also have spread to Long Melford, to Lavenham, to Colchester even?

In the back of a long deep drawer in the kitchen dresser Vivien had found two large, heavy spoons. They had been in a section of the drawer at the back, the front divisions containing carving knives, a fork and a sharpening stone. Rufus had once seen a pair like them on the table at a regimental reunion dinner to which his father had taken him.

'They're stuffing spoons,' he said. 'For hoiking the stuffing out of chickens and whatever.'

Adam said they looked old, they looked valuable. 'Isn't that a Georgian bead pattern?'

The trouble was that they were afraid to hawk them around any of the local towns, just as they were afraid to hawk the dozen liqueur glasses, the two hexagonal salvers and the mask jug, all scheduled to be disposed of next. Money was getting very short. Zosie said she would steal food for them, she would steal bottles of wine, but Adam stopped her. He was afraid she would be caught and he would lose her.

'I could sell my ring,' she said.

She wore it on the little finger of her left hand. Zosie's fingers were very small and delicate and Rufus frankly doubted if the ring would fit anyone but a child. It was of gold, of several strands of gold, fine as wire, and plaited together in an intricate braid. Zosie had only recently taken to wearing it. For the first weeks from her arrival it had lain in her back-pack along with the sweater and the boots and the studded belt. It used to turn her skin black, she said, there was something about her skin that when she wore gold made a black streaky deposit. She kept studying her hand to see if this was happening again but so far it did not seem to be.

'I don't want you to sell your ring,' Adam said, putting his arm around her.

Shiva had a look at it. 'Besides, who would it fit? An Indian girl perhaps. The English mostly have thick fingers. And I don't think you would get much money for it, gold or no gold.'

That made Adam cross. 'I should think it would fetch at least £50, but I don't want her to sell it. I hate the idea of her selling it. There are other ways of getting money. It may be that we'll have to take some stuff to London. Somewhere like the Archway Road is full of places offering good prices for silver.'

They were a commune in only one way but that perhaps not an insignificant one. What they had they shared. Of course this mostly meant that what Adam had they shared, but at this point Rufus contributed something. He pawned his gold neck chain. Strictly speaking it was not his but his mother's. Rufus rather fancied himself in a shirt open to the waist with the gold chain and pendant hanging against his deeply tanned chest. His mother never wore it so he helped himself. He said nothing to the others about pawning the chain. Indeed, he did not know if you could still pawn things, or if the practice had become obsolete. He went to Colchester to the pawnshop in Priory Street, doubting the validity or significance of the three brass balls, but it was all right, there was no difficulty, pawning still flourished apparently, and the pawnbroker gave him £100 for the chain.

Thinking about those last weeks, the weeks of August, Rufus recalled for the first time that he had never redeemed that neck chain. Probably it was still there. It might by now be worth £500. His parents were both dead, had died within a year of each other four and five years ago. They had not been young, approaching forty, when he and his brother were born. If his mother had missed the neck chain she had never said.

The money he handed over to Adam and Vivien with the proviso that some of it be spent on wine. Meanwhile, Zosie kept her ring. After a day or two the black streaking reappeared and she was always taking the ring off to wash her hands. The ring was often to be found on the edge of the kitchen sink or in the bathroom or lying anywhere about the kitchen, jumbled up with utensils.

Rufus tried to remember when it was that Adam, and Zosie with him, had gone to London to sell the stuffing spoons, the liqueur glasses and the mask jug. Not then, not until nearly the end of August, for Adam had been reluctant to go to London at all on account of his neurotic fear that he would encounter one or other of his parents. Rufus told him he was like those Antipodeans who, when one of the neighbours is off on holiday to London, tell them to say hallo to their cousin or friend, should they meet these people in the street. But the fact that there were about nine million people in London, that he was going to Highgate and his parents lived in Edgware, had little effect on Adam's fear. He wanted to go, he needed the money, but he kept putting it off. Rufus did not allow himself to indulge in what his father had used to call 'jobbing backwards'. It was useless to regret and say, if only he had never gone.

Much later in August, nearly at the end of the month, the London trip with all its consequences had taken place.

He was jumpy and nervous, he didn't trust Adam. Adam was one of those people who go to pieces under stress. In an emergency they are useless. Look at what happened on that last morning when the postgirl came. Adam had already been in a panic over footsteps he imagined he had heard circling the house in the small hours and had actually stalked that invisible, non-existent intruder with a shot-gun cocked. And the gun had come readily to his hands again when they saw the red flash of the bicycle, heard the letterbox make its double rap sound. He panicked. Hysteria bubbled up in him and erupted.

Rufus told himself to keep calm, he at least was not one of those people, he wasn't the sort to jump when the phone rang. But he did, this morning he did. His receptionist was very selective about which calls to put through to him while he was with a patient, but if Adam were to plead urgency . . .

Adam couldn't stand on his own feet, he couldn't hold out alone, never had been able to. He needed constant support and then kicked you in the teeth. He had no patience either. What must he be like with this daughter of his? Rufus could not imagine, could only see Adam as he had been at nineteen, humping the carrying cot up the stairs at Ecalpemos and never bestowing a glance inside it, Adam who had loved Zosie, who said he wanted to live there for ever with her in their Garden of Eden, but who when she began crying had shouted at her:

'Shut up or I'll kill you!'

Rufus held himself still, told himself to be cool and calm, to be optimistic, but he was not totally under control. He got hold of the wrong notes for Mrs Hitchens and was about to tell her that her symptoms were menopausal when he looked up and saw he was addressing a girl of no more than twenty-eight.

It was just before one when Adam phoned and by then Rufus had given him up for the day.

'I'm sorry but I had to tell them I went to Greece with you. If I wasn't at Wyvis Hall they wanted to know where I was and who with. I had to say, I couldn't just invent someone.'

'Thanks very much,' said Rufus.

'The ironical part is that after I'd made the statement I rang up my father and asked him exactly what he had said about me to the police and he'd never mentioned me being in Greece.'

'Ironical is what you call it, is it?' Rufus's nurse was going off to lunch. He waited till she closed the door behind her. 'You've involved me in this quite unnecessarily. Why the fuck didn't you phone your father first?'

'I didn't think of it, that's why. And why shouldn't you be involved anyway? I don't see why I should carry the whole burden of this alone.'

'You shot her, that's why. You fired the bloody gun.'

Rufus crashed down the receiver. The blood was pounding in his head. He sat down and made himself breathe deeply, regularly, he began telling himself that the worst which could happen would be for the police to ask him to confirm that he was with Adam Verne-Smith in Greece during July and August 1976. As far as he could see they couldn't prove he hadn't been. The passport he had had then had expired and been renewed but even if they asked to see the old one and he showed it to them, as often as not passport control officers did not bother to stamp the passports of other Europeans.

'A little place called Ecalpemos,' he could say if they asked him precisely where he had been. 'It's very small and obscure. You won't find it on your map.'

Of course he wouldn't say anything so risky. The really worrying thing was that Adam was unreliable, Adam would crack. If he had blurted out Rufus's name the minute they had asked him to name a travelling companion, what might he not say if they became actually suspicious? Suppose, for instance, they told him the antique dealer with the Welsh name or the coypu man or the farmer from Pytle Farm were all prepared to swear that Adam and a group of friends had been living at Wyvis Hall with two girls among them? Suppose the council refuse collectors had seen them? True, they had always taken their rubbish – wine bottles mostly – up to the top of the drift on whenever it was, Tuesdays or Wednesdays, because Hilbert had done so, Adam said, but one of those men might remember collecting it week after week. What would Adam say if the police confronted him with that? As likely as not he would break down and confess everything. The best thing would have been to have refused to answer when asked where he had been. He had a right to refuse, everyone had. Rufus, who would have liked to do that, realized that now he

452

couldn't, for this would incriminate Adam and therefore, by association, all of them.

Since he had started permitting himself to think about her he thought about her all the time. She came into his dreams, entering in strange guises, once in a nurse's uniform of blue dress and white cap to tell him Abigail was dead. She, Zosie, had taken the greatest care of Abigail, had watched over her and sat by her bed and loved her, but nevertheless she had died. She had turned her face into the pillow and died. Out of that dream he awoke fighting, flailing at the air. Anne said:

'You're ill, you're sick. For God's sake go to the doctor.'

He got up and at two in the morning was driving down Highgate West Hill. He took the turn into Merton Lane and left the car halfway down, carrying with him Hilbert's shot-gun, which, after taking careful thought about this he had wrapped up first in strips of rag, then in part of an old brown curtain that in the past had been used for covering up furniture while he painted a wall. Secured with string, this made an innocuous looking parcel. At least it no longer looked like a gun. The rags, he reasoned, would disguise the identity of the gun but not protect it.

There was no one about. It was dark but there were street lamps on all night. He walked down to the ponds where he lost his nerve. If he merely put the gun into the shallow water it would soon be found and he did not dare throw it so that it fell in the centre. He could imagine the splash. There were too many houses and flats around here. He went back home again. Anne was sitting up in bed with the light on.

'Where have you been?'

'Not to the doctor,' said Adam.

Next morning which was Saturday he drove around until he found, north of the North Circular Road, a huge used-car dump, a mountain of broken, torn, rusted, disintegrating metal. It looked abandoned, was quite unattended. All the piled dumped vehicles were far beyond rescue, rejuvenation. All that could happen to them would be either that they were simply left here, an eyesore, an awful detritus, for ever, or that individually they were picked up and crushed flat or, by means of some marvellous machine that could do such things, compressed into a small cuboid block of metal.

Adam walked in among the metal mountains where there was no vegetation and the ground was hard and dusty. On either side of the central walkway rose hills in which the strata were blue and red and cream with here and there outcroppings of black rubber and slivers of glass and spars of chrome. There was an all-pervading smell of motor oil which contains a high proportion of metal filings, a bitter, unnatural odour.

He poked the gun through the broken rear window of what had once been a Lancia Beta saloon. It was unlikely that it would be found there and if it was the finder was most unlikely to take it to the police. But probably, when the time came, it would be crushed up in the compressor along with the metal shell which now housed it.

Walking back to the car, he found it impossible to remember why he had ever brought the gun away from Ecalpemos in the first place. Why had they not buried it in the Little Wood along with the lady's gun, the four-ten? Had he actually thought the time might come when he would *use* it again?

He had not known anything about cleaning or oiling guns but on 12 August he had gone into the gun room and taken this one down from the wall, 'broken' it and begun his cleaning operations. After all, cleaning was cleaning. There was presumably only one way you could do it. Zosie came in and watched him.

'Today is the glorious twelfth,' he said.

'I don't know what that means.'

'It's what they call the day grouse shooting begins. It's the twelfth of August, which is today, and it's called the glorious twelfth.'

'I wouldn't know a grouse if I saw one,' Zosie said.

'There aren't any here. I don't think there are any south of Yorkshire. I'm not planning to shoot grouse anyway. I might shoot pheasants or pigeons or something. Or a hare. I expect Vivien could cook jugged hare.'

Rufus said you couldn't shoot pheasants before 1 October.

'You mean there are secret gamekeepers hiding in the wood to stop me?'

'You're right. No one would know,' said Rufus and he laughed.

But Vivien had been appalled at the prospect of his attempting to shoot a hare. She made more fuss about it than Mary Gage had about the coypu man. So Adam promised to confine himself to birds and did actually succeed in shooting a couple of pigeons which they ate, though the purple-brown flesh was tough. But it taught him to like the feel of the twelve bore in his hands and after that he took it out every day, aiming at squirrels or pigeons or sometimes at a hole in a tree trunk. He could imagine himself becoming an English country gentleman, a landed squire, living here with Zosie. In a couple of weeks' time Vivien would be gone and Shiva with her. A further week would see Rufus's departure. Adam could hardly wait. All that worried him was money. What were he and Zosie going to live on? They had nothing.

'We shall have to get jobs,' he told her as they lay at dusk on the bed in the Pincushion Room. The windows were open and the sky, just after sunset, was a soft rich violet-pink, not clear but covered with innumerable tiny flecks of cloud as if overspread with flamingo feathers. 'We shall both have to work.'

'I can't do anything,' said Zosie. 'What could I do?'

'Can you type?'

She shook her head. He felt her hair rub silkily against the sensitive skin in the hollow of his elbow.

'You could work in a shop.'

'I'm bad at counting up,' she said. 'I'd get it wrong. I'm best at stealing really. I can't do honest things. I told you I should have to marry a rich man. Do you know what my mother calls me? Well, *called* me. She called me Lady Muck because I'm idle but I like nice things. Why doesn't my mother come and look for me, Adam?'

'She doesn't know where you are.'

'No, but she hasn't tried to find out, has she? I'm so young, Adam, you'd think she'd be *concerned*, wouldn't you? Why doesn't she love me?'

'I love you,' said Adam.

'You love screwing me.'

'Yes, I do, yes. But I do love you, Zosie. I adore you. I love you – with all my heart. Don't you believe me? Say you believe me.'

'I don't know. It's too soon. If you're still saying it in a year.'

'I'll still be saying it in fifty years.'

She turned to him with trembling lips, in tears that seemed to him shed from no understandable cause. He made love to her in the pink light that muted to purple, to dark. It was warm and humid and he tasted on her skin the salt of sweat and the salt of tears. Afterwards she sat up and said,

'I won't hide myself on the floor when next we go out in Goblander.'

He smiled and held her, pleased by this sign of rational behaviour.

'We must think about working next. We must think about money.'

'Do you know at school they were always reading out that bit from the Bible at prayers about the birds of the air not sowing or reaping but your heavenly father feeding them just the same. Only he doesn't, does he? Birds die and so do people and he doesn't do anything. I don't understand that.'

'Nobody understands that, my sweetheart,' said Adam.

One evening, in a pub in Colchester, Rufus picked up a girl who was the wife of a serving soldier. The soldier was away somewhere on a course. Someone had told Rufus that Colchester was unique among English towns in having at the same time a port, a garrison and a university, and it was perhaps in consequence of this that it had the highest rate of venereal disease in the country. He repeated this to the girl because it amused him. Later on they went back to the girl's house in married quarters. Now he was uncertain of what her name had been, Janet or perhaps Janice.

There was no uncertainty in his mind though as to whether he had ever taken her back to Ecalpemos. He hadn't. They had met on half a dozen more occasions but he had always spent the night at her place. Rufus had not been averse to the others knowing where he had been and what he had been up to. His *amour propre*, his machismo, had suffered through his being seen to lack a woman while the other men (less attractive to or successful with women than he was, he thought) had girlfriends. Adam had seemed relieved, was even congratulatory. Rufus guessed he felt guilty about Zosie, as if he had stolen her from Rufus instead of, as was truly the case, Rufus himself voluntarily relinquishing her. But Shiva had been shocked. One good thing about that, Rufus remembered, was the effect it had of stopping Shiva constantly asking him about his chances of getting into medical school. Instead Shiva settled down at last and applied to every teaching hospital they could jointly think of, consulting the public library in Sudbury for the required addresses. From time to time he eyed Rufus as one might eye the Antichrist if one were so unfortunate as to see him.

That August, on the 17th, Rufus had had his twenty-third birthday.

Ten years ago and two months. But that twenty-third birthday had been the first he had not looked forward to with pleasure at being a year older. He had thought how much better pleased he would have been to be twenty-two.

'Another year older and deeper in debt,' Adam said, quoting something no doubt, on the birthday morning. And that was true too. There was scarcely a tenner left out of the pawnbroker's money.

It was hotter than ever the night they went out to celebrate his birthday, first in the Chinese restaurant in Sudbury, then in the pubs where Rufus remembered he had given up wine for that night and drunk brandy. The tipple for heroes, Adam had said, quoting someone else. He had sold to the man called Evans or Owens a Flora Danica wall plate to raise money for this spree and Rufus was grateful. Together they had gone to Hadleigh, to the shop, and now Rufus, with a sense of chill, remembered the old man saying:

'Settled in at Wyvis Hall then, have you?'

And Adam had replied with some enthusiasm that he was happy there, that he intended to go on living there. Had Adam forgotten that? Had he forgotten the old man going on to say – and he had not been so old, he had been a spry and vigorous sixty-odd – that he must come down again in the next week or two:

'Try and twist your arm about that cabinet I've got my eye on.'

The cabinet in the dining room with the curve pattern in the veneer that he called 'flame-fronted'. Adam hadn't wanted to sell and didn't want to sell now.

'I'd make it £300, you know, and don't tell me that's not a tempting offer.'

It hadn't tempted Adam. Why hadn't it? What was there about possessing all that old furniture that meant so much to him? The lord of the manor syndrome, thought Rufus, it probably wasn't all that uncommon. Rather than sell Owens or Evans an old cupboard he never looked at from one week to the next he preferred to do that stupid terrible thing that brought retribution down on all of them, and out of which in any case he never made a penny.

He hadn't done it for money, of course, he had done it for Zosie, because he was in thrall to Zosie. The idea of the money had come from Shiva. Ten thousand pounds. It didn't seem so much today but things had changed a lot and he had changed and his circumstances. It was fairy gold anyway, at the end of an impossible rainbow, while Evans' or Owens' £300 would have been notes pressed into the hand.

A lively little man with an undercurrent of Welsh in his voice that a lifetime of living in Suffolk hadn't got rid of. He had walked about the house as if he had some sort of right to buy, as if their poverty and his comparative affluence and expertise gave him the right to what he wanted. And in the shop he held the Royal Copenhagen plate in his hands and looked at it and then at them as if he wanted to possess it yet despised them for selling it.

It may be crazy but I'm going to go there, Rufus thought, I'm going to go down there. There are things I have to know. Thank God it's Saturday.

And thank God too for a woman who did not probe, who was not apparently sensitive to his moods or any more aware of apprehensiveness in him than she was of his inner sighs of relief. He could have an affair or a nervous breakdown and she would be none the wiser. That he would himself have to pay for this by a lifetime of being misunderstood, he judged a fair bargain.

It took him a little while, though, to think up a convincing lie. He had a private patient rushed in as an emergency to a hospital in Colchester, he told Marigold. Of course he did not especially want to go down there and visit her but he thought he should. He would have been surprised if Marigold had asked any questions, yet at the same time it seemed to him faintly odd that she didn't. It would have been natural for a wife only three years married to demur at being left alone all day on a Saturday.

Nor did she say how she would herself spend it. She was wearing her new Edina Ronay sweater and Rufus noticed how long she had let her hair grow. It tumbled down over her shoulders, beautiful, thick, shiny blonde hair, and she had washed it when first she got up. She appeared neither glad nor sorry he was going to Colchester. Certainly she was not relieved. But still, Rufus thought, suppose if I had been here she had said to me that she was going to her mother's, or to someone's coffee morning, or made any excuse for going out, I would have thought nothing of it, I would have accepted. She won't have to say that now. It may even be a source of satisfaction to her that because I shan't be here she won't have to go out.

With all these minutiae of reactions he felt he could not concern himself now. The abyss between them that they bridged with 'darlings' widened a little further, that was all. By ten he was on the motorway whose approach road was only a quarter of a mile from where he lived.

The yellow-brick pile by Colchester station that might have been a hospital or a children's home or some sort of institution for the mentally handicapped, was gone and a high fence put up round the site. It was there, on this spot, just beyond the bridge, that he had picked up Zosie. For the first time Rufus was really aware of the difference between himself now and the Rufus of those days, a lifetime seeming to separate them, not a mere ten years. That clapped-out van, the drugs under the back seat, his hair long and shaggy, a stubble growth on his chin, naked to the waist, nicotine-stained hands, a predatory way with women. He felt a hundred years older, he usually did feel old for his age. The Mercedes glided smoothly, purring as it did its automatic gear-shift. He put up his hand to his face involuntarily, felt the smoothness of the skin and felt too the deep indentation which now ran from nostril to jaw.

Nunes might have changed but he didn't know, he couldn't be sure. He had no eye for things like that. That house might be new, that one extended. What altered it most was the season, the greyness of autumn, the leaves falling and the leaves that had already fallen, a sodden mat of them everywhere. A notice on a pole had been planted outside the church, asking for donations for repairs to the roof. He drove past the Fir Tree and the phone-box to which he had taken Vivien to make her call to Robin Tatian. There had been a police car parked by the phone-box, the parti-coloured green and white kind they called a panda car, and if not exactly alarmed they had both been made wary by the sight of it. Of course its presence there had nothing to do with any of them but they had both thought of Zosie who must be classified as a missing person and of the things she had stolen.

But he had parked Goblander behind the police car which was in any case without driver or passenger, and Vivien had gone into the phone-box, this very phone-box, to say the phone was damaged and not working. So he had driven on and found another box outside a cottage converted for use as doctors' surgeries and waiting-rooms. There had been a plaque on the gatepost, Rufus remembered, and here it was, still the same, though doubtless some of the GPs in the

459

group had gone and others come. There, on the grass verge, now glistening with water and scattered with shed leaves but then dry springy turf, he had sat and waited for Vivien because it was too hot to stay inside the van. And people had come by and looked at him, two women and a bunch of children and a dog. Rufus was glad now that he had never succumbed to the prevailing fashion of the time and painted Goblander with moons and stars and flowers and hieroglyphs.

He slowed, pulled in and consulted his road plan, though he had no need to. He wanted to appear to passers-by as a man consulting a road plan. But there were no passers-by. It was desolate October and here in the country everyone ate lunch at noon, everyone was indoors. He lifted his eyes to the red phone-box, the length of brick wall hung with ivy.

Vivien had come out and given him back what remained of his change, down to the 2p pieces. She was always meticulous about money, over-conscientious. And she had told him that Robin Tatian had himself been at home, had answered the phone. Yes, of course she could have the job, he had written to her. Hadn't she had his letter? Vivien wouldn't tell lies, even of the whitest kind, and confessed she had inadvertently given him the wrong address. Rufus had not asked if at this point she had given him the correct one. There had been no reason to ask, no need then for prudence or caution, any more than Adam thought he had needed those things when Evans or Owens asked him if he were settling in at Wyvis Hall. But Robin Tatian might even now, he thought, be reading in his newspaper about the prospective identification and seeing the name Wyvis Hall and the name Nunes, remember that his children's former nanny . . .

'I'll stay for a year,' she had said. 'By then I'll have enough to get me to India and once I'm there – well, if I starve in India I won't be alone, will I? The thing I dread is that I may get too fond of the children.'

'The children?'

'The Tatian children, Naomi and Nicola. I may get to love them, in a way I hope I will, but then it will be such a wrench to part.'

'It's just a job, surely?' Rufus had no special feeling for children, had not had then or now. 'You'll look on it simply as work, won't you?'

She gave him a strange look.

'You think it's that easy?'

He misunderstood her. 'I didn't say it was easy. It's badly paid, bloody hard work but it's your choice, presumably.'

'That's not what I meant, Rufus. I'm afraid I shall naturally come to love those little girls because I'm a woman with a woman's feelings and I'm afraid too that they may come to love me and be even more upset than I when we have to be separated. I'm afraid that if that happens I may not have the strength to go. Have you ever thought what a nanny's life must be? A succession of bereavements, joy succeeded by loss.'

'You exaggerate,' he said.

He had never liked her. She was a tiresome woman, uncomfortable to be with. He could not remember her ever laughing and her smiles were not occasioned by wit or amusement but by wonder at some remarkable sight, a bird or a flower or a sunset. Well, those ambitions of hers had come to nothing, broken, lost, destroyed. The trouble was that he could easily have imagined her sitting at the feet of some dirty, emaciated fakir or with a begging bowl or robed as a nun. Things do not work out as we expect them to, though they had for him.

If he was going to Hadleigh he had better get on with it. Hadleigh, as he remembered it, more or less closed down after lunch on Saturdays. No one went shopping and half the shops closed. He drove past the post office and the Hampstead Garden Suburb houses, postponing enquiries there till later. What he hoped for was that the shop kept by Evans or Owens, a shop whose position in the High Street he could perfectly remember, would be gone and replaced by a hairdresser's perhaps or a florist. And the florist would tell him the old man had died and left no children to take over the business.

They seemed to stretch before his mind's eye in a procession, those people who might remember the company at Wyvis Hall, and as soon as one was discounted – as in the case of Bella – another rose up to take her place, just as threatening, just as dangerous. He had seen something like that in a play, a line of dangerous people, kings perhaps, whose numbers were endless, but he couldn't remember what the play was. Adam, no doubt, would know. Bella was gone but now he remembered the men from the council's refuse department who emptied each week the dustbins they took up to the top of

461

the drift. Someone must have come down to read meters too, even if they had never been admitted to the house . . .

Hadleigh was changed, seemed more cared for, made more consciously ancient, preserved, precious. There were traffic lights at the approach to the town which he couldn't remember from before. He drove in, over the river bridge. Down there on the right it had been, past the wine shop but before you reached the butcher, a low shop you went down a couple of steps to reach . . .

And still was.

He parked the car on the opposite side, outside the vet's, crossed the street and walked a little way along. Outside the shop he paused and looked in through clouded windowpanes at polished furniture within, elegant, sparse, a porcelain leopard, brown spotted golden glaze, lazing in the centre of a circular mahogany table, and behind it, standing there and talking to a customer, a brisk-looking very young man, a mere boy.

Rufus went down the steps and into the shop. The woman was leaving, hastened her leave-taking when she saw him. Rufus said:

'I see you've changed hands. There used to be someone called Evans or Owens . . .'

'Mr Evan, that's right, not Evans. That's my father. What made you think we'd changed hands? I mean it doesn't matter but I'd be curious to know.'

Before Rufus could reply Evan himself had come into the shop from a door at the back and was standing there spry and slightly smiling, looking not a day older than he had ten years before.

— 15 —

The riots of the night before dominated the morning paper. Two of the eastern suburbs. It had begun when police went into a house in Whiteman Road to arrest a man suspected of robbery with violence and in the scuffle a woman had been knocked unconscious. The inhabitants of the house were black and one of the policemen was Indian and this had contributed to the outbreak of violence. A photograph showed the name of the street which was itself an irony. Down the road they had overturned cars in Forest Road. Nearly every window between Mersey Road and Blackhorse Road Station had been broken and a fire started down one of the side streets.

Anne, who liked to go shopping near there on a Saturday morning, was afraid to go near the place, so Adam went alone. But in places the damage was so bad that whole areas of street had been closed and the traffic diverted and Adam found himself in Hornsey, passing Hornsey Old Church, a route he had always consciously avoided, for this was the way he had come into London with Zosie.

This time, of course, he was driving in thick traffic in the opposite direction and it was the church itself which alerted him to where he was, the church which looked as if it might be Victorian Gothic but was in fact a single medieval tower. It was a key in his memory which immediately gave access to the file of those last days. Here, with the church ahead of him on his left, he had nearly turned left and headed down to Holloway, Islington, the outskirts of the City. Zosie had the street atlas on her lap and he had said,

'I don't know why I'm going so far west. It might be better to go down to Holloway.'

And she had said, 'Go on then. *You* know. I've never been here before.'

But, 'If I was going to I should have turned down the Seven Sisters Road.'

So he had driven on and changed his whole future. If he had turned left Zosie and he would have married and been living together at Ecalpemos still. Why not? And the turf in the cemetery would have lain undisturbed and the guns still been hanging in the gun-room, Abigail unborn but other children born to him, and he would not have been a murderer in daily expectation of arrest.

Adam reached the shopping precinct and managed at last to park the car. He thought he had put Anne's shopping list in his pocket but he couldn't find it. He would have to do his best from memory but it seemed that all his memory could *do* for him at the moment was dig into the documents of the past. Later Anne's parents were coming to them for supper. It would be the first time since the previous Christmas so they could hardly get out of it. Then there had been a family gathering with his own parents among the company and his sister and Anne's sister. They had been summoned to arrive in time for a present-giving ceremony before lunch. Anne's father had given her mother a mask jug. She collected Victorian porcelain.

Anne's father knew nothing about antiques and boasted of this, saying that the woman in the shop had vouched for its authenticity and value – well, he could vouch for that by what he had had to pay. The jug was of pale cream and yellow china, its spout a face in profile with hair depicted in gold as flowing back round its rim.

'That's called a mask jug,' Adam's father had said. 'You can see why. It's on account of the spout being in the form of a mask.'

Everyone already knew this. They could see. But his father went on instructing them, taking the jug from Anne's mother's hands and holding it up to the light, swinging it about and tipping it upside down until Adam was in a sweat that he would drop it. It was only the second mask jug he had ever seen in his life.

'My old uncle, the one that had this rather splendid house in Suffolk, a mansion really, he had one of these jugs. White it was, white picked out in gold.' He remembered then that Adam must have inherited the jug along with the other contents of Wyvis Hall. 'What became of it, I wonder? Got it over at your place, have you? Or did you sell it along with all that other priceless stuff?'

'I don't know,' Adam muttered. 'I don't remember.'

But he had, only too well. Back at that time he was in the habit of escaping from or cancelling Ecalpemos thoughts. So good was he at this that on that Christmas Day, even if he had tried, he would have had difficulty in recalling the shape or colouring of the jug. Now there was no such difficulty. He could see it: about twelve inches high, a high white glaze, the spout or lip a smiling Silenus face with flowing locks lightly gilded, and on the almost spherical body of the jug a fernleaf pattern in gold. Zosie had wrapped it in tissue they found lining a drawer and then in newspaper. Whenever they went anywhere she bought a newspaper to see if her mother had told the police yet and there was a hunt on for her. There was quite a pile of newspapers mounting up. They used more sheets to wrap the stuffing spoons and the delicate glasses etched with a Greek key design.

Vivien found a cardboard box to put the things in. It was one of Rufus's from the wine shop. Rufus had considered coming with them, Adam remembered. What had stopped him? He had a date with that girl, the married one, that was it. It would be his last chance to see her before her husband came back.

'He is doing a wicked thing, I think,' Adam overheard Shiva say to Vivien. 'Like your King David.'

'Rufus didn't send her old man into the forefront of the battle,' Adam said. 'He's only gone on a gunnery course.'

'How would Rufus feel if he got killed?'

'Bloody awful, I should imagine, only the chance is a bit remote, don't you think?'

So Rufus had stayed behind, though his date wasn't till eight-thirty. Things would have worked out differently if he had come. If he had stayed at home past eight o'clock they might well have worked out differently. There had never been any idea of Vivien or Shiva accompanying them. Shiva meant to go on one of his nature walks and Vivien always baked bread on Mondays. She was setting out her things just as they were leaving, scales, a big earthenware bowl, a measuring jug, a large bag of wholemeal flour, a lump of yeast. She poured flour into the bowl, started cutting up the yeast to drop it into warm water and just in time saw Zosie's ring stuck on the underside of the lump. That little ring of plaited gold strands was always lying about getting caught up on dough, scooped into vegetable peelings, threatened with being washed down the sink.

It was odd what Zosie did then, though not perhaps so odd when you knew Zosie. She put the ring on her little finger and put her arms around Vivien's neck, hugging her. Vivien held her, having little regard for her floury hands which made mealy marks on the back of Zosie's pale blue T-shirt.

'What's the matter, lovely?'

'I don't know, I feel so funny sometimes, as if I'm not anyone, as if I'm a shadow or a dead petal that's dropped off and someone will sweep me away. When I put my ring on I feel a bit more real, I get to be the person who wears the ring.'

Adam hated her to talk like that. He felt bereft because she had gone into Vivien's arms and not his. 'The usual tradition about rings,' he said, 'is that they make the wearer invisible, they don't *reveal* them.'

She seemed to shrivel. She edged away from Vivien, drawing her arms back, pulling in her fingers like an animal retracting its claws.

'I'm not invisible, am I?' She looked from Adam to Vivien and back at Adam, her eyes vague and strange. 'You can see me, can't you? Say you can see me.'

'Don't be a fool,' Adam said roughly. 'Of course we can see you.'

Vivien spoke his name warningly.

'Zosie, love . . .' he said.

'Am I your love?'

It embarrassed him being spoken to like that in front of Vivien. It was almost as if they were in the presence of his mother. 'You know you are.'

'If I went away would you tell the police? Would you look for me?' She harped on that always.

'If you'd only tell me where your bloody mother lives we could go there and find her and find out the truth of it.'

'I will one day, I really will.'

'In the meantime,' he said, 'we're supposed to be going to London. It's past one now and if we don't get on with it it'll be too late.'

'I'm coming,' she said. 'I'm coming.'

He could see that tiny ring on her tiny finger now, the plaited gold. It must be a child's ring, he said to her, it must have been made for a child.

'It was. It was made for me when I was little. I wore it on one of my big fingers then.'

The idea of her having big fingers made him laugh. She took off the ring and showed him a Z engraved inside.

'So you really are called that. I did wonder.'

She sat beside him with both arms round his neck and her head on his shoulder and it was beautiful (If we find each other that's beautiful, if not it can't be helped) only he wasn't a good enough driver to contend with distractions like that. Her right arm she left along the back of his seat, her hand resting against his neck, the other with the ring on in her lap. It really was a lap because she had a skirt on, the first time he had ever seen her in one. It was a wraparound thing, white with pale blue checks. Perhaps it wasn't a skirt at all but a curtain she had found somewhere. She looked older dressed like that and less like a pretty boy. He had made love to her only two hours before but seeing her like that, her brown polished thighs showing where the hems of the curtain parted, feeling her fingers in his hair, made him want to drive into one of those fields and carry her to a hedge bank where the wild clematis was in bloom and the tall weed flowers gone to seed.

It was hot, oppressively hot, but not as it had been. This heat was humid, making you sweat as soon as you went out into it, causing breathlessness. There was air all around you but you wanted air, you gasped for it. The horizon was lost in a foggy blueness. It did not need a meteorologist to forecast that the long-enduring, fine, dry weather was drawing to its end. They had all the windows of Goblander open but the heat was still thick and enveloping. Adam knew she had fallen asleep when he felt her hand drop. How she must trust him, he thought. There was no one he could think of he would let drive and go to sleep beside them.

He drove on down the A12 and still she slept, breathing with a gentle, childlike rhythm. For a while he thought about words, about two words no one could spell, desiccated and iridescent, even the good spellers could not spell them, and then his mind had drifted back to Zosie and he wondered as he often did if she loved him, if she really loved him, and if his lovemaking gave her pleasure. Did she enjoy it or was her response an act put on for some secret purpose? How could one know? Adam wondered if it were possible she played this game *because she wanted him to go on loving her* even though she might feel no love for him.

He had driven into London along Forest Road, through Walthamstow and Tottenham. There was a smell of oil and soot and stagnant water. By this time Zosie was awake, staring out of the window, saying she had never been here before in these ugly north-eastern suburbs. Riots had been unheard-of in those days, apart from the old troubles in Notting Hill and the occasional fracas at a football match. Zosie had the street atlas open on her lap and she wanted to know where all the reservoirs were (she called them lakes) and the parks and open spaces she could see on the area plans when everything outside was just buildings in a grey heat haze.

At Hornsey Old Church he had gone straight on and up Muswell Hill towards Highgate Wood. If on that journey he had passed within sight of Archduke Avenue where he now lived he did not think he would have considered buying the house. But he had not and there was nothing about his house or the street in which it was situated to remind him of that drive. Only the grey stone tower had reminded him of it and reading of the riots along the route they had taken.

Adam took a shopping trolley and began walking dazedly around the store.

It had not been their Evan but his younger brother. Their Evan was dead. It seemed to Rufus that his adversaries were being bowled over

467

and swept away in rapid succession, first Bella, now the old antique dealer.

'I was always about,' he said to Rufus, blandly. 'We were partners. Pure chance we never met, it must have been, though the fact is my brother tended to be the one that went about buying while I minded the shop.'

He drove back to Nunes, absurdly relieved, dying for a drink. Of course there was no question of having a drink when he had seventy or eighty miles to drive home. He lit a cigarette. In those people's place, he thought, in the shoes of the coypu man or the meter reader or the farmer or the postgirl he would have gone to the police and volunteered what information he had. He would have thought it his duty, would even have *enjoyed* it. For the first time he saw himself and Adam and Shiva and Vivien and Zosie as the local people must have seen them, wild, feckless, curiously dressed or half-naked, driving about too fast in a dirty, dilapidated van, hippies, drug addicts, the kind it was a pleasure to tell the police about. If they remembered. If they made the connection.

On the Hadleigh side of the village stood the four Hampstead Garden Suburb houses. They seemed far smaller than he remembered. Ten years ago he had not noticed the name of the little curve of road: Fir Close. It was separated from the main road by a half moon of grass on which were planted four or five saplings, sticks without branches that had shed their few leaves. He drew the car in along Fir Close, but found he could not remember on which garage drive he had seen the Vermstroy van, on one of the two centre ones, he supposed, but he had no idea which. Nor could he remember what the coypu man looked like. He had only glimpsed him once and that had been when he, Rufus, was lying on the terrace and the coypu man had appeared on the further shore of the lake, a distance of some two hundred yards.

'Like a brigand,' Adam had said. 'Fierce-looking with a big black tache.'

But Adam had a too-vivid imagination. A woman came out of one of the houses and Rufus wound down the window of the car and asked her if she could tell him where it was the pest-control people operated from. He could see at once she didn't know what he meant.

'We've only been here two years,' she said. 'The people at the end have got something to do with a hardware firm in Sudbury. It wouldn't be them? The man next door to us committed suicide but that was years before we came and the widow moved anyway. Did you say a white van? The people at the end had a white van but it was more a mobile caravan.'

They had no real reason to believe the coypu man had lived there. It was an assumption that had been made on very thin evidence and somehow become part of Ecalpemos mythology. Rufus got to the post office ten minutes before it was due to close until Monday morning.

Ten years before it had not been there. The post office had been a pre-fabricated hut which none of them had ever gone into. After all, they had bought no stamps, sent no letters. This was a shop that took up part of the ground floor of a cottage almost opposite the Fir Tree. Rufus had already noted that the present landlord of the Fir Tree was not the same man who had kept it ten years before when he had met Janet or Janice there for the last time. The landlord's name was printed above the door to the public bar and Rufus knew it was not the same, though he could not remember what the other one was.

He went into the post office with no story prepared, trusting to inspiration. There was a kind of cubicle with a wire grille behind which a middle-aged man in glasses was intently performing those mysterious tasks with forms and slips of paper and rubber bands that postmasters everywhere seem to spend their time at. A youngish woman, stout and smiling, tired-looking, was behind a sweet and newspaper and postcard counter. Rufus picked up a copy of the *Daily Mirror*. There were no other papers remaining, perhaps there had been no others.

'Where would you recommend me to get some lunch?'

She hesitated, looked at the postmaster.

'I don't think the Fir Tree, do you, Tom?' The Suffolk accent was strong, a coarse intonation with glottal stops and what Adam had once called a 'concavity of vowel sounds'. 'No, I wouldn't recommend that. That's the best place, the Bear at Sindon.'

'He doesn't know where that is,' said Tom in the voice of a retired army officer.

'It's a long time since I was round here,' Rufus said quickly. 'A good many years. Did you know a Mr Hilbert Verne-Smith at a place called Wyvis Hall?'

'Everyone knew him,' she said. 'A friend of yours, was he? My uncle helped him out in the garden, used to go down there to see to the garden twice a week year in, year out. But the young fellow who came in for it, the nephew, he didn't want him, turned him off with just what was owing.'

Rufus had an immediate picture of an old man with a knotted handkerchief on his head. 'Is he dead?'

'Mr Verne-Smith? He died a good ten or eleven years back, didn't he? I said the nephew came in for it.'

'I meant your uncle.'

'Dead? No, he's over to Walnut Tree on account of needing a bit of care but he's as fit as a fiddle really.'

Seeing Rufus's puzzlement, Tom said, 'Geriatric ward in Sudbury.'

'Oh, I see. Yes.'

'He never went back,' the woman said. 'Never set foot on the land again. It as good as broke his heart. Except for just the once, once he went back, to pick up the tools what was his own, his old spade and his dibber, and he went down there five one morning so as not to disturb folks and took a look at that garden – his garden, like he called it – and it was gone to rack and ruin, all burned up and the weeds gone mad and grass like a meadow. Mind you, it was that hot summer we had, whenever it was, 1976.'

'So as not to disturb folks', Rufus repeated in his own mind. He understood now whose the footsteps were that Adam had heard very early on that last morning. And Goblander had been outside and Vivien's washing on the line. He was in a geriatric ward, the old gardener, but fit as a fiddle really.

'The Bear at Sindon, you said?'

She began giving him elaborate confused instructions for finding his way there. Rufus looked at her face while she bent over the counter, drawing maps with her forefinger on the cover of the *Radio Times*. There was something familiar there, something that recalled a red bicycle to him, a waving hand, solid legs pumping pedals up the steep drift . . . He could think of no way to ask her if she was the postgirl who had brought the rates demand to their door and then the electricity bill, and without asking he could never be certain.

There was no question of going to Sindon to find some lunch. He had no appetite. And he felt that he had accomplished nothing. He had complicated matters. Driving past Pytle Farm he thought, the farmer may already have been to the police. They would certainly have been to him when the enquiry began. 'So as not to disturb folks' – the phrase ran through his head. It made him appear in his own eyes naïve, as if he could reasonably have supposed for a moment that they could have lived down there for two and a half months and no one would know.

Down here.

He stopped at the top of the drift. A sign on a post, roman lettering on a piece of oak, bore the name Wyvis Hall and under this: *Private Road*. It came to Rufus quite suddenly that not the Evans, father and son, nor the woman at Fir Close, nor the postmaster or the woman who might or might not have been that postgirl, had mentioned the animal cemetery to him or what had been found in it or said a word about police. He wondered why this should have been but came up with no answer.

Simple fear prevented him from turning down the drift and driving to the house. Not normally imaginative, he pictured curiously a reception committee down there, the owners of the house – Chipstead, were they called? – police of course, the real postgirl, eighteen still, the meter reader, the farmer, the coypu man . . .

After a little while he began the drive home. Rain had started to fall as on that last day, the day of the expulsion from paradise. It was the same sort of rain, the kind that comes in spurts, wind-driven. And dismal rain had continued to fall in the ensuing days after he was back home, keeping him indoors, lying low and staying silent with his parents and his brother, waiting always for something to happen.

Just as now, he read the papers carefully every day, read everything about the baby, his tension mounting when the papers said the police had a clue, a shaming relief flooding him when it seemed they were farther than ever from finding the truth. He used to wake in the night and wonder if he would ever go back to medical school, if he would be free to go back. He had done nothing really, he had only been there, but he never tried to deceive himself into believing he had no share in the collective guilt, the collective responsibility. It never crossed his mind, though, to break the undertaking they had all given and attempt to see the others. He didn't want to see them, he wanted to be rid of them for good.

There had been some sort of old school reunion around that time but he hadn't gone. He avoided Highgate from then on, sometimes making quite elaborate detours to keep clear of the Archway Road and North Hill and the Highgate police station on the corner of Church Road.

Adam and Zosie had driven along the Muswell Hill Road where it winds and dips up and down between Queens Wood and Highgate Wood and up to the lights at the crossroads where the Archway Road runs northwards and becomes the A1. There he turned right and started looking for somewhere to park Goblander. This would not have been possible in the Archway Road itself. Adam had not been here since he left school some thirteen months before but the little antique and secondhand and junk shops were here as he remembered them and he even saw in a window a notice inviting customers to bring their silver to sell.

He had turned left into Church Road. Any of those wide roads would have done, he had thought since, but he had had to choose Church Road and that in spite of what Zosie said.

'That's a police station on the corner. You're not going to leave it outside a police station!'

'Why not? We're not doing anything illegal.'

God help him . . .

'Drive a bit further up,' she said.

So he had taken Goblander to the other side of the junction with Talbot Road. He didn't want Zosie coming with him. Ideally, he would have liked her to sit in the van and wait for him. At that time he had the beginnings of an awareness that what he would really like would be to keep her utterly to himself, shut her away for his exclusive society, an Albertine to his Marcel.

She looked up at him, large clear golden eyes, childlike and innocent.

'Do you know what? That's View Road over there. On the other side of what's-it-called, North Hill.' She had been studying Rufus's street atlas. 'That's where Vivien's going to be a nanny. We took her there, Woof-woof and me.'

'Oh, yes?' he said, not interested.

That was it, he hadn't been interested. He was glad Vivien was

472

going, he would be glad to see the back of her and Shiva, but where she was going he didn't care about.

'I'll be about half an hour,' he said. 'Maybe a bit more. Say three-quarters of an hour.'

She nodded, back at her map-reading. He got out of Goblander, carrying the wine-shop box with the liqueur glasses in it and the mask jug and the stuffing spoons. That was when he heard the first of the thunder, a long way off like muffled drums.

'You never told me,' Lili said to Shiva, 'how they came to take the baby. But I suppose that's something you don't really know.'

It was not she who had started on the subject but he. Traffic was diverted down Fifth Avenue away from Forest Road and he stood watching the streams of it, comforted because his street was a safe place and off the beaten, broken, dangerous track. All the glass down here was intact and last night it had been peaceful and even the exodus from the Boxer orderly. And then, abruptly, not knowing why really, he had turned away and come to Lili in her pink sari and Marks and Spencer's cardigan, and said he wanted to talk about that time, about Ecalpemos.

He shook his head. 'I know all right. My goodness, *I know*. But I didn't at first, not on the first day.

'You see, when they came home we thought the baby was Zosie's baby. It sounds a bit crazy, you'll say, but we knew Zosie had had a baby and we knew she wished she'd kept it and when they came back with a baby we just took it for granted it was hers. That is, Vivien and I did. Rufus wasn't there. He was with that woman who was deceiving her soldier husband. A fine thing that, wasn't it? Rufus was a bad person, through and through, I don't think he had a redeeming feature.'

'Never mind Rufus, Shiva. You mean they just walked in with this baby and you accepted it? Just like that?'

'You have to understand that Zosie was always mysterious. There were all sorts of things we didn't know about her and new things were always coming out. When they came home Vivien and I had finished our evening meal and I was out on the terrace reading and she was doing something to her herb garden. She'd cleared a patch and planted this herb garden and she had to water it every night or it

473

would have died. We heard the van come, or I did, and then a bit later I heard a baby crying. Vivien came round the house with her watering can and said what was that. I said it sounded like a baby. Then Zosie appeared. Was there any milk? She wanted it for the baby. She had a feeding bottle in her hand and she was – well, she was absolutely *alight* with happiness and excitement. That's why we thought, I'm sure we both thought, that it was her baby.'

'Did she go to London deliberately to kidnap it?'

'It wasn't like that,' Shiva said. 'It was more an accident, a chance happening. It was like this – or that's what they told me. It was about three-thirty when they got up there and Adam parked the van down a turning off the top of the Archway Road. The road where he parked was a sort of continuation of the road where Vivien was going to work but I think that was just coincidence. I went there once, months afterwards, it had a sort of fascination for me, dreadful though it all was, I wanted to see for myself. And when I got there I could see it wasn't all that much of a coincidence. If you wanted to go shopping in the Archway Road that's where you would park, down one of those side streets up there, that would really be the only place.'

'So Adam left her in the van. Why didn't she go with him?'

'He didn't want her going in those shops. You can understand why not. He thought she'd take things. "Unconsidered trifles", he called them. He thought she wouldn't be able to resist "nicking" things – his word. That business in Sudbury was in his mind, you see. Anyway, he took his box of stuff and went off to look for the shop that had the notice in its window about high prices paid for silver. He left Zosie sitting in the van. She said she might walk around a bit. It was too hot to stay in there.

'She was mad, you know. She had a sort of post-natal insanity. Her thought processes didn't work like other people's, she wasn't rational.'

'You mean you think most people are rational, Shiva?'

He paused, remembering the night before, the noise of it, the shattering of glass that seemed to go on for hours, the shrieks and animal roars that punctuated the continuous cacophony of the sounds of destruction. The loud but dull and meaningless crunch, a reverberating noise of dissolution, that was a car being overturned. Brakes screaming, the pounding of running feet, far off a dull explosion. No, men were not rational. 'They have some idea of reality,' he said, though doubtfully. 'Some notion. Zosie thought of a baby as a doll she could have to comfort her. But no, that's not quite it. It was more as though she thought that what she had done was no worse – no different really – from, say, a kiddy stealing a doll from another kiddy. And yet it wasn't as if she didn't look after the baby. She loved the baby.'

'Little girls love dolls but they get bored and then they stick them on a shelf.'

'She didn't do that. She didn't neglect the baby. Of course she didn't really get the chance.'

'But how did she come to take it in the first place?'

'Her,' said Shiva. 'It was a girl. She went for a walk, you see. She got out to stretch her legs and walked along to the house where Vivien was going to work. She had been there before. I don't think she had any idea then of stealing Mr Tatian's baby but she knew there was a baby there. The house looked as if there was no one at home. Remember it was so extremely hot, but all the windows were closed nevertheless. She walked round to the edge of Highgate golf course and then she came back. She hadn't a watch, you know, but she calculated it was more than half an hour since Adam had gone.

'This time there were windows open upstairs in Mr Tatian's house and she saw a woman come out with one of those things you transport babies in, what do you call them?'

'A carrying cot?'

'That's right, a carrying cot. Zosie said she didn't look at her, she didn't see her, and she can't have done. She put the carrying cot on the back seat of the car and she left the car door open, because it was so hot, presumably. Anyway, she went back into the house, in by the front door which she didn't close behind her. It was as if she'd forgotten something, Zosie said, or gone back to check on something.

'Zosie said she couldn't help herself. She didn't think of what she was doing, not of the dangers anyway. She had to have that baby and she took her. It was the little boy in the department store all over again, only this time Rufus wasn't there to stop her. There was no one to stop her. She put her hand into the car and pulled out the carrying cot and walked off down the street with it. The baby was asleep and she went on sleeping. She was a remarkably quiet, sleepy sort of baby, I suppose, but I don't know anything about babies.' Shiva looked up at Lili and quickly away again. 'The traffic was at a standstill at the lights at North Hill, she said. She went over and down Church Road. She didn't meet anyone. I suppose the drivers of the cars that were stopped must have seen her but if anyone saw a girl in a blue check skirt holding a carrying cot they didn't come forward. She put the cot on the back seat of the van and sat in the passenger seat in the front and in a matter of seconds Adam came back.

'He got into the driver's seat. He said to her, "That was a bloody waste of effort," and he started up the car, turned into North Hill and headed for Finchley and the North Circular Road. Zosie looked to her left and down View Road. The car was still outside with its rear door open and she saw the woman coming back down the path.'

'You mean Adam didn't know? He didn't know the baby was there?'

'He didn't know until they were right out Enfield way. They were parked at some lights and the baby woke up and started to cry.'

– 16 –

The road sign pointing to the garrison recalled to Rufus that girlfriend he had had for a few days or a couple of weeks or whatever it was and whose name was tantalizingly present to him in two alternative forms. Had she been Janet or Janice? It was rather like the way Adam couldn't remember whether the antiques man had been Evans or Owens. He had turned out to be Evan, so perhaps Rufus's girlfriend had been Janine or Jeannette even.

He would never remember. She had had dyed red hair and been rather thinner than he liked a woman to be. He was sure he had never given her his address at Nunes and he had had no phone number for her to wheedle out of him. Certainly he had never brought her back to Ecalpemos. In any case, she would be the least likely person to go to the police with her story of ten years in the past, especially if she were still married to the soldier, perhaps had children by him.

He associated her somehow with the taking of a taxi home. And with the only time he had ever gone on foot into the village of Nunes there to meet her in the Fir Tree and for some reason or other read the name over the public bar doorway of the landlord, now certainly changed. But why should he have walked when he had Goblander?

Janet or Janice (Janine or Jeannette) had come in her own car, or her husband's, to that last rendezvous they were ever to have, and he walked there, not greatly enjoying this very non-macho activity but even then, he remembered, being unwilling to let her know precisely where he lived. Very likely he had been apprehensive of her confessing to her husband in a moment of frankness or guilt and the soldier hunting him down.

And, of course, yes, that was it – he had not gone to this date in Goblander because Adam and Zosie had gone to London in Goblander. That was the evening they had brought the baby home. He had not been there, he had not seen the homecoming, for he had been with Janet or Janice first of all in the Fir Tree and later in some other pub or restaurant where they had quarrelled nastily over the meal because Rufus had nothing but the tenner which remained of the pawnbroker's money and he had made it plain he expected her to fork out for the rest of the evening's drink.

But they patched things up and made all well again in her double bed with the photograph of the soldier turned face-downwards on the bedside cabinet. And said goodbye next morning with no regrets, Rufus only hoping there was more relief on his part than on hers. She hadn't offered to drive him back to Nunes though. In fact she had gone so far as to say she couldn't afford the petrol, it being something like a twenty-four-mile journey there and back. That was why he took a taxi, of course it was, and when he got back to Ecalpemos he had had to keep the driver waiting with his meter running while he went inside and got the money for the fare off Adam.

Only he hadn't gone inside, or only just, for Adam had either been in the hall or the porch. He had started moaning about how badly he had done trying to sell that stuff down the Archway Road. He had got less than a hundred quid for the stuffing spoons and the mask jug put together. No one wanted spoons like that, he had been told. What use were they nowadays? The liqueur glasses he hadn't even been able to sell. Rufus got the £4 for the taxi out of him with difficulty, but he got it.

Would the taxi man remember? He had been young, no older than Rufus himself. It had been a mistake to let him drive down the drift, for some reason he had felt that at the time, but there had been no help for it. He would hardly have consented to wait at the top for his money.

Of course he would have had dozens of fares that week, many of them in rural places too. There would be nothing specially memorable about driving down the winding lane through the wood to Ecalpemos. Unless he had heard the child cry . . .

No, that was impossible. Rufus himself had not heard it until the departing taxi was almost lost to sight. And young he might have been and even observant but he would not be able to identify Rufus after ten years or Adam, come to that, who had stood there holding out the money and looking, in the expression current at the time, 'spaced-out'. Rufus had even thought he might have been smoking dope, only he couldn't have been because they hadn't been able to afford any more.

'Are you OK?' he had said as the taxi went off up through the hedge tunnel. 'Or is it merely a king-size hangover?' (How we judge others by ourselves.)

Adam didn't answer. They walked down to the front door which stood open. It was then, for the first time, he heard the baby's crying. It greeted them plaintively, as unlikely a sound in that house at that time as a lion's roar. Or perhaps not, perhaps not . . .

'Christ,' said Adam.

'I take it that this means Zosie has brought her child here.'

'You said that in a glacial voice,' said Adam. 'That's what novelists would call it, "glacial".'

'Only very bad novelists.' The crying stopped. 'I suppose one will have children of one's own one day and be obliged to put up with that sort of thing but I do rather draw the line at now. However, it's your house.'

Adam didn't say anything and then he said, 'Later on I'd like to explain about that. Well, I wouldn't like to but I'll have to.'

Stiff and haughty Rufus had been. 'Not on my account.'

'How did you know Zosie had had a baby, anyway?'

'How do you think?' said Rufus. 'It's my business to know things like that or it soon will be.'

It must have been the middle of the afternoon before he saw the baby. Adam, very nervous and jumpy, had been telling him about his

478

attempts at selling the spoons, when Zosie came out on the terrace with a swathed bundle in her arms. Zosie had been at Ecalpemos nearly two months and the baby had presumably been born about a month before she came. That was how he had reasoned that afternoon. Not much of its face showed between the folds of Vivien's dark red shawl in which it was wrapped but enough to tell him it was very young, very tiny, three months old or so. Vivien followed Zosie, carrying a feeding bottle and one of Lilian Verne-Smith's embroidered towels, with Shiva bringing up the rear, looking mystified, out of his depth. Quite a retinue.

Of course they all (except Adam) thought the baby was Zosie's. What else could they have supposed? And what amnesia, or even aphasia, was Adam subject to that he did not realize what Vivien's innocent approval implied? But perhaps that did not especially matter, for a kidnapped child is a kidnapped child.

For the time being, Adam thought he was done with the police. Or the police were done with him. He had answered their questions and made that statement. Of course he could imagine they might come to his house again, this time to arrest him, that idea was with him always, constantly haunting him, but never imagined he might receive a phone call from them.

He was at home and the evening paper which he had bought but not read lay on the arm of the chair beside him. He did not feel himself equal to looking through it, to searching for the small item of news which might, in plain print, reveal the identity of the adult bones found in the grave. Some extra sense of *fingerspitzengefühl* told him it would be there and while he knew that if it were not there, that he had another twelve or even twenty-four hours to wait for it, he would feel relief, he still could not bring himself to look. His parents-in-law were coming, he could not remember for what reason Anne had invited them, but he resisted the notion of having more to conceal, more company from whom to conceal it, a greater load to bear and still to present a casual relaxed appearance.

When the phone rang he was alone in the room, for Anne was preparing Abigail for bed and had not yet brought her down to him. He thought it was Rufus phoning, he was convinced it must be. Rufus was phoning to tell him he had spoken to the police and confirmed the details of the Greek trip and they had seemed completely satisfied, had perhaps even told him it was unlikely he would hear any more from them . . .

He picked up the receiver. It was the policeman called Winder. Adam went cold, his throat contracting.

'Oh, Mr Verne-Smith, just a few small further enquiries. I won't keep you.'

His voice sounded as if he had a bad cold. 'That's all right,' he said while thinking what a stupid and meaningless rejoinder this was.

'I wonder if you can remember. It's a long time ago.'

'What?' said Adam.

'While you were living at Wyvis Hall in the summer of 1976 . . .'

'I told you I never lived there,' Adam said. 'I stayed there. I stayed there for a week.'

'Well, live, stay, it's all a manner of speaking. What I wanted to ask you was: can you recall ever being called on by some pest control people called Vermstroy?'

This was it then. The coypu man had remembered. He had remembered the encounter at the back door and the sight of Rufus on the terrace and Mary Gage's pursuit of his van and her shouted remonstrances.

But 'No,' he said, 'no, I don't remember.'

Holding his breath, he waited for Winder to tell him they now had proof he had not been there alone, that another man had been there and a girl, when he had assured them no girl was ever there. What could he do but deny it? He would always deny it, he would never admit.

And Winder persisted, though not yet taking the tack Adam expected.

'A biggish, dark man with a moustache? You've no recollection? We understand he used to destroy vermin for your – grandfather, was it? Uncle?'

'My great-uncle.'

'Oh, yes. Your great-uncle. Rats and moles too, I believe. Oh, and those peculiar things – what are they called?'

Adam knew he wanted him to tell him but he wouldn't be caught out like that.

'Never mind. It doesn't matter. Well, Mr Verne-Smith, if you can't help us you can't and that's all it amounts to. You'll be glad to hear that in any case our enquiries are almost complete. Sorry to have held you up. Good-night.'

Adam sat holding the receiver in his hand, listening to the dialling tone which droned from it. After a moment or two he put it back. They must be thinking the girl the coypu man had seen was Vivien. He imagined the coypu man voluntarily going to them with his information.

'He asked me if it was an acro-something and I said, no, it's a rat, isn't it? And there was this fellow lying asleep out on a sort of terrace along the back and a girl that came chasing after the van. End of June, July, somewhere around then . . .'

Perhaps he had come at other times, later times. Who knew? And there had been the bill, paid to an Ipswich address. Up into the wood he had gone and there, no doubt, had come upon the animal cemetery which he could testify had at that time been untouched, undisturbed. Possibly too he had returned in September and seen the newly dug grave, the squares of turf replaced. Flittermus, ottermus, myopotamus . . . How young I was, thought Adam, how carefree, how *frivolous*, to invent these artless rhymes. Was I the same person?

Adam knew he should phone Rufus and tell him what had happened but he lacked the will and the vigour to do this. It had been a shock, that phone call from Winder, and it had debilitated him, a shock almost as great as that which he had felt when his father came to meet him at Heathrow or as on that evening when he and Zosie were driving back to Suffolk from Highgate.

He allowed the memory of it to flow back into his mind. The heat of the evening first, the unbreathable thick air, his hands slippery on the wheel, the droplets of sweat gleaming on Zosie's forehead and upper lip, sweat gumming his body and his clothes to the car seat. He thought of it, feeling everything that had happened before, remembering, avoiding for a moment the recollection of that shocking sound that had broken into tranquillity and disrupted a world.

It nearly made him go into the back of the car in front of them. The cry was a sudden wail with no murmur or whisper to herald it. The van was in bottom gear, the clutch half out, and the shock made him let the clutch in and jam his foot on the accelerator. It was lucky for them the amber light had come on with the red and the man in the car in front was one of those quick ones at a getaway.

Goblander shot forward. He stamped on the brake and she bounced out of her seat, nearly hitting her head on the windscreen.

'For Christ's sake,' he said.

'Please don't be angry. You mustn't be angry.'

He looked into the back and saw the cot, no head or face, but a tiny hand upraised. He could see it now, that starfish hand. The truth didn't occur to him then, what she had done didn't occur to him. As all the others were later on to believe, he believed it must be Zosie's own child. In his case, of course, the delusion was brief. But momentarily, as he pulled in to the side of the road and stopped the van, he had some sort of idea that during the bare forty minutes he was away Zosie had somehow repossessed herself of her own baby.

She gave him her fearful look, her mouse look, eyes bright and round and desperate, darting to him and darting away. Her lips were pursed into a little mouse mouth. She got down from the van as if she were running away from him, as if she were going to run and scream for help. But all she did was open the doors at the back and pull the cot out. She came back with the baby in her arms. It looked very small, too small to be crying so loudly.

Zosie spoke confident words but spoke them nervously. 'What a bit of luck that this was in the cot with her.' She was holding a feeding bottle half full of milk. 'Otherwise we might have had to go into a shop and buy one. I expect I can manage all the rest of the stuff we'll have to have.'

Adam, closing his eyes, thought this must be what people meant when they said they felt faint.

'What do you mean, luck?' he said. 'What do you mean, "in the cot with her"?'

'I took the cot as well. When I took her, I took her cot too. She was in it. In the back of Mr Tatian's car.'

That told him everything. Or he thought it did. 'Zosie, we have to take it back. We have to turn round and take it back where you found it.'

'"Her". She's a girl. Her name's Nicola. Vivien said she was called Nicola.'

'OK, now we turn round and take her back where you found her.'

Zosie started crying. She and the baby sat in the front seat and cried noisily, Zosie's tears falling on to the baby's face. Adam couldn't bear to see her cry. It killed him. Oh God, and he had left her behind

482

in the van because he was afraid of her stealing things in shops. How much better would that have been than the theft she had actually indulged in!

'We must take it – her – back. Her parents'll be doing their nuts. You can imagine. Zosie, please don't cry. Please don't, I can't bear it. Zosie, you can have a baby of your own. You and I, we'll have a baby.'

It embarrassed him now to remember it, his pleadings, his promises. He had come close to tears himself. They were children themselves, their combined ages no more than thirty-six, and life in its most awful aspects had attacked them and they could not fight it off. He had felt as if it tore him apart. He loved her, he longed for her happiness, yet he was almost hysterical with fear.

'I won't give her up,' Zosie screamed at him. 'If you turn round I'll throw myself out of the van. I'll jump out and throw myself under a truck.'

'Zosie . . .'

'I want her, I love her. I took her and I won't give her up.' She was nearly ugly in the ferocity of her expression, her snarling mother tiger face. 'I want her to love me, don't you see? If I look after her she'll have to love me, I'll be first with her. Don't you know what it means to want to be first with someone?'

'I love you,' he said, levels in his mind falling away, down, down to a bottomless pit. 'You're first with me.' His voice strangled, he croaked the words out. 'I'll love you for ever, I'll never change, I promise, Zosie, but please, please, for God's sake . . .'

How had it happened that he had given in, had fallen in with what she wanted, and had driven on? He no longer knew, he was not the boy he had been then. Since then a hardness, a tired indifference, had encrusted his character. Perhaps it was not her pleadings which had won him but fear of returning, of the reception awaiting anyone who came back with their story – with what story? So he had started the van and gone on, driving slowly on the inside lane because his hands were shaking. Zosie lay back, spent, and the baby lay in her lap, on the skirt that was a blue checked curtain, sucking at the bottle teat, later relinquishing it and falling asleep. Zosie's face was beautiful and curiously matured in its maternal placidity, her tears dried on her cheeks in little drifts of salt.

The heavy sultry day drew in to a stuffy evening. Great clouds rose in mountain shapes and the moon sailed among them like a white galleon moving through the straits that divide volcanic islands. The clouds were blown by a warm wind that came in sporadic gusts. In front of the house the cedar flapped its rough black arms like a living creature, like a witch in black skirts, Zosie said. It was the last night of his life on which he had been happy, he thought, the last time he had known joy.

Of course that couldn't be so. It was an exaggeration. He must have been happy since then, oblivious, euphoric, he must have been, but he couldn't remember any specific occasion. That particular night he could remember, though, in all its strange details, their homecoming down the drift and the wind blowing the branches that met overhead, Zosie running into the house with the baby in her arms and himself following with the cot. Like young parents, first-time parents bringing their child home from the maternity hospital, and with as little idea of what to do and what life would bring. Only when this had happened in his own life, when Abigail was brought home, he had been at work and Anne's mother had gone to fetch her.

The baby gave one single sharp cry which Vivien must have heard. Vivien was watering her herb garden, nursing along sad little sprigs of parsley and coriander, but she came into the house and helped Zosie prepare the feeding bottle. Zosie took the baby straight upstairs to their room and pulled a drawer out of the walnut tallboy to make a cot for her. She put a big oblong cushion from the drawing room into it for a mattress and she covered the baby with her own bedclothes and Vivien's red shawl. She tore up one of the towels to make napkins. Adam could hardly believe it when she said she was going to bath the baby but she did bath her in the bathroom washbasin and pinned a clean strip of towelling round her and then put her back into the pink Babygro she had been wearing, lamenting that she had nothing fresh to dress her in. The baby cried but not distressfully. Zosie held her in her arms and fed her with milk.

Adam went downstairs and fetched glasses of milk for both of them and some of Vivien's fresh bread with cheese and their own early apples, Beauty of Bath, striped red on wrinkled yellow skins. They sat on the bed and ate the food while the baby slept in her drawer and Adam managed somehow to forget for the time being the awfulness of what they had done, not to think about the misery that must come about through this theft, and anguish and panic. The wind shivered away, had blown itself out, and left a purple sky, clear as some dark streaked petal, the clouds in distant ranges. He opened the window on to the ruined, dried-out garden. Shiva was standing by the lake, holding a book in his hand, though it was too dark to read, looking up at the stars. It was early still, no more than ten. They had never been to bed so early. They were parents now, Zosie said, and parents had to go to bed early because their baby would wake them at dawn. She was mad and he knew she was mad but he did not care.

He took her in his arms and made love to her and for the first time – the first and the last, the only – she made love to him, she responded. She was passionate and lascivious, wet and soft, and the warm crumpled bed smelt of salt flats and fresh-caught fish. Her tongue was a small slippery darting fish but inside her was a warm pool of space that grew and enclosed him in warm weeds and as he drowned caught him up and threw him on the shore. She caught him with a shock that was almost pain, that made him cry out as she did, made him close his eyes and arch his back and sink on her with a sigh and a rattling gasp. She was looking at him when he looked at her, smiling she was and surely satisfied.

Or was she? Had she been? How did he know? How does any man ever know? Besides, he knew now that it was the baby, the possession of the baby, that had brought her to this, not he. Already the baby, *her* baby for only the past four or five hours, was more to her than he was. But he made love to her again, he stirred her and himself into excitement again, then and later in the night, in the small hours. He was young, he had thought it was always like that and always would be at all ages. And he had believed too that love lasted and he would love her for ever.

Adam sat with Anne and Anne's parents who were drinking whisky and coffee. A sickly mixture, he thought, but he hated both anyway. Winder's questions and sly taunting comments rotated in his head. In the conversation he took no part, keeping silent, bolstering his reputation as 'not very talkative'. On these occasions he often wished Abigail would wake up so that he could go upstairs and comfort her, cuddle her. But it was a long time now since she had wakened of her own volition in the evenings, but slept undisturbed, in a beautiful noiseless serenity. It had been different with that other baby who in her sleep made faint whistling sounds and occasionally soft irregular clicks. Was that why Anne's clicking in her sleep had so enraged him?

The clickings had grown more frequent and there had been a grunting and whimpering before she awakened. And then cries. That crying had been disconcerting, bringing him a feeling of incipient panic, very like what he felt now. At first he had wondered what it was, where he was. And it had been the same the next morning, the sky he saw when he opened his eyes, red as if somewhere a great fire was burning, and it had taken him a moment to realize that this was the dawn.

'I suffer from eosophobia,' he had once said. 'An irrational fear of the dawn.'

Zosie went down and got milk for the feed. She changed the baby's napkin, she knew how to do that, they had made her do that in the hospital where her own baby was born, even though they knew she was giving it up for adoption. They slept again, all three of them. And outside the world was going mad looking for that baby, outside the charmed circle that enclosed Ecalpemos, outside the invisible walls the shutting spell had erected.

By the time they got up there were four wet napkins in the bucket Zosie had brought up from the kitchen. Vivien washed them because she had to wash her own blue dress. She looked at the baby and talked to it and held out one finger which the baby got hold of in its own tiny pale fingers, but she asked no questions, desisting as a very caring, kind mother might. And even then he had not thought what this meant, what Vivien's acceptance meant.

They had no newspapers and if they had the radio on, no one ever listened to the news. If Vivien, going about her work, had heard talk of a missing baby, would she have made the connection? She and Rufus accepted that the baby was Zosie's, concluded presumably that she had had the adoption order set aside now that she had a home of her own and a man of her own.

He was only a little bit afraid, that day. When the car with the lamp on its roof came down the drift – albeit a yellow lamp and not a blue one – he thought for a moment it was the police. It was only Rufus returning and without enough money to pay the cab-fare. And he was strangely intimidated too by the weather. It seemed crazy to say the weather frightened him but it did because it was different. Overnight it had grown cold, the temperature falling from over ninety degrees – they still thought in Fahrenheit then – to less than sixty. And he could not help seeing it as an omen of a change in their fortunes, as an end of the good times and the beginning of an encroachment of disaster.

What else had they done that day? Nothing much. When he looked back on it he remembered Zosie as inseparable from the baby, cuddling the baby and feeding it and changing it, and himself as restless and nervous, glad of the night coming, of being able to go to bed early. The baby woke up and cried and he thought, Oh, God, what a drag, is this what my life's going to be?

The new cold made him bad-tempered. The morning was dull and stormy and Zosie cuddled the baby and talked to the baby and suddenly he knew the baby would have to go back. Of course she would. How had he ever believed they could keep a kidnapped baby and not be found out?

He considered reasoning with Zosie, a pointless task at the best of times. He couldn't just grab the baby and take her to London on his own. The help of the others might be enlisted, except that the others didn't know.

They were soon to find out. Once Shiva gave him the lead, handed him the opportunity, he wasn't going to stay silent. Not even for Zosie's sake. Besides, it wouldn't be for Zosie's sake in the end, it would be better for Zosie to relinquish the baby – or he thought so, he couldn't see further than the moment, the cold, increasingly alarming present.

It was Shiva who asked.

'Whose baby is it, Zosie? Is it yours?'

Vivien smiled and nodded. Rufus wasn't there, he was lying hopefully out on the terrace where once the sun had shone. Shiva sat at the kitchen table, looking from one girl to the other. Now Adam had his chance and he took it.

'She isn't Zosie's,' he said. 'She's someone else's baby.'

'She's mine,' Zosie said.

'Only,' said Adam, pedantic to the last, 'in the sense that she's presently in your possession.'

Shiva said, 'I don't understand what you mean.'

Zosie, who had been heating milk in a saucepan, stepped away

487

from the stove, her shoulders hunched, her eyes the eyes of the mouse in the corner, its back to the wall. The baby was in Vivien's arms. She and Zosie had been, as it were, joint priestesses of some maternal mysteries, performing together the rites of an ancient cult, and Vivien had smilingly confirmed Zosie's motherhood in a way that excluded males. But in all this she had been deceived and at Adam's denial she sprang back, clutching the baby tightly to her, her face a mask of shock. Adam had a feeling that anyone else, at this revelation, might actually have dropped the baby but Vivien held on to it the more firmly, as if by the mere utterance of certain words it was placed in danger and required her special protection.

He spoke steadily, without emotion. 'She's a baby Zosie took out of a car when we were in London. She kidnapped her, if you like.'

'I don't believe it,' Shiva said in a slow wondering voice.

'Of course you do. You know people take babies, women do when they've lost their own. It's a well-known fact.'

'She just took a baby out of a car? Didn't anyone see her do this?'

'Obviously not. Look, we've been through all this. I'm sick of it. I know it was wrong and terrible and all that, I know that. I'm not feeble-minded. I know the baby's got to go back and the sooner the better, as far as I'm concerned.'

Vivien spoke. She still held the baby. She wouldn't relinquish the baby. 'It was a wicked thing to do, an evil thing. I think you are feeble-minded, both of you, that's just what you are. This baby has to go back to her parents now, immediately. You have to drive back to London now with her and give her back.'

'I quite agree,' Adam said wearily.

'Do you know who her parents are? I suppose you don't. You took her out of someone's car, you say? You're mad completely, you're sick in your minds.'

'Oh, shut up.'

'Rufus will have to know about this. Rufus should be in on it.'

It must have been the first time Vivien had ever made an overture of any kind to Rufus. Still carrying the baby, she put her head out of the window and called him.

'Rufus, would you come in here, please?'

Zosie had filled the bottle and was holding it under the cold tap to cool it. She dried the bottle on a cloth and came to Vivien lifting up her arms. For a moment it seemed as if Vivien would hold on to the baby, for she briefly raised her left arm to shelter face and head from Zosie.

'She's a human being you've stolen,' she said in a wondering voice. 'A *person*, not an animal or a toy. Do you realize that? Do you *think*?'

The baby broke into wails at the sight of food held tantalizingly a yard from her. Vivien said:

'I thought she was yours, I thought this was your own child you'd somehow got back.'

'Please give her to me, Vivien.'

Cigarette in mouth, Rufus walked in just as the changeover was taking place, Vivien putting the baby into Zosie's arms while turning her head sharply away. Shiva had begun to laugh, not wildly, but softly, ruefully, while shaking his head. Rufus said:

'What's going on?'

'Zosie's stolen this baby out of someone's car. She just took it yesterday afternoon. She's mad, of course. Presumably she thinks she can get away with kidnapping. I know you thought it was hers, we all thought it was hers, but it's not, it's someone else's. They don't even know whose baby it is, they don't even know who the parents are.'

'Oh, yes, we do. It's Tatian's, it's that man's you're going to work for.'

Vivien looked at Adam. She put her hands up to her face which had gone as pale as the cream cotton of her dress. The baby in Zosie's arms sucked away at the teat, its miniature hands, pink as shells, holding on to the shoulders of the bottle. Vivien took a step towards Zosie, in a threatening way, it seemed to Adam, and he half-rose, but she was only looking at the baby, staring into the baby's face.

'Are you saying you think this baby is Nicola Tatian? Is that what you thought? Nicola's *nine months old*, she's big, she crawls about. I ought to know, I've seen her. God knows who this is, God only knows. What made you think you'd taken Robin Tatian's child?'

Zosie didn't speak. She doesn't care, Adam thought, she doesn't care whose it is, it's hers now, that's the way she thinks.

'It was in a car outside his house. Zosie naturally thought it was his.'

Shiva's had been a nervous giggling and had ceased now, though the shaking of the head continued. But it was simple raucous laughter

Rufus gave vent to, peals of laughter that shook him so that he had to sit down at the table and bury his face in his arms.

'Put the radio on,' said Vivien. 'Keep it on till we get some news. There's bound to be something on the news. You're useless, aren't you?' she said fiercely to Rufus. 'You'd think anything was funny. You'd think murder was funny.'

'Maybe I would,' he said, throwing back his head. 'Maybe I would.' But he did not when the time came.

Shiva put the radio on and rock music thrummed out. Almost at the same time, as if the radio had started it or the music had provoked it, thunder rolled out of the distance, a sound like a load of stones being rattled out into a pit of stones. And then the music stopped and a man's voice began speaking the news bulletin.

His father-in-law was talking about Wyvis Hall. Adam, lost in his reverie, his hearing shuttered, had missed whatever it was that triggered this off. He sensed though that it might be some news item his father-in-law had read or heard but which had escaped him, something fresh which the media had just got hold of, and while one part of him burned to know what it was, the rest cringed from it, would have given anything not to know it, covering eyes and blocking ears. Nor did he want to answer the questions which were now being put to him about his ownership of the place, what sort of a house it was, what was the extent of the grounds, what kind of people lived in the neighbourhood.

He did answer, though, in an abstracted kind of way, thinking all the while that he had only to enquire what made him ask for Anne's father to revert to whatever had begun it. Those lines in the evening paper he was afraid to look at, perhaps, or even something on television. But he did not ask. Instead he found himself saying abruptly that it was an unpleasant subject, it was something he didn't want to talk about. Anne was looking at him with those suspicious narrowed eyes that seemed a habitual expression with her nowadays. And suddenly Adam thought, my marriage won't survive this, we shall split up over this. In a way it would be the least of evils. If the sole result of all this were to be the break-up of his marriage he would have got out of it lightly. But it could not be the sole result, not now, not with the coypu man appearing on the scene and saying his piece.

*

490

Adam remembered lightning, a bright flash of it, flaring in the kitchen. It was only then that they realized how dark it had become. It had given them an illusion of night time but it wasn't night, it wasn't even evening but three in the afternoon. He had gone to the window and looked out on a grey and purple sky where the clouds were mountain ranges capped with snow. Like the Himalayas, warm and close in the foothills, clear and icy on those distant peaks. A tree of lightning grew out of the blue horizon, branches forking through the cumulus, and the thunder cracked this time, a sound like gunfire.

He listened to the voice coming out of the radio, they all listened, even Rufus. 'The missing Highgate baby' was the way the voice referred to the child in Zosie's arms, not by name. Zosie rubbed the baby's back, cuddling it against her shoulder. For a few seconds she held her head on one side, listening to the words which the announcer delivered in ominous tones, but not as if it had any application to her personally, with no more interest than she might have given to news of an earthquake taking place on the other side of the world.

She had torn up another towel and was changing the baby's napkin. Shiva recoiled from this with wrinkled nose and downturned mouth.

'I'd like to go to Sudbury, please, and buy her some clothes. She ought to have another Babygro and vest and things. She ought to have real napkins.'

Adam wondered what it was this reminded him of. He closed his eyes. Of his sister, yes, of Bridget when she was a child of seven or eight, and had for a few days become obsessed by a birthday doll.

'You're not going to Sudbury,' Vivien said. 'You're going to London to take that baby back.'

She was mother, she was in charge, hers was the voice of authority. Only it no longer worked so effectively. And Rufus surely had been father. Why do we need these roles, Adam had wondered then and wondered now, why do we cast ourselves in them?

'A small local difficulty,' said Rufus, 'is that we don't yet know who it belongs to.'

'It'll have been in the papers. It'll have been in this morning's paper.' Adam was beginning to see what he must do. 'I'll take Zosie into Sudbury and buy a paper and find out whose it is.'

'I don't see why,' said Zosie, 'seeing that I'm not taking her back.'

Adam put his arms round her. He put his arms round her and the baby, the baby was between them, keeping them apart. For more reasons than one, he wanted to be rid of the baby.

Shiva, who had been silent, who had seemed only to be listening intently as might someone whose grasp of the English language was imperfect but who needed to understand every word, now said slowly:

'Do you realize it's fortunate it wasn't Mr Tatian's baby you took? You would have been found by now if you had, the police would have found you.'

They all looked at him. It was the first mention of the police.

'Because they will want to know about everyone connected with the Tatian family. Mr Tatian would have said he had this new nurse for his children coming on Thursday but he didn't know much about her, it was his sister-in-law who had interviewed her. He would have said there was something odd about her address, she had given him a false address. There was no such place as Ecalpemos but it might be true that she lived at Nunes in Suffolk. What do you think they would have done then? They would have been here by now, they would have found us, they would have called at every house here.'

'Congratulations,' said Rufus. 'One of these days you will make a great detective, a credit to the force.'

A flush came into Shiva's olive face. 'It's true, though, isn't it?'

'My guardian angel was looking after me,' Zosie said.

'How about this baby's mother's guardian angel? He was on leave, was he?'

'I thought you were on my side, Rufus.'

The radio was playing music, rock, not very loud. Rufus turned it off. He lit a cigarette.

'Did you now?' he said. He was looking at Zosie in a speculative kind of way and yet as if he found her an astonishing creature. 'I'll tell you whose side I'm on. Rufus's. And that goes for always.'

Adam had an uneasy feeling that the grown-ups had come. He looked at Rufus, needing him, needing him for guidance, for direction. And what Rufus said next struck him like a blow under the ribs. He felt the blood run into his face and the skin grow hot.

'Frankly, this is no place for me. Not any longer. It's time for me to quit.' He smiled at Adam but not pleasantly, without camaraderie. 'So if you'll excuse me, I'll be on my bike in the morning.'

Adam had to maintain a cool manner. He had to put up his eyebrows and shrug.

'As you like. It's your decision.'

'Right. But I'm afraid I shall have to deprive you of the van.' He said 'the van' and not Goblander and this twisted a knife in Adam. 'So if you want to buy newspapers and baby clothes I suggest you run into Sudbury now while the going is good.'

Very laid-back was Rufus, cool as a cucumber and with a cutting edge to his voice. He didn't have to put it into words. It was plain what he was thinking: I am a medical student at a great teaching hospital with a future before me. And I am good, I am going to be good, I am going to be a success. I have two years still before I qualify. I have far to go up the ladder but up it I am going and be damned to the lot of you. The last thing I mean to do is jeopardize my career for a crazy girl with kleptomania – the kind of kleptomania that has babies not things as its object.

From goodness knows where Rufus produced a big square bottle of gin Adam didn't know he had, poured himself a generous measure and drank it down neat. He didn't say any more but went off through the house, carrying his bottle. As soon as he was gone Zosie started telling them about the little boy she had tried to abduct from some shopping centre when she and Rufus and Vivien were all in London together. It was the first Adam had heard of this and it turned him cold. The baby would have to be returned. Rufus could go, he would soon be going anyway, and all Adam really wanted was to be alone with Zosie. Without the baby.

Some time, later on, if he could divert her, if she would go to sleep, say, he might be able to take the baby back. And what would that do to their relationship? What would keeping the baby do to it?

The empty carrying cot was on the back seat of Goblander. Zosie sat holding the baby, wrapped in Vivien's shawl. Her childlike hand on which the plaited ring gleamed stroked back the cobweb-fine hair, touched the round satiny cheeks. Her face was rapt and her guardian angel sheltered her with his wings. She no longer reminded him of his sister but of girls he had seen in paintings, Renaissance madonnas whose ardent faces and shining eyes had nothing to do with piety.

Like a small, ill-treated animal begins to trust the first human being who is kind to it, the first who does not kick it or desert it, she trusted him. She wasn't afraid to leave the baby in his care.

He supposed he should be flattered and in a way he was. It pleased him, it meant that later on he could do what he had to do. But first he left her with the baby, went into a newsagent's and bought the *Daily Telegraph*. The missing baby story was big on the front page and the name was there. The child which slept in the carrying cot on the back seat of Goblander was called Catherine, her surname was Ryemark and her parents whose guardian angel had been on leave lived on the other side of Highgate, in the area called the Miltons.

Her arms full of packages, a carrier bag hooked on one arm, Zosie came back, came dancing back in spite of her burdens. The shopping she had done must have made a big hole in the mask jug and spoons money.

'Catherine,' said Zosie when he told her. 'I like Catherine better than Nicola.'

The baby seemed to smile at her. It was very quiet, placid, staring. The large blue eyes were calm and mild, not wandering but fixed on Zosie's face. Adam read aloud a minute description of the carrying cot, cream with a white and cream check lining, the linen white with a pink blanket and a pastel coloured patchwork quilt. He wondered why all the people passing by did not look into the van and see the carrying cot and rush off to denounce him.

A few drops of rain had fallen, widely separated, each the size of a large coin. They watched the sparse rain with surprise, almost with curiosity. It was so long since they had seen it, it came as a phenomenon.

'It says here she's fourteen weeks old,' Adam said as they began the drive back.

'Doesn't that seem tiny? You can't imagine being fourteen weeks old.' Zosie sat in the back with Catherine. She had taken her out of the cot and held her in her arms. 'My baby was a little girl. I haven't told you that before, have I? The funny thing is I feel just the same about her as I did about my own little girl, just the same, no different. Do you know, Adam, it won't be long before we forget she's not our own baby.'

Adam didn't say anything. He would have liked more information than the newspaper gave, but he did not like the sound of a 'nationwide hunt' for Catherine Ryemark. There was nothing in the story about motorists stopping to let a young girl in a blue top and blue and white check skirt holding a carrying cot go across the pedestrian crossing at North Hill. Perhaps no one had seen her.

At Ecalpemos Vivien was waiting for them, standing under the front porch waiting. The rain had never really come, though the sky was still a rolling mass of cloud and the thunder growled distantly. A wind had risen, swaying and shivering the trees. She began telling them before they got in the door how the baby must go back, how they must not even bring her in but take her home at once.

Adam agreed really but he knew that if he was to accomplish the child's return he must seem not to agree. He pushed angrily past Vivien. Rufus was nowhere about, probably he was up in the Centaur Room. Because she had been awakened at dawn and after that had only dozed briefly, Zosie was sleepy and yawning, putting her fists into her eyes as children do. It was no more than five but it was as if dusk had come and the rooms had a gloomy, almost wintry look, though stuffy and close. They had closed all the windows on account of the threatening storm and Adam went about opening them again.

Upstairs in Pincushion he found Zosie lying fast asleep, stretched out on the bed, and close beside her, not in the carrying cot but on the mattress, the baby Catherine Ryemark lay also sleeping in the crook of her arm. Adam bent over and kissed Zosie softly on the forehead. It was done almost as if he intended to wake her, as if he would in this way prevent himself from betraying her. But she did not wake. His kiss had an effect of assisting him in his purpose, for it disturbed her enough to make her whimper quietly, turn herself towards the wall and withdraw her arm from under the baby's head.

Adam picked up the baby, put her into the carrying cot and carried the cot along the passage towards the Centaur Room. None of them had ever been into the others' rooms. How odd that was! It had almost been prudish of them, an old-fashioned and unexpected respect for privacy. Adam did not know whether he should knock or not, but he needed to speak to Rufus to ask if he could borrow Goblander to take the baby back to London. Preferably, would Rufus himself drive him and the baby to London? Holding the carrying cot, he stood indecisively outside the door. Then he did knock but there was no reply. He opened the door and looked inside. The room was empty, the bedclothes tossed back on to the floor and the windows wide open.

Adam looked at the reproduction of the Böcklin painting, *The*

Centaur at the Forge, and noticed for the first time that among the crowd of curious bystanders eyeing the man-horse who had come to be shod was a woman holding a baby in her arms. He turned away. He would have to find Rufus and quickly. It would be just like Rufus to have gone off to the pub.

He went back along the passage, thinking about where they would take the baby. The best way would be to leave it on the steps of a church or some public building. Provided the storm did not come, of course. Well, they would have to take care to leave it under cover.

The house was darker at this hour than he could ever remember having known it, though of course he had been here in the winter and it must have been darker then. A momentary uneasy feeling came to him that it was here, at the top of the back stairs, that Zosie had seen Hilbert's ghost, or said she had seen it. Of course there was nothing and no one, only Vivien throwing open the door of the Deathbed Room and starting on him again.

'OK, the baby goes back tonight,' he said. 'But don't keep at me. I have to think of ways.'

Where had she disappeared to? How was it he had gone into the kitchen alone and found Shiva there, sitting at the round deal table, reading with great concentration the story of the stealing of Catherine Ryemark? He could not remember, any more than now as he said perfunctory goodbyes to his parents-in-law, preparing to explain to Anne his silence and his 'rudeness', he could remember where Rufus had been. Not out in Goblander, for from a side window of the kitchen he could see the van parked on the drive. In the drawing room perhaps with what he called his Happy Hour drink and the secret drink too that he thought (through the only naïve chink in his armour) no one knew about.

Shiva looked up and at the carrying cot and then he quite simply told Adam about this idea of his. He smiled as he spoke, looking roguish.

'We couldn't do that,' Adam had said.

'Why not? You have the name, the address, everything. It will take a load off their minds, be a relief.'

'I don't know,' he had said. 'I don't know.'

But he did.

Abigail awoke crying just as he was getting into bed. He got up and comforted her, changed her napkin, fetched her orange juice in a bottle which Anne said was wrong, encouraging bad habits. It would be bad for her teeth, but she only had one. All the time he was thinking that the occasions on which he would perform these simple paternal tasks were numbered, could perhaps be counted on the fingers of one hand. As he laid her down again he seemed to see the baby Catherine's face instead of hers, a face that was more infantile, more feeble and vulnerable, the eyes glazed and not quite in focus. He twisted his head away, closed his eyes. When he opened them again it was his own child he saw who looked gravely at him and then favoured him with a radiant smile.

In the suburban dark that is not dark he lay listening to Anne's steady breathing and the soft clicks that came irregularly. They no longer annoyed him. It was rather as if these sounds were visited upon him as a kind of retribution, because he had agreed to Shiva's suggestion. All sorts of fanciful ideas came to one in the night. At this hour it was quite possible to believe the dead child's spirit made those soft delicate clicks through the medium of Anne's slightly parted lips. Or, more readily if one understood about guilt and fear, that Anne never made them at all, that there were no sounds, they did not exist, but that his fevered imagination re-created them from that night ten years ago when at last the rain came and the air grew cold. When he lay listening to the rain fall and abate and fall again and then to the baby's breathing, the occasional just audible click, the whimper which seemed a threat of crying that never came.

He remembered but he did not dream. He knew he would not sleep. It was raining now, the sluggish drizzle of winter. He could just hear the whispering patter of it. That night they had fotgotten to shut the window and one of the things they found in the morning was water lying on the broad oak sill.

One of the things.

The Sunday paper came early and he got up and went down to fetch it, praying please, please, please, touching wooden surfaces all the way, banisters, the front door, the architrave of the front door. Abigail cried out but for once he left it to Anne to go to her.

The page where the home news was. His hands trembled. When he saw the paragraph, homing onto the headline, he couldn't look. He closed his eyes. Opening them, he stared, not understanding what he read, thinking anxiety must have broken his mind. The bones from the grave at Wyvis Hall had been identified as those of a Nunes girl and her infant daughter, the identification having been made by a Mrs Rita Pearson of Felixstowe.

That was all.

— 17 —

The police must have come for him, Shiva thought, when the two men came into the shop just before closing time on Monday and one of them held out his warrant card on the palm of his hand. He too had seen the paragraph in the paper, indeed had known of this piece of news since the previous morning when Lili herself had pointed it out to him, tucked away inside the *Sunday Express*. It had not stopped him sleeping, for he was no longer anxious. He was resigned. Lili had withdrawn herself from him, it had been too much for her, as she had warned him it might be. If he said too much it might destroy her feeling for him and he had said too much. There had been nothing else for them to talk about, they had talked about it all the time, and he had told her the ultimate which tipped him over the edge of her love.

But it was not for him that the police had come. They wanted the pharmacist. They wanted to talk to him about a tip-off (Shiva guessed) they had had that Kishan had been buying suspect-source drugs, re-packaging them and selling them at the current retail price. Shiva suspected he had been but he did not intervene, turning the notice inside the glass door to Closed, saying good-night and going home.

Home where Lili would be – would she be? – waiting for him with eyes no longer tender, with no more reassurance and practical comfort. He had received the last of that last night before he told her.

'You weren't to blame,' she had said. 'You just happened to be there. Unless you mean you should have told the police off your own bat.'

'I don't mean that. It isn't that. I was to blame. If I hadn't put up this idea of mine to Adam he would have taken the baby back then

498

and there. As soon as he found Rufus he would have taken her back to London and if he had taken her back she might not have died.'

'Would he have taken her back?'

'Oh, yes, he was ready to do that. He was going to get in the van and do that – but I stopped him.'

Lili said nothing but a change came over her face. Without actually moving she seemed to shrink from him. It was as if her spirit, her soul, her mind, or whatever you called it, receded more deeply inside her. She was wearing a dress of Indian cotton, embroidered and with bits of mirrorwork, not unlike the one he had given Vivien from his father's warehouse. Did Lili know Indian women never wore clothes like that? He found himself wondering about it with supreme irrelevance. She put her hand up to her face and rubbed her pale, Austrian cheek.

'When you told me about this before you didn't tell me that.'

'No.'

'Did you really do that, Shiva?'

'It seemed a harmless thing. I swear I thought it couldn't do any harm. It wasn't hurting anyone, I thought, it wouldn't even make them more anxious. At least the parents would know the baby was alive. I didn't suggest it for myself, Lili, I was going to leave there almost immediately. When Vivien was due to go I was going too. I wanted to get home. I thought there might be some replies from the medical schools I'd applied to. I swear to you it wasn't for myself. Adam needed money and I thought this was a way of getting money.'

'You were always trying to get in with those two. You would have done anything to make them like you. But they despised you really.'

'I don't know. Maybe. They are the sort of Englishmen who always think themselves superior to someone like me. They can't help it, it's ingrained.'

Walking along to the bus stop, he found he was nodding to himself. Adam had seen him at Heathrow but had deliberately not seen him. Of course that could be explained away. They had made a pact not to recognize each other and that was before this business began in the newspapers. (Shiva thought of it as 'this business in the newspapers', though he knew very well there was a reality, a series of physical happenings, behind the printed lines.) But he sensed that the pact not to communicate had since been broken and Adam and Rufus were following events together. He imagined one of them phoning the other, their meeting, their perhaps daily colloquies. But neither of them had been in touch with him. Manjusri was an uncommon name, he and his family were the only ones in the London phone book. They could easily have found him. But they thought him insignificant, of no account, an unnecessary third he would have been, at their conferences. Shiva felt very alone and an end to his isolation would not come when he reached home.

It was true what Lili had said. He had been making a bid for Adam's attention. In all the time he had been at Ecalpemos he had never felt more left out than in that hour or so before Adam came into the kitchen with the carrying cot. The facts about the snatching of the baby he had had to get secondhand from Vivien or pick up himself from the conversation. No one had explained anything to him, still less consulted him. He had got hold of the paper Adam and Zosie brought back from Sudbury and sat at the table reading it, making himself conversant with the facts. And Adam had come in and asked where Rufus was. Or had he asked that? Had he spoken at all? Adam was always going about asking where Rufus was, so it might be that he was remembering wrongly and Adam had said nothing, had not even glanced at him as he passed through the kitchen on his way to the back door with the baby in the carrying cot.

'It had started to rain,' he had said to Lili, 'and Vivien had gone out on to the terrace to bring the quilts in. The terrace had been like a great bed covered with quilts from end to end. She was out there and Rufus was in the study listening to the radio and drinking gin.'

'What did Adam say?'

'When I suggested the ransom? First he said we couldn't do it and then he said he didn't know and then how would we do it. He put the cot on the floor and sat down at the table. I thought they'd trace a phone call and anyway we didn't have the number and we couldn't very well ask directory enquiries for it. So I said send a letter, cut words out of this newspaper and stick them on paper. Adam said we mustn't ask very much. I mean not some huge sum. He said we should ask ten thousand pounds because any ordinary middle-class people could raise ten thousand pounds if they had to.'

'I don't suppose we're middle-class then, are we?' said Lili.

'Adam took the kiddy upstairs again. We cut the newspaper up sitting in our bedroom, Vivien's and mine. The Deathbed Room, Adam called it, because of this picture on the wall of a dead child and its parents crying. When we'd done the ransom note Adam took the picture down and said he was going to take it out of the frame and burn it. But he didn't. Not then, not till later on.

'We'd decided to post the note in London but we couldn't do that till next day. Adam said he'd get Rufus to post it since Rufus was going back to London anyway, and he was sure Rufus would do it, it was the kind of thing that would tickle him. I'm only quoting, Lili, that was what he said. But he couldn't tell him then because Rufus had gone out, he'd gone off to the pub in Goblander on his own.

'Vivien was standing in front of the stove drying herself. Her dress was wet but the other one, the blue, that was wet too, still out on the line. Adam told her he was going to take the baby back that night.

'What happened after that was rather strange. Vivien didn't seem to know Rufus had gone out. She went up to have a bath and when she came down I was there on my own – as usual – and Adam and Zosie were off together somewhere, in their room maybe. I didn't exactly tell Vivien Adam and Rufus had gone out together to take the baby back but I let her think it. She asked me if that's where they were, you see, and I said that's what I understood, though the ransom note was in my pocket all the time and the kiddy was upstairs. I don't know what I thought would happen when the baby cried but I didn't think of it. You don't when you're not used to babies.'

'I suppose not,' said Lili.

'Vivien sat sorting out her flower remedies and she went to bed early. We all did – except Rufus. You see, we'd lived outside in the sun and warmth all the time we'd been there and suddenly there was no sun and no warmth any more. We didn't know what to do with ourselves. The baby didn't cry, or if it did we didn't hear it. Zosie came down to the kitchen for some milk just as I was thinking of going to bed. She was just like a young mother, she was changed, happy and practical and looking tired. I lay awake for a long time and so did Vivien. We talked and she kept saying how relieved she was they'd taken the kiddy back. She wanted to know where they had taken her, what plans they had made. They would be sure to have taken her somewhere safe, wouldn't they? Did I think they would have thought of phoning the parents to let them know? All that sort of thing. She went on and on and then, somewhere around midnight or later, we heard Goblander come back.

'Rufus used to go to pubs that didn't keep to licensing hours, they'd stay open till one or two sometimes, it was all a fiddle, you know, pretending they were the landlord's private guests. Rufus didn't care about it being illegal. Vivien thought Adam was with him, she thought they'd come back from London, and I didn't contradict her. I wanted to go to sleep and I thought it would all sort itself out in the morning.'

'Well, it did,' said Lili. 'And now you blame yourself because if you hadn't suggested asking for a ransom they really would have taken the baby to London and been coming back.'

'Yes.'

'I think you're right to blame yourself,' said Lili.

He had thought she would adjust to it and hold him in her arms but she had not. And later on she had said she did not think she would come to bed but he should go, she wasn't tired, she would sit up for a while. It had been a very quiet night, humanity and the elements equally silent. Shiva lay in bed in that silence remembering noise, remembering the sounds of Rufus's return, his running feet slapping on the wet gravel, the front door slamming behind him as he came into the house. Vivien had turned over and sighed and murmured, 'Good-night, Shiva,' and slept immediately, her breathing gentle and regular. All their nights except one cool one had been warm, moonlit or starry, blue velvet nights, the curtains flung back, the windows open. That night was cold and from time to time rain slapped against the glass . . .

A rain so fine that it hung rather than fell, misted Fifth Avenue. Shiva walked along the deserted street. At the Forest Road end all the windows were boarded up after the riots of two nights before, giving the street a strange look, as if it were scheduled for demolition. No one spoke to him, no one catcalled him as sometimes happened. But as he passed the Boxer and was crossing the road a stone no larger than a piece of gravel struck him on the cheek. It struck him with a sharp painful sting and Shiva put up his hand to feel the place.

Another stone, uncannily describing the arc of the first, stung the back of his raised hand. Shiva wheeled round in the misty dark. A door slammed somewhere. The street was empty but he sensed, or imagined, many watching eyes. At least it had happened to him and not to Lili. He stopped outside his own house and stared at the fence.

The graffiti, done with aerosol paint, read: 'Go Home to Pakistan.'

Shiva stretched his mouth into a bitter smile. He was remembering forebears of his, his grandfather and his father's uncles, who had hated the name of Pakistan more than any Walthamstow Jamaican or Irishman could conceive of. Tomorrow he would try to clean that off or maybe spray over it, he would have to think about that. What he disliked was the knowledge it would be there overnight, it marked his house, it located him and Lili as enemy-victims or potential victims.

He went in, closing the door quietly behind him. A letter, waiting to be posted, addressed to his mother-in-law in Salzburg, lay on the shelf where the phone was, where Lili had laid down her gloves. He thought, when women leave their husbands they go home to their mothers, they write and ask their mothers if they can come home to them. It was nonsense he was thinking, he told himself, as he went through the little house to find her.

Adam had not told Rufus about the ransom note that night. This was because he had a half-formed idea that he might be able to get Rufus to post the letter without telling him what it was. Rufus had shown no interest in the parentage of Catherine, had not even glanced at the newspaper, as far as Adam knew, and now the paper was not available for him to look at, for after Adam and Shiva had cut the words out they had stuffed the remains of it into the kitchen range.

Rufus would wonder, though, why Adam had printed the name and address on the envelope and used a disguised, back-sloping printing at that. It was no good hoping Rufus would not bother to look at the envelope. He would be bound to because he was going to have to buy a stamp for it. Neither Shiva nor Adam had any stamps. Adam thought Rufus might not want to be involved, even remotely, in what would be, after all, a criminal act. When he thought of it like that Adam himself felt quite sick and at the same time he felt it was all unreal and he could not truly be involved in it, not he. On the other hand they were going to have to hand the baby back some time and however they did it at some risk to themselves, so why not get paid for that risk?

For a long time that night Adam had lain sleepless, listening to the rain, the thunder that grumbled softly like a beast stirring in its sleep, the light breathing of the baby and the uneven clicking in her throat. It was cooler than it had been at any time since they came to Ecalpemos, so they had a couple of those quilts over them as well as the sheet, and for the first time Adam was able to hug Zosie in her sleep, to hold her in his arms and rest his head against her fragile shoulder. It was also the last time and if he had known that he would have luxuriated in it more, given himself totally to the joy of it, instead of worrying about Rufus and stamps and printing on an envelope.

Now, ten years afterwards, he could not remember what the ransom note had said. It must surely have told those Ryemarks how to contact him or have said how he would contact them. Instructions must have been contained in it, a location proposed for where the money should be taken, a prohibition on calling the police, and so on. But all he could now recall of it was the sum named, the ten thousand pounds.

He and Zosie could have lived on that for two years, he had believed, and naïve as he was, green as he was, he had still somehow known that this would suffice him, that if he could have her at Ecalpemos for two years it was the best he could hope for or ask, and then he would return to the real world, sell the house, go back to college. What he had felt was impossible would have been to return home when the others returned, give up the house, become a student again, for somehow he knew that his relationship with Zosie, his love for her, would not survive out there in the harsh light but only here in the dream country of Ecalpemos.

He held Zosie, her back curled against his chest, as if lying down she were seated in his lap, and he held her right hand in his right hand, feeling the gold ring on her little finger. They would soon be alone here together, everyone else gone and perhaps the baby gone too. They could have a baby of their own if Zosie wanted one – why not? Zosie might be pregnant with his baby already for all he knew. He had done nothing to stop it.

Downstairs the front door slammed. That was Rufus coming in. He heard Rufus mount the stairs and go to the Centaur Room and after a while he was aware that the rain had stopped. The only sound was a steady drip-drip-drip from the guttering on the corner of the house and that too slackened, the gaps between the drips growing longer, finally ceasing altogether. A profound silence spread over land and sky, the air washed clean and sharply fragrant, the wind fallen. It was black-dark but the open window showed up dimly as a grey, very faintly luminous, rectangle. His legs felt stiff and his left arm ached but if he turned over he would have to relinquish his hold on Zosie and he could by no means be sure that she too would turn and put her arms round him. Was that a test of love? If in your sleep you instinctively turn to embrace the lover, was that a test? He had not come up with an answer but had turned over just the same, though Zosie, he recalled, had not turned with him to hug him in her arms.

For all that he had slept quite quickly once he was on his right side. The Romans – or was it the Greeks? – made their slaves sleep on the right side so as to rest the heart. There was something soothing and reassuring about the black silence which was not broken by any sound from the baby sleeping in the drawer.

An old Morris Minor van stopped at the lights ahead of Rufus. He drew the Mercedes up behind it. The van was the same dark green as Goblander had been, the same age too, judging by the registration plate, so therefore very old by now. Holding up well though, Rufus thought, it had probably been carefully looked after while Goblander would long ago have perished. Things were always going wrong with it even in those days.

Because he expected it to be rickety and uncomfortable – and because, let's face it, he was very drunk – he hadn't noticed anything particularly amiss when he came home alone from the pub. It had seemed a bit bumpy coming down the drift but it was always pretty bumpy. He woke up next morning about ten with a dry mouth and banging head, though nothing like the hangover he would have had today after the amount he had drunk. He got dressed and carried out a bundle of his stuff to put in the back of Goblander, intending to leave around lunchtime. By then, he remembered, he'd been looking forward to getting back to London, a better place to be when the weather was grey and wet. The flat tyre was a nuisance but no worse than that. By a piece of luck, when he had had that big service done back in June, he had replaced the spare tyre with a new one. He was standing there, making up his mind to start changing that wheel, when Shiva appeared carrying an envelope.

He came out of the front door holding up an umbrella and he was very formally dressed for any inhabitant of Ecalpemos, in grey flannel trousers and grey and white striped shirt and black leather jacket.

'"The rain it raineth every day,"' Shiva said in a way that sounded a bit like Adam.

The umbrella had a gold band round the handle and was probably Hilbert's as was the grey Pringle sweater Rufus had found in a drawer and pulled on over his T-shirt. He took the envelope, read the printing.

'What's this?'

The rain had started to come down quite heavily and Shiva held the umbrella over Rufus. 'Adam wants you to post it for him when you get to London.'

'Does he now? What is it, some sort of ransom note?'

Now that had been guesswork on Rufus's part and even as he said it he did not really believe the envelope could actually contain a demand for money. He could not believe this of Adam. His disbelief was founded not on moral grounds but on simple incredulity that anyone he knew as well as he knew Adam would do anything so foolhardy. He was not even sure that he believed the account he had been given of the stealing of the baby. There was more to it than he had been told, or less to it. A very strong instinct for self-preservation was sending him home that day to a safer environment, but at the same time he had never accepted that he or any of them were in very great danger. Games were being played, that was all, and games of which he was largely ignorant and wished to remain so. If he had been aware of the whole truth he would not have slept the previous night but he had in fact slept soundly. If he had known what had actually happened and what Adam and Shiva were up to he would not have waited till the morning but have gone the night before. Or tried to.

'You've a flat tyre,' Shiva said.

'Yes, I know.'

'I will give you a hand.'

'Not dressed like that you won't,' said Rufus. 'Who are Mr and Mrs Ryemark and why has someone printed this address?'

So Shiva explained. He was careful to explain that the ransom idea had been his own, and he seemed proud of it. Rufus said:

'Come back into the house.'

They went into the drawing room because Vivien was in the kitchen. She had the radio on and a burst of music and then a man's voice were just audible.

'What's in this letter?'

'Adam is asking for ten thousand pounds. The mother is to bring it to Liverpool Street Station, one hundred yards along platform twelve. One hour later she'll find the baby in the station mothers' room.'

'I don't believe it!'

'No one will be hurt, Rufus. Adam won't hurt the baby if they don't pay. And when they pay why is it worse than ordinary stealing? I don't see why it's different from Zosie stealing that silver bracelet or that camera. Except there's more money involved.'

'I'll have nothing to do with it,' said Rufus. 'And if you take my advice you won't either. What are you thinking of? You want to do medicine as a profession, don't you, yet you'd get yourself into this shit?'

'I'm not going to take any of the money, Rufus.'

'For Christ's sake, there won't be any money. There'll be a policewoman with a suitcase full of paper and another one to go and get the baby.'

'If that's what you think, Rufus, you'd better tell Adam. But I can tell you he's sold on the idea.'

'I shan't tell him anything,' Rufus said. 'I shall change the wheel on my car and take myself off out of it.'

But he had got no further than the front door when Adam came down, wild-eyed, his face working, white as a sheet, and from upstairs came a long keening wail.

SIDS, Rufus very well knew, ranks after congenital abnormality as the most usual cause of death in very young babies. Generally it affects infants from two weeks to one year old but its peak incidence is between two and four months. All classes are affected by it, though there is a statistical relationship to poor home conditions and a degree of neglect or mere inattention. About 1,200 babies in Britain die of SIDS every year.

This much he had known then while he was still a student but he had never seen a case. Catherine Ryemark was the first and because of her, when he saw another as a house officer in an East End of London hospital two years afterwards, he was able to diagnose at once. But his hand had trembled and his mouth gone dry.

That day, that first time, he had gone up the stairs two at a time and run into the Pincushion Room and snatched the child out of the cradle Zosie had made for her in a drawer. Zosie was sitting naked on the bed rocking from side to side, an unearthly unhuman sound issuing from her closed lips, a thin, cat-like wail. The baby felt cool but not cold, her face waxen but not blue, her blue eyes clear and staring but empty of their vital force. Rufus tipped her upside down and began compressing her chest with his thumb. He gave her kisses of life, his mouth over her cold pearly lips.

'She was lying with her face down,' Adam kept saying. 'She was lying with her face down.'

Zosie's keening rose an octave.

'Make her shut up,' Rufus said. 'Take her away.'

She wouldn't go, she clung to the bedpost. Rufus continued to work on the baby, but he knew she was dead, it was useless, hopeless, she had been dead before he began. He could feel what little warmth remained in the tiny fragile body receding under his hands.

'What is it? What happened to her?'

Rufus didn't stop even then. He didn't look at Adam.

'Sudden Infant Death Syndrome,' he said. 'Cot death to you.'

– 18 –

They were not experienced parents. They didn't know about babies, how they don't let you sleep on until ten or eleven in the morning. Adam had not even thought about it. He would have been surprised and even angry if the baby had disturbed him in the night or wakened him early but he wasn't at all troubled by these things not taking place. Nine years afterwards, when he was married and Abigail was newly born, he scarcely slept, he was too afraid, and when he grew hopelessly exhausted and fell into a doze he would wake and jump up in horror, certain Abigail had died while he slept. For nearly three months, until Abigail had passed the age of Catherine Ryemark, he had made Anne take turns with him in staying awake to watch over her. Or, rather, he had tried to make Anne take turns, and it was her unwilling half-hearted compliance and her ridiculing of his fears which had caused so much damage to their marriage. It made an abyss between them, only Adam knew that it was his own past experience and personal knowledge which had really caused this rift.

He had fallen asleep that night while it was still very dark, two or three hours before dawn probably. Just before he woke up he dreamed he was out with Hilbert's gun in the wood when a large animal appeared between the trees in the distance. Adam saw, though without surprise, that the animal was a lioness, a beautiful nervous beast of a pale straw colour. He lifted the gun and took aim but before he could fire someone seized him. He woke up to find Zosie shaking him.

'You were making awful noises. You were snorting.'

The room was full of clear grey light. It was broad day but for the first time for months there was no sun. He turned over and put his arms around Zosie and she cuddled up to him.

'Isn't Catherine good? She's slept for hours and hours. She must like it here, she must like us.'

'I don't suppose it's very late. It's probably only about six. Go to sleep again.'

'I've had enough sleep,' said Zosie. 'I do feel happy. Are you happy?'

'Of course I am.'

'I wish I could show her to my mother. But I don't suppose I can.'

'Don't even think of it.' Worries of the day ahead had begun to crowd into his mind, pushing sleep away. Rufus was going and with him they would lose their transport. He couldn't remember what he had done with the letter, brought it up here with him or left it with Shiva. He put out his hand to the table by the bed, feeling blindly for the envelope he might have left there, encountered instead his watch. 'You were right,' he said to Zosie. 'It's ten past eleven.'

She sat up. In seconds she was out of bed and across the room. 'Poor Catherine will want her breakfast!'

What fools they had been, what children, not to know that when a healthy baby wants breakfast it yells for it. It doesn't lie meekly waiting, like some elderly hospital patient. Zosie knelt down, she bent over the drawer, gave a shocked gasp, then a long high scream. He would never forget the sound of that scream nor his own sight of the baby, her face deep into the pillow, her body utterly still, and the feel of her skin, cool and waxen.

They got Rufus, or he did. Zosie sat on the bed, hugging herself, swaying back and forth, making a noise like a cat howling. Adam meant to try to explain lucidly to Rufus but all he could say was, 'She was lying face-downwards, she was lying face-downwards.'

Rufus turned the baby upside down and massaged her chest and gave her the kiss of life. She had been dead long before he got to the Pincushion Room, before they even woke up, perhaps before dawn. If he had looked at her while he lay wakeful listening to the rain and the dripping gutter, could he have saved her then? He knew it was what they called cot death before Rufus told him.

Zosie pushed him away screaming when he tried to get her out of the room. She knelt at Rufus's feet and put her arms round his knees and said in a little, thin, mad voice that the baby had died because she had swallowed her ring.

'She did *what?*'

'Of course she didn't swallow your ring,' said Adam. 'You've got your ring on.'

It was the only thing Zosie did have on. He pulled the sheet off the bed and wrapped it round her. She began keening again. In a sing-song voice she said, 'I put my ring on her but her little fingers were too small for it.'

'It's nothing to do with your ring,' said Rufus. 'It's not known what causes cot death but it may have something to do with the respiratory centre in the brain that controls breathing shutting off.'

Adam was trying to control a desire to scream himself. 'What makes that happen?' he said, stammering.

'It could be some sort of infection or have something to do with inhaling food – I mean milk in this case. Perhaps she had a cold. Did you hear her wheezing?'

Adam couldn't remember. He said helplessly:

'What are we going to do?'

Rufus didn't answer him. He said something which Adam would never forget, which would haunt him for ever, whatever the outcome of all this. And he said it to be cruel.

'There is a theory that cot death could be due to fear. Things are not the way the child has been used to. The tranquillity of routine has been disturbed. It isn't the mother's face that the child sees when first she wakes.'

Adam shuddered. He felt himself shrink in pain. They both looked at the demented girl rocking herself this way and that, her head flung back, animal sounds trickling from her half-open mouth. Rufus's words had not touched her. She hadn't heard them.

'I've got something I can give her.' Rufus meant a sedative drug. 'And we ought to make her a hot drink.'

It was then that Adam caught sight of the envelope with the Ryemark's name and address printed on it sticking out of Rufus's pocket. He made a sound of pain and put his hands up over his mouth.

'Christ,' he said, 'that bloody letter.'

'It doesn't matter now.'

'Did you mean that? Is it true? I mean about the baby being afraid because it's the wrong face it sees?'

'It's what I've heard. It's a theory I read somewhere.'

'Why would she die because she was afraid?'

'I'm not saying she did. It's only a theory. No one's proved it. You know how animals play dead? Pretend to be dead to deceive a predator? The theory is that it's something like that babies do and then they really do die.'

Adam turned away his face.

'You're not making me feel any better.'

'I'm not in the business of making you feel better,' Rufus said roughly. 'I'm telling you what I think, what the possibilities are. Right?'

'You won't go, will you, Rufus?' Adam said like a child, pleading like a small child. 'For God's sake don't go and leave me with this lot.'

'I won't go,' said Rufus.

Zosie had stuffed the end of the sheet into her mouth. Her head hung down over her knees. The sounds she was making were like the grunts of a gagged person.

'What are we going to do?' Adam said again.

'Stay here. I'll get her something.'

Adam tried to put his arms round Zosie. He tried to pull away the sheet from her mouth. The muffled noises she made turned to a thin choked scream emerging from the folds of sheet. He turned away, twisting his hands within one another, wringing his hands. He looked at the dead little baby with mixed feelings of terror and pity and disbelief. She lay on her back, her eyes wide open, her skin bloodless, pale as ivory. Remembering something he had read of or perhaps seen in films, he pulled Vivien's red shawl up to cover her face.

Rufus came back with something hot in a mug. He had got barbiturates from somewhere, 'downers' that he had bought from Chuck, Adam thought. Zosie hit out at the mug and Rufus nearly dropped it, tea splashing everywhere. But after a while he did manage to calm her, easing the sheet from between her lips, talking softly to her, not comforting her but telling her screaming and crying wouldn't help, would make things worse. He held the two red and black capsules out on the palm of his hand and offered her the half-empty tea mug and, silent now, white and aghast, she took the capsules and drank, gagging on the tea with a sob, but drinking it down.

Watching Rufus's every movement, Adam realized he was relying on him utterly. Rufus would save them, Rufus would be their rock.

'Don't ask me what we're going to do, please,' Rufus said. 'Don't ask me that again. I don't know yet.'

'Can we keep it from the others?'

'Shiva knows,' said Rufus.

Zosie went to sleep very quickly. She had already slept for about twelve hours and a couple on the previous afternoon, but that didn't stop her sleeping again.

'If she's never had these things before,' said Rufus in a tone of satisfaction, 'she'll probably sleep all day and half the night.'

They told him nothing. Shiva had minded more about that than about the baby's death. Well, then he had, at that particular time. Remorse came later. At the time his exclusion from the drama, the tragedy being enacted at Ecalpemos, mattered more to him than anything.

He and Rufus had been talking about the ransom note and Shiva had felt quite sufficiently put down and admonished. Rufus was going back to change the wheel on the van and he, Shiva, was thinking he would offer to help and thereby – yes, he admitted it – get himself back into Rufus's good graces. Up till then, up till that moment, he still cherished dreams of Rufus saying, 'Let me know when you get into medical school. Give me a ring. We might meet and have a drink.' But then Adam had come running downstairs saying he wanted Rufus, Rufus must come because he thought the baby was dead.

Shiva just stood there in the hall. Then he walked through the house to the kitchen and started to make tea. He made all the movements mechanically just to have something to do, to keep moving. Besides, he felt the need for strong hot tea. At that time he thought Adam – or Zosie – had somehow killed the baby. He decided he would tell Vivien – to be revenged upon them presumably.

In a little while Rufus came in and saw the teapot on the stove and said:

'Pour me a cup of that, would you?'

Distant, doctor-like, indifferent.

'What's happened?' Shiva asked.

'You heard Adam say, didn't you? The baby's dead.'

Rufus took the note out of his pocket, opened the door of the stove and thrust the envelope inside, on top of the glowing coke. He went back the way he had come without another word, carrying the tea mug. Shiva went outside and into the garden, looking for Vivien.

He had told all this to Lili last night, before he made his confession, how he meant to find Vivien and tell her everything. The two of them together could go to the police and explain everything that had happened. The ransom note seemed unimportant, an irrelevancy. It was destroyed now anyway, burned, and it might never have existed.

And then, as he walked along the grass below the terrace, passing the stone figures he had always thought ugly and anti-erotic, he realized that Vivien would ask him why Adam had not taken the baby back on the previous night as he had undertaken to do and he, Shiva, would have to explain that it was he who had stopped him. A glimmering of that feeling of self-hatred began in that moment. He stood still, his hand to his forehead, looking about him, looking at the garden.

'If I had been asked,' he said, 'I would have said the garden was a blaze of colour, a mass of flowers, but in fact by then there were no more flowers. They were all over, finished, or else dried up. I looked at the place that morning, I looked with new eyes, I suppose, and it was just a wilderness I saw, a desert. The rain had come too late. There were dead trees with the leaves shrivelled on them and plants dried up like straw. The apples were being eaten up by wasps and the plums Vivien brought in from the fruit garden were full of worms.

'We sat in the kitchen cutting up the plums for stewing, cutting out the maggoty bits. It made you feel sort of sick, you didn't feel like eating them. I knew I wouldn't eat them when Vivien had cooked them anyway. I just went on doing it mechanically. What I wanted to do was run away. I wanted to run away and hide, cut myself off absolutely from that place and everyone in it. It was dreadful being in that kitchen with Vivien and hearing her talk so – well, innocently. Rufus had told her the baby had been taken back to its parents, that Adam and he had taken it back, and she was relieved in a grave sort of way. She said to me she didn't think she could go to Mr Tatian now, though. She couldn't take the job after what she knew, the Ryemarks being people he knew, you see. It would be wrong, it would involve deceit.

'Vivien was so circumspect in every aspect of her life. She daily examined her motives and her actions, it was all-important to her. Although she wasn't prepared to tell lies she thought she could go so far as to phone Mr Tatian and tell him that circumstances beyond her control prevented her from taking the job. That was true, after all. It grieved her to let him down at the last moment but as she saw it she had no choice. The fact that she would have nowhere to go, no income, didn't affect her decision at all. She made up her mind that she would get Adam or Rufus to take her to the village and from there she would phone.

'I felt responsible for her and I didn't want to be. I just saw all this as adding to my troubles. If she didn't go next day what would Adam do? I was afraid all the time too of the police just turning up.

'In the middle of the afternoon I packed the two bags I'd brought with me. I didn't have much and they weren't very weighty. I'd made up my mind to walk to Colchester. It was twelve miles but I thought I could walk twelve miles as I'd been having a lot of exercise lately, I was quite fit. Some motorist might stop and give me a lift, I thought.'

'What about your responsibility for Vivien?' said Lili.

'I'd tried to dissuade her from phoning Mr Tatian, I'd tried telling her that sometimes she should put herself first. It was useless. And I was no good to her any more. She took up with me in the first place because I was Indian and she had some sort of mystical feeling about Indians, that they had something special to offer her, that they were more civilized than other people. But she'd found out that I was just ordinary, just like anyone else only inside a brown skin. I wasn't a prophet or a poet or a saint.

'I told her I was going, I didn't just sneak off. Rufus I couldn't get hold of, he had shut himself up in the Centaur Room and locked the door. She didn't put up any objections, I think she was glad to see the back of me. I walked off up the drift carrying my bags and when I got halfway up I met Adam coming out of the wood.

'He begged me not to go, he implored me. It was flattering, that, to be wanted at last. He said he relied on me to take Vivien away. If she was allowed to do what she wanted and phone Mr Tatian and give up the job she would stay at Ecalpemos, he would never get rid of her. So I went back to the house with him. I gave in.'

'Did you try to get Vivien to go?'

'Where could I take her? That was the trouble with all of us. We had nowhere to go except back to our parents. We could either stay where we were or go back to our families. And Zosie, or so we thought, didn't even have that. In the end Rufus drove Vivien to the village to phone Mr Tatian but she couldn't get a reply. There was nothing for it but for her to try again next day.

'You know what happened next day. I've told you before.'

'I know what happened,' Lili said.

'And after that I went home and straightaway I got ill. It was a sort of nervous breakdown, they said. I was ill for a year and by then I'd given up the idea of being a doctor. I gave up the pharmacology too. You see, I could never make myself see it as all inevitable, as something I couldn't have prevented. If I'd stuck by Vivien in the first place Rufus would have supported us, he was nearly there. If I'd said the baby must go back we'd have taken her back somehow.'

'And Rufus – and Adam – might have had some respect for you.'

Shiva shrugged. 'Perhaps the baby wouldn't have died. Rufus thought she wouldn't have if she'd been at home or with people who knew how to look after her. Adam and Zosie neglected her, though that was the last thing they meant to do. They didn't know, they were ignorant.

'I could have taken Vivien to my auntie. It would have been a hassle, there would have been a lot of explaining but I could have done it. It seemed easier to try to persuade her to go to Mr Tatian as she had undertaken she would. I thought I could talk her into it. I didn't see what harm waiting another day would do . . .'

It was a windy cool evening of sporadic rain. Of all of them the only one who was innocent and tranquil was Vivien, who cooked a lentil dish and made a salad. The plums had been turned into a sort of mousse. While the food was cooking Vivien stood in the kitchen ironing the blue dress. And upstairs, drugged by Rufus's barbiturates, Zosie slept on.

Adam could remember very clearly destroying the radio. He took it up into the wood in the afternoon, smashed it with a heavy stone and buried the pieces under the thick soft leaf mould. Coming back he had met Shiva sneaking off, running away really, but he had made him stay on. When she had finished her ironing Vivien started looking for the radio. She wanted to hear what the Ryemarks' reaction had been to the return of their child, she wanted to rejoice with them, she said. Adam went upstairs to look at Zosie. Every five minutes he went in to look at her. She was still asleep and he didn't like it in spite of what Rufus had said, he didn't like her sleeping on and on like that, dead to the world.

Vivien thought she hadn't come down because she was too upset at parting from the baby. She said she would go up and talk to her and offer her some of her Bach rescue remedy and when Adam said no, not to do that, she was asleep, she said:

'Will it be all right if I stay on a bit, Adam, just till I find myself a job?'

'You've got a job,' Shiva said. 'Why don't you just go ahead and take the one you've got?'

'I've told you why. It wouldn't be right. I should be deceiving him. Mrs Ryemark might come to the house with her baby and I should be acting a lie even if I wasn't telling one.'

'Life is too short to be so circumspect.'

'How do you know it is, Adam? You're no older than me, you're not as old, so how do you know better? I think life's too long to do anything that we know is wrong before we begin.'

She had been so earnest, yet so meek too, never aggressive but talking in that soft low serious voice, humourless, utterly sincere. He saw her as one of those incubi that appear along life's route, clinging, insinuating, almost impossible to shake off.

'You can't stay here,' he said, surly, short, looking down at the plate of food she had cooked.

She was terribly taken aback. This was not what she expected. 'I mean for only a week or two.'

'I am staying here alone with Zosie and that's final.'

She looked at him, her hand going up to her mouth.

'OK, so you think I'm ungrateful. I'm not. Thanks very much for all you've done. But it's over, right? The party's over, the summer's over. Shiva's going and Rufus is going and I'm afraid you'll have to too. Now excuse me, will you?'

He just made it to the bathroom. He held his head over the lavatory pan and was repeatedly sick. *Mal au cœur* was what the French called feeling sick and that was about right, that was how he felt, sick at heart. In the Pincushion Room Zosie slept, lying on her back, breathing regularly. He thought, suppose she isn't asleep, suppose she's in a coma? But he had to trust Rufus, he would trust him.

In the Deathbed Room where the newly-ironed blue dress hung on a hanger from the wardrobe door handle, he unhooked the picture from the wall and with the dusty paper backing outwards and the painted scene turned against his chest, he took it downstairs and outside into the garden. He was going to make a fire.

The site for it was just this side of the fruit-garden wall. Adam had never before made a bonfire but he thought paraffin might assist him and he found some in a can in the stables. The gale had blown dead branches and twigs down from the big trees. He went about gathering them up, looking with dismay at his wrecked garden. His lost Eden. The picture he threw into the flames without removing it from its frame. There was nothing subtle or ominous about its burning. A sheet of fire leapt from the shellac on the frame and engulfed glass and picture in seconds. The carrying cot burned less easily. No doubt it was purposely made from some non-flammable material.

Later on, because he could not bear to think of sleeping – or even just remaining – in the same place with it, he took the drawer and its contents into the Room of Astonishment. He couldn't even remember why they had called it that, for there was nothing astonishing in there except a staircase which wound up into the loft from a wall cupboard. The room was on the opposite side of the passage from the Deathbed Room but north-facing and always rather dark. No one went in there.

He did not immediately get into bed beside the still heavily sleeping Zosie. His fire was still burning. He had lit it too close to the wall of the fruit garden and the smoke had blackened the bricks. That much could be seen from the window in the lasting glow from

517

the fire. The night was dark, gusts of wind rising from time to time, moving black branches against a faintly paler sky. Earlier, before they separated for the night, he had said to Rufus that a kind of poetic justice would have been for the flames to spread to the house and set it on fire. At this point there would have been a rightness about the destruction of Ecalpemos.

A light moved on the lawn. It was someone with a torch. Adam saw that it was Shiva going up to look at the fire and obscurely he resented this, seeing it as interference. But he did nothing, only watched, saw Shiva take hold of a dead branch and poke at the fire, sending cascades of sparks into the air like fireworks.

Lili had left Shiva a note. It wasn't that sort of note, the sort he dreaded when first he saw the white square held firm on the table by a small vase with two chrysanthemums in it, but the customary line or two she sometimes wrote to remind him she had gone to her Bengali lesson.

He got himself some food from the fridge, tried to watch television. There was nothing about Wyvis Hall on television but there never had been since that first time. If he wanted an evening paper he would have to walk the length of the street to get it and he did not much care for the idea of that. He had not looked at himself in a mirror since he reached home but now he did and saw that his face was cut on his right cheekbone, a dried trickle of blood running down from the punctured skin.

Lili would be home by nine. He decided to meet her. The presence of the graffiti made him decide that, though he was by no means sure how he would be received, whether or not she had rejected him. The idea dismayed him and if he had not clenched his hands and set his teeth panic would have taken hold of him. He turned the television on again and made himself watch a panel game. At about a quarter to nine he went out into the hall and picked up the letter to Sabine Schnitzler. There was no stamp on it. Shiva had a stamp in his wallet, he had several, eighteens and thirteens. Neither would be sufficient for a letter to Austria but two thirteens would be. He stuck two 13p stamps on the envelope and thought, suppose she is writing to her mother to ask if she can come to her when she has left me, I should be carrying, so to speak, my own death warrant to the executioner. But he took the letter with him just the same and posted it on the way to Lili's friend's house which was in Third Avenue.

He had timed it so that she was just coming down the steps from the front door. Salwar and kamiz she was again wearing this evening with her brown tweed winter coat over the pink silk trousers. In the dark the pallor of her skin did not show. If she took his arm, he thought, he would know all was well. She did take it, but lifelessly, and he knew nothing. They walked along in silence and there were no flying stones, no catcalls, no other people even.

The graffiti on his mind as they turned into Fifth Avenue, Shiva nevertheless decided not to point out the spray-paint letters to Lili. Approaching from this direction she might not see them. Of course she would see them tomorrow but things were different in daylight. They came up to the gate and Lili wasn't looking to her left and didn't see them. In the distance Shiva heard someone make a whooping sound and then the noise of a tin can being kicked again. He hustled Lili quickly into the house and drew across both bolts on the front door.

As they were getting ready for bed he forced himself to ask her if she had forgiven him.

'I don't see that it's for me to forgive you things you didn't do to me,' she said, quite reasonably.

'All right then. Can you forget?'

'I don't know,' she said. 'I haven't forgotten,' and that was all she would say.

Shiva lay in bed beside her – at least tonight she had not stayed up till goodness knows when, saying she wasn't tired – and thought what a fool he was to talk of forgetting when things had not really begun yet, when the gathering forces were only just starting the work of retribution. She would not be *allowed* to forget, he thought.

The sound of running feet awakened him. Feet came running down from the Forest Road end of Fifth Avenue, pounding on the pavement – two pairs of feet, he thought, but there were no vocal sounds. And that was odd, for those people never moderated their voices or restrained their words because it was the small hours and others were sleeping. The footsteps slackened, it seemed outside his own house, and it came to him that they might be writing more words on the fence. But then his letterbox, the box on the front door, gave a double metallic snap and he knew that they, whoever they were, had put something through it. Not something disgusting, he hoped. He heard feet stamping and the gate banged. Once before a parcel had come in this fashion and though he had never opened it, from the feel and the smell he guessed it was full of viscera, the insides of a chicken probably.

The feet that stamped kicked at a tin can. The clanging the can made, not merely kicked but kicked from one gutter across to the other, woke Lili. She sat up and held him. Shiva put a bedlamp on. Even in his fear he was happy that it was to him she turned instinctively, holding on to his arm, looking up into his face.

'Something came through the door,' he said. 'I'll go down.'

'Don't go down.'

The sound of the rolling can went on and on, growing fainter but still audible. They had left the window open a little way at the top and the curtains quivered.

'I suppose the morning will do,' he said. 'It won't go away, will it?'

He put the light out. He felt the tenseness slowly go out of her, knowing that as soon as she relaxed she would sleep. Her back just touched his back and he was pleased because she did not flinch away. The deep silence that had succeeded the clatter came into the room and filled it with peace and filled Shiva's head too, bringing the beginnings of sleep, the first hesitant waverings on the edge of unconsciousness.

It was the smell that brought him back from the brink and into total wakefulness. Because he was confused he thought for a moment that he was smelling the contents of the parcel. And in a way, of course, he was.

A crackling sound ripped through the house, a mindless chattering. Shiva got out of bed, smelling the burning which was strong enough to make him cough, to choke him, sucking the oxygen out of the air. He ran across the room and threw the door open and saw the whole hall on fire, a pit of fire down there, the flames strong and thrusting and greedy as if fire were eating the house.

He gave a cry which was lost in the roaring of the fire. The flames came to climb the stairs and eat the banisters. Through it he could not see the door to the living room, which they had left open and through which the fire had burst and driven. A cascade of sparks broke over the burning staircase. Shiva retreated into the bedroom, slamming the door behind him, covering his mouth with clamped hands.

Whimpering, crying out, calling to Lili, he threw up the window sash and as he did so a great tongue of flame shot up from the burning bay below him. It seared his face and he backed, his hands up, as the long, curling, crackling flames licked into the room.

He turned blindly back to the bed and picked up the sobbing Lili in his arms.

— 19 —

The sombre photograph of the blackened house, the account of the preceding fire and the search for arsonists, served only to remind Adam of that last night at Ecalpemos. He recalled how he had half-hoped, half-dreaded, that his own house would catch fire. It was an Indian man and his wife who had lived in that little terraced box in the east London street and they were both dead, the man dying in an attempt to save his wife, she surviving for an hour or two after the ambulance reached the hospital. A deliberate racist act, some policeman said on television. Adam did not catch the name of the couple nor bother to read about them in the newspaper.

He fancied that during the previous night he had heard the sirens of fire engines. But would such vehicles be permitted to have sirens on at that hour? He didn't know. Perhaps he had imagined it, just as, ten years ago, he had imagined the sound of footfalls circling the house on that last night, or had dreamed of them.

Sometimes he thought that it was then he lost the ability to sleep soundly. His sleeping since had always been light, precarious. The footsteps passed beneath his window, went on, stopped, continued towards the corner of the house where the Centaur Room was and Rufus slept, and went on to the stables. The sky was lightening, with dawn not sunrise. A bird cried, it could not have been called a song.

What had he feared? That they had tracked the kidnappers of the baby here? If so what he did was foolhardy in the extreme. But he had not known what he was doing, he was overwhelmed and conquered by his instinct for self-preservation. He ran downstairs and into the gun-room and took Hilbert's shot-gun down off the wall. He loaded the gun and stepped into the dining room, approached the window, hiding behind the curtain.

There was no one there. He went into the hall and listened. The birds had begun their chorus, the twitterings of autumn, not spring birdsong. But there was no other sound. He opened the front door and went outside, the gun cocked. He must have been mad. Suppose it had been the police out there, for who else would have come searching for Catherine Ryemark?

Ecalpemos lay grey and barren in the grey morning. It was rather cold, the air having a chilly, humid feel, and he could smell stale woodsmoke. Still carrying the gun, he went to look at the site of his fire. It was dead, a sprawl of grey ash with the blackened metal frame of the carrying cot balanced on a half-burnt branch. He was aware of an awful silence, the deep silence of the countryside at dawn which the sound of birds does not seem to mitigate, as if the birdsong were something else, were on a different level of perception.

Had he dreamed those footfalls? It would seem so. He had no inclination to go back to bed but took himself into the gun-room and huddled there in the Windsor chair with the gun beside him. He must have dozed off, for he awoke freezing cold in spite of Hilbert's old shooting-coat he had slipped his arms into. From the kitchen he could hear Vivien moving about and singing. Perhaps she always sang when she got up in the mornings. He had in the past been too far away to hear. It was 'We shall overcome' that she was singing, the hymn of resistance, and the sentiments expressed maddened him, the simplicity of it and the assumptions.

He went upstairs. At last Zosie was awake. At the sight of him she gave an inarticulate cry and burst into tears, clinging to him, sobbing into his shoulder. It was strange and horrifying what had happened to him in those past twenty-four hours. He had lost his love of her. Overnight really it had gone. He had thought his feelings everlasting, profound, a reason for existence, as if he and she were all those things true lovers were supposed to be, one flesh, two halves of the one whole, all in all to each other and the world excluded. Twenty-four hours before he had wanted nothing so much as to live here at Ecalpemos with her, the others gone, the two of them in solitary bliss. She had been all sexuality to him but she had also been his high goddess. He was miserably aware now that it was a poor little frightened girl he held in his arms, an infantile creature, not very bright, not even very pretty.

'Stop crying,' he said. 'Please. Try and get yourself together.'

She sobbed and shivered.

'Where's Catherine?'

'In our room. In the other room. She's to stay there, you're to leave her there, Zosie. Listen, we have to take her away from here today, we have to hide her somewhere. Yes, stop, please . . .' for she had begun to cry out in protest, 'Zosie, she's dead. You know she's dead. She's not a baby any more, she's not *there*. It wasn't our fault but we have to look after ourselves now. You don't want them to put you in prison, do you? You don't want us all to go to prison?'

He had meant to say that they would do what they had to do and then they must start to forget, come back here, just the two of them, and start forgetting. But he couldn't say it because he no longer wanted this. He didn't want to be here alone with her or anywhere with her. As for the two of them living together, having their own child . . .

Her face was swollen with tears, almost ugly. She smelt of sweat. He would have liked to shake her till her teeth chattered. It was your fault, he wanted to say to her, you brought all this on us, you with your crazy hunger for babies, your kleptomania, your lies. But he only set her upright on the bed, wiped her face on a corner of the sheet, handed her clothes to her item by item, helping her to dress.

'I'm not meant to have babies, Adam. Why are all my babies taken away from me?'

He was impatient with her.

'It wasn't yours. You'd no business with it.'

'*She*. With *her*. She was a person.' She pulled the grey sweater over her head, pushed her fingers through the fine pale hair. 'Where are her things? Her clothes?'

'I burned them. I made a fire and burned everything.'

As he looked again at the photograph, the skeleton of the house, its girders a blackened ribcage, he seemed to hear her wail again, her keening cry, fists clenched and shaken in the air. The shell of the carrying cot had looked not unlike the burned bones of that house, reared up on a bed of smouldering ash with a soot-bleared wall behind.

Vivien was in the kitchen in her cream-coloured dress, making tea in the big brown teapot Adam could remember his Aunt Lilian using. And Shiva and Rufus sat on either side of the table, Rufus slicing up one of Vivien's smooth round loaves of brown bread topped with poppy seeds. It was like any other morning, any other day, only everything was happening much earlier. And outside a little thin rain was blown in gusts against the windowpanes. He sat Zosie down at the table and put food in front of her, a mug of tea, a piece of bread with butter and honey. She began picking off the tiny blue poppy seeds and placing them on her tongue. She's mad, he thought, she's lost her mind.

Somewhere in the house a chiming began. A clock was striking. Adam started and shuddered. None of Hilbert's clocks had been set going since they came there.

'What the hell's that?'

'I wound up the grandfather clock,' Rufus said. 'On an impulse.'

'Fuck you,' Adam said, trembling. 'Why can't you mind your own business?'

Ten times the clock struck. Last week he had hardly known there was such a time as ten in the morning. Vivien pushed a mug of tea over to him.

'Have a drink, Adam. It'll make you feel better.'

Like a half-drowned kitten, Zosie looked, a rescued creature for whom there is yet no hope. She had her forefinger in her mouth, pulling down one corner of it. Vivien said,

'Would one of you drive me to the village? I should like to phone Mr Tatian.'

Shiva looked angry. 'You're still insisting on that? You realize how you are letting the poor man down, don't you? He is relying on you to come and be nurse to his children. What will he do? Have you thought of that?'

'It's impossible,' Vivien said. 'I can't go there. Anything is better than my going there.'

'I shall leave here without you then. I have my future to think of even if you haven't.'

Adam could tell Vivien was waiting for him to say she could stay, that she would be welcome, but he wasn't going to say it. The bread they were eating she had made. Because of her the house was clean and everything smooth running. By her housekeeping and her management she had probably saved him from denuding the place of

524

furniture but he couldn't ask her to stay. Rufus hadn't looked at him since that outburst over the clock but now he did and Adam thought he could read a lot into the glance, especially when Rufus said, addressing himself to Vivien:

'I'll take you back to London with me, if you like. If you want to go back to that squat you were living in, I don't mind taking you over to Hammersmith.'

But Catherine Ryemark? What was Rufus indicating here? That he would take the tiny body with him or that he, Adam, left alone, was somehow to conceal it?

Rufus said, 'Do you want to go into the village now?'

'The sooner the better, I suppose.' Vivien looked troubled. She was making a decision to act quite against her personal desires, Adam could tell. She was doing this as she did so many things for an abstract principle. It mystified and mildly annoyed him. 'I'll just go up and get my shawl,' she said. 'It's got quite cold. We've forgotten it gets cold but it does.'

It was at this point that the postgirl came. Shiva was the first to hear her. He sat quite still at the table, his head turned.

'What the hell's that?' Adam said.

They all thought it was the police, even Rufus. He got up and moved to a yard or two inside the window. The letterbox on the front door made its double rap and by that time Adam had been into the gun-room and come back with Hilbert's shot-gun. Shiva jumped up.

'My God!'

The red bicycle passed the window, a flash of red and silver only, as a bird might have flown by or a flag been pulled out by the wind. Rufus came in from the hall with an envelope in his hand.

'It was the post,' he said. 'A bill. Are you crazy?'

'Jesus,' said Adam, 'I thought it was the fuzz.'

'We all thought it was the fuzz. What were you going to do if it was? Kill them?'

'I don't know. Did they see you?'

'It was that girl again. How do I know if she saw me?' Rufus looked at the gun that Adam held pointing at the table. Limp, pale, wide-eyed, Zosie stared apathetically into the muzzle of it. 'Put the bloody thing down. Christ, the sooner I get out of this madhouse the better.'

From upstairs, a long way off, Vivien's voice came to them in a strange, drawn-out cry. Not a scream or a howl but a round O sound immensely protracted, a cry of sorrow.

They knew what had happened, what she had found. She had gone to look for her shawl. Adam, too late, remembered where that shawl was, that it had been used to cover the body in the tallboy drawer. Unable to find the shawl in her own room, Vivien had gone looking for it, recalling no doubt that she had lent it to Zosie for the baby.

They found themselves moving closer together, taking up a united stand along the back and the head of the table. Zosie got up and held on to Adam. There was silence in the kitchen but for Shiva clearing his throat, a nervous muffled sound. Adam thought of the postgirl, still not far off, no doubt having to push her bike up the drift . . .

Vivien's footsteps sounded, running, along the passage, down the back stairs. Zosie began to whimper.

'Shut up,' Adam said. 'Shut up or I'll kill you.'

Vivien opened the door and came in, her tanned face bleached as if she had jaundice. Her eyes had become big and staring, the whites showing all round the irises. She was goose-fleshed and the down on her arms stood erect. He felt the hair rise on his own neck.

Incongruously Vivien said, 'What are you doing with that gun?' And then, 'Haven't you done enough damage?'

'It was cot death, Vivien.' Rufus took a step towards her but she recoiled from him. 'It was no one's fault. These things happen. It would probably have happened if the child had been in her own home.'

'I don't believe you.'

'Why should I tell lies about it? We're all in this together. There's no point throwing the shit around.'

'You've lied to me once. You said you'd taken the baby back.'

It was unanswerable. 'OK,' Adam said. 'We lied to you but we're not lying now.' He wished he could keep his voice steady, he wished he could control the muscles of his mouth and throat. Rufus could. 'D'you think Zosie would have hurt the baby? She loved her, you know that.'

He had made a mistake in mentioning it. Zosie let out a wail and rushing to the back door began pounding on it with her fists. If people are allowed to have guns, in an extremity or even in any sort of danger, people will use them. Adam had read this but never before put it to the test. He found himself raising the gun and pointing it at Zosie.

'Put that down,' Rufus said.

It was brave of him not to be deterred by Adam's shout to mind his own business and keep out of this. He simply reached out and took the gun and laid it on the table. Vivien went over to Zosie and got hold of her arms, pulling her to her and holding her. She walked her back to the table, sat her down, sat beside her. Adam heard himself give a heavy sigh, a release of long-held breath.

'You must be brave, Zosie,' Vivien said. 'We're going to the police to tell them about this. I think you know that, don't you? The only thing now is to be open and honest about everything, tell them how you took the baby because you hadn't been well, because you'd lost your own baby. They won't be horrible to you and I'll be there. We'll all be there. We'll tell them how good you were to the baby, how you looked after her but she died just the same. Rufus will tell them it was cot death she died of and they'll listen to him because he knows about medical things.'

'You have to be joking,' said Rufus.

Vivien was measuring out drops from a little phial to give Zosie. They were her Bach rescue remedy. 'There isn't anything else to be done, Rufus,' she said gently. 'We have to do it. We have to go to the village now and phone the police, or it might be better to drive to one of the towns. Yes, that might be best.' Zosie was looking at her in fear. She smiled at her, gave her the cup with colourless liquid in it, the panacea that was supposed to be a restorative in any emergency. 'They won't do anything bad to us, perhaps put us on probation at the worst. Zosie may have to have some sort of treatment, that's all they can do. You see, we didn't mean any harm, none of us did. The worst is that you three rather supported Zosie in keeping the baby, that's all.'

Rufus had been watching Vivien's pouring of the rescue remedy with contemptuous distaste. 'They'd kick me out of medical school, that's *all*. I could say goodbye to all my prospects.'

Shaking his head, swallowing, Shiva seemed to have difficulty in speaking, but he did speak, lifting his hands up to his neck in a curious gesture as if he were holding his head secure on his shoulders. 'And what about me? My father? I am supposed to be getting into a teaching hospital.'

527

'Do you really think those things important compared to what's happened here? This was someone's child, a precious child, and she's dead.'

'They'd think we'd done something to her. We could go to jail for life,' Adam said flatly.

Rufus shrugged. 'Come on. Things are no different from what they were half an hour ago except that Vivien knows. So we go on as we planned. The first thing is for Shiva and Vivien to get ready and then I drive them to Colchester station. Right?'

She wouldn't have it. She stood firm. 'No, it isn't right. I can't have anything to do with this, Rufus. I can't go in with you all. If the rest of you won't come with me I shall go alone. There's a police house at Sindon.'

'You're no driver, Vivien,' Rufus said and he came up to her and took her by the arm, a tall strong man, her weight and half as much again.

She shook him off. 'I can walk.'

'I'm afraid you can't. There are four of us to one of you. We can keep you here even if that means manhandling you.'

One of the terrible things was that Vivien had said no more after that about going to the police, about telling anyone at all. She had declared her intention but had not repeated it after Rufus said that about manhandling her. Perhaps she had changed her mind and would not have gone. Adam could hardly bear to think this, even now. At the time, if he had thought coherently about anything at all, he had thought only that she must not be allowed to leave. But it was possible she never would have gone to the police. Though she hated what they had done, or what she believed they had done, she would not have shopped them, she would have been loyal. Alone, she would not have stood against them.

On the other hand, she had no bag with her. So in leaving the house she had not had the simple intention of escaping and making her way to London. Her clothes and her carpet-bag were still upstairs, the box of flower remedies still on the table. But she prised off the hand Zosie had put out to clutch at her skirt and she pushed Rufus away. Her eyes lingered on Shiva, just looking at him without expression, but that blank gaze made him wince. She put up her hand and tore the Gestalt Prayer down from the wall. Still holding the piece of paper, she opened the back door, but without a word, still not saying she would go to the police.

Somehow or other Shiva had got between her and Rufus, so that to reach her Rufus would have had to push him aside, and did not in fact reach her, did not come within feet of her. There was a rush of cold damp air into the kitchen and Vivien was running out across the flagstones . . .

News from Wyvis Hall had disappeared underground. There had been nothing since Sunday. Adam thought he had observed this kind of thing before in the progress of a murder enquiry – or the progress that is made public knowledge – how day after day small paragraphs or a few lines would appear in newspapers to be followed by an ominous lull. A week might pass during which time guiltless readers would forget, dismiss the case completely from their minds. And then, suddenly, would come the short piece about the man helping police with their enquiries, succeeded next day by the announcement of an arrest, a court hearing.

Rufus phoned to tell him the police had not come or been in touch. Adam was aghast to hear of the visit to Nunes. He felt he could never have dared approach it or that an invisible wall surrounded it and kept him out. As to the police, it was not worth their while to seek confirmation, for they had never believed his story. It was the coypu man they were interested in. He imagined Winder or Stretton or both of them closeted for long hours with the coypu man and the postgirl and the farmer and Rufus's taxi-driver while these people told them of the group of people living at Wyvis Hall, two girls among them, of the sounds of shot-gun fire, of a baby heard crying, of a gardener peremptorily dismissed, of wine bottles, dozens of them, put out for the refuse collection each week, of a hasty departure, of new-cut turf in the clearing in the pine wood . . .

There was nothing in the papers on Thursday. It was Anne's birthday and they were going out to dinner. She had asked his parents to baby-sit because she couldn't find anyone else, she said, but Adam was annoyed by it. He didn't want to go out because he was afraid of coming in and finding the police waiting for him.

Lewis said, 'Funny, that business at Wyvis Hall seems to have died a natural death.' He sounded disappointed.

'Which is more than the people in the grave did,' said his wife.

'Absolutely. You're right. I don't suppose we've heard the end of it.' He said that Adam could offer him a small sherry if he liked, very dry if possible, but amontillado would do. The sherry glass did not have a Greek key design round its rim but Lewis asked just the same if this was 'by any chance one my poor old uncle's glasses'.

Adam didn't answer.

'It's a bad business, all of it, I don't suppose that little cemetery will ever be restored. That little dog Blaze, a West Highland, you know, Anne – we had quite a funeral for him, do you remember, Beryl? I've a very strong notion you were there too, Adam, but no more than a babe in arms. Your Aunt Lilian read a piece of poetry, something of Whitman's about wanting to live with animals, and we laid the poor little fellow in the earth. Your Aunt Lilian was a strange woman.'

'Why do you call her my aunt? If she was anyone's aunt she was yours.'

Lewis went on as if he had not spoken. 'Who would have imagined on that sentimental but rather charming occasion that the cemetery would be put to such a use?'

Adam said recklessly, 'A girl I knew saw that dog's ghost on the back stairs.'

Anne gave him a look of disgust. This time Lewis did reply. 'Absolute rubbish. A load a twaddle. What girl?'

'Come on,' Adam said to Anne. 'We might as well go.'

In the car she said to him, 'Are you losing your mind or is there some purpose behind all this?'

A movement of his shoulders was all the answer she got.

'Why are we going out together like this? It's a farce.'

'We're celebrating your birthday by quarrelling in a restaurant instead of at home.'

'I hate you,' said Anne.

Those had been Zosie's words to him too. He had forgotten, or thought he had forgotten, but those words were the key that when touched gave entry to the last file of all.

'I hate you, I hate you . . .' as she tried to get hold of him, clutching at his clothes, tumbling over as he pushed her away.

He parked the car, the engine died. He sat at the wheel with his eyes closed. Then he made a great effort. He didn't want to remember any of this, he wanted to escape out of it to a blank screen. Anne had got out of the car and slammed the door. Adam also got out, lifting his face to the cold air, the thin sprinkling of rain.

It was the postgirl on her bicycle he had been afraid of, that she had not gone, or not gone far enough, or was there waiting, her mercy to be thrown upon, her bicycle to be borrowed, her consent obtained to be a witness . . .

But there was no one. He had seen no one. The drift was empty, windswept, under a grey tumbled sky. There was no one but the figure in the pale cotton dress running across the flagstones. And voices shouting and Zosie's voice raised in a thin wail. Following Anne across the pavement towards the doors of the restaurant, he found the escape key failing, the past inescapable, the present lost. He had raised the gun to his shoulder, braced himself for the kickback and fired. She screamed and he fired again and this time she whirled round, shot full of arrows, fountaining blood, blood exploding from the little body, breaking in great scarlet splashes all over the cream cotton.

Now, as then, he stumbled, grabbing just in time the lintel of the door. In the dark entrance to the place he shook himself, opened his eyes wide, forced his mouth into a grin. Then after the third firing of the gun, he had fallen down, had lain spread-eagled on the stones, crying:

'Stop, stop, stop, stop!'

— 20 —

When he came back from Nunes, or from his visit to his patient in a Colchester hospital, Rufus had found Marigold at home waiting unquestioningly for him. And he had not questioned her about her day either, though aware of how unnaturally they were behaving towards each other. It had been a precedent, he knew very well. Now she would never ask him and he would never ask her, they would get into the habit of doing separate secret things, bland and smiling and calling each other darling more often than could be sincere. But that evening, eating supper with friends who were another young married couple, he could not help feeling that her behaviour with the husband was constrained. They behaved, he fancied, as if they intended to seem indifferent to one another while last time they had all been together there had been flirtatiousness. It was probably all in his imagination.

The days passed and he phoned Adam. He waited, as Adam waited, for more news from Wyvis Hall. As soon as he saw the name on the front page of the *Standard* he knew it was Shiva's. Manjusri. He remembered now. It was Shiva's house that had burned down and Shiva who had died trying to save his wife. A shop assistant, the newspaper called him, but it was the same one. Rufus, secret drink at hand, scoured the paper for what he had got into the habit of looking for every morning and every evening, and found nothing. But it was only a matter of time, he was sure of that now. Too many witnesses had been revealed for him to have much faith any longer in the possibility of escape. He had not begun making contingency plans, for there were none he could make, there were no options open to a doctor, a consultant, who had been concerned in murder and concealing deaths and concealing bodies. All he could do was psych himself up to behave with coolness and decorum when they came for him. But he was past feeling relief at the death or disappearance of witnesses, at the departure of Mary Gage, Bella's death and Evan's. For Shiva, looking once more at the photograph, he felt something almost alien to his nature, a kind of horrified pity. Yet in a way Shiva was better dead than facing what Rufus now saw as inevitable.

For Shiva had been even more deeply concerned than he. Shiva had thought up the ransom idea and his too was the idea of burying the bodies in the woodland cemetery. Sitting silent with the paper before him, Rufus thought of it now. He was too silent and Marigold's cheerful acceptance of his silence was almost unnerving. Weakening, Rufus had a vague absurd dream of being able to tell her, of weeping in her arms and of her weeping too, and of love and commitment, but he steadied himself. That wasn't what he had ever wanted, certainly not what he would get. Almost better to contemplate poor Shiva than an alternative life he didn't have and never would . . .

'We could put them up among the children – I mean the animals,' Shiva had said. 'No one would think of looking there, they'd be hidden there.' And he had been pleased – *pleased* at that moment – because they had listened to him and agreed.

Or Rufus had and Zosie. Adam lay on the stones in the rain. He lay there till Rufus shook him and said, 'Come on, get yourself together,' and Rufus pulled him up and he covered his face with his hands. Shiva it was who carried the body into the house, covered it with one of those absurd, heavy, stiff monogrammed sheets. Already the rain was washing the blood off the stones. Rufus dragged Adam inside and stuck him at the table and gave him gin. Of course he had a secret bottle, a thick square bottle of Geneva he had bought with some of the gold-chain money.

No one asked Adam why he had done it, then or later. He had done it, there was no point in asking. And the rest of them were already conniving, covering up, sticking together, planning how to survive. I never felt guilty, Rufus thought, only afraid of being found out. That's all I feel now. But Zosie who took the baby, Shiva who tried to get a ransom for it, Adam who shot and fired that gun, how had they felt? Well, Shiva was dead.

Tears ran down Adam's face. He didn't try to stop them, nor did he seem ashamed of crying. How long had they just sat there in the kitchen, Adam and he and Shiva? Hours, minutes, half an hour? In retrospect it seemed a long time, it seemed as if they were waiting for something, and perhaps they were, perhaps they were waiting for Zosie to come down with the baby.

She took off her ring of gold plaited strands with the Z inside it and put it on the baby's finger. On the baby's thumb rather, for it was too big for any of the tiny fingers but not too big for the thumb. In that curious way her own finger was stained black where that ring had been. It was a pointless act of sentiment, having no special relevance to the baby's situation or her relationship with it, whatever that might be. Rufus had been impatient.

'Let's get on with it.'

The rain had eased up a little. In procession they went up into the pine wood, not yielding to the idea of using the heavy old wooden wheelbarrow which stood in the stables but carrying the wrapped bodies, Rufus taking Vivien on his shoulders, and Zosie with the baby. Adam and Shiva each carried tools, the heavy spade and a fork, the lighter spade they had used to bury the coypu in the Little Wood being unaccountably missing. Or it had been unaccountable then. Now Rufus knew it had been taken by the gardener who came to Wyvis Hall at dawn and whose footsteps sent Adam to the gun-room and the gun, who was in a way responsible for Adam's using the gun.

Adam woke very early on Thursday morning, at about five. Waking had been preceded by a dream in which Hilbert and Lilian, with himself and Bridget and their parents in attendance, were burying the body of their only child in the cemetery in the pine wood. The body could not be seen, for it was sealed up in a tiny coffin of walnut, veneered in a flame pattern. Lilian and Hilbert looked less like themselves, or after a time began to look less like themselves, than like the parents in the picture. Adam knew he had dreamed this because of what his father had said to him the evening before about Blaze's funeral. He lay in the dark wondering if this was the day on which his world would end. He had taken to wondering this every morning.

In the dream Hilbert and Lilian had been doing the digging themselves, having selected the plot next to where Blaze was buried, and they were digging deep. They dug deeper than their own height, so that not even the tops of their heads showed above the brink of the grave. When they had dug, Shiva and Rufus, and then he had taken over from Shiva, they had not been so thorough, but had gone down no more than three feet. If we had dug deeper, thought Adam, if we had dug the statutory six feet down, none of this would have happened . . .

But it had been three feet, not six. Even so it took them a long time and the worst part was putting the earth back, seeing the earth trickle into the folds of cloth, the strands of hair. If the grave had only been deep, deep enough for a man as tall as Rufus to stand in and his head not show above ground level. They had been oppressed with fear, and cold and wet, shivering in the rain, wanting to get on with it and get it over. A morning at the end of summer and the end of the world . . .

Up there you could just hear the traffic, what there was of it, a car or two passing, and once, horse's hooves. Shiva had cut the turf back carefully before they began digging, cut it out in squares with the spade. He had laid the squares on one side ready for replacement when the grave was filled. Rain, which had been falling intermittently all the time they worked, now came down in a glassy sheet. Yet it was as if the rain were on their side, falling swiftly on the grave to make the grass grow over it.

In the pine wood, among the dense growth of black tree trunks, they took refuge. It was bone-dry in there, dark, scented and close. You could hear the rain but not feel it. Hours seemed to have passed since anyone had spoken, it was as if they had all been stricken dumb, but inside the pine wood Adam spoke to Zosie.

'Are you all right?'

She moved out of the circle of his arm. 'Oh, yes.'

They put the turf back and trod on it, pressing it down. The sky was all clouds, the treetops swinging. The cedar was doing its witch-like dance, clapping its branches in their black sleeves, when they came out of the wood and approached the house.

Shiva hung up the fork in the stable where the tools were kept but Adam held on to the spade. He went into the house, into the gun-room where the turtle was and the fox came bursting out of the wall, and fetched the four-ten, the lady's gun, and then he and Zosie went down to the Little Wood and buried it near the spot where they had buried the coypu. He had meant to bury both guns, the lightweight shot-gun and the heavier pump-action one, the one he had used, but when it came to the point he was afraid.

Up in the cemetery he had spoken only to remark on the rain falling, the rain being on their side. But Rufus had said:

'We should all go our separate ways as soon as we can. We should pack up now and go.'

'I haven't got a separate way,' Zosie said.

Alone upstairs with Adam she said it as they bundled up their clothes into bags and Adam put the gun into Hilbert's golf-bag. Zosie wrapped up the belt with studs in her pink T-shirt and put them and the rest of her clothes and the jeans she had made into shorts into her back-pack.

'I shall go to my mother.'

'But how will you? Where is your mother?'

She gave him a timid sidelong look, the small frightened cat, the hare that hears a stick break underfoot.

'Here,' she said. 'In Nunes.'

'In *Nunes*?'

'They moved here from Ipswich a week before I came.'

'Zosie, were you on your way to Nunes when Rufus picked you up?'

'Yes, of course. I did say to him to go to Nunes, though I didn't want to. I was scared. I knew they didn't want me. Well, they couldn't have. Look how they never searched for me.'

Adam had had that feeling of faintness again that came from terror slipping out of control. He put his hand up to his head, pressing on the bone with cold fingertips. There was a cough, a knock, and Shiva came in. He was carrying Vivien's carpet-bag.

'What am I to do with this?'

'I don't know. God knows.'

'Can Rufus take me to my mother?' said Zosie.

Adam knew it was impossible. He tried to explain why. Their future safety lay in its not being known they knew each other or had been here. But Zosie would be bound to come out with it. Where would she say she had been? But even as he explained to her he felt that the responsibility for her should be his. Was he to abandon her? Where would she go. She had nowhere and no one. She had less than Vivien who at least had had the squat and then the job with Tatian . . .

Adam went downstairs, Shiva following him. He filled a glass with water and drank it, hoping it would stop him being sick. His stomach was empty and felt hollow but he knew that would not prevent him from vomiting.

Rufus sat at the table, his things ready, the van keys in front of him. He had emptied the fridge, packed the food into a box, switched the fridge off and left the door open. Someone had washed and dried up the breakfast things. Shiva, presumably. And Shiva had put Vivien's flower remedies into the carpet-bag. No one had eaten anything since breakfast. It would be a long time before any of them could eat, Adam thought.

He said, 'Rufus, listen, what are we going to do about Tatian? He'll expect Vivien to come today. When she doesn't turn up he's going to wonder, isn't he? I mean he's not just going to accept she's changed her mind.'

'He's not going to tell the police either,' said Rufus.

'He might tell them.' Shiva had been a sick yellow colour since the morning. He looked as if he were recovering from an illness or about to succumb to one. 'It's his friends whose baby has disappeared. If Vivien doesn't come they may connect her with that.'

Adam sat down opposite Rufus. He felt weak, drained of all

strength. The rain lashed the windows on a sudden gust and the start it made him give brought a sob up into his throat.

'Steady,' said Rufus, quite kindly for him.

'I'm all right. I'll be all right.'

'Sure you will. We're going to have to phone Tatian.'

'Oh God, no!'

'I'll do it,' Rufus said quickly. 'What else can we do? We're going to have to tell him Vivien's been taken ill or something like that. He knows where she lives, you see.'

'He knows where she lives?'

'She told him Ecalpemos, Nunes, Suffolk. He's going to remember that when she doesn't come, and because the police will have interviewed him and asked him to let them know anything odd that has happened or does happen, he's going to tell them about her. And they'll be down here at every house. There aren't many houses in Nunes so it won't take them long to find this one.'

'That's what I said,' said Shiva. 'I said they'd question him.'

Rufus's eyebrows went up. 'So you did.'

'Who's going to do the phoning?'

'Not you,' said Adam. 'You've got an accent. You sound Indian – or Welsh. He might be suspicious.'

'Oh, I'll do it,' said Rufus.

'And would you – I mean is it at all realistic to think of Zosie going home? She wants to go home to her parents in Nunes.'

'In *Nunes*?'

'Yes, I know. She thought you might drive her home. I've told her it's impossible but what alternative is there?'

She had provided it herself, coming quietly into the room and standing on the threshold wearing Vivien's blue dress.

The instant he heard Abigail Adam got out of bed, went into her room and picked her up. He prepared orange juice for her, changed her napkin, loving to do these things, wondering how many more mornings he would be there to do them.

The paper came. He heard it fall on the doormat and the letterbox give a double slam. Like when the postgirl brought the rates bill that time and then the electricity bill. The red flash of the bicycle past the window, the slam-slam of the letterbox.

Abigail sitting in the crook of his arm, he picked up the paper, stomach clutching, heart making it apparent to him that he possessed a heart in there in the cage of his ribs, sensations he had every morning now. He opened the paper at the home news, scanned both pages. Nothing, still nothing. There had been nothing since Sunday.

He wasn't interested in the post. He didn't receive any letters at home anyway. Bills would come and the occasional postcard and junk mail. This morning it was Anne who fetched the letters in, wordlessly, cold-faced, putting the envelope down by his plate. He was giving Abigail her breakfast and it was ten minutes before he opened it.

Rufus was shaking hands with Mrs Shaw who was still enthusing over the success of her hormone replacement therapy when the special messenger arrived. His name was sprawled on the envelope and Rufus, though he hadn't seen it for ten years, recognized the handwriting as Adam's. It took all the nerve he had and all the resources to continue making amiable rejoinders, but he did continue, a paralysed smile stuck on his face like a mask he had put on, and at last she was paying up and going and he could take the envelope – and its contents, whatever they might be – back into his room. With ten minutes to spare before the next patient.

You do not put off things because they threaten you, because you are afraid. It was a rule of life he had made his since before Ecalpemos. He opened the envelope with a paper knife, making himself breathe regularly. When he saw it was newsprint inside he quailed but he unfolded it. Scrawled across the top of the sheet by a hand that had trembled were the words: *The Coypu Man*.

Instead of coming over to speak to him, Rufus had gone first to the bar. He saw Adam sitting in the corner and he raised his hand to him, went to the bar and now approached, carrying two glasses. It was almost a week later. There was an intimacy in Rufus's manner which showed itself in the absence of any greeting or formal enquiries, and an extreme casualness too.

'I can drink them both if you don't want one,' he said.

'Oh, I don't mind having a drink,' said Adam.

Rufus lifted his glass. 'Absent friends!'

That seemed to Adam in atrocious bad taste. He did not echo it. He said, 'Most of it was in our own heads, wasn't it? There was never much in the papers, little paragraphs, a line here and there. Of course there was that bit on television while I was still away but nothing more. I suppose the police had an idea of the truth from the first. They never really suspected us or my great-uncle or Langan. They knew from the first it was the coypu man.'

Rufus was looking strangely at him. 'But it wasn't.'

Shaking his head as if he were shaking off a delusion, Adam said, 'I don't mean that. I mean all that questioning of me wasn't to find out about me but about the coypu man. Only I saw it back to front.' He muttered softly, 'My guilt made me see it back to front.'

He looked terrible, Rufus thought, aware that he himself was looking particularly well. Only that morning a Mrs Llewellyn (polyps and a partial prolapse) had told him he looked too young to be a consultant in Wimpole Street. Adam was gaunt and hollow-eyed, grey-skinned. And he couldn't keep still. Instead of relaxing now all was over, he was fiddling with his glass, making those interlocking wet rings.

Rufus took the cutting from the *East Anglian Daily Times* out of his wallet, unfolded it and laid it on the table. His glance picked out a few salient words, words he knew by heart anyway: 'Zoe Jane Seagrove ...' '... infant daughter ...' '... stepfather Clifford William Pearson, died November 1976. An inquest verdict was recorded of suicide while the balance of his mind was disturbed. A police spokesman said that the Wyvis Hall case is closed and no further enquiries will be made.'

'Do you want this back?'

'I shouldn't think so. I don't know who sent it to me but it must have been someone who knew I'd be – interested is a bit of an understatement, isn't it? I suppose it was Shiva. There was nothing to show, just the cutting in an envelope.' Rufus said nothing, knowing it couldn't have been Shiva, suddenly averse to guessing who it might have been. 'What do you think made her mother sure it was Zosie in that grave?' Adam said.

'The ring, surely. She put her ring on the baby's hand.'

'Yes.'

'There would have been pellets of shot too, mixed up with the gravel. Even if they had found it by sifting the gravel, those woods must be full of shot. Or perhaps they think Pearson shot her.'

Adam said in a low voice, 'She said to me once, "He kills little

539

things, he has no mercy." All the time she must have known the man we called the coypu man was her stepfather. She must have been afraid he would come back and find her, hurt her as he had threatened to, put her mother against her. Had he been her – lover? The father of her child?'

'Who knows?' Rufus said dismissively. 'It's an interesting thing that the story didn't even make the national papers, it got no further than a provincial daily. It wasn't important enough.'

Adam didn't seem to find it interesting. 'All that about Zosima was lies too, wasn't it? She was called Zoe Jane.'

'Was?' said Rufus.

Tasting the sweetish contents of his glass, cold, lemony, tingling, Adam wondered if it were gin or vodka Rufus had brought him. He was very ignorant about these things. Already the stuff was making his head swim. It was a good thing he had not brought the car, though he had thought of doing this, his parents' house being such a long way out. For a while, until he found a flat, he would be staying with his parents.

'In a sort of way,' Adam said, 'I suppose I forget that it wasn't Zosie in the grave but Vivien. I forget it wasn't Zosie who died. It makes you wonder what became of her.'

'Didn't you wonder before?'

'Not much. I didn't want to know. I used to switch it all off, blank my mind.'

'I think she wrote to her mother or more probably phoned her, told her she'd had the baby and could she come to see her. If you remember, she used to fret about her mother not caring much for her. But she didn't go. Perhaps she was afraid of Pearson or afraid of not having a baby to take with her. When she didn't come her mother reported her as missing. We don't know anything about Pearson or his relations with Zosie, but the police do. They know his business was going wrong, he'd maybe threatened suicide, was perhaps a bit mad. He killed himself a couple of months later but when the bones were found and the ring . . .'

'Where do you suppose she is now?'

'She was a disaster person,' said Rufus, thinking of Mrs Harding and her daughter. 'She wasn't a survivor. She's probably on hard drugs. Or in jail. Remember the camera and the bracelet? She tried to steal a little boy once, too. Did you ever know that?'

Adam nodded. He pushed his empty glass away.

'Do you want the other half?'

'You can't say that about spirits,' Adam protested. 'I mean, about beer you can but not about spirits. The other half of what would it be?'

Rufus laughed. 'Still the same old Verne-Smith. Remember the Greek verb "to rub"? I'll remember that to my dying day.'

'Yes, so you said before.'

'That doesn't make it less true.'

'No. No, it doesn't. I don't really want another drink.'

'I should have expected you to be – well, euphoric, to say the least. Aren't you even relieved to be off the hook? I mean you have realized, haven't you? This is the end of it. It's over. No punishment. This time society fails to take revenge?'

'Oh, I've realized. I've got away with it.' Adam picked up their glasses. 'I'll get you a drink, I ought to. I just never seem to think of it, that's all.'

Rufus watched him make his way to the bar. What sort of curious nature would it be that never thought about drinking or that others might wish to drink? It seemed to him that Adam didn't know about Shiva, that he had not made the connection between the man burnt to death and the man they had known at Ecalpemos. There was perhaps no point in enlightening him. It might lead, Rufus thought with a hint of recoil, to quasi-philosophical speculations on the nature of retribution or even God not being mocked. No, he would say nothing.

Vodka and tonic was put down before him. Adam had bought himself something that looked suspiciously like neat Perrier.

'We drank a hell of a lot of wine at Ecalpemos,' said Rufus. 'Muck most of it. Plonk. It apparently did us no harm.'

Adam looked up and said in an aggressive way, 'Isak Dinesen said that life is no more than a process for turning healthy young puppies into mangy old dogs and man but an exquisite instrument for converting the red wine of Shiraz into urine.'

Rufus gave a bark of laughter. 'What brought that up, for God's sake?'

Adam muttered something about random access, so Rufus didn't pursue it but started talking about his plans to move house, about a house far beyond their means really that Marigold had found in Flask

Walk but which he supposed they would stretch themselves to the limit to buy. But euphoria was making Rufus enthusiastic and even expansive. He had been on what he called a high for five days now, doing his best to keep up there on it too, because somewhere inside him a little tiny nasty voice was whispering that once he came down he would have to think about his wife, and his wife's friend's husband, and whether he was buying an astronomically priced house to please or even to *buy* his wife. So he said fulsomely to Adam:

'We mustn't lose touch again. I mean, the point is we don't *have* to lose touch again. We can all meet up now. I'll get Marigold to give your wife a ring, shall I?'

At one point Adam had felt like explaining. He had felt like opening his heart to Rufus but the moment had passed or all that breezy insensitivity had made it impossible. So he nodded and said OK and because he didn't know what else to do, stuck out his hand and shook hands with Rufus. Rufus offered him a lift but Adam said no thanks, he would get the tube.

Marigold could ring Anne, he thought as he walked towards Tottenham Court Road, and be told what would put an end to any possible cosy get-togethers: that Adam and Anne were no longer together. She had left him, or rather, had asked him to leave so that she might remain in Abigail's home with Abigail. It was the only possible way, anyone could see that. Adam was on his way to get the Northern Line up to Edgware where his parents lived.

It was that remark of Rufus's about no punishment, about society not taking revenge, which had finished him. It was an irony, he thought, that all through the anxiety it had been his removal from Abigail that had worried him, never her removal from him. There was no doubt that they would be given joint custody and he would get to take her out on Sundays . . .

— 21 —

A clearing in the pine wood was how you would have described it now, the turf as smooth and level as a croquet lawn. Meg Chipstead, standing on the green ride and looking at it from a little distance away – she still did not care to go too close – thought not for the first time that perhaps they should replace the monuments. It seemed a pity that something which was historic really, an interesting rural curiosity, should be destroyed because of that one horrifying act. The gravestones had been placed in two neat stacks in the stables: Pinto, Blaze, Sal, Alexander and all. Of course she would have no idea where to re-site them, except in the case of Blaze. That could never be forgotten.

Meg called out, 'Sam, Sam!' and the little dog, the Jack Russell, Fred's replacement, came running out of the deciduous wood. No dog would venture in among the pine trees – at least, Fred never had. There was no point really in putting the gravestones back, now they had decided to leave the place. Let the new owners replace them if they chose. Meg and Alec had decided they must tell all to those new owners, whoever they might be. They would find out anyway.

It was May and the bluebells were out. Drifts of them gleamed between the trees like ground mist, like shreds of sky. The beech leaves were a pure pale green, each an unfolding cocoon of silk. A breeze moved the shafts of sunshine, or seemed to do so, making fluttering dapple patterns on the fallen leaves of last autumn. Last autumn . . . Whenever Meg thought of that she knew there was no use saying the place was beautiful and they would regret selling. She could never forget those days of disinterment and investigation, the spoliation of sanctuary and peace. They had made up their minds to go and would keep to this resolution.

She began to walk back to the house, the little dog running through the brakes of bramble, the uncurling green fern, chasing a squirrel across the drift. Meg called him, 'Sam, Sam!' because she could hear a vehicle coming down. It would be the people with an order to view, the prospective buyers. A Range Rover in an olive-green colour, darker than the new leaves, came into sight under the arch of branches and lumbered down the tracks.

Meg waved to show they were expected, to show they had come to the right place, and got in return a hand raised in a salute. This unfamiliar presence started Sam off barking.

'Shut up,' said Meg. 'Come on, race you to the house.'

She threw a stick to speed him on his way. Of course he was off in a streak of white and tan, boomeranging back to her with the stick in his mouth. This time he forgot the stick and went to yap at the people who were getting out of the car in front of the house. Meg came jogging down over the lawn, under the branches of the cedar tree. The front door opened and Alec came out, holding out his hand.

But what a lot of them there were! Meg was rather appalled. The old woman who lived in a shoe, she thought, as from the rear doors of the Range Rover one child after another appeared. A stream of children, little steps, as her mother would have said. In fact there were five and the young woman, the wife, was pregnant. She looked a lot younger than her husband, close on twenty years. He was tallish with grey curly hair, thin, a bit worn, as well he might be.

She hadn't quite caught their name on the phone, Lathom or Heysham or Patience or something, and she wasn't to learn it now, only to have her hand shaken and told, what a lovely house, really he had had no idea!

Rob, his wife called him. She was a little plump woman, in perhaps her sixth month of pregnancy. Her hair was streaked in rose pink and blonde and she was still young enough to wear the fantastic loops and frizzes into which it had been tortured. The two older children, the girls, couldn't be hers. The elder of them was at least fifteen.

'Rob, we can leave this lot outside, can't we?' she said. 'It's a lovely day. I mean they could have a little look round the garden if Mr and Mrs Chipstead wouldn't mind.'

'Oh, please,' said Meg. 'Whatever they like. I expect it would be boring for them inside anyway.' She said to the children, the smaller ones staring at her, 'Only you will be careful of the lake, won't you? You won't go near the lake?'

'I'll just take the baby in with me, if that's all right.' A flicker of some indefinable emotion seemed to cross her face. 'I don't like leaving him, not just yet.'

The 'baby' was a big boy of about eighteen months, able to walk but not steadily. His mother yanked him on to her hip, shaking her head when her husband tried to take him from her. They went into the house where after the outer brightness, the gentle breezy warmth, it seemed as if a dark chill met them.

But this sensation lasted only a moment and the house unfolded itself in all its eighteenth-century elegance. They walked through the drawing room, where the pink marble was admired and the fireplace, and on into Alec's study that was more a library. The Chipsteads had had the room entirely lined with bookshelves and stuck to oak and leather for the furnishings. Meg was proud of the views across the garden from this room, the flint walls of the kitchen garden, the green slope down to the lake where the kingcups were in bloom and yellow flags. The two girls and the two little boys were squatting down at the water's edge trying to persuade a duck to approach them.

Their father tapped on the window and when the elder girl looked up, shook his head in an admonitory way. If they did decide to buy Wyvis Hall, he said to Alec, something would have to be done about that lake, fence it in perhaps.

'Or teach them to swim,' said his wife. 'And I could learn too in case I fell in.'

He gave her an indulgent smile, tender, somehow, sexual. It made Meg feel slightly embarrassed. To cover the faint confusion this glimpse into their private life had brought her, she asked him if they planned to move permanently to the country.

'Oh no, we should keep on our London house. My company is there. I shouldn't fancy three hours' commuting a day, though I know people do it.'

On the stairs she handed the boy over to her husband, stood for a moment getting her breath. She laid her hand on the swollen belly.

'It does lurch about so. It gave poor Dan an awful great kick just now. No wonder he wanted to go to you.'

The master bedroom, the pink room, the lilac room, and the *en suite* bathrooms. Alec and Meg had had two new bathrooms put in soon after they came there. Just one for a house that size was ridiculous. An eye was kept on the children from the window of the turquoise room (green carpet, peacock-feather wallpaper, green and blue striped duvet) and their father called out to the eldest:

'Take the little ones up into the wood, Naomi.'

'And pick some bluebells if you like,' said Meg.

'How kind of you! You are nice!' Dimpled hands were pushed through the pink and yellow confection of hair, not very clean hands either, Meg noticed with surprise. The finger with the gold wedding ring on it was all streaked with black. They all stared at her when she said, 'There's a staircase in that cupboard that goes up to the loft.'

'Absolutely true,' said Alec. 'There is.'

Meg opened the cupboard door. 'More convenient than a trapdoor and a ladder. But how did you know?'

'My wife spent some time in this part of the world before we were married. You've never been in this house before though, have you, Viv?'

She looked with a kind a nervous wonderment, it seemed to Meg, at the pretty green silk curtains, the Klimt reproductions. 'Not *this* house, no.'

'Would you like some tea, shall I make a cup of tea? I think we have some squash for the children.'

'Thank you very much but no, we must get back. Our nanny comes back from holiday today, thank God. We like the house. Actually we saw it advertised in the *East Anglian Daily Times*, we take it, my company has an office in Ipswich, but I suppose we shall have to go through the agent? I don't mind telling you we like the house very much.'

'We *love* it,' his wife said.

The children came running across the grass from the wood with fistfuls of bluebells. The smaller boy gave a bunch to his mother.

'And we ought to tell you,' she said, 'we do know about all those grisly things up in the wood.' She smiled, holding out her arms, her swollen body swinging under the full loose skirt, child-like no longer but powerful suddenly, a ruling force. 'And we don't mind a bit.'

The House of Stairs

To David

I

The taxi-driver thought he had offended me. I pushed a five-pound note through the opening in the glass panel and said to stop and let me out. The lights were changing from red and as he pulled in to the side he said in a truculent way,

'I've a right to my own opinion.'

He had been talking about forcible sterilization of the unfit, a subject resulting from some newspaper controversy, and he was all for it, voraciously and passionately for it. I might have been offended, I especially might have been offended – if I had been listening, if I had taken in more than the gist of it.

'I didn't even hear you,' I said, realizing as I said it that this would only make things worse, and I risked the truth, though I knew it wouldn't help. 'I saw a woman I know, a woman I used to know. On the crossing. I have to see her.' Out on the pavement, I shouted back at him, 'Keep the change!'

'What change?' he said, though there was some, a reasonable tip. He was one of those men who think women are mad, or tell themselves women are mad, this being the only way to explain otherwise inexplicable behaviour, the only way to defend themselves against the threatening regiment. 'You want to get yourself seen to,' he shouted, and – who knows? – perhaps he was reverting to his original subject.

It wasn't malice that had made him set me down on the south side of the Green. It only seemed like it as I stood there, imprisoned by the flow, the running tide of traffic, that at the same time had the effect of a door constantly slamming in my face. All the while the lights remained at green Bell was slipping away farther and farther from me. The metal tide, the slamming door, bore a great exodus out of Wood Lane and the Uxbridge Road, from the West End by Holland Park Avenue, out of the West Cross Route, and the emerald light pulled it on, summoned it to a swifter onslaught, a more tumultuous roar. It cut off my view of the Green on which she must now be – walking which way?

Through the taxi's windscreen I had seen her on this crossing. With her characteristic gliding walk unchanged, back straight, head held high as if she carried an amphora balanced on it, Bell had passed northwards from the Hammersmith side. I gasped, I know I did, I may even have let out a cry, which to my cab-driver had sounded like a protest at his words. She disappeared from my sight towards Holland Park so quickly that she might have been an hallucination. But I knew she wasn't. I knew that strange though it was to find her in this unlikely place, it had been Bell I saw and I had to follow her even after all these years and after all the terrible things.

Enforced waiting when you are in a desperate hurry, that is one of life's worst small stings. It didn't seem small to me then. I jogged up and down, bouncing on my feet, praying, begging the lights to change. And then I saw her again. Buses moved, a red wall of them, and I saw her again, crossing the Green, a rapidly retreating figure, tall and erect and looking straight ahead of her. She was in black, all black, the kind of bunchy clustered clothes only the very tall and thin can wear, the waist that looks breakable contained by a wide black belt as if to keep it from snapping in two. From the first sight of her I had noticed something startlingly different. Her hair, which had been very fair, had changed colour. Although I could no longer make it out across the expanse of grass and paths as the figure of Bell grew smaller, I understood with a sense of shock, with a kind of hollow pang, that her hair was grey.

The lights changed and we streamed across in front of the impatient, barely stationary, waiting cars. Or fled in my case, fled on to the Green and across it in pursuit of Bell whom I could no longer see, who had disappeared. I knew of course where she had gone, into the tube station, down into the tube. A 50p ticket out of the machine and I was going down on the escalator, forced now to face alternatives and make a choice, the ancient but everlasting choice of which of two paths to take, in this case westwards or eastwards? Bell had been a Londoner once. Before she disappeared from all our lives into the limbo years, into no man's land, the cloister fort et dure, she had been a Londoner who, in spite of sojourns in exile, boasted she would lose her way west of Ladbroke Grove or east of Aldgate. West of Ladbroke Grove (simply The Grove to her and all of us then) she had been this evening but visiting only, I thought. Somehow I knew she was going home.

So I turned to the platform going east and the train came in at the same time, but before I got into it I saw her again. She was a long way along the platform, walking towards the opening doors, and her hair was as grey as ashes. It was ash grey and done up like Cosette's had once been, done in the very precise style of hers, piled loosely on her head in the shape of a cottage loaf with a knot in the centre like a bun of dough, the way it had been when first Cosette came to the House of Stairs.

There was something dreadfully disturbing about this, so upsetting indeed that I felt a real need to sit down and rest, close my eyes and perhaps breathe deeply. But of course I dared not sit down. I had to station myself just inside the doors so that I could see Bell when she left the train and walked past my carriage to the way out. Or even briefly go out on to the platform at each station in case her exit took her the other way and I missed her. I was very afraid anyway that I was going to lose her, but not so preoccupied that I couldn't examine the situation as I stood close up against those doors. For the first time I wondered if Bell would want to see me and I wondered what we would say to each other, at least to begin with. I couldn't imagine that Bell blamed me, as for instance Cosette had blamed me. But would she expect me to blame *her*?

I was thinking along these lines when the train came into Holland Park. The doors opened and I leaned out, looking along the length of the train, but Bell didn't emerge. It was about half past seven by this time and although a lot of people were about, the crowds had gone. Doing what I was doing, or trying to do, would have been impossible in the rush hours. The next station would be Notting Hill Gate and I was almost certain Bell wouldn't alight there, for this was the station we had all of us used in those days, all of us that is except Cosette, who went everywhere by car or taxi. Bell, for all that she had loved these particular parts of west London, wouldn't have been so insensitive as to choose a return to those streets and that tube station when she came out of prison.

There it was, I had said it, silently and to myself, in my own head, but I had uttered the word. Not cloister nor limbo nor no man's land, but prison. It made me feel weak, dizzy almost. And this thought was succeeded by another, very nearly equally tumultuous: I hadn't expected her to be free, I had thought another year at least, I am not prepared for this. Had I expected her ever to be freed? But I had to be prepared, I had to get out of the train in case I was wrong, in case Bell was not living here but only visiting and was obliged to use this station. I stood on the platform, watching for her, but again she did not appear.

She left the train at Queensway. I got out and followed her, certain now that I must catch up with her in the crowd that stopped to wait for the lift. But when the lift came it could accommodate only so many of the waiting passengers. I saw Bell get into it, her fine ashen head held high above all but two of the others, but had to take the second lift myself. However, before I did so, before the doors of the first lift closed, Bell turned to face this way and looked straight at me. I don't know whether she saw me or not, I have been puzzling about this but still I can't say, though I think she didn't. The lift doors closed and the lift rose up, bearing her away.

It was sunset when I came out into the Bayswater Road, the sky a pale red but tumbled with ranges of cloud that were rust-coloured and crimson and nearly black. The skies of cities are so much finer than anything you see in the country and London has the best of them, though I know Americans would make that claim for New York and I will gladly give it second place. T. H. Huxley used to look down Oxford Street at sunset and see apocalyptic visions, and that evening I too seemed to see wonderful configurations above the Park and Kensington Palace Gardens, great swollen masses of cloud stained with the colours of ochre and dried blood, dividing in the wind to lay bare little limpid lakes of palest blue, closing again in vaporous surges dark as coal. But Bell I couldn't see, Bell I had lost.

I walked back and looked up Queensway. I looked along the Bayswater Road in both directions. There was a tall woman in black a long way ahead, walking westwards, and I think even then I knew in my heart it wasn't Bell, though her waist was small and her hair was grey. I deceived myself because what else was I to do? Go home empty-handed and empty-hearted? I should have to do that sooner or later, but not now, not yet. And the moment the woman had turned out of the Bayswater Road into St Petersburgh Place my conviction that it was Bell, it must be Bell, returned – for how could she have escaped and hidden herself so fast? – and I pursued more eagerly, up St Petersburgh Place, past the synagogue and St Matthew's, along Moscow Road and into Pembridge Square, across Pembridge Villas. By then, of course, we were nearer Notting Hill Gate tube station than Queensway and I was telling myself that Bell deliberately avoided it, took this long way round to her home because it was as hard for her as it was for me, or harder, to face the old associations.

I lost her somewhere this side of the Portobello Road. I say 'somewhere this side' as if I didn't know the place like the palm of my own hand, as if I could have been indifferent to any inch of it, forgotten any yard of it. It was in Ledbury Road that I lost her and found her again on the corner of the Portobello Road where she had met a friend and stopped to talk. And then I saw it wasn't Bell, as that part of me which would recognize her blindfold had always known. It was an older woman than Bell, who would now be forty-five, that I had been following and the girl she was talking to on the corner was a small dumpy blonde, her shrill laughter echoing in that empty ugly glamorous street. I walked on past them and saw the red sky was no longer red but a wild stormy grey of heavy jostling clouds and black with thunder over Kensal Town.

Few people were in the streets. It had been different when first I came here nearly twenty years ago and all the youth of England was on fire, and most, it seemed to me, in Notting Hill. Now there were cars instead, cars which swallowed up the people and transported them in protective capsules. The houses here have gardens and in May they are full of blossoming trees so that the place smells of engine oil and hawthorn, honeysuckle and petrol fumes. It was French cigarettes it smelt of in Cosette's day, any old cigarettes come to that, French and English and Russian and Passing Clouds even, and marijuana in the Electric Cinema. I walked along, not the way I had come, but further south than that, along Chepstow Villas, and I knew where I was going, there is no possibility I can claim I was tending that way by chance, that I didn't know Archangel Place lay in that direction.

But it was of Bell that I was thinking as I walked, wondering who there was that I could find to lead me to her; who would know. My certainty remained that she had been going home, was very likely home by now. It was the sight of me from the lift at Queensway station which had sent her hurrying, hiding even. She had only to slip inside the entrance of the Coburg Hotel or even into Bayswater tube station, just a few yards along Queensway, to have eluded me. And of course she didn't live in Notting Hill, but somewhere in Bayswater. There must be someone I could find who would tell me where. But that she should have wanted to elude me . . .? I who never walk anywhere if I can help it had been walking fast and running in pursuit of the real and the false Bell and my legs began to ache.

It is inescapable always the feeling that this may be it, this time it is no ordinary tiredness but the early warning itself, and the usual unease touched me, the usual quiver of panic. I am not old enough yet to be out of danger, I am still within the limit. But oh, what a bore it all is, how dreary and repetitive and simply boring after all these years, yet how can something be a bore and a terror at one and the same time? I have told no one, ever, but Bell and Cosette. Well, Cosette knew already, naturally she did. Does Bell remember? When she saw me in the station did she remember then and wonder if it had caught me yet or passed me by and left me safe?

I told myself, as I always do, your legs ache because you're not fit (the muscle in your chin jumps because you are tired, carelessness made you drop that glass) and I thought what a fool I was to go out in high heels, in pointed shoes that pinched my toes. It scarcely helped, nothing helps except the ache, the tic, the weakness, going away. I thought I would hail the next taxi that came round one of those narrow leafy corners, out of a crescent or a terrace, for this region of West Eleven is a tight-knit confusion, a labyrinth of alleys and mewses, blown fields and flowerful closes, green pleasure and grey grief.

No taxi came and I was fooling myself when I said I would have taken it if it had. I had come to the narrow lane that leads into the mews and thence into Archangel Place, a lane which, for all its overhanging tree branches and dense jostling hedges, could never be in the country. Slates, polished by the passage of town shoes and their friction, pave it, and there is privet in the hedge and catalpa among the trees. It smells of a city, of staleness and use, and underfoot is dust rather than earth. Between the mews and the street stands the church called St Michael the Archangel, Victorian Byzantine, unchanged, not closed and boarded up, not transformed by one of those vaguely blasphemous conversions into a block of flats, but just the same and with its doors flung wide to show the archangel in the sanctuary with his outspread wings.

I paused on the corner, bending down to rub the muscles in my calves, then looked up and stood up, stood there looking down the narrow, straight and rather short street. From there the House of Stairs also appeared unaltered. But it was dusk now, the long London summer dusk, gloomy and cool, and changes might be hidden. Slowly and deliberately, as if out for a stroll, I walked down on the opposite side. On summer evenings when Cosette lived there people used to sit on doorsteps and when it was hot sunbathe stretched out on the flat roofs of porches. But Archangel Place has come up in the world and I suspect that behind the varied façades, Dutch, Victorian Baroque, neo-Gothic, Bayswater Palladian, are rank upon rank of neat flats that are called 'luxury conversions', with close carpeting and false ceilings and double glazing. It was soon clear to me that number fifteen was such a one, for where Cosette had a twisted wrought-iron bellpull is a row of entryphone buzzers with printed cards above each one.

How could I have had the bizarre idea that Bell's name might be on one of them? It was this at any rate that made me cross the road and look. The House of Stairs has become six flats, from basement to attic every floor economically used by occupants with Greek names and Arab names, a Frenchman by the sound of him, an Indian, a woman who might be German-Jewish or just an American, but no Bell. Of course not. The colour of the house had changed. From the corner of the street this had not been discernible, but now it was, this new, doubtful shade that might be quite different in broad day from what the lamplight showed me, a darkish buff. When Cosette bought it the house was painted the dull green of a cabbage leaf but the stonework remained its natural cream colour, as it still is now. The windows, five sets of them above ground level and one below, you can see for yourself in Ruskin's *The Stones of Venice*, the plate that shows the arch masonry in the Broletto of Como. Whether the architect went there to see for himself or simply copied these windows from Ruskin's drawing I don't know, but they are very faithful renderings, each consisting of three arches with a knot like a clove-hitch half-way up the two double shafts which are surmounted by Corinthian capitals. You can get a better idea from the picture.

There were lights on in these windows and not all the curtains were drawn. I retreated across the road and stood under one of the plane trees that line the street. It was shedding from its dying flowers the pale fluffy stuff that Perpetua used to say gave her hay fever. The new owners or the builders had changed the front door which when Cosette lived there would also have been to Ruskin's taste, having a pointed arch and its woodwork ornamented with ears of corn and oak leaves enclosed by fillets. The new one was a neo-Georgian monstrosity and the arched top of the architrave had been filled in with a pane of ruby-coloured stained glass. But no one had changed the garden – the front garden, that is, for the back was invisible from where I stood.

It is a very small area of garden, between the pavement and the deep recess that separates it from the basement window. What always made back and front gardens remarkable was that they were grey gardens of grey flowers and grey foliage, cinerarias and sea holly, rabbit's ears, lavandula lanata, the silver dwarf lavender, lychnis coronaria with leaves like felt, cardoons that are sisters of the globe artichoke, artemisia with its filigree foliage, ballotas and senecios. I who knew nothing of gardening learnt the names of all the plants in Cosette's garden. Jimmy the gardener taught me, was delighted to find someone who cared enough to learn, and those names have stuck with me. Did Jimmy still come? He used to say that lanata was frail and would scarcely survive without his care. The plants looked thriving to me and the pale silver irises were in full bloom, their papery petals gleaming in the greenish lamplight.

Without being able to see it, aware that I couldn't have borne to see it, I knew that the back garden would be different, would have undergone some tremendous change. Whoever had the house after Cosette, and after I refused it, must have known, must have been discreetly told and have decided to accept the facts and live with them. But along with this decision would have come a need to alter the garden, change the positions of things, perhaps plant trim box bushes and sharp-pointed conifers, bright-coloured flowers. All this would be designed to exorcise the ghosts that some say derive from the energy left behind after an event of violent terror.

I tried to see between the houses, to make my eyes penetrate brick wall and high hedge, black, nearly solid, masses of evergreen foliage. But if the eucalypt had still been there its thready branches with fine pointed grey leaves would by now far exceed in height the hollies and the laurel, for gum trees, as Jimmy once told me, grow tall quickly. If it were still there it might even by now have reached close to that high window. It wasn't there, it couldn't be, and before I turned my eyes away I imagined its felling and its fall, the powerful medicinal scent that must have come from its dying leaves and severed trunk.

There are two balconies only on the façade of the House of Stairs, on the windows of the drawing-room and principal-bedroom floors, and they are copies of the balconies on the Ca' Lanier, bulbous at the base, somewhat basket-like. This disciple of Ruskin was not averse to a hotch-potch of styles. As I stood there the central window on the drawing-room floor opened and a man came out on to the balcony to take in a plant in a pot. He didn't look in my direction but down at his plant and, re-entering, swept aside the curtain to afford me a glimpse of a gold-lit interior, mainly a tiny twinkling chandelier and a dark red wall no more than ten feet inside the window, hung with mirrors and pictures in white frames. It was a shock of a physical kind, clutching at the centre of my body. And yet of course I knew the drawing room must have been sub-divided; must, for it had been thirty feet deep, now comprise the whole flat. The curtain fell and the window was closed once more. I had a sudden vivid memory of returning from some time away, some visit to Thornham perhaps, and of climbing the first flight of stairs to open the drawing-room door and seeing Cosette seated there at the table, her head at once turning towards me, that radiant smile transforming her wistful face, her arms out as she rose to receive me into her unfailing welcoming embrace.

'Darling, did you have a good time? You don't know how we've all missed you!'

A gift for me there would be from that clutter on the table, a homecoming present carefully chosen, the strawberry pincushion perhaps or one of the gemstone eggs. And she would have wrapped it in paper as beautiful as William Morris fabric, tied it with satin ribbon, perfuming it as she did so by chance contact with her own skin, her own dress . . .

My eyes were tightly shut. Involuntarily I had closed them when the tenant or owner of the first-floor flat allowed me a sight of his living room, and I conjured up Cosette where the red wall now was. I opened my eyes, took a last look at the changed, re-ordered, spoiled house and turned away. It was dark by then and as I began walking towards Pembridge Villas, refusing for some melodramatic reason to look back, a taxi came out of one of the mewses and I got into it. Leaning back against the slippery upholstery, I felt curiously tired and worn. You will think I had forgotten all about Bell, but she had only temporarily been pushed out of my mind by remembering Cosette and by all the other emotions the House of Stairs awakened. What I had truly forgotten was the pain in my legs and this had gone, I was reprieved, the bore and the terror would be gone for a week or two.

Of Bell I now thought in a new mood of tranquillity. Perhaps it was all for the best that I had lost her, that there had been no confrontation. Again I wondered if she had seen me over the heads of those people in the lift and again I couldn't make up my mind. Had she fled from me or, innocent of my presence behind her, left the station and gone directly into one of the Queensway shops? It might even be, and this was disturbing, that, emerging, she had followed me, unaware of who I was. Or indifferent? That too had to be faced.

Perhaps she would want to know no one from those old days but start afresh with new friends and new interests, and that (as I now decided must be the case) was borne out by her living in Bayswater or Paddington, areas of London I believed she had never lived in before.

But all this made no difference to my decision to find her. I would find where she was and how she lived and what she now called herself, and obtain a sight of her, even if I took it no further than that. My heart sank a little when I contemplated the prison years, insofar as I could imagine them, the waste of life, the loss of youth. And then, just as I had had a kind of vision of Cosette at that drawing-room table, loaded as it always was with books and flowers, sheets of paper and sewing things, the telephone, glasses for seeing through and glasses for drinking from, photographs and postcards and letters in their envelopes, so I seemed to see Bell as she was almost the first time I ever saw her, walking into the hall at Thornham to tell us that her husband had shot himself.

2

I was fourteen when they told me. They were right, they had to tell me, but perhaps they could have waited a few more years. What harm would it have done to wait four years? I wasn't likely to have married in those four years, I wasn't likely to have had a baby.

Those were the words I used to Bell when I told her this story. She is the only one I have ever told, for Elsa doesn't know, even my ex-husband Robin doesn't know. I confided it all to Bell on one dark winter's day in the House of Stairs, not up in the room with the long window, but sitting on the stairs drinking wine.

It wasn't that my mother's illness was apparent. They weren't even sure she was ill, not physically that is. Mental changes, which is how the books describe her condition, could be attributed to many causes or to none in particular. But they had set fourteen as the age and they stuck to it and told me, not on the birthday itself, which is what happens to the heroes and heroines of romance initiated into family rituals and family secrets on some pre-set coming of age, but two months later, on a wet Sunday afternoon. They must have known it would frighten me and make me unhappy. But did they understand what a shock it was? Did they realize they would make me feel as much set apart from the rest of humanity as if I had a hump on my back or was destined to grow seven feet tall?

I understood then why I was an only child, though not why I had been born at all. For a while I reproached them for giving me birth, for being irresponsible when even then they knew the facts. And for a while, a long while, I no longer wanted them as parents, I no longer wanted to know them. The rapid progress of my mother's illness made no difference. There is no time in our lives when we are so conspicuously without mercy as in adolescence. I turned from them and their secret, her distorted genes, his watchful eyes and suspenseful waiting for the appearance of signs, to someone who was kind and didn't cause me pain. I turned to Cosette.

Of course I had known Cosette all my life. She was married to my mother's cousin Douglas Kingsley and because we are a small family – naturally, we are – the few of us in London gravitated towards each other. Besides, they lived near us or near enough, a walk away if you didn't mind long walks and I can't have done in those days. Their house was in Wellgarth Avenue, which is Hampstead – almost Golders Green. It faced the ponds and Wildwood Road, a thirties Tudor place, huge for two people, which was meant to resemble, but didn't quite, a timbered country farmhouse. When people told Douglas that Garth Manor was very large for just two people he used to reply simply and not in the least offensively, 'The size of a man's home doesn't depend on the size of his family. It's a matter of his status and position in the world. It reflects his achievement.'

Douglas was an achiever. He was a rich man. Every morning he was driven down to the City in his dark green Rolls-Royce to join the queue of cars, even then, in the fifties and sixties, rolling ponderously down Rosslyn Hill. He sat in the back going through the papers in his briefcase, studying them through the thick lenses of glasses in dark solid frames, while his driver contended with the traffic. Douglas had iron-grey hair and an iron-grey jowl and the shade of his suits always matched hair and jowl, though sometimes with a thin dark-red or thin dark-green stripe running vertically through the cloth. He and Cosette led a life of deep yet open and frank upper middle classness. When I was older and more interested in observing these things I used to think it was as if Douglas had at some earlier stage of his life compiled a long list or even a book of upper-middle-class manners and pursuits and chosen from them as a life's guide those of the more stolid sort, those in most frequent popular usage and those most likely to win reactionary or conventional commendation.

All this was reflected in the magazines that lay on Cosette's coffee table, *The Tatler*, *The Lady*, *Country Life*, in the food they ate – I have never anywhere else known such an enormous consumption of smoked salmon – the clothes from Burberry, Aquascutum and the Scotch House, his Rolls-Royce, her Volvo, their holidays in Antibes and Lucerne and later, as the sixties began, in the West Indies. But at fourteen I didn't of course see it like this, though I couldn't help being aware of their wealth. If I thought about it at all, I saw this lifestyle as the choice of both of them, willingly and happily entered into. It was only later that I began to understand that their way of living was Douglas's choice, not Cosette's.

I began going to see her in those summer holidays after my parents told me of my inheritance. She had invited me while on one of her visits to our house. I was a child still, but she talked to me as to a contemporary, she always did this to everyone, in her smiling, vague, abstracted way.

'Come over next week, darling, and tell me what to do about my garden.'

'I don't know anything about gardens.' I must have said it sullenly, for I was always sullen then.

'My lilies are coming out, but they're not happy and it seems a shame, because they have such lovely names. Gleaming Daylight and Golden Dawn and Precious Bane. It says in the catalogue, "thriving in all garden soils, tolerant of both moisture and drought, they can be grown in full sun or partial shade . . ." but I must say I haven't found it so.'

I just looked at her, bored, not responsive. I had always liked Cosette because she took notice of me and never fussed or inquired, but on that day I hated all the world. The world had been injuring me without my knowing it for fourteen years and I had a lot of revenge to take on it.

'We won't have to do anything,' said Cosette, evidently seeing the offer of idleness as a great inducement. 'I mean we won't have to dig or plant or get our hands dirty. We'll just sit and drink things and make plans.'

They had told her I had been told and she was being tender with me. After a while she wanted my company for myself and kindness didn't come into it. But at that time I was just a young relative who had been given a terrible burden to bear and whom she felt she could uniquely help. Cosette was like that. She welcomed me to Garth Manor and we sat outside that first time on the kind of garden furniture the other people I knew didn't have, chintz-upholstered sofas that swung gently under canopies, cane chairs with high backs that Cosette called 'peacocks'.

'Because they are supposed to look like the Peacock Throne but without all the jewels and everything. I wanted to have a pair of peacocks to strut up and down here – imagine the cock bird's lovely tail! But Douglas didn't think it would be a good idea.'

'Why didn't he?' I said, already resentful of him on her behalf, already seeing him as an oppressive, even dictatorial, husband.

'They screech. I didn't know that or of course I wouldn't have suggested it. They screech regularly at dawn, you could set your clock by them.'

There was a glass-topped table of white rattan, sheltered by a big white sunshade. Perpetua brought us strawberries dipped in chocolate and lemonade made out of real lemons in glasses that by some magical means had been coated with actual frost. Cosette smoked cigarettes in a long tortoiseshell holder. She told me how much she liked my name. She would have called a daughter of her own by it if she had ever had a daughter. It was she who told me how it was that Elizabeth became a perennially popular name in England. Since then, though not at the time of course, I have often thought of the trouble she must have been to, gathering this information and a great deal more, just to please me and put me at my ease.

'Because if you say it over and over to yourself, darling, it really is quite a strange-sounding name, isn't it? It's just as strange as any other from the Old Testament, Mehetabel or Hephsibah or Shulamith, and any of them might have got to be as fashionable as Elizabeth if a queen had been called by them. Elizabeth became popular because of Elizabeth I and she was called Elizabeth because of her great-grandmother Elizabeth Woodville, that Edward IV married – so you see! Before that it was as rare as those others.'

'Cosette must be very rare,' I said.

'It means "little thing", it's what my mother always called me and it stuck. Unfortunately, I'm not a little thing any more. I'll tell you my real name, it's Cora – isn't that awful? You must promise never to tell anyone. I had to say it for everyone to hear when I got married, but never, never since.'

I wondered why Douglas hadn't given her an engagement ring and a wedding ring made of something superior to silver, not knowing then that the element was platinum, the latest fashion when Cosette was married. The big diamonds looked sombre in their dark grey setting. At that time Cosette's only excursion into cosmetics was to paint her nails, and these were the bright reddish-pink of one of the clumps of lilies. The gesture she made when she pointed was peculiarly graceful, and somehow swan-like – only that is absurd. Swans don't point. But we think of them as moving with a slow fluidity, a delicate poise, and this too was Cosette.

The flowerbed she indicated was shaped like a crescent moon and the lilies in it looked perfect to me with their red flowers and yellow flowers and flowers snow-white printed with a coffee smudge. The gardener had planted them and ever since tended them. Cosette might direct operations here and in the house, but I never saw her perform with her own hands any domestic task. I never heard anyone, not even my father who was rather carping, call her lazy, and yet lazy she was with an unruffled, easy idleness. She had a tremendous capacity for doing absolutely nothing, though her sewing was exquisite and she could draw and paint, but she preferred to sit for hours in quietude, not reading, without a pen or needle in her hand, her face gentle and serene in repose. For in those days, and she must have been rather older than I am now, something over forty, the sadness I have spoken of had not come into her expression. Simone de Beauvoir, in some memoir, laments age which causes the face to droop and therefore take on a sad look. It was this sagging of the facial muscles which later gave Cosette an almost tragical appearance, except when she smiled.

To me, then, she was old, so old as almost to seem of a different species. Unimaginable that I might live to be as old as that – and unlikely too, as I sometimes thought with bitterness. She was then a large fair woman, overweight, fat even, though in those days she never showed signs of minding about her weight. Her eyes were a pale greyish-blue that seemed to look at you uncertainly, with a wistful and perhaps timid regard. For there was shyness in Cosette as well as confident generosity.

'You think my hemerocallis is quite happy there then, darling?' she said. The names of plants presented her with no difficulty. She might never plant them or pull out the weeds that threatened them but she knew exactly what each one was called. I said nothing, but that did not deter her. 'I suppose I'm being unduly impatient, expecting great things when the poor dears have only been there six months.'

Even I, young as I was, miserable as I was, couldn't help smiling at the notion of Cosette as an impatient person. Her tranquillity was the essence of her. In her company, because of this almost oriental placidity, I – and others – inevitably felt eased of burdens, curiously enfolded by a sweet meditative calm. It made you think in a strange way of its opposite, of the restless briskness so many women of one's mother's generation had and which made people of my age feel nervous and inadequate. She was always the same and always there, always interested, always with nothing better to do.

I soon began visiting her three times a week at least, then staying overnight. I was at school in Hampstead Garden Suburb and it was easy to explain that it was far more convenient for me to live at Cosette's during the week than to go home to Cricklewood. Or that was how I did explain it, an explanation which would soon absurd to anyone aware of the distance between the Henrietta Barnett and Cricklewood Lane. Only the existence and frequent presence of Douglas stopped me attempting to live at Garth Manor. Everyone knows couples of whom one is congenial, the other unsympathetic. For me the return home of Douglas each evening, heralded by the sound of the Rolls's wheels on the gravel drive, cast a blight over the companionship I enjoyed with his wife. He was so male, so stiffly elderly, so stockbroker-ish, much of his talk incomprehensible, and he seemed, without actually asking for it, to require a measure of grave silence in his house while he was in it. And at the weekends he was there all the time.

Cosette changed not at all in her husband's company. She was the same sweet, smiling, calm yet effusive creature, the same woman whose great gift was as a listener. To his accounts of deals and negotiations she would listen with the same rapt attention that she gave to my own outpourings, the retailing of my dreams, visions, frustrations and resentments. And she really listened. It was not that she closed off her mind and wandered in thought to other regions. I marvelled at the intelligent replies she made to his mysterious diatribes and looked with suspicion and lack of comprehension when, getting up from her chair to move swanlike across the room, she allowed one plump white hand to rest softly against the side of his face. When she did this he would always turn his face into it and kiss the palm. This caused me a furious embarrassment. I know now that I didn't want Cosette to have any life of her own, any private life, that was not directly concerned with making mine easier and happier.

She didn't mention the terror and the bore but waited for me to do so. Cosette seldom raised subjects or showed curiosity. I spoke of it – it burst out of me in a passion rather – after a neighbour of hers, a woman called Dawn Castle, had been in the garden with us on a warm October day when the lily flowers were dead and gone and it was the late dahlias that Cosette and I were admiring. Dawn Castle was always talking about her children, what a worry they were, the youngest had just been expelled from school, something like that, and another one had failed an exam. She finished, as she always did, with the old cliché.

'Still, I suppose I wouldn't be without them.'

It never occurred to me that this often-repeated remark might be hurtful to Cosette. I saw it only as profoundly silly and said rudely, 'Why not if they worry you so much?'

She looked shocked, as well she might. 'One day you'll have a baby of your own and then you'll feel differently.'

'I shall never have a baby, never.'

I had spoken very abruptly, and I felt Cosette's eyes on me.

'I'd like a pound for every girl who has told me that,' said Mrs Castle with her hard little laugh, and after that she went home, being one of those people who are only at ease in an atmosphere of small talk and are quickly frightened away by what they call 'unpleasant-ness'. Cosette said, 'That was fierce.'

'It's cruel,' I said. 'People ought to think before they speak. If she doesn't know about me surely she knows about you, she knows Douglas is my mother's cousin.'

'In my experience no one ever remembers about other people's family relationships.'

'Cosette,' I said. 'Cosette, is that why you never had any children? Didn't you want children?'

She had a way of smiling in reply to a question she intended not to answer in words. It was a slow, mysterious smile that overspread her face, vague and gentle, but it somehow always put an end to further probing. I got it into my head then, for no reason, that Douglas had married Cosette without telling her of his inheritance. There was no foundation for this belief, you understand; I read it or thought I read it in her rueful eyes, in a kind of resignation. Adolescents do that, weave impossible romances around the lives of their older friends. I taught myself to believe Douglas had deceived Cosette, denied her children when it was too late for her to retreat, had attempted to compensate by showering her with opulence. That winter they went to Trinidad and I went home, where I found myself watching my mother in an almost clinical way. One day she dropped a wineglass and I screamed. My father came up to me and smacked my face.

It was a light slap, not painful, but I received it as an assault.

'Never do that again,' he said.

'And you never do that again to me.'

'You had better learn to control yourself. I have had to. In our position you have to.'

'Our position? What position? You've got one position and I've got another. I'm the one people are going to scream about, not you.'

Strong stuff for a fifteen-year-old. In the spring I went back to Cosette and Garth Manor from where I could walk to school across the Heath Extension and where I had in my large bedroom with its view of the woodlands of North End such luxuries as my own television and electric blanket and bedside phone. Though I must say, in my own defence, that it was not these things which attracted me. Why do young girls, at this particular stage of their development, enjoy the company of an older woman? I should like to think it wasn't stark narcissism on my part, it wasn't that Cosette, very nearly thirty years my senior, presented no competition, or that my own good looks showed up more delightfully by contrast to her ageing face and body. For as ageing I certainly saw her, aged in fact, past hope as a woman and sexual being. The truth was that I had made Cosette into another mother for myself, the mother I had chosen, not had thrust upon me, the mother who listened and who had infinite time to spare, was prodigal with a flattery I believed and still believe sincere.

In those days she never seemed to mind being taken for my mother. That came later, in Archangel Place, when though she might not express it aloud, the pain she felt and a kind of humiliation at the frequent assumption made that I (or Bell or Birgitte or Fay) was her daughter, showed in her eyes and the wry twist of her mouth. But Mrs Kingsley of the Townswomen's Guild, the Wellgarth Residents' Association, school governor, purveyor of Meals on Wheels and occasional volunteer social worker, had no such vanities. Sometimes, in the holidays or on Saturdays, we would go shopping together and in Simpson's or Swan and Edgar, then still dominating the corner between Piccadilly and Regent Street at the Circus, an assistant would sometimes refer to me as her daughter. The same thing happened in the restaurants we dropped into for the cups of coffee Cosette seemed to need every half hour in order to survive.

'That would suit your daughter,' said an assistant in the Burlington Arcade, and across Cosette's face would come an almost adoring look of appreciation and pleasure.

'Yes, that would suit you wonderfully, Elizabeth. Why not try it on?' And then, as happened so often, 'Why not have it?' which meant she would buy it for me.

I had no impression then that she wanted to appear younger than she was. But would I have had, at fifteen? She dressed in suits which she had made by a tailor, an unheard-of thing today, and something which was old-fashioned even then. They were formal suits, 'costumes' made of cloth very like that which Douglas himself wore, with square shoulders and box-pleated skirts, the kind of garments least suited to someone of Cosette's type. She should have worn floaty dresses, cloaks and draperies. Later on, of course, she did, and not always to happy effect. On the shopping expeditions it was underwear she bought for herself, cruel ineffective girdles and slips of shiny pastel satin, clumping lace-up shoes with two-inch heels, blouses with big bows at the neck to show between the lapels of those worsted suit jackets.

As I grew older I, who had never judged Cosette, but loved her in a simple unquestioning way, became critical of her appearance. I never put this into words, or at least not into words I uttered to her. Sometimes, though, I am afraid I would make these comments to my friends and there would be giggling in corners. Cosette was one of those people whom others laugh at secretly, behind their backs. How cruel that it should be so, how painful! I wince as I form the words. But I am trying to tell the whole truth and it was true that when I brought a friend home (you see how I was then thinking of Garth Manor as 'home') and Cosette appeared, flushed and hot perhaps, untidy as she often was, that bird's nest of greying gold hair a mass of fluff and strands, collapsing and shedding pins, the hem of a silk blouse escaping from the waistband of a tailored skirt too tight over her jutting stomach – then we would glance at each other and giggle with sweet soft contempt.

Quite often, and especially when Douglas was away on a business trip, Cosette would take me and the friend out to dinner in Hampstead. First, though, a preening session took place in her huge and sumptuous bedroom (white four-poster with organza-covered tester, curtains festooned and window seat cushioned, dressing-table with organza petticoat and triptych mirrors) and there in her admiring presence we tried on, like little girls, the clothes Cosette no longer wore, her fur capes and stoles and scarves, belts and artificial flowers and jewels, I always taking care never verbally to admire, for I knew

569

from experience what the result would be. But my friend, out of ignorance or concupiscence, exclaimed, 'Oh, I love it! Isn't it lovely? Doesn't it look nice on me?'

And Cosette would say, 'It's yours.'

It was among these treasures of Cosette's that I first saw the bloodstone. It was a ring, the dark green stone flecked with red jasper embedded in a setting of densely woven gold strands. A ring for a strong hand with long fingers, Cosette said it was, and when she put it on it looked clumsy on her very feminine hand with the shiny pink nails.

'It belonged to Douglas's mother,' she said. I knew what had become of Douglas's mother and the cause of her premature death, but said nothing. I only smiled, the smile that grows stiff as the lips are held unwillingly stretched. 'She was born in March,' said Cosette, 'and heliotrope is the birthstone for March.'

'I thought heliotrope was a flower,' said my friend.

And Cosette smiled and said, 'Heliotrope is anything that turns to face the sun.'

I may not have been as kind to her as she was to me but I loved her, I always loved her. The nastiness of adolescence is ironed out as the senior teens are reached and, just as I now regret with a kind of agony the lack of compassion I had for my mother, so then I looked back with shame on my laughter and contempt. I was able to feel relief that Cosette had never known. For she asked nothing from those she loved except to be able to trust them. Perhaps that is not nothing, perhaps it is a great deal. I don't know, I can't say. She only wanted to feel she could surrender herself, her heart and mind, into the loved person's keeping and be safe there, not be betrayed. Years later, when I saw a college production of *The Maid's Tragedy*, two lines especially struck me, reminding me of her: 'Those have most power to hurt us, that we love. We lay our sleeping lives within their arms.'

Douglas she could trust. Whatever earlier doubts about that I had manufactured, he had never deceived her. He had loved her and made her safe and in exchange she had only to accept the way of life he had imposed on her: the neighbours to dinner and dinner with the neighbours, meetings of the Wellgarth Society in her dining room, Perpetua coming daily to clean, Maggie to cook, and Jimmy to weed the lilies, a view of North End in one direction and the Heath

Extension in the other, inexhaustible money and unending placidity, Dawn Castle running in to drop platitudes from clacking lips, a surrogate child and six bedrooms. Of course it was not unending, nothing is. Cosette was fond of a story supposedly about the dying Buddha and I often heard her tell it in that soft unhurried voice.

'His disciples came to him and said, "Master, we can't bear to lose you, how can we live when you've left us? At least give us some word of comfort to help us after you have gone." And the Buddha said, "It changes."'

I used to smile because nothing ever changed for Cosette. Or so it seemed in those years while I lived most of the time with her and Douglas, her life an unvarying round of small, pleasant tasks, the high spots those holidays in conventionally exotic places, her excitements the dressmaker's delivery of a new evening gown for some livery-company dinner or, I selfishly flattered myself, my own satisfactory A-level results. It changes, but in some lives change is a long time coming.

One autumn morning, when the traffic was particularly heavy in Hampstead and the Rolls-Royce stationary in the queue above Belsize Park station, Douglas looked up from the document he had been reading, laid his head back against the seat and died.

The driver knew nothing about it. Douglas was not in the habit of talking to him unless something untoward happened and a traffic jam would not qualify as that. He had heard a sigh from the back of the car and a sound like throat-clearing, which was later how they were able to pinpoint the time at which death came. When they were down in the City, in Lombard Street, the driver came round to open the door and saw him reclining there with his head back as if asleep. He touched him and the skin of his face already felt unnaturally cool.

Douglas was fifty-three and therefore had almost certainly passed the time when his inheritance could have appeared in him. His death had nothing to do with this particular hereditary disease, for it was quick and merciful, not the long drawn-out torture that awaited my mother. Some kind of vascular catastrophe had wrecked his heart. The doctor told Cosette it happened so fast he would have known nothing about it.

3

They stood in the rain, Cosette and her brothers and their wives, a reception line of mourners under black umbrellas. Douglas, naturally, had had no brothers or sisters. We shook hands with the brothers and sisters-in-law and kissed Cosette on her cheek. I saw everyone else do this, so I did it too. I was there at Golders Green Crematorium with my father, my mother being past going to funerals by that time, or indeed going anywhere. A great many relatives of Cosette's were pointed out to me, but there was only one member of Douglas's family there apart from myself, his and my cousin Lily, an unmarried civil servant, who at the age of fifty was so deliriously happy at realizing she must now have escaped the scourge that even on an occasion like this she could scarcely suppress bubbling high spirits. She came up to my father and laid a hand on his arm.

'Tell me, how is poor Rosemary?'

No one ever asked a man after the health of his dying wife in more cheerful tones. Me she eyed with unconcealed speculation, for she knew, none better, that you can't get it unless one of your parents has it, that if the parent who carries the gene reaches fifty without it, you too will never get it.

Perpetua, who was there with a grown-up son, had told me when I called to see Cosette that she had screamed and sobbed at the news of Douglas's death, had wept hysterically and threatened to kill herself. When I saw her she was crying. I was no longer staying at Garth Manor even part of the time, for by then I was twenty and away at college. If you are at university in Regent's Park you will scarcely live in Golders Green if you can help it. But I rushed to Cosette as soon as I heard Douglas was dead, yet once there hardly knew how to comfort this woman who had nothing to say and who cried without ceasing. I come from a family that makes almost a fetish of not showing emotion and although I would have liked to be able to show it myself, I didn't know how. A friend that I envied – it was that same friend who had benefited from admiring Cosette's jewellery, a girl whose name was Elsa and whom naturally we called Lioness – used to tell me that throughout her childhood her parents shouted and raved at each other, all barriers down, all claws bared, but at least they showed their feelings. From this she believed she had derived the ability to show her own.

So I watched Cosette warily as the tears streamed down her cheeks, without an idea of what to say or do. And a week later her face was still red and her eyes still swollen. Standing there under her elder brother's umbrella, wreaths and crosses of dripping flowers at her feet, she looked as if she had been crying until the moment she entered the crematorium chapel, to stop abruptly only when Douglas's coffin disappeared and was consigned to the fire. She was in deepest black. Her suit was not one of those timeless tailor-mades, but dated from the period of the New Look, post-war, contemporaneous with my own birth, a long flared skirt which I suspect she could only have got into with the zip undone, a jacket with a peplum. I think she must have bought it for the funeral of her own mother, who had died about that time. It smelt of mothballs. Cosette, who was a rich woman, who had inherited from Douglas something in the region of a million, a huge sum in 1967, had not thought to buy a new suit for her husband's funeral. She disliked black, Perpetua told me later, and refused to waste money on something she would never wear again.

This was the first thing about Cosette that ever surprised me. It was the forerunner of many surprises.

There was speculation as to what she would do now. I have since learnt that relatives and neighbours are invariably ready with advice for a woman in her situation, while never suggesting the kind of things they would want to do themselves. The courses they propose always seem designed to keep the subject out of mischief.

No one less likely to get into mischief than Cosette could be imagined. She was forty-nine, but she looked older. Her hair was iron-grey. Her face was drawn and haggard, but she had put on weight, being a woman who ate for comfort. It was Easter and I went to stay with her. Once there, I made up my mind I would follow the example she had set me and be a good listener. I would listen and let her talk about Douglas and her life with him, for some intuition told me she would want to do this, that it would be a catharsis. My intuition was wrong. Bemused, looking slovenly and distracted, breaking off pieces of chocolate and putting them absently into her mouth, she asked me in a vague way what I had been doing, what my plans were.

'I want to know about you,' I said.

She responded with that mysterious smile, slightly shaking her head. It was as if to say her affairs were not important. I read into her look and her gentle insistence on my talking and her listening, an abnegation of a future, as plain as an utterance that her life was over, all that remained a slow decline to old age and death. And this attitude seemed supported by the visitors who came in a constant stream, relatives and friends, the usual widow's advisers with their glib counsel to move to 'a little place by the sea', a country cottage, a 'nice flat' in the Suburb.

'Not too big,' Dawn Castle said. 'Something compact for just you on your own. You won't want to wear yourself out keeping the place clean.'

Perpetua was even at that moment using the vacuum cleaner out in the hall, which made me think Mrs Castle must be deaf or else (more likely) one who never gave a second's thought to the sense of what she said. Cosette's brother Leonard suggested she move nearer him and his wife. They lived in Sevenoaks. A small house or bungalow near Sevenoaks, preferably a bungalow, said his wife, because as Cosette grew older she wouldn't want to climb stairs. She might not be able to climb stairs, this woman hinted darkly, watching Cosette helping herself from a biscuit tin. The other brother lived in one of those huge barrack-like blocks of flats in St John's Wood, an enormous place with four bedrooms he always called an apartment.

'There's a compact little one-bedroom apartment just come on the market in Roderick Court.' He added persuasively, 'It's on the ground floor, so you wouldn't even have to use the lift,' as if Cosette would soon be too decrepit to step across a hallway and press a button.

She listened and said she would think about it. I never once heard her protest when they treated her as if she were on the threshold of senility. Of course women were older then than they are now, even twenty years ago they were. Middle-age then began at forty, but today at nearer fifty. The women's movement has had something to do with this change by altering the significance of beauty. It is no longer vested in youthful bloom, it is no longer even an essential part of attractiveness and attractiveness itself no more the essence of female existence. Cosette had never worked for her living, she had never even worked in the home, her life had been very near that of the concubine, and for twenty-eight years she had been the comfort and support of Douglas, his to be loved or left, to await his homecoming and listen while he talked. They would have been shocked, those callers with their advice, if they had heard this put into words, but they all knew it in their hearts. With Douglas's death Cosette's usefulness was over, just as the harem woman's is over when her lord dies.

She made no promises. Cosette hardly ever rejected any suggestion categorically, but she had her own kind of stubbornness. A refusal to study orders to view, to telephone estate agents, to be shepherded around show houses, is just as much a refusal when indicated by a smiling shake of the head as by an outright no. She was listening more and speaking less then than at any time I could remember. Grief had stricken her dumb, I thought, but later I came to understand she was silent because she had so much on her mind. She had so much to think about, and it was not her past with Douglas. She was making up her mind how to manage what she had set her heart on.

Men call to visit widows in the hope of getting into bed with them. Widows are ready, widows are grateful. Men who have been married for twenty years to the widow's best friend, apparently faithful husbands who have scarcely up till then ever called the widow by her Christian name, turn up sheepishly and make a pass at her in the kitchen while she is putting the tea-bags in the pot. Or so I have heard.

If this happened to Cosette it wasn't while I was staying there. Perhaps my presence put them off. The only possibilities anyway were Dawn Castle's husband Roger and the president of the Wellgarth Society. I have a photograph of Cosette taken in the garden that summer, and it looks like the kind of thing women's magazines use of some reader who wants advice on her appearance. On the opposite page is the same woman after the depilator and hairdresser and make-up artist, and plastic surgeon maybe also, have been at work. I can produce that photograph of Cosette too.

But reclining on the swinging seat, under the floral canopy, she looks blowsy, with her features taking on a blurred look and her hair hanging in disordered loops, lipstick apparently applied in a dark, mirrorless room, sunglasses hanging round her neck on what looks like a piece of elastic. She wears a dress like a cotton tent. At least she had abandoned the tailored suits, perhaps she could no longer get into them, the only change she seemed to have made in her appearance or way of living. For she still sat on her board of governors, went to meetings of the society, had the neighbours to dine and went to dine with them, they making a point of inviting her as if conferring on her enormous favours. No one, however, she later told me, went so far as to produce an unattached man for her. She was fifty, her birthday was that August, and we were living through a period of the cult of youth.

The notion of Cosette having a man friend, a lover, to me was grotesque. For that you had to be young. You might not have to be exactly good-looking, but you had to be attractive in some indefinable way or somehow charming, young and not fat. I had no idea I might be insulting Cosette in having these thoughts about her; I would never have had them at all, I would have supposed attracting a man was alien to her wishes as adopting a child or beginning a career might be, had Dawn Castle not said to me, 'The only thing for poor Cosette would be to marry again.'

Like a Victorian, I was shocked. 'Douglas has only been dead six months.'

'Oh, my dear, it's a well-known fact that if people are going to marry again they do it within two years.'

'Cosette would never want to marry again.'

'That's what you think, but you're young. Someone who's been married that length of time, of course she wants to be married.'

That conversation I remembered when a year later or less Cosette, alone with me, said in a burst of frankness,

'You're always hearing of men being womanizers. I'd like to be a manizer. Do you know what I'd like, Elizabeth? I'd like to be thirty again and steal everybody's husbands,' and she laughed a soft, hopeless, bitter laugh.

But there was no hint of this on the fiftieth birthday she quietly celebrated with a dinner in a restaurant to which she invited my father and me, her brother Oliver and his wife Adele. The Sevenoaks brother was away on holiday. In the taxi back to North End I was alone with her; she cried for Douglas and I put my arms round her, thinking of what Dawn had said, the absurdity of it.

In this house where I live in Hammersmith, in Macduff Street, are things which Cosette gave me. There are probably more things Cosette gave me than came from any other single source, certainly more than any other person ever gave me. For a long time they reminded me of her so sharply, with such pain, that I put them all away so as never to see them, but things changed, as things do – 'It changes,' said Cosette – and I got them out again and spread them about, in the living room, in the bedroom, in the room where I work. This is a little house, mid-Victorian, in a terrace. There is a garden which I am thankful to say is small, a box enclosed by walls like all the other gardens in this street and the next street, so that looking down on them from a helicopter would be like looking into a grocer's box when all the tins have been taken out. The two cats come and go over the walls, never venturing out into the front where the Great West Road threatens, not even knowing it is there or that it is possible for cats to go near it.

The three eggs Cosette gave me, one of chrysolite, one of agate, one of amethyst quartz, sit together in a round glass bowl on the living-room window sill. I had once had an idea of collecting gemstone eggs, but never collected more than these three. On the bookcase is Hans Andersen's Little Mermaid in Royal Copenhagen porcelain, a copy of the one in Copenhagen, which Cosette gave me for my twenty-fifth birthday. It comes in the category of disappointing things, she said, the things that are so much smaller and more insignificant than we expect.

'The Mona Lisa,' Mervyn said, and Gary said, 'The Commons Chamber, a little green box.'

'Niagara Falls,' I said, 'especially now they can turn them off.'

'The Central Criminal Court,' said Marcus.

We all looked at him.

'The Old Bailey, to you,' he said. 'Inside. It's little, it's not imposing. You expect something much grander.'

Strange, aren't they, these remarks of appositeness, of light-hearted, mild cleverness, uttered without thought that they might have an awful appropriateness, with no knowledge of the long shadows they cast before them?

'When were you at the Old Bailey, Mark?' Cosette asked him, and she looked so concerned that we laughed. Well, Bell didn't laugh, but the rest of us did. I think Bell had stopped laughing by this time. Mark said a friend of his who was a journalist, a crime reporter, had got him in. It was a manslaughter case, a man had killed his girlfriend.

'I thought it would be awe-inspiring,' said Mark. 'I wasn't exactly disappointed. I kept thinking about people being there on criminal charges and how it would make them feel less frightened, not more.'

'And would that be a good thing?'

Bell stared intently at him. 'Of course it would be a good thing,' he said. 'Of course it would.'

In the room where I work is a pen jar made of agate, a hollowed-out lump of red and purple and brown and green striped stone, which Cosette brought back from a holiday in Scotland and in it, among the pens, is a curious paper-knife whose handle, also striped in those colours but somehow a different kind of stripes, Cosette swore was carved out of a heather root. Or a bundle of compressed heather stalks or a fossilized heather root, something like that. In this room too are a cigarette-lighter with a blue-and-white Wedgwood base that Cosette gave me because she had it and I saw it and said I liked it. The old, generous, 'It's yours' response, that savours of the lavish hospitality of some clan chieftain or head of an emirate. On a table in the corner is the old manual typewriter on which I wrote my first book at Archangel Place. This machine, a Remington, had belonged to Douglas. When I said I meant to write a book Cosette got a room ready for me, without telling me in advance, she just got it ready for me, she and Perpetua, and led me up there, showing it to me proudly, the desk she had bought in the Portobello Road, the swivel chair, the sofa for 'resting between chapters, darling,' and on the desk the ream of paper, the agate jar full of sharpened pencils, ballpoint pens, the heather-root paper-knife and Douglas's type-writer.

I no longer use it. I use an electronic one, not having yet moved on to a word-processor. Douglas's waits there for when I run out of cassettes for the electronic one, or it breaks down, or for the power cuts that seldom come, though they were frequent enough in the Archangel Place days. The bookcases in this house contain a lot of books Cosette gave me. A complete *Remembrance of Things Past*, a complete *A Dance to the Music of Time*, the complete novels of Evelyn Waugh. A whole set of the novels of Henry James, with *The Wings of the Dove* present, showing no sign of special wear, bearing no marks of time or pressure or pain. But why should it? It was not this copy in tooled blue leather, stamped with gold print, which Bell picked up and looked at, idly turning the pages, inquiring of me indifferently what it was about, Bell who never read anything more demanding than the *Evening News* or a fortune-teller's manual.

The Complete Works of Kipling, the Macmillan red-leather edition, tooled in gold. How Cosette loved sequences and sets! They enabled her to spend more money, be more giving, to overwhelm with a multiplicity of gifts. A dictionary of obscure quotations, a dictionary of psychology, a dictionary of modern Greek which Cosette bought me one Christmas, being unable to get a classical Greek one. And I was cross, I remember, I wasn't grateful or even resigned.

'But I told you,' I said, 'I told you over and over. I said not to get modern Greek. I told you not to get anything at all. What am I going to do with a dictionary of modern Greek?'

And poor Cosette said humbly, 'I'll get you the one you want. I've ordered it. They're going to get it in for me, they're going to get it next week. You'll have two that way. Wouldn't you like to have two Greek dictionaries?'

I stand here in my room looking at the dictionaries and at the sets and novel sequences. I look at my pictures, the water-colours my father gave me from our old house when he moved, the Fulvio Roiter poster of the Venice Carnival, the Mondrian reproduction and the Klee reproduction – and I look at the space where I tried hanging the Bronzino but couldn't, couldn't face the sight of it. Douglas's typewriter is dusty and should be covered up, but there is no cover for it, the cover was lost long ago, probably while Cosette was still living at Garth Manor – pretentious, absurd name; if ever there was an instance of belonging in a category of disappointing things, this was it! – or lost in the move. On the desk, which is not the one Cosette bought in the Portobello Road, I have a London telephone directory and a list of numbers, not in London, that I wrote down from other directories while I was in the public library this morning. The London directory is an old one, but Cosette Kingsley isn't in it. I don't know why I look for her name, for something so impossible, but I do.

The Castles' number I have found, at the same old address in Wellgarth Avenue. It would be useless to phone them anyway, they won't know. But I could ask them for Diana's number, I could ask them where she is now, if she has married. I don't want to speak to them, that is the truth of it, I don't want to have to parry their innocent inquiries or offers of help. Fay's number is written on the piece of paper and so is Ivor Sitwell's. Fay lives in Chester and Ivor in Frome, in a kind of farming commune I gather, a place where they grow organic vegetables. I couldn't find the dancers' number, there was no number either for Llanos or Reed. There is only one Admetus in the phone book, initials M. W., but it must be Walter and he must have moved from Fulham up to Cholmeley Crescent in Highgate. But why should any of them know the whereabouts of Bell, whom they have no reason to care about, whom they may hate?

Also on the piece of paper is Elsa the Lioness's number, not because she lives outside London, but because she is ex-directory and I have had a succession of secret, closely guarded numbers of hers written down in my personal phone-book for years. The latest is on the paper now because it seemed more convenient to have all the numbers together. I have not seen her or spoken to her for a while, a month or two, but it is not the first time months have elapsed without our seeing or speaking, and when I do get to speak to her it will be all right, there will be no reproaches or accusations or grumbles, I know that. The Lioness has been married and divorced and married again and now lives on her own in a flat in Maida Vale. I dial her number but get no answer.

Her cousins, Esmond and Felicity, with whom we used to stay, she and I, live outside the area covered by London phone directories. Or they did and probably still do. I find it hard to imagine anyone willingly leaving that house. But then, of course, people leave houses unwillingly, they leave because they must, as Walter Admetus may have done, because they cannot afford them any more, or find them impossible for physical reasons, because of their staircases and steps up to the front door, their different levels, long passages, heavy doors. I should know that if anyone does. I should know. Then I remember that these cousins had a *pied-à-terre* in London, a studio in Chelsea they hardly ever used, the address of which I don't know, have never known, but in this case that doesn't matter because these cousins have a name so odd, so unique even, that in any phone book in the entire world anybody named Thinnesse is going to be one of them or closely related to them.

It is quite hard to pronounce correctly, that is to pronounce with both those middle n's separately enunciated as Esmond and Felicity always did. 'Thinnis' is the best other people usually attain to. I find their Chelsea number in the phone-book and dial it and, miracle of miracles, someone actually answers. It is not really a miracle at all, it is only what I should have expected. I knew their children must be in their early twenties by now, must be of an age when people are desperate to find accommodation in London away from parents, hostels, tiny furnished rooms. Perhaps I am not very happy admitting to myself that those Thinnesse babies who were three and six when I first went with Elsa to Thornham Hall are now grown up, are of an age to be taken by shop assistants and waiters for my children, just as once I was taken for Cosette's child.

It was the girl who answered my call, the girl Miranda. It is amusing to think that if this girl reads Beatrix Potter to her children it will be because I read Beatrix Potter to her when she was six. Of course we do not mention the Beatrix Potter sessions in the bedroom whose window overlooked the garden of Bell's cottage. She has forgotten them and I have forgotten everything about them except that they took place and that once, while readng *The Tale of Samuel Whiskers*, I saw Bell come out into the garden and peg ragged-looking, greyish washing out on a clothesline.

She tells me, this girl Miranda Thinnesse, that her parents still live at Thornham Hall and she gives me their number, a number which I wouldn't have been able to find in the directory for Outer East London and West Essex (or whatever it is called) because it has recently been changed to deter an anonymous phone-caller who said obscene things to Felicity. For all she knows, since she can't remember ever having heard the name Elizabeth Vetch, I might be the obscene phone-caller myself.

I can't bring myself to speak Bell's name to her. As she talks about her parents and her brother and the first her brother has just taken at Cambridge, I tell myself she will never have heard of Bell, her parents will have forgotten Bell. And then she says, what did I want to ask her parents? Did I just want to have a chat? Or was it something about that woman who killed someone – what was she called? Christine something?

'Christabel Sanger,' I say, and my voice sounds all right, sounds quite normal, as it might if I were speaking any other name, any name at all. And I say it again, to hear myself say it. 'Christabel Sanger,' and then, 'but we called her Bell, everyone called her Bell.'

'Did you want to talk to my mother about her?'

I sound remote, almost indifferent, or I think I do. 'I want to ask your mother if she knows where she is living.'

'Well, all I can tell you is she phoned my mother. She'd just come out of prison, an open prison I think, and she phoned home. I don't know why. It was a while ago now, I mean weeks. I think she phoned a lot of people. My mother could tell you more. Now you've got the number why don't you phone my mother?'

I say I will and thank her and say goodbye. It is strange what it does to me, this confirmation that Bell is back amongst us, that therefore it really was Bell I saw. It makes me feel a little sick, nauseous, no longer looking forward to the dinner I am being taken out to. Weeks ago she had phoned Felicity Thinnesse and 'a lot of people', but she hadn't phoned me. Me she had fled from along the streets of Notting Hill, had hidden from to elude me, had seen and stared at without smiling, seemingly without recognition. Or had not seen, had never seen, had not eluded, had merely gone into a shop outside Queensway station to buy a paper or a pack of cigarettes or a flower. Me she had perhaps tried to phone, had dialled my number many times, while I was away. For I have been away, was away first in Italy and then for a week staying with my father, who lives in a bungalow at Worthing now, the kind of bungalow they wanted Cosette to buy when she first became a widow.

I have gone upstairs into my bedroom to change my clothes, telling myself that I have no time now to speak to Felicity, telling myself that when I do speak to Felicity she will want to know all kinds of things I may not want to talk to her about. She may, for instance, ask me about Marcus, or even something about what the set-up was in Archangel Place just before Bell did what she did. She may invite me to Thornham Hall, and I am not sure whether or not I want to accept such an invitation. Probably I don't. Or suggest a meeting when next she and Esmond come to London. I move about my bedroom opening cupboard doors, opening drawers, looking at the phone extension and deciding to postpone the making of this call until tomorrow morning. Now I have in my hand a pincushion Cosette made me. It is in the shape of a strawberry and made of red silk, with the seeds on the strawberry's satiny outside embroidered in pale yellow thread. The pincushion is heart-shaped and fatly padded and it has never been used for the purpose it was designed for because I have been afraid to spoil the texture of the silk.

The cameo brooch in the jewel box was one of her birthday presents to me. The face in profile on it, carved from rosy-cream, strawberry-cream, coral is like Bell's, a classic profile, high of forehead, straight of nose, the upper lip short, the mouth full, the chin of perfect depth, and the hair, loops and tendrils of it arranged in careless Regency fashion, disarrayed and tumbling, ringleted and tangled, is Bell's hair. I was taken by Cosette to choose this cameo and chose it because the face was Bell's, wore it expecting everyone to notice, to comment, to say, 'The girl on your brooch looks just like Bell,' but only Cosette noticed, only Cosette remarked on it.

I shall wear it tonight, going out with this man I haven't known very long, but like well enough. He is taking me to Leith's, something I have known for days and dreaded. How could I go to Notting Hill, the taxi perhaps passing the end of Archangel Place? How could I, in company, revisit those streets which were once my world, where everything that ever happened to me happened? All is changed and I no longer feel like this. I have been there, I have been back, following Bell. I am even excited. And I know the excitement does not stem from the prospect of sitting in a taxi with Timothy, eating dinner with Timothy, but because, up there, where Kensington Park Road meets Kensington Park Gardens or Ladbroke Square, I may see Bell again.

Tonight may be the night I shall find her.

— 4 —

After my mother was dead I went home to live with my father. I hated it and he hated it and both of us, I think now, saw it as our duty, I to be there and he to take me in. The arrangement endured only from the end of June until the end of September, my long vacation. He returned to work long before September came, before August came, I spending my days with Elsa and at Garth Manor with Cosette. Near the end of it my father suggested I go away for a holiday, without thinking perhaps that there was no desirable foreign place to which I could get a package he would pay for at such short notice. Most of the people I knew had already filled up the minibuses and Bedford trucks making for Turkey and India. His dreadful suggestion that he and I should together have a few days in Colwyn Bay caused his voice to falter with dismay even as he was making it. I compromised and went for a week with Elsa to her relations in Essex.

She used to talk of these relations, an aunt, a cousin and his wife and their two children, and somehow gave me the impression that it was north Essex where they lived, the Stour Valley, Constable Country, or the marshes, Great Expectations land. Or that was how I received it, which is nearer the truth. Essex is a big county. When we set off towards the Central Line tube, I thought at first this was merely the first leg of our journey, that we should change trains at Liverpool Street, but no, Elsa bought a ticket for herself and a ticket for me to Debden, which is getting on for as far as the line goes. A huge council estate lay outside the station and my disappointment was bitter.

Elsa laughed and said, 'Wait a little, said the thorn tree,' a very nearly incomprehensible remark which was a favourite of hers and had something to do with Africa and the lioness personality she cultivated at that time.

Esmond Thinnesse came to meet us in a Morris Minor Estate car. He was older than I had expected, fair-haired with glasses and, fortunately with that name, extremely thin. Felicity was thin too and so was his mother, Elsa's Aunt Lois, and I used to wonder if there had ever been a fat Thinnesse and if so what misery and humiliation had he or she suffered. Or did Thinnesses keep themselves thin by rigorous diet and exercise and mortification of the flesh? There was no sign of this while Elsa and I were there, large, lavish meals being provided and partaken of enthusiastically by everyone. And no one was made to go out for healthful country walks.

For country it was, as deep I am sure as that to be found on the other side of Chelmsford. The Morris Minor took us no more than two miles away from the Debden Estate but the little red-brick terraces stopped and the straight white dual carriageway stopped, and the shiny opal-green roof of the factory where they make notes for the Bank of England disappeared behind the trees, and the lanes became narrow and winding, the hedges high, the river Roding running between willows and alders. Thornham Hall had no place in the category of disappointing things. It was a real hall, with fifteen bedrooms and a library and a morning room. I sometimes used to think about those houses, so many of them, Jane Austen puts her people in and describes as 'new-built, modern'. Thornham was one such, about 170 years old when first I went there, austere, elegant, square, a balustrade running round its shallow roof, wide bays on either side of its flat, porchless front door. It stands on an eminence commanding a view of the winding Roding, of Epping and the villages, someone of incredible foresight having planted a screen of scotch pines and Wellingtonias, six trees deep, to conceal the houses for East End of London overspill no less-inspired person could have imagined ever being built. Now, I suppose, Thornham also has a view of the M25 motorway cleaving a long white wound through the meadows.

Its own estate, with vestiges of the feudal, stood near to it: stables, a cottage or two, a farm with barns at the foot of the hill. And there were huge trees, horse chestnuts and limes, fan-shaped screens of elms that must be gone by now, felled by the disease that changed the face of the countryside. I had never before stayed in a house of this size and eminence, have not done so since. It was almost in the class of houses you are taken round on conducted tours. Esmond's father, a merchant banker, had bought it just before the Second World War, so in no sense was it a family home, he being really the first generation of Thinnesses to live there.

Today, in similar circumstances, I think we girls would have called his mother by her first name, but then she was Aunt Lois to Elsa and Lady Thinnesse to me. Her husband, Sir Esmond, had been rewarded with a knighthood for some particular merchant-banking service two years before he died. To me she was very old, though I suppose no more than in her late sixties. A rather carping though good-natured woman, she lamented the changes in her environment, notably, obsessively, the building of the Debden Estate. These moans dominated her conversation and went along with an often repeated regret that Sir Esmond, on their marriage, hadn't bought a house farther out in the countryside. She would ask me, or anyone else who happened to be with her, why he had failed to foresee that the London County Council, as it was then called, would take over some of the most beautiful pastoral land in the Home Counties for their 'slum clearance'. I was unused to such reactionary talk and her terms shocked me. She gave the impression that her marriage, at least from about 1950, had been permanently soured by her disillusionment over Sir Esmond's lack of prevision.

Also staying in the house was a friend of hers, an old woman called Mrs Dunne, who came from another, more rural part of Essex, and who was worried about proposals to extend the capacity and area of Stansted Airport. No conservationist except where her own immediate interests were involved, Lady Thinnesse showed a bored indifference to poor Mrs Dunne's anxieties and wound up any discussion of Stansted with the advice to her friend to move.

'It isn't as if you had a big house, Julia. You aren't trapped like I am.'

Felicity Thinnesse, who was a tease and liked showing up in company the follies and insensitivities of her mother-in-law and her mother-in-law's guests, used to enjoy what she called 'winding up' this old woman in front of us. In fact I think Mrs Dunne liked it, had no idea Felicity was anything but serious, and rather appreciated attention from 'the younger generation'. Julia Dunne had once been a Master of Foxhounds and such had been her life and the narrow circle she had always moved in that she had no notion there were people existing – at any rate middle-class people in England – who might consider blood sports cruel or degrading. At the same time she loved animals. Certain horses had played a more important part in her life than her husband had, as far as I could tell. She had once had a pet fox which she had reared from a cub when its mother had been killed by the hounds.

'Didn't you ever think of that as being a bit odd?' Felicity asked her, innocently interested. 'I mean, hunting foxes and keeping a fox as a pet?'

'Oh, no, dear. I was very careful about that. I always shut him up in the stables when the hunt came by,' said Mrs Dunne.

Grave-faced, Felicity said she found it hard to understand this new disapproval of the keeping of battery hens when it was obvious they were safest while in those boxes. No fox could get them there. Julia Dunne was enchanted by this defence of factory farming. You could see she was storing it up for future use. Later Felicity told me that back home in north Essex Mrs Dunne used to crouch behind hedges with a stout stick in her hand, ready to club down any rabbit that might start eating the plants in her flowerbeds.

Felicity found the presence of her mother-in-law as a permanent resident and her mother-in-law's friends as temporary ones a cross to bear. Life was a laughing matter to her, sometimes a sick joke, and she demanded amusement, entertainment, as her daily food. Her husband was a quiet, dull, rather clever man, religious in a conventional Anglican way. Just as Lady Thinnesse usually had someone staying so did Felicity, but Felicity demanded more of her guests, far more; she expected wit and stories and even contributions such as young ladies made at Victorian parties, she expected visitors to play or sing or recite something. And she expected us to take part in the quizzes she set and the debates she instituted in the evenings and which would continue long into the nights. Elsa told me that on a previous visit, just before the Act of Parliament which made homosexuality legal between consenting adults in private, Felicity had organized a debate that 'This House will abolish outrageous laws that purport to interfere in the private sexual behaviour of adults'. Lady Thinnesse had had some other old woman guest with her and this person had immediately said that if this kind of thing were to be discussed it would be 'above her head' and she would go to her room. Lady Thinnesse had soon followed her. The debate had gone on until three in the morning, only breaking up when one of the children was heard crying upstairs.

On that occasion, Elsa said, the people from the cottage had come up for the evening and had taken part. They were friends of Felicity. Silas Sanger had in fact been an old boyfriend of Felicity's, they had parted on the best of terms, Felicity to be courted by, become engaged to, eventually marry Esmond Thinnesse, Silas Sanger to live with and later marry (or not marry, as Lady Thinnesse appeared to believe) Christabel. He was a painter, but not the sort who ever made much or any money by his painting, not the sort of 'artist' that Lady Thinnesse had known and approved of in her younger days. He had had nowhere to live, had been through some kind of breakdown, and Felicity had persuaded Esmond to let him and his wife, or non-wife, live in one of the cottages near the house, the one that was in the better state of repair.

There he continued to paint, feverishly sometimes, at others sporadically, gloomily, from time to time doing nothing, lying on his bed all day, suffering what Felicity rather inaccurately called a dark night of the soul. He was a ferociously heavy drinker and the substances he drank were bizarre. What Christabel did no one seemed to know, at any rate no one said, and she appeared as something of a mystery. These people were due to come up to the house for dinner – a dinner that would be cooked by a woman who cycled over from Abridge – and remain to join in the debate, scheduled to be on the subject: 'This House deplores the present divorce law and would make divorce possible between consenting parties after two years' separation'. Such a provision was, of course, to become law in 1973. I couldn't imagine there would be any dissenting voices, unless Lady Thinnesse and Julia Dunne consented to take part, which they had already declared with shudders to be out of the question, and I was surprised when Esmond said in his mild way that as an Anglican he must disapprove of any kind of divorce in any circumstances. Did Felicity remember that gently uttered but decisive statement when she ran away to Cosette's?

The painter's wife I had already seen. Reading to Miranda, the two of us sitting on the window seat in her bedroom, I could see the garden below and around us, the fans of high elms full of chattering starlings, the small meadow with the two horses and the big meadow shorn of its barley crop, the giant conifers that hid so much, that were always, at any time of the day, black silhouettes. I could see all this without raising my head and it was all curiously like what I was reading, all like the illustrations to *Samuel Whiskers*, the same sleepy windless pastoral, the same birds going to rest, the same sky of very high, small myriad clouds. To the right, on the slope of the hillside, stood Silas Sanger's cottage and its garden, a fenced plot of shaggy grass with nothing in it but two clothes posts with a length of dark-grey rope sagging between them. The cottage and its surroundings had an air of neglect. If Beatrix Potter had drawn it and been faithful to its true appearance, she would have used it as an illustration of the home of some villain of her animal world, a fox perhaps, or Bad Mouse. Curtains there still were at the window, but these were torn or coming down or, in the case of those at one downstairs window, apparently refusing to be drawn back, had been looped to either side of the frame with what looked from my vantage point like string.

Out of this hovel and into this small wilderness, as the sun was setting and those tiny clouds coloured with pink, came a tall girl too thin and too decorative to be one of Millet's peasants but having an air about her of some Fragonard woman. This was in the carriage of her elegant head with its crown of soft, fair, untidy piled-up hair, in the length of her narrow neck, in the bunching of her clothes, a long full underskirt, an overskirt clenched in at the waist with a scarf wound round and round, a low-necked blouse, a jacket over it of thin clinging stuff, the sleeves rolled up, a ribbon or two hanging in streamers, the whole in a variety of tones of brownish-pinkish-dusty-beige. No such personage ever entered the pages of Beatrix Potter. She carried a tray, not a basket, an ordinary tea tray laden with wet washing, which she proceeded to peg out on the clothes line.

I paused in my reading and said to Miranda, 'Who's that?'

On all fours she clambered over me. 'That's Bell.'

'She lives there with the painter?' Lady Thinnesse's view had almost unconsciously communicated itself to me.

'Silas is Mr Sanger and Bell is Mrs Sanger. Her washing looks as if it hasn't been washed, don't you think?'

It was all the same sort of light grey and there were big holes in something that might have been a pillowcase. I said it didn't look very clean, only to be reprimanded by Miranda.

'I'm not supposed to say that and especially you're not because you're grown up. Mummy says it's despicable to say things about people's washing being dirty. Go on reading, please.'

The girl in the garden, the girl called Bell, pegged her clothes out on the line with a kind of weary indifference. You could see her heart was not in it. Her whole stance, her attitude, the way she held her body, spoke of something worse than boredom, of encroaching despair. I had the impression those wet clothes had been lying about all day and at last, at an absurd time to hang out washing, at the close of the day, when the sun was setting, she had forced herself to drag the pile of it out here and rid herself of it, committing it to whatever fate awaited it from the dews of night. The tray empty, the line filled, she stood with the tray held loosely against her, stretched to her full height, gazing down into the valley, raising one hand to shade her eyes from the red sun's glare in a pose so Fragonard-like that she might have learned it by studying a reproduction in a magazine. But somehow I sensed she had no idea she was observed. Miranda reminded me once more that I was supposed to be reading to her and I reluctantly drew away my eyes.

The debate party was two days after this and in the event neither of the Sangers came to it. There was a phone in their cottage, according to Miranda, but they had had it cut off or it had been cut off due to non-payment of the bill. A note was put through the letter-box of the Hall rather late in the afternoon, certainly after the time the cook from Abridge had already arrived. Felicity read it aloud to us with a kind of exasperated resignation. She wasn't cross, she was amused – disappointed but amused by the way Bell did things like this.

'"Felicity: Sorry, we aren't going to come. I am not equal to it. Yours, Bell." She's proud of always saying what she means, not telling social lies – well, not any lies really.'

Felicity smiled at us, flinging out palm-upwards the hand that was not holding the note. She truly believed Bell never told lies, that Bell told the truth on principle no matter what the cost or how much moral courage was required. She believed this and we, hearing her tone and seeing her expression, believed too. Thus do utterly false testimonials of character and probity spread.

'She'd hurt someone badly rather than lie to them,' said Felicity. 'She'd involve herself in endless trouble. It's admirable in a way, you have to admire it.'

Yes, we had to admire it and did. I am not at all sure that Lady Thinnesse and Mrs Dunne admired it. They had looked at the small, torn, dirty piece of paper, written on in pencil, and then glanced at each other and Lady Thinnesse said, 'What does she mean, she isn't equal to it? Isn't she well? Does she mean she isn't up to it? Your debates can be rather strenuous, Felicity.'

'Living with Silas can't be any bed of roses,' was all Felicity said.

I was disappointed. I had looked forward to meeting the Fragonard woman who carried her washing about on a tray and hung it on the line at dusk.

'Wait a little, said the thorn tree,' said Elsa.

'That's all very well,' I said, 'but we've only got two more days here. Can't we go and call on her?'

'I don't think we could do that, I really don't. He is rather strange, Silas Sanger. Rude, you know, and often drunk. He wouldn't ask one in if he was in one of his moods, and he mostly is. In a mood, I

590

mean. He doesn't like anyone much except Felicity – he adores her.'

'Doesn't he like this Bell?'

'I've only seen them together once,' said Elsa, 'and he didn't take any notice of her at all, not any notice. He didn't speak one word to her.'

'Are they married?' It was more important in 1968 than it became soon after that.

'Frankly, I wouldn't think so.'

The debate was postponed and we went home without meeting Bell or Silas Sanger, Elsa promising to take me there again soon. This I didn't take very seriously. I knew I should have to spend the Christmas holiday with my father. Or try somehow to manoeuvre my father to spend Christmas at Cosette's. For Cosette was still at Garth Manor, withdrawn, quiet, grieving it seemed, and apparently unable to make up her mind whether or not to move. Then she told me she meant to take the holiday she and Douglas had intended to spend together in Barbados. It was arranged for Christmas and the New Year, she had never cancelled those arrangements, and she would go. This announcement was curious in that it was a preparation for another announcement she was to make as soon as she returned, something far more momentous, something to stun us all. In the meantime I could comment to Elsa and to Dawn Castle's daughter Diana how very odd it was of Cosette to return to the hotel on Barbados where she and Douglas had stayed twice before, to return there alone and a widow, anticipating the pain and bitter nostalgia surely such a revisiting must evoke.

I thought I was condemned to sharing my father's Christmas and then he told me, with apparent insouciance, that he had been invited to spend it with my mother's cousin, that Cousin Lily who had been in such high spirits at Douglas's funeral. And he wanted to go, he was looking forward to it. I hadn't been asked, he said, but he would inquire if he could bring me. This was spoken in such a tone of gloom and grudging unwillingness that I almost laughed out loud. Please don't, I said, please don't trouble, you'll have a great time without me, you'll be better on your own. He gave me a sidelong look, he asked if I thought it would be all right. And then I understood he felt he was doing a daring thing, a thing likely to give rise to gossip, for my father belonged in that generation, the last perhaps to think this way, who believed there was something improper and even scandalous in sleeping under the same roof alone with a member of the opposite sex. Times had changed, I said, no one would care. He seemed disappointed.

Thus I was free to go to Thornham Hall with the Lioness.

Two memorable things happened that Christmas. The first was Felicity's quiz.

Felicity was apparently as famous for her quizzes as her debates. She composed them herself, using the *Encyclopaedia Britannica*, *Brewer's Dictionary of Phrase and Fable*, Steinberg's *Dictionary of British History* and the *Oxford Dictionary of Quotations*. The quiz forms were typed by her and she did as many carbons as the typewriter would take, this being before the days of ubiquitous photocopying. We were to undertake this particular quiz on the day after Boxing Day, 27 December.

The Thinnesses' house was full. Mrs Dunne was there and Lady Thinnesse had also invited an ancient brigadier and his wife. He had risen to this rank during the First, not the Second, World War, which gives some idea of how very old he was. Felicity had her sister and her sister's husband and their twins and a friend called Paula she had been at college with and the friend's daughter and everyday local people from Chigwell or Abridge or Epping came as well. On the day in question there might be as many as fifteen of us doing the quiz, the children being excluded. No mention was made of the Sangers, Silas and Bell, and I concluded they hadn't been asked. I concluded more than that, that a coolness now existed between the Thinnesses and the Sangers, and this was confirmed by Jeremy Thinnesse, aged three.

'My daddy wants Mr Sanger to go away and live in another house.'

'Really?' said the Lioness. 'Why would that be?'

'It's despicable,' said Miranda loftily, 'to wheedle information out of children who are too young and innocent to know better, Mummy says.'

It was not clear whether she referred to Elsa's conduct or possibly Silas Sanger's, but it had the effect she aimed at, that of stopping the conversation. No more inquiries were made. I found myself often looking in the direction of the cottage, but saw no one. The clothes line had gone and the two posts and the place looked unoccupied. Whether Silas and Bell celebrated Christmas I didn't know and don't know to this day, their life inside there was a mystery, their ways secret and surely wildly unconventional. Sometimes smoke could be seen rising from the cottage chimney and this fretted Lady Thinnesse, who seemed to think the house would catch fire.

After lunch on 27 December we all sat down in the hall to do the quiz Felicity had prepared, our twenty questions typed on two sheets of paper, foolscap size. This room, rather than the drawing room, was chosen because the latter being enormous took a great deal of heating and the weather was very cold. The hall at Thornham is itself very large, with the two-branched staircase mounting to a gallery at the back of it, but this area can be closed off with double doors, making a cosy chamber at the front where the fireplace is. A big fire of logs had been lighted and chairs and two sofas drawn up in three hundred degrees of a circle round it.

Thornham Hall has no porch and there is no inner lobby or vestibule, so draughts tend to come in round the front door. The long windows on either side of it rattled in the wind, but it was warm enough round the fire. Lady Thinnesse wore only a thin silk dress and seemed to take it as an insult to her household arrangements that Mrs Dunne had a shawl round her shoulders and Felicity's sister had put on fur-lined boots. I remember precisely where I was sitting in the circle: on the right-hand side of the fireplace and directly facing the front door. Felicity's brother-in-law sat on one side of me and her college friend on the other. It had been tacitly arranged that the old people should have their seats nearest to the fire, and between the college friend Paula and the fireplace were sitting the ancient brigadier, the ancient brigadier's wife and Mrs Dunne, with Lady Thinnesse and an old couple from Abridge facing them. The children were all up at the other end of the hall playing with their Christmas presents and warmed by a portable electric radiator.

Felicity handed out the papers, our names written on the top of them. I think it was at this point that I began questioning what I was doing, what we were doing, taking part in an examination we were not obliged to sit, giving up our leisure to an absurd general-knowledge test, vying with each other in a pointless contest. And for what? For what? A quarter bottle of brandy was the first prize and a box of chocolates the second. The force of one woman's personality dictated our obedience. No one had considered demurring, though those old ladies certainly must have feared failure and humiliation, that, in Bell's curious phrase, they would not be 'equal to it'.

Felicity had a chair at that point of the circle furthest from the fireplace, directly facing the fire, where for a few moments she had ensconced herself between her husband and Elsa the Lioness. To that chair she never returned, but stood watching us as we turned our eyes to our papers, a tall, strongly built yet slender dark woman, Juno-faced with massy black hair and the faintest black down on her upper lip, miniskirted as was the fashion, though not a fashion designed for a woman as strapping as she. Thirty minutes we could have, she said, precisely half an hour, the maximum possible score fifty points. Then she went over to the children, turning on lights as she passed the switch.

It was three-thirty but already dusk. The red light from the fire had been inadequate to see by. Some of the contestants were already writing, but I did what I had been taught to do and read through the questions on the paper before I began. I don't remember all the questions, only the first and the fifth. The first inquired what were Germinal, Brumaire and Fructidor and what did they have in common? I think the second question was something to do with architecture, the third with Second World War battles and the fourth with Shakespeare. The fifth question required contestants to explain what were Pott's disease, Klinefelter's syndrome and Huntington's chorea.

It gave me a shock, I felt the blood rush into my face, and that everyone must see that crimson blush. Inescapably, paranoiacally, I thought it was deliberately set for me, geared for me, designed as some kind of mockery of me. At the same time almost, or immediately afterwards, I knew of course that it couldn't be, that Felicity was not a cruel or vindictive woman, and moreover she didn't know, couldn't know, no one knew but my father and his Cousin Lily and my mother's doctor and Cosette. Elsa the Lioness didn't know. There was nothing to show, nothing in my appearance, my face, eyes, bodily movements. I had even been told (and my mirror told me) I was good to look at, beautiful even. If it was there waiting for me as it had waited for my mother, my grandmother, her father, it lurked silently in my central nervous system, hidden, static, resting, biding its time.

I looked up to meet the eyes I expected to see fixed on me, but all of them were looking at their papers with varying degrees of comprehension, lack of comprehension, pleasure, dismay. Most of them were writing. My eyes returned to the paper. Huntington's chorea. The words stood out of the rest of the text as if executed in boldface. My hands were shaking, the hand that held the pencil and the hand which, trying to grip the sheets of paper, failed and trembled as if Huntington's had already struck, had sent its first tremors down the nerves.

For once, of course, when experiencing trembling or lack of coordination or ordinary failure of manual dexterity, I had no real fear that this was the onset of Huntington's, I knew it was the effect of shock. But I told myself that I must exercise control, I must behave as if nothing had happened. And after all nothing had happened, everything was the same as before I read the questions on the paper, nothing had changed. 'Huntington's chorea' were words I repeated to myself if not every day of my life, almost as often. But for all these reassurances, trying to steady my still-shaking right hand, I found myself quite unable to answer the questions, unable to write a word. I knew, for instance, that Germinal, Brumaire and Fructidor were months in the French Revolutionary calendar, knew even (because I had had occasion to look this up not long before) that these names had been invented by Gilbert Romme, but when I brought the pen to the paper my hand felt paralysed. I tried to read the remaining questions but the print danced before my eyes, and when I forced myself to eye the lines of type as coolly as I could, the sense of what was there failed entirely to communicate itself to my brain.

It was almost funny. I didn't see it at all like that then, but later on, much later, I did. I saw it as an extreme irony that I, whom Felicity had certainly picked along with Elsa and Paula and her brother-in-law Rupert as her white hopes, her high scorers, would end up with a blank exam paper while the brigadier's wife, a self-confessed ignoramus, would certainly have answered three or four questions correctly. And this had happened to me not through simple exam nerves or drinking too much wine at lunch but solely as a result of the emotive, almost occult, power of a question composed by Felicity with a view only to demonstrating the superiority of intellect of those she saw as her own personal friends over her mother-in-law's cronies.

I looked up. I met Elsa's eye and she winked at me. She had been busily writing away and I could see she had a good chance of winning the brandy. I was wondering what to do, whether to admit to a sudden onset of blankness of mind or, more deceitfully, feign illness and escape upstairs to my room. I was wondering this and at the same time letting my gaze wander vaguely about the room, from Felicity kneeling on the carpet and helping her nephews build a fort from plastic bricks, to the tall, over-dressed, candle-laden Christmas tree in the corner diagonally opposite the fire, to the two long windows and the unrelieved misty dusk outside, back to Elsa feverishly scribbling, her head bent and her lower lip caught under her upper teeth. The room was silent but for an occasional crackling from the fire, a clearing of the throat from Felicity's sister, who had a cold. Even the children, raptly attentive to new toys, made no noise.

I had decided. I would stay there and face it out. What did it matter? People are made happy by such defeats of others. I had turned the papers over, so that the name would no longer leap black-lettered out at me, was reaching out to return my pencil to the box of pencils on the low table where the triumphant Elsa, her quiz completed, had already returned hers, when the front door flew open to let in a gust of wind and Bell Sanger.

The front door at Thornham was locked only at night. I expect things are different today. Then it was always unlocked and everyone knew it, but still Bell's eruption into the hall was a shock. The wind blew the papers the contestants were holding and actually blew Lady Thinnesse's quiz out of her hand and straight into the flames of the fire. She jumped up with a little shriek. Bell stood there, on the rug, in fact some kind of animal skin, just inside the door, her clothes and hair blown by the wind, a wild woman with staring eyes. Felicity got up from her knees and said rather crossly, 'For God's sake, shut the door.'

And Bell did. She reached behind her and pushed the door which slammed. The whole house seemed to shake. Bell said, 'Would someone come please? Silas has shot himself.'

Someone said, 'My God,' but I have never known who it was, one of the men. Esmond got up, pushed his chair aside to let himself out of the circle, and took a few steps towards her. Bell didn't wait for him to speak.

'He was drunk,' she said. 'He was playing one of his games. He shot himself. I think he's dead.' She hesitated, looking at us all with a kind of dawning dismay, realizing who we were, as if we were the last people she would want to communicate this to, to share this with.

But what could she do? What choice had she? We were there, we were the only people, it was unavoidable. 'He was playing,' she said, addressing these words to Felicity. 'You know what I mean,' and, incredibly, it seemed that Felicity did.

She nodded, one hand going up to her mouth. Esmond said, 'Felicity, phone Dr Thompson, will you? And perhaps the police, yes, we have to phone the police.'

Felicity said, 'Christ, what a thing! What a thing!' She seemed to realize she was surrounded by staring children. 'Come with me, all of you,' and she scooped the children up, putting each arm round two or three of them.

My eyes met Bell's. She looked at me, I thought, as if I might be the only one there she could like, who might have some sort of affinity with her. Or that is how I took it, how I received her steady, aghast, long, grey-eyed stare. Esmond opened the front door and held it for Bell to precede him out into the dark. I got up and followed them.

— 5 —

Stiletto fatalis, far from being some sort of weapon, is the Latin name for the flaw worm, an agricultural pest. The entomologist who devised it must have had a sense of humour. There were posters in the Thornham village shop warning farmers to beware of this creature, and Felicity got hold of the name and made a tremendous joke of it. That Christmas, at any rate before the shooting of Silas Sanger, she was always talking about *stiletto fatalis*. If she had included a question on it in her quiz everyone would have been able to give the right answer. Stiletto heels were in fashion that winter and at parties, especially in houses with woodblock floors, you were given little plastic heel caps to keep the spike heels from making stab marks. All the floors at Thornham Hall were of wood, scattered with small carpets and large rugs. Felicity always examined the shoes of newcomers and gave a verdict on them, whether they could be classed as *stiletto fatalis* or not.

This aspect of her, which I thought I had forgotten, which I hadn't thought of for fifteen or sixteen years, the last time I saw her, comes back to me in the morning as I am making up my mind to phone her. I remember *stiletto fatalis* and how it and all its successors had given place, by the time Felicity was taking refuge at Cosette's, to a new conversational obsession with Selevin's mouse. Nothing much had evidently occurred in Felicity's life since then if she was, as it appeared, still married to Esmond, still chatelaine of Thornham, no longer perhaps much resembling the dramatic intense girl in a mini-skirt who had confided in Cosette evening after evening. I regard the piece of paper on which I have written down the number Felicity's daughter gave me. I dial it. For last night, though I went to Leith's, though I got the taxi to drop me on the corner of Pembridge Road and walked the rest of the way, I didn't see Bell, of course I didn't.

Felicity answers the phone herself, using, as soon as she knows who it is, her unchanged characteristic greeting.

'Hallo, there!'

I once heard Esmond introduce himself to some newcomer as 'There', saying his wife had re-christened him. She sounds just the same and as if the the last time we spoke was a couple of weeks ago. There is no marvelling that I haven't been in touch before, am in touch now, am still alive, and there are no reproaches. She doesn't even say what a surprise it is. I have no recollection of her being so wrapped up in her children twenty years ago or when she abandoned them for nine months to the care of their father and grandmother. But now she talks of them. She talks of them immediately she has been through the polite requirement of asking how I am, taking my 'How is everyone?' *au pied de la lettre* and telling me all about Miranda's amazing job with BBC Television and Jeremy's history first. She even follows this up with genius's mother's cliché number one:

'And do you know we despaired of him, he didn't do a stroke of work!'

I let her go on a bit, then tell her I have spoken to Miranda.

'Oh, did you manage to catch her? What a relief! You've actually taken a load off my mind. I haven't spoken to her for days, you know what they're like, so elusive and of course quite indifferent to one's very real terrors. It's a simple relief just to know she's around and in possession of her faculties, answering the phone and so forth. And now tell me all about you.'

598

That can easily be avoided. 'Miranda told me you'd spoken to Bell Sanger. I thought you might give me her address.'

A silence. Then the voice changes, becoming stagey. 'Oh, my dear, I don't have it. I have a phone number. Do you remember those wonderful London phone exchanges, Ambassador and Primrose and Flaxman? So easy to remember. This is six-two-four something. What on earth would six-two-four have been?'

'Maida. It's Maida Vale and Kilburn.' So that is where Bell lives. I feel a little bit faint; I am breathless to know more, afraid we shall be cut off, that I shall never learn those four remaining digits. 'Six-two-four what?'

And I am right to be afraid, my fear is justified, for she has it written down somewhere but just where she can't remember.

'You know the size of this house, Elizabeth!'

'How was she?' I say, unable to keep this back, unable to contain it. 'How was Bell? Did she seem – well, not happy, no – resigned?'

But Felicity isn't going to answer this, perhaps has no opinion on it. She was, and no doubt is, a self-absorbed woman, interested not in the feelings of others but only in her own feelings about them. 'I wish I could have seen you to have a good talk when all that happened,' she says. 'After the trial, ideally. I had such a lot of things to tell you, inside stuff really. I mean there was such a lot I knew about Silas, personal, intimate things, though of course she was always a mystery. But you disappeared and one does have some reticence. Running you to earth wasn't really on. Oh dear, that does remind me! Do you remember that awful old woman I used to wind up about fox hunting? My mother-in-law's still alive, can you believe it? Eighty-six and sound as a bell – O God, you wanted Bell Sanger's number, didn't you? Look, I'll have to find it and call you back.'

'I would very much like you to do that, Felicity.'

'Of course I will. I'm going to ask you something and if you think it's too awful of me just don't answer. Don't put the phone down but don't answer, you don't have to. Now then. Did it ever cross your mind Bell might have shot Silas herself?'

I do reply. I say in a silly, faint, mealy-mouthed sort of way, 'Not then.'

'Well, no, not then of course. But at the time of the trial? I mean when all those other things about Bell's past came out. It did mine, I can tell you. And I knew all about his games. I knew all about what he got up to and his drinking and I still thought Bell might have shot him. Oh, Elizabeth, I wish we could meet and really talk this through. I mean it's fascinating, don't you think? Are you ever down this neck of the woods?' Mercifully, she goes on without waiting for an answer, 'No, I don't suppose you are. We shall have to meet in London sometime. We still have the flat, but of course you know that if you've talked to Miranda. Look, I'll call you back without fail and give you that number and then we can fix something. I can't promise when but it'll be today absolutely without fail. Goodbye till later. We'll speak again soon.'

She has always had that power of exhausting those she is with or just talking to. With some people it may be enjoyable, but it is also a wearisome battle to be in their company. And there are others, like Cosette, who revive their companions, revitalize them, leave them feeling restored and content simply by their own attentive listening and ability to ask the right small questions at the right time. When I got home from Thornham after the death of Silas Sanger – and Elsa and I were peremptorily dispatched by Lady Thinnesse on the following day – I gave an account of all of it to Cosette. And she listened, she was interested, she seemed really to want to know. By that time Elsa and I together with Paula and Felicity's sister had been amply regaled by Felicity on the subject of Silas's games.

Silas had two guns, a twelve-bore shotgun and a Colt revolver, which he claimed to have bought from a stallholder in the Portobello Road market, a man who sold silver. He had a passion for guns, which was not easy to gratify in this country where to collect guns and have the appropriate licence and so forth you have to be a respectable person with no criminal record and one who doesn't mind visits from the police. Silas, of course, had no gun licence. Felicity told us he used to play Russian roulette with the Colt and that was the least of his games.

'They don't kill themselves, those people, but they don't care for their lives the way the rest of us do. They do reckless things, they tempt fate.' I thought she looked wistful, as if she rather hankered after being that kind of person herself. 'You know how Carmen goes to the most dangerous places, sets herself out to get the dangerous men?' We didn't know. I at least had never heard *Carmen* then, not even on records. 'And at the end she doesn't have to get herself killed, she can easily avoid it, but she's too proud to avoid it and anyway, what else is there for her?'

Was Felicity saying Silas was like that? And if you take the analogy with *Carmen* as far as she took it, to the end of the last act, what was she implying?

She said Silas liked to play firing squads. It was never quite clear whether she had been the partner in these games or had only heard of them. If she had been I could understand she might not want the rather strait-laced High Anglican Esmond Thinnesse to know about it, and therefore could not risk telling us. What she did tell us was that Silas would get his woman, in this case presumably Bell, to gag him and tie him up, he having previously loaded one of the guns, the Colt or the shotgun. She wouldn't be told which one was loaded. She was to choose one and shoot him as a member of a firing party might do. Of course neither Bell nor her predecessors were good shots; he had taught them the basics of handling a gun and that was all. Felicity said that after her affair with Silas came to an end she met him once with his arm in a sling and he said he had been shot. She concluded some woman had picked the right (or the wrong) gun, but the shot had gone a bit wide.

He never shot animals or birds, that didn't interest him, and he was a vegetarian. Another one of his games was to get his girls to shoot at a target with the aim of improving their marksmanship, and just as whoever it was – and I believe at least once it was Felicity herself – took aim and fired, dash across in front of the target. He liked the naked terror, the loss of control, the screams.

'But was it something like this he had been doing that last time?' said Cosette.

'I don't know. I don't think anyone knows.'

'This girl called Bell must know.'

'If she does I don't think she'll tell.'

We walked across to the cottage, Esmond, Bell and I, through the wind and darkness. Can it really have been so dark at four o'clock even in December? I remember it as dark and the shock I felt at seeing the cottage in darkness, at observing that Bell had left no lights on. She had not at any rate locked the front door but left it on the latch as the front door to Thornham Hall was always left. We went in and lights were switched on and there was Silas Sanger lying dead on the floor.

I think it was at this point Esmond realized I was there. You see, no one had spoken a word since we came out of the Hall. Esmond realized and turned to me and said something about it not being right for me to be there, for me to see such things. But by then it was much too late. I had seen and Esmond had seen and he had gone very pale.

It might have been worse. I remember thinking that. Silas's face was intact. He had shot himself through the neck, severing, it later transpired, the spinal cord. He lay in a lake of blood and his face reminded me of paintings I had seen – they are legion – of John the Baptist, or rather the head of John the Baptist, in a dish of blood, being held by Salome. His face was a translucent greenish-white, white-lipped, the red-brown curly hair and beard and moustache looking very soft and somehow young. I thought I could look at this dead man with detachment, with simple interested curiosity, and I had no feelings of nausea, no physical revulsion. Or so I thought until my knees sank earthwards and a terrible faintness overcame me. I don't think the others saw. I sat down and breathed deeply, my eyes closed, and heard Esmond say, 'What happened?'

'He'd been playing with the Colt. It's there on the floor, in the – in the blood. He said he was going to fire it once, out of the window. To see what happened. He meant to see if you'd come out, I think.' When Felicity, later, was telling us about Silas's games she also told us that his indiscriminate letting off of the Colt and the shotgun was the reason for the quarrel between him and the Thinnesses. Esmond had been horrified, had had no idea of Silas's propensities. Silas must go and at once. The difficulty was that he and Bell had nowhere to go. And now she had nowhere to go. 'I went upstairs then,' she said. 'The bugger didn't fire out of the window. He was playing Russian roulette instead.'

She was very calm. It was despair, perhaps. She sat down on the only other chair in the room, looked at me and performed that action known as casting up the eyes, a curiously inadequate gesture in the circumstances. It suggested not so much shock or grief as exasperation. That day she was dressed in assorted garments of browns and greys – Bell's clothes were never like other people's, though a few years later they were to become wildly fashionable in the alternative mode – and the bundled layers were caught in at her thin, stalk-like waist by what looked like a luggage strap. There was blood on her left sleeve.

She said to Esmond, 'Cover him up!'

Esmond looked round the room for something to serve the purpose. It was a sparsely furnished, squalid little room with linoleum on the floor and cut-off pieces of carpet serving as rugs, two upright chairs and a horsehair sofa, a gate-leg table with a broken leg propped up on a flowerpot and bookshelves made of planks resting on bricks. A shawl, hand-crocheted in shades of mud and granite, obviously Bell's, was draped over the back of the sofa and this Esmond covered the body with, an action for which the police later reprimanded him. But everything felt better; the atmosphere didn't exactly lighten, yet it was like a sigh of relief. It was possible to keep one's eyes open, to breathe, now that face and that awful neck were hidden.

'You had better come back to the house,' Esmond said to Bell. 'You had better let Elizabeth take you back. I'll stay here.'

'I'm staying here,' she said.

I went back alone and in a few minutes the police came. Cosette, when I told her all this, asked me what Bell was like to look at and then what age she was. She had become, I noticed, very interested in other women's ages.

'Like an actress in a Bergman film.'

Cosette, dating herself, revealing the preoccupations of her own youth, mistook my meaning. 'Ah, yes. *Intermezzo. Casablanca.*'

'Ingmar,' I said. It was the era of the director. No one any longer knew the names of stars. 'Like a Swedish actress, tall and thin and with a long neck but very soft features, a little straight nose and full lips, big eyes. Masses of sort of dusty fair hair. About, I don't know, twenty-five?'

'As young as that?' said Cosette.

I thought she meant Bell was very young to have experienced so much, and perhaps she did. But it was from this time, I believe, that Cosette's obsession with age began to grow. It was as if she had slept away her life, or most of it, and had woken up in a panic to find it gone and irrevocable. The sad, wistful look came into her face. It had nothing to do with her grief over Douglas and not much to do with the sagging of facial muscles, which came later. It was a change wrought in her by that awakening. I think she saw Bell in her mind's eye and thought that to be twenty-five again and tall and beautiful would be worth any amount of suffering and tragedy and poverty and deprivation. But of course I don't know what she thought, I can only guess, I can only hazard ideas about her in the light of what happened later.

'And they sent you home next day?' she said.

'Well, you can understand that. We must have been in the way. They sent everyone home and took Bell into the house and I think they were very nice to her.'

'There would have to be an inquest, wouldn't there?'

'I don't know. Perhaps. Yes, of course there would. She told us what happened, you know, later on. She wouldn't stay in the room with him when he started playing with the gun. She went upstairs and sat in the room where all his paintings were. It must have been very cold, it was icy in that cottage, and there were only oil stoves heating it. He had been drinking, the stuff he usually drank, cheap wine with methylated spirits in it. She told us in a very matter of fact way. And the thing was she told all of us, I mean Elsa and Paula and Felicity's sister and brother-in-law, that didn't seem to bother her, the fact that we were strangers.

'She sat up there, looking at his paintings. Apparently she had some idea his paintings might be saleable; I mean, in the sort of way he would have scorned. Some of the landscapes she thought she could take down to the local pub and ask them if they'd hang them in the bar to see if any of the customers would pay five pounds for one of them. It seems they were desperately poor – to the extent of not getting enough to eat, only he always had his wine. Anyway, she was sitting up there thinking like this when she heard the Colt fired, she heard a shot. It wasn't specially unusual, that, but what followed was. She heard a sort of gurgle, an awful sound, she said, between a groan and a gurgle. So she went down and she found him and if he wasn't dead thirty seconds before, he was by the time she got there.'

Not a very credible story, was it? But I believed it then and Cosette believed it. Cosette wasn't the sort of person to ask the question Elsa asked me some months later: why couldn't Bell have got a job if they were so poor? Jobs were to be had then, it was different from now. But I never knew Bell to keep a job of any kind, then or later or ever. A very strange thing happened to make employment for her not essential: a few hours before Silas died his father had died of heart disease. He wasn't a rich man and he had no savings, but he owned the house he lived in and though he had made no will, he was a widower and Silas his only child. It came automatically to Bell, for Silas and Bell had been married, she was as much his wife as Felicity was Esmond's. She sold the house for £10,000 and this sum, when invested, brought her just enough to live on, just enough to scrape by on without working, to hang on by the skin of her teeth.

All this was in the future. I knew nothing of it when I was relating my story to Cosette. I awaited a verdict from her, a summing-up. I meant to receive it, discuss her conclusions, then (on the grounds that it would be good for my psyche) if my mood could be rightly established, confide in her question number five of Felicity's quiz and confess my foolish tremors, my spontaneous terror. I was so entirely accustomed, you see, to Cosette as listener, Cosette as recipient. When Cosette talked about herself it was almost an affront. As, instead of pronouncing on the probable fate of Bell or the curious cerebral processes of a man who played firing squads with his wife, she now did:

'I have bought a house.'

It was hardly an astounding act but only what everyone expected her to do sooner or later. I looked inquiringly.

'I made an offer for it before I went to Barbados.'

She could have a very childlike look sometimes, the look of a child who expects to be reprimanded. I asked her where this house was.

'It's in London.' She lived in London already. I waited. 'It's in Notting Hill. You'll like it, it's a big tall house on five floors with a staircase of 106 stairs. I counted. I call it the House of Stairs.'

I must have looked rather blankly at her. It all seemed to be out of character, so unlike Cosette, whose two weeks in the heat had reddened her skin but done nothing to reduce her weight. One of her cotton tents enveloped her. The chignon her hair was done up in was very like Bell's but on her not Fragonard-like, only untidy. The flesh-tinted transparent rims of her glasses had been mended with a piece of sticking plaster. All I could think of was, how was she going to manage climbing all those stairs?

'You won't have so far to come to see me,' she said.

'Notting Hill?' I said. It was still, at any rate the northern and western parts of it, a slummy, shabby, dirty and dangerous area of

London. The street carnival, an annual event that had begun a few years before, led to trouble, recalling the violence of the riots of the fifties. I asked her why she wanted to live there.

She said naïvely, 'It's in the best part. It's Bohemian.'

'Why do you want somewhere so big?'

'I don't suppose I shall be on my own – much. People will come.' She was looking at me anxiously now, doubtfully, in need of reassurance. 'Don't you think people will come?'

What people? Dawn Castle and her husband? Elderly Maurice Bailey, president of the Wellgarth Society? Her brothers? 'Well, I suppose. If you invite them. They all expect you to live in a flat or a bungalow.'

'There are a lot of young people in that part of London,' said Cosette.

It seemed irrelevant. 'But what will you do?' I said.

'Live,' said Cosette, smiling, and then, perhaps because she thought that sounded pretentious. 'I mean I will just live there and – and see.'

It is absurd the way I am waiting for Felicity to phone. I am waiting with the breathless anticipation of someone expecting a call from an unreliable lover. What will happen if she phones while I am out? Will she call back again? I dare not take the risk so cannot go out. This should be a good opportunity to get on with the book I am currently writing, and I might with truth say that I have at least sat in front of my typewriter all day, or on and off all day. And the sheet in the typewriter is not blank. No doubt though what is on it is rubbish and will all have to be done again. It and its contents, its theme and plot and personages, fail to distract my thoughts from Bell. And when I abandon it, though still sitting there, looking from Cosette's agate jar and the curious heather-root paper-knife to Douglas's old Remington on which my first books were typed – with such enthusiasm, with such excitement – when I turn my attention from it and try to think instead of my first visit to Archangel Place when Cosette took me there on a bitter day in February, concentration is impossible and this too fails. Remembering the House of Stairs as it was that day, the yawning icy rooms that seemed to branch off that winding trunk of staircase like leaves from a twisted bough, goes no further than remembering this, evokes no consequent memories of acts and activities, of the changes that came, of the people that came, of Cosette's 'salon'. Bell alone occupied my thoughts. I remember her in those early days, or rather, I remember what I heard of her, what Elsa and Felicity told me of her, for she vanished from any scenes of mine for more than a year.

But then, after Silas had been covered up with that shawl (a shawl Bell later calmly went on wearing) I went back to the house and left them there, Bell and Esmond Thinnesse. And after a long while, several hours, after the police had been and a doctor, and all sorts of adjuncts of the police, Esmond brought Bell back to the house and she walked into the drawing room where we all were. It was almost palpable in the air, the embarrassment everyone felt, everyone that is but me and Felicity, who doesn't know what embarrassment is, and Elsa. I could tell the others were wondering what they were to talk about, how the rest of the evening was to be passed, now Bell was among them. But their difficulty was momentary. She stood there and said in a voice of cold disdain, a voice that made nonsense of what she said, 'I am sorry to be the cause of so much trouble.'

An odd thing to say, wasn't it? Surely poor dead Silas was the cause, he and what he had done? She said it and immediately turned and went upstairs. Felicity was later obliged to go after her and ask her if she wanted anything, a drink, for instance, or something to eat, a share in the supper of cold Christmas leftovers we were all picking at downstairs. Bell refused everything. Next day the police were back, talking to her, and after being closeted with one of them for a long time in Esmond's study, she walked in among us.

She was all in black. But I later came to know she often was, it had nothing to do with mourning for Silas. I had never seen anyone like her, never before encountered that air of indifferent confidence and tragic poise. Sorry for her, pity for her, I never felt, though perhaps I ought to have felt it. After all, she was a widow, she had lost her husband only the day before in the most appalling circumstances of violence and horror. I felt only admiration, the kind of hero worship I had not had for anyone since I had a crush on the music mistress some seven years before. What I would have liked was for the two of us to go away somewhere and talk. I would have liked to be with her, alone with her, to talk and learn about her and tell her about me.

Of course this was impossible. Elsa and I were going back to

London, were due to be driven to Debden tube station by Esmond in about half an hour's time. Felicity's sister and her husband and children had already gone by car, taking Paula and her daughter with them. Bell came close up to the chair where Felicity was sitting with the little boy Jeremy on her lap. She laid her hands lightly on the back of the chair, holding her head high, that mass of untidy fair hair, hair the colour of tarnished brass, plaited and tied up on top of her head with a piece of string. Without looking at Felicity, looking at the plaster mouldings on the ceiling, the cornice, the elaborately pelmeted tops of the windows, she asked if she could remain at Thornham a little longer.

'Not in the house. In the cottage. Just until I find somewhere.'

Felicity was beginning to say, 'But, my dear, of course, of course you must, I wouldn't dream . . .' when Bell said, 'I know Esmond doesn't like me. I know you don't any of you like me.' Did I imagine her roving glance coming to rest for a moment on me and the slightest change, a softening, in her expression, as if she made an exception of me? 'But I have,' she said, 'nowhere else to go.'

She had a reputation for being honest. On the way to the station Esmond said to us, 'It's true I don't much like her. Frankly, I didn't like him. But one can say for Bell that she's a totally honest person. She is incapable of deceit.'

It is interesting how such reputations are built. They come about through confusing the two kinds of truth-telling: the declaration of opinion and principle and the recounting of history. Bell always expressed her feelings about things, her beliefs, with frank openness. It wasn't in her, for the sake, say, of politeness or social ease, to say she was pleased about something when she wasn't or that she liked something or someone when she didn't, or that she didn't mind when she did mind. And because of this, because of this well-known honesty of hers, it was assumed – no, taken for granted – that she also told the straightforward transparent truth about what she had done, what her past was, what had happened. I came to know, and it was a hard lesson, that Bell was in fact one of the world's grand liars, who tell lies from choice and, I think, for pure pleasure.

On that occasion she told Felicity she had nowhere to go and Felicity, first denying for all she was worth the plain truth that no one at Thornham much liked Bell, offered her the cottage rent-free for as long as she might want it. Bell nodded and said thanks in that laconic way of hers that she could make sound as if she had little to be grateful for.

'What shall I do about the blood?' she said.

Felicity nearly screamed. She put her hand over her mouth. Jeremy was staring, big-eyed, mouth open.

'Someone will have to clean it up.'

'The police will see to that, Bell,' Esmond said. 'You can leave that to the police.'

That was the last time I saw her, as I have said, for two years. Elsa told me that she had no relatives to take her in. Her parents were dead. She had no profession, was trained for nothing, her life since she was nineteen had been the wretched sharing of Silas Sanger's poverty and the homes he had contrived for them, a cottage that was no more than a hut on an estate in the Highlands of Scotland, a room in south London, a coachhouse loft in Leytonstone, finally this cottage of the Thinnesses. The knowledge that she was to inherit Silas's father's house took her away from Thornham and translated her to that house, first to live in it, then to sell it and realize from the sale a skimpy income. She moved out of the orbit of Esmond and Felicity and such lesser moons as Elsa and Paula who circled about them, and for quite a long time was lost among the unnumbered galaxies that made up the youth of London in the late 1960s.

It occurs to me as I wait for the phone to ring that it is possible Bell herself will still phone me. When the phone does ring it may not be Felicity, whose voice I longed for, but Bell, who would be much the greater prize. In moments of stress, when alone, I always talk aloud to myself. Does everyone? Do you?

'Are you mad?' I say aloud to myself. 'Are you mad to care like this, to need like this? What do you want and what do you need after so long, after receiving so little, after knowing everything? Are you mad?'

But I don't pursue that one. Madness is something we don't speak of lightly, frivolously, in our family, for madness of a kind we are also heirs to, the schizoid delusions associated with our inheritance. I don't pursue it and, strangely, when it gets late, too late for anyone reasonably to phone, much too late for Felicity, I feel a curious unexpected lightening of the heart.

Of the figures who come into our dreams, according to the Jungians, the only ones whose identity we can be certain of are ourselves. When I first read of this I wanted hotly to deny it, for hadn't I often encountered Bell in my dreams? And Cosette and even, once or twice, Mark? But I came to see that they were not in fact themselves, but only figments that exhibited aspects of those people, that often metamorphosed, changing into unknown personages or half-forgotten acquaintances or even animals. Why this should be, taking into account how little we really know of those who are closest to us, is no mystery, but a warning not to be hasty with our assumptions about the nature of others or complacent about our knowledge of the human heart.

So it wasn't Felicity I dreamed about last night but only someone who looked and sounded like Felicity, and that not for long; someone who, once she had led me into the grey garden in Archangel Place, turned her head and showed me a changed face, the face of someone I can't name but connect with that time, a face I find it hard to say was a man's or a woman's. Before that happened we had been in the House of Stairs together, and from Cosette's table Felicity had picked up the sheets of paper on which her quiz was typed. Some were untouched, some half-completed. She said, as I never remember her saying at the time, as I would remember if it had happened, 'That woman is such a fool, she has identified Huntington's chorea as a geography book. I suppose she thinks the Isles of Langerhans are off its coast.'

Freud's dream theory has been much ridiculed. But no one disputes the wisdom of his suggestion that in trying to understand our dreams we should write accounts of them as soon as we wake up, keeping pencil and paper beside the bed for this purpose. Felicity's remark didn't pain me in the dream as it would have done had I been conscious and she real. I was amused by it in the dream, and hastened to write it down. Then I reflected on the rest of the dream, how she and I had gone outside where the plants in the grey garden were taller and more luxuriant than I remember them, where even the flowers were not yellow or white but a metallic, silvery grey. We stood looking up at the back of the house, a tall house of five storeys and a basement, but not as tall as in the dream, in which it had become a tower whose pointed top was half-obscured by the lowering London sky.

But the windows were the same. These wide apertures, one on each of the four middle floors, pairs of glazed french doors really, opened on to narrow balconies with low plaster walls. But on the basement floor and on the top the windows were simply long narrow sashes. It wasn't Mark who came out on to the fourth-floor balcony from the room that was once mine, it wasn't Bell or Cosette. The figure who stood up there leaning perilously over the wall was a child's, a child I didn't recognize but that Felicity knew, that Felicity or the possessor of the changed face she turned to me recognized as one of her own. She began shouting at the child to be careful, to go back.

'Go back, go back, you'll fall!'

And now I am reading my account of this dream along with Felicity's remark, which no longer seems so brilliant to me, so witty, as it did at first. Written on the paper too is Bell's phone number which she gave me when she phoned me this morning, accosting me with her cheerful, 'Hallo, there!'

I asked her what I had not been able to bring myself to ask her yesterday. (How much joy do we miss through cowardice?) I asked her why Bell had phoned her.

'Oh, Elizabeth, I thought you knew. Didn't I say? She wanted your number.'

Joy, indeed. Immediately I reproached myself for feeling such a surge of happiness. I should know better, I should have learned something in all those years, after so many friendships, a marriage and other loves.

'Didn't you give it to her?' I realized as soon as I said this that there was no reason why she should have known it. It is a long time since we have spoken, though something to Felicity's credit perhaps that it doesn't feel long, that she, maddening woman though she is, has that quality of taking up the reins of friendship and driving merrily along as if no lapse of years had ever been. 'No, you couldn't have. I'm in the phone book in my married name. My publishers wouldn't give my number.'

'I didn't try them. Frankly, I thought Bell would be the last person you'd want to be in touch with. After all that happened.'

I realize now, after some hours have passed, that she thinks I was in love with Mark. Maybe others thought so too. That, they suppose, is what accounted for my unhappiness and my withdrawal. I contemplate this number that begins with the three digits six-two-four, the Maida number, but I do nothing more with it, I only look. Strangely, the last thing I need to do at this moment is dial it, speak to Bell. I am so supremely content to know she wanted mine, that her sole purpose in phoning Felicity was to ask for my number, that I feel no need to proceed further – yet. I feel, sitting here in my workroom in front of the typewriter, rather as I felt on the very few occasions in the House of Stairs when I smoked the cigarettes Bell passed to me at the window's edge: at peace, serene, there is no tomorrow or if there is it is of no significance, there is only the everlasting, delicious, tranquil now.

In which to recall Cosette seems to come naturally.

She didn't mean to live alone in the House of Stairs. She was going to have Auntie with her and Dawn Castle's daughter Diana.

If I haven't mentioned Auntie before it isn't because she was unknown to me or played a small part in Cosette's life, but because it is so hard to know what to say about her. She was a cipher, a little old woman who seemed without character or opinions, almost without tastes, who seemed to dislike nothing yet enjoy nothing. I have never known her Christian name. Cosette always called her 'Auntie', though she wasn't her aunt but I think her mother's cousin. We – I mean the crowd of the young – were supposed to call her Mrs Miller, but no one ever did for long and she became 'Auntie' to us too. To her we were all 'dear', because our names eluded her memory, even Cosette's.

Two or three years earlier Auntie had been living in a miserable room in a run-down part of London. Somewhere in Kensal Rise I believe it was. She was being harassed by a landlord who wanted the house vacated so that he could sell it, and was plagued too by the four-man jazz band who occupied the top floor. Cosette had always looked after her, paid her some sort of allowance, had her shopping done, taken her out. She and Douglas rescued Auntie and bought her a tiny one-room flat near them in Golders Green. From this flat Cosette removed her and carried her off to Notting Hill.

She gave no reason for doing so. Auntie had seemed quite happy where she was, though it was always hard to make any sort of assessment of the state of her emotions, and if Cosette could have gone from Golders Green to Kensal Rise to tend to her she could probably have made the journey equally often in reverse. It may have been a simple act of kindness. I shouldn't express surprise at Cosette's kindness, which was so frequent as not to be remarked, and yet I came to believe there was another motive. I came to see that Auntie was needed in the House of Stairs for her role in the attempted recapture of Cosette's youth.

Her presence had no effect on me one way or the other. It was different with Diana Castle. My reactions to her being asked to live there, given a room there, were I am afraid those of jealousy and resentment. You have to understand that, without being fully aware of it then, I had replaced my mother with Cosette – and this not just since my mother's death but long, long before. Of course I should have known that Diana's being there didn't exclude my being there, that I was always welcome, that there would always be a place for me, that Cosette took it for granted and supposed I did too, that her home was my home whenever I chose to make it so.

I sulked a little. I had my degree and I wandered about Europe, meeting nomadic people like myself, thinking of the books I meant to write. The first of these was in fact written in Cosette's house, but not yet, not then. Instead, I went off to do a year's post-graduate teacher training, something I have been glad of since, but which was undertaken as a result of the injury I felt Cosette had done to me, a result of sulking.

The House of Stairs I had seen once or twice and had responded to it in a way which might have been more justly expected from my own father, say, or Mrs Maurice Bailey. I saw it as big, old, dirty and cold, the stairs a curse and a handicap, the arrangement of the rooms – the kitchen was in the basement, all the best living and sleeping space loftily high up – seemingly designed to be as inconvenient as could be, the steep staircase and windows dangerous. The second time I saw it Cosette had moved in, had been in three weeks, but the furniture still stood about where the removers had stuck it, the crates of books and china and glass remained unpacked, the windows uncurtained and the phone not yet connected.

But the third time I went there all was changed. I had been away and Cosette had been busy, though this is the wrong word to use about someone so gently and contentedly indolent. Others had been busy on her behalf: Perpetua who still came to her, travelling down each day on the 28 bus, Jimmy the gardener and handyman, a troop of carpet fitters and curtain hangers. The rooms hadn't been re-painted, that was something she refused to have done, and their faint faded shabbiness suited them, keeping them from a glossy *Homes and Gardens* look, though there was never much danger of this *chez* Cosette. But the windows had been festooned with curtains in slub silk and curtains in velvet, with Roman blinds and Austrian blinds and Chinese bead curtains that were mêlées of rainbows when they moved and showed pastoral pictures, remote and oriental, when they hung still. I don't think Cosette any longer knew there were such colours as brown, as beige, as fawn, as grey. The house gleamed with rich blues and reds and purples, with emerald green, with dazzling white. And in her own wardrobe gone were the tailored suits and gone the cotton tents in tablecloth patterns. That day when I came in, when I used the key she had sent me and mounted the stairs, carpeted now in blood red, came to the top and found her seated at her table, she was in yellow silk on which blossomed white daisies and red roses and sprays of green fern. And that was by no means the only change in her.

She put out her arms and without a word I went to her and into that embrace and we hugged each other. Being sent the key had touched me, had moved me near to tears, the trust it implied. I hugged Cosette and felt her warmth and smelt her scent and felt the new thinness of her under the slippery silk.

'I've been on a diet.'

'I can see,' I said.

'The doctor told me to lose weight because of my blood pressure.'

It was a shy look she gave me, her eyes not meeting mine. I had a curious feeling that though she was telling the truth, it wasn't the whole truth. This wasn't her honest and entire motive for losing weight.

'You've done something to your hair.'

Cosette put up her hand to the reddish-brown coiffure. 'First of all they tint it to your natural colour and then every time you have it done,' she said confidingly, 'they tint it a slightly paler colour until you end up nearly blonde. That way all the grey gets sort of absorbed and doesn't show.'

'Yes, I see,' I said.

Had that ever been her natural colour? Come to that, had it ever been anyone's natural colour?

'The hairdresser says it takes ten years off my age.'

I wasn't going to deny it, though I couldn't see it myself. The strange coppery colour made Cosette's face appear tired as the grey never had, and worse than that, her hair looked like a wig. I told her heartily that she looked very nice, it was all an improvement, and this seemed to make her happy. She said I must come and see upstairs, I must see 'my' room, and I half-expected her to jump out of her chair with a new lightness of step. But she was the same languid Cosette, apparently with all the time in the world at her disposal.

We climbed up, looking into the rooms as we went. Auntie was out in the garden, sitting in a deckchair, sleeping probably, so we looked into her room up on the next floor, a big room full of old lady's things, a strange radio from the forties in a polished wooden case, silver-paper pictures and a collage of sepia postcards, antimacassars on the two armchairs. A flypaper hung from the central light. I looked out of the window which, being at the back, was one of those glass-doors-opening-on-to-a-balcony arrangements. Among all that grey foliage the top of Auntie's head looked rather like a white chrysanthemum. She was sitting with her hands folded and her legs up and stretched out. If she had been doing anything, sewing for instance or even reading, I think I should have been very surprised. But she was doing nothing, just existing, basking in a mild autumn sun, the grey leaves all around her. Later I came to learn that the smoke-coloured tree which made dappled shadows was a eucalypt, but I didn't know it then, I didn't know the names of anything in that pale, ghost-like garden.

Cosette had allotted me a room on the floor above, but at the front. It had one of the Venetian bays. I have harped rather on windows, I see, as if I noticed them more than I noticed the proportions of the rooms and their sizes. Of course I didn't. It was what happened later that makes me think I must always have been more aware of the windows than of any other feature of the House of Stairs, even the staircase itself, aware not only of their size and shape but of the danger to which they exposed those inside them. The ones at the front were safe enough, with their deep sills or guarded by their graceful iron baskets, but at the back of the house

– what careless architect had designed windows that were in fact glass doors out of which you stepped almost into the void, on to at any rate a narrow ridge of plaster with a low wall a child could have stepped over? And one at the top which, when open, was just a doorless doorway?

The room that was to be mine had a bed in it and crates and crates of unpacked articles. I began to wish I hadn't committed myself to that teacher-training course. For some reason, and this sort of attitude isn't typical of me, I wanted to start unpacking and arranging immediately. The sun was shining, the last sun before the winter came perhaps. On the balcony in a house opposite, an austere Parisian angular balcony very unlike the ones on this side, a woman was watering geraniums. There were more trees in the street than cars.

'You can come every weekend,' said Cosette.

Going downstairs, we met Diana Castle and a boy coming up. Their appearance had been heralded by the front door slamming and making the house shake, shivering on its spine of stairs. Diana kissed Cosette and to my surprise the boy did too. They went on up into the room that became known as the room of the 'Girl-in-Residence'. Who coined the expression I don't know, perhaps Cosette herself. The door up there slammed too. Cosette smiled in a way I knew meant she was glad Diana could make herself at home in her house.

She said to me, 'I like the idea of having a girl living here. I'd like it to be you, but until it can be I'll have someone else. People do seem to like it here. I *am* pleased.'

Diana was supposed to look after Cosette a bit, do some shopping, clear up after parties, count and pack up the laundry, things like that, but not cleaning. Perpetua did the cleaning. But if Diana started off doing these tasks she soon gave it up, just as her successors did. With the best will in the world it is almost impossible to wash dishes, tidy up, go down to the shops, when someone (the someone you are doing it for and in lieu of rent) keeps telling you not to bother, to leave it, that it isn't important, but to sit down and talk to her instead. Already an enormous untidiness, a jumble-sale clutter, had begun to accumulate in the house around Cosette, covering the surfaces and lying in heaps on the floors. But it was a somehow pleasing disorder, it was the kind of delightful mess that puts visitors at ease.

A great deal of it was strewn across the large circular rosewood table at which Cosette had been sitting when I arrived, at which I was to learn she sat for a large part of every day. It was the reception point of her salon, the place from which she held court. I remembered this table from Wellgarth Avenue where, with two leaves inserted in its centre and twelve chairs around it, it had nearly filled the dining room. There it had been kept polished to an immaculate glossiness. This gloss was already dimmed, the surface already marked with white rings and dull rings, water spots, the indentations made by handwriting on thin paper without a pad beneath. And this somehow, of all the observable changes in Cosette's style of living, more than anything expressed to me the break she had made with the past, the revolution in her life.

And, of course, because this is the way with human beings, I felt a twinge of fear and more than a twinge of resentment. When we are young we want ourselves to change, but everyone and everything else to remain the same. She didn't mention Douglas. Perhaps that wasn't unnatural, but by no oblique word or hint or adumbration did she refer to her loss or her widowed state. There was no photograph of him in the house that I could see or ever did see. Later that day we went into her bedroom, a lavish boudoir new-furnished with a big oval-shaped bed, a Hollywood-style dressing-table, the circular mirror surrounded by light bulbs, Chinese screens in ebony inlaid with mother-of-pearl. The rich-man's-bride furniture of Wellgarth Avenue, the honeymoon bed with its frilly white canopy, was distributed about the house, a piece here, a piece there, a couple of chairs for Auntie, the bed itself, stripped of its flounces, donated to the Girl-in-Residence. The silver-framed photographs Cosette now had were of me, of her St John's Wood brother and sister-in-law and a niece's wedding.

That evening people came, all of them young, students, hippies, I suppose. Someone must have set this influx in motion, started it off. Cosette can hardly have advertised or stood in the street crying the house's amenities like a barker. Perhaps Diana was the moving spirit behind it originally and her friends told their friends. I think even then I knew they came because it was free, what they got there, drink, at any rate tea and sometimes wine, food if they wanted it, unlimited cigarettes, talk or silence, and an offer if not of a bed of a floor to sleep on. But it was also because of Cosette herself, her capacity for loving. She should have had ten children.

These people came like the flies came to Auntie's flypaper, lured by the sweetness of the gum, but unlike those flies paying no penalty for their attraction. And Cosette sat at her table with the books on it and the phone-books, the sheets of paper, the empty cups and glasses, the phone and the radio, the dying flowers in the vase, her bulging handbag, glasses, cigarettes, powder compact and her nail varnish, but no biscuits or chocolates because she had to retain her new figure. For Cosette was looking for a lover.

I didn't know it then, I couldn't have guessed. To me she looked like these people's mother, an impossibly indulgent one of course, for what mother in the late sixties would have permitted a daughter to take a boyfriend off to bed or a son to roll a joint and as it was passed round, partake of it? These things Cosette not only allowed but seemed positively to promote with her all-permissive smile. Did she smile with greater warmth on those passive bearded boys, the silent one who sat with bent head over Kahlil Gibran or the frenetic one who for hours on end plucked tuneless vibrations from a guitar? If she did I would have attributed her smile to some other cause; I would never have guessed at a loneliness and an almost agonized longing that made her consider boys thirty years her junior as potential lovers. It was only later, at Christmas, when by a miracle we actually found ourselves alone together one evening, that she explained to me. It was then she talked about being a 'manizer', about stealing husbands.

'If I was thirty again, Lizzie. I'd been married for eleven years when I was thirty. I'd never worked, you know. Lots of girls didn't in the thirties, it wasn't just married women who didn't. Girls stayed at home with their mothers till they got married and you were lucky if you got married young, the younger the better. You never heard any of that talk you hear now about waiting to get married till you're older, about having to be mature and all that. I was envied, everyone thought I was fortunate to be engaged at eighteen and married at nineteen – really, I was the envy of all. It seems mad now, it's all changed.'

'Do you wish you hadn't?' The conversation made me feel a little uncomfortable.

'In the climate of the times what else could I have done?'

'I suppose it was what sociologists call a culture-specific,' said I, being clever.

She lifted her shoulders, said very quietly, looking down, 'I ate my cake and now I want to have it.'

Even I, at twenty-one, knew better than to tell her she wasn't thirty any more and never could be again. She leaned forward and looked hard at me, then placed her fingertips on her cheekbones, raising the facial tissues until the lines on either side of her mouth disappeared and the jawbone was defined. I had no clue as to what she was doing, although I knew she was waiting for some comment from me. I looked up and then down, feeling my eyes flicker, feeling the embarrassment the young do feel when the old exhibit desires discordant with their years. I didn't know what Cosette meant, only that it seemed to involve a loss of dignity. She took her hands down, letting her face sag once more.

'I've got a lot of money,' she said. 'I'm rich. I think I should be able to do what I like with it within reason, don't you?'

'Sure,' I said on firmer ground. She led me back to the quicksands.

'Lots of middle-aged women find men to love them. A woman in her late forties isn't what a woman would have been when I got married. My father used to say that you were middle-aged at thirty-five and elderly at fifty. That sounds absurd to you, doesn't it?'

Not specially. It sounded about right. Knowing Cosette was already past fifty I said I thought she looked very nice, lovely, I loved the way she looked, and I meant all that. I did love her tired, gentle face, made haggard by the dieting, her still plump, unused hands with their pink polished nails, her dry reddish hair which the hairdresser, true to his promise, was gradually bleaching to a rosy blonde, her dress of midnight-blue lace. It didn't occur to me to tell her what she wanted to hear, the only thing she wanted to hear; it didn't occur to me that she would have been delighted if, for instance, I had said she looked awful or ugly but young, if I had said I hated her hair, her dress, the colour of her lipstick, yet reluctantly admitted how young she looked for her age. I would gladly have lied if I had only thought of it.

Soon after that Auntie came into the room. She invariably knocked before coming in, though Cosette tried very hard to stop her doing this. There was a chair she always sat in, far from the table, near the window, a rather stiff and upright wing chair upholstered in Cosette's favourite red velvet. Cosette always fussed around her, making her comfortable, looking in vain for the Girl-in-Residence – still Diana

Castle, who was of course out somewhere – to fetch a small sherry or a cup of tea. In this particular instance I fetched Auntie's drink and when I came back with it a crowd had arrived, five people whose combined ages probably added up to a hundred, and whom Cosette was in the process of presenting in a measured and formal way to her old second cousin.

'This is Gary, Auntie, this is Mervyn, Peter, Fay, this is Sarah, Auntie. I want you all to meet my Auntie.'

It must have made her young in their eyes, you see. Elderly people, even middle-aged people, don't have aunts. There was exploitation in it but no cruelty, no harm. It was scarcely comparable, say, to the conduct of those Spanish Habsburgs who kept dwarfs at court the better to show off their own height and looks. Auntie suffered no loss of dignity, no humiliation. She looked well on it, this court-dwarf role; she, ironically enough, actually did look younger than when I had seen her last. Placid, complaisant, almost totally silent, she sat in her wing chair at the window, not looking out into the night, for the red velvet curtains were drawn, but staring as if mesmerized at the soft, cherry-coloured folds.

When I saw Cosette again, a month later, she had had her face lifted, and, newly done, it was purple and yellow with bruises so that poor Cosette looked as if she had been in a fist fight. By Easter all these efforts had had their effect and the man who called himself Ivor Sitwell was her lover.

– 7 –

It was he who, indirectly, led me back to Bell, or who brought Bell back into my life, though that was a while ahead. At first there seemed no possible good that could proceed from that source. I remember the shock I felt at finding him in the House of Stairs, the self-control I had to exert to stop myself telling Cosette exactly what I thought of him.

She hadn't told me about him in advance. But this was at first unnoticeable, because after a fashion she had achieved her salon and there were always people coming and going, the red stair-carpet was already showing signs of wear. Some had even moved in to occupy the empty bedrooms and on your way to Cosette in the drawing room it wasn't unusual when passing the ground-floor rooms to see beyond an open doorway four or five unknown people sitting on the carpet in a circle with a candle in the middle and someone playing a sitar or ocarina.

Cosette herself had submitted to, or enthusiastically taken up, the sixties' candle craze. (It came in useful for those seasons of power cuts a few years later.) Though there was a light on the stairs, in the drawing room the gloom was pierced only by candle flames. Candles stood in the pair of iron and bronze candelabra she had bought in the King's Road, and in saucers too and even the screwtop lids of jars. I could just make out the shape of Auntie, in her red wing chair but facing into the room, and the shadowy candlelit forms of several others sprawled on floor cushions or seated at the round table. The huge ornate chandelier hung unlit but faintly luminous in its thickening drapery of cobwebs, a ghostly object growing out of darkness.

I knew better than to comment on Cosette's new face in that company – in any company. I liked the old one better, but I wasn't a lover and Ivor Sitwell had never seen the old one. Somewhat egg-like and with less expression, tautly pulled and faintly polished, the new face broke into the old smile. I was reassured. I kissed the smoothed-out skin and it felt the same as the old crumpled skin, or perhaps I mean there was the same smell, the sophisticated flowers of Patou's Joy. Cosette's hair had nearly reached the desired shade. It was the colour of dry sand. On the third finger of her right hand she was wearing the bloodstone ring. It had become very fashionable but it still didn't suit her.

People were introduced, but I forget their names. If Ivor alone was introduced by his Christian and last names that, perhaps, was only because his surname was a distinguished one, at any rate one that someone like me was bound to notice if not remark out loud on. For the sake of suspense I might keep this a secret but I won't. A long time afterwards I found out that Ivor was not 'a' Sitwell, was not connected with the family and Sitwell was not even his real name. He had picked it himself when he shook the dust off his feet of his parents' semi-detached house in Northampton. One of the Sitwells – Sacheverell, I think it was – had happened to live in the manor house of a village not far away.

Ivor was a poet. Cosette told me so when she told me his name. She also told me his poetry was wonderful and she would show me some of it next day. He was a thin, unhealthy-looking man with a bony sallow face and very long brown hair. Most young men were wearing their hair long then but Ivor wasn't very young, he was getting on for forty, and he had a bald spot on the top of his head. He said, 'Hi', which was what everybody said then, which if you still say it brands you a child of the sixties, but Ivor murmured it without looking up from the book with which he was preoccupied. I say 'preoccupied' and not 'reading' because he was standing up, looking down at the book which was open on the table. It was one of those books which are collections of the best work of some photographer, interesting enough if the photographs are of people but boring (to me) if they are merely of artefacts. These photographs were of objects in incongruous juxtaposition to each other and Ivor Sitwell was staring with a look of rapture at the picture of two empty milk bottles, the milk scum still clinging to their insides, standing next to a dead fish in a birdcage.

He was one of those people who have made up their minds which members of the company are worth bothering about and which are not. I was not and Auntie was not and, with the exception of the prettiest girl, the people on the floor cushions were not. It was Cosette he spoke to. 'That sensuous, tender curve,' he said, indicating the side of one of the milk bottles with a dirty finger, 'don't you find that almost unbearably exciting?'

Cosette smiled at him and agreed. 'Yes, it's lovely, darling.' I knew that smile. It indicated only a sympathy with the inquirer, a desire to please, to be kind.

'Lovely, yes, but doesn't it make your juices flow?'

I thought I detected a movement from Auntie, a start of astonishment, but then I saw that she was fast asleep, she had jerked in her sleep. Ivor picked up the book and set it in Cosette's lap. She was to look, she was to study it. He stood behind her instructing her, holding the candle. It was soon after this that the candle grease spilt. People used to think Cosette clumsy, probably because she did things slowly, but in fact she never was, she was manually dextrous, delicately so. She reached up the hand with the green and red ring on it and Ivor made to thrust the candle into it. Perhaps it was not for this reason she raised her hand, perhaps it was to take his, but whatever it was, between them they dropped the candle on to the open book, letting fall before it went out a long stream of grease.

'You clumsy cow,' Ivor shouted. 'Look what you've done!'

That was when I knew he was her lover.

A mere visitor to the house wouldn't have spoken like that. Of course it was indefensible in Ivor to do so and I wasn't yet used to his ways. But Auntie must have been, up to a point. His voice woke her up and I saw her sleepy old eyes fix themselves on him in a kind of innocent bewilderment. The people on the floor took no notice and nor did the two at the table who were setting out the Tarot. Cosette said, 'Oh, darling, I'm terribly sorry. I can't think what made me do that.'

Ivor was holding the book up close to his face. 'Do you know what I sometimes think? I sometimes think you've got one of those nervous diseases, Parkinson's maybe, something like that.'

Inwardly, I trembled. How could I not? Cosette caught my eye, as she would, she must, when such things were said. I knew her look of anguish and the faint swift shake of her head were for me, but he took them as a reinforcement of her apology.

'A normal woman wouldn't be so awkward, even a woman in the throes of the menopause.'

Auntie got up, gathered together her book, her bag, her glasses, and began making her way to the door. I had never before known her signify disapproval of anything and perhaps she wasn't disapproving, perhaps she was only tired. Cosette, of course, intercepted her with a strained fluttery, 'Are you all right, Auntie? Can I get you anything?'

'No, thank you, dear. I'm off to bed.'

The door closed the way Auntie always closed it, extremely, exaggeratedly slowly, with the faintest whisper of a click, as if the house were full of sleeping invalids. I sat at the table, watching them, Cosette and Ivor. She was telling him in her most soothing tone that she would replace the book, she would buy him another copy tomorrow. I didn't know then that the one damaged by candle grease had been her gift, as was almost everything portable Ivor possessed, including the clothes he stood up in. If this didn't of course justify her spoiling it, it did make his abuse the more outrageous. But I sat there dwelling on my discovery, the revelation that had been made to me. I was shocked.

My reaction, I suppose, was close to that of a child who finds out

623

that its mother is having a love affair. The foundations of life are shaken, security slips from under one's feet, is pulled away. Did it make a difference that this lover of Cosette's was such an odious person? Perhaps, but not entirely. Anyone in that position would have been shocking, for the position itself was shocking. Cosette might have told me she would like to be a 'manizer', to be thirty again and steal husbands, but I supposed there was a natural gulf fixed between wishes and reality. Naïvely, I believed the slimming and the hair dyeing and the face-lifting undirected to any other end but her own self-esteem. A curtain was lifted and I looked out into a world for which I felt distaste, a world where those I thought of as old had desires and excitements to 'make juices flow'.

She never told me he was her lover in so many words. And certainly he never said he was. His attitude was one I had never seen before but have since. She was thirteen years his senior and therefore had no rights, no claim upon him, and he no obligations of fidelity or the duty even of courtesy. In other words, she was lucky to get him and he had the right to use her as he chose and get out of her what he could. A while later, when he had decided I was worth taking a little notice of, not so much due to my daughterly role in Cosette's life as to the fact that I was young and good-looking, he remarked to me in one of his pensive moods, 'You see, I have no sweetheart at present, no one to make music with.'

Cosette, supposedly, didn't count. Yet they shared a bed, the big new oval bed in Cosette's bedroom. I even saw them together in it. One morning a man came to the front door delivering a piece of furniture I was sure had been mistakenly sent; it seemed very unlike Cosette's taste, the old taste or the new. Cosette, of course, was still asleep. Like her young guests she so much wanted to resemble, in this new life she slept late and was seldom up before noon. I went upstairs, up the four flights to the second floor, and knocked diffidently upon her door. I was actually shrinking at what seemed to me the enormity of what I was doing, the intrusion.

But Cosette, of course, wasn't sorry to see me. Had she even feigned sleep so that I was obliged, when I had knocked repeatedly, to open the door and go inside? She was gratified that I should see her with her young lover, in a situation to prove their sexual involvement. He lay on his front, bundled up in bedclothes, a selfish man who grabs the sheet and blankets to himself, his bald head showing. Her hair, which she had formerly been in the habit of pinning up overnight, flowed loose on to her shoulders. She wore a nightgown designed for a young mistress, black lace and thin straps.

'Don't make a noise, darling. We mustn't wake Ivor.' Her finger to her lips, she climbed with exaggerated care out of bed.

He turned over, snorting as he did so. I felt quite shaken by the sight, by this encounter. Sometimes, in the past, as adolescents do, I had tried to imagine Cosette and Douglas in bed together. And I had succeeded in imagining the two of them engaged in the sexual act, a love-making carried out in a stately way with the minimum of movement, without speech, in darkness, to their mutual, quiet, unexpressed satisfaction. It is only recently, in the past couple of years, that I have come to understand this is the way most children imagine their parents making love.

To envisage Cosette and Ivor together – this was harder, this was to be shied away from. And I was too old to indulge that kind of curiosity. I pictured Ivor as merely servicing Cosette and with less enthusiasm than an animal at stud, but I may have been wrong. In the light of what happened later with another man I may have been quite wrong. Ivor may not have been in love with Cosette, may have been waiting for some young 'sweetheart' to come along, but he could still have been attracted by her. That languor can be very attractive, that slow sweet gentleness, that air of issuing invitations to love in idleness. And no doubt the pains Cosette had taken with her appearance had paid off. I alone still saw her as she had been before the transformation, stout, grey-haired, in her tailored suits. I alone saw her as a mother.

Nor was she in love with him. At the time I couldn't face so bleak a notion, but now I know she wanted a man of her own, a man to show off to others, a man to go about with, perhaps too a man to sleep with. Strange that I could accept such a concept quite naturally when it applied to my contemporaries, to myself, to Diana Castle, say. Diana and Fay, the pretty floor-cushion girl Ivor flirted with, had taken full advantage of sixties morality to sleep with anyone they fancied. Love didn't come into it. Why should it? They had discovered it isn't necessary to love someone in order to enjoy yourself with him. And that was all right, I understood that, I felt the same. But that Cosette might feel the same – that was too much for me, that was something I didn't want to confront. I know now that while

Cosette had loved Douglas dearly, had been a good and faithful wife to him and mourned his death with great bitterness, she was only in love once in her life, and that was neither with Douglas nor Ivor.

I wish, I really do wish, I could say something in Ivor Sitwell's favour, could have found in him some redeeming feature. It would have reconciled me to his presence in the House of Stairs, it would have gone some way to explaining Cosette's unaccountable partiality. He was ugly and mean-spirited, ungrateful and rude, as discourteous to Auntie as he was to Diana and me, capable of caressing Fay in Cosette's presence and then walking up to Cosette and asking her for money in front of all of us. He did nothing to help in the house and used Perpetua as if she were a servant in a Victorian household. Perhaps he was a good poet. I can't say, I don't know. Cosette had shown me, as she promised, a volume of his verses. They had been published but had he, as I was sure at the time, paid to have them published? Or, rather, got some woman, some predecessor of Cosette's, to pay for their publication?

These verses weren't bad in the way Patience Strong is bad. They weren't doggerel, they didn't express stale emotion in clichés. That I found them incomprehensible is nothing against them. I might not do so now if I were ever able to get hold of any examples of them. After all, people in the sixties found Pinter incomprehensible and fraught with *non sequiturs*. Once or twice, in the evenings, Cosette read them aloud to whoever might be there. It was only while she was reading his poetry that I ever saw Ivor look at her in a lover-like way, look at her, that is, with neither indifference nor anger.

That spring I stayed with Cosette for several weeks. I had teaching practice to do as part of my course and had, by a lucky chance, been sent to a school in North Kensington. Times have changed, but even then it was a rough area, shabby and sordid by day and dangerous by night. The children, then as now, were a mixed lot and in order to teach them satisfactorily one should really have been proficient in Gujarati and Bengali. But it had the great advantage of being within walking distance of Archangel Place.

In the evenings Cosette used often to take us all out to dinner. Perhaps the truth was that Ivor didn't specially want to spend time alone with her. They hardly ever went out alone. Instead Cosette would gather up whoever happened to be around, myself and Fay who had become the Girl-in-Residence – Diana having gone off to Cornwall to live with her boyfriend – the boy with the sitar and the boy with the ocarina, Perpetua's brother, an Irishman from County Leix who had come to London to seek his fortune and been given a room in Archangel Place, 'just until you find somewhere, darling'. And, of course, Ivor. We always went to expensive, exclusive places: the Marco Polo in the King's Road, San Frediano's, The Pheasantry, the Villa dei Cesari. On the few occasions Cosette found herself dining at the Hungry Horse in the Fulham Road she thought she was slumming.

She had brought the big old Volvo with her from Wellgarth Avenue and she left it parked in the street. It was still possible to do this at that time in the little streets of Notting Hill. An old-fashioned woman in some ways, she never drove the car herself when Ivor was with her but handed the keys to him before we left the house. He was a terrible driver. Already the Volvo, which Cosette's years of slow, skilful driving had left unscathed, was scarred and marked and chipped and one of the rear lamps smashed. To drive eastwards to the Edgware Road and then south along Park Lane is neither the easiest nor the shortest way to get to Chelsea, but it was the way that Ivor took. Perhaps he took it in order to drive along Moscow Road and give himself the opportunity of pointing out to all of us the house in which Edith Sitwell had once had a flat. 'Cousin' Edith, he called her. To other Sitwells he referred in a similarly familiar way, speaking of 'Sachie' and 'Georgie'. I didn't then know that he had absolutely no right to claim this relationship. Interested, I even asked him if he had any special memories or anecdotes to relate of the celebrated three. He then told several tales which I later came across pretty well word for word in Osbert Sitwell's *Laughter in the Next Room*.

It showed me one thing. That if you wanted to put Ivor in a good mood you either had to praise his poetry or ask him about these people we all believed were his relatives. Nothing else would do it. We went to the Marco Polo that evening, as we often did then, and it was there that I received, without knowing it at the time, news of Bell.

Chinese restaurants were not common then as they are now. At least, good ones were not. It felt very grand to sit round a table big enough to accommodate us all and fiddle about with the dishes that make up what was then a rarity for London, Peking duck. I sat between Dominic and a boy called Mervyn, and on the other side of Dominic was Fay and on the other side of her, Ivor. I sat there enjoying it but thinking how strange it all was, recalling the decorous dinner parties at which Cosette and Douglas had entertained her relations and the Wellgarth neighbours. Some of those people had occasionally called at Archangel Place and their astonishment, expressed in wandering eyes, hesitant inquiries, was greater than mine. They were older and more set in their ways. They thought Cosette had gone mad.

Eating at the Marco Polo, or wherever it might be, produced the same sort of astonishment in some of Cosette's young guests. You could see they wondered what it was all about, why Cosette did it, and in the case of some of them, what price were they going to have to pay? This was specially evident in the Irishman, youngest of Perpetua's large family of siblings. Dominic had come to London to find work and when his sister told him she had found a place for him to stay, must have expected a miserable room in a comfortless house, an exigent landlady, a shabby neighbourhood. He could scarcely believe his luck or overcome his terrible suspicions. Like the streetwise beggar picked out of an alley to attend the rich man's feast, he seemed always on the watch for the reckoning. Sooner or later Cosette's motive must emerge. What was surely some gross and elaborate practical joke would end in his humiliation, or else she was mistaken in him, believed him other than he was, and when she discovered the truth, that he was a labourer by necessity not inclination, poor and nearly illiterate, accustomed to a diet of fried bread and chips at his mother's kitchen table, she would expose him and fling him out of doors.

Or so I suppose. This is what his expression told me, for at that time he never spoke except to say thank you, and later on when I might have asked him, I didn't. His wild beautiful dark face was anxious in repose, marvellous when he smiled, as he did whenever he was spoken to, his eyes, the bluest I have ever seen, positively glowing with gratitude and apprehension. On the other hand, the boy called Mervyn was out to get what he could. I think Fay was too. I think it now, though at the time I never quite believed in people actually and purposefully having an attitude of this sort. I thought it was something come upon in old novels whose authors were not conversant with the subtleties of human nature. I had never read Balzac. I hadn't yet begun reading Henry James.

So when I saw Fay raise and lower her long eyelashes at Ivor Sitwell, stretch her bare arms behind her head to lift her breasts, smile at him and whisper something indecent and provocative, having apparently waited for the moment Cosette left us to go to the bathroom, I thought it done in innocence and by chance. And these factors of accident and random acts I thought operating again when she later turned her back on him and concentrated on Cosette, pinning up Cosette's back hair that was flopping out of its pins, complimenting her on her perfume, sniffing with eyes closed as if ravished by it, going off to find a waiter and demand a jug of water because Cosette had asked for it. Mervyn had different methods: eating and drinking as much as he could get, far more than any reasonable person would want to eat and drink – Cosette always asked for the bill and paid it without a word, with scarcely more than a glance at it – remarking that he had run out of cigarettes, observing loudly and often how much he liked the jacket some man on the other side of the restaurant was wearing or how he had always longed for a certain kind of pen or cigarette lighter. I believed it all artless, but I learned.

At Cosette's table, whether at home or in a restaurant, there was always excess, too much food, too much wine, a bottle or two left half-empty, cigarettes stubbed out half-smoked, cigarettes left in packets on the cloth, liqueurs left in glasses, chocolates on dishes. If Gary, the boy who played the various exotic musical instruments was there, he would gather up all these leftovers and put them into a carrier bag he kept with him for this purpose. For all I know this may have been the first doggy bag to make its appearance in London. As well as the bag, Gary carried a Tupperware box to put beansprouts and noodles in, including those that other people had left on their plates.

It was a few days after this that I first witnessed this spooning up of leftovers, and saw him, green in the face after drinking four glasses of kirsch, stagger to the bathroom to be sick. On this occasion Ivor burned the five-pound note to show his contempt for money.

'Can you let me have a fiver?'

Cosette didn't hesitate. The banknote, worth so comparatively little now, would then have paid a week's rent of a better room than

Dominic could have afforded. Ivor took it out of her fingers. He had been discoursing on the wealth of 'his' family and how happy he was that, due to some legal mix-up, none of it had come the way of the particular branch to which he belonged. He talked about money corrupting and about selfishness. I have since then noticed that it is only deeply selfish people who point out the selfishness of others. Earlier that day, it appeared, he had proposed that Cosette should back the founding of a poetry magazine of which he would be editor. She hadn't refused outright, only said it would be hard for her to lay hands on such a large sum at short notice.

'Now why do you suppose we refer to people who oppose innovations in the arts as Philistines?' he asked us, still holding up the banknote in his fingertips.

No one answered him, no one knew or cared.

'Possibly because no documents in the Philistine language are extant,' Ivor said. 'Equally possibly because the Philistines long held a monopoly in smithing iron, their only known skill.' He looked at Cosette, drawing towards him with his free hand the candle a waiter had just lit. 'But how did the use of the term in its modern sense arise?'

Cosette was very tolerant, very easy-going, so well able to conceal hurt that you might think she scarcely felt it. Betrayal was what she feared and Ivor, who had presumably made her no promises, given her no guarantees, couldn't betray her. But she liked things to be pleasant, she was one who poured oil on troubled waters.

'You've just told us how, Ivor,' she said. 'It's very interesting. I didn't know that.'

'The use of the term for people deficient in liberal culture and whose chief interests are material was first applied by German students in the nineteenth century to those who hadn't been to a university. People like you.' He might equally have said people like himself, since his claims to have been to Oxford, or indeed any seat of learning after he left Northampton High School at the age of sixteen, were without foundation. The information about Philistines I later discovered he had purposely mugged up in advance. Cosette didn't in the least mind these insults, having no inflated image of her own intellect, indeed very much under estimating it. He too saw this, he saw he had misjudged his victim and her vulnerable area, and now, unerringly, he aimed at her tender place. 'Not that I blame you for that, you can't help it. You were born too soon.' He said to the rest of us, 'Women of her age just weren't allowed higher education.' And leaning forward, he thrust the folded note into the candle flame and lit his cigarette with it. 'Naturally their chief interests would be material, but there's no harm in showing them how' – pause – 'little' – pause – 'these' – pause – 'things matter.'

His efforts were largely wasted, for I think it was only I who saw Cosette's deep blush. The others were too busy watching, like animals hypnotized by headlights, the consumption in flames of the five-pound note. All except Gary who, in an agony at the wicked waste of it, actually making a wailing sound, lunged forward and tried to snatch the burning paper from Ivor's hand. All across the restaurant people were looking. Ivor was laughing, holding in his fingers the burnt fragments of paper, snuffling smoke out through his nostrils. I looked to see if the strip of metal, allegedly embedded in every genuine banknote, had survived the fire, but could see only rags of dark brown ash. It seemed to me in that moment, as Fay leant back, resting her head against Ivor's shoulder, crying, 'Oh, magnificent, magnificent!' as Gary with tears on his cheeks sulkily shovelled leftovers into his plastic box and Dominic, thunderstruck, murmured, 'Holy Mary and Joseph,' it seemed to me then that I saw in Cosette's face the flash of fear that says, 'What am I doing here, what have I got myself into?' I think so, but I could be mistaken.

She paid the bill, as always, with the merest glance at it. She added her usual excessive tip. We walked out into the King's Road and Ivor suggested we all go on to some drinking club he knew in South Kensington, a place called the Drayton. Cosette had a headache and I could see she was being overtaken by pain. Under the harsh acid lights, dressed in the bright colours she now favoured – that night a red skirt and red silk sleeveless jerkin over a flowered blouse – she looked old and tired. The 'lifting' had done little to prevent a droop at the corners of her mouth. It wasn't for me to resist going to this club, no one would have taken any notice if I had, and besides I wanted to go on there, I was young, I wanted to live. At that time I was passing through one of those phases of recklessness that perhaps come to everyone over whom hangs the sword of a fatal disease that may strike next month or next year or tomorrow.

Cosette wouldn't have considered refusing. She had taken on the role of youth and she must play the part in all its aspects. But she was unable to fake enthusiasm, and Ivor saw this at once, he was sensitive in his way; he saw that she was tired and in pain and not able to disguise it, able only to acquiesce. It was one of the things about her that made him angry, her complaisance, which I think he saw as a rich woman's indifference. If you have that much money you need scarcely trouble yourself about anything or make yourself interesting, you need merely be supine. I think he saw it this way. He was consumed with envy, with covetousness for her money, and would without a doubt have married her for it. Someone had told Bell who told me later that he couldn't marry because he was already married to a Catholic woman who wouldn't give him a divorce. And this was a couple of years before the new, easy, divorce law came in.

He was angry and anger always made him vindictive or silky. That night he was silky. In the car on the way to Drayton Gardens he began talking about women, about the types of women he admired. For some reason he least admired the type in which I belong, small, slender, dark, brown-skinned. By the time we were in the club, which Cosette was obliged to join and pay a membership fee, for no one could be found to support Ivor's claim to membership, he was describing this type in detail as anathema to him. Since I disliked him so much I was rather amused, and I was touched to see how Dominic resented it on my behalf.

Fay's looks were the kind he most appreciated.

'Tall and not too thin,' he said, 'lots of very light hair but not yellow hair, never yellow. Grey eyes, large grey eyes, and a little short nose and a sensuous mouth.'

The ironical thing was that though he was describing Fay and looking at Fay, he was also describing Cosette, or the way Cosette had tried, and with some success, to re-make herself. She saw this, if no one else did, and it revived her. Her eyes brightened, she smiled a little. Not, I think, because she much cared what Ivor said, she was passing beyond caring what he said or did, his days were numbered, but because he was after all a man talking about a woman like her, talking of her as desirable, placing her by definition in a stage of youth.

Fay enjoyed it too. Fay thought she was being individually praised and perhaps knew she was being flattered, for she wasn't very tall and her nose turned up. We were all sitting round a table, drinking a mixture called Singapore Sling, and a girl had come on to the little stage to sing Edith Piaf songs in what Ivor said was very bad French. It sounded all right to me and I said so. He cast me one of his poisonous looks, so ridiculous as to arouse derisive laughter. I had never laughed at him before. Had I been a coward and did I now sense his star was setting? Perhaps. Anyway, I started to laugh and after a while Dominic laughed too, tentatively at first, then with uninhibited uproarious mirth. Ivor watched the girl leave the stage.

'I've met her,' he said coldly. 'I met her in a friend's house at a party and the most beautiful woman I've ever seen was there. She rents a room from my friends.' He warmed to this. I thought he was making it up. I was sure he was as his vindictiveness increased. 'She would make any woman in this room look a clapped-out old slag.' Cosette grew still, stricken. He had shocked Fay, whose face had become a joke-mask of drunken incredulity. A kind of hysterical giggling afflicted me and it took all the control I had to suppress it.

'A daughter of the gods,' said Ivor, 'divinely tall and most divinely fair.'

'Did you make that up yourself?' said Mervyn, awe-struck.

'Of course I didn't, you stupid arsehole. I'm a real poet. I tell you, she has that face I've described, only she has it to perfection, as if all the others' – he looked at Fay – 'were just bad copies, as if they were waxworks. A Scandinavian face, the face of a Viking maid – "a face to lose youth for, to occupy age with the dream of, meet death with" – and I didn't write that either.' I realized he was terribly drunk, but weren't we all, except Cosette? Something was striking a chord in my consciousness and there came back to me a conversation Cosette and I had once had. I looked at her to see if she remembered, but saw in her tired face only pain and perhaps regret, as if there had come into her mind a memory of peace and of lilies in a garden and her high-powered, dull husband.

'You could imagine her in *Smiles of a Summer Night*,' said Ivor. 'You could imagine her in Strindberg.'

I said suddenly, 'What's her name?'

He was too taken aback by the abruptness of it to attempt cleverness. 'Christine Something. They call her Chris. Why?'

'Nothing,' I said. 'It's not the same one,' for I had forgotten Bell's name was Christabel; I had forgotten it entirely.

They were dancing now to the dull tuneless jungle beat of rock. Gary had fallen asleep with his head on the table. Mervyn was doing a kind of solo caper as if for the edification of the band. Perhaps because Cosette sat staring at the art nouveau wall panels with what looked more like indifference than despair, Fay put out one hand to Ivor, fearful that he would refuse her. But instead of refusing he got up and with his arm round her walked precariously up the length of glassy floor.

I said to Dominic, 'Come and dance.'

– 8 –

Something over a hundred years ago George Huntington described a disease which he had observed affected families in New England. These people were descendants of seventeenth-century immigrants from the Suffolk village of Bures. I have heard that an ancestor of mine, from far, far back, was a Bures woman.

There is a test you can have now to determine whether or not you will fall victim to Huntington's. It is very complicated and involves not only taking a sample of one's own blood but also that of a number of one's relatives, at least seven. I haven't got seven living relatives on the appropriate side of the family. They have all died of Huntington's.

Once there were quite a lot of us. My grandmother had six children. Her own father had died aged thirty-five, not of Huntington's but of poliomyelitis, then known as infantile paralysis. Her mother vaguely remembered her mother-in-law afflicted with what she mistakenly called St Vitus's dance which made her limbs jerk and her hands fly out, but she didn't know it was hereditary, she didn't know her own husband would have succumbed to it had he lived. She didn't know her children might inherit it. Three did. My grandmother's choreic movements began soon after her sixth child was born, soon after her thirtieth birthday. Of her six children each had a fifty-fifty chance of succumbing to it. That is the genetic ratio, neither more nor less. If one of your parents had it, you are fifty per cent likely to have it and fifty per cent unlikely to have it. If neither of your parents had it you can't have it. My mother showed the first symptoms, inconsistent behaviour and malaise, when she was thirty-six. One of her sisters had died of diphtheria as a child. Would she have developed it? Two others did, a brother and a sister, and both died before her. The other sisters never had children, never even married, they dared not, though in fact neither of them have developed it and both are still alive. They alone are alive, though if the test had been in existence twenty years ago probably enough could have been mustered to supply blood for me: Douglas, who was the son of my afflicted grandmother's afflicted sister, Cousin Lily descended from my grandmother's other afflicted sister, my mother, her sisters, one dying, insane uncle – well, it would have been a near thing but maybe sufficient could have been found.

And if they had, if the test had existed, if I had dared take it, if it had shown negative, would it have made a difference to my life? Would I have done more and done less and done differently? Would I have had children, written other, better things? What is the use of talking about it? It didn't exist and now that it does there aren't enough people left and I am balanced on the final ridge – only two or three more years and I shall know for good or ill, I shall know for ever.

I wrote my first three books in Cosette's house. The first one I wrote on Douglas's old typewriter in the room at the top of the house with the window that had no real balcony and where there could be no noise above my head to disturb me. It was written rapidly and badly and with the maximum injected sensation and violence and crude sex. I couldn't blame Ivor Sitwell for saying some time later, 'Still churning them out, are you, Elizabeth?'

But all this was a way ahead. I was going to be a teacher. I was going to write a thesis on Henry James. And Ivor was still living with Cosette and sharing her bed and insulting her and trying to squeeze money out of her for his poetry magazine. Over this she proved exceptionally stubborn. There was a stubborn side to Cosette and, surprisingly, a businesswoman side. It must have rubbed off on her from Douglas. At any rate, she wanted to see figures and estimates and meet the people who would be involved with Ivor in this venture before she was prepared to do what she called 'come across'. Two others were concerned. One of them was a woman, now married, Ivor said had once been his 'sweetheart' and who had written a libretto for a musical that had actually been performed somewhere in America in theatre-in-the-round. The other, who had some connection with *Private Eye*, was called Walter Admetus, and it was in his house that the woman who had so enchanted Ivor, the woman called Chris or Christine, rented a room.

I don't know why I behaved the way I did, I don't know why I suddenly became devious. I had already made up my mind the beautiful woman couldn't be Bell, having got it into my head that 'my' Bell was really Isabel, and yet Ivor's description tallied with her so closely, matched her feature for feature, colouring for colouring. I could easily have asked Elsa the Lioness whom I often saw, who was a regular visitor to the House of Stairs, to find out from the Thinnesses if Bell Sanger was still in their cottage. Come to that, I could have rung up Felicity Thinnesse myself. We had encountered each other once or twice since that Christmas, we had all met at a party at Elsa's. If I didn't do this I think it was because I wanted to enjoy a shock of recognition, I wanted some rapture of the heart. I think it was that but I don't know. Certain it is that although I had seen her so little my emotions were already involved with Bell and her life.

So when Cosette suggested that Walter Admetus and the woman he lived with were invited to dinner in Archangel Place, I opposed it. She suggested it to me first, we were alone with no one there but Auntie, and this was a piece of luck – or so it seemed, so fatefully it seemed – for if Ivor had been there he would have jumped at the chance, as he always did, of getting something, anything, out of Cosette for himself or anyone connected with him. I have often wondered since then what would have happened if Cosette had refused me, if when I said it would be better to phone Admetus and suggest a meeting at his house, then later if she liked him he could be asked to dinner, if then she had rejected this idea, as with her hospitable ideas she well might have done, she all too well might have done. Would I have made my way alone to the northern reaches of Gloucester Place where Admetus lived to seek out Bell? I don't think so. It would have been hard, it would have required a brashness I don't possess and never did. I would have left it, I would have forgotten Bell – and Cosette would never have been granted bliss nor had her life broken nor come with the rest of us to the high window with the narrow ledge.

'I don't think I could do that, darling,' Cosette said. 'I couldn't invite us to someone's house – ' and, doubtfully, ' – could I?'

636

It was so funny coming from her, to whose house everyone invited themselves, that even Auntie laughed. She caught my eye and daringly, fearful of giving offence, she laughed her old woman's thin, throaty laugh.

'I don't mind phoning him,' I said. 'I'll say I'm your secretary.'

'Oh, no,' said Cosette, shocked. 'Then he'll expect the sort of person who would have a secretary. I suspect he's very Bohemian.'

This archaic term would have earned Ivor Sitwell's ridicule and the incomprehension of the other inhabitants of the house. But I was used to it, it had been one of Douglas's words. 'If he's Bohemian,' I said, 'he won't mind us inviting ourselves.'

Only then did Cosette catch on. 'Do you mean you'd come with me, Elizabeth?' There was something touching in the way she spoke, that she who conferred so much love and largesse should also be shy, be fearful of intruding, be inordinately grateful that I would spare the time to give her my company. 'That would be very kind of you.' Her face took on the look it wore when she was making plans of generosity, a mischievousness, an almost youthful anticipation. 'We could take him some nice wine. Or Madeira – should we take him a bottle of Madeira?'

I did my best to persuade her that it would look very odd indeed to take presents of wine to someone with whom she might never be on more than a business footing, someone in any case who would be offering her a glass of lemonade, since Cosette herself rarely drank. She looked doubtful. It went against the grain with her not to be giving; instead to be, as she saw it, taking. But in fact she was to give and take nothing, beyond that lemonade, for the magazine never came into being. The libretto woman disappeared to South America and Ivor went off with Fay. Of course he intended to come back, as Fay also intended. Because Cosette was kind and generous, because she never lost her temper or sulked, because she seemed endlessly forgiving, people who were not very percipient thought her gullible. They thought her foolish and ripe to be deceived.

Ivor told her he was going to Northampton to see his mother who was ill. Fay just went without a word. I believe they borrowed a room in Putney which belonged to someone they knew who had gone away on holiday. Cosette, taking Auntie out for a drive, saw them lying in each other's arms in Richmond Park. She showed a side of her

637

character which I had not suspected if I call it vindictiveness, but if I call it something else, not spite, not revenge, but a horror of being betrayed, then I had always known of it.

She had her man from Golders Green come in – Jimmy the faithful handyman who had done all these odd jobs for her in Wellgarth Avenue and now came to Archangel Place – to change the locks and have new keys cut. However, if she didn't change her phone number this was because she hardly ever answered the phone herself. I used to think that if she got anything out of having a houseful of freeloaders it was that there was always someone to answer the phone, an operation she very much flinched from. Mervyn, whom I had never suspected of having a particular dislike for Ivor, took intense pleasure in telling him when he phoned that Cosette had 'given orders' he wasn't to be admitted. Cosette was horrified when she heard about this, but by then Mervyn, and Gary too, had had enormous fun telling Ivor Cosette 'knew all about him', had 'an important friend at Scotland Yard' and was at that moment 'with her solicitor'. Ivor, supposedly, took this to mean that among other things his deception about his family origins had been rumbled, though in fact none of us then suspected he was not as much a Sitwell as the late Sir Osbert himself, whose funeral the year before he claimed to have been invited to.

But before all this happened Cosette and I went to Walter Admetus's house, having arranged to meet Ivor there. We went in the big, old, dusty navy-blue Volvo which gobbled up petrol and which it was Gary's job, never performed, to clean in lieu of rent. Its interior was like an extension of the House of Stairs, being full of Cosette-style clutter, full and half-full and empty cigarette packets, bottles and sprays of Joy, boxes of pink tissues, new novels with torn dust-jackets, shoes to be worn for driving and shoes to be put on after driving, and all those parcels to be taken somewhere that never got there, laundry and dry cleaning and things to be sewn and things to be mended. I felt excited and my excitement communicated itself to Cosette who took it for anxiety that she shouldn't be gulled or lured into parting foolishly with her money.

'When I'm in danger of not being prudent,' she said gravely, 'I think of Douglas. I remember how he worked hard to make all this money for me and it does restrain me.' It was the first time for many months I had heard her mention him.

Elegant-appearing Georgian houses can be just as much tips inside as anywhere else, a fact which was new to me then. Fifteen Archangel Place, though untidy, was not squalid, thanks to the efforts of Perpetua. Walter Admetus's house was. It looked as if it had never been cleaned and it smelt. The upholstery on the furniture was greasy, or rather encrusted with some kind of sticky deposit, the accumulation of years, to which animal hairs adhered, in places as thickly as the pile on a fur. The smell was of fried onions or sweat – which smell much the same – of clogged sink waste-pipes and of old dog and sick cat, though we saw neither animal while we were there. Even Cosette, the least fussy of women, hesitated a little before sitting down on the spot indicated, a stained, hairy sofa cushion on which a blowfly crawled.

Walter Admetus is the only man I have ever known actually to introduce his girlfriend as his mistress. He was a courtly person, with a small, pointed and prominent beard, the kind of beard that turns up and sticks out, and she was very prettily dressed in early Laura Ashley with shiny hair and a pink hair-ribbon. It was a mystery how people could come out of that place and yet be so spruce and groomed.

'Admetus,' he said, holding out his hand and close to clicking his heels. He behaved like some German or Scandinavian aristocrat, though he is as English as I am. 'May I introduce my mistress, Eva Faulkner?'

I was wearing the cameo brooch Cosette had given me for my twenty-first birthday, the one with the head of a girl on it that looks like Bell. I found myself fidgeting with this brooch as I sat rigidly on the sticky filthy velvet of my chair seat, watching Cosette hand over the bottle of red Graves she must have secreted in one of her always huge handbags. It had occurred to me for the first time that Bell simply might not appear, most probably wouldn't appear, might not be at home, and even if she was in was only a lodger here, not a friend. I wondered what I should do. Walter Admetus took the bottle with extravagant expressions of gratitude. His manners were at any rate a far cry from those of Ivor. He insisted on pouring glasses of the wine immediately, although it was very much the sort of stuff to be uncorked in advance, stood about at room temperature and served with food.

'I'm afraid I haven't anything for you and your daughter to eat,' he said.

Cosette winced. I said quickly that I wasn't her daughter. Admetus made things worse by saying with extreme cloying courtesy that no doubt Cosette wished I were. Cosette's face was fixed in that gentle, dreamy smile she could hold for several minutes without relaxing her mouth or blinking her eyes. There seemed absolutely nothing to say. We had arrived rather late, so by now Ivor was very late. The sun poured through the dirty windows, making bars of dull yellow light in which dust motes swarmed like insects. It fell on Eva Faulkner like a purposely directed spotlight and she sat silent and bored, reminding me of the description in *Antony and Cleopatra* of Octavia as a statue, not a breather. I began to realize that I had made a mistake in not telling Cosette that I expected Admetus's lodger to be Bell, for how could I now ask Admetus about her without revealing my duplicity?

I also began to doubt once more. What had I really to go on? A description that I had perhaps distorted in my own mind to suit my wishes and a name I had no real reason to connect with Bell. Cosette had begun a conversation, stilted and very much of the small talk kind, on the amenities of the neighbourhood. Rigid in her sun bath, Eva Faulkner made no replies, gave no sign of having heard, but it seemed just the kind of exchange of pleasantries to appeal to Admetus, who responded with a positive eulogy of the backwoods of Notting Hill, so that you wondered why he didn't immediately move there. His beard wagged and his eyebrows worked up and down and his hands waved like fans. I began to feel angry, we had been there three-quarters of an hour, and I was about to say to Cosette we shouldn't wait, it was hopeless, Ivor wasn't coming, when I heard the front door open and Ivor's voice.

It was disquieting to observe Cosette's reaction to the sound of Ivor's voice in those days. Her expression would become one of resignation, even of stoicism. I couldn't distinguish the words, nor did I speculate as to whom he might be speaking or, come to that, how he happened to possess a key to this house. I was only wondering if he would break the apparent rule of a lifetime and apologize.

The door to the room opened and he came in with Bell. Typical of him was the way he pushed his way in first and left her to follow.

I don't know if she recognized me, remembered me or if Ivor, who immediately began telling us how he had encountered her in the street outside, had already told her who would be there when they reached the house. I could have asked but I didn't, I never did. She looked at me and said very calmly, 'Hallo, Lizzie,' as if we had last seen each other the day before.

She was all in black – like James's Milly Theale. I never saw her in any but dark or dull or muted shades except the time I made her put on the dress of 'wasted' red like the one the girl wears in the Bronzino painting. This was before the antique-clothes cult, before the knitted-cotton revolution, before long skirts. Bell's clothes had probably been bought at a jumble sale, the long, narrow, black wool skirt with box pleats front and back, the man's black cotton shirt, its sleeves rolled up, its waist defined by a black 'locknit' scarf tied round and round, the rope of black and brown wooden beads. Her fine, thin ankles, the long shaft of the Achilles tendons, just showed below the hem of the skirt. Her feet, brown and long-toed, were in Greek rope sandals. It looked as if she had tied her hair on top of her head with a bit of picture cord. Tendrils of it hung alongside her cheeks and down the long straight nape of her neck, hair that was the colour of pale unvarnished wood, but leaving the high smooth forehead bare. She held her head aloft, poised, as she always did, as if balancing on it a heavy vessel full of liquid.

A great deal of marvelling now took place on the part of Cosette, Admetus and Ivor – though not of Eva Faulkner, who apparently took all such coincidences as a matter of course – that Bell and I already knew each other. Once Admetus had gone through the elaborate process of introducing Bell to Cosette, only he called it 'having the honour to present', Ivor began praising Bell's beauty in her presence, walking round her, his head on one side, pointing out with a curved index finger each exceptional feature, as if she were an item on sale in a slave market.

'Look at that chin, look at those dear little ears like shells, and that skin. Have you ever seen such a carriage? A plumb line could pass through her from the crown of her head to the soles of her feet.'

The pointing finger just brushed Bell's neck. She didn't recoil. She said quite slowly, almost casually, but absolutely without amusement, 'Take your hands off me, you ugly bastard.'

She was frank and open, you see, honest they said, she always spoke her mind. Cosette gasped. Admetus gave a nervous titter. To my extreme pleasure I saw that Ivor had gone quite white. Bell said to me, 'Come up and see where I live.'

I didn't hesitate. I left the room with her. Therefore I never knew what actually happened at the tripartite discussion between Cosette, Ivor and Admetus. I know only that Cosette never handed over any money for the founding of the magazine and Ivor was soon to depart, though we went on seeing Admetus, he became a friend and visitor to the House of Stairs, and for a little while, after Eva had left him, I even wondered if he might become Ivor's successor with Cosette. That was before Marcus of course, that was before the coming of Marcus put all other men, any other man, out of the question.

So I went upstairs with Bell and she showed me the little room where she lived, where she had been living ever since she sold the house she inherited from Silas Sanger's father. There was very little in it apart from the bed and a table and a chair, for Bell, then and perhaps now too, has no feeling for domestic comforts or for the appearance of her home. But Silas's paintings were there, canvases stacked against the walls.

'I take them with me wherever I go,' she said. 'He was a really shitty painter, but that doesn't mean a thing. One day there's a chance he'll be recognized and then I'll have an exhibition and sell them for huge sums.'

She spoke to me as if we were old friends. She spoke of Silas without emotion, coolly, practically, as if she were a gallery owner and he a painter she had discovered and invested in. I was awed, remembering the dead man, the blood on the floor and on her.

'Did you stay long with Felicity?' I asked her.

'Two months, one week and two days,' she said. 'Then I went and lived in the house the old man left until I sold it.'

Another question. I asked her a lot of questions that afternoon, though none of the ones I ought to have asked, none of the vital questions. 'What do you do? I mean for a living. What do you work at?'

'I don't.' She looked pleased to be able to say that. 'I don't work at all and I never shall. I'm *never* going to work.'

'Then you're rich?'

Her eyes opened wide. They are sea-grey, her eyes, and very large and clear. 'I'm not, I'm not rich. But I hate working. I've got just enough to exist on without working if I live in a hole like this.' She had a way of dismissing subjects when she had had enough of them, turning her head quickly from side to side, lifting her shoulders, changing on to a new topic. 'Who's that shit I came in with? I've seen him here before.'

'He's a man who lives with my friend you were introduced to.'

'That's a relief. I thought maybe he lived with you.' Too bad if he did. It hadn't stopped her calling him a shit. 'What a turd,' she said. 'Isn't he a bit young for her?'

'A bit stupid for her,' I said. 'A bit ugly and selfish and bloody. I don't know about young,' and, untruthfully, 'I never thought of that.'

She laughed. 'I shall have to see what I can find out about him.'

It was the first time I'd heard her laugh, and it was a surprisingly deep, rich, gurgling sound. Her pale face glowed and she was beautiful. I found her exciting in a disturbing way, a soul-shaking way, without knowing in the least what I wanted of her. That we should be friends? That we should meet and talk and be together? And what did she want? Not of me, but of life? I know now, of course I do, I have known for a long time, but I didn't know then. It mystified me, later on it did, it puzzled me that someone young and beautiful and healthy and intelligent should be content to live in that mean little room in that dirty house, she and all her sparse worldly goods contained in a space twelve feet by twelve, with no job, no career, no prospects, no apparent aims. She was a childless widow of twenty-seven, skilled at nothing, trained for nothing but more beautiful than any model whose photograph graced magazine covers, who dressed in rags, who – I discovered this a while later – had no lover and scarcely a friend.

Of course she was waiting, looking about her, biding her time. That was what she wanted of life. We opened her window on to the white sky, the plane tree with its branches on which pink-bronze pigeons perched, its thread-like twigs and fine silky leaves hanging still in the windless air. We leant out on to the broad windowsill. So many of my memories of Bell concern windows, sashes, casements, glass and draughts and drops, but there was no draught that summer's day. The air smelt fresh from Regent's Park, it smelt like the air of a spoiled countryside. Bell took a tobacco tin from a drawer in the table and, without asking me, taking things for granted, began to roll a joint. It was the first time for me. She showed me how to draw in the smoke and hold it in my lungs until my head began to swim and curiously to expand, and with the exhalation feel the arrival of a deep, tomorrow-less peace.

*

643

That September Cosette and I went to Italy together. She had meant to go with Ivor, but by that time Ivor had gone.

'You come,' she said to me. 'I'd rather it was you than him anyway. Really. I was dreading going with him.'

I had seen Bell a few times. She had been to visit me at the House of Stairs and we had gone to the cinema together, to the old Electric Cinema in the Portobello Road, and I would have liked her to come to Italy with us.

'I've only once been to a foreign country,' she had said to me, 'and that was to France with Silas. We were at a place called Wissant which is so near it's practically England.'

It made me marvel that someone young and fit preferred to forgo so many pleasures rather than work. Bell had enough to live on but not enough for holidays. One word to Cosette and she would have been invited to join us, her fares and hotel bills paid as a matter of course, for it was taken for granted that any friend of mine partook of Cosette's largesse just as I did. That was the reason why I couldn't say the word. I couldn't even mention that Bell had scarcely been abroad or had no holiday plans this year. I even had to go further and, against the grain as it was, say to Cosette, 'Bell never wants to leave London. She's got to make up for those years she was with Silas out in the sticks.'

In Florence, at the Uffizi, hangs Bronzino's portrait of Lucrezia Panciatichi. This is the painting most critics have agreed inspired the one Henry James describes in *The Wings of the Dove* as hanging in 'the great gilded historic chamber' at Matcham and calls 'the pale personage on the wall'. It resembles, of course, the doomed Milly Theale in her 'eyes of other days, her full lips, her long neck ...' With its 'face almost livid in hue, yet handsome in sadness and crowned with a mass of hair, rolled back and high', it also profoundly resembled Bell.

I wish I could remember whether I saw it there on my first visit to Florence when I went to Italy with Cosette. We must have gone into the Uffizi. I have certainly seen the portrait on subsequent visits but it is no use, try as I will, I can't remember whether I saw it that time. It was a print of that portrait which, walking along the Arno with Cosette, near the Trinità bridge, I saw in a shop window. Cosette was struck by the resemblance – remember that only Cosette saw the similarity between Bell's face and that on my cameo – and standing in front of the print, said that we should buy it.

I concealed my enthusiasm. Although I knew how sensitive to the wishes and secrets of others Cosette was, how she would readily have fallen in with any plan of mine concerning the fate of the picture, I somehow imagined it framed in stainless steel by the 'little man' in Kensington Park Road, hung on the drawing room wall and pointed out to all comers.

'A postcard then,' Cosette said. 'Do you know, I have a dress very much like that somewhere that I had made for the Chelsea Arts Ball. I was supposed to be Lady Jane Grey. I wonder if I could still get into it?'

But Cosette couldn't find a postcard of Lucrezia Panciatichi. Next morning, while she was still asleep, I went out on my own and bought the print of Bronzino's painting which I carried home secretly and for a long while kept in a hiding place.

— 9 —

I was standing in front of my small version of this portrait when Bell phoned.

For a long time the print lay in a drawer of that desk Cosette bought me. I had it framed as soon as I could afford things like that and hung it in my bedroom. If Cosette ever saw it she didn't remark on it. A little while before the murder I took it down and put it away once more, but I never considered ridding myself of it and it travelled with me, first to the flat I had on Primrose Hill when the House of Stairs was sold, then to Hampstead where it again hung on the wall, out to Cambridge for a year or two during my brief marriage, back to London and this Hammersmith house. Though telling myself I am not superstitious, I nevertheless came to associate displaying it on a wall with the coming of bad things.

All the bad things but one thing have happened to me, yet I have put the picture back in the drawer. But three days ago, in the study here, I took the framed Roiter poster down from the wall and hung up the Bronzino in its stead. It is many years since I have looked at it and I seemed to see among its reds and blacks and golds things I have never observed before, the fact for instance that Lucrezia, though well bejewelled, wears only a single ring and that with a very dark stone in it which may even be a bloodstone. Her hair, whatever Henry James may say, is not really red but a very pale copper colour. Of course, he speaks only of a Bronzino, of a pale red-headed lady in red, not of this specific portrait and he would have known very well how many people sat for Bronzino, that this Florentine Mannerist was as distinguished a portraitist as a painter of allegories. Looking at the picture, I was reminded of course not only of Bell herself but of other aspects of our life when Cosette had the House of Stairs, of Bell's interest in *The Wings of the Dove,* of her surprising request to hear the plot of it, of the conspiracy.

In a moment, I thought, I will make that phone call. I will call that number on the six-two-four exchange and put an end to the fearful impasse I have been in this past week, for it is nearly a week now, put an end to procrastination and doubt and persuading myself it is too early or too late to phone, that she is bound to be out, that it is too soon, that it is not soon enough, that tomorrow is the best, destined, most appropriate, day. Lucrezia was returning my regard with her calm, reposeful look – not 'handsome in sadness', surely, not 'livid' – was meeting my eyes with her own large, limpid eyes so that I now saw a resemblance there not only to Bell but also to the young Cosette of early photographs, when the phone rang.

It never crossed my mind it would be Bell. But although all she said, when I had given the number, was 'Hallo', I was in no doubt even for a second who it was. My silence was due to the stupefaction of shock, a shock I felt even though I was prepared, even though I had seen her and knew she had asked for me.

'It's Bell.'

'I know,' I said. 'Oh, I know.' I sat down, feeling a sudden great tiredness. It was a few seconds before I realized I had closed my eyes. 'I saw you,' I said. 'I followed you but you disappeared.'

Bell was never one for explanations if she didn't want to make them, never one to apologize. It was much later I learned that Felicity Thinnesse had rung her up and told her I wanted to be in touch with her.

'Will you come and see me?' she said.

Which is why I am here facing her now across a room which is very like the room in Walter Admetus's house where I was first alone with her. There is a bed with a dirty white cotton cover and a table and a wicker chair and a couple of suitcases as well as two tea-chests. It is a warm spring day and Bell has opened the window, but no fresh breeze from Regent's Park penetrates here, there are no plane trees outside and no Georgian terraces. This house is squeezed up against a railway bridge, crushed so close as to be absurd, all light surely excluded from its front bays, while the back rooms, of which this is one, overlook a scrapyard. Bell tells me that when she was first released from the open prison where she served the final year of her sentence, she was obliged to live in a hostel. Then her probation officer found this room for her. This woman had also found her a job. It is due to start next week and is in a shop where the owner has of necessity been told who and what she is.

'I don't know if I shall be equal to it,' she says, but whether this is because she has scarcely had a job before or because the job is in, of all places, Westbourne Grove, I don't know and she doesn't say. She is very changed in appearance, though still slender and straight with that high-held head on her long neck. Her hair is iron-grey and coarsened by its greying. A tracery of lines lies on her face as if a cobweb had been spread there, and I remember what James said about the portrait in relation to Milly Theale as 'a face . . . that must, before fading with time, have had a family resemblance to her own'.

She wears black, a skirt and a sort of tunic that seems to be no more than a length of material with a hole cut for her neck and the sides sewn up, sandals, no stockings. Her legs have become very thin. I haven't touched her yet, I haven't shaken her hand or kissed her. Shock prevails, and pity and wonder. Will I ever get used to her? Will I ever be able to say calmly to myself, this is Bell?

When I came to the door and she answered it and brought me up here, when the door was shut, she remembered. All these years she has remembered. And she said to me, 'Are you out of the wood yet?'

I was immensely grateful to her. It seemed the greatest kindness, more than any valuable gift.

'Coming to the edge,' I said.

She nodded. I haven't yet seen her smile. 'I often thought about it,' she said. 'I used to wonder.'

She sleeps a lot. She told me she couldn't sleep in prison and since she has been out – over two months had passed before she got up the nerve to phone Felicity – she has slept all night and half the days. 'That's why I mayn't be equal to this job.'

'I don't work at all and I never shall,' she had once said to me, 'I'm never going to work again.'

On the evening I saw her she had been to see the therapist in Shepherds Bush she goes to for her counselling. On the way back she got out of the tube to look at the shop where she is destined to work, vanishing into a tobacconist's in Queensway as I emerged. For while the rest of us gave up cigarettes in the seventies, Bell still smokes. Living on social security, she goes without food to buy cigarettes. Her clothes smell of them and her hair and this room, just as they must have done in Admetus's house, only we all smelt of smoke then, so none of us noticed it.

'Do you mind if I sleep for a while?' she asks me. 'You can stay if you like, or go. I know where you are now and you know where I am.'

But as she stretches out on the bed under the open window, as she curls up and lays one hand under the pillow, she reaches out with the other and takes mine. Like a sick person or a child she means me to hold her hand while she sleeps.

When we came back from Italy, Cosette and I, Bell had moved away from Admetus's house and disappeared. She had gone, leaving no forwarding address, no message for me. To this day I don't know where she went and I no longer care, it no longer matters. Perhaps she was with a man – or a woman – or the simple truth may have been that she could no longer afford the rent Admetus asked.

Somehow, though, I knew she would reappear and find me, that out of the blue or by some other kind of coincidence we would confront each other again. And yet, apart from Felicity, I knew no one who could be called a friend of Bell's, I had never then heard her speak of any friend, or, come to that, of mother, father, siblings, any relatives. She had been married, been widowed, had never worked, always spoke her mind with what seemed like transparent honesty, and that was all I knew of her. Whereas, so thoroughly already had I confided in her, that she knew all about me, my family and, yes, my horrible inheritance, my dead mother, my special regard for Cosette and hers for me, and even the affair, though I am afraid I called it a relationship in those days, I was having with Dominic.

I shouldn't have done it, I know that now. It was one thing to flirt with him, to dance with him, quite another, when we all reached home in the small hours after that dinner at the Marco Polo and that visit to Ivor's club, to go up to his room with him almost as a matter of course. I fancied him, you see. He was so beautiful. It not only didn't seem important then that he was Perpetua's brother, a country boy nearly illiterate, naïve, lacking in almost any kind of sophistication; I also didn't even think about it. I must have known he was a devout Catholic, too. Hadn't I seen him go off to mass every Sunday, every Day of Obligation? I didn't think of that either. I made him my lover because he was slim and tall and straight, because he had the bluest eyes I ever saw and the silkiest raven's-wing hair (the kind that turns grey before any other kind) and a face like one of El Greco's young clerics. Also, and this is more excusable, because of the terror and the bore, because of the thing that hung over me, so that I believed I must take everything I wanted, do everything, live, before an end was put to living for ever.

We were drunk that first time. We didn't talk. But in the morning we made love again and afterwards he said, 'How can someone like you love me?'

I felt a little chill, for I didn't love him, but I didn't understand then either. I didn't understand his simplicity, that from his innocence and his strict life, he believed not only that a woman would sleep with a man solely if she loved him, but also that this man would be the one she had chosen for ever, to be her life partner, almost as though human beings were as monogamous as certain birds who, imprinted in early youth with the image of a mate, remain exclusively bonded to this one for always. Instead, I asked him what he meant. Humble, shy, without self-confidence, his attitude of mind entirely at odds with his splendid, even arrogant, looks, he said that I was clever, educated (had 'been to college' was what he said), was of a 'different class'.

'I'm just an ordinary working fellow,' he said in that voice that was like the *Playboy of the Western World*, that was like Christy Mahon's.

'What,' said I with incredible insensitivity, 'does any of that matter?'

Later on I made him read that bit out of Synge about the holy bishops straining the bars of paradise to catch a glimpse of Helen of Troy, and her walking abroad with a nosegay in her golden shawl. Only he couldn't read it very well, he stumbled over the words, and I had to help him. Oh, I have been too fond of literature one way and another, and produced too little of it myself!

So when I came back to the House of Stairs there was Dominic waiting for me like a husband, calling me 'dear' and telling me he had changed the sheets on the bed for my homecoming. And my heart sank as had begun to happen whenever he came home to me or I to him, for I had wanted a sensuous tumultuous adventure lasting a few weeks and he, it grew ever more obvious, wanted an exclusive lifetime's partnership. Cosette, romantic and with that Wife of Bath side to her, who had rather encouraged our affair in the beginning as she would have encouraged almost any affair, especially one between the young and good-looking, now saw it all.

'The next thing will be he'll want you to marry him,' she said. 'In Brompton Oratory, I expect, or even the Cathedral.'

'I thought it was women who clung and men who wanted to be off,' I almost wailed. 'How can someone look like Don Giovanni and have the soul of a milkman?'

'You can't judge a sausage by its overcoat,' said Cosette.

She had shifted her enthusiasm from my sex life to my career, or at any rate to my immediate project. The idea that I should write a book in her house was delicious to Cosette. What kind of book hardly mattered. Almost without critical judgement, she came close to worshipping anything made by someone she was fond of. Thus, Diana's typing was the fastest and most accurate in London, Gary was the world's greatest virtuoso of the sitar, and the section of the Underground tunnel dug out by Dominic was the best bit. To her the only flaw in my writing project was my insisting on having a job as well, though working in an after-school-hours play-centre wasn't much of a job, and if I am honest about it I shall have to admit it brought me in enough to live on only because I lived rent-free.

The writing room was created in secret during the two or three hours I spent at work in the early evening. It was almost the only room in the house vacant at that time, Gary and Mervyn having one each, Dominic his and I mine – I had never consented to move in permanently with him – Cosette with her grand chamber and Birgitte the new Girl-in-Residence, a real au pair girl this time, in Fay's old room. The top floor of attics, where the high, balcony-less window was, remained unfurnished, a depository for cardboard crates and tea-chests. The room Cosette and Perpetua prepared for me was directly below this one, its window having one of those narrow balconies without a railing which overlooked the grey garden.

A quiet woman with an intense devotion to Cosette, Perpetua would have probably done anything she asked, did in fact put herself out tremendously for her, travelling all that distance daily by bus and cleaning up after a troop of careless, untidy people. Otherwise I doubt if she would have consented to carry furniture upstairs for my benefit, lay carpet and hang curtains for me. She saw what everyone but poor Dominic now saw, that I had been using him and was not in the least in love. And twenty years his senior, a sister grown up before he was born, she resented it as a mother might. Her resentment took the curious form of her ceasing to use my Christian name when she spoke to me. How I was to recall this later when the woman who failed to use my name meant so much, so infinitely much, more to me!

Instead of, 'Coffee's ready, Elizabeth,' she would say, 'There's coffee if you want it,' or, calling upstairs, 'Are you there?' and waiting until the appropriate voice answered.

The desk was delivered and the typewriter unearthed and dictionaries placed in a new bookcase. I stood and admired, was effusive in my gratitude. Cosette, a good as well as a generous giver, took a simple, innocent pleasure in being thanked and enjoyed an enthusiastic reception of her gifts. It was then that I said how much I should like a dictionary of classical Greek (which I intended to teach myself and later did) and then that Cosette promised me one for Christmas, failing, producing instead a modern Greek dictionary, and earning from me those unkind reproaches I am for ever ashamed of having made.

So that winter, the winter that was the bridge from the sixties into the seventies, I sat down to write my novel, beginning on a glorious day at the end of October when it was as hot as midsummer. With the example of Henry James before me, knowing James as thoroughly as I did, I might have at least tried to write something that was an examination of the human heart, but I didn't. I wanted money, I was after the fast buck, the quick return, because I was an inheritor of Huntington's chorea and I had to live now while I could, I had to have it all now. So I embarked on a cheap, sexy, romantic adventure story about people of the kind I had never met and set in places I had never been to but could mug up well enough for my purposes from travel books and other people's novels. That is the sort of book I have been writing ever since.

Cosette treated my endeavours with reverence. In her eyes I had become almost overnight an 'artist' and she had the attitude the French have towards those who create, almost irrespective of what they create. My work must be looked on by others as the most important activity going on in the house, they must creep up the stairs, forbear to play their records and musical instruments, lower their voices, and never, never interrupt me by coming to my door. Naturally, after a while, this discipline slackened and the old hubbub returned, but Cosette herself never changed, continuing to treat me in this area of my life in a way appropriate to a Balzac, say, or at any rate a Graham Greene.

One afternoon, when I had been writing for most of the day and was nearly due to go off to my play-centre job, I had a phone call from Felicity Thinnesse. She sounded excited and distrait.

'I got your number from Elsa. The woman whose house you're living in, she takes paying guests, doesn't she?'

I was unreasonably incensed. Poor Felicity of course had asked me in good faith, probably like most people being unable to imagine anyone giving board and lodging to a host of freeloaders like Gary and Mervyn and Fay and Birgitte.

'Why do you ask?'

'I've left Esmond. Well, I will have left him when I've found somewhere to go. I have to find a room.'

I don't know why I thought of the children. I remembered Miranda repeating her mother's strictures on right behaviour. 'For three of you?' I said doubtfully.

'I can't cope with Jeremy and Miranda. They'll stay with Esmond. Then,' Felicity added very oddly, 'he won't have so much to make a fuss about.'

I told her I would ask Cosette, promising to call her back 'before Esmond gets home or after he's gone out to the Conservative Association'.

I found Cosette in the drawing room accompanied only by Auntie and Maurice Bailey from Wellgarth Avenue. Now he was a widower he used to spend a lot of time pottering about in Harrods and the big

Kensington High Street stores, and at teatime he would take a taxi through the park and look in on Cosette for half an hour. The purpose of these visits seemed to make comments on the wretchedness of Cosette's lifestyle by contrast to what she might have had. Therefore the question I had to ask Cosette only served to inflame him further. I made it in his presence because I knew, or thought I knew then, that Cosette rather enjoyed what Felicity would have called 'winding him up'.

'Another sponger,' he said. 'This place must be notorious as the local doss-house.'

Auntie, enjoying it, looked timidly from one to the other of them. Cosette appeared rather splendid in a totally unsuitable blue brocade caftan. Since the departure of Ivor Sitwell she had been wearing less make-up and had regained some of her lost weight, so that she looked younger and quite well and flourishing. Her hair was by then a very pale golden blonde. I told her, quoting Wilde, that at the loss of Ivor it had turned quite gold from grief, and she liked this so much that she repeated it to everyone. Now, mildly to rile Maurice Bailey, she began to enthuse over the coming of Felicity.

'Of course you must tell her she can come here, darling. How awful to be obliged to stay with a man because you've nowhere to go; can you imagine?'

'I'll call her back then, shall I?'

'Yes, do that, and tell her she'll be most welcome. I don't know where we'll put her, one of the rooms at the top, I suppose. Perpetua will organize that, you know how marvellous she is. Don't look at me like that, Maurice.' She put one of her beautiful hands out to him, lightly touching his jacket sleeve. Unused all her life, Cosette's hands were still girlish, plump and white, taper-fingered, with nails like blanched almonds, heavily be-ringed. 'Maurice,' she cajoled. 'Haven't you a smile for me? Felicity will pay me rent, you know, or at least she'll make it up in kind. There'll be all sorts of little jobs for her to do.'

As there were for Mervyn and Gary, who had long since ceased to carry out their functions of floor-polishing and car-cleaning; as there were for Birgitte, the Danish au pair who, perfectly willing to work for her living when first she arrived, had rapidly been persuaded by her employer that there was nothing for her to do, told it was a shame

653

for someone so young and pretty not to have a good time while she could and why not enjoy herself in Carnaby Street and down the King's Road?

So Felicity came a few days later. Subdued and chastened at first, fearful that Esmond would find out where she was and come after her, she took to Cosette immediately and poured out her heart to her. A tête-à-tête was virtually impossible, there were always too many people around for that, people used to follow Cosette into her bedroom at some ungodly hour of the morning, at three or four, and continue their conversations or their musical renderings sitting on her bed. But Felicity, undeterred, would commandeer Cosette, corner her and talk, sometimes sprawling at her feet with her head in Cosette's lap, sometimes opposite her at the table, leaning forward, gazing into her eyes, and snatches of what she said would reach the rest of us, or those who cared to listen, isolated words and phrases: 'my bloody husband', 'his old bitch of a mother', 'prison', 'buried alive', 'living death', 'frustration', 'pain', 'misery'.

At that period there were living in the House of Stairs: Cosette, myself, Dominic, Mervyn, Gary, Birgitte, Mervyn's girlfriend Mimi, Auntie and now Felicity. Nine people. At Christmas Diana Castle and the man she lived with came up to stay for the holiday and stayed on for several weeks. That made eleven. Those two were obliged to bed down in sleeping-bags on the floor of the top front room. Cosette, of course, was prepared to buy a bed to accommodate her visitors, except that no one, not least the shop delivery people, could be found willing to carry it up a hundred stairs. Even Perpetua rebelled, saying darkly that any more lifting would give her a prolapse.

She and Dominic had transported a convertible sofa-bed upstairs for Felicity, for which service they each got extravagant praise and a fiver from Cosette. The room was the one above what Cosette called my 'sanctum' and Felicity, when she arrived, was very politely requested to be 'as quiet as a mouse' during the sacred hours of ten till three, while I was working. It had once been for a maid or maids and was a shabby chamber with sloping ceiling, very different from the rooms on the lower floors. By the look of the walls and woodwork, no one had painted it since the house was built. Cosette was all for getting Gary to paint it before Felicity moved in and gave him some sort of extravagant payment in advance, but in fact it was a long time before he got around to the painting and by then Felicity had gone back to Esmond and her children.

A few days in the House of Stairs and of confiding in Cosette set her up splendidly and she was soon her old self, teasing, fascinated by everything, censorious, dispensing useless, inconsequential information, contemptuous of the slower-witted. I was invited up to her room to look at the view and pronounce on whether the dome she could see was Whiteley's or the Greek Orthodox Church. That window was alarming when you stood close up to it and looked out. Even worse when you looked down through the sheer drop of forty feet or so to the garden, its grey-leaved plants sodden with rain or nipped by frost. Directly below the window was an area paved with York stone that Cosette called the terrace and Perpetua the patio. Somehow the window would have been less frightening if there had been lawn beneath it or a flowerbed.

Felicity said she had been out of the window on to the narrow ledge. You have to understand that this was a window, not a glass door or pair of doors, but coming very low down, to no more than six inches or so from the floor, a sash window which could be opened to create an aperture four feet deep either at the top or the bottom. Outside, Felicity said, on the stone or ashlar or whatever it was surrounding the window frame, there were deep holes, each with a trickle mark of iron stain under it, to which, she was sure, the bars of some kind of cage or grille had once been attached. It was long gone by Cosette's time. We speculated as to why the foot of the window should be so close to the floor and Felicity suggested, rightly no doubt, that at some time the floor had been raised. For sound-proofing? To make a greater space between the floor of this room and the ceiling of the room below? Because the maids, rising early, might have disturbed a sleeper in the 'sanctum'?

'No one ever opened their windows in those days,' Felicity said very sweepingly, and lingering with relish over the word, 'so there wouldn't have been any risk of defenestration.'

I don't believe I had come across the word before. 'Haven't you ever heard of the Defenestration of Prague?' said Felicity. 'I expect that was when it was first used. "Defenestratio" would be the Latin, you know. It was in the Thirty Years War. Some Protestants threw two Catholic bishops out of a window in Prague, but they weren't really hurt, they fell into the moat.'

'You mugged that up for one of your quizzes,' I said.

'I'll tell you what, Elizabeth, I never did another quiz after the one we couldn't finish because that woman Bell Sanger came in telling us Silas was shot. It put me right off.'

'I never heard what happened at the inquest,' I said.

'Suicide while the balance of his mind was disturbed. It was more the balance of the gun, if you ask me. He'd been playing Russian roulette.'

'I don't exactly know what you do in Russian roulette,' I said.

'It's something White Russian officers used to play to alleviate boredom,' she said, true to form. 'You've got six chambers in the revolver, you see, and you put a bullet in just one, so in theory you've got one chance in six of killing yourself, which makes the odds pretty high. But if the chamber's perfectly balanced the weight of the bullet will generally carry it to the bottom, so the chances of surviving are a lot greater than you'd expect. That's why they say Russian roulette cheats death.'

'Only Silas's gun wasn't perfectly balanced,' I said.

'That's what they said at the inquest, but I don't know, I thought it was jolly fishy. Silas was mad about guns, he was always messing about with guns, he really knew about them.'

'Maybe he wanted to die.'

'Maybe he did, poor Silas. If he'd lived another day he'd have known he'd inherited his father's house and have had something to live on.'

I didn't tell her I already knew that. She opened the window, raising the sash from the bottom, and we looked down the long drop, I crouching on the floor for safety's sake, Felicity, who had no fear at all of heights, standing there in her miniskirt, her long, long legs in red tights, glancing idly down as anyone else might at an object dropped on the pavement. The cold drove us back and we shut the window once more on the flurry of sleet the wind carried.

— 10 —

Once I would have held Bell's hand until she woke, I would have held it the night through. Even though my fingers were numb I would have held it. But not now. Once I would have been fearful she would never phone, no matter what promises she made, but now I knew she would. It changes, as Cosette said. She slept, relieved I think that she had found me and that I was willing to speak to her, visit her, know her. I extricated my hand, touched her cheek lightly with my finger, and went home.

In the spring I went with Dominic to one of the performances given by a company that called itself Global Experience. I had an idea that poor Dominic would find the whole thing incomprehensible and even frightening and that was why I wanted him with me. Unforgivable this was, shamefully unkind. For what Global Experience put on was the ultimate in audience participation. Dressed in cheesecloth robes which were conspicuous for being without buttons or zips, the company danced and mimed, took partners from out of the onlookers and each pair then stood or sat gravely face-to-face, experiencing each other by touch, stroking arms and shoulders and hair, but being quite prudishly careful to avoid erogenous zones. Objects were also examined by each couple together, with a view supposedly to seeing them in a new light, and I remember me and my partner (not of course Dominic) going into raptures over the texture, colour and scent of a very ordinary and rather battered Jaffa orange.

It was months since I had seen Bell, but she was in the audience at Global Experience that night. For some reason, perhaps because stroking a stranger and exploring an orange demand great concentration, I didn't see her until afterwards, when Dominic and I were in the theatre's cafeteria, called Food of Love, drinking apple juice and eating sticks of raw carrot and celery. We were just about to leave, poor Dominic by then bewildered to the point of being seriously upset, when I saw Bell sitting at a table in the far corner with two other girls and two men.

One of these men was very much like her to look at, darker but with the same sort of features, the same straight carriage and graceful way of moving. Before I reached the table and said hallo to her he had got up and gone to the bar or food counter.

'Is that your brother?' I said.

She turned to look at him, hesitated, nodded. 'Yes. Yes, it is. Good-looking, isn't he?'

'He's like you.'

'You could say that. D'you fancy him then? Shall I see what I can do?'

'I'm with someone,' I said, 'and I do have to go.' And then I said, 'I wish you'd come round, I'd love to see you.'

That was my first sight of Mark. Perhaps it was true that I fancied him, that I admired him desirously at that first encounter, briefly, for a matter of seconds. Any woman would have. And Dominic took it upon himself to be jealous, accusing me of only going to Global Experience for the opportunities he said it gave for wanton behaviour. His words, not mine. He was an Irishman, after all, and though often silent, never inarticulate. I forgot Mark within minutes, hardly supposing I would ever see him again, naturally having no prevision of the part he was to play in all our lives. It was Bell alone I held in my mind, hoping she would come.

A week or so later she did. There was a crowd of us in the drawing room with Cosette: Diana Castle and her boyfriend, who were back again, Mervyn and Mimi, Dominic, Birgitte and Felicity. Mervyn and Mimi were one of those couples who can't keep their hands off each other for five minutes. You seemed to come upon them all over the house – it was almost as if they could be in two or even three places at once – standing on a bend in the stairs kissing, lying mouth to mouth and hip to hip on a sofa or someone else's bed, just inside an open door, with hands on each other's shoulders, gazing into eyes. Cosette, true to form, had seemed to like it at first, but by then most of us, for various reasons, resented Mervyn and Mimi. They served to show us what we all lacked. I would have liked someone to love me, but not Dominic. Dominic wanted me and no one else. Diana and her boyfriend were on bad terms, they quarrelled all the time. And Cosette, poor Cosette, was no nearer finding the lover she longed for than she had ever been. As for Felicity, she was dying for a love affair but afraid to have one, 'woefully out of practice' was how she put it to me, scared all the time Esmond would come and haul her off before she had had a chance to make up for all those years of repression. That evening she was talking to us about Selevin's mouse. This had been quite funny at first and Cosette, particularly, had been enchanted.

'It's a Russian rodent that lives in the desert, and can you imagine, it was only discovered in 1939. I mean, think of them, millions of them probably, little fat animals with grey fur, all living in the deserts in Russia, and no one knowing they were there. They only come out at night, you see. The really amazing thing about Selevin's mouse is that it can't stand more than a few minutes' exposure to the sun without becoming ill.'

'I don't believe it, Felicity,' Cosette said. 'You're making it up.'

'I swear before God,' said Felicity with unnecessary melodrama, 'I can prove everything I've said. Look it up in the *Encyclopaedia Britannica*. That's all you have to do, look it up.'

'We haven't got *Britannica*.'

'You can go to the library in the morning and look it up.'

'I do believe you really, darling, only it seems so odd. I think it's lovely really. I think it's enchanting. The poor little loves being ill when the sun shines.'

This had been a day or two before. Felicity, however, went on and on about it, she couldn't leave it alone. When Auntie had admitted the day before to not feeling very well, Felicity said that, like Selevin's mouse, she must have been out in the sun. Someone, Gary I think, happened to mention he was an only child, whereupon Felicity said he was like Selevin's mouse, the only member of the family *Selevini-idae*. To her it was all uproariously funny. Dominic sat there eyeing her uneasily, having an unfounded notion that all this was being done to mock him.

That was the evening Cosette was wearing the bloodstone. I had seen it on her finger only once before. This time she must have put it on to match her rather grand and dramatic new dress, a long-skirted robe of dark green shot silk which showed a red or green gleam according to the way the light caught it. The ring still seemed too heavy for her hand, but it no longer looked out of place. In candlelight – and Felicity was going about lighting candles – the red in it glittered like sparks against the deep green of the chalcedony.

'Haematite,' Felicity said, picking up Cosette's hand to look at it.

Cosette said gently, 'No, heliotrope, I believe, Felicity. I think that's the term in – what do you call it? Petrology?'

Felicity wouldn't have that. 'Oh, no, absolutely not. It's from the Greek for blood as in haemorrhage, haemophilia and so on. "Haema", meaning blood and "tite", stone.'

'Yes, but not this stone, darling, that's quite another kind, a sort of red rock.' Cosette was right, as it happens, I looked it up next day, but she didn't insist, she wasn't the kind to insist, having a horror of

659

seeming superior to anyone. She was quite capable of apologizing for being right, just as she was of spending much of her time (as Henry James has it) making excuses for obnoxious acts she had not committed. Afflicted by no such scruples, Felicity was going on in her didactic way about Greek and the ignorance of people now they seldom learned it any more, going on much as she did about the lifestyle of the Russian dormouse, when the doorbell rang.

'That will be Walter,' Cosette said.

It was the sort of time we often saw Admetus, around nine-thirty in the evening. I went to the window. It was the end of April and not really dark. If I appeared on the balcony the courtly Admetus could be relied on to strike an attitude, to step back, place his hand on his heart and declare that this window was the east and Juliet the sun. For some reason I liked the idea of that. It came to me in that moment that if Admetus and I were to get something going, it would free me from Dominic. I opened the french windows, stepped out on to the balcony and, looking down over the Ca' Lanier railing, saw Bell looking up. The lamplight shone on her pale hair. She was in black, but with that mud-and-granite-coloured shawl wrapped tightly round her, the shawl I had last seen draped by Esmond over Silas Sanger's dead body. I swear it was the same, I recognized it at once.

Bell came upstairs with me and, seeing Felicity as soon as the drawing-room door was opened, receiving her rather surprised, 'Hallo, there!', seemed thunderstruck.

'What are you doing here?'

'Thanks very much,' said Felicity. 'I suppose I can be here as much as you can.'

'Is Esmond here too?'

Nobody answered her. Mervyn and Mimi were lying locked in each other's arms on the carpet in a corner. Dominic had picked up some musical instrument of Gary's and sat disconsolately plucking the same note over and over on a string. With a glance at the couple on the floor, Bell lifted her thin straight shoulders, loosened the shawl, looping it over her arms. Rather to my surprise, she went up to Cosette, shook hands with her and asked her how she was. But no more time was to be wasted. She had come to see me and, being Bell, made no bones about it.

'Can we go up to your room?'

For some reason I took it that she meant the room I wrote in rather than my bedroom. On the stairs – there were 106, remember, to the top, ninety-five to my writing room – she said, 'They're all on the make, aren't they? Getting what they can out of her? Does she know?'

'I don't think she minds,' I said.

'I should mind those two wanking around on the floor. I'd throw them out.'

'Cosette would never do that.'

Bell never read a book. I don't think she had read a book since she left school, whenever and wherever that had been, but if there were books lying about she would pick them up and scrutinize them in a wondering, curious sort of way, as someone else might examine an ornament. We lit cigarettes and she walked about the room looking at everything, astonished that I was writing a novel, glancing at *The Princess Casamassima*, which I was currently reading, picking up a couple of works of reference that lay on my desk, surveying the dictionaries Cosette had provided, at last turning her back on literature and its mysteries, back to me and to reality, which was what she understood.

'I suppose Felicity has left Esmond. When they had rows she always said she would leave him before she was thirty-five. He'll come for her though, you'll see, and she'll go back to him.'

I couldn't go along with that. Felicity was adamant that she would never go back. Even if she never saw her children again she wouldn't go back. She had even found herself a waitress's job at a café in Shepherds Bush. I had yet to learn that when it came to human behaviour Bell was almost always right. She knew people and how they were likely to react. Not being addicted to literature, scarcely knowing that literature existed, she had not had her perception suppressed under its narcosis or her assessments of human nature distorted by its false reality.

'She's going to divorce him,' I said.

'Esmond will never let himself be divorced.'

'Under this new law,' I said, 'he won't have much choice. She can do it without his consent after five years.'

Bell didn't answer directly. She had lit another cigarette from the stub of the first, was sitting on the floor with her back against the wall. Comfort never meant much to her. 'Who knows where we'll all be in five years?' she said.

It was pouring with rain when the time came for her to go. I suggested she stay the night, though in the present state of over-crowding that would have meant another sleeping-bag. But she wouldn't stay, though it was nearly midnight. Nor would she tell me where she was living. That is to put it rather too strongly, for of course she didn't actually refuse to tell me, just as I didn't ask her outright. I asked her for her phone number and she said she didn't have a phone. But she had walked, she told me when she first came, to Archangel Place. Now Bell was a great walker, unlike me, and it would have been nothing out of the way for her to undertake three or four miles, which gave a pretty wide radius for her to be living within.

'You aren't going to walk back?' And I added, 'To wherever it is?'

'Sort of that way.' She waved in a vague north-easterly direction. 'I could get a cab, only in my budget I don't allow for cabs.'

We would phone for a cab, I said. Cosette was always phoning for cabs.

'Then she'll pay for it. I don't want that.'

I was struck by this, a very rare attitude for anyone in Cosette's orbit to take. There was a purity about Bell, I thought, a rectitude. She gave me one of her cool smiles. All she wanted, she said, was for me to lend her a mac or a raincoat or even just an umbrella. And that was how we came to go into my bedroom.

Descending, we encountered on the third-floor landing, standing within an alcove like a pair of statues in the half-dark, Venus and Adonis perhaps, Mervyn and Mimi locked together. I opened the door of my bedroom, having forgotten for the moment what hung on the wall facing us. The light came on and Bell, entering, looked straight at the Bronzino. She approached it slowly, stood silent in front of it while I grubbed around in the cupboard for something to cover her. Then, 'That's me,' she said.

I prevaricated. 'It was painted about 400 years before you were born.'

'It's still me. Where did you get it? Did you put it there because it looks like me?'

'Yes,' I said.

I held out my thin, silky black raincoat for her to put her arms into. She drew it round her, shawl and all, her back still to me. I had never closed the door, it still stood ajar. From downstairs came the weird plucked notes of the sitar. Bell took my face in her hands and kissed

662

my mouth. It was a mouth-to-mouth kiss, but it might just have been received and interpreted as a woman saluting another woman in friendship and affection, except that it lingered rather long and I thought – I was not quite certain but I did think so – I felt the tip of her tongue touch the rim of my upper lip. The sound of a door opening downstairs and the volume of the sitar music increasing parted us. In a little while, after she was gone, I would begin to tremble but not then, not then. I said, very lightly, 'There's an umbrella down in the hall. You mustn't get wet.'

But she changed her mind about the taxi, one happening to come cruising along Archangel Place as we splashed out into the wet windy dark. I hadn't a key and I let the door close behind me so that Cosette had to come down and let me in.

'Darling, you're cold,' she said. 'You're shivering.'

Until they came and took her away I never lost Bell again after that. Let me correct that and say she never went off again and disappeared.

A lot of things happened that summer. My book was accepted by a publisher. Felicity found a lover. Cosette gave the first of her big parties. Birgitte left and went home to Odense. Mervyn and Mimi departed to set up house together in a caravan.

Cosette said she never had any doubt I would find a publisher. She had read the typescript and went about telling everyone, to my mild embarrassment, what a wonderful book it was. A sort of cross between *Gone With the Wind* and *Murder on the Orient Express*, she said, without irony and intending high praise. She wasn't, in fact, far wrong. Now, I thought, having received a much bigger advance than I expected, I should be able to get down to my critical work on Henry James. That was before I had really looked at my contract and seen my publishers had an option on my next work of fiction, which they had been led to expect within twelve months. I hadn't known until then that in life there are traps in which one gets caught where one is obliged to pedal round and round in a squirrel cage.

Birgitte had been caught shoplifting in the food hall at Harrods. It can't have been because she didn't get enough to eat at home, but perhaps for some neurotic or compulsive reason. If meals were irregular in the House of Stairs and mostly you had to get what you wanted for yourself, the fridge and the larder were overflowing with food, splendid food of the luxury kind, out-of-season vegetables, salmon and pheasant and caviar and paté and profiteroles and cream and strawberries. Cosette was in the habit of taking Auntie out for drives, and while they were out they always went shopping. Birgitte had gone into the food hall carrying two empty Harrods carriers. With incredible naïvety she must have believed they would therefore think she had paid for what she had in them. She had helped herself to tins of biscuits and boxes of chocolates and a jar of some sort of candied fruit before she was caught. It made me wonder if she had got the idea from Gary's habit of filling bags with leftover food in the restaurants Cosette took us to dine in. He too was gone by July, off like so many others at that time on the golden road to India. And Mervyn had departed for his caravan, no longer able to endure, he told us, any company but that of Mimi and hers too in isolation. We were missing two bottles of brandy and six of claret after he left, but I said nothing about it to Cosette, though I think she knew.

Felicity's lover was called Harvey something. He was one of those tallish, thinnish, thirty-ish men with dark shaggy hair and moustache and beard, in much-worn crew-neck sweater and patched jeans, who thronged the streets of west London then and still throng them today. He hardly spoke and was shy, being more Auntie's type, one would have thought, than Felicity's. I never heard how she met him or witnessed his introduction to the house. He just appeared in her company. One day she was alone and the next Harvey was with her, sitting beside her holding hands. To be fair to her, she had probably asked Cosette if he could stay, could move in with her that is. It just happens that I didn't hear her ask.

You could see she was very proud to have secured a man of her own. She was like Cosette had been when she first landed Ivor Sitwell. I remarked on this to Bell as we sat side by side on one of the flights of stairs at Cosette's party. Bell was very dressed-up, wearing a feather boa and artificial pink roses with a dress of black crêpe de Chine and lace, bought for seven and sixpence at a jumble sale at St Mary The Boltons. It was then that she told me about Ivor not being a real Sitwell, though she seemed to have no actual idea what a real Sitwell was.

'Brothers and a sister who were writers, Eva said.' For it was Eva Faulkner, Admetus's stand-offish ex-girlfriend, who had spilt the beans. 'She's well rid of him,' she said of Cosette. 'Do you think she'd like someone else?'

'She'd like someone she could love and who would love her. Wouldn't we all?'

Bell gave me a strange, sidelong look. She didn't reply. Perhaps she thought I didn't expect a reply, or more likely because she herself did not come into the category I spoke of. There had been no repetition of that kiss. We were cool, friendly, chain-smoking, with a bottle of wine between us on the stairs, half a French stick and a piece of Brie. We sat there commenting on the guests who came up and down, who sat five stairs below us, who congregated on the landing beneath.

Dawn Castle and her husband had come, out of place but determined to enjoy themselves. Even Maurice Bailey had come. He spent the evening in the dining room talking to Auntie. Walter Admetus was there with a new woman – so much for my ideas of seducing him – and Fay, long forgiven by Cosette, there with a new man. A pair of ballet dancers, Cosette's latest acquisition, had arrived early. They were husband and wife. Perdita Reed was as beautiful as Bell but in a different way, tiny, white-skinned, with classic ballerina looks, the raven hair drawn back and centre-parted. She had been approaching international fame when she fell in love with a dancer from Madrid. Apparently she wanted him to appear in everything she was in, it might be thought to the detriment of her career. I overheard Fay's new man say something slighting about Cosette, and if Luis Llanos gave no reply beyond a smile, he didn't spring to her defence either. Though inhabiting a borrowed flat in Hampstead, though grandly and gorgeously dressed, they were poor and needy.

A lot of people at that party, as Bell pointed out, were there for the purpose of freeloading. 'Everyone comes here,' she said, 'on the gravy train to Cadgeville.'

It reminded me of *The Great Gatsby*, the bit about all the world and its mistress going to Gatsby's house and where the young ladies are saying nasty things about him while picking his roses and drinking his champagne. Of course it didn't remind Bell of any such thing, she never having heard of Fitzgerald, or almost any other novelist, come to that. Sometimes I think it would have been better for everyone if I never had, if it had been history or political economy I had read at university.

Caterers had done the food but everyone was left to help themselves. They were left to help themselves to drink too because this was Cosette's way, she who seldom drank more than half a glass of wine, but it was a mistake. A lot of them were well away by ten-thirty. It was at about that time too that the sweet reek of marijuana crept up the stairs from somewhere down below. Auntie followed it up, carrying with her all the things old ladies take to bed with them, a book and glasses and a handbag and a knitting bag. To my surprise Bell jumped up and gave her an arm. Auntie had been rather dragging at the banister, her face grey with a kind of tired bewilderment, and Cosette, watching her from the landing below, seemed about to follow and help her. I had never seen Bell do anything like that before, I had never seen her take a scrap of notice of Auntie before. She seemed to know which room was hers though, for she opened the door and escorted Auntie in, saying, 'Good-night, Mrs Miller,' and telling her to sleep well.

We went downstairs in pursuit of what Bell succinctly called 'dope'. The landing on the drawing-room floor was more spacious than the others and there stood on it at one side a scroll-ended sofa and at the other a kind of day-bed with no back but vertical sides. I once possessed a postcard photograph of Proust seated on just such a day-bed which so enraptured Cosette that, at enormous expense, she got an antique dealer in Kensington Church Street to find this one for her. Seated on it now were Felicity and Harvey who, perhaps following Mervyn and Mimi's example, were kissing and nuzzling and fondling each other. Admetus was sitting on the sofa opposite, drinking brandy, his girlfriend stretched out with her head in his lap.

People sat on stairs all the way down, most of them drunk and a lot of them engaged in what I once heard Ivor pompously define as 'the preliminaries to sexual congress'. Maurice Bailey had had enough of it and was going home. Having donned his summer hat of white straw, he was shaking hands with Cosette just inside the front door and telling her in a very repressive way not to over-tire herself.

For a little while Bell and I joined the circle of smokers in the dining room, passing round the joint speared on a hatpin with a marcasite rose on it, which must have belonged to Cosette, if not to Auntie. The doors to the garden were open. It was a warm soft night and a big orange moon was slowly rising behind the roofs and spires of Notting Dale. But the light it shed was mysteriously pale. As it rose, revealing itself like a large, glowing, not quite spherical, fruit, a light breeze came with it, ruffling all the grey foliage and making the leaves of the eucalypt shake with a soft rattle. A group stood watching it and commenting on this moonrise with extravagant admiration. There were a lot of people around at that time who raved about nature, about almost any natural phenomenon, about a common flowering weed even, and they were always those who were entirely ignorant of natural history. Over in the corner, on the stone seat, behind which the macleaya grew tall with its bluish vine-like leaves and feathery orange blossom, Gary and Fay were supervising a friend of theirs who had embarked on an acid trip. They had given him the LSD in a spoonful of jam, and now that it was too late, though nothing had so far happened, he had remembered a good reason for not experimenting with hallucinogens.

'I'm a phobiac,' I heard him say nervously. 'I have arachnophobia. Suppose I start seeing spiders. I might see spiders on me. I'll go mad if I get spiders on me.'

Dominic, somehow isolated in this crowd, stood watching them with the unhappy near-disbelief of a crypto-Christian at a Roman orgy. When he saw me his expression changed from incredulous dismay to reproach. I knew he would soon be leaving, that his sister had found a room for him in Kilburn in the next street to where she lived, and, coward that I was, I hoped to avoid a showdown, an explanation, telling myself it was an ugly rather than a dignified parting that I feared. So I looked quickly away, I turned away, and taking Bell by the arm, was leading her back into the house when two things happened simultaneously. The clock on the tower of St Michael the Archangel at the end of the street struck midnight and the doorbell rang.

It didn't just ring, it rang insistently, as if whoever it was had put finger to bell and kept it there, pressing hard. I thought it was more guests arriving, or rather gatecrashers, for as many of the people there were uninvited as invited. How could you tell, when Cosette had said to Gary and Fay and Dominic, to Felicity and Harvey and even the ballet dancers, to ask anyone they liked?

'Most likely the neighbours complaining,' said Bell.

But it wasn't the neighbours or gatecrashers. It was Esmond Thinnesse.

Neither Bell nor I let him in, but we were the first people he saw that he knew, indeed, apart from his wife, the only people there that he

667

knew, for by then Elsa the Lioness had married and gone to live in France. He had been thin before, but now he was much thinner. He had an ascetic, even priestly, look. In fact, that was essentially the way he did look, like some monk long subjected to a severe discipline or fast. I remembered he was supposed to be particularly religious, and now his face had the rapt, trance-like look of a holy martyr in a Renaissance painting. Or so it appeared in the mixed moonlight and candlelight which was the hallway's only illumination.

He said to me, 'I've come for my wife. Where is she?'

Someone behind me gave a nervous giggle. I was momentarily stunned. It was the oddness of it that astounded me, that a man as conventional and in many ways old-fashioned as Esmond should for any purpose whatever come like this to a stranger's house without warning in the middle of the night. He seemed to sense what was passing through my mind, for he said, 'I have been in London all day on business. I have the motor with me. Finding myself at Marble Arch, I had an impulse to come here. It seemed the best way.' He spoke rather remotely, like one who has suffered such terrible unhappiness that it has drained him of all emotion. Or perhaps like someone who has done as his faith adjured him to do and cast his burdens upon God. 'We can't,' he added in the same tone, 'go on like this.'

I was beginning to say, 'She's upstairs somewhere . . .' but Bell was quicker and, recalling no doubt what Felicity had been doing upstairs, was half-way up the first flight before I had finished my sentence. Esmond followed her and I him, a crocodile of people following me, all of them somehow sensing melodrama, growing bored with the party, wanting a new stage for it, a climax or at least a diversion. But a curious silence fell, at any rate on the stairs and that first landing where faces appeared over the curve in the banisters. Above, of course, the hubbub continued, augmented at that moment by music from the record player in Gary's room on the second floor where someone had put on, at full volume, a Rolling Stones record.

Bell, in any case, was too late. Not knowing what all this signified or who had arrived, Felicity and Harvey, having long before this gravitated from the day-bed to a real bed, came out of Cosette's bedroom carrying empty wine glasses and in a state of extreme dishevelment. Felicity persisted in wearing her mini-skirts, though the fashion for them was past, and the one she had on, of black

668

leather, had its zip undone. Her long dark hair hung loose over her shoulders, and her face – she always made up heavily – was like a painter's palette at the end of a hard day's work. Harvey had his arm round her shoulders, his hand scooping up and squeezing her left breast as if he were trying to express milk from it.

Cosette whispered to me, 'Who is he?'

'Her husband.'

'Oh dear. It's all like the worst excesses of the Roman Empire, isn't it?'

Felicity screamed when she saw Esmond.

I said afterwards to someone, Cosette I think it was, that it must have been dreadful for him, her screaming like that. He must surely then have remembered moments of passion and tenderness between them, perhaps those first moments of love beginning or the time when the sight of him, far from causing her to scream and hide her head in another man's arms, brought her running to him with joy. But his face showed nothing of this. He said, 'Felicity, I want you to come home with me. Come with me now and we can be home in an hour.'

You could see Harvey didn't want any part in this. Felicity was clinging on to him, but he wasn't holding her. He whispered something to her and then actually began backing away. She lifted her head from his chest and turned slowly round, cringing, with her shoulders hunched. People were coming down the upward flight now. I don't think Esmond was aware of them, I don't think he was really aware of anyone but himself and Felicity and perhaps a few vague, scarcely human, presences, a faceless chorus in a tragedy.

'Come with me now, please,' he said. 'This has gone on long enough.'

I thought he would say something about the children, but he didn't. He simply repeated his request to her. The landing was still lit only by candles and moonlight but now Esmond, who had never been in the house before, put out one hand and pressed the light switch as if he had been doing so in this particular place every night for years. A kind of chandelier of metal branches bearing spheres of etched glass hung there and the light it gave was so bright that Cosette avoided having it on. When the brilliance flooded us all, making people blink and showing up their untidy hair and crumpled clothes, Felicity gave another cry, but this time it was a piteous, yielding sound. Esmond approached her, putting out his hand. She hesitated. She said, incredibly,'What about all my things?'

I wouldn't have been surprised if someone had laughed, but there was utter silence except for Mick Jagger upstairs. Bell's and mine were the only names of those present that Esmond knew and he said, without looking at us, without taking his eyes from Felicity, 'Elizabeth or Bell will send them on.'

She took his hand and went with him. They passed me and went down the stairs. On her face was a look of total defeat. Her freedom had lasted nine months, and I should think it was a matter of doubt whether she had enjoyed it. Esmond spoke not a word to anyone and nor did she. The front door closed quietly behind them and I heard a car start.

I had a note from her two or three weeks later, thanking me for sending the two packages of her clothes, and after about a year, or a year and a bit, she phoned to invite Cosette and me to Thornham for Christmas. For various reasons, though rather touched at being invited, we refused. Later on Elsa told me Esmond had bought the flat at the World's End, very much the 'in' place to live at that date, to afford Felicity a kind of bolt-hole. I heard about her, but I never heard from her nor spoke to her until two weeks ago.

The party began to break up after they left. That kind of thing casts a blight on merry-making, in much the same way as a ghost might, coming to the table and sitting down in an empty chair. We never saw Harvey again. Though he had been living in the House of Stairs, sleeping with Felicity in her room on the top floor, he must have had somewhere else to go, for he disappeared along with the crowd that went when the dancers went.

Only Gary and Fay and their phobiac friend remained, still out in the garden, still on the stone seat, and looking now in the moonlight like a group of statuary on a fountain after the water has been turned off. Arms round each other, heads lolling, they sprawled in attitudes of abandonment, even the acid-freak in a peaceful, stupefied doze. Bell and I looked down at them from the dangerous window of the top room, the room which had been Felicity's. I had conducted her there, offering her the bed, when she said it was too late for her to go home. We opened the lower sash and leaned out, lying on our stomachs for safety's sake. The sky was clear but no stars were visible. Cosette's garden had become a tip of empty bottles and broken glasses and cigarette ends and heels of loaves.

'I don't understand why people get married,' said I, who was to do so myself three or four years afterwards.

'Women get married to have someone to keep them,' Bell said quite seriously. 'They get married to be safe.'

'Felicity's got a degree, she could get a job. Why does she need someone to keep her?'

Bell laughed a little at that, a small, dry laugh. 'You know my feelings about that. Not everyone's into working the way you are, as you could see by the gang here tonight.'

Emboldened by the night and her niceness, I asked her why she got married. Why had she married Silas?

She was at art school, she told me, Leicester College of Art, and she met Silas there. He was her supervisor, she a first-year student. They got married because she was pregnant, but afterwards he made her have an abortion. Then Silas got the sack, or got warned he would get the sack, or something like that, on account of his propensity for doing dangerous things with firearms, so he left and tried to live by his painting alone.

'So you didn't marry to have someone to keep you,' I said.

'Yes, I did. Partly. I knew he'd got an old dad who was ill and who'd leave him something. As a matter of fact, I thought it was more than it was. But I wasn't far wrong, was I? I did get it and it does keep me – just.'

We said good-night soon after that and I went down to my own room, congratulating myself on having at last found out something of Bell's history. I had no idea then – naturally I didn't, believing her, as everyone did, as Esmond Thinnesse had once said he did, because of her honest and direct manner, to be totally truthful – that most of what she told me at the window that night was false. The important bits – none of those were true. When people tell lies about the past, they nearly always distort it to flatter themselves. That is why they lie. The truth isn't glamorous enough, it doesn't make them into the exciting, experienced, successful people they wish to appear. Bell was unique. She invented a past that showed her in an unsympathetic light.

I think she rejected the truth out of mere caprice.

II

In Venezuela there is a village where half the population has Huntington's chorea. Such a high incidence is brought about by the inbreeding in this remote place where the poor people until recently have been quite ignorant about the hereditary nature of their sickness and have intermarried regardless of a parent's disease and the disease of a partner's parent. In their lakeside village they also thought Huntington's – though not knowing it by this name – exclusive to their locality and were amazed when told it was worldwide.

I have been reading all this in today's paper and can't help wondering if Felicity has read it too. Unless she has changed greatly, it is right up her street, just the thing to regale her family with the way she used to regale us with Selevin's mouse and *Stiletto fatalis* and the Defenestration of Prague. But she may have embarked on it long before today, for the newspapers and television and magazines have been full of Huntington's lately, Huntington's has become a fashionable disease, displacing multiple sclerosis and even schizophrenia in the public's curiosity. I glanced at the piece again before I got ready to go and meet Bell, at the photographs of the poor bewildered people, and re-read the paragraph at the end of the article about the test that can now be done and the counselling for potential victims that can be sought.

If the sixties were the age of the sexual revolution and the seventies of the destruction of our environment, the eighties are the decade of the support group and the counsellor. I doubt if there is any problem, physical or mental, confronting modern man and woman, for which counselling can't be obtained. If I had been able to talk to a counsellor in the sixties, would the course of my life have been different? Who knows? As it was I did so much of what I did in the expectation of grotesque paralysis and encroaching death: writing for financial gain my bad, sensational, insensitive books, so as to live and enjoy the present; making love with whom I chose, often promiscuously, on the dubious ground of not missing anything; marrying, criminally, dishonestly, in the hope of pretending none of it was true, and giving a false reason for my refusal to have a child. And then, of course, there was Bell . . .

It sounds insane, but can you believe me when I say, half-truthfully, more than half, that if Huntington's had come, at least it would all have been justified, at least I could say, I acted in the fearful expectation of this and I was justified? I was right not to have a child, I was right not to give birth to another being with a fifty-fifty chance of Huntington's. I was right to produce twenty-five sexy, romantic, sensational adventure books in seventeen years, so that I could live those years in comfort. I was right not to struggle half-starved and alone in a rented room creating the literature I know I could have created and on the dream of its being published one day in the sweet or paralysed by-and-by. (Though in fact the gain was never as great as at first I anticipated, I never made a fortune, or achieved great success or fame, as perhaps writers don't, even the purveyors of adventure and passion and crime, unless they write from the heart.)

I shall be forty next week and as Bell said I am very likely out of the wood. To speak, as I am sometimes inclined to do, with the truest deepest pessimism, I have made a mess of my life for nothing. But it is useless to brood on it, pitifully absurd to maunder like this. I have been to meet Bell, as I hinted just now, I have been to meet her after her first day at the shop in Westbourne Grove.

It wasn't that I much wanted to. Nor did she ask me, though she rang up the morning after I left her sleeping to remind me rather dolefully of when she was starting and where the shop was. I went because I thought I ought to. A poor woman who has passed years in prison – the least an old friend can do is keep an eye on her, give her some kind of support until she adjusts to her new world. Anyone who has loved passionately and now feels an obligation to the object of her love, that where desire once impelled, duty now dictates, will know how I felt. For that renewal of excitement, of passionate need, which I experienced when I pursued Bell on the tube train and through the streets, that was ephemeral after all, was a false fire, and now what I feel is more a wariness and a dread of something I can't define.

She was surprised to see me but very pleased. How ecstatically grateful I would once have been for those signs of pleasure, the lighting up of her whole face, her hands stretched out to me! Once, of course, I wouldn't have been late but waiting for her to come out ten minutes before the shop was due to close. As it was, the phone rang as I was leaving and then I found one of the cats on the front doorstep, a place neither of them is supposed to know exists, and had to stop to put him inside, so when I met Bell it was on the corner of Ledbury Road, I having raced down from Westbourne Park station.

I spotted her before she saw me and it seemed to me that she was walking aimlessly, and if she was making for Notting Hill Gate, in the wrong direction. But before I spoke to her I understood, or thought I understood. She was avoiding Archangel Place. The extent or depth of this I didn't realize until she said simply, 'I can't exactly remember where it is.'

You would think that anyone who had done such things and known such things, would have the place where they happened indelibly printed on the memory, so no matter what was forgotten that could never be forgotten. There would be a map in the mind, a street plan with fearful corners and ominous landmarks and signposts that warned what to shy away from. But, 'I think something has gone wrong with my memory,' said Bell. 'I expect I could find it in the London guide. Anyway, it's all changed round here.'

It hadn't – much. Apart from some smartening up, nothing had changed in this immediate vicinity. Together we walked westwards, towards Ladbroke Grove.

'How was it?' I said.

'The shop? I don't know if I shall be equal to it.' Bell laughed the laugh that was always dry and faint but has now become ghostly, a whispered giggle at the far end of a passage in the dark. 'She doesn't like me handling money, you can tell that. I nearly told her it wasn't for helping myself from the till I got sent to prison for.'

'Perhaps you had better not say that.'

'Oh, I won't. I am not so open as I used to be, I can tell you.'

I had no clear idea of where we were making for. It seemed that, considering our separate destinations, we were both going in the wrong direction. And then it came to me both that Ladbroke Grove station would do for me as well as Westbourne Park and that Bell intended to come home with me. What else had I had in mind? A cup of tea in a café and then dispatching her back to Kilburn? She was a ghost, I thought, and not only in her laugh. We always think of ghosts as pale, as white and glimmering, and Bell has faded, has bleached to pallor, her skin and her hair and even her eyes, vague now, leached of their colours. Only her clothes remain deepest black. I wonder what has become of the shawl she wore the first time she came to Cosette's and which once covered Silas's body?

674

She smoked as she walked, by the station going into a tobacconist's to buy more cigarettes. In the train she fell briefly asleep but revived once we were home and walked about my house, admiring it. The cats homed in on her, loving her for some reason, clambering over her and the ash-scattered folds of her bundled black cotton. I fear the reason may be that they love anyone who smells strongly, no matter what of, and Bell reeks of stale cigarette smoke, she smells like something raked out of the ashes of a fire. She is sleeping again now, her long pale hands hanging over the arms of the chair like empty sleeves.

I am sitting opposite her with a glass of gin and dry vermouth in my hand. Bell has only sipped hers and her cigarette has burnt itself out in the ashtray. It seems strange to me that though we have been talking for the best part of two hours she has never once mentioned Cosette, or for that matter, Mark. But perhaps that isn't so strange.

Cosette and I had refused Felicity's invitation but Bell accepted, spent Christmas at Thornham and reported back to me that everything was just the same as before Felicity ran away. Even the children seemed unaffected by her long absence, and Miranda was still quoting, with proud sententiousness, her mother's opinions.

'My mummy says it's revolting to eat quails' eggs,' or 'My mummy says only old ladies wear stockings.'

The party was run on the same lines as those of the one the year Silas died. Only there was no quiz on the day after Boxing Day. There was no quiz at all. But the same people were there, more or less. At any rate, old Julia Dunne was there and the ancient brigadier and his wife and Rosalind and Rupert, Felicity's sister and brother-in-law. And Lady Thinnesse, of course, was there, behaving towards Felicity exactly as she had always done. On Bell's last evening Felicity organized a debate, the subject being the possible reintroduction of capital punishment, in which, Bell said, Esmond stood up stoutly for the noes and Mrs Dunne became quite rejuvenated and vociferous for the yesses.

One of the things I liked so very much about Bell, I mean one of the definable things, was that she was quite as interested in people as I was. She was the only person I have ever known who really wanted to get inside people's heads and know how they worked and the only person who could talk about other people for hours on end without getting bored or tired. Without any tutelage or training, she had a fine grasp of human psychology. I learnt a lot about people from Bell, though I never had the wisdom to put any of it in my books, preferring to use stereotypes for my characters. And of course she had, has, will always have, a wonderful imagination.

By this time I had found out why she hadn't wanted me to know where she was living or to go there. It was her mother's flat in Harlesden. Bell often said how she didn't really think of anywhere west of Ladbroke Grove or east of the City as being London at all, so I could understand her detestation of West Ten and all its subdivisions. Besides, it was her mother herself. She said she wanted to be totally open about it now she was on the subject and the truth was she would have been ashamed for me to meet her mother.

'If you saw her in the street you'd think she was an old baglady. She doesn't even keep herself clean. She's an old cockney' – and here Bell laughed her dry laugh – 'who carts her false teeth about with her in a tobacco tin.'

'She can't be that old,' I said.

'She's old to be my mother. She was a lot over forty when I was born. The thing was, when I left Admetus's place I hadn't anywhere to go but to her. She's not well anyway. She needs someone with her and there's no one but me.'

I hesitated. Still, why not say it? 'But you've a brother, haven't you? I've seen your brother; I saw him at that Global Experience thing.'

She laughed. It must have been at the memory of those dotty happenings. 'Oh, Marcus, yes.'

'Is that what he's called?' I was enchanted by his name. A person couldn't be that bad, I suggested, who would call her children Marcus and Christabel.

'She probably wasn't as bad then but she's very bad now.'

I told her she couldn't live with her mother for the rest of her life, meaning her mother's life.

'Don't you worry, I won't,' said Bell.

Soon after that conversation I remembered Elsa the Lioness telling me just after the death of Silas that Bell had nowhere to go and no relatives to take her in. Her parents were dead. But since she was so ashamed of her mother, wishing to keep her existence a secret from most people, no doubt she would have said she was dead. It seemed reasonable enough. How strange and sad that she should so detest her mother and I so love mine – well, my adoptive mother. For that was the year, or the spring, Cosette was ill. In fact, she wasn't really ill at all, she had a scare and gave me a scare, but because I loved her so much I magnified it out of all proportion. I was sure that because she was having uterine haemorrhages she must be dying of cancer and I confided my worries to Bell.

'When will you know what she's got?'

'In about a week,' I said.

I imagined losing her, I imagined her own fear of death. I talked to Bell about it, about Cosette's long, half-asleep life, and the chance that had come at last, too late perhaps, for her to live. How terrible if freedom, so short-lived, not even surely enjoyed, should so quickly end in death! Bell listened, calmly attentive. Sometimes she looked as if love was something she didn't quite understand and, lips parted, head held slightly on one side, was considering it as a subject for possible research. But I am not sure if I thought like that then, if I was as wise as that then.

Cosette went into hospital, it was the Harley Street Clinic, and they scraped something from the inside of her womb and found she had a benign polyp which they removed. I think – no, I know – Cosette was proud of all this. You see, it made her seem young. It made her seem as if she still had active reproductive organs and when I went in to see her along with the crowds of other people who gathered round her bed, I was embarrassed by her talk. I was embarrassed when she said to Dawn Castle and Perpetua that they hadn't 'taken anything away', that her insides were still in 'working order', they hadn't made her sterile. Because of this I said not a word to other people, not even to Bell, telling myself that because the worry was past so must any interest in Cosette's condition.

We welcomed her home with flowers and a feast. We put flowers in the drawing room and flowers in her bedroom and in the big jardinière that stood at the top of the first flight of stairs. Bell helped me fetch the flowers and arrange them and she helped me lay the table in the dining room and shop for food. It was Cosette's money, of course, for she had an account at the delicatessen and an account at the florist's, and because she was always more or less on a diet, she ate less than anyone, but as she would have said, it was the thought that counted. She looked tired when she came home and rather bemused. It occurred to me – too late – that someone ought to have gone to fetch her in her own car, not left her to be brought back by an unknown minicab driver. But I wasn't able to drive then and as for Gary and Fay and the acid-freak Rimmon (his real name was Peter) who had come to live in the house without invitation, none of them offered or were even at home when Cosette left the clinic.

People of Cosette's kind, generous, selfless, patient, disproportionately grateful for any little thing that may be done for them, these people are always used, taken advantage of and neglected. Nineteenth-century fiction is full of them and this had led us to believe that they and their fate are the invention of novelists. But they exist, to endow others and be trodden on by those who owe them the most. All of which makes Cosette's subsequent life and eventual fate the more bizarre. Her life to come and her fate were what no one could have expected, they seemed a contradiction and a defiance of the rules that say, such a woman will never find passionate disinterested love, tragedy, violent death and final irony, but only exploitation and disillusionment.

None of us young ones had given much thought to Auntie while Cosette was away. It is only now, looking back, that I understand she must have seen Cosette almost in the light of a protector. She was so mouselike, so quiet and creeping, that even to Bell and me with our never-satisfied hunger to know what went on in people's heads, our constant examination of personality, she seemed a person without feelings, certainly a person not worth wasting conjecture on. That she might be afraid in Cosette's absence, afraid of us all with our habits acquired in a revolution she had never understood, of our youth and our music, our comings and goings and our sexual freedom, never crossed our minds.

Perpetua, of course, was sometimes there. Jimmy the gardener would always put his head round the door with a word for her. But Cosette's old friends from Wellgarth days, though visiting the clinic, never thought of visiting Auntie. Bell had been kind to her on the night of the party, but if she paid her any particular attention while Cosette was away, I wasn't aware of it. Did anyone actually speak to the old woman while Cosette wasn't there to speak to her? As I try to imagine the drawing room as it was without Cosette I also see it without Auntie and this makes me sure Auntie kept to her own room most of the time, hiding herself from us and the challenges and dangers and shocks we offered, longing surely for Cosette's return. And when Cosette walked into the drawing room Auntie had taken care to be there. For once she showed emotion, getting up from the red velvet chair and coming to Cosette with her arms out.

'Why didn't you come to see me?' Cosette asked her when the embrace was done.

Auntie had no answer, perhaps didn't care to say the means were not at her disposal, that none of us had offered to take her or even call a taxi and direct the driver. She could only shake her head and frown mysteriously, in the way old people do when they want to keep their needs and shortcomings a secret from the young.

We all assembled in the dining room for the meal, Cosette and Auntie, Bell and I, Gary who had just come back from India, and Fay and Rimmon. It was a small party for the House of Stairs, no one having come to take the place of Mervyn or of Felicity and Harvey. There was no longer any Girl-in-Residence, a function as empty and free of duties as being a Gold Stick or Steward of the Chiltern Hundreds, but still a role with a room that no one filled. Cosette had tried to persuade the ballet dancers to take over the top floor as their home but they, naturally, were reluctant to give up rent-free occupancy of the Hampstead flat whose owner, with luck, might never come back from South Africa. A girl called Audrey, who was a cousin of Admetus's new girlfriend, had said she might take up the vacant post and vacant room. I don't think she quite believed she could have that large second-floor room for nothing and live there without performing any services beyond talking and listening and making cups of coffee, and that was making her hesitate. Cosette talked wistfully about this during the meal.

We finished eating and, as usual, got up without thought of clearing the table or washing up. Perpetua wouldn't be there next day and it was Bell who said in a very uncharacteristic, housewifely way that she and I should do the dishes.

'Oh, leave it till the morning,' said Cosette, not at all uncharacteristically.

'I shan't be here in the morning.'

'But, darling, I thought you were living here now!'

She sounded not just polite. She sounded appalled that the number of her household was therefore even smaller than she had supposed.

'Bell has to live with her mother,' I said. 'For the present anyway.'

'I'm sure we've room for your mother too. Look at all the room we've got!'

Of course this was absurd. Cosette could be absurd, her liberality taken to ridiculous lengths, and to insensitive lengths too. Even supposing Bell's mother was very different from the grotesque description I had been given, why should she want to give up her home and come to live in a strange woman's house? Bell gave her dry chuckle.

'I'll bear your kind offer in mind, Cosette.'

No kind offer had been made, of course, only an assumption. But now the idea was in her head, Cosette wanted Bell. Not in the Girl-in-Residence's room, that was reserved for Audrey, but why not in the top room above the place where I worked if she wanted some privacy? We even had to go up there and look at it, the lot of us, though Auntie disappeared into her own domain on the way. Cosette, sitting on the bed that had been Felicity's, breathless from all that climbing, apologized for the room, its location up 106 stairs, its slanted ceiling, its dangerous window.

'I'll have bars put on that window. I'll have a kind of cage made to make it safe.'

She never did. Because Gary said how awful it would be, you would feel you were in prison? Or because Bell said not to do that for her, she couldn't leave her mother's house in Harlesden at present? Apparently, though, she was well able to leave her mother for a night or two, for she stayed and slept up there and next day, when I came home from the play-centre, told me that she had met an old friend of her mother's who might just be willing to come and share her house.

It was not that evening but a week or so later that I dressed her up in Cosette's gown of 'wasted' red. I had forgotten those remarks of Cosette's, when she first saw the Bronzino reproduction, about still possessing somewhere a dress that looked like Lucrezia Panciatichi's. But Cosette had been invited to Glyndebourne by the Castles and it was still obligatory then to wear a long evening dress when you went to hear opera there. Very seldom did anyone take Cosette out. I was happy that the Castles had thought of this, even though I knew it was done to show Cosette a contrast to the House of Stairs. At a party Cosette gave for Admetus's fortieth birthday, I had chanced to hear

Dawn's husband murmur to his wife, 'I wonder if she knows the life she gave up for this circus is still going on?'

The Glyndebourne evening was two months off but Cosette took it into her head she must root out a suitable dress to wear, or in default of this, buy a new one. It reminded me of the old days at Garth Manor where Elsa and I used to try on Cosette's jewellery and she would say when either of us admired something particularly, 'It's yours!'

'Have it, have it,' was what she kept saying to me if I lingered a little over some thirties 'frock' or post-war floor-length creation. But I laughed at her and shook my head. What did I want with a shawl-neck dress in powder-blue rayon crêpe or a black ballerina skirt with bead embroidery? Then we came upon the Bronzino gown and it was very much like the one in the painting. Lucrezia's low-cut neckline is of course filled in with gold lace and the lower parts of her sleeves are of a rich, ruffled black satin, but otherwise the dress was the same, tight bodice, puffed sleeves, full skirt, and all made of silk the colour of a ripe Victoria plum.

'Have it,' said Cosette. 'You'll be doing me a favour, darling. I'm such a hoarder, can't bring myself to throw things away.'

Bell was in her rusty, dusty black. Looking at her now, as she sleeps in my armchair, I can see no difference between what she wears today and what she wore on that momentous, tremendous, wonderful day, when she arrived at the House of Stairs in the early evening, except that, because it was March and cold, she had a black cape on and the shawl wrapped round her. Cosette was taking us out to eat and Rimmon and Gary were coming too. I don't remember where we went, though it may have been that Russian place down in Brompton. Later events must have obscured my memory of such things as restaurants and food and drinks.

The house was nearly empty. Auntie, who would never eat out in the evening, had long gone to bed. Gary and Rimmon had gone off to see a friend in Battersea and if it seems strange to me now to hear of people going out visiting at eleven-thirty at night, it didn't then. I don't know where Fay was, staying perhaps with her new lover, an Indian who kept a sordid hotel, a kind of house of call, near Paddington Station. Bell and Cosette and I were alone and Cosette, at only midnight, talked of going to bed. She easily got tired, debilitated still from her not very serious operation.

'Though it isn't a delightful prospect,' she said, embarrassing me, 'getting into that great big bed on one's own. Sometimes I pull down one of the pillows and hug that.'

'I want you to put the dress on,' I said to Bell.

At first she wouldn't. She said it was silly, her hair was wrong and she hadn't any jewellery. But as she stood there looking at the picture, the idea grew on her. It would take a little while, she said, for she would have to braid her hair and wind it round her head, and I mustn't be there, I must come back when it was done. I gave her the cameo that was herself and fastened it to a string of pearls, for it is a necklace rather like this that Lucrezia wears.

While she was changing I went down to Cosette's room. Cosette, in a Hollywood thirties bedjacket with white feathers on it, was sitting up in bed reading my book, which had been published the week before. She had already read it in manuscript and proof, but she swore it would be different because I had dedicated it to her. I now had to listen to a lot of extravagant praise of what I knew even then was worthless trash; it made me wince, and serve me right.

In her bed with its piled satin-covered cushions and its pink pillows, its pink silk and white lace counterpane all covered with magazines and tissues and pairs of glasses, white telephone, telephone directories, address-book, writing paper, fountain pen, Cosette, rising from befeathered fluffiness, scented with Patou's Joy, looked much younger in the flattering pink lamplight, looked almost girlish. Since the coming of Ivor Sitwell she had abandoned the plastering of her skin with greasy cream at night and the pinning up of her hair and these exercises had never been resumed after he left. Her hair, now a silvery-gold, lay smoothly on her plump white shoulders. The lines on her face scarcely showed, and the sad look, which came now that the tissues had begun to droop once more, gave her an appearance of wistfulness, not age. And those words someone speaks of Cleopatra at the end of the play came into my mind, that 'she would catch another Antony in her strong toil of grace'. Or I think they did, they should have done, but could I really have had such foresight?

We were talking about the book, I with reluctance, for I should like to have taken the money and forgotten it, Cosette with enthusiasm, when the door opened and Bell came in. Or Lucrezia Panciatichi came in – or Milly Theale. She was wearing the pearls and the cameo and had found a gold chain of mine as well and a string of beads to wind round her braided coronet of hair. The red dress was loose on her, but you couldn't see that from the front, she having skilfully pinned it down the back and at the waist. Her skin had that very pale luminous brownness that gives Lucrezia her glowing look. Instead of smiling at our delight – Cosette actually clapped – she stood gravely between the Chinese screens, then sank softly into the high-backed chair and became entirely the portrait, her left hand closing over the carved arm, her right holding open the little leather-covered book she had brought with her.

Cosette wanted to take a photograph of her. She even got up and started poking about the room in a fruitless hunt for flashbulbs. I think she did take some sort of picture in the end, a picture that we all knew would never come out. Though she couldn't find the flashbulbs, she found the bloodstone. She tried the ring on Bell's hand, but Bell's fingers were very long and slender. It was too big for the third finger and had to go on the middle one. Bell sat there, curiously serene, not laughing at Cosette's efforts, not even smiling. It was as if Lucrezia or Milly had entered into her, infecting her with an old-fashioned placidity. After a while, when Cosette was back in bed, Bell joined in the conversation, idle midnight talk it was, about fashions and how uncomfortable it must have been to dress like that all the time, but she didn't smoke while she had the red dress on. My cigarettes were on the green-room-style dressing-table with its mirror ringed by light bulbs, but Bell didn't take one.

Cosette was tired and falling asleep. It wasn't in her nature to say she wanted to sleep now, to shoo us away. She nodded off, smiled, shook herself, her head dropped again. We took pity on her and left, turning out all the lights at the door. Bell slipped the ring off her finger and left it on the dressing-table.

It was a black night, starless and with no moon. I was aware of the quietness of the house, for at this time there would usually still be music coming from somewhere, the murmur of voices, the sound of languid laughter. That night there was a deep silence, and even the perpetual hum of distant traffic seemed hushed. For a long time the light bulbs on the staircase had needed replacing, a job for Perpetua if only she had known it needed to be done, but she was never there after dark. As our ancestors had done, we took candles to light us to bed.

But Bell in the red dress had come down from my room in the dark, guided by the light from the doorway above and the doorway below. On the stairs she took my hand in hers and led me. The long stiff skirt of the dress rustled as we made our way up. In my room the light was soft and dim, coming from the bedlamp. The painted Lucrezia looked down at the living Lucrezia. I thought – but not then, next day – how strange it was, how infinitely mysterious it would have been to that cinquecento girl if she could have imagined, while she sat to Bronzino in all her beauty and finery, the picture he made reproduced and the copy, no less brilliant and true, hanging in the room where two women, one of them surely herself, entered each other's arms and made love.

Bell pushed the door closed with her toe, a naked toe that had not previously made itself visible under the red silk. Oh, there was such a silence! No words, no sound of breath, after our mouths parted and our eyelids half closed, then like a roar in the quiet, the rustle of cascading silk and the tinkle of gold and stones, as the dress fell and the jewels fell. A shivering and a rapture of silky skins touching, and we moved into the pool of light shed by that single lamp on to the bed.

– 12 –

Today is Sunday. I never write on Sundays and Bell hasn't to go to work in the shop. It is time for us to talk. By whose decree? It was a decision we both seemed to reach simultaneously, as if each knew at the same point that the time had come and there was nothing else left to do.

Working in the shop wears her out. She falls asleep as soon as she gets home, and by 'home' I mean my house, for it is here that she has returned every day. On the second evening and the third, when she woke up at about ten, I had a taxi take her home to Kilburn and the house under the railway arch. But it seemed a cruelty, perhaps because she was so malleable and so meek, allowing her arms to be pushed into the sleeves of the old black coat she wears, letting herself be led out to the waiting cab, lifting her face to be kissed on a cold cheek. So on Friday I made up the bed in the spare room for her and there she has been sleeping, fourteen, fifteen hours at a stretch.

And all this sleeping, the cumulative effect of it, has at last refreshed her so that when she came down this morning, smoking her first cigarette of the day, she seemed less ghostly, more present, younger and fresher looking, even managing to smile. And when the bigger, friendlier cat climbed on to her lap, she began stroking him instead of pushing him listlessly away. Facing each other later on, we came to this joint decision. We must talk. The things that had been waiting so long for utterance must now be said. It was only on which things should take precedence over which other things that we differed. I believe it was Felicity's phone call as much as anything which directed the turn our talking took. Yesterday evening, quite early in the evening, while Bell lay upstairs sleeping and I was sitting in the study reading for the fourth or fifth time *The Spoils of Poynton*, she phoned from the World's End flat.

I had truly supposed I should never hear from her again. All that about our meeting in London, about our having unanswered questions to discuss, I had taken as so much flannel, the stuff of small talk. But no, she meant it. Here it was, Saturday night, and she and Esmond up in town planning to eat at a little French restaurant round the corner when she suddenly thought – 'Why not ask Elizabeth to join us? We did actually book a table for four but of course the chances of Miranda and Jeremy actually wanting to eat with us were pretty well nil from the start.'

There was something attractive about it. What is she like now? What is he like? What, above all, are they like together? As she spoke I could again hear her scream when she saw Esmond come up Cosette's stairs, I could see her turn her face away into Harvey's shoulder. But I had Bell to think of, Bell who slept because I was there, a reassuring presence downstairs. I lied to Felicity, I told her I had already arranged to go out. My refusal seemed not to distress her.

'Some other time then,' she said, and then, incredibly, so that I had to suppress my laughter, 'As a matter of fact it's our wedding anniversary, so perhaps Esmond wouldn't have liked it.'

'I should think not.'

'I'll ring you again, I shan't let you go as easily as that. Did you ever hear from Bell Sanger?' Poor Bell has acquired a permanent surname in Felicity's speech. This sets her apart, puts her outside the friends category in which she may no longer be allowed a place.

Why did I lie again? For the usual reason for all our lying. It makes things easier. 'No,' I said. 'Oh, no.'

'What did she want?' Bell asked me when I told her about the call. Through her half-sleep, half-waking, she heard the phone ringing or dreamed she heard it.

'Me to go out with them.'

She jumped up and the poor cat shot off her lap. 'She isn't coming here!'

'She isn't. Don't worry. But would that be so bad? You've spoken to her.'

Touchingly, she said, 'Only to find out about you.'

But Felicity's name brought her into an area of her past that isn't the part I want to know about. These revelations, the ones she made this morning, are not those I longed to hear. At least she has begun, though. She has begun to reveal.

'Has she said anything to you about Silas?'

I asked her carefully, 'What sort of thing?'

'Anything. Has she mentioned him? I can see in your face she has. Did she ask you if you ever thought I might have been responsible for Silas's death?'

What was the use of denying it? I nodded, pursing my lips, as if perhaps it was too bad, too awe-inspiring, for speech.

'No one mentioned it at my trial, did they? Did you notice? The prosecution didn't even say I'd had a husband who killed himself. But all that stuff about me as a child came out, all that. And I'd forgotten it, did you realize that? I'd forgotten everything about it. I had to think for a moment who Susan was. It might have been some other person, some other twelve-year-old they were talking about. But that's why I got such a long sentence. Isn't it terrible to go to prison for all those years for something you've forgotten? They found it out, all the dirt, but they never found out about Silas, or if they did they never questioned that he shot himself, even though by then they knew what I was.'

She took another cigarette and lit it, shaking the match too slowly to extinguish the flame, having to drop it burning into the ashtray. 'I did kill him,' she said. 'Well, isn't it obvious, knowing what we all know?'

'You're making it up, Bell,' I said.

'Why would I? Haven't I got crimes enough and notoriety enough? Why would I make it up?'

'Why did you ever make anything up?' I said, and I know I said it bitterly.

'To make things better, of course. To make them go the way I wanted them to. Do you know anything about Russian roulette?'

'Only that you use a revolver, put a bullet in only one of the chambers and then spin it round. Felicity told us that much.' I was reluctant to talk about it. It is an unpleasant feeling to think you may be encouraging someone in her lying. It marks you as a dupe. 'I never thought about it again,' I said. 'I wasn't interested.'

'Not even when you met me again? Didn't you wonder?'

'I thought I was living in a society where people might commit suicide but not where they killed each other.'

She laughed her distant dry laugh. 'In Russian roulette,' she said, 'what do you think the odds are? Come on, don't look so – pained. You know most of the things I did, you ought to be tougher. You know now you were living in a society where one person anyway was capable of killing. So what do you think the odds are, using a revolver with a six-chamber cylinder?'

'They must be five to one.'

'Oh, no. That's the mistake most people make. Because, you see, in a well-balanced gun, if you are loading only one cartridge, when you spin the cylinder the chamber with the cartridge in it will be heavier and will naturally tend to fall to the bottom. So the odds are much much higher than five to one, perhaps, if you know just how to spin, as much as a hundred to one.'

This seemed to echo something I'd heard before; but: 'What has all this to do with Silas?' I said.

'Silas taught it to me.'

'Among other things he taught you, I suppose. At art school. Before he got you pregnant and married you and you had your miscarriage.'

'Is that what I told you?'

'Oh, Bell, don't you even remember?' I realized I was carping pointlessly. It was hardly cruel, since she showed no sign of suffering, seemed almost to enjoy my sarcastic reminder of one of her prime lies. But it was useless and it was too late, she would never see. 'What exactly did Silas teach you?'

'About spinning the cylinder and the heaviest chamber falling to the bottom. And then he said if you got a lead bullet, a blank but not a cartridge, a solid lead bullet, and loaded it into one of the other chambers, that would be quite an interesting situation. Because now when you spun the cylinder that one would fall to the bottom, not the one with the cartridge in. If you calculated which chamber would be brought into line with the barrel when the chamber with the lead bullet fell to the bottom, say the one next but one to it on the left, you could load a cartridge into that chamber. Or if the cartridge was already in the revolver you could calculate which chamber to put the lead in to bring the cartridge into line with the barrel.'

'Would you say that again, slowly,' I said.

She said it again. She offered to draw it.

'No, don't bother. I can see it without that. But barring mistakes or unless, say, the revolver wasn't well-balanced, it wouldn't be a matter of odds then, it would be a certainty.'

She nodded. 'Yes.'

I looked up at her. Her face had the impassivity of Lucrezia Panciatichi's, bland and composed, Lucrezia aged but still Lucrezia. 'I don't understand what you did,' I said.

'Silas put a cartridge into one of the chambers and he left the revolver and went to get a drink – you know that filth he used to drink, wine with meths in it, one part purple meths to two parts red wine. While he wasn't there I put the lead bullet into the next chamber but one.'

There was silence. Bell took another cigarette and held it between her lips unlit for a moment. She reached for the Wedgwood lighter Cosette gave me, watching me speculatively.

'The police would have found it,' I said.

'I took it out after Silas was dead and before I went over to the Hall.'

I didn't know whether to believe her or not. All that stuff about well-balanced revolvers and the heaviest chamber falling to the bottom – how would I know if it is true or false? I know nothing of guns. I know no one I could ask. Would a man load a gun and then just lay it down somewhere while he went to get a drink? He might, if he were Silas Sanger. For one thing, he might have had a lot to drink already. I couldn't believe it but I could see Bell doing it just the same. Oh, I could see her.

'Accepting that you did, which I don't accept, why did you?'

'I was so pissed off with him, I was so bored; he was driving me insane. He married me to get a slave and that's what I was, a slave and a drudge, a thing to use, a servant to serve. When he married me I was grateful, I thought that was the life, ten times better than anything I could expect with what was behind me. I didn't know anyone else, my mother and father wouldn't have me near them, I hadn't seen them for seven years. I hadn't any friends. I only knew social workers and one or two kids from the home. You know all that, it all came out in court. I thought I was lucky to get a life with Silas, but I learned, I did a lot of growing up and learning in my six years of married life.'

'There's such a thing as divorce,' I said.

The look she gave me brought it back, that sidelong calculating look brought back to me my old delusion that money meant nothing to Bell, that she was uninterested in material things. But I am no longer deluded, that went long ago, I just remember with wonder and self-disgust the faith I had in the purity of her aims. 'His old father was dying, wasn't he? And he was rich. Well, he wasn't as rich as Silas boasted, but his house was worth a bit. I knew what Silas would do with it, he'd told me often enough. Go and live in bloody Java and paint. He'd been there, he liked the climate. That's why we were hanging on at Thornham, even though Esmond wanted us out. We were waiting for his old dad to die so that Silas could flog the house and go to bloody Java like some old French painter he was always wanking on about.'

'Gauguin,' I said, 'and it was Tahiti.'

She took no notice. She always hated those interjections of mine, what she called 'boring bits of culture'. 'He didn't care whether I came or not. But if I didn't he said he wasn't going to keep me. I could go out to work. He'd kept me for six years, what did I expect? So when the telegram came saying his father was dead I didn't show it to him. I kept it to myself and put the lead bullet in the revolver.'

'You can't send telegrams any more,' I said stupidly. 'Well, you can but they won't get there any faster than letters.' Had there been a telegram sent up to Thornham? It was possible but who would remember now? 'I don't believe any of it, Bell,' I said.

'Suit yourself.'

'I can believe you wanted him dead.'

'What's the difference?'

'There is a difference.'

'I wasn't there when he did it,' she said. 'I was upstairs like I said. He wouldn't have known anything about it or if he did for a split second he'd have thought his time had come, the way you must be sort of expecting your time to come when you play Russian roulette.' She picked up the little cat and began stroking him, long hands pushing hard down the length of his body the way he loves. 'His liver had gone rotten anyway. He wouldn't have lived long. One glass of that red muck of his and he'd be staggering. His liver couldn't handle it any more, he was going yellow all over. God, I hated him.' Another cigarette, and the little cat flinching from the lighter flame. 'Felicity saw the telegram come, you see.'

'What do you mean, Bell?'

She didn't answer at once. 'If Silas had died before his father I wouldn't have got the house, I was only his daughter-in-law. At any rate I'd have had to fight for it. But once he was dead it was sort of automatically Silas's. Only as soon as Silas could get his hands on it he was going to be off to Java. And he mightn't even have bothered to take me. Why would he? He was as sick of me as I was of him.' She drew on that cigarette then and puffed the smoke out through her nostrils as if there was a fire inside her face. 'You'd finished lunch,' she said, 'and Felicity was upstairs fetching the quiz papers that were in her bedroom. She looked out of the window and saw the boy come up on his bike. I don't think she made the connection for quite a long time, not till just before I was going to leave in April. She got me talking about the old man and his death – I was moving into his house, you know. She just said, "But didn't you get a wire an hour or so before it happened?" I didn't know what she meant at first. Have you ever heard a telegram called a wire?'

'Only in books,' I said.

'Sorting that one out gave me a chance to think. I told her the boy had come to the wrong house but I could tell she didn't believe me. Funny, at my trial I thought she might be a witness. And then I thought that if I got off they'd get me back again on another charge, on killing Silas, and Felicity would be there ballsing on about that telegram.' She sighed, looking at her fingers that were beginning to turn yellow with nicotine. 'Have you still got that picture?'

'What picture, Bell?' Though I knew, of course I knew.

'The one of the girl in the red dress that whoever it was wrote a book about?'

Not the same words, but the same kind of words, the same lack of comprehension, the same wonder. The wonder to me is that she can speak of it after the part it played, the role it had.

'It's in the study,' I said.

'I haven't been in there yet,' she said, and then, 'Can we go out? I should like to go down to the river and go in a pub. Could we find a pub and eat there? Isn't there a pub where some guy wrote the words to "Rule Britannia"?'

'James Thomson and it's The Dove. How did you know?'

'You once told me,' she said.

We didn't talk about it but we each made assumptions. Or so I suppose. I made assumptions and all Bell's behaviour showed that she must have done so too and that they were of the same kind. But there was no talk of why.

I would have told anyone who asked me that I was heterosexual. I had only, till then, had affairs with men. A few men. Several. I would like to say I didn't count their number, that it wasn't in that sort of light that I looked on them and back at them, but it wouldn't be true, for that is a number we all know. After Dominic, there was a man at my publisher's, an editor, though not my editor, and for one night there was Gary, just once. We weren't drunk or high on anything, we just happened to be alone together in the house, talking, experiencing a sudden mutual warmth, fellow-feeling, shared knowledge, all those things and being young. But it was something like that, something of the same kind only magnified a hundred times, that brought me and Bell together that silent night.

I have never wanted any other woman before or since. On the other hand, I never felt it was a shocking thing we did or wrong or perverse. It seemed natural. Homosexual men who have occasionally slept with women have told me it was enjoyable, they liked it, but they felt it wasn't the real thing. Doesn't Proust say somewhere that the homosexual man only sins when he sleeps with a woman? So

691

afterwards I half-expected my love-making with Bell, though delightful, though immensely pleasurable, not to be like the real thing. But my reaction was very different, for 'delightful' and 'pleasurable' were not words to be used, other hitherto undiscovered words had to be found, and as to the real thing, this was more real than whatever the real thing is. And so I come up against an inability to express my feelings, my desires and my fulfilments, a blankness like a sheet of dark water, a pool on which float dazzling mysterious memories and whispered words, a drowning place where the thin branch I clutch at is the recollection that I was in love. I was in love with Bell with the kind of fierce, jealous passion experienced by girls ten years younger than I was for someone they are at school with.

Psychologists would say – oh, I know what they would say – that I had been arrested in my sexual development by a shock, a trauma-making revelation. This there had certainly been, and perhaps the knowledge of my possible legacy of Huntington's did freeze me in some inverted phase. But it didn't feel like that, it felt like passion, it felt like being in love, it *was* being in love, it was the kind of thing you delude yourself that, if all goes well, will last a lifetime.

Things, of course, didn't all go well. When do they?

On a high and glorious plane it lasted a little while. The girl called Audrey had vanished, so Bell moved in and became the Girl-in-Residence. I have never known if Cosette knew but I tend to think she didn't. Cosette had an attitude towards lesbians characteristic of her generation: 'Don't leave me alone with her, darling. Whatever would I do if she made a pass at me?'

Did she then suppose that all heterosexual men she was alone with would make passes at her? Hoped it perhaps, poor Cosette. I never felt the hint of a recoil when I kissed her or saw her flinch when Bell came near her. No doubt she saw us only as 'best friends' and the jealousy in her that I observed was due to this, that Bell took me away from her and – incongruously perhaps, but who really understands people? – I took Bell away from her.

She was very alone that summer which was Bell's summer and mine, she must have been, though I was aware of it only afterwards. Being in love and having, at least supposedly, one's love returned, there is nothing like it for making one oblivious to the loneliness of others. I was a little dismayed, I am sorry to say a little fastidiously disapproving, when I understood Cosette was sometimes sleeping with Rimmon. She was fifty-five and he was twenty-seven, he had no money and she had a lot. If I didn't understand about loneliness I understood even less that in middle age the heyday in the blood does not always grow tame. Going to Glyndebourne with the Castles and taking Auntie for drives in Richmond Park were not enough for her.

Bell has never read any of my books. She has scarcely read any books by anyone. If I am to be very honest I will say that in a secret corner of myself I was glad she never read mine, for my books are not the way I talk, they don't reveal real emotion, real sensitivity, they are not about people in the way Bell and I talked about people. Anyone who knew me the way she knew me would, after reading them in the spirit in which Bell would necessarily have read them, be disillusioned about me and see me as a hypocrite. Useless to talk to someone so unacquainted with books as Bell is, of the dichotomy between the writer's art and the writer's life or, as she would have put it, other balls like that.

She was in my room just as I finished my stint of writing for that day. It was late summer, early autumn, and she was in white cheesecloth, a kind of robe with huge sleeves, the waist caught in to its tiny span by a belt of plaited leather. Above my head, while I typed the last of my requisite 2,000 words, I had listened to the movements she made prior to coming down to me, the closing of that window, the window which had never been protected by the promised cage, her footfalls muffled by the carpet, then touching the wood surround which did not at all muffle the clack-clack of Indian sandals, the door shutting, the creak of the 104th stair as she began to descend. These are the stuff of love's obsessiveness, in which I was up to my neck.

She never read a book, as I have said. But she would walk about picking up books and examining them. I have said that too. It is such a strong image in memory. I was still intending to write my paper on Henry James, between books I would write it, and eventually I did. It was *The Awkward Age* that Bell picked up off my desk, a copy from the library in Porchester Road, and, looking at it with interest, feeling the texture of it, assessing the number of its pages, reading its spine, rather than even glancing at its text, said, 'Is this the one that's about the girl that looks like me?'

'No, that's *The Wings of the Dove*.' I found my copy and gave it to her, taking the other book out of her hand and kissing her hand, holding it against my face. She was so touchable, Bell, her skin sweet-smelling, like a child's. We stood close together for a moment, the sides of our bodies pressing. 'It's the painting that looks like the girl and you look like the painting.' She turned her face into mine, smiling close to my cheek, said in that light way she had, teasing, incredulous, 'When did he write it, this guy you're so keen on?'

I had a shot at it, but was a year out, '1901.'

'I don't see how she can be in a painting you say was painted in fifteen hundred and something if he didn't write it till 1901.' She was looking at *The Wings of the Dove* now, and if there was ever a novel to daunt the non-novel reader, the dipper into magazines, the desultory scanner of newsprint, this is it. The pages of text scarcely broken into paragraphs, uninterrupted by dialogue, as she viewed them with increasing dismay, brought such a look of horror to her face that, stepping back to get a clearer look at her, I burst out laughing.

'What's it about?' she said. 'It doesn't even make sense, it might be in a foreign language.'

So, sitting there cross-legged on the floor, Bell dropping to sit beside me and be close to me but still with the book in her hand, still disbelievingly turning its pages, I told her the plot of *The Wings of the Dove*. That was all I ever did, all. It wasn't even the only or the first novel plot I had told her, for I remember some weeks before she had wanted me to go with her to the Electric Cinema where they were showing *The Wanderer*, which is the film version of *Le Grand Meaulnes*, and I had given her a kind of précis of that too. But Milly Theale remained in her memory, Milly Theale and Merton Densher and Kate Croy, though I don't believe I ever told her their names. That wasn't necessary, the plot was enough, the melodramatic central spring of the novel which James somehow makes not sensational but subtle, tenuous, like life. I suppose it was the painting that anchored her to it, the Bronzino that looked like her and which poor doomed Milly Theale looked like.

She said slowly, wonderingly, 'What a clever idea!'

'James was clever. There's never been a cleverer novelist.'

'He could have fooled me,' she said, typically Bell, 'the way he goes wanking on.'

The first time Mark came to Archangel Place there were living in the House of Stairs Cosette and myself and Auntie, Gary and Fay, Rimmon and a Filipino friend of his and, of course, Bell. In the autumn of 1972 she had gone back to Harlesden for a while because of some crisis in her mother's household. I know now, and have known for years, that Bell had no widowed mother in Harlesden, that her own mother and father were living together in Southsea, attempting to put their unhappy foray into parenthood as far behind them as they could. But I didn't know it then. I believed Bell when she said she had to go 'home' to 'sort things out'.

Though an adept at self-delusion of many kinds, I have never deluded myself about the moods and climatic changes in love affairs. I know at once when something is going off the boil. That first tiny break in the lover's absorption, not rejection, nothing as plain as that, more an air of distraction, a vagueness, then the unavoidable painful observance that it is always the other now who is first to end an embrace, withdraw the tongue, harden and retract the lips, the other whose laughter ceases to be slow and conspiratorial and whose fingers no longer have all the time in the world at their tips. I am aware of these things, I don't delude myself that they are not there. Where the self-deception comes in is in my ability, notwithstanding all this, to persuade myself of its being a phase, a stage in a progress, or a mere lapse.

Bell's passion for me, which I am sure, am still sure, in spite of everything, was once as real as mine for her, had begun to slacken its intensity. She became abstracted, withdrew herself a little. My second book was published, there was some press attention this time and talk of it as a candidate for an adventure-novelists' prize; American publication was assured, and I was busy with all this, but not so busy as to be unaware of Bell's absences, of some business she had that was private from me. What could she have to do that took her away from the House of Stairs so much? Where was she when occasionally she phoned me or Cosette to say she would be late, she was 'held up'? She did nothing – ever. In this way she rather resembled Cosette, as in so many others – and what does that say about Mark and about me?

Bell had no occupation, hobbies, interests. Her interest in people and their behaviour absorbed her. She liked to look at beautiful things, in shops and in exhibitions; not at clothes, though walking through fabric departments, stroking the more extravagant stuffs, gave her intense sensuous pleasure. Mark told me later she sometimes went to look at the crown jewels in the Tower. Was that what she was doing, in all those absences, looking at the people and the lavish artefacts in Bond Street? Stroking damask in Liberty's? Strolling round the V and A?

Then she went back to her mother's. There was an awful evening when we sat together in the grey garden, Cosette and Auntie and I, each feeling our peculiar individual loneliness, not even a warm evening, but humid and cool and smelling of soot and the leaves of the eucalypt. Anyone who looked over the high walls of brick and flint might have taken us for the representatives of three generations in one family, daughter, mother, grandmother, but no one looked over the walls. The sky was like white marble, the night long in arriving. Once, I remember, Cosette said, 'Why does no one come any more?'

That shy, half-fearful smile trembled on Auntie's lips. She seemed to understand less and less as time went on. Her bewilderment was of the kind that is afraid no sincerity remains, everything is becoming a joke, but a joke that to her is meaningless. In another way she was like one of those poor zoo animals that, accustomed to living in a group of their peers and in a particular habitat, are imprisoned in an alien one and alone. I went indoors, ostensibly to fetch a sweater and, mounting the stairs, hearing with the first of many twinges of pain my foot set the 104th creaking, entered Bell's room to hold one of her dark wraps to my face and smell her sweet child's smell. *The Wings of the Dove*, unread, never to be read of course, lay on a chair. I took it away downstairs.

Another time, when Auntie had gone off to bed, Cosette said to her reflection in the drawing-room mirror,

'Is this the form, she made her moan,
That won his praises night and morn?
And, Ah, she said, but I wake alone,
I sleep forgotten, I wake forlorn.'

I put my arms around her, I hugged her. How that would have flustered her had she known about Bell and me! But she laughed at Tennyson and herself.

'Isn't it dreadful? Ivor wrote better poetry than that. Well, marginally better. "My life is dreary, he cometh not, she said . . ."'

He cometh not . . . The inexpressible, absolute he, the non-pareil of he's she has waited for. She had been reading *Washington Square*, lent to her of course by me, and she identified with poor Catherine Sloper. Women are usually shy about admitting their need of a man. They deny this need, dismiss it; they could easily, they say, get themselves a lover, a husband, if they wanted one. But why go to so much trouble? Why bother? They are content as they are. Not Cosette. Frankly, she would declare it, not just to me but to almost any listener, to Perpetua, to Auntie, that she was sick for a man's love, a man's companionship. Her life was dreary, he cometh not, she said . . .

But two days later he did come. He arrived like the answer to a prayer, or like the answer one dreams of but doesn't expect to get. He arrived like the prince that some fairy messenger brings, and he wasn't even in disguise. Or not apparently so. It was Bell who brought him. There was no fanfare of trumpets. Very casually, she gave notice to Cosette of what was about to happen, announcing this event that was to prove so momentous in her usual offhand way. She had reappeared in the House of Stairs after an absence of two or three weeks — why do I say two or three weeks when I know the length of time precisely, when I know it was exactly eighteen days? — and sauntered into the drawing room as if she had never been away. She was wearing her white cheesecloth, carrying her cigarette packet and matches in her hand. I never saw Bell with a handbag. Us three, Cosette, Auntie and I, she glanced at us as if we were equally casual acquaintances, people she tolerated in an indifferent good-humoured fashion.

'My brother's coming this evening. Is that all right?'

But Cosette spoke to her as if she were her daughter. 'Darling, how can you ask? Of course it is. We all long to meet him.'

Mark — how can I describe him? He was simply the best-looking man I have ever known and one of the nicest. Or so I thought for a long time, marginally, at last, changing this view of him. He was one

697

of those people you at once feel at ease with, who are 'always the same', without vanity or apparently the knowledge they have anything to be vain about, clever and amusing without cruelty, unfailingly kind, seductively charming without any of the slyness or conscious affectation this implies. Yet when I look back on this I see I have given an impression of someone quite unlike Mark, for the point with him, I might even say the point *of* him, was his naturalness, that all these most delightful possible attributes of a young handsome man had come into being and coalesced by a happy chance and he was not even aware that they were there. Even the things he said seemed never the result of calculation but the expression of a warm and gentle nature. Have I made him sound like a fool? I don't think he was a fool, for a long time I thought him intelligent, but that view too I revised. Let me say only that Mark was exceptional to look at but intellectually nothing out of the common way.

Older than Bell by several years, he was thirty-six that winter. By then I had put him and Bell down as probably being of Scandinavian origin, but Mark's looks were really more of the Slavonic kind, the wide, high cheekbones, the nose that was perfectly straight but rather short for a man's nose, the short upper lip, the full but firm mouth. His skin was brown and his hair nut-brown with a streak of silver running from one temple across the crown. How Cosette came to love that silver streak, how important it was to her!

She wasn't looking particularly nice that evening. Her hair needed doing and the roots showed grey. Staying thin wasn't just a losing battle with Cosette but a series of skirmishes in which about fifty per cent of the time her side won. Necessarily, therefore, the other half of the time fat was the conqueror and he was in the ascendant now, positively crowing his victory on the scales that morning. She had a silk caftan on, in a shade of light red that didn't suit her, and she had sprayed on too much Joy. Fay, on the other hand, with twenty-five years' advantage over her, was looking gorgeous. She went through phases, did Fay, times of indifferent, rather shabby looks when she would be washed-out and stringy, and times of glory, each dependent on the attention she paid herself. She must have been attentive lately, for she glowed under make-up as heavy but more skilfully applied than Felicity's had ever been, and instead of her usual jeans, she was in a skirt which showed off her legs and fine ankles. Perdita, the dancer, who had been left there by her husband while he went off to some charity performance, also presented an appearance with which Cosette couldn't have competed. She was always exquisite, like an exhibit in a little girl's glass case of dolls, waxen-faced, raspberry-fuchsia mouth, hair that might have been painted on with lamp black and a fine brush, every gesture learned and every pose rehearsed.

I mention competing because that was the impression they gave, those three women, when Mark walked in. Bell had gone out on to the balcony to check that it was he when the doorbell rang and then she went down to let him in. He was the only man and there were we five women. You could see at once what an impact he made. His grace as much as his looks did that. He was very thin and he walked like a dancer – imagine Nureyev entering a London drawing room incognito – or perhaps he walked like an actor, which is what he was. It would have been amusing, the reaction of those three, if it hadn't been sad, for in the few seconds before Mark went over to her and shook hands, you could see Cosette, bowed and humbled, retire from the contest. It was as if she took in for the first time without self-delusion the appearance of the other two, as if the shock of it struck and pained her, her fifty-five years and her weariness smote her, and she put out her hand to him with a half-smile in which was self-mockery and defeat.

It was not she whom he approached first. Mark was Mark and he knew what was due to the obviously eldest lady there. Auntie was the first of us he shook hands with, Auntie who was so accustomed to being ignored by pretty well everyone except Cosette – you see how, even here, I said that we were five women, not six – that she was too stunned to reply when he said how do you do to her. Bell made no introductions, I should have been astounded if she had, she simply waved a hand at him and said, 'This is Marcus.'

He said quickly, almost apologetically, 'No – Mark, please.'

And of course I found out long afterwards that it was Bell, with her fondness for pretentious fancy names, who had Latinized him. Cosette told him who we all were. Something like this had happened the first time Walter Admetus came round, the first time Luis Llanos did. The dancer had merely bestowed on all his charm-laden smile and a 'Hi!' while Admetus went from person to person, carefully enunciating names – 'How do you do, Gary?' 'How do you do, Mimi?' Mark said how do you do only to Auntie, an individual hallo to all the rest of us. I saw no special glance of admiration rest on

Perdita or on Fay. Bell, too, was watching, with the same passion for the finer points of human behaviour.

Mark didn't talk about himself and it was from Bell that I found out what he did. He had a part in a radio serial, precarious work since there were constant threats to kill off the character he played, but it was more secure than his past, which was a history of tiny parts in television drama, as a film extra and repertory work in places such as Colchester or Gateshead. It took me just as long to find out where he lived, in a studio flat in the neighbourhood of Brook Green, and his age, and that he was single and had never been married. But Mark was a listener, at any rate not one to fill the conversation with his history and his opinions, and for a while we knew of him only that he was charming and interesting and 'an addition to our circle', as Cosette put it in a kind of parody of Victorian talk.

'Why have you kept him to yourself for so long, Bell?' Cosette asked her when we were all down in the dining room, eating one of those luxury cold meals the fridge disgorged.

She shrugged but she looked at him with the modest satisfaction of someone who has brought unquestionably the most stunning exhibit to the show. 'He could have come before. He knew it was here.'

'Don't you believe her. She never said a word about all this.' He put out a hand to encompass Cosette's art nouveau hanging lamp, the walls all laden with Flora Danica porcelain, the purple curtains not drawn but carelessly flung back to show the grey garden made yellow and shiny and glittering by shed lamplight and winter wet. Later he was to say he had always hated the House of Stairs, but there was no sign of that then. 'She never said a word about you, all of you. I just knew she had a room here and a friend.' His glance lighted on me charmingly, it seemed to me admiringly. 'For all I knew, it was another glory-hole like old Walter's tip where the cat fleas can be seen nightly, dancing on the carpet.'

'The origin of the term "entrechats" perhaps,' said Cosette with a smile at the dancer who, not understanding, returned her look with her usual one of wistful wonder.

Mark laughed. Cosette's gratitude for his amusement fairly blazed in her face. She wasn't sitting next to him, she would have thought it selfish to have placed this prize next to herself, but now that we had finished eating, though two just-opened bottles of wine remained, we followed one of our customs of changing places at table and Bell, who had been between Mark and me, got up and invited Cosette to take her chair. In my turn I moved to change with Fay, ostensibly to sit beside Gary who had come in just as the meal began, but really to be in a position to observe Cosette and Mark. I was afraid for her, I was already afraid.

They talked about Walter Admetus. Though he had been to his house to see Bell, he had never actually met Admetus, but he was far more familiar with the pieces he wrote for *Private Eye* and the *New Statesman* than Cosette was. With the kind of intellectual approach actors rarely have, he told Cosette what a good critic he thought Admetus was, how considered and searching, never going in for the cheap jibe for the sake of raising a laugh and at the expense of truth. Did Cosette know he had written a novel which had never received the attention it deserved? This, of course, led Cosette into fulsome praise of my own imperishable works. I was embarrassed, of course I was, but to my surprise I found Mark knew I was a writer, had in fact read my first book and the only good review I had ever had – almost the only review – and instead of Ivor Sitwell's sneering remarks or Admetus's manner of ignoring entirely that I had ever written or published anything, said, 'I sat up all night to finish your book, I had to know what happened. You deserved that prize.'

I muttered some sort of thanks. 'Did Bell tell you about it?'

If she had he would have answered directly, but, 'Oh, Bell's illiterate and proud of it,' he returned. 'And I'm not one of your readers who get your book out of the library and then expect you to go down on your knees to me for graciously borrowing it.'

This was so accurate I began to laugh. 'Did you actually pay down good money?'

'The best,' he said.

Cosette fell in love with him that evening. It happened as quickly as that. I was dismayed to see it, I watched aghast as, when we returned to the drawing room to drink, for some forgotten reason, champagne, she turned on him a look I had once seen on another face in very different circumstances. This had been when Cosette and I were together in Italy and into this café in Bologna came an itinerant musician with a guitar. There was a child in the café with her parents and older sister, a girl of about eight. She fell in love at first sight with the guitarist, following him in worshipful silence round the restaurant from table to table, watched with unconcealed amusement by her mother and father and the older girl. When he became aware of her attention he turned to her and performed only for her, seating her on a chair at a table alone, playing for her a grotesque pluck-plucking version of *Santa Lucia*, and receiving with evident kindly delight her gaze of adoration. Cosette, of an age to be that girl's grandmother, wore that look identically, as for a long moment when he brought her a glass of champagne she met his eyes with undisguised wonder and glory in her own.

It would pass, I thought, it *must* pass, it must be no more than a 'crush', an evening's infatuation that with nothing to feed on would die, would become for poor Cosette no more than a piece of nostalgia on which to look back with a, 'Do you remember that beautiful man who came here once and was so nice to us? I was madly in love with him for a whole week . . .!'

But she wasn't going to give that a chance to happen. She wasn't going to let him get away. Bell she rightly knew as evanescent, unreliable, an occasional 'disappearer'; one not to be trusted to bring her showpiece back again. And Cosette was aware of the invalidity of the vague invitation that postulates another visit 'sometime soon' or 'when you're passing'. Mark had to be summoned back for a specific occasion and he was: a party; she would give a party – for what? For Bell's birthday, her thirtieth it was going to be. This seemed tremendously young, of course, to Cosette, thought I am less sure of how Bell felt about it. Not too happy to have this milestone advertised, I suspect.

'If I could be thirty again, I'd be a "manizer", I'd go about stealing everyone's husbands.'

I remembered that then. I remembered that when she invited Mark to Bell's birthday party, including Fay in the invitation, of course, and Perdita. Her face was radiant still. It was like the little Bologna girl's face in that there was no disguising her joy, as if she had seen no men before, never been married and had her two or three lovers, but had slept her youth away in the depths of a wood or wasted it in a nunnery, and like Miranda, cried, 'O brave new world, that has such people in't!'

That night, later, lying in bed beside Bell, I said to her, 'Cosette is going to fall in love with Mark.'

'She's in love with him already.'

'You saw that?' I said.

'Didn't you? Of course you did.'

'I wish there was something we could do to stop it.'

'Why? Why ever? Because you're afraid for her? But he'll be different, he won't be like that bastard Ivor Thing. Mark doesn't fuck women over.'

'I mean he won't feel the same as she does, he won't be able to return what she feels.'

'He'll be kind to her, though. That'll be the difference, you'll see what a difference that makes, he'll be so kind.'

'I'd rather he didn't get the chance,' I said.

'Would you? Cosette wouldn't.' She turned over, pulling herself away from me, 'I'm going to sleep now. Good night.'

This morning we went shopping together, Bell and I, down to the supermarket where I buy food for my cats. As we waited in the queue at the check-out, I pointed out to her the pictures in bright gilt frames the supermarket offers for sale at £9.95 apiece. In one of them was represented a favourite subject of Silas Sanger's, an animal walking across a clearing in woodland, though this animal was a retriever in a sunlit grove, whereas Silas's would have been a bloody-jawed predator in a rain forest.

She thought of him too. 'Silas used to freak out when he saw things like that,' she said. 'They're obscene, they make me feel sick.'

'That's the Leicester Art College view, is it?' I said. I know I shouldn't make these scathing remarks to her every time we come near places in the past where she lied to me, but I can't help it. Still, I must, I must resist. She doesn't seem to care though, she takes it as if I have a right to try and settle scores, and perhaps I have.

'You know I was never there. It's a wonder you ever believed all that crap in the first place.'

'Curious as it may seem to you, people do tend to believe what they're told.'

Her laughter is as dry now as sticks crackling when they start to burn. We paid for the cat food and lugged it out and waited for a taxi. She hasn't after all found herself equal to that job in the shop in Westbourne Grove and has moved in with me, she lives with me now. Not that this has actually been said, not in those words, and rent is still being paid for that room under the railway arch. How she expresses it is that she is staying with me, but I know she means to remain. The irony of it amuses me greatly, for I remember how ecstatic I would once have been to have Bell living with me, to know Bell wanted to live with me – wanted it more than I wanted it. But such a state of affairs was unthinkable, unimaginable.

Now, frankly, I don't want it at all. I don't want Bell as some sort of temporary but long-term guest in my house. She is too much for me, her past is too much, the things she has done. I jib at that. Who wouldn't? It has made me nervous, all of it, it is causing me the kind of stress that always results in – well, you can guess what, can't you? In a tic, a twitching, a jumping of the muscles. The more I worry about it the worse it gets. This is not the way Huntington's begins, but I don't like it and I worry about it, I know I am still not too old.

My fortieth birthday has passed and gone. Bell and I went out to dinner and celebrated. We go out together a lot, several evenings a week, often to the cinema, for there have been so many good films lately, *Mona Lisa* and *A Room with a View* and *Prick Up Your Ears*. I haven't been to the cinema so much for years. And last week we went to see *Antony and Cleopatra* at the Olivier, the finest performance this century some say, and had our supper at the National Film Theatre by the river. Two rather good-looking women in early middle age, people must think us, not sisters, too dissimilar for that, and not suburban neighbours either. No one could think Bell in her black layers, her different black textures all bunched and bundled and tied, anyone's suburban neighbour. She wears nothing but black now. Like Chekhov's Marya perhaps, she is in mourning for her life.

'What bollocks,' she said when I told her this. 'Half your trouble is you've read too many books.'

'You mean half *your* trouble is I've read too many books.'

You see, I want to get her to talk about Cosette and Mark. Sooner or later, if she fails to respond to all these hints, I shall have to say their names to her, talk about them myself, but I don't want to do that yet. No, that's not true. I'm afraid to mention them. When we got home the phone rang and it was Timothy. Do you remember Timothy, the man I was having dinner with in Leith's the day after I first saw Bell? He doesn't mean much to me, I am not in love with him or he with me, but he is a friend and I can't see him now, not at present. I can't ask people to meet Bell, I can't introduce her to them. They may not know who she is and what she has done, there is no need for them to know, but I know and it inhibits me.

Bell smoked all the way back in the taxi in spite of the driver's notice saying 'Thank you for not smoking'. She couldn't believe this wasn't a joke when she first read it. The driver coughed ostentatiously and when we got to my house said, 'I'd have put you out of my cab, only I've got old-fashioned ideas about what's due to ladies. Pity others aren't so considerate.'

I thought Bell might swear at him, but she didn't, she didn't say anything, hardly seemed to have heard. She walked up to the front door and waited for me to unlock it and when we were inside said, 'Shall I tell you how I really met Silas?'

'Suit yourself.'

'Come on,' she said, 'that's me, that's what I say. You're pinching my lines.'

I started laughing. 'Tell me how you really met Silas.'

'It was in the children's home. The home was a big house that was a sort of experimental unit – experimental fuck-up, actually. I mean they mixed up big kids with much younger ones and really little ones. It was supposed to be like a family, Christ. Give me my cigarettes, will you?

'They put me in there when I was sixteen. You know where I'd been and why. Well, they put me in there sort of secretly, it was all supposed to be very progressive, in tune with the changing times and all that, it was 1958, not a word to get into the newspapers. There wasn't much else in the way of media then. But they weren't progressive enough to think I ought to be at school. I went out to work and lived at the home and in the evenings I used to have to help put the little ones to bed. Yes, really, that was a laugh, wasn't it? I was dying to get away but I didn't know when I could, if I ever could, being me, whether it was eighteen or twenty-one then or what, or whether it was just another kind of prison. Well, it wasn't.

'Silas had a relation with a kid in care but they used to let the kid go home at the weekends. Sometimes it was Silas who brought her back. Felicity was his girlfriend then. She was at college and I reckon she thought it ever so wild and daring screwing around with a schizzy soak like Silas. OK, so I got him away from her and I really did get pregnant and the superintendent that ran the home made him say he'd marry me. They told him who I was and made it look like he'd done something really awful even touching me, like I was a leper, and now we'd both have leprosy but we'd have to have it together. I had a miscarriage on my wedding day. I started bleeding in the Registry Office.'

'Is that true, Bell?'

'Is what true?'

'All of it.'

'Of course it is. You said yourself even liars tell more truth than lies.'

The muscles were jumping in my neck and shoulders. I tried to control them, breathing deeply. 'Where was Mark then?' I said. 'What was Mark doing?'

She jumped up and ran out of the room, banging the door.

Mark came to the party Cosette gave for Bell's birthday. For some reason, it was a far more decorous affair than the one Esmond Thinnesse interrupted to take Felicity away. People got drunk, of course they did, and Rimmon went on one of his acid trips, but these had become habitual to him, were a weekly indulgence. As far as I remember no couple disappeared into a bedroom as Felicity and Harvey had on that previous occasion. I have sometimes thought that this party was less of a saturnalia than previous ones simply because Mark was there. Of course I am not implying that he had prudish views or that there was anything repressive or disapproving in the way he behaved. There was nothing like that. It was more that his presence seemed to make people feel that it was possible to have a good time socially without getting drunk or high or pawing others about, that conversation and being nice to fellow-guests was a reasonable, if out-dated, alternative. Of course I realize I'm making a pretty high-flown claim for Mark and maybe I'm quite wrong, maybe the party was the way it was because Admetus wasn't there and nor were Felicity nor Fay nor Gary.

Cosette urged Bell to invite her own friends. She was very anxious that Bell and Mark's mother should be invited and in fact wanted more than that. Because it was for Bell's birthday, she wanted Bell's mother asked round in advance, she wanted her actually to take some part in organizing the party. Bell invited no one. I can quite see why not now, but at the time it seemed strange to me. Apart from Mark, the guests were all Cosette's old gang, the usual Wellgarthians, Oliver and Adele and the ballet dancers and Perpetua with a lot of her family, including Dominic, and Mervyn and Mimi, and some neighbours from Archangel Mews.

At that party, for a birthday present, Cosette gave Bell the bloodstone ring. She said it suited Bell's hand much better than her own and she was right. Bell said thank you and looked at the ring on her finger and then up at Cosette, but without smiling or showing any special signs of pleasure. Almost anyone else would have kissed Cosette for that, thrown her arms round her and kissed her. I wasn't surprised when Bell didn't do this, but I was sorry. I was sorry too that she never wore the ring afterwards, or if she did it wasn't when she was with me. The next time I saw her and I think every time since then, her hands were bare.

Mark didn't stay till the small hours. He went home a little after midnight. Cosette pressed him to come back the following evening to dinner when they would talk about the party.

'I don't think I should come tomorrow,' he said.

There was something in the way he put it that made it far from a direct refusal. Cosette seized on this.

'If you mean you ought not to come because you've been here twice, that's nonsense, you know. Everyone else comes just as often as they want. We don't stand on ceremony here. Please come.'

He smiled at her. 'Just the same, I won't come tomorrow.'

I was angry with him. It seemed to me he was playing hard to get. Why follow these rules with a rich woman old enough, nearly old enough, to be his mother? It was unkind. Or it was deliberately making himself elusive, unattainable and therefore the more longed-for. He said no more. Cosette watched him go down the street, watched his long thin shadow the lamplight cast. She closed the door. We were alone in the hall, the party and the music still going on upstairs.

'I'd give everything I've got to have my youth back,' Cosette said. She said it in a fierce, intense whisper. 'I'd give all the future and take death at the end of it if I could have one year of being thirty.'

It was nearly a week before she heard from him again. In that week, what was she like? Sad, I suppose, just sad. She didn't talk about him, she didn't say anything, but you could imagine her thoughts. If only, they must have run, I could have been just a handful of years younger and he just a fraction older, if only we could have met with no more than five or six years between us – ah, then! As it is I can do nothing, I can't even phone him as I would Walter, say, or Maurice Bailey or some other man, I can't do it because of the way I feel, I can't face the humiliation of a refusal. So she must have thought. Sometimes I caught her looking at Bell as if there lay her only hope. Bell was the key to Mark. What questions could she answer, what histories give, what analyses of his past behaviour? But Cosette never asked, and I didn't ask either. It seemed to me – quite wrongly, of course, as I now know – that perfect confidence had existed between Bell and me and the coming of Mark spoiled it. I was afraid to ask and she was not willing to explain. It erected a barrier between us, or so I thought. In fact it did erect a barrier, it was through Mark that we began to be drawn apart, but not at all in the way I supposed.

– 14 –

There is a limit, said Henry James, to the impunity with which one can juggle with truth.

I could question that. He never knew Bell, he never knew the arch-juggler in the circus of the world. It is a strange thing the conclusions we draw not from the impressions we are given but from the impressions we take. I took it for granted Bell was experienced, sophisticated, richly travelled in all kinds of sexual regions, as street-wise as could be, as tough. Yet she never told me so. Did she act these things, or did I choose to see her as acting? Certainly she told me she had been at art school, had lovers long before she went there, grew up fatherless and with a strange mother who had been a concert singer. Her maiden name, of course, had been Mark's name, Henryson.

I reached a conclusion: life with Silas had compounded her distaste for men. Even while with him, married to him, she had turned to women as lovers, probably a series of women. And after he was dead and she was free she was able to indulge her love for her own sex. I thought it likely that this accounted, more than a need to be with her mother, for those absences of her and that disappearance which took place soon after our meeting in Admetus's house. She had had a lover, a woman, to whom she was deeply committed but with whom she had finally broken in order to come to me. For, looking back over our life together and the multitude of things we had talked about, I could recall no mention of any man she was involved with except Silas, no mention indeed of any man at all except her brother Mark, and on the subject of him she was not communicative.

I thought we would never see him again, and I was surprised when I answered the phone to hear his voice. He recognized mine at once. Mark wasn't one of those people who, though they have met you, when they phone treat you, with their 'Can I speak to so-and-so?', like the secretary or the housekeeper. Mark called me by my name and asked me how I was and then sounded taken aback when I said Bell wasn't in.

'It isn't Bell I want. I hoped I could speak to Cosette.'

He had rung to ask her out to dinner. Just the two of them, not a party, just he and she because he thought it would be nice to entertain her for a change after he had twice been her guest. Her reaction wasn't at all what I expected. It wasn't what Bell expected either. I won't say I knew Bell by that time. In view of how tremendously I was deceived, that would be stupid, but I knew sides of her, I knew what it meant when she watched someone in that cold interested way of hers. She was making mental notes of their follies, how far they would go. Having seen Cosette – well, let me make no bones about it – having seen her simper at Mark and bridle and gaze with adoration, hang on his words and defer to his opinions, she was waiting for some fresh ridiculous display. Isn't it strange that I was beginning to understand that Bell disliked Cosette? Hardly anyone ever disliked Cosette, you see, it was nearly impossible, so I had discounted the signs I had seen before, only keeping in mind the kindnesses and politenesses Bell had rendered Cosette when first they met. Now I saw in Bell's eyes a mild scorn, and I saw disappointment that when Mark asked her out to dinner Cosette didn't get into a panic about what to wear, when to have her hair done, what to do about her face, and cry, oh, if she could only be a little bit younger!

You see, I think Cosette had given up the battle. Probably she had taken a good, hard, long look at herself in the glass and decided it was no use. *This man was too important for it to be any use.* Ivor Sitwell was one thing, the kind of man you had your face lifted for and dieted for and bought new clothes for, but only to get back into the running. Rimmon – well, what was he but what Bell called a snack-fuck, something to have between proper meals? There had been another man, I think, some pal of Admetus's, no more than a one-night stand. But Mark was the real thing and because he was the real thing it was no use. Better to have him as a friend, to have his respect, his delightful company, than make a guy of oneself, an over-scented, over-painted show, and thus earn his contempt.

'I am trying to teach myself not to mind when the people in the restaurant take me for his mother,' she said to me. 'No, I'm doing better than that. I'm teaching myself to expect it and like it. I mean, I'd have loved to have a son like Mark. Imagine how different things would be for me now if I had a son like him.'

'You never liked it when I was taken for your daughter and he's ten or eleven years older than me.'

'I would like it now. I'm changing, I've got to. I'm going to grow old gracefully.'

The interesting thing was that she looked a lot nicer and a lot younger for not going in for all that make-up and rigid hairdressing. She wore her hair in a simple loose knot on the back of her head (the way Bell wears hers now), touched her face with a little soft colour, put on a plain, dark-green dress with the pearls that had been Douglas's last present to her. Handsome and dignified she looked and only a very unobservant person would have thought her old enough to be Mark's mother, unless she had mysteriously been reared in a society where girls get married at twelve.

Over-courteous in Admetus's way, obsequious and deferential, Mark never was. He had arranged to meet her at the restaurant, not call for her. And it was a little bistro in Queensway to which he was taking her, none of your *grande cuisine*. I didn't see her go or return. Bell and I were invited to Elsa's divorce 'thrash', the party she was giving to celebrate extricating herself from her French Catholic husband. Next morning, late because we had got home in the small hours, Mark was there in the drawing room with Cosette and Auntie, and he and Cosette, facing each other across the table, were engaged in animated conversation, their eyes fixed on each other's faces. I caught a sentence or two of it. Cosette was saying, 'But I don't know anything about Schoenberg,' and Mark rejoined, 'Neither do I – yet. We can learn. We can learn together.'

They – at any rate, Cosette – didn't seem too pleased to see Bell and me. Of course she put up a show of being pleased because she was like that, but I could tell. They went out soon after that, they were taking Auntie somewhere. It was Cosette's day for taking Auntie for a drive and Mark had said he would come too. Auntie went along obediently, in the rather zombie-like way she did most things, just doing what she was told, but I fancied she looked less bewildered. Mark was a person she could understand, not curiously dressed or using words she had been taught it was a crime to utter or smoking strange things or making discordant music. And he talked to her, he didn't pretend she wasn't there.

I went out on to the balcony to watch them go, wondering if Mark would drive the car, but he didn't, not that time at any rate. He sat in the back.

'He must have stayed the night,' Bell said in the curious, uninflected tone she sometimes used.

'I'm certain he didn't.'

'Why not?'

'I just have a feeling he didn't. They would have been different, Cosette would have been different.'

And it turned out the way I supposed. Bell asked Gary directly. I thought it a strange thing to do, to ask him outright like that. Gary never slept much, going to bed very late always and seldom staying in bed much after seven. Mark had come in with Cosette at eleven the previous evening, he said, stayed ten minutes, come back at ten that morning. Gary had let him in himself.

'You sound like you're his wife's spies,' said Gary.

'He hasn't got a wife,' Bell said.

'Do you want to know if he kissed her good-night?'

'For Christ's sake!' I said, trying to put a stop to it. 'This is Cosette we're talking about, *Cosette*.'

'So what?' he said, rather unexpectedly. 'The wine she drinks is made of grapes.'

'Maybe, but he's not likely to drink the same wine, is he?'

Bell said slowly, 'I don't see why not, I really don't see why not.'

'Cosette's well into her fifties. She doesn't expect it, she doesn't dream of it.'

'I bet she *dreams* of it,' said Gary.

Mark was just a friend. How could it be otherwise? At least he wasn't on the gravy train to Cadgeville. He took Cosette out to meals or else he came to the House of Stairs when dinner was over. Very occasionally, when all of us were taken out by Cosette, he would join us, but he behaved rather austerely at these dinner parties, drinking sparingly, eating cheaply. He didn't smoke, he didn't drink spirits. When he was present you could feel the lavish days were past, the days of green chartreuse and burnt banknotes.

I had got it into my head, on the strength of once having seen them together, that he and Bell were close. This seemed not to be true. It was plain, at any rate, that he didn't come to the house to see his sister. They took no more notice of each other than each did of Gary or the ballet dancers, less in fact, for Mark was always polite and pleasant to Cosette's friends. Bell was the only person I ever saw him apparently indifferent to. And he was more than indifferent to her, he was capable of ignoring her when she walked into the room. Sometimes I saw him look up, realize who it was that had come in, and look away again without a nod or a word. I don't know why, but somehow I thought this must be Bell's fault, this must be something Bell had done.

I asked him one day what she was like when she was a little girl.

He smiled. 'I haven't the least idea.'

'You must have. You're her brother.'

In Cosette's presence, out of a compliment to Cosette supposedly, he often added unspecified years to his age. 'I'm so much older than Bell.' He made it sound as if the age gap was twenty rather than six and a half years. 'I was away at school.' It was plain he didn't want to talk about it.

That same day I looked up Henryson in the phone book. Mark was there at Brook Green, a Riverside number, but there was no Mrs Henryson in Harlesden. Why would there have been? I had never known Bell to phone her mother; no doubt she didn't have a phone. I was naïve, I was gullible. I believed in Bell, confusing frankness with honesty.

Her frankness has led her to talk to me about Silas and their life together. We have moved on. Not to Cosette or Mark, she reacts to their names like an animal when it hears a gun fired, but to herself and me.

'No, there weren't any women before you,' she said. 'There haven't been any since, come to that.'

'Am I hearing what I think I'm hearing?'

'I'm not a lesbian. Sometimes I've wished I was. There was a lot of that going on in prison.'

'Then why . . .?'

She said simply, 'Because you were.'

'Never, till you.'

Her dry laugh rattled in her throat. It is the kind of laugh that used to be called 'dirty', scathing, self-mocking.

'Something came over me,' she said, 'that night when I put the dress on. I thought you'd like it, and you did, didn't you?'

'Didn't *you?*'

'Oh, sure. I loved it, but it was never quite the real thing. Did you feel that?'

'No,' I said. 'It was the real thing for me. But I've heard other dabblers say what you say.'

'What do you mean, dabblers?'

'Queers trying it straight and straight people trying it queer.'

'Have I upset you, Lizzie?'

'You've given me a shock,' I said.

I couldn't look at her. I was wrong, wasn't I, about her having been as much in love with me as I with her? But this is the kind of thing which must often happen to certain people, finding out that a lover made love to them only to please them or to gain a particular end. It must happen to rich old women and rich old men, to ugly rich people. But I had been young and poor and some said good-looking . . .

'Were you ever in love with me?' It took me a good hour to work myself up to ask that question and when I asked it my voice sounded strange, hoarse and horribly anxious. 'I was in love with you. Were you with me?'

Something has softened her, the dreadful prison years supposedly. She takes pains not to hurt me too much. 'I don't know. I was very fond of you. I liked the sex. I liked the feeling of doing something – outrageous.'

Has she always been so grossly insensitive? Was she then, when we were together? She laid her hand on me. She touched my

713

shoulder, my neck. I stopped myself jumping up, shrieking, the way Cosette said she would if any woman made an advance to her. I just picked up the hand and threw it off, though not as fiercely as you would throw off an insect that fell on you out of a tree. I cast it away as Cosette once cast my hand off her arm.

'The last thing I want,' I said. 'I'm not sure what you're offering but I don't want any part of it. Not if you and I were the last people on earth and marooned somewhere.'

'That's all right then. I'm sure I don't. I don't mean you specially, not anyone, man or woman; it makes me shudder, the mere thought.'

As Mark's visits grew more frequent, as he came more to the house and he and Cosette went out more together, spending a lot of time in each other's company, so Bell and I grew apart. You must remember that I didn't know then what I know now, that she didn't love me, had never loved me, looked upon me – well, it is true, isn't it, it must be faced? – as a sort of perverse indulgence, a co-player in a naughty game. I thought she had loved me but that her love was passing, she was getting tired of me. Perhaps, anyway, that isn't much of an improvement on the truth. Never to have been loved – that is somehow more acceptable than being the kind of person a lover quickly tires of.

We talked less, too. The confiding stopped, the discussion of people in the house, the way they behaved, the things they said. It was Bell who stopped it. I would begin with a question as to why Gary had done such and such, what Cosette's brother Oliver had meant by some remark, and my answer would be a shrug or, 'Who cares?'

Cosette, rather late in the day, had bought a television set. Ostensibly, it was for Auntie. It wasn't in the drawing room, Cosette wouldn't have that, but in the front room on the ground floor, a place that had never before had any particular function except sometimes as a centre for musical or hallucinogenic rites. A sofa and chairs were set out in it and Cosette had bought a huge, gilt-framed mirror to hang on one wall. Bell spent a lot of time in there, watching television. It was as if the television was my victorious rival, drawing her away from me. She and Auntie, who had nothing else in common, who had scarcely spoken to each other, were now usually to be found down there in armchairs side by side, a sporadic, totally screen-focused conversation carried on between them.

'Shall I switch over to the other channel?'

'Yes, if you like. It's our serial tonight.'

Auntie was usually off to bed by ten. Bell stayed up watching until midnight or beyond, if there was any beyond. And I would lie in bed waiting for her, first hearing Cosette and Mark come in, Mark sometimes but by no means always coming up to the first floor for a drink or a last word with her, then the front door closing on him, then finally Bell's footsteps mounting the first flight and the second, but passing my door and going on up, up, up, to her room on the top.

My heart was sore. I had had my dreams and made absurd plans. Our affair, or whatever you liked to call it, couldn't of course go on, I knew that, but I had a romantic idea that a special bond would always be there, each of us as the years passed would be first with the other. And some ritual would come into being, we would for instance meet and make love once a year, we would always have a unique friendship, our secret closeness would enrich our lives and there would arise between us a special empathy so that, as separated twins are said to do, we would sense from a distance whenever the other was enjoying good fortune or in danger.

For this to happen there would have had to be something to alter things and wrench us apart. Cosette's moving, for instance, or illness afflicting me or Bell's mother needing her. Now I saw that there were other ways of parting a pair like us, evanescent, subtle things that took away the substance and left – nothing. For, as if we were true gays, we had always behaved with the utmost decorum in public. Homosexual couples invariably do, I have noticed, except in the society of others like themselves. When with straight people they never touch each other, exchange glances, or even sit side by side. So there were no changes for Bell and me to make in our social behaviour. We had never touched and caressed in the sight of Cosette and Auntie. Now we no longer did so by night, in private. I knew only that I had no human rival, for Bell hardly ever went out and never received or made phone calls. She watched television.

She said so little to me that spring and summer, whole weeks seemed to go by without a word from her, that I remember only one remark of any significance. We passed on the stairs. I was on my way to see my agent – to be told no one was interested in publishing my monograph on Henry James – and she had come up only from the hall where she had been to pick up the household's post from the front doormat. Bell had grown pale and sickly looking from never going out. The weather was warm, sultry, windless, but she preferred to be indoors, lying on her bed for hours on end up there, the dangerous window open to its fullest extent. And the dusty black she wore reminded me of the clothes of Middle Eastern women.

'I feel like escaping, but where would I go?'

I said, and immediately wished I hadn't, 'We could go away somewhere together. We could go for a holiday.'

She looked me hard in the eyes. 'I don't mean that at all.'

Sisters can be jealous of brothers – anyone can be jealous of anyone – and I thought it might be that she minded Mark's spending so much time with Cosette. Had Cosette separated them? Was that the event which had taken place since I first saw them together and had changed their relationship? I fancied Cosette might have taken a sister's place in Mark's life. His own sister had perhaps been cold, uninterested, no longer the comrade of earlier years, and Cosette had slipped into that role. Certainly there was no sign of her and Mark being anything to each other but friends. Mark, who after his first few visits seemed cast for Ivor Sitwell's part, had never stepped into it, but had rather retreated. And Cosette, who gave him at that same period so many languishing glances, who seemed set to fall deep into adoration, looked at him and spoke to him in the same tone she might use to Gary or Luis. The promise she had made, to teach herself that sexual love between them was impossible, to grow old gracefully, it appeared she was keeping. Her reward was his affection.

He liked her for herself. She was his dear, special friend. Or that was how it looked. Very likely, he was the son she had never had and she the sort of mother he would have liked to have. There are plenty who would see it in that light. Young men do have older women friends and go about with them in an apparently sexless relationship. Of course it is impossible to generalize and insensitive to try. They liked each other.

They went to concerts, presumably to learn about Schoenberg, as I had overheard Mark say they would. They went to the cinema. They took Auntie out for drives. Eating out as a way of life was

becoming fashionable and they usually ate out together. Only sometimes would Cosette be assailed by guilt feelings that she was doing
unfairly by the rest of us and then we would be gathered together
into rather a formal dining-out group and shepherded off to the
Marco Polo or even somewhere very grand like the Écu de France,
on which occasions Mark would conspicuously not be present. It was
very different from Wellgarth days and as different again from that
early wild, decadent, chaotic time in the House of Stairs.

I remembered Cosette's dying Buddha story: 'It changes.'

Mark never stayed the night, though, not even in the spare room
on the top floor next to Bell's. I was as sure as one can be of such a
thing that he had never slept with Cosette, never even kissed her
beyond putting his lips to her cheek. Had he even done that? Once
he spoke of her to me. We were alone together, it was a rare event,
and very short-lived. Bell had refused to go out, Gary was away
somewhere, it was all too late for Auntie, but Mervyn was back, he
and Mimi still together, though used to each other by now and as
comfortable together as an old married couple. The two of them,
Mark and Cosette and I were all dining out and Mervyn and Mimi
were dancing. Cosette got up to go and pay the bill. It was a discreet
way of doing this which she had learned, a way which made it seem
as if there was no bill to be paid. Mark sat watching the dancers and
I watched him. I have said he never cared what he wore, he was
indifferent to clothes, but he was always decently dressed for the
place he was in, and that night he was wearing grey flannel trousers
and a jacket of some sort of loose-woven dark-blue stuff, far from
new but not shabby either. Men were wearing their hair long then,
but his was short by the standard of the time. He was very thin and
this gave him a look of particular elegance. There is something
sexually moving about a man's upper back when it is straight and the
bones are barely covered with flesh. Mark had tremendously attractive shoulder blades. I was very aware of it at that moment as he
leaned forward across the table, lifting his head. His hands were long
and slender but not at all effeminate, the bones of the knuckles too
prominent for that.

He turned his head and spoke to me.

'It seems so strange that all this time Cosette and I were both
living in London and we never knew each other. It seems such a
waste.'

717

'You can make up for it now,' I said, reflecting that it wasn't so long since Cosette had had a husband who I was sure wouldn't have welcomed Mark among the visitors to Garth Manor.

'We are making up for it.' He looked over his shoulder quickly. To try and find her in the crowd or to make sure she wasn't coming? Mark's eyes, the deep dark blue of lapis, had the clarity of water, but water that flows over a multitude of living things. 'I've never known anyone like her,' he said. 'She is the most wonderful person; she has everything.'

Except youth, I thought, and I thought he was going to say it. I thought he was going to say, with rue, that if only, if only, she had been a bit younger. He didn't. He pursued his theme.

'Every gift, every grace. It's rare to find a woman who's never bitchy. Cosette envies no one.' I would have taken issue with him there. She envied all the girls she met, only without vindictiveness. He made nonsense of my thoughts. 'Of course there's nothing she could be envious about.'

Cosette came back. I thought she looked tired and worn, the make-up she wore runnelled and smeared, her hair lank, and that red dress – the one she had been wearing when first she met him! But her face lit at the sight of Mark, lit as if there truly were a lamp of great brilliance inside her head and his smile had switched it on. He said, rather crossly for him, 'It's time you went home, you're tired. Come, let's go.'

'But, Mark, they're still dancing, and look, you can see they're enjoying themselves so much . . .'

She never called him darling. 'Darling' was for all the rest of us. But her face betrayed everything, the love in it at that moment was naked, stretching out its yearning arms. He said, 'They can either come now or get home by their own transport.'

She loved it, you could see that, she loved a man who would be masterful and put her wants first. Had anyone, even Douglas, done that before? But when we reached Archangel Place, Mervyn and Mimi naturally with us, willing to sacrifice any pleasure rather than pay a bus or tube fare, Mark came only as far as the hall where, in a curiously formal way, he placed Cosette in my charge, asking me with his usual simple courtesy please to see she went to bed now, that she had a good night's sleep. He would phone in the morning and see how she was.

718

He always did exactly what he said. If he said he would phone, he phoned. I happened to take the call, it was made a bit early for Cosette and she was still asleep. How, anyway, would he be cognisant of Cosette's retiring and rising habits? He seemed amused and strangely delighted – 'tickled to death' is the expression my father would have used – to hear she was still in bed. On no account must I wake her. Just tell her he had phoned to ask how she was.

'And give her your love?'

There was a pause. 'Whatever you think she'd like,' he said.

Cosette always listened to the radio serial he was in. He had quite a significant part in it and certainly could be heard at least three out of the five nights of the week it was on. She hadn't possessed a radio, but she bought one after she had known Mark for about a week. Alone, she would sit listening to his voice while Bell and Auntie stayed downstairs, preferring the television. I came into the room to hear him utter the last sentence of the episode. He had been in private conversation with the heroine and the words he had to speak struck me as immensely strange in the circumstances. They had a thrilling effect, and an embarrassing one too. It was disquieting, it was shiver-provoking, to hear Mark's voice say, 'You must know I love you. I've been in love with you for ten years, ever since we first met . . .'

This was the signal for music to swell, to break like a wave on a beach. There would be no more till tomorrow when that music would begin afresh. Cosette switched off her transistor and there was a deep silence, until into that silence, dully fragmenting it, came the thud-thud and mutter of Auntie's television from below.

You have to understand that Cosette didn't talk about herself, she wasn't always airing her feelings. The concerns of others seemed more important to her, formed more of the substance of her converse. I have told you of that vague mysterious smile she put on when asked questions she wasn't happy to answer. She was an adept at shifting interest from herself on to others. I believe she genuinely thought that in her sphere and at her age she was no longer an object to provoke interest or excite curiosity. But that evening, at that moment, when we had heard Mark's voice and she had abruptly cut the music off, I had a premonition confiding was to begin and revelations to be made.

Suddenly she said, her voice fierce – it was as if she clutched at me, though she hadn't moved and we were yards apart – 'I'm so much in love with him I think it will kill me.'

'Mark?' I said stupidly. Yet, was it so stupid? I had convinced myself by then that they were friends, the best of friends but only friends, that the desire for no more than friendship was hers as well as his.

'I didn't know what it was,' she said. 'I never had it for anyone before. No, not for Douglas, never, never, I didn't dream of it. Don't look like that, Lizzie. Why are you looking at me like that?'

'I'm sorry,' I said.

'I think of him day and night. When he's not with me I'm thinking of him and talking to him. I have these long imaginary conversations with him in my head. You needn't look like that, darling, so pitiful. You don't have to be sympathetic. It doesn't make me unhappy, it makes me happy. I've never been so happy in my life. Is there anything so blissful as being in love? I couldn't stand not being now, I should die.'

I didn't remind her that five minutes before she had said that being in love would kill her. Instead, prudently, I advised caution.

'You'd better go a bit easy.'

'Why? Why should I?'

I hesitated. I was remembering what Stendhal says somewhere about wishing he were in love, his longing for the bliss of that condition. Though she might be the ugliest kitchenmaid in Paris, that would be of no account provided he was in love with her and she returned his passion. I said, with care, 'Perhaps being in love isn't all that great if it isn't returned – I mean if the other person doesn't feel the same.'

Her reply shook me; I seemed to feel the floor beneath my feet quiver. Cosette was soft-voiced, but she almost shouted, 'Who says he doesn't feel the same?'

Her beseeching face, turned up to me, her hands curiously stretched out to supplicate, induced in me a chill and a nausea that were quite physical. 'Cosette . . .?'

'Cosette what?' she said. 'Is there any reason why I shouldn't be loved? Aren't I lovable?' Her face wasn't haggard then, it was young. It was as if, briefly, a young Cosette had crept out of the skin of age.

'I don't want you to be unhappy,' I said, the words wrenched out of me.

Her voice trembled. 'If I were a man and Mark a woman no one would think anything of me being fifteen years older.' Poor Cosette had entered her phase of reducing when she talked about it the span of years between them. After the same fashion she had taken to pointing out the silver streak in Mark's hair. 'Why does it matter so much the other way round? We live longer than men. Why do we have to be old for so much longer?'

In the years since then things have happened to redress that balance. Elsa married a man eleven years her junior and everyone said how lucky he was. I said to Cosette, lamely I'm afraid, 'Everyone can see how fond he is of you.'

'How I hate that word!'

I could think of nothing more to say, so I went over to her and hugged her. We held each other in a strong warm embrace which I can easily think myself back into now and feel again, which I can remember more readily than any of those love passages with Bell.

— 15 —

We have had two visitors, Bell and I. It is two weeks since she came to stay and in all that time, until yesterday, no one has come to the house. We have been alone together and every morning I have gone into my room and tried to write – that is, I have tried to write the novel I am supposed to be working on, a tale of international intrigue and sexual adventure in Vienna and Mauritius. I haven't written a word of it. All I write is this account or record or whatever you care to call it. What Bell does while I am in here I don't really know, but I hear her go out, so I suppose she walks, ranging the west London streets. Never since she has been here have I heard a word scorning suburbs or about my house being too far west for her.

But yesterday my father came. Twice a year he comes to London for a medical check-up. He has a pacemaker to regulate his heart and although he could easily and far more conveniently go for his examinations to a heart specialist in some hospital on the south coast, he has an idea in his head that everything in London must be better. Especially in Hammersmith, where the hospital enjoys a glamorous reputation in matters of the heart. He is spry and energetic for his seventy-three years, but London and its crowds confuse him and I always go to meet him at Waterloo and take him to the hospital. After his check-up he comes back here to stay the night.

It may seem strange, when Bell and I were so close, that he should know nothing of her, not even know until yesterday that she exists. But I wasn't called upon to give evidence at her trial, there were other witnesses to do that. And although he must have heard of her, for, briefly, every newspaper reader and television viewer heard of her, there is no reason for him to connect the sombre and austere woman in her mourning clothes, whom I introduce to him simply as Bell, with Christine Sanger. Did I tell you Christabel was another of her inventions, that instead of Christabel she was really Christine, that Ivor Sitwell in giving her that name was unwittingly correct? I am telling you now.

My father has changed. His tragedy he has put far behind him. If he knows that there is still time for his daughter to go the way his wife went, he never gives a sign of it. Sometimes he even talks of the distant future, *my* distant future, and with satisfaction of the good fortune that awaits me. For although he has, and has had for years, a woman friend a few years younger than himself, a widow living on the same senior citizens' estate, in the same street three bungalows away, he declines to marry again because thereby he would deprive me of my rightful inheritance. His bungalow and the few thousand pounds he has in unit trusts are destined for me, and it is in vain that I have told him over and over that I don't need them, that they are his to dispose of as he pleases, to leave to a wife if he likes.

He reverted to this subject, as he always does whenever we meet, while we were all watching television, during a commercial break. A banking advertisement set him off.

'It's all in my will, it's all set down in black and white,' he said. 'I've done that so that you don't have the fuss and bother of applying for Letters of Administration.'

'That's a long time off,' I said.

'Easy to say at your age and when you don't know what illness is. There's a chap I've seen at that hospital every time I've been there for the past three years, he always had his appointments the same day as me, a curious coincidence, really. Well, he was missing today and why do you think? He'd dropped down dead a month ago on his way on holiday to Ibiza, fell over and died in the duty-free shop.'

We turned our eyes back to the screen, Bell rather more slowly than my father and I. She had been watching him in wonder. I supposed it was his refusal to recognize my continued danger that she found astonishing, but perhaps it wasn't that, perhaps what he said recalled to her the evening she asked me about Cosette's will. I didn't inquire. When he went off to bed and for half an hour or so we were alone, I didn't ask her. I am not yet prepared to force a discussion of Cosette or of Mark. They must wait a little longer.

This morning I took him to catch his train. As I walked back along the street where I live I saw ahead of me a taxi stopped outside my house and a woman getting out of it. I didn't recognize her. She was a big dark woman, tall and heavily built, with one of those figures in which the stomach has become very prominent, jutting out nearly as protuberantly as the bosom. Her hair had been dyed raven black and dressed in such a bouffant way that it would have given the impression from a distance that she was wearing a wide-brimmed black silk hat. She paid the taxi-driver and turned to face my house, looking up at the roof and down to the little front garden in an appraising way as someone might who was surveying the place with a view to buying it. She opened the gate and began to walk up the path. My footstep behind her made her turn. I may have changed as much as she has, but she had the advantage over me, she knew that living in this house I was more likely to be Elizabeth Vetch than not. The voice I recognized, when she had spoken my name.

'Felicity,' I said.

I was at the typewriter in my working room in the House of Stairs, listening to Bell's movements above me, listening with pain to the closing of the door and the creak of the 104th stair, for I knew that what would happen was what always happened now. She would pass my door without slowing her pace. It was late summer, a weary dusty time, the London air stale and still. Below, in the grey garden, when I went as I now did to the window, I could see the top of Auntie's white chrysanthemum head in one of the deckchairs and, resting lightly back against the canvas of the other, Cosette's freshly blonded chignon on to which a silver eucalyptus leaf had fallen, seemingly pinned there like a hair ornament.

But this time, instead of passing my door, Bell's footsteps slowed. She must have stood there for a long moment – doing, thinking, what? Wondering perhaps about the enormity of what she planned to ask? I held my breath. Bell knocked on the door, causing me pain, more pain than I want to write about. She had never before knocked at the door of any room I was in. My whispered 'Come in' was so low I had to repeat it.

She entered the room without any awkwardness, unless to pause just inside the door and light a cigarette is to be awkward. If she felt she owed me some explanation for repudiating me, she never showed it. The paperback books on the desk and on the table were not those that had been there last time she was in my room. It was a long time since she had last been there. She picked up *What Maisie Knew*, turned it over, looking at it in the way one might look for an assay mark on a piece of silver. At the window she glanced downwards, no doubt to check that Cosette was still far away, still well out of earshot.

'I suppose,' she said brusquely, 'Cosette will leave everything she's got to you.'

'*What?*'

'In her will, I mean. You must know what I mean. When she dies this house and all her money will go to you.'

'I *don't* know. I don't suppose she has made a will. Why should she? She's not going to die.'

Bell went once more to the window. The casement was opened a little way. She closed it, stood there with her back to the window. 'She's got cancer, hasn't she?'

'What gave you that idea?'

She didn't say anything and her silence spoke terrible things to me. I jumped up out of my chair.

'Who told you? Are you keeping something from me?'

'I don't know anything you don't. I thought they found cancer when they scraped her out or whatever they did.'

'They didn't find anything, she was perfectly clear. She's been for a check-up since and she was fine. She'll probably live for thirty years, she'll live longer than I will.'

Bell said slowly, as if she were thinking deeply and enormously, laying out options and rejecting them, biding her time, 'I see,' and again, 'I see.'

From that moment I date my anger with her, my distaste for her, my near-hatred of her. All those things are quite compatible with love, aren't they? I was angry with her because what she had said seemed to confirm my fears that she disliked Cosette, that Cosette's generosity inspired no gratitude in her, that living on Cosette's bounty, rent-free, with heat and food freely provided, had provoked no affection, aroused no warmth. I said, speaking to her as I never had before, 'I was working and I'd like to get on. So would you mind going?'

After she had gone I couldn't work. I repeated to myself, carefully, word for word, all the things she had said, and though I read into them a suggestion that she expected and indeed wanted me to inherit Cosette's property, my anger wasn't cooled or my hurt less painful. I only saw her as inquiring in order to make sure of the future good fortune of her 'friend', under whose protective umbrella she meant to shelter. With luck, by playing her cards right, even when Cosette was dead a home here would be secured for her, an even freer and more spacious home in fact, with me as owner. I felt I was being used, perhaps had always been used to this end. Was it possible that Bell had got to know me, had then engineered our relationship into what it had been for those few months, solely because she saw me as a rich woman's adopted child and necessary heir?

Of course I was quite wrong. I was even flattering myself; I was attributing to myself an importance I didn't have. Bell's motive for asking those questions was outside the bounds of my imaginings. I heard her go down the stairs, down all the stairs to the bottom, and then I heard the front door close after her rather harder than usual. She had nearly slammed it. I used to wonder where she went, perhaps only to walk, or to visit those corners of London where the beautiful things are displayed, to range Kensington Church Street and the King's Road and Camden Passage. She was back again by six, watching television with Auntie, while Cosette, on the floor above, listened to Mark in his serial, the character he played newly married and just returned from his honeymoon.

That evening, an hour or two later, Auntie died.

I wasn't there, I wasn't in the house, my bitter anger against Bell having sent me to the telephone to ring up a man I had met a week before at a party, a man who had phoned since and left a message for me with Mervyn. His name was Robin Cairns and three years later I was to marry him, but I foresaw nothing like that then. He was just a useful person to keep thoughts of Bell away.

Auntie sat in the armchair next to Bell's and they watched an episode in a serial about policemen in San Francisco. At some point during the car chase up and down those switchback hills, while guns were firing and tyres bursting, rictus-faced men doubling up to clutch gunshot wounds, Auntie lay back against the cushion and died. It was a death not dissimilar to Douglas's. If we might all die so gently, so quietly! Bell saw her glasses fall off her nose, but since they were attached to a chain round her neck, they didn't fall far. She never took any particular notice of Auntie, and though I suppose she answered if Auntie spoke to her, it seemed she was herself never the instigator of an exchange, it was never she who was the first to remark on a programme or an actor.

Mark came at nine, but he didn't look into the room where Bell was, though the door was always left ajar. Mimi let him into the house and he went straight through the dining room into the garden to find Cosette. It was darker than dusk, for by then it was September, but it had been very hot that day, hot as July, and the heat still hung in the air. There must have been a strong pungent smell of eucalyptus out there, as always on warm nights. I know there was a moon, for Robin and I saw it and watched it rise, a smoky red harvest moon, unusually large and glowing, as we walked along Kensington Gore.

It was Mimi who told me what happened. She preceded Mark into the garden and went back to the corner where she had been lying beside Mervyn on a blanket spread out on the paving stones. They had been smoking, of all things, locust beans. Mervyn had heard that kids in Philadelphia hallucinate on them and had got someone to bring a bagful back from a trip to the United States. Like Rimmon, those two would smoke or chew anything they thought capable of changing their consciousness. They had even tried the eucalyptus leaves, though to no effect. Mimi saw Mark go up to Cosette and kiss her cheek, sit down in the chair facing hers across the white-painted iron table and heard him say something to her about the stars which were peculiarly visible that evening, bright punctures of light in the dark blue sky which often, in London, seems to cover and conceal them. Some constellation hung brilliantly above them and they were both looking up at it, their chairs pushed close together, their shoulders touching, Mark pointing with one lightly extended forefinger, when Bell came out into the garden.

She came across the paved area quickly, though not running, and went up to Cosette. I am sure there was no deliberate cruelty in the way she behaved. It was only thoughtlessness, only insensitivity. She had no feeling for Auntie and, on account of her eighty years and her reserve, scarcely considered her a human being. And I, perhaps wrongly, had once passed on to her my theory about Cosette's only having her there to seem young in contrast to Auntie's age. So she stood in front of Cosette and said, 'Auntie just died. She's dead.'

Bell, of course, was familiar with death. She had seen death of more frightening sorts, the death of Silas and that other death I haven't yet told you of, though I shall, I shall. Auntie's was a quiet affair compared to those, all in the day's work, something to be communicated much as one might retail a somewhat unexpected item from the television news.

Cosette gave a cry and put up her hand to cover her mouth. Mark turned on Bell and said roughly, 'What do you mean?'

'I just told you, Auntie's dead. She lay back and died while we were watching TV.'

'Are you absolutely unfeeling, coming out here and telling her like that?'

Mimi said Bell didn't care for this. It made her wince. She stepped back, frowning, holding her hands up to her head. I could imagine her doing that, I could see that gesture of hers, as if her mass of fair hair were a wig and she was holding it on in a high wind. Cosette, silent, turned her face to Mark. They had both stood up. Mimi didn't expect him to do what he did. She too had accepted he and Cosette were friends only, a son for a mother who had never had one, a mother for a son whose own was inadequate. Mark took her in his arms and held her and she put her arms round his neck and held him. They stood there very close, embracing for comfort, for solace, and Bell watched them.

When I came in about two hours later the doctor had been and gone, had certified Auntie truly dead. A massive stroke had killed her. He and Mark moved her and laid her body on the sofa lest rigor should set in before the undertaker came in the morning. The sofa was rather less than five feet long, but it was more than big enough to accommodate Auntie's small, shrunken body. I found Cosette desolate, not crying, not giving way to any transports of grief, but shattered with sadness, already shadowed by the guilt that was soon to oppress her. She had nothing to be guilty about. If Auntie had been a mother to her these past few years, she had been a good daughter. It was all of us who had neglected Auntie, treating her like a bit of furniture, who should have felt guilt, and of course none of us did. And for some reason, with very misplaced pity, Cosette was worried about Bell.

'Poor girl,' she said to me, 'I wouldn't have had that happen for the world. Imagine what it must have been for her, finding Auntie dead. I should have been there, I shouldn't have left her on her own.'

Useless to tell Cosette that for one thing she wasn't on her own and for another that Auntie adored television, that only exhaustion could drag her from it. I did tell her that the year during which Auntie had had television had probably been the happiest of her latter life, only to have Cosette retort that this made things worse, that she should have given Auntie television five years before.

Mark came in and told Cosette she ought to go to bed, there was nothing more to be done till the morning. She should go to bed and try to sleep and he would come back first thing in the morning. Cosette turned to him and said with a kind of artlessness, as innocent as a small girl, 'You're not going, are you? I somehow counted on your staying.'

It was then that I noticed, in spite of the shock and sorrow which had left tearmarks on her cheeks, how much younger she had begun to look. I mean, how much younger than, say, a year before. And I remembered what she had told me about loving Mark, about being in love, being killed with love, and I thought, killing or no, it's done this for her, it has taken the lines away and the shadows, it has made her eyes shine and her face glow, it's put a spark of youth back, I don't know how.

'Of course I'll stay if you want me to,' he said.

It stabbed me, the shock of it. I thought he meant with her, in her room, in her bed, and I didn't want that, I was afraid of it. It was important to me to go with them up the stairs to Cosette's door, to observe them. Bell, someone had told me, Mimi probably, had long ago gone to her room. Even she, Mervyn remarked, wouldn't keep on watching television over Auntie's dead body. I was hurt by that, struck by the unfairness of it, for he in that household had been no shining example of altruism.

Cosette took Mark's arm up the stairs. Not like an old woman might, though, more like a young girl who has received some injury. It astonished me that he wasn't even sure which of the doors was the one to her bedroom. She opened the door and stood there, said suddenly, 'I've this stupid feeling we shouldn't be leaving her alone down there.'

'It is stupid,' Mark said, but very gently.

'I'm sorry to be such a fool. Don't look so concerned for me, I shall sleep. I'm only sorry to say I shall sleep soundly.'

She drew herself away from him, took a step into the room, still holding his hand. Their hands clasped more tightly for a brief moment, then each let the other go free. I knew it was going to be all right. Mark said to me, 'There's a room I can sleep in at the top, isn't there?'

I nodded. 'Next to Bell. The right-hand door, Bell's is on the left.'

He didn't kiss Cosette. They looked at each other with a strange grave regard and he said, 'Good-night, Cosette.'

Her voice was very quiet. 'Good-night, dear Mark.'

It was a great relief to me, all of it. I watched him mount the next flight and pass out of sight on his way to the top. I knew it was all right then. Cosette slept in her own room and Bell in hers and Mark next door to her in the room that had been Felicity's and everything was as it should be. Or so I thought then.

I lay in bed having fantasies about their future, Mark and Cosette's. She would always have a special place in his life, a unique role. One day, of course, he would marry and she would suffer bitter pangs, but she would adjust, she would acclimatize, ultimately coming to love his wife too. I imagined her godmother to his children, an honoured matriarch in his home. Not to make myself out too great a fool, in fairness to myself, I must say here that I also imagined retailing this to Bell and Bell saying, in typical utterance, that it was all a load of shit.

Next day the undertaker did come and Perpetua came, commiserating with Cosette as perhaps no one else could, and something else bad happened. Mark lost his job. Or, rather, they decided to write out the character he played in the radio serial, to kill him off by the end of the following week. According to Bell – Mark never went into details himself – the actress who had the role of his wife had landed a Hollywood contract and the producer had decided the best way to handle this was to have them both die in an air crash.

Cosette listened to the last instalment he would ever be in. We listened to it together. With not too much verisimilitude the script had had the character Mark played offered a wonderful job (too wonderful for him to dream of refusing) in the Far East. In this final episode for Mark, his brother-in-law and parents-in-law were seeing him and his bride of two months off at Heathrow. The next day's would have the news of the air disaster brought to these relatives. We decided not to listen to it.

'Mark won't have any trouble in finding work,' Cosette said to me after she had switched the set off. 'He's such a marvellous actor.'

It might have been true, but from her it was no reliable testimonial. Everyone close to Cosette, whatever it might be that they did for a living, in her eyes did it to perfection. And, in some ways, no one had ever been as close as Mark, in the way of passionate love, that is. I agreed with her, I said I hoped so, but I wasn't really confident.

'He'll move on to television,' said Cosette. 'He's ready for that now, it's a step he ought to take.' She spoke as if Mark had never made his unsuccessful foray into this medium and as if a move now was entirely a matter for his own decision.

I expected her to have an enormous showy funeral for Auntie, partly as a remedy for guilt. But one of the interesting things about Cosette was her way of behaving unexpectedly. She would act in character for a long while, until you thought you knew her thoroughly, could predict any move she might make, then perform the startling. It was Bell who once pointed this out to me, during the conversations we had used to have about people and their ways. So, instead of announcing to the household that the funeral service would be at such and such a church and the cremation wherever it might be and the post-funerary food and drink at this or that particular hotel, Cosette only gave the necessary information quietly to me, and no doubt also to Mark. There was no fussing about what to wear, no lavish ordering of flowers. Cosette surprised me further when she said, 'Would you very much mind not saying anything to Bell?'

'You mean that the funeral is today?'

'I don't suppose she would want to come but I'd – well, I'd prefer her not to be there.'

I might have said there was no fear of that, but I didn't. It was the nearest Cosette ever got to intimating not so much that she didn't like Bell or found her uncongenial but rather that things about Bell deeply upset her. I promised not to mention it, but I think that by that time, a week or so after she had found Auntie dead, Bell had forgotten she had ever existed. Cosette and Mark and I went to the crematorium together. Her small cross of white chrysanthemums – a coincidence it must have been, their resemblance to Auntie's pretty white curly hair – lay alone on the coffin. There were no other flowers and no one else there – who else could there have been?

'The whole Archangel Place circus,' Mark whispered to me when I put this question to him. 'Very sensibly, Cosette didn't tell them.'

A bit of a nerve, I thought he had. Who was he to talk in that patronizing fashion about her friends when he was no more than one of them? Mark out of work had subtly shifted his position in my estimation. One of the reasons I had looked on him in a different light from the 'circus' was the fact that he worked, he supported himself. As the weeks passed and he found no work, refusing, as I understood from Cosette who was hotly indignant at the suggestion he should, any jobs outside acting, I found myself watching him with suspicion. I was waiting for him to borrow money from her (though I might not have known if he did), instigate once more the big dining-out parties which would include himself and for which as a matter of course Cosette paid, move in, and of course, at last, do the inevitable at this stage and sleep with her.

That autumn Cosette suddenly became far richer than before.

I haven't said much about Cosette's income, her fortune, rather giving the impression perhaps that she just possessed a lot of money. But it wasn't quite like that. Douglas had left all kinds of assets, including defunct companies which still however had stock exchange quotations, and a certain amount of apparently undesirable real estate. By that I mean it was in the form of land in outer suburbs with derelict industrial buildings on it, that sort of thing. One of these companies had already been bought out, the purchaser being in need of the stock exchange quotation, and paying something in the region of a halfpenny a share. That was just before decimal coinage came in at the beginning of 1971. Of course that didn't bring Cosette in much money, but the piece of land she owned did. She had forgotten she owned it, these few acres somewhere on the edge of south London. A firm of accountants administered everything for her and they were pleased to tell her that an enormous offer had been made for this land by a garage and petrol-station chain. A new road was going through and Cosette's old industrial site would abut on to it.

The precise figure I never knew. Perhaps Cosette didn't know it herself. It wasn't in her nature to be discreet and she broadcast the news of this 'windfall' as she called it to all the visitors to the house.

'Hundreds of thousands of pounds,' was the nearest she got to exactitude. 'It will make me a real millionairess.'

Bell was there to hear it and so was Mark – inevitably. I looked at her, expecting to meet eyes turned to meet mine as she calculated the benefits of staying friends with me, but she wasn't looking in my direction. She was looking at Cosette. It struck me then that, for one who prided herself on her powers of observation, she had made a curious mistake in supposing anyone who looked like Cosette to be suffering from cancer. For unhappy on one level as Cosette might be, guilty that is and really sorrowing for Auntie, missing her as one might miss a mother, on another level she was quite obviously rapturously happy and her happiness made her beautiful. People tend to eat less when they are in love and Cosette had got slimmer without effort. Her skin glowed, her hair shone. I don't suppose it's really possible for happiness to tighten up the muscles of the face, but that was the way it looked. I am sure Mark never went shopping for clothes with her, but since knowing him her dress sense had improved. It was a surprise to me what good legs she had, but I had never before seen her wear very fine denier stockings and plain high-heeled shoes. She had bought some simple dresses in silk or fine wool with which she had taken to wearing that jewellery that had been the envy of Elsa and me. She had become elegant – a word no one would have thought in the past of applying to Cosette. But of those who were assembled in the House of Stairs I alone remembered the stout, sturdy woman whose iron-grey hair matched her tailored suits.

Bell, who had been watching Cosette in silence while Mervyn made some hopeful remark about going out to celebrate, now got up, pushed her fingers through her tangled, tendrilled, bird's-nest hair, and announced that she would be going to Felicity's for the holiday, she would be going next day. And Cosette, as if to neutralize this cold tone with an extra warmth in her own voice, said, 'Oh, darling, we *shall* miss you. It has become quite a regular thing for you, going there for Christmas, hasn't it?'

Bell looked at her, lifting first her eyebrows, then her shoulders, her expression remote. As if someone walked over her grave? Or as if she had a strange prevision this would be the last time?

It wasn't, anyway, to invite either or both of us for Christmas, that Felicity came to visit me this morning. Even for her July would have been a little early. And Bell she will never want again, whatever her feelings about me may be. She was astonished to see Bell, so surprised that she actually jumped at the sight of her, recognizing her at once, with no difficulty. Before going into my living room, where I supposed rightly that Bell was, I tried to whisper a warning, to utter simply the three words that would be enough, 'Bell is there!' but Felicity, who has become far more overbearing and dictatorial, gave me no chance, walking rapidly ahead of me and remarking loudly about how sweet these little houses could be made, how delectable mine was, what wonders could be done with these former artisans' cottages. For Bell there was no escape, the artisan's means not having stretched to two exits from the living room.

Being on what Henry James calls almost irreconcilable terms with the printed page, Bell was watching television, some abysmal late-morning offering. The little cat lay in her lap, watching the big one who sprawled on top of the set. Or possibly watching the lion on the screen that slowly stalked a wildebeest. Bell still has that enviable poise. No jumping for her, no attempt at rising even. She looked at Felicity in a way that made me doubt for a moment if she knew who this was.

'My God,' said Felicity. 'Surprise, surprise.' How did I know, even then, that whatever it cost her, she wasn't going to utter Bell's name?

'Why?' Bell said. 'I talked to you on the phone. You knew I wanted to find Elizabeth.'

'Oh, true, true.' Felicity gave an unpleasant little laugh, a laugh I couldn't remember from the old days. 'When I said "surprise" I meant I was surprised on Elizabeth's behalf, not yours.' It was the kind of silky rudeness Cosette used to hate so much and it is from her I have derived my hatred of it. Felicity sat down, her skirt riding up, showing a lot of plump leg and black stocking top. It is horrible, for she isn't in the least like Cosette, never has been, but the way she dresses, showily and unsuitably, *coyly*, reminds me of Cosette's early efforts, between the departure from Wellgarth Avenue and the coming of Mark. 'I'm having lunch with a friend in Barnes,' she said to me. 'The taxi almost had to pass your door, so I thought, why not? I'll never get to see her if I wait for her to phone.'

A strange route for a taxi going from Glebe Place to Barnes to take. I didn't say so though. I was relieved she wouldn't expect to lunch here. 'I knew I'd catch you because you'd be doing your writing at this hour.' It was said with a fine, artless regard for the writer's self-imposed disciplines.

'You were wrong, weren't you?' said Bell, her first contribution, and a hard cold one. 'About her writing, I mean, not about you catching her.'

I explained about my father. It was something to say. I didn't know what to say with the two of them there, Bell seemingly so despairing of her life that she didn't care what she said, consequences being of no account to her, Felicity revengeful and disapproving of Bell's very existence. I was afraid Felicity would say something about Cosette, it seemed so obvious that she must, though I doubted if she would go so far as to refer to Mark. And now I noticed for the first time that she was carrying, along with her large black patent leather handbag and a pair of absurd white gloves, the early edition of the evening paper, the *Standard* which had been on the streets a couple of hours. I had already glanced at it while at the station, at the lead story which was that of the murder by a child of a child. With a dreadful feeling of heart-sinking I saw Felicity lay her handbag on the table, place her gloves beside it, so that this newspaper, though still folded, lay alone on her unattractively bulbous lap, the large bold print of two words only of the headline exposed, but the two words of greatest significance: 'child' and 'killed'.

Bell perhaps also saw it. I don't know if she did. Felicity said, 'Do you think we could possibly have the television off?'

Carrying the little cat, pendulous from her forearm as a muff might be, Bell got up and made the most offensive response to this request there is, not excluding refusing it. She turned the sound down to a low murmur. Felicity was unfolding her paper, I don't really know why, I can hardly imagine what she intended to say or do. To read that story? To ask Bell in her didactic way (teaching always, reverting always to the vocation she had missed) what comments she had on it? Listing, for I am sure she still lives in a world of quizzes, a catalogue of mini-monsters, adolescent and sub-teen assassins?

But Bell forestalled her. Still standing, still with the cat draped over her arm as if boneless, a stretchy rubber sling sheathed in sable fur, Bell said, 'It looks to me as if you've come a long way since you were sponging on Cosette and that ponce with the beard was screwing your brains out.'

I was more shocked to hear her speak Cosette's name than by the actual content of what she said. She had got back into the dangerous country, she had taken some terrible plunge, was swimming the river.

You could see it in her face, too, in the width of her eyes, the recoil, as if someone else had spoken those words. Felicity, of course, looked terribly offended. But she didn't jump up and leave the house in dudgeon. I think people very seldom behave quite like that. They like to have options left to them. In fact, she managed a breathy deprecating laugh.

'Sponging!' she said. 'Oh, dear, what a word! As if people, some of them not too far from here, didn't sponge on me year after year. Inevitably, that's your lot if you happen to be rather better off than the run of the mill.'

She got up then, taking care to display the entire front page of the paper and the headline: *Tyneside Victim Killed by Child, 10*. Then she dropped the paper on the seat of her chair. 'Oh, no, you keep it,' she said sweetly when I reminded her. I used rather to like Felicity, her enthusiasms, her rebellions, her intensity, her passions. All that seems to be gone now. No doubt it was necessary, if she was going to live with Esmond at Thornham and have a modicum of contentment, to ditch all that. Perhaps it was a case of ditching it or going mad. Who knows? I saw her out and we made cool, careful farewells, with of course no added riders of meeting again.

I was afraid to go back in there, I was really afraid. But you can hardly avoid going into your own living room for the rest of your life. I braced myself, opened the door. The newspaper was on the floor by Bell's chair. The little cat sat on one edge of it washing his face. Bell had her head in her hands, the fingers plunged into her grey, wiry, coarse hair. I didn't know what to do. So I sat down and waited and said nothing and thought of the peaceful, quiet, reasonably industrious, life I had been leading before she came out of prison and I found her. Presently she took her hands down and looked at me and said in quite a normal, ordinary voice, 'Am I a psychopath? I suppose I must be, they all said I was. But I don't feel like that, I just feel like anyone else.' What she had said must have struck her as absurd or shallow, for she corrected herself. 'Or I think I do.'

– 16 –

Since Bell has been here I have got into the habit of looking at people and wondering which of them, if any, are like her. I mean, like her in that they have killed someone and been sent to prison for it, served their sentences and come out again. It is a new phenomenon. Murderers used to be hanged.

Now they are set free and come back to live among us. Or to exist. I look at people and I wonder. Think of the number of murders we read are committed each year. Give it ten years – Bell was exceptionally long incarcerated and that for a particular reason – and their perpetrators (as the police say) are out again, ordinary people looking like everyone else, having ordinary jobs, perhaps living next door. But that woman I find myself sitting opposite in the tube, she may have shot her lover. That man with his dark scowl, arms folded across a thickly muscled chest, leaning against a wall on a street corner, may have knifed someone in a street brawl. How many have smothered the baby in its cradle or helped the elderly encumbrance on its way? People like me and Felicity and Elsa know them and go on knowing them and learn to adjust. Yet you would think murder the one act no one could adjust to, no one could make allowances for.

She had asked me if I thought she was a psychopath – well, she had asked the question, of the air perhaps, or of God. I could only shake my head and say I didn't know. I have always understood psychopaths to enjoy tormenting animals. Having uttered her question and made her half-despairing remarks, Bell turned away from me and coaxed the little cat back to her. It jumped on to her lap and she began stroking it in the way it likes, long hard movements of the hands, strong enough to push it to a crouching position. Then, as it folded itself up and curled into the thick black bunches of her skirt, she let her hands rest with the softest and most caring of movements on its sleek back. I would never have associated tenderness with Bell. Sensuousness, passion, a kind of tragic grandeur, all those, but not tenderness. Yet she is tender with my cats, as wondering and appreciative and absorbed as some women are with babies.

'I was never with animals before,' she said, as if reading what I was thinking. 'I didn't know I liked them.'

'Admetus had a cat,' I said, 'with cat fleas,' and I remembered Mark, and Cosette's anxious witticism about the 'entrechat'. 'There were dogs at Thornham.'

'Big and loud and domineering like their bitch of an owner. She would have invited you down there if I hadn't been here.'

'I wouldn't have gone,' I said, and, 'What was it like that – that last Christmas?'

We used to talk of people, she and I, why someone said that at just that moment, why someone else did that particular thing, what their motive was, and wasn't it all strange? I see little sign that this still interests her. People have been too much for her and now she likes animals better.

'Just the same, only without the quiz,' she said. 'The same as the year before. It always was the same. I don't know why I went.'

'Don't you?'

She looked at me with a sort of cold stubbornness. Why should I talk if I don't want to, she may have been thinking, why should I explain? 'You went so that you shouldn't see those two together,' I said, 'so that you wouldn't be there when *it* happened.'

'You're as bad as me,' she jeered at me. 'You'll no more say their names than I will. Only I will, I will. Mark and Cosette – there!'

'All right,' I said. 'You needn't shout.'

'When *it* happened – you're like some mealy-mouthed old woman, like *her* auntie. Why don't you say what you mean, that I didn't want to be there the first time he fucked her? As if I cared. I only wanted him to get on with it. Christ, he was so slow, like some fellow in those old-time books you read. The truth is I thought he'd get on faster if I wasn't there.'

'It made no difference whether you were there or not.'

She shrugged. 'It doesn't hurt any more,' she said. 'None of it does, nothing does.'

'I want to know something. If nothing hurts you I can ask it.'

She looked at me, smiling now. 'Ask what you want. I don't have to answer.'

'Did you,' I said, choosing words with care, 'mean to kill Cosette? I mean, were you planning it even at that early stage?'

'I got it into my head she'd die naturally.'

'But when you knew she wouldn't, were you planning it then?'

It was so open, her response, a frank scoffing. 'Planning it? Making a sort of plot? You know I don't do that.'

'Oh, Bell,' I said. 'What was all your time at the House of Stairs but a plot?'

'I mean plan to kill someone. I do that' – she spoke quite proudly as if talking of some arduously acquired special skill – 'on the spur of the moment. Even Silas – I thought about it often but I was only planning for about five minutes. It's only when things get intolerable or I – I want something very, very much.'

She got up, carrying the little cat. The big one, which was still on top of the television set, she scooped up and hung over her other arm. It is something she has taken to doing when she goes up to her room, at bedtime or to rest. 'I don't want any lunch,' she said. 'I'm going to lie down.' She is such a curious figure in her black and with that crown of ashen hair, saved from appearing absurd by her tragic slenderness, the cats entwined round her arms like a boa of living fur.

Here, in my house in Macduff Street, she once again has the room above my work room. That is where my spare room happens to be. The difference, one of the differences, is that it happens to be sixteen stairs up, not 106. As I sit here at my desk I hear nothing but a single murmur of the bed springs when she lays herself down on the mattress, a sound like a heavy sigh. The cats will stay with her for a little while, then climb out of the window while she is asleep, get on to the slate roof of the kitchen and try to catch starlings. They are never there when she wakes up.

That last Christmas I missed the sound of her above me, the creak of the 104th stair as she came down, even the murmur of the television she had taken to watching alone now Auntie was gone. The house was full. Diana Castle had come with a new boyfriend, and Birgitte, though having left under a cloud, reappeared with a boy she said was her cousin. The dancers and Walter Admetus went home only to sleep. Cosette refused to allow any visitor to occupy Bell's room, she thought that wouldn't be right, so with Gary and Fay, Mervyn and Mimi and Rimmon as permanent residents, when her niece, Leonard's daughter, turned up, she had to sleep on the sofa in the television room. Rimmon, trying to get the niece to sleep with him by telling her that sofa was where Auntie had been laid out, only succeeded in driving her from the house.

But the days of the big parties were over, the evenings of the great restaurant gatherings. When Cosette and Mark went out they went alone together. Without the least element of saturnalia, with no resemblance to those orgiastic parties, there was an atmosphere in the house of high romance. Winter, whatever may be the accepted view, is a more sexual season than summer, a bedroomy season of curtained windows and soft upholstery and artificial heat, of cold shut out and warmth enclosed, of faded, dwindling days and long, long nights. You notice these things more when you have no one of your own, for Robin wasn't my own or much to me then. Had there ever been so many lovers all together in the House of Stairs?

Picture how it was. Gary and Fay, for a start, who having for a long time been no more than fellow-lodgers, had embarked on a stormy, intense relationship. They were always parting for ever and then being marvellously reunited. Diana and Patrick, newly in love, at the touching stage, the ardent eye-contact stage, were apparently unable to bear the rupture that occurred each time flesh was sundered from flesh; Birgitte and her 'cousin', a giggly pair, babes in the wood who had sex as well as cuddles under their leaves; Mervyn and Mimi, a couple with that rare quality, an air of there being no one else in the world who mattered half as much as the other. Of all the lovers I knew then, only they are still together. I saw them a couple of months back, walking down North End Road hand in hand, she holding the hand of a boy of about eight and he of a girl about six. I waved, but they didn't see me.

And, of course, there were Mark and Cosette. If you saw them together you would have taken them to be in love, he with her as much as she with him. They were more decorous than the other couples. They were not to be come upon in corners, rammed almost painfully together, bones bruising flesh, open mouths devouring mouths which themselves ate lips and tongue, fingers prising as if to unearth where and what that essence was which created appetite and produced love. I never saw more than hands touching or a finger laid against a cheek. Their age made dignity harder and they seemed to strive for dignity. *Their* age? Mark was only a year older than Diana's

Patrick. But just as Cosette seemed to have grown younger to meet him, so he had aged to meet her; not so much in looks, he retained altogether his handsome, somehow Slavonic appearance, his lean straight figure, but in his bearing, so that without losing any of his grace he appeared more staid and more deliberate.

They weren't lovers in the sense that we use the term. I don't think they were. Of course Cosette went out with him and they were gone for hours and they may not have been in theatres or cinemas or restaurants. They may have been in Mark's flat in Brook Green. But I have, and had, a very strong feeling this wasn't so. At home, in the House of Stairs, Cosette was after a fashion chaperoned by day and night. Naturally, I don't mean anyone would have interfered with what she did, tried to stop her for instance, but they would have known, everyone would have known. It was a curious situation. Here was this house full of lovers, by night everyone a lover except me, love in the air of the place like an all-pervading perfume, languorous and sweet and strangely exhausting, but Cosette, who looked more in love than any of them, whose whole manner, restrained though it was, spoke of a dying for love, remained unfulfilled, remained a kind of reconstituted virgin.

I speculated about it; I couldn't understand why. She had gone to bed readily enough with Ivor and, come to that, with Rimmon, men she had scarcely cared for, men who were stopgaps. Every gesture of hers, every word uttered in and out of his presence, testified to her passion for Mark. And she was no cold woman and no moralist, adhering still to the prejudices of her youth. Love to her, she had said often enough, was something to be consummated as soon as possible. Was it Mark then who hung back? And if he didn't want her, what did he want? Because I was lonely, finding myself in that situation when I wasn't first with anyone in the world, I consoled myself by watching them, how they behaved to each other; discreetly I did it, I hope. Of course I was jealous of Mark. In Cosette's affections he had taken my place as no predecessor of his ever had. So much for those who believe I was myself in love with him . . .

For a long time I had been telling myself he wasn't pursuing Cosette for her money. She happened to have money, a lot of it, but he would have liked her and wanted to be with her whether she had or not. So I believed. Yet who was paying for all these dinners they ate and all these plays they saw? He still had no work. He had no prospect of work. I remembered Ivor asking for money in the restaurant and, on one occasion, a cheque being palmed to Rimmon to spend on acid. Mark seemed beyond all that, having a curious, pure containment, walking tall and keeping himself distant from all these fleshpots.

The position changed and all was altered as openly as on any wedding night in the past when the bride is brought to bed, the bridegroom fetched to her and the guests, barely excluded, are witnesses of a necessary ceremonious rite. It was a few evenings after Christmas. The air was cold and thick with mist and it had been dark since soon after three. With the great feast only a few days past we had all been lazing indolently, no one had got up till late, and it was Walter Admetus who woke me, ringing the doorbell at noon. There was talk of going back to his place for an improvised party and to drink the case of Spanish champagne he had somehow come by. He had a place in Fulham by then, a converted coach-house, and had taken up with Eva Faulkner once more. I didn't want to go, I knew it would be the sort of party it didn't do to be alone at, and I worked on my new book until late in the evening. Gary and Fay went but Cosette and Mark, who were the prizes it seemed Walter was seeking, said they were going out for dinner, just the two of them.

It was very late when they came in. We were all in the drawing room. Those of us not compulsively enraptured by another's body, myself, Mervyn, Mimi and Rimmon, were gathered round Cosette's table drinking wine. The air must have been thick with cigarette smoke in those days, only no one seemed to notice it, or no one seemed to mind. Wrapped in each other, locked together like pieces of a human jigsaw, Diana and Patrick possessed the sofa with a heavy, silent, very nearly unmoving occupancy. Birgitte and Mogens lay side by side, lips sometimes touching, whispers passing, each with a hand on the back of the other's neck. From time to time Mervyn had been playing to us on Gary's ocarina, sometimes accompanying music from the record player. I had never heard him play before and he surprised me. He was good. After a little while he got up and put on an LP of *Carmen*, and when it reached the appropriate passage Perdita, who was there without her husband, who had been sitting in her quiet poised way in the red velvet chair that had been Auntie's, rose and without a word began to dance the *seguidilla*.

It was seldom she would dance for us and when she did I think we all felt privileged that we had had the chance to see in private this once-great dancer who had spoiled herself, who had backed down from the last unscaled height of success, for the sake of love, for, if you like, the folly of love. It was flamenco, I suppose, the dance she did. I only know that all of it, the music, the dance, the single lamp and the candlelight, the wine and the warmth and the lovers, was enormously romantic.

She was a little tiny woman, but as straight as a flame, black-haired as Carmen should be, the dress she wore having a flounced skirt of many red frills. She wanted us to clap to the music while she danced but we couldn't, it seemed to interfere with the air of it, the distance of it from us, the otherness. The ancient ceremonial steps, the stylized movements, the slow twirls, followed their prescribed order, and the music its pattern, and Mervyn's instrument made a strange haunting overtone, and the candle flames fluttered with the stirred air. And into it, the door opening very gently, came Mark and Cosette, pausing just inside when they saw what they had interrupted. It was scarcely an interruption, for the dancer didn't pause. And they stood side by side, watching, moving almost imperceptibly closer and closer together until their bodies touched and Mark slid his arm round Cosette's waist.

We all clapped when it was over. I poured a glass of wine for Mark and one for Cosette, who, rarely for her, didn't refuse it. There was no conversation. This wasn't unusual for the House of Stairs, where everybody knew everybody else and knew their views and didn't feel the need to make small talk. It was a place where people sat reading books in company. But that evening, it seemed to me that there was a peculiar wordlessness, as if communication was being made by other means, by touch and sight and music. The lovers were together, absorbed in each other, and we three who were each alone had our own interior worlds in which to lose ourselves. Rimmon was already slipping into that narcosis with its horrible fantasies from which he was never truly to recover, the dancer perhaps had her memories and her sacrifice and I thought of Bell and remembered Felicity saying that, like Carmen, Silas had had nothing left to do and nowhere to go but to die.

The music was changed, replaced by something of Massenet. The doorbell rang and it was the dancer's taxi-driver, come to take her home. I thought Mark would go at the same time, but he only went downstairs to see her into her cab, and although he had no proprietorial air about him, it was the first time, I was sure, that he had behaved in this manner of a host. He returned, but not to his chair. He sat on the arm of Cosette's, drew his hand very softly across her golden head and let his arm rest across her shoulders. She looked up at him, but not smiling; whatever it was they had come to was too serious for that. The music had become gentle and warm and seductive. Instead of returning this long rapt gaze of hers, his eyes ranged the big, warm, candlelit room, passing from the locked jigsaw couple on the sofa to the finger-patting, butterfly-kissing couple on the rug, to Mervyn and Mimi at the table, she with her head on his shoulder and his arm holding her. The light gleamed on the silver streak that banded his brown hair. Mark turned his head and let his eyes meet Cosette's. I could swear that at that moment they might have been the same age. I could have sworn it was a mutual passion.

He bent and kissed her lips, not drawing away but holding the kiss for a little time. You won't believe me if I say I was shocked, but remember it was the first time I had ever seen them kiss. I found myself first staring, then looking away, glad of the wine I had drunk that fuddled me a little, that blurred the hard edges of painful things. Cosette was flushed a rosy red when the kiss was done, proud in that company, the leader of it. She smiled, spoke his name only, 'Mark . . .'

He gave her his hand. 'Time to go,' he said, and pulled her lightly to her feet.

I thought he meant he was going home. She would go to the front door with him if he let her, he didn't always. Sometimes he would shake his head at her and with a movement of his hand indicate to her to stay sitting where she was. She invariably obeyed him. But that night she put her arm into his, for all the world as if they were going out for a sedate walk. And it seemed to me, though this may be hindsight, that the faintest shyness came into her face and made her manner a shade diffident.

But when she said to me, 'See that all the lights are put out, darling,' her voice was steady, and she added in that abstracted way of hers, 'The candles, I mean. You know how I worry about the candles.'

She looked as if she worried about nothing on this earth. She

743

turned her face into Mark's neck and he bent his head, his lips on her forehead, looking like some picture I have seen of Paolo and Francesca.

'Good-night,' she said, and Mark said, 'Good-night.'

They didn't quite close the door behind them. Doors weren't closed much in the House of Stairs except those to bedrooms. I really thought, I still thought, I would hear their footsteps descend the stairs and only one set return. But they mounted. We were all silent in there, listening, even love forgotten, even desire, in the silent press of listening to *know*. Her door shut and no one came down. Mimi released her breath in a long, shuddering sigh.

We were mad, weren't we? This was just a couple breaking the ice of the first time, getting through or over the awkwardness and rapture of a first time that was the more fraught with awe and tension for having been so long postponed. We were insane to make so much of it. But I am telling you how it was and that is how it was, as important somehow as a monarch's wedding night. I trembled at the thought of Bell, I began immediately to fear for Cosette.

But the fearing and the trembling, the sighs and the awkwardness, were all broken into by the arrival home of Gary and Fay, who banged the front door no more than five minutes after Mark and Cosette departed. They came up the first flight quarrelling bitterly, shouting insults and imprecations at one another, only to be hushed by us, fingers to lips, as they burst into the drawing room, as if upstairs were babies we had at last managed to rock and sing to sleep.

— 17 —

To catch Bell and warn her before she saw for herself, seemed to me important. I wasn't sure when she was coming and knew better than to expect her to let us know. She would walk in when she was ready, climb the stairs, all 106 of them, wearily perhaps or energetically and without pausing at the landings, and shut herself into her room. I might only know she had returned by the sound of her movements above my head.

As it happened, I intercepted her quite by chance. It was early and the household was asleep. I went down to pick up the post, expecting a letter from my publisher. Time doesn't mean much to Bell, she knows no regularity in her hours, perhaps because she has never worked for her living, perhaps for other reasons. She is as likely to get up at five as to go to bed at that time. On that particular morning she must have left Thornham at seven in order to be here by nine. It was cold, early January, and she brought a gust of raw, bitter air with her as she unlocked the front door and came in. She had a carpet-bag with her, they were a hippie fashion then, but hers was worn and discoloured, and over her black and brown layers she was wearing a coat of synthetic fox fur which I recognized as an old one of Felicity's. It was plain what had happened. Bell had turned up at Thornham with her usual ragbag of cotton skirts and jumble-sale jumpers and nothing to keep her warm but the shawl which had done duty as a shroud for Silas.

I was standing by the table, reading my letter. We looked at each other and Bell said, falling back perhaps on that perennial staple at moments of awkwardness, the weather, 'Christ, it's bloody freezing.'

Unprepared now that the time had come, I hunted for suitable words. She dropped the carpet-bag, unwound the long grey scarf that wrapped her head and pushed her fingers through that flaxen, tangled, curly hair. It is a noble face Bell has, Lucrezia Panciatichi's, aristocratic, serene, the proportions of small straight nose in relation to full folded lips, wide eyes, high forehead, almost perfect. How can someone like her have a noble face?

She held up her arms. 'What do you reckon?'

'Of the coat? Did Felicity give it to you?'

'I had to have something. She's got so many she won't miss it. That was what she said, she actually said those words. It's hideous, isn't it? But beggars can't be choosers. It's not half as warm as the real thing.'

'Felicity wouldn't wear the real thing, I suppose,' I said, and then, because I still hoped for something, for love or friendship, 'I'll buy you a coat, Bell.'

'No,' she said. 'No, thanks.' She made things clear. 'If I can't have something wonderful and wicked, if I can't have snow leopard, something *you* couldn't afford I mean, I'd rather have Mrs Thinnesse's cast-offs.'

'That's frank.'

'Well, I am. No point in being otherwise, is there? I'm very poor – did you know? I don't suppose you ever thought about it. That money I got from Silas's dad's house, it's not worth what it was five years ago. What it brings in isn't worth what it was. I've been talking to Esmond about it. He says going decimal has done it and it hasn't half begun what it'll do in the next few years.'

It was a muddled way of putting it but I dimly saw what she meant. 'Talking is pointless,' she said. 'I often think talking about anything is pointless.' She picked up the bag and walked past me to the stairs, beginning the climb that with that bag and in that coat would be a slow, long haul. I followed her, saying, 'Bell . . .'

'What?'

'I thought you might want to know, I mean I don't want it to be too much of a – a surprise to you.' I nearly said a shock. 'Mark is up there. In Cosette's room.'

I don't know what I expected, but not what I got: a pleased smile, the first smile since she had come in, a look of genuine delight someone might wear when you told her of a friend's good luck or forthcoming marriage. 'How long has that been going on then?'

'A week.'

'About time too.'

We began going upstairs together. She took off the mock-fur and I carried it. 'Tell me about it.'

'Tell you what?'

'Well, how it came about, what they did, how you knew, all that. You *know*.'

It was like the old days, when we used to talk and share with each other views and opinions no one else might know. But we were outside Cosette's door and I put one finger to my lips, as we had hushed Gary and Fay that first night. Bell mouthed at me to come on up to her room. The house was as still and silent as other houses would be by night. Even Gary, who nearly always got up early, was sleeping in. We climbed on up to the top. Outside her door I told her how Cosette wouldn't allow anyone else to sleep there while she was away, though we had a house full to overflowing, and Bell only said that was nice of her but she wouldn't have minded. Why should she mind? And when we went in I wondered of course why should she mind, it was such a barren place, with no imprint of its occupant on it, unless Silas's paintings with their backs turned were an imprint.

No pictures on the walls, no books, no magazines, no ornaments, no garments scattered, only the bed, a chair, an ashtray as big as a soup bowl, that had once *been* a soup bowl, empty but still smeared with ash, on the bedside cabinet. The air smelt stale and musty, but it was too cold outside to open the window. It presented, from where I stood, a view only of sky, white but veined with grey and shedding a thin, fine drizzle that might have been rain or snow.

I told her about the night of the *seguidilla* and she listened with approval but laughing sometimes, giving whoops of laughter, at places in the account I hadn't found funny. She was unpacking the carpet-bag, throwing aside those unidentifiable lengths of dark cloth, crumpled and faded, in which she dressed herself. Then she locked the door. She came and sat on the bed beside me. She lay on the bed beside me.

'It's all very good, isn't it?'

'For them?'

'For everyone!'

She took me in her arms. It was the first time for months and the last time for ever.

Mark was living in the House of Stairs, though I believe he still kept his flat on. In February, which is about the worst time of the year to do such a thing, though I suppose it doesn't much matter when you're on your honeymoon, he and Cosette went to Paris for a couple of weeks. Cosette must have paid, of course, and they stayed at the George V. I couldn't stop thinking about that aspect of things, I was always thinking of it, how Mark, like the others, had become her kept man, though, without being explicit about it, he had made it plain he never intended to be.

On the subject of the 'others', who should turn up soon after they got back but Ivor Sitwell. He just arrived early one evening without warning. Cosette was too happy for recriminations. He had betrayed her and treated her shamefully, but who cared now she had Mark? It was Fay he had betrayed her with and she had long been good friends with Fay. She seemed delighted to see him and was soon arranging for us all to go out to dinner together. No one could have been in their presence for more than five minutes, not even anyone as insensitive as Ivor, without realizing Mark was Cosette's lover. An outsider might have been with her and Ivor for hours without being aware of the situation, but things were different now. It wasn't just the way she looked at Mark but the way he looked at her. Even I, fearing him bought, corrupt, prostituted, had to admit he looked at her as if money didn't come into it, as if he were passionately in love.

Advance copies of my new book had come and Cosette was looking at the one I had given her when Ivor arrived. She, of course, was being extravagant in her praise and Ivor, taking the copy from her, remarked that I was 'still churning them out'. He was as objectionable as he had ever been, though making no references this time to the Sitwell family. No doubt he had been rumbled, and by others apart from Bell and her informant. He tried to get a flirtation going with her while we were in the restaurant, but you can imagine how far that got him. All the time he was living with Cosette he was never so nice to her as then, when he saw her with another lover.

We were a big party, eleven of us round the table, and by some mischance I had been seated next to Ivor. Bell was on the other side of him, Mark next to her, and Cosette next to him. When Bell had put an end to his compliments and tentative advances with her own brand of devastation ('Why don't you fuck off?') he turned to me and said how nice it was for Cosette to have such a charming 'sweetheart'.

'It's nice for him too,' I said.

'Sure it is. I don't doubt he knows it. What does he do?'

I told him. Ivor said he was sure he must have heard his voice, but it wasn't like being on television, was it? 'Resting at present, I imagine?'

We talked for a while. I didn't have much choice. Bell would have had a choice, she simply wouldn't have replied. She sat isolated, eating, drinking rather a lot of wine, not talking because she had no one to talk to, having rejected Ivor and been rejected by Mark – at least, temporarily deserted by him. He had eyes and conversation for no one but Cosette, had finished his meal and, having twisted round in his chair, was talking to her in a low, loving, intensely intimate voice not much above a whisper. I remember thinking then how alike she and Bell were, like enough at any rate to seem related, Cosette looking far older of course and far less beautiful – that wasn't a mere matter of age – but of the same physical type, with the same fair, northern beauty, a kind of Valhalla goddess cast of face, a Freya or a Brunhild. Her right hand lay on the tablecloth, a plump, white hand not at all like Bell's, and Mark laid his tenderly over it. She made some reply to him and his own response to it the entire table might have heard, a gratified, delighted, ardent, 'Darling!'

Ivor said dryly to me, 'Of course, he's an actor.'

It was cruel, but it was only what I was thinking. And yet, and yet ... When I was at school and I read Thackeray's *Esmond* I used to wonder how Lady Castlewood who is 'old' and made ugly by smallpox could quite suddenly grow beautiful. Well, Cosette had grown beautiful and no doubt for the same reason. She paid the bill and Mark let her. He didn't have much choice. Cosette told me a little while afterwards that he had recently done some auditioning for television but he didn't photograph well. Perhaps I should say he didn't film well, which was astonishing with those cheekbones and that mouth.

'He's too beautiful,' she said. 'You see, he couldn't get a big part, I mean he's not a star, and he's too good-looking for supporting parts, he'd steal all the scenes from the stars.'

Perhaps this was true. It sounded a bit like a Hollywood thirties verdict. Mark might just not have been a very good actor and after that, as far as I know, he never worked again. But he was a man of many interests: he read, he walked, he worked out in a gymnasium before this was a fashionable thing to do, he was passionately fond of the stage and he took Cosette to lunchtime theatre and fringe theatre; he cooked, so that those meals of expensive delicatessen became a thing of the past. Strangely enough, he seemed to have no friends of his own, or if he did have friends, none of them came to the House of Stairs. But he became, in a way neither Ivor nor Rimmon had approached becoming, the master of the house.

I don't mean he was domineering or even masterful. He didn't suddenly start dictating to everyone or telling Cosette what she should do. It was nothing like that, rather that when it was a case of making a decision, he made it. And in a way that I know sounds sinister, though it wasn't because Mark himself was about as far from sinister as anyone could be, he began to make it clear that not all the occupants of the House of Stairs were welcome guests.

Gary, for instance, and Fay. 'He asked if I ever in fact cleaned Cosette's car,' Gary said to me. 'That was the arrangement when I first came here, he said.'

'It's not that Gary minds having that sort of thing said to him,' said

749

Fay. 'He's not paranoid. But it's a question actually of who says it. He wouldn't mind if Cosette said it.'

'Except that you can't imagine Cosette saying it. I might have cleaned the bugger sometimes if Cosette hadn't always told me to leave it.'

Birgitte and Mogens he got rid of more easily. How I don't know but I suppose he simply told them to go. They were very young and Mogens was one of those rare Danes who don't speak much English. They had nowhere to go and very little money and Birgitte was actually crying when they left, escorted out of the house by Mark, reminding me of an 'Expulsion from Paradise', Adam downcast, Eve in tears and avenging angel driving them ahead of him. Cosette knew none of this, he kept it from her, and when she found out she was upset. He told her they wouldn't come to any harm, they could throw themselves on the mercy of the Danish consul.

'All good things come to an end,' he said.

Cosette looked anxiously at him. 'Oh, don't say that!'

'I meant them, not us.'

Since they had only come for a protracted Christmas holiday, Mervyn and Mimi had already gone. Rimmon was rather ill. It wasn't that he was addicted to any particular drug, but rather that he had poisoned himself in some way with all the things he had swallowed and injected over the past two or three years. He was extremely thin and he ate very little, he had no appetite, and he wandered about the house, pale and hollow-eyed, doing absolutely nothing. Mark refused to call him Rimmon but insisted on addressing him by his real name, Peter. Almost anything that was said to him, even mildly critical, upset Rimmon, and when Mark told him he couldn't go on like this, he obviously needed psychiatric treatment, he started crying. Of course Mark was never loud or aggressive, far from it, he was always gentle and with an air of thinking carefully about what he said, but Rimmon cried just the same and couldn't seem to stop, the tears falling in a permanent slow trickle. At last Mark got a doctor to him – naturally, Cosette had her own tame private doctor – and poor Rimmon went into a psychiatric ward, disappearing for ever from our knowledge, at least from mine.

I began wondering who would go next. Gary and Fay were still there, but by then they understood they were there on sufferance, indefinite marching orders had been given them, and the sooner they found a flat or room elsewhere the better. Towards Cosette's friends from outside he reacted very differently. Admetus and Eva Faulkner, who were married a few months afterwards, he made very welcome, as he did Perdita and Luis and the Castles and Cosette's brothers. They were all respectable people, more or less, they had jobs or at any rate they had callings, they didn't use drugs or keep peculiar hours or buy their clothes at jumble sales or make love in public. Sometimes I saw Mark's eyes rest speculatively on Bell as she lay on Cosette's sofa, chain-smoking, or repaired to the room where the television was, or he encountered her coming upstairs, wrapped in Felicity's synthetic-fur coat. And then I wondered if it wasn't too far-fetched to think her days in the House of Stairs might be numbered.

'They'll get married,' she said to me one evening when we found ourselves alone in the drawing room, Mark and Cosette having gone off to see a play in some suburban theatre. 'You'll see.'

'It's what she wants, I suppose.'

'It's what they both want. You know my views. Marriage is an economic arrangement. You'd realize that if you weren't so sentimental.'

'You mean,' I said, 'that she wants him and he wants her money.'

'That's my kind of blunt speaking,' she said, 'but yes, OK, that's about it. I told you, he'll be nice to her, he'll treat her right.'

'She's nineteen years older than he is. When she's seventy he'll only be a bit over fifty.'

Bell gave me an odd sort of look when I said that. It was as if I had said something incredible, as if I were talking about some contingency not just remote but beyond the bounds of possibility. I didn't understand it then. I thought she was implying something quite different.

'Are you saying that won't matter because he'll have other women?'

'It's not likely he'll stay faithful to her for the rest of their lives, is it?'

'It would kill her.'

'People aren't so easily killed,' said Bell, as if she regretted this. 'It'd solve a lot of problems, wouldn't it, if people died of jealousy or being rejected? Imagine if it was a fatal disease – "She's got terminal jealousy," or, "He won't last long now he's been rejected."'

I didn't ask her what she meant. I thought she was thinking about Silas or even Esmond Thinnesse. But when Mark and Cosette came in a couple of hours later I half-expected them to announce to us their impending marriage. It wouldn't have surprised me if one or the other of them said they had something to tell us and then invited us to Kensington Registry Office on the following Saturday; or, because Cosette was romantic and there was that formal, ceremonious side to Mark's nature, to a marriage service according to the rites of the Church of England at St Michael the Archangel.

Nothing like that happened. The room was full of smoke from our cigarettes and Mark opened the windows on to the balcony. It was April and cold and the wind lifted the red velvet curtains and made them belly and shudder. For someone to do that today wouldn't be exceptional, what would be is such excessive smoking, but it wasn't then, it was normal, everyone in the house smoked, except Mark himself. His gesture, followed by a fanning of himself with his hand, seemed a reproach – more than that, for he looked at Bell with distaste, as if he knew very well that the majority of the cigarettes had been smoked by her. He looked at her as if he wished she weren't there.

Bell returned this look with a classic one of her own, impudent and defiant. It seemed to say, I brought you here, I put you in the way of all this good fortune, and just you remember it. You won't turn me out the way you got rid of Birgitte. Of course all this was in my imagination and in fact I was quite wrong. Bell's look meant a great deal, but not that.

She left the room soon after they came in. I had noticed she didn't like being with them and I had even asked her why she now disliked Cosette. Her reply had a chilling effect.

'I don't dislike her. I'm indifferent to her.'

I ought to have asked her how, this being so, she had the nerve to go on living on Cosette's bounty, but I didn't. I didn't because I loved her, I needed her, to be with, to talk to sometimes, to maintain for myself the illusion she was still my closest friend. And I had begun to be afraid she would leave, either of her own volition or because something would drive her away. Mark would drive her away; I was very afraid of that.

It was soon after this that he asked me to have dinner with him.

The evening he named was one on which Cosette would be at a niece's wedding. This was the niece who had stayed in the House of Stairs and been told by Rimmon she was sleeping on the sofa where

Auntie had died. It was to be a big wedding down in Kent with a disco in the evening and Cosette had promised to stay for part of this. Mark hadn't been invited. Leonard and his wife knew him, had met him at the House of Stairs, and Mark had treated them with great courtesy, but I think they found the whole set-up rather awkward. They hadn't liked to ask if he were a friend or a kind of servant-companion or Cosette's 'fiancé' or what. Probably they didn't realize he was living with her. Anyway, he wasn't asked to the wedding. I was very surprised that the first evening he found himself without her he was asking me out. Briefly, I remembered what Bell had said about the unlikelihood of his being faithful to Cosette for the rest of their lives. But I couldn't see myself as a possible candidate, he being, I was sure, as unlikely to fancy me as I was to be attracted by him.

Then of course it occurred to me that this was a party he must be arranging. 'Have you asked Bell?' I said.

Was it my imagination or did the mere mention of her name these days make him, if not quite wince, somehow withdraw himself, brace himself, force a response?

'It will be just you and me,' he said. 'There's something I want to say to you.'

The chances were that this was to be an ultimatum. I was the next member of the household he wanted out. Over an elegant dinner paid for with Cosette's money, I was to be asked, with charm and tact because of my special position and place in her affections, if I didn't think it was time I quitted my two pleasant rooms and looked about for somewhere of my own to live.

You will see that I had come very near to disliking Mark. He was a threat to me, a thief of love, who came between me and Cosette. As they wished me to do, I was seeing everything inside-out.

– 18 –

We lived in the same house but we didn't go together. We met in the restaurant. It was a bistro not far from Paddington Station, not at all grand, but not shabby either. For some reason I didn't say anything to Bell about dining with Mark – the reason probably was that I

753

didn't get the chance, I didn't see her – and later on I was glad I hadn't. I took it for granted Cosette didn't know this meeting was going to take place and I was surprised when Mark said to me, it was almost the first thing he said, 'It was Cosette's idea we meet away from the house. You know how it is, you can never be sure if you're overheard.'

His smile and raised eyebrows had a rueful air. All those crowds of people, he seemed to infer, lurking behind doors, listening, sponging. And there was something in what he implied, for Gary and Fay still hadn't moved and to his dismay Diana Castle and her boyfriend had suddenly arrived, begging Cosette to put them up for just a week, it wouldn't be more than a week, and Cosette of course had consented. But this declaration of 'Cosette's idea' made me immediately anxious. I could hardly believe she would depute Mark to turn me out, yet his influence with her was great, was growing greater with every day that passed. She was in thrall to him, and that would not be putting it too strongly.

'What did you want to say to me, Mark?'

'Several things, really.'

He waited. Usually very articulate, he seemed at a loss for how to express himself, and my apprehensiveness grew. It seemed to me that his look had become almost ominous, like that of a messenger come to break bad news. In those moments my expectations changed and in spite of what he had said about our meeting there being Cosette's suggestion, I had a sense that he was going to tell me of a coming breach with her, of his involvement perhaps with someone else, even of his coming marriage to that other woman. His silence was heavy and, unable to bear it any longer, I leant forward and said in the voice one uses to jerk someone from a trance state, 'Mark, what is it?'

He smiled, shook his head. 'Oh, nothing, nothing to look like that about. I find some things hard to say, that's all.'

And then he did say it. It gave me a greater shock than if he had told me he was leaving the House of Stairs, never coming back, going to the other side of the earth. The words came rapidly, almost in a rush.

'I suppose you must realize how much in love with Cosette I am.'

I just looked at him. I didn't say anything.

'It wasn't like that at first,' he said. 'Of course I liked her, I liked her enormously. And then – well, I fell in love.' He laughed a little.

'I couldn't quite believe it at first. It seemed so – improbable.' Why? Because she was so much older? Because he wasn't the falling-in-love kind? He didn't explain, but he forgot his reticence and what might have been embarrassment. 'I tried to stop it, I told myself it was ridiculous. I couldn't stop it. Of course I wouldn't want to stop now – the idea of stopping is impossible, it's laughable. You look surprised. Couldn't you see? I thought it showed in every word I spoke and every way I looked.'

He meant what he said utterly. He was as moved with passion as Cosette herself had been when she told me she loved him so much she would die of it. He leant across the table and gazed at me with an ardour the waiter who came up to us must have thought was meant for me. I was so astonished I just sat there shaking my head. When someone says 'I am in love', we know at once what is meant even though we may find it very hard to define. It isn't the same as 'I love', not just in degree but in kind, it isn't weaker but far stronger than the extravagant expressions, 'I adore', 'I am mad about'. It implies obsessive commitment. It includes thraldom, blindness, total acceptance, absolute fidelity, involuntary exclusiveness. In it lies security. Outside it is the world that cannot get in. When I had got over utter disbelief and into absolute belief, I felt enormously relieved. My relief was for Cosette, that she was safe.

'I don't,' he said, 'actually want it to show.' This was a confession of some significance that I was to appreciate later.

'Is that why you said it was ridiculous?'

Because she's old, I thought, because she was such an obvious pushover. That wasn't what he had meant, as I later found out, but he seemed to have forgotten saying it.

'Did I say that? Ridiculous at my age, I suppose.'

Then what about hers? 'Why are you telling me?'

'Because you're more than just a friend of hers. You're almost an adopted daughter.'

We began eating. I was astonished by what he said and growing more and more pleased by it, yet somehow it had taken away my appetite. I picked at my food. I drank my wine.

'There are things I mean to do,' he said, 'and not to do. I thought it would be right to tell you. What others may think is irrelevant. For one thing, I'm not going to get married.'

So much for Bell, I thought.

'It would seem the absolutely right thing to do when you feel like I do, make a public statement of one's commitment. The reason I'm not going to do it is because Cosette' – he paused for word selection – 'is very wealthy. I don't think it would be quite – well, honourable for me to marry her. Do you understand what I mean?'

I nearly burst out laughing. I knew a lot of people, older people, my father and Cosette's brothers for instance, who thought practically the only honourable thing a man could do by a woman was marry her. Once a woman lived with a man he'd never marry her, was what they would say, he wouldn't make an 'honest woman' of her. And here was Mark telling me that in his philosophy it wouldn't be honourable to marry a rich woman. But I saw what he meant. I even thought it quite admirable and saw him in those moments as a strong-minded, disciplined man.

'Some would think you married her for her money,' I said.

'To put it brutally, yes.' He obviously hadn't liked the way I put it. 'Of course, in the nature of things, if I live with her – and I intend to live with her for as long as she'll have me, for ever I hope – some of her wealth must rub off on me. I must benefit. But at least I won't – have a right to it.' He talked as if the Married Women's Property Acts had never been passed, but again I knew what he meant. The waiter came over and he asked for another bottle of wine. We were drinking ferociously, to combat emotion I suppose. Mark looked at me and with a quick shiver shed his pomposity, like someone slipping off a cloak. He said simply, 'I'm so happy. I've never been so happy.'

'I can see,' I said.

'The next thing I want to say is that we shan't go on living in Cosette's present house.' He had never called it the House of Stairs. I was suddenly, for the first time, aware of this. 'I've never liked Number Fifteen Archangel Place.' He gave the address a stagey emphasis. The enthusiasm he showed on his first visit was apparently forgotten. 'It's very inconvenient. It costs Cosette a fortune to run – mainly for the benefit of other people, I don't mean you, Elizabeth – and what is it, after all, but a damned great staircase with rooms sprouting out of it? It's a folly, really.'

'Cosette used to love it.'

'It's interesting why Cosette bought it. It was as an antidote to loneliness, the principle being that if you have empty rooms they'll be filled. And they were, they were. Now she wants to be with me just as much, thank God, as I want to be with her.'

'Alone with you?' I was thinking of Bell but he, of course, thought I meant myself. He said quickly, in a cliché to which it would have been hard to find an alternative, 'There will always be a home for you with us, Elizabeth.'

It seemed to put me rather in Auntie's role. I didn't care for the idea of living with these lovebirds. 'Where will you go?' I said.

'A little house in a mews, we thought.'

There would be no room for Bell. And I should lose her once and for all. This would be the rupture and it would be a parting without a promise of reunion, I sensed that. 'Bell will be happy for you,' I said. 'She thought you'd get married, so she wasn't entirely right, but she was right in principle.'

A shadow touched his face. It was as if all the happiness, the glow of it, was cut off by a shutter closing. His gaze had been a room filled with light and happy people celebrating and then the door was shut. 'I wonder if you'd mind not saying anything to Bell just for the moment.'

'About moving, d'you mean?'

'About any of it. It doesn't matter if she thinks we're getting married. I'm not surprised to hear she thinks that.'

'You mean she's one of those people who might think you were marrying for money?'

The lowering of inhibition through drink made me speak like that. It didn't please him. 'I said it was irrelevant what other people think.'

'You don't want me to tell Bell you're in love with Cosette and you're going to live with her and you're not going to get married and you're going to leave the House of Stairs?'

He had to say yes, that was right, but he didn't like it. I had thought of Mark as strong, the way he talked, his peculiar articulacy, his seeming always to know his own mind, his decision-making when Cosette vacillated, but now I understood this wasn't so. He was weak. He was only strong where there was no effort to be made, no barriers to overcome. Cosette was far stronger than he. I had a strange idea. Could it be the vigour of Cosette's love, a love of consuming strength into which she put her whole self, body and soul, could it be that this was so powerful that it had reached out and drawn an answering love

757

from him, ignited a passion where previously there had been no more than a spark? He looked weak as he sat there, he looked young and afraid and curiously wistful, as if he had found what he had been seeking all his life and now feared dreadfully that it would be dashed away. Cosette was a mother to him, of course, and he a son to her, that was part of it and important, but only a small part of the complex whole. That indecisive, apprehensive look passed from his face and it hardened perceptibly. He smiled.

'Of course we'll tell Bell in time. It's just that we'd rather you didn't mention it at present. As a matter of fact, Cosette feels she'll have to make it up to Bell in some way. She's thinking of buying her a flat – well, a studio flat, you know the kind of thing.'

I didn't say any more. I don't think we talked much more about it. We never did have much to say to each other, Mark and I. For the sake of politeness, I suppose, he did his best to be host while we ate our cheese and finished the third bottle of wine. He was no drinker and his voice had thickened as he talked to me about this actor he knew and that actress and some play he had been on tour in and how the author had to cut some scene out so as not to offend the sensibilities of Middlesbrough. Along with the Brie and biscuits I digested what he had said, that Cosette would compensate Bell for the loss of her room by buying her a flat. I found it, at first, nearly incredible.

Not incredible that Cosette would do it. That was typical, exactly the kind of thing she would do, if she thought the projected recipient was in need. Remember, after all, Auntie. But someone would have had to put the idea into her head first. Why should she even have supposed it was her duty to compensate a young, healthy woman who was nothing to her, who even disliked her, for the loss of a room for which she had never paid a penny in rent? Had Mark asked her to do it? I felt a momentary gratitude that at least there was no proposal to provide me with some *pied-à-terre*.

So Bell was not to be told, not to be told any of this, not even, it seemed clear, that the notion of marriage she had got into her head was wrong. She must be allowed to continue in delusion. But when the House of Stairs was sold she would be informed and then fobbed off with the deeds of a bed-sit with kitchen and bathroom in north Kensington. I decided to ask Cosette about it; I wasn't going to be instructed by Mark. Going home alone in a cab – he had gone off in another one to Victoria or Waterloo or somewhere to meet Cosette's train – I found myself making rather wild plans to buy myself a home and ask Bell to share it with me. She would say no, of course, she wouldn't do it. I imagined her disappearing once more, walking out one day and not coming back, and in ten years' time I would go to someone's party and she would walk into the room, heralded perhaps by an Ivor Sitwell look-alike saying the most beautiful woman he had ever seen was about to arrive . . .

I was in error there. I was in error about Cosette and Mark too when I created a picture of them in my mind, living in their shared future. I had even decided on the street they would live in, a little alley of houses like country cottages up north of Westbourne Grove, one of those houses would be right for them, perhaps the one with the great yellow flowering tree growing in its garden. Since then – a long while afterwards, because for years I stopped myself thinking of any of it – I have sometimes wondered what their life together would have been like.

It would have been a life together, they would have stayed together, of that I am sure. And Mark would have married her, if for no other reason than that she would have come to want it so much. He could never bear to disappoint her. He would have dedicated his life to making her happy, as he had already begun to do. I think it would have been a rather cloistered partnership, one of those of which people say that the couple are 'very wrapped up in each other'. Certainly there would have been no more rent-free tenants, non-paying guests, visitors who came for a night and stayed for a year. There would have been few guests of any sort, myself, Bell of course, Luis Llanos and Perdita Reed, Walter and Eva Admetus perhaps, Cosette's brothers, those friends of Mark's he sometimes mentioned but we never saw. Sometimes they would have been seen, Mark and Cosette, dining alone together at some exclusive restaurant, the Connaught perhaps, or Le Gavroche, celebrating an anniversary, the day they first met, the night they first made love, their wedding day, oblivious of the presence of others, eyes fixed with ardour upon the other's eyes, hands touching, fingers enlaced upon the tablecloth. And by that time it would of course be Mark who paid the bill, went through the motions that is, the signing of the cheque or the presentation of the credit card. For by then she would have become so accustomed to deferring to him in all practical matters, to leaving it all to him, that they would have largely forgotten whose money it had been in the first place.

'Are you really going to buy Bell a flat?' I said to Cosette.

'I'd rather buy you one, darling.'

'I shall manage for myself,' I said. 'Thank you, but I really will. It will be good for me to stand on my own feet, as they say. Time I did. But do you mean to do that for Bell?'

'Well,' she said, 'Mark seems to think it would – soften the blow.'

'What blow?'

'He seems to think she won't like us selling this house and moving. Or I suppose that's what he means. It isn't altogether clear what he means. I think he's rather confused. He seems to think that if bell were – well, compensated, she wouldn't feel so bad.'

'Why should she feel bad?'

'She'll lose her home, won't she? He's got hold of this idea that she loves this house. Well, I can understand that, I love it, but it was a phase in my life really, something I had to do, and now I'm moving on. It was a kind of dream I had to make come true and the dream I have now is of living alone with Mark in a little house where we have to be close together because there isn't room for us to be apart. Do you think I'm quite mad? You see, he feels exactly the same, and we can't both be mad, can we? And when I think how I said I loved him so much I'd die of it! I love him so much now I want to live for it. Oh, Elizabeth, I'm so lucky, I can't believe it sometimes, I can't believe anyone can be so happy and it can go on and on and he can feel just the same as me.' Cosette, who had seldom talked much about herself, who had always put others before herself, now, transformed by love, deflected every conversation to her own feelings and, of course, to Mark's. She had forgotten Bell.

It wasn't hard for me to do what Mark had asked, for I hardly ever saw Bell. I only heard her, the droning monotone of the television in the ground-floor room, the creak of the 104th stair, her footsteps moving above my head. She avoided me, I think she avoided everyone. I began to make preparations for acquiring a home of my own. I could easily afford to buy somewhere, I was doing well enough out of my books, much better than if I had followed the career I was trained for and become a teacher, better than if I had been a head teacher or taught in a university. Spending a lot of time peering into estate-agents' windows, I graduated at last to getting them to send me details of flats.

The House of Stairs had become a quiet, even decorous place. Sometimes, in the past, when I had been in my room trying to write, I had been exasperated by noise, music, footsteps running up and down, voices calling and voices shouting, doors slamming. So perverse are human beings that now I missed it. Loneliness drove me to Robin (in one of my novels I would have said it drove me into his arms) and to grow closer to him than would naturally have happened, given our very incompatible temperaments. And then Elsa came to stay.

I think I prefer the company of women.

This was something you didn't admit to in the early seventies. If you said you liked being with women it was taken to mean you made a virtue of necessity, you put up with women because you couldn't get a man. Of course things are quite different today and it's acceptable, recognized as perfectly reasonable and indeed intelligent to prefer women's company. I was overjoyed when Elsa came. She had always been my best friend, is still. For the first time I took it upon myself, took advantage of my daughter-of-the-house status, to ask someone to stay without asking Cosette first. It was unimaginable, anyway, that Cosette would say no.

Elsa had been renting a flat while waiting to move into the place she was buying. Things were getting easier, but for a divorced woman on her own to buy a flat on a mortgage wasn't the straightforward operation it usually is today. There were delays and her three months' lease came to an end without the option to renew.

'It might be a month or longer,' she said when I invited her.

'Cosette will hope it's longer – you'll see.'

Mark didn't. He wasn't very pleased. But you could see he was thinking that all this sort of thing would come to an end soon enough, would necessarily come to an end when they had a house without spare rooms. Well, I could see it, but Bell didn't seem to. Bell seemed to be waiting for something to happen, she had an air of biding her time. She watched Mark, but Mark no longer ever looked at her.

We gave Elsa Auntie's old room, on the floor below mine. All

Auntie's things were still there, the antimacassars on the chairs, the radio in its veneered wood case. Elsa said to leave them, she liked them, but Perpetua took down the flypaper. I was interested in what was happening in the House of Stairs, I would have liked to talk about it, but Elsa isn't like Bell, people's acts and motivations aren't of much concern to her.

'It doesn't matter, does it?' she would say when asked why she thought someone had said or done what he had said or done. 'I expect he had his reasons.'

Bell was making it plain she no longer wanted to know me. It was as if I had fulfilled some requirement of the moment, served my purpose, and now her needs had changed, I was superfluous. If she passed me on the stairs she would say a casual 'hi'. At the big table down in the dining room she would pass me a plate and ask me if I wanted something. If I addressed her she answered. That was all. My consolation – if consolation it was – was that no one received more from her than I did. When we gathered together in the drawing room, as we still sometimes did, she would never be one of our number. One day she walked into the drawing room while I was there with Elsa and Mark and Cosette, drinking coffee Perpetua had made and brought up to us after lunch.

She said to Cosette, 'Can I take the telly up to my room?'

Down there, in the room where Auntie had died, no one ever watched it. Cosette seemed grateful for the request. I think she was grateful Bell had spoken to her. These cold, laconic people, you can be almost elated by a sign of warmth from them, an ordinary remark even.

'Of course you can, darling, if it will work up there. Will it, Mark?'

'I've no idea,' he said.

'And you mustn't attempt to carry it on your own,' Cosette said. 'Mark will give you a hand with it.'

He didn't refuse but he didn't say he would. His voice sounded strained. 'If you want television, Bell, why don't you buy a set of your own?'

'I'd like to speak to you,' she said to him. 'In private.'

I thought he would say there was nothing she could say to him she couldn't say in front of Cosette, but he didn't. Elsa and I were there, of course. He hesitated and then he got up and left the room with her.

'It's about having a key to her room,' Cosette said. I was very sure it wasn't. 'She mentioned losing it the other day.'

Elsa helped her carry the television set up those 106 stairs. Later that evening I came upon her in the kitchen going through drawers, supposedly looking for the lost key to her room.

'Why bother?' I said. 'I won't come in.'

It was the only time I ever saw her blush. She left the drawer open, walked past me out of the kitchen and slammed the door. Above me, as I worked, I would hear the television. She had it on at all hours, whenever there were programmes, though luckily for me there weren't nearly so many then as now. Elsa said to me, sitting in my work room, while some cartoon for children chattered and squeaked overhead, 'Mark is a weak sort of character, isn't he?'

It was unlike her to comment on people's natures. 'Why do you say that?'

'For one thing, he's afraid of Bell. He's got someone coming to look at this house tomorrow, to value it, and he doesn't want her to know. He wants me to take her out somewhere so that she's not in when this man comes. He says only I can do it because I'm the only one here that's on good terms with her.'

'He'll have to tell her sooner or later.'

'There's something more than that he'll have to tell her,' said Elsa. 'I don't know what it is but I sense it. She asked me yesterday if I'd heard anything about their marriage plans, but I could only say I didn't know they were getting married.'

'I wish I knew,' I said, 'just what was going on.'

She shrugged. 'Wait a little, said the thorn tree.'

Bell half-guessed. She knew at any rate that something had gone wrong. Aware of people's ways as she was, she must have known his weakness, the sponginess at the core of him, which made him amenable to her suggestions in the first place. She must have known it was this which now held him back from making to her some great revelation. That was what she wanted to talk about to him in private, and at that private conversation I am sure he lost his nerve again and told her only that things were going well, she must be patient. I can't ask her all these things now. I can't. I think she half-guessed and the half she guessed was only that Mark wasn't going to get married. But what she believed was that he was unable to persuade Cosette to marry him. He may even have told her this at their private talk, that she must wait a little, thorn-tree-like, while he tried his powers of persuasion.

Imagine, though, what it must have been like for him, poor weak Mark, having to do this and talk like this while loving Cosette with all his heart.

— 19 —

'What became of Silas's pictures?' I said.

It was this morning and we were in Bell's room in Kilburn under the railway bridge.

'When I went to prison my solicitor said what would I want to be done about my things and I said burn them, so he did. He said he would, so I expect he did. They would never have been worth anything.'

'I'd have looked after them for you.'

She smiled at me. Sometimes she has this way of looking at me as if I am an eccentric child, given to making artless statements of a charmingly innocent kind. When she was first in prison I got a monthly Visitors' Order and used to go in and see her, but after a while she asked me not to come any more. She didn't want visitors, there was no one she wanted. Well, things have changed and she isn't like that now. She wants me. Irony of ironies, she now wants me. We are here in her room, clearing it out, packing her very small and some would say pathetic quantity of possessions into one of my suitcases. For Bell is moving in. She has told her probation officer and she is coming to live with me, not for a week or two or for months, but for ever. Because she wants to and I don't know how to say no. The past won't let me say no; it would seem like an act of violence done to the past, to my old feelings and vows and desires, to refuse her.

It isn't something I look forward to with relish. If I could afford it I would sell my house and buy a bigger one so that we wouldn't have to live in, as they say, each other's pockets. But I can't afford it. Bell and I will have to live side by side in four rooms. She is destitute and depends solely on me. I haven't yet actually handed cash over to her, I haven't given her pocket-money for her cigarettes, but no doubt that will come. Is she drawing social security benefits? I haven't asked, any more than I asked what happened to the money derived from the sale of Silas's father's house. She told me.

'I spent it on my defence. They wouldn't give me legal aid when they found out I had a private income.'

We began packing her things into my suitcase. Among them I recognized a necklace Cosette once gave her, a long chain of amber beads. I don't suppose they are really amber, they are only amber-coloured, and I have never known Bell to wear them. They were in a box, a long shiny black box that I think is called 'japanned' and which was probably once used for keeping long gloves in. No doubt the beads were in this box when Cosette gave it to her. Also in there, wrapped in one of the remnants of cloth that constitute Bell's garments, was the bloodstone.

The dark green is chalcedony and the red spots are jasper. This gemstone was much in demand by painters in the Middle Ages for flagellation scenes, and to symbolize the blood of martyrs. I sound like Felicity, I probably got that from Felicity. I laid the ring in the palm of my hand, looking closely at it for the first time. The setting is composed of many strands of gold, laid parallel to form the band itself, twisted and plaited where these surround the stone. Examining it, I wondered where it had come from, if it had passed down in our family, perhaps from one afflicted member to another, until it finally came to Douglas's mother, who was my mother's aunt. And I remembered Cosette giving it to Bell for her thirtieth birthday, at the party when Mark came to the House of Stairs for the second time, and how Bell took it indifferently with a muttered word of thanks.

'Have you ever worn it?' I said.

She didn't answer my question, but said to me, 'You can have it. Why don't you have it?'

'All right,' I said. I expect I spoke ungraciously, for I thought of it as Cosette's to give, not hers.

Her action, her words, surprised me. She put the bloodstone on my finger. 'With this ring I thee wed,' she said, and laughed her dry as dust laugh. I don't understand her, I often don't, I don't know what she wants. She can still astonish me. For instance, it always surprised me how little of the paraphernalia of living she needs in order to live. We filled that one suitcase and a single plastic carrier and the room was emptied.

'And think what someone like Felicity has,' I said. 'That great house filled with her things and the flat they have that must be filled with them too.'

'If I can't have the things I want,' Bell said, 'and I can't because I can't afford them, I'd rather have nothing.'

It wasn't the first time I had heard her say that. But the first time I heard it I didn't know what I know now. Someone walked over my grave; I felt a small, cold thrill, but she wasn't looking at me, she had forgotten ever saying it before. She looked round the room with indifference, the indifference I believe she has felt to everywhere she has ever lived. So much for Mark, who tried to make me believe she loved the House of Stairs and would mind leaving it. We went downstairs and out into the street, looking for a taxi. At certain times of the day taxis come down from Cricklewood, making for the West End. This wasn't one of them and we walked southwards along Kilburn High Road, I carrying the suitcase and she the carrier bag, but they weren't heavy and it had been a warm humid day of thick air and hazy sunshine. Even if no taxi came we could have got into the tube at Kilburn Park. It was Bell who, looking down the long slope towards Maida Vale, mentioned the friend we had who lived there.

'Now we're here we could go and see Elsa.'

I was more likely than she to have made this suggestion. Up till today she hasn't spoken of wanting to see anyone from the past, and when Felicity came she was almost violent to her. She has asked about no one, reacts with perhaps natural terror when I speak the names of Cosette and Mark – that I can understand. But Admetus? Eva? Has she no curiosity about the fates of Ivor Sitwell and Gary and the dancers? I had made no reply to her and she said with suppressed violence, 'I should never have come out of there, out of prison. I was best in there. I could cope in there, maybe I ought to go back.'

There is no answer to make. Platitudes and placebos, which I was once quite good at offering, are alien to my present mood. Instead I said, pointing down Carlton Vale, 'Elsa lives down there. Do you want to ring her first?'

'Why, when we're on the doorstep? If she doesn't want us she can tell lies to our faces just as well as on the phone.'

'She won't tell lies to me,' I said. I was aggrieved and glad to be, glad to feel something more than dull indifference. The suitcase suddenly felt heavy and I wondered what I was doing, carrying it. 'Your turn,' I said and I swung it at her, the red sparks in the bloodstone flashing. 'Give me the bag.'

Elsa keeps me informed of things – and people. Certain people I never see any more whom she does see she tells me about, and that is the only way I know. She is my best friend, yet months pass by without our seeing each other. I hadn't even spoken to her on the phone since Bell reappeared in my life. I don't believe there is anyone left but me who still calls her by that school name, Lioness. One of my books is dedicated to her, the one about the safari park: 'To the Lioness, with love.'

She looks like one, strong and lithe and muscular, with amber cat's eyes and a mouth that tilts up at the corners. Of course she must have known Bell was with me, Felicity would have told her, for Felicity is her cousin. Or, rather, Esmond is and he once gravely told us, 'A cousin's wife is a cousin. Husband and wife are one flesh.' She answered the entryphone and said nothing to my announcement of who it was but 'Come up.' At the top of the first flight of stairs where her flat is she was waiting for us, a towel in her hands and her sandy-orange lion's hair wet from washing. Bell didn't even wait for her to speak a word but said, 'I can see you don't recognize me, I'm so changed. An ugly sight, aren't I?'

For some reason I wanted to hit her. I wanted to scream out. It is a new mood for me and devastating. Of course I did nothing – that is, I said nothing, only made eye contact with Elsa and cast up mine, while a kind of panic hatred of Bell made my whole inner self tremble, though outwardly I was icicle-like, still and stiff and cold. Elsa spoke graciously, reminding me that she was indeed Esmond's cousin, 'It's good to see you, Bell. I hope you and Elizabeth will stay and have lunch with me.'

In this gracious way she spoke to a woman who has done murder and put herself outside the pale of any civilized society. And with aplomb she preceded us into her flat.

It isn't the same place as the one she was waiting to move into while staying at the House of Stairs. That was a very long way down in Chelsea, practically Fulham, even further west than where the Thinnesses have their *pied-à-terre*. Since then she has married again and is waiting to be divorced again. She was not particularly interested in people's motivations, but she was interested in sexual relationships. And she loved Cosette, she was pleased to see Cosette happy.

'He doesn't seem to have any friends of his own,' she said to me.

'If he has they don't come here.'

Of course you might have said that Bell had no friends either, but that wouldn't quite be true. The Thinnesses were her friends and the Admetuses, at least she knew them and associated with them; I was her friend and Elsa. But Mark appeared to have no one, nor could I remember his speaking the names of friends in conversation, but only of his referring vaguely to people he knew. He never talked about his past either. He might, for all that was known of his origins, have been born two years ago, aged thirty-six, or been created by Pygmalion-Bell and had life breathed into him specially for me to see him across the room at Global Experience. It was quite a shock for me, though a pleasant one, when researching one day in the British Newspaper Library and looking (for something quite different) through old copies of the *Radio Times*, to find his name among those in the cast list of a play heard five years before. Ibsen, it was, *Rosmersholm*, and Mark Henryson had been cast as Peter Mortensgaard.

He had told me nothing of his past, but why should he? Cosette he had probably told. Cosette very likely knew his whole history from childhood to the present day. How would I know? I was hardly ever alone with her; Mark was always there.

Elsa refused to fall in with Mark's plan to get Bell out of the house while his valuer came, for Elsa is truly honest, truly open. She might – as Bell suggested today – tell a social lie or two, but she wouldn't consent to deceive a friend for an unworthy purpose. She no more believed than I did that Bell was too deeply attached to the House of Stairs to bear the idea of leaving it. By this time I think she had gathered how little Mark had wanted her to come there even for two or three weeks, though she was one of the few of Cosette's visitors who bought food for the house, contributed to the wine stocks and saw to her own laundry. Clearer-sighted than I, fresh of course to the situation, she suspected Mark, and said in a sweet tone that took the sting out of it, 'You'll have to do your own dirty work.'

In the event he did nothing, the valuer when he came didn't want to go into every room and Bell was shut up in hers with the television on. Three days later a man representing a property company – shades of things to come! – came to look at the house with a view to buying it. It was a happy coincidence for Mark that Bell happened to have gone out for one of her long walks, the first she had taken for weeks. Before she came back Mark and Cosette had gone out house-hunting, or I believe they had gone out for this purpose. They made a big secret of this because Bell wasn't supposed to know.

'Short of killing her,' I said to Elsa, 'I don't see how they're going to get out of it.' I was writing a novel in which someone had to be disposed of by murder. It was the only possible way for the life of the book to continue. I suppose I had it on my mind.

'I doubt if they'll do that,' she said.

That night we were all to be taken out to dinner by the dancers. Entertaining Cosette was something they did about once a year, to make up for all the entertainment they received from her. Since they dined with her at least once a week and were taken about by her to plays and concerts and cinemas, it didn't even begin to make up for it, but I expect it eased their consciences. They were resigned to the company of whoever else might be in the house, for Cosette would have contrived, very gently and tactfully, to decline their invitation unless she could take what Ivor had rudely called her 'entourage' with her.

I remember so much, but I don't remember the restaurant we went to. In Soho it may have been, or Charlotte Street. And Luis and Perdita were lucky, for they only had five guests, whereas in the past there might easily have been ten. Bell had consented to come, much to my surprise. It was curious how she had got herself into the position of the odd person out, the third in the two's-company-three's-none situation, almost the spectre at the feast. We paired naturally into Cosette and Mark, Luis and Perdita, Elsa and me, and then there was Bell. She must have been the worst-dressed woman in that restaurant – she was by far the worst-dressed of our party, a tied-up parcel of layers the colour of brown paper – but heads turned to look at her. They always did. It was the way she walked, so straight and her head so perfectly carried, and that crown of disordered gleaming pale hair and that indestructible face, the profile carved for a cameo.

It is worth telling you how we were seated. They put three tables together for us and Luis sat at the head of them with Cosette on his left and Bell on his right. Mark was next to Cosette – they always sat like that, they would never be parted – and Elsa next to him. Opposite them, Perdita sat between Bell and me, so that Elsa and I faced each other.

We ate nothing that evening, we none of us reached the point of having dinner. I think Luis actually ate a few pieces of a bread roll and we all had drinks of the aperitif kind. Bell had brandy. It's strange how clearly I remember that. Everyone else had wine or sherry, and Cosette of course had her orange juice, but Bell had brandy, a double brandy which she asked for in a desperate voice as if she were dying for lack of it. Cosette was wearing a new dress of pale yellow lawn with a pattern on it of sprinkled white daisies, and she was looking very nice, her face serene and happy. The dim lights in the restaurant flattered her. Her hair had been done that day and looked as fine and as silky as Bell's. For once she wasn't talking with Mark, behaving, as they so often did, as if no one else existed, but had got into a mild argument with Luis about, of all things, whether Gibraltar should or should not be Spanish.

A waiter came and took our orders, Luis had just finished telling a joke that was going the rounds about Franco having said Britain could keep Gibraltar if she would give him back Torremolinos, when a woman came up behind Mark and touched him on the shoulder. She was about forty, dark, attractive, more conventionally and conservatively dressed than any of us. He looked round, immediately pushed back his chair and got up. She kissed him on the cheek.

It would somehow be satisfying to say that he turned pale. In the fiction I write all the colour would have drained from his face or he would have flushed 'darkly'. Mark simply looked blank. He said, 'Hallo, Sheila,' and then spoke our names rather slowly and monotonously. It was as if he was struggling to recover from a shock. 'Cosette, Elsa, Elizabeth, Perdita . . .' but she interrupted him with, 'Of course I know Bell!'

She was looking at Bell and smiling. Bell was holding her brandy glass in both hands, just staring ahead of her. By this time it was clear something was very wrong, or something was about to go wrong. At least it was clear to everyone at our table but not to the woman called Sheila who, swivelling her head to the left and to the right, having uttered shrill hallos and how-do-you-dos, said, 'I'm Sheila Henryson, I'm Mark's sister-in-law.'

She turned round and beckoned to a man who was sitting with a party almost as big as ours. He got up and made an excuse to the woman next to him. He wasn't in the least like Mark in feature, and he was much heavier, but as soon as you knew you could see he was Mark's brother. Which meant, didn't it, that he must be Bell's brother too?

Sheila Henryson must be a very insensitive woman. The silence at our table was almost palpable now, but she seemed unaffected by it. Her husband came up, muttered something to Mark and gave him a pat on the back. Isn't it strange that I never learned what Mark's brother's name is and I don't know now? She began making explanations. They lived abroad, Riyadh or Bahrain or somewhere like that, were home for a few weeks' holiday, had tried to write to and then phone Mark but had, as she put it, 'got no joy of that', which wasn't surprising since Mark never went home to Brook Green any more. She began making plans for the two parties to unite, we must all contrive somehow to sit together, the management would fix it, they were with people Mark knew, she said, and who would love to see him again . . .

Cosette was the first of us to speak. She had been looking simply confused. Not unhappy, not that, but bewildered. She interrupted Sheila Henryson's flow in a way quite uncharacteristic of her, and said to Mark's brother, 'Then Bell is your sister?'

'No,' he said. 'What makes you think that?'

I heard Bell make a sound. It wasn't distress but more like exasperation. Cosette didn't turn pale or flush either, but age got hold of her face, she aged before our eyes. She put out a hand as if to touch Mark. He was still standing up, standing quite rigid, with his eyes fixed on a point on the other side of the restaurant. The way he was standing with his brother on one side of him and his sister-in-law on the other, made him look like someone about to be arrested. Cosette put out her hand and withdrew it without touching him. Mark's brother gave a nervous laugh.

'I can tell I've said something I shouldn't,' he said.

It was at this point that a waiter appeared with a plate in each hand, the first of the hors d'oeuvres we had ordered. Cosette looked at the artichoke hearts he placed in front of her, put her hand over her mouth, got up and walked out of the restaurant. She walked fast and clumsily and as if she were blind, bumping into people and pushing chairs out of her path and fumbling with the door and letting it bang behind her.

Everybody began talking at once, Luis and Perdita inquiring what had gone wrong, Elsa casting up her eyes and saying she wished to God she hadn't come, Bell drumming her fists frenetically on the table and saying, 'Fuck, fuck, fuck, fuck – oh, fuck!'

The brother said to Mark, 'But what on earth did I *do*?'

Mark didn't answer. He went after Cosette. I sometimes wondered if poor Luis and Perdita had to pay for that uneaten meal, for I don't think even they ate any of it. I heard Luis say something to the waiter about bad news, about its being impossible to stay. I never saw Perdita again, though Luis I did – but that is another, later story. Murmuring that we were sorry, sorry, that we too must go, I left them there with the brother and his wife now imploring them to explain what had gone wrong, and followed Elsa and Bell. Cosette had disappeared and so had Mark. Elsa said what I hadn't been able to find the words for, 'Why did you say he was your brother?'

Bell heaved up her shoulders in an exaggerated shrug. She cocked a thumb at me. 'It was her idea. She said, is he your brother, and I thought, why not? I thought it'd work better and so it did till that stupid bitch put her spoke in.'

'What do you mean, work better?' I said.

She didn't answer that one. 'He's my lover,' she said.

I think I gasped. 'Since when?' I too had a vested interest – nearly as much as Cosette did.

'Years.'

Cosette and I, then, were in the same boat. When was it I had first seen them together at Global Experience? Three years ago . . .

I said fiercely, 'He's not still your lover.'

'There's had to be' – she paused, in search of a phrase, found one that was wildly unsuitable – 'a temporary suspension of that.'

We were walking along the street, wherever it was. A street of restaurants and clubs and little shops. The weather was warm and sultry and it wasn't anywhere near dark, but high summer and as light as at mid-afternoon. That sort of shock gives you a pain, the kind they call a stitch, that you can get from hard running. I felt as if I had been running. I wanted to sit down and I did. I sat on a doorstep. Elsa stood and looked at me, her face kind and concerned but very puzzled, and Bell stood a little apart. If I had to describe the way she looked I'd say she looked awkward, which was very unusual for her.

'I don't feel equal to this,' she said.

Elsa looked as if she would have liked to hit her. 'Shut up,' she said. 'Why don't you piss off somewhere?'

Which Bell did. She just walked away from us, her head held high. She came to a street that turned off to the right and walked down it, disappearing from view. Elsa and I stayed there for a while, sitting on the step, while I thought about what it meant to me, Mark being Bell's lover, and what it would mean to Cosette, and then we got a taxi and went home in it. The house appeared to be empty. I went outside again to look for Cosette's car. It was still a Volvo, though not the one she had had when she moved there, the successor to the successor of that one. Parking in Archangel Place was getting more and more difficult, but it was always possible to park somewhere down there or in the mews. I looked up and down the street and down into the mews but the car wasn't there, and that obscurely made me feel better, it made me think Cosette and Mark must have gone out somewhere in it together. At any rate it made me feel better for Cosette.

Elsa and I got ourselves something to eat and we waited. She asked me no questions but took one of the new novels Cosette had on the table and started reading it. I believe she guessed I had an emotional involvement with Bell quite different from my friendship with herself. But I didn't care then, I didn't care about hiding it. I couldn't read, I could only lie back in my chair and stare at the ornate, complicated ceiling and the cobweb-festooned chandelier and think and think and be wretched. When it got to midnight, I said, 'I have the feeling we'll never see Bell again.'

'Who cares?'

I didn't answer her. She knew very well I cared. 'She won't come back here,' I said. 'She won't bother about her things, they don't matter to her. She'll go to someone, she'll go to her mother.'

'Are you sure she's got a mother?'

No,' I said. 'No, I'm not,' and then, 'I thought she had a brother.'

Elsa said, 'She told me a long time ago, when I first met her at Thornham, that she had no parents. She had had no parents since she was twelve. I thought it was a bit fishy when you mentioned her mother.'

773

'What she told you might equally well be a lie.'

'True, but they can't both be.'

'What happened when she was twelve? I mean, did she say her parents were killed in an accident or something? What happened to her?'

'She told me only that she lost her parents. She went into some sort of institution.'

'A children's home, d'you mean?'

Elsa gave me a strange look. 'I don't think it was a children's home, not at that stage, that came later. I don't know what it was.'

As she was speaking, reluctantly, doubtfully, as if the words were dragged out of her, we heard the front door close downstairs. We were sitting in the drawing room and I think we both thought it was Cosette or Mark or, best of all, Cosette *and* Mark. The footsteps, a single set, came up the first flight and passed the door. It must be Bell. We heard her go on up the stairs, walking heavily for her, and because of this we weren't positively sure it was she, and we went out on to the landing to listen. Like personages in a ghost story who have heard some sound that shouldn't be, some unnatural footfall, we stood there clutching each other by the arms and staring upwards. It was absurd, it was hysterical behaviour, but we seemed to be involved in some high drama, and we held our breaths. Even from down there you could hear that 104th stair creak. Her bedroom door closed.

Elsa smiled her crooked ironic smile and broke the tension with, 'She hasn't got a mother.'

In the drawing room again, having no thought of going to bed, though it was past one, we opened the french windows and went out on to the balcony. It was a warm night and very quiet. But after a while of listening you could hear distant music of two sorts, and other sounds, a faint throb of traffic, a light rhythmic hammering as of someone who, because he worked all day, had to build his shelves and cabinets by night. The foliage was as dense as in a country lane, the trees heavy hanging masses of unmoving leaves. On a house opposite a vine grew and grapes dangled from it, gleaming pale green in the lamplight.

It came as a shock to see that the Volvo was there. It filled the space which had been empty when Elsa and I came in. We could see only the roof of it and we had no idea how long it had been there. The notion came to me to go back into the room and put the lights out. Whether this worked or whether the extinguishing of the lights went unnoticed I can't tell, but after a moment or two, the driver's door opened and Mark got out. I nearly gasped, I felt an almost intolerable constriction of the throat. What had become of her? Where was she? It seemed possible he had never found her, that he had come back here only to fetch the car and search for her.

He went round to the passenger door and opened it. I should have remembered his unfailing simple courtesy. Cosette got out without assistance from him, without taking his hand. But they were together, they had returned together. He closed the car door and they stood looking at each other and then, there in the street where anyone could observe them, indifferent perhaps as to whether they were observed or not, they went into each other's arms and pressed their faces together with their cheeks touching.

He put his arm round her waist and led her out of our sight up to the front door and into the house.

Elsa is as courteous and friendly towards her as if Bell had done no more than travel on the tube without a ticket. Does she remember that dinner and Bell's flight and my misery? We have all grown decorously into the preliminaries of middle age. After lunch, over coffee, I watched Bell who sat stately and dignified, cool and – harmless. It was absurd what she had said to Elsa about being an ugly sight. Perhaps that was why she had said it, for she has lost years and years since that day I followed her on the tube, since that day I went to see her in her room in Kilburn. She is growing young again, is being rejuvenated, revitalized. I could see Elsa glancing from her face to mine. It may be only conjecture, it may be my imagination, but I fancied Elsa was making comparisons, was thinking, how can Bell look the way she looks after suffering so much and Elizabeth the way she does after so little?

Of course she said nothing and it may be she never thought it. We had talked about everything that was innocuous, we had talked for about two hours, and still I hadn't asked the question I always make a point of asking Elsa when we meet, for I have no other means of finding out the answer. She had told us about her new job and her new man that may be the one she has been waiting for, though she won't marry him, she will never marry again. We spoke of our morning's task and our future plans, our intention perhaps of taking a holiday together. I mentioned my father and his visit. And then Bell got up and asked Elsa where the bathroom was.

'Do you have a bathroom?' was what she asked, as if the chances were that the occupant of this charming and prettily furnished flat had to use a communal lavatory and the public baths.

Elsa smiled at me after she had left the room and I knew the same thought was passing through her mind. Whatever else Bell was, had become, she remained tactless, insensitive and, about such small social niceties, quite uncaring. Quickly, I asked my question.

Elsa seemed to understand. Her eyes went to the closed door. 'Very well, I think. We spoke on the phone a couple of weeks ago.'

'I'm glad,' I said. 'I'm always glad. I don't suppose' – How often I ask this and always so awkwardly! – 'anything is ever said about me?'

That English passive is enormously useful, isn't it? You can thus do without names, should anyone be listening at the door.

'Nothing, Lizzie, I'm sorry.' I nodded a little. 'I get the impression even mentioning you would – cause great pain.'

'Bell hasn't asked,' I said. 'I don't want to say anything until she asks.'

I could hear her coming back, heard her pause outside before bringing her hand to the door handle. She is quite capable of listening. Elsa and I fell silent, looking at each other, waiting for her to come in, awed by her, knowing she stood on the other side of the door in the hope of hearing secrets she was not meant to know.

— 20 —

The phone was ringing when we came into my house. That was three days ago, but it seems a lifetime. The widow my father likes but wouldn't marry for fear of depriving me of my inheritance had rung me to tell me he was ill, he had had a stroke. Bell was behaving strangely. She had been quiet, bemused, ever since we left Elsa's. When she heard my father was ill, that I was going immediately down to Worthing where he was in hospital, she said, 'Is he going to die?'

'I suppose so.'

'I shall be all alone here,' she said. 'I shall be alone in the house. I don't know if I'm equal to it.'

'You'll have the cats,' I said.

At present I am staying in my father's house, which is on an estate where the average age of the inhabitants is said to be seventy. I am used to it, I have come down here to stay every year for a week, but in the past I have tried to pick a time when the Arundel Festival is on or there is good theatre at Chichester, so that I have something to do. And once, fourteen years ago, shortly after he had bought it, I lived here with him for a whole month, I and my typewriter, trying to write, trying to seem normal. Poor man, he must have wondered if he was to be saddled with me for years, for a lifetime. I could hardly explain that I had lost my home, my friendships, my life, but I made a convincing enough case for myself with my excuse of not wishing to stay in a place where murder had been done.

Most of each day I spend at the hospital where my father lies half-paralysed and with his face grotesquely twisted. No doubt it is natural to feel as I do when one's father is dying. Just the same, I have never before experienced a depression so deep as to cause physical malaise. A great weariness has taken hold of me and, as was the case with Bell when she first came out of prison, I sleep a lot. I fall asleep in the chair at my father's bedside and, returning to his house in the evening, fall asleep in my armchair in front of the television. But I don't sleep well at night. At night, with my head aching, I lie awake and think about things. And I see figures and shapes form in the darkness whether my eyes are open or closed, I see men and women then that I have never seen before, strange faces like the faces of unknown people we see sometimes in dreams. One of the oddest things, it has always seemed to me, is that our minds can invent people for our dreams. Or are they not invented? Have we seen them all somewhere before and has some camera of the mind photographed them? Between the unknown faces, emerging from a great crowd of them, I sometimes see Cosette's and sometimes Mark's, but they are never together, they are always separated by a multitude of strangers.

That night fourteen years ago I fell asleep quickly, the sleep of relief. But I awoke to understand that though things might come right for Cosette, they couldn't for me. She still had Mark, but I had lost Bell. He had been Bell's lover. When, I asked myself, when was the last time? When was the last time Mark had made love to Bell? And

777

suddenly I knew when it was. It was the night Auntie died, when Cosette begged Mark to stay and I, in my innocence, directed him up to the top of the house, to the room next to Bell's.

That other night, after the scene in the restaurant, while he and Cosette were out in the car, driving and parking and driving again, getting out to walk, sitting on park benches, he told her everything. He had to, he couldn't do less, there was nothing else for it. He laid it all before her, as Bell had conceived it and he, with increasing reluctance, had tried to carry it out. And Cosette forgave him. Why wouldn't she? It isn't hard to forgive someone who tells you he was kept from the ultimate baseness by love of you. But in these instances someone has to be blamed. Not the abject, ardent lover, but the lover's scapegoats. Mark, in those long hours of explanations and excuses, had been obliged (in his methodology) to lay the blame elsewhere, to confess that if some of the action had been his the strategy was not, the original conception was not.

It wasn't in Cosette's nature to send for someone, to seek an interview designed to extract an explanation. She suffered, but in silence. She suffered, but she had Mark, who would mitigate any suffering for her, soften any blow. I was innocent then, unaware that I might be involved in Cosette's immediate trouble. I even felt excluded, an unnecessary presence in the house. That she might have any feelings towards me then beyond an affectionate but abstracted warmth, a mother's feeling for one of her children when, for once, her own concerns have become paramount, never crossed my mind. I had an idea only that when I next encountered her I would hug her and hold her close to me.

The next day, in the early afternoon, I met her on the stairs. There were so many stairs and the staircase was so big in relation to the size of the house that when the place was full meetings took place on the stairs every time you went up or down. There were only five of us now, and Bell had been up in her room ever since she returned in the middle of the night. Elsa was at work and the house was still and silent. I was coming down from my workroom, having finished my morning's stint rather late, and Cosette was coming from the drawing room back to her bedroom. She had a dressing-gown on, it was a Japanese kimono, green with white flowers, and her fair shiny hair hung loose to her shoulders. Her face was pale and drawn and you

778

could see she had been crying, but a long time since, before she slept.

She would have gone past me without a word, without even that look of reproach which itself implies future forgiveness is possible. I put out my hand to touch her arm. You must understand I had no idea then that I could be thought guilty of any offence. If I saw myself as in any way culpable it was only in having been, among others, a witness of that scene on the previous night. She would have passed me without a glance but she was tired, drained of feeling, and when you are as close as she and I, living side by side, mother and child, must there always be greetings, inquiries, signs? Love, as against being 'in love', is about taking for granted. But I spoke to her.

'Are you all right, Cosette?'

She stood there and she looked at me. Behind her head hung that branched and bead-hung chandelier of Murano glass which had been so bright that night when Esmond switched the lights on. She pulled my hand off her arm, plucked it off, the way someone might pluck off a leech. Her eyes looked into mine, but dully, without feeling, without care. If it were possible to use such an expression in connection with Cosette, I would say with indifference.

I rephrased my inquiry. 'What is it, Cosette? What's the matter?'

It's strange, isn't it, that when those you love speak your name, your given name, you know all is well? You know things will be all right. Cosette didn't speak mine, she never spoke it again. She said, 'You brought that woman here.'

'Bell?' I was already cold with fear. 'But I didn't know,' I said. Even then I didn't want to speak of the deception she had practised. 'I didn't know; I was as much taken in as you.'

Cosette moved her shoulders. She was holding quite tightly on to the banisters, and she looked up the staircase, up the winding shaft of it, to the top. Her voice remained gentle, she couldn't change that.

'It was your idea Mark should pose as her brother.' I shook my head but she went on, 'You gave her some book to read.'

'Bell? She's never read a book in her life.'

Cosette said with quiet bitterness, 'She didn't need to read it. You told her the story. You gave her the whole marvellous idea. I suppose you told her what a close parallel there was to the situation here. Only I'm not young and beautiful and I wasn't dying.'

It was a lot to take in, and it took me some seconds to receive it, to begin the process of understanding. While I stood looking at her and she brought her gaze down from that spiralled height, right down, to fix it on her own white hands that side by side clutched the banisters, Mark's voice came from the bedroom above, calling from behind the door that was narrowly open: 'Cosette, where are you?'

She ran to him and let the door slam behind her. I stood where I was for a moment and then I went on slowly down. I had had a shock and knew myself the victim of a great injustice. Perhaps, just because of this, I was even then – so quickly do we rally our forces – sure I could explain, I could make things right. She had had a shock too. Wait a little, as Elsa might have said, wait a little.

Down in the kitchen, where I had been on my way to make myself a late lunch, I sat at the table and thought about what Cosette had said. My appetite had gone but I poured myself some icy-cold white wine that had been opened the day before, a glass drunk from it and the rest left in the fridge overnight. I drank my wine down, poured another glass and thought, you can understand why people take to drink. Mark, of course, had betrayed me – no, not that, for in order to be betrayed in this context I would have had to have done something wrong. Better to say he had shopped me, or borne false witness against me, sold me down the river. Plainly, he had told Cosette I had recommended to Bell that she and he do what the conspirators in *The Wings of the Dove* do, I had advised it as a practical plan. Sitting there with my wine, I remembered Bell picking up the book in my workroom and asking what it was about, and I remembered my answer.

'This man and girl are engaged but they can't marry because they haven't any money. There's a young girl called Milly Theale who's terminally ill and enormously rich. James doesn't say what's the matter with her, but he does say it's not what you might think, meaning tuberculosis. I've always thought it must have been leukaemia. The engaged girl proposes to her fiancé that he marry Milly. Then when she dies she'll leave him all her money and he and she can marry and enjoy it.'

Bell had thought Cosette had cancer. Mark would marry her, she would die and he inherit her money. Then he and Bell would live on it. It came into my head how Bell said if she couldn't have nice things she'd rather have nothing. She would have nothing now. It was no wonder, I thought, that she had positively wanted Mark to sleep with Cosette, had been irritated by his delays, had expected him speedily to marry her. But what had her discovery, late in the day, that Cosette didn't have cancer, wouldn't die from natural causes, done to the plan? Not much. Doubtless, she saw herself still Mark's lover after the marriage (or the relationship at any rate resumed) and in that role able to enjoy Cosette's bounty as much as he did. Perhaps that too was part of the plan. Or had she intended to deal with Cosette?

I didn't think of that then. These ideas came to me much later, when I knew what Bell was, when the facts about her sister Susan were known and Silas's suicide came in question. On that summer's day in the House of Stairs I thought only that Bell and Mark had tried to re-live the plot of a novel and it had failed – as indeed the conspiracy in *The Wings of the Dove* fails.

Have I said that it was a very hot day? I don't believe I have. That kitchen, down in the basement, was the coolest place in the house. I went about opening windows, but without making much change in the atmosphere. It seemed only that blocks of hot stuffiness moved in to displace the blocks of hot stuffiness inside. No breath of wind stirred the curtains as the french windows were pushed open to bare the balconies. On the opposite side of the street a man and two girls came out on to the flat roof above the porch, spread out a blanket and lay on it, drinking wine. I had my wine bottle with me in one hand and the glass in the other and as I ascended the staircase, pausing at each open window, I poured myself wine and drank it, a very unusual thing for me to do, very out of character. If you live under the threat of Huntington's chorea you don't do things that will bring about a loss of dexterity, a vagueness, a failure of coordination. The wine began to give me a headache and dry up my mouth, but I wanted more, I thought of starting on another bottle, drinking myself into a stupor.

Cosette and Mark went out together at about three-thirty. I don't think they saw me. I watched them from the drawing-room balcony where I had finally stationed myself, by then with a glass of water. The sun had reached a stage of glare, close and dusty, as if it shone through a sheet of grey gauze. Cosette wore a loose flowing dress, sleeveless, in pastel-flowered voile. Mark was in jeans but with a jacket and a tie. They got into the car, Mark driving as usual. It must have been blazing hot inside the car, for I saw Cosette flap the passenger door back and forth, back and forth, before she closed it and they drove off. Later I found out that they had gone to see the registrar. They were fixing a date for their marriage. He was so weak, Mark, he was as weak as water, unable even to stick to that bold and honourable resolve of his not to marry where it might be thought he had married for money.

After a while I went out into the back garden, hot and dusty and scented by the eucalypt, and looked up at Bell's window. It was wide open, the two sashes pushed up to the top. I thought of calling out to her, but I didn't. I went up instead. By then I had got the idea that my best hope with Cosette was to make Bell explain that none of it was my fault, that I wasn't in on the conspiracy. I must have been drunk to have imagined Bell doing this. I called to her from outside the door. There was a movement from inside, as if she had been lying on the bed and had swung her feet to the ground, but she said nothing and she didn't open the door. I went down again. How many times, I wonder, did I climb and descend the staircase in the House of Stairs that long afternoon? How many times did I retreat to the garden and return to the drawing room? In times of stress I find remaining still very difficult, I need to fidget, to sit down, stand up, pace, wander to windows and gaze out of them.

On the drawing-room balcony, that Ca' Lanier basket, on to which this past year I saw the new occupant come from his red and white streamlined segment of drawing room, I paused, looking down through leaves of plane and laburnum, sycamore and sallow, leaves that flagged in the heat of the day, on to the dusty roadway, car roofs that reflected the sun's dull glare, yellowed grass growing out of splits in the pavement. I felt the heat laid on my arms like a thick soft cloth.

Do you remember in the Old Testament how the sun stood still for Joshua? The sun was stilled upon Gibeon and the moon in the valley. I could see no sun, it was lost in its own white pool of heat, a molten source of burning, but time stood still for me the way it stands still when you long for it to pass. I went back into the neither cooler nor hotter interior, again pointlessly essayed the stairs, and tried the garden that looked to me as grey as mildew. There I sat at the stone table where in days that seemed long past, long gone and lost, I had sat with Cosette and Auntie, and Cosette had been Mariana in the

Moated Grange and had asked so plaintively why no one came to visit any more.

As I sat there I understood something. I understood that to lose Cosette would be the worst of all possible losses, to which separation from Bell would be a mild deprivation, to which my own poor mother's death would be nothing, to which no loss of lover or friend could compare. I could even define it. It would be the heart of loneliness. For Cosette, whatever nonsense I told myself about Bell, it was Cosette I loved, Cosette was this house to me, she was my home, it was she I had chosen to be my mother.

I couldn't lose her. It must be possible to explain to her and make her see. But a kind of panic took hold of me, a primitive fear, closely linked with self-preservation. It was as if, without Cosette, I could not preserve myself, my self. If she had truly been my mother I could never lose her, for no matter what abuses have been heaped on them, what betrayals, insults, neglects, mothers can always be got back, brought round, retrieved. Mothers will always forgive. My terror lay in the fact that Cosette, though chosen, though loved more than any mother, was not my mother and between us there existed no flesh and blood bond of parent and child. The bloodstone, passed down through Douglas's family, had not passed from her to me.

You will see that I was growing hysterical. I returned to the house, went back to the garden, climbed the stairs to the drawing room and the balcony, and still they didn't come back or Bell come down or Elsa return from work. I hung over the balcony in the heat, and what caused this release I don't know, but sweat began to stream off my skin like bath water, as if I had stepped from a bath.

A taxi came down the street. It stopped outside and Luis Llanos got out of it. He had tight white trousers on and a loose white shirt made of some very thin transparent embroidered material and he looked very cool. He also looked, and all he needed to complete the picture was a black hat, like a bullfighter. When he had paid off the taxi he looked up at me and waved, very casual, serene really. Of course I understood he knew nothing, he didn't know the world was coming to an end.

I went down to let him in.

Two days ago, at nine in the morning, my father died. I have done all the necessary things, registered his death, notified the funeral directors, seen his solicitor. And I have done the unnecessary things too, comforted the widow who would like now to be *his* widow, phoned Bell.

I can scarcely imagine what words of sympathy from Bell would be like. What would she say? I shall never know, for now I have no more to lose and the occasion for condolence will never arise. What she said, yesterday afternoon, when I told her my father was dead, was: 'A good thing that didn't drag on.' And then, 'When are you coming back?'

I would have been made very happy once by such an inquiry from her. Now I find it mildly repulsive. Curiously enough, I don't much want to go home, it is quiet here and removed from anything I have ever known, a placid life among the old whose blood is tame and passion spent. We will have the funeral, and I and the widow will attend it and one or two of my father's neighbours, I expect.

It will be the first funeral to come within the scope of my care since that one fourteen years in the past and that I didn't attend. I was told it would be an outrage for me to be there. Bell, of course, was also excluded, but for other reasons. Murderers only attend the funerals of their victims if their crime has yet to be detected, and there was no detection in Bell's story. Surprisingly, that brother and sister-in-law of Mark's who had caused so much of the trouble, were there to show something for him – love or respect or, more likely, accepted behaviour. And Perdita and Luis, both in unrelieved but glamorous black, like participants cast for a dance of death. I saw none of it, I wasn't, as I have said, there. Elsa I think it was who told me, though surely she can't have been among the mourners. Luis Llanos I saw for the last time on that unbearably hot, still, dust-laden afternoon, when he arrived in a taxi to ask after Cosette.

Unfairly, perhaps, I took this inquiry when correctly translated to mean: What was going on last night? Give me all the dirt. Angry with the world, sore with resentment and beginning anyway to feel ill, I tried to force him to say what he really meant.

'Why should there be anything wrong with her?'

'Happy people, people who are having a good time, they are running away out of restaurants in the middle of their dinners? No, Elizabeth, you know they are not.'

Sickness saved me. I said, 'Excuse me, please, Luis, excuse me a minute.'

As I ran from the room I could see him nodding, nodding and smiling, saying with awful complacency, 'Yes, you are throwing up, I think.'

I was throwing up. I had got to the bathroom just in time. Dehydration followed with swift ferocity and, leaving him alone, not caring, I went down to the kitchen to drink glass after glass of water. He had followed me down and was standing in the doorway watching me.

'Where is Cosette now?' he said.

'I haven't the least idea,' and then, because there was no point in being antagonistic, no point in providing the occasion for more explanations, 'Let's go out into the garden. It might be a bit cooler out there by now.'

'Why are you drinking, Elizabeth?'

He meant: why were you drunk? Luis was always, no doubt still is, asking questions. It is something people tend to do when they have a less than perfect command of the language they are obliged to speak. I have done it myself when trying to communicate in French or Italian. Real conversation in English was beyond Luis. He asked questions instead and, I must say in his favour, listened intently to the answers. If one was prepared to give them. I wasn't, not on that afternoon, and I shrugged my shoulders impatiently. I wasn't prepared to make tea for him either or open wine that I was in no fit state to share. Orange juice from a jar was all he was getting. We took it outside on a tray with two glasses.

Thus it was that Luis Llanos was also a kind of witness to the death that was shortly to take place.

By that time the sun had moved enough to leave half the garden in shade and the light in the other half wasn't bright, but hazy and subdued. There was stillness and there was dryness, a scattering of leaves from some pre-autumnal drop lying on the surface of the stone table. Ribbons of silvery bark hung as if flayed from the trunk of the eucalypt. The greyness looked as if it were the result of drought, not a natural property of those leaves, those stems, those effete flowers.

I never remember a single insect in that garden, not even a common cabbage white butterfly, not a bee, nor some bright-bodied blowfly. There must have been birds, if only sparrows, but if there were I have forgotten them. Once I lifted a large, marble-like whitish stone, a giant pebble, and from underneath scuttled away a family of woodlice. But these after all are not insects any more than spiders are. The walls, of brick, of stone, of flints in places, were tall enough to keep out all sight or sign of neighbours except for branches and leaves which showed over the tops of them, their foliage greenish or yellowing. All the grey was inside, grey of flowers and leaves and urns and faded furniture, grey shade and above us a sky of great brightness but a grey sky just the same.

It was the last time I sat there, just as it was almost my last day in the House of Stairs, the last time I spoke to poor, tiresome, irritating Luis with his vanities and his poses, his interminable questioning that had moved on to a series of inquiries as to why Cosette had this garden, kept it like this, had ever bought this house. He gesticulated with his long beautiful hands, naming the House of Stairs as 'an elephant, an absolute elephant', terminology incomprehensible to me until I understood he had omitted the significant adjective.

I hardly listened to him anyway. Looking upwards, I had seen Bell's head appear at her wide open window, appear strangely at floor level, edged out over the sill almost as if not attached to her body, as if it were a decapitated head that had rolled there. It lay, cheek downwards, on the window frame, nest of fair hair outside on the narrow shelf of stone. Of course she was simply lying on the floor, but that was not how it looked from down there. I was to see her again, but not for long and not to speak to − words that seem incongruous, more than absurd, grotesque.

The car returned. I heard it. Luis might have noted a taxi, not the individual engine sound of Cosette's car, a sound familiar to me but not to him. He had reached a point of saying, 'Why aren't you speaking, Elizabeth? Why don't you talk with me?'

I said: 'I'm not feeling well,' and I lay back against the chair and closed my eyes. I was filled with an enormous yearning for Cosette, for her to come out and tell me it was all a mistake, stupid, she didn't know what had come over her, all was well, would I − would I forgive her? A need for action screamed at me, to move, to leap up and rush indoors, to cast myself upon her. Something told me not to do this, it would be wrong to do it, it would be disastrous. I must make myself wait if I could, if I could.

By now, I thought, they would be in the house. Surely, surely, they would come out here and speak to us? All the windows stood open, the garden doors. Then, of course, I knew nothing of the purpose of their outing, but I sensed it was something momentous. I sensed they had news to impart, perhaps the purchase of a house. And Luis knew nothing. I opened my eyes and saw him looking at me aggrievedly. I said, 'I think Cosette is back. I think I heard the car.'

He asked if she would know he was there. It exasperated me. I felt like asking him if he had left evidence behind, unravelled a ball of string as he passed across the hall and the dining room and out through the french windows. But all I said was, 'Why don't you go and tell her?'

I waited there for Cosette to come back with him, I waited and the sun stood still. Hours passed, five minutes passed. The sickness I felt had nothing to do with wine. I remember throwing my arms out across that table and laying my head in them. And Luis, at last, came back alone.

It seems unlikely that I shall ever return to my father's house. I came home yesterday, having asked his solicitor to see about the sale of it. Incredible the sum I find may be asked for it and probably obtained! Astonishing too the small fortune my father has left, his amassed £20,000, give or take a little.

'Take,' says Bell, when told about it. 'Unless you feel like giving some of it to me.' She laughs, so that I shall know she is joking. But, 'You could buy a bigger house for us now.'

It is an idea. I could buy a house big enough for her to live in one half of it and I in the other. Or I could buy her a flat and put her in it and be rid of her for ever. But this I don't think I shall do. A sense of fatality colours the depression I live in now, colours it grey. I am stuck with Bell for better or for worse. She has abandoned black at last and is dressed in grey herself today, garments in shades of lanata and senecio and eucalypt made of fine knitted cotton, but they don't suit her, they make her look like a witch, one of those beautiful witch-queens or malevolent fairy godmothers.

I am being silly, I am imagining things, for she is very gentle with me today, kinder than perhaps she has ever been. She tells me she has been to see her probation officer, agreed with this woman that she must look for a job, find herself a gainful occupation.

'I said I would. It's easier than giving an outright no.'

The cats have both draped themselves on Bell, the little one reclining in her lap, the big one half on the back of her chair, half on her shoulder. They have taken to her completely and now they prefer her to me. She strokes the big one's head, pushing his face into the curve of her neck.

'Of course I shall never work again. They made us work in the town when I was in the pre-release place – did I ever tell you?'

I shake my head, unbelieving.

'In a hospital, cleaning wards. I got paid. I spent all the money I got on cigarettes.'

I know she is stalling. She is filling up emptiness with talk that will provoke me to question her, so that she may postpone what it is she has to ask. I don't react, I am not to be tempted.

'Don't you want to know what else I did while you were away?'

'I know you want to tell me.'

'Elsa phoned and asked me round and I went. I went for walks, I walked all the way to Archangel Place and looked at the house – there!' She looks at me sideways, lays a hand on each cat as if prepared to spring away, carrying them with her. 'I watched telly. I saw Mark.'

My voice comes all ragged and rough. 'What do you mean, Bell? What do you mean, you saw Mark?'

'I saw Mark on telly.'

'He was hardly on it, only radio, you know that.'

'He made just that one film – don't you remember? Before you knew him. They were doing this Michael Caine season and he had this small part in a Michael Caine film. It was funny seeing him, it was really strange. Do you remember we all once talked about the category of disappointing things? It wasn't much of a film, it was a disappointing film.'

We looked at each other, into each other's eyes. I had this feeling of my thoughts being read or that the force in them was so great as to transmit them into her mind. For I could see another watching that old film – with unchanged love? With indifference? Or in tranquillity?

And for once the thought-reading or the will to have thoughts read has worked.

'Lizzie,' she says, 'Lizzie, what became of Cosette?'

'I wondered when you'd ask.'

'Is she dead?'

'No, she's not dead. She married Maurice Bailey and went back to live in Golders Green.'

I have shocked her and she has gone quite pale.

'I thought she was dead, I thought she must be.'

'Why? She's only just seventy.'

'And she married that funny old man?'

'He was only eight years older than she. I believe people thought it very suitable. People like the Castles and Cosette's family must have thought it the best thing that could possibly have happened to her. They must have thought she had come to her senses at last. He was a widower and very comfortably off and he had a house that was even bigger than Garth Manor.'

'Why do you say "must have"? Don't you know?'

'No, I don't know, Bell. I can guess. I can gather things from what Elsa tells me. Elsa keeps in touch with Cosette but I don't, I can't.'

'Why don't you? What do you mean?'

I may as well tell her. I have never told anyone but Elsa. No one has been interested. Why should they be? We fall out with our friends, everyone does, friendships come to an end through disuse and neglect mostly, but sometimes through the violence of a quarrel.

'Cosette hasn't spoken to me since, Bell. She never spoke to me again, she has never forgiven me. She thinks I betrayed her, you see, and that was the one thing she couldn't bear.'

'You could have explained.'

'I didn't get the chance. After it happened, you see, that same evening, she didn't stay in the House of Stairs; her brother Leonard came and took her away to Sevenoaks. I phoned her there and Leonard's wife answered and said Cosette was too ill to speak to anyone. I meant to write but I didn't know what to say. Elsa and I were still in the House of Stairs, alone there. A solicitor wrote to me on Cosette's behalf . . .'

Suddenly I find it desperately hard to speak of this. I am near tears and my voice is failing. But Bell presses me and Bell has got hold of the wrong end of the stick.

'You mean Cosette got a solicitor to write to you and tell you not to get in touch with her? Did she? I wouldn't have believed it of her!'

'No, Bell, he wrote to tell me Cosette wanted to give me the House of Stairs, she wanted to make it over to me by a sort of deed of gift.'

Her face has changed, it has become greedy, rapacious, the eyes glittering with need. 'She gave it to you? It must have been worth a fortune even then.'

'Don't be silly. Do you imagine I'd have taken it? I wouldn't have dreamed of taking it. She meant it as compensation for herself, for losing her. I understood that. I wrote to the solicitor and told him I didn't want the house or what it would fetch or anything, I didn't want compensation for losing Cosette.'

'And you never got in touch with her again?'

'After your – trial, after that, she went away somewhere and when she came back I couldn't find her, I couldn't find where she was. Perhaps I didn't try very hard. I knew her, you see, I knew how she felt about betrayals. Being betrayed was the only thing she couldn't forgive. Then Elsa told me she'd got married and I got married too and it was all too late.'

When Mark and Cosette came home from the registrar they went straight up to the drawing room, where Luis found them. They told him their news, they had no need to keep it a secret. They were getting married. They had given notice of their marriage to take place three weeks from that day. I don't know what was said, of course, I only know what Luis, coming back into the garden to say goodbye, told me was said, and he had no gift for reportage. But Cosette had referred to the difference in their ages, he told me, and I can imagine her saying, 'We had to put our ages on the form, Luis, and it was a bit humiliating, but not so bad as having to say them out loud.'

Luis, with unusual sensitivity, must have understood his company wasn't exactly the fulfilment of their desires at that moment. Not that Cosette would ever have said so or have failed to press him to stay, go home and fetch Perdita, all go out together and dine. Probably it was Mark who put up no dissuasion when Luis said, half-heartedly, that he must go.

Left alone, the two of them brought to crystallization the flow of doubt, hesitancy, half-decision, which had filled their talk, running between islands of love and love-making and future plans, ever since the night before. Mark must tell Bell. Or they must both tell Bell. Bell must be told.

The thing, the awful thing, was that Cosette never really knew what Mark had to tell Bell. Cosette never knew the magnitude of it, what being told that her lover was truly 'in love' with her would do to Bell. Because, you see, she thought the worst of it was that Bell must be informed of their intention to marry and of the loss of her home, a blow which she had persuaded herself would be much softened by compensating Bell with a substitute. What a one for compensating people with houses Cosette was, incurably generous, undaunted!

But this she saw as the worst of it. Mark, of course, knew better. Mark had some idea of what he faced in confronting Bell. No doubt he was afraid she in her turn would confront Cosette and pour out to her all the early plans she and Mark had made, an intrigue not qualified by loving apologies and excuses (and laying the blame elsewhere) as had been Mark's own policy when confessing to Cosette, but raw and ugly, with every greedy word quoted, every yelp of laughter recalled, every callous aspiration exposed.

You understand that I am guessing, don't you? You understand that I was not there, that Luis was not there, that Elsa wasn't yet home, that he and Cosette were alone? But if I had been there, could I have seen into Mark's heart? No one knows precisely what he thought or what he feared, though what he said when he was in Bell's room, that is known. He was very afraid to go up there. He would have liked to postpone it for ever, to have sat for ever in that close, warm, still drawing room, side by side with Cosette on the sofa, his arm round her and her head on his shoulder, from time to time turning her face to kiss her lips. But for the most part silent, at rest, the awful events, the alarms and excursions of the past twenty-four hours, by a miracle of love – and, yes, of exertion too and passionate hard labour – smoothed into serenity, forgiveness asked and granted, levelled into a kind of rich peace.

But for Bell. But for the task that remained. He probably told Cosette that he was afraid, he wouldn't have minded telling her that, though not precisely what he was afraid of. Wasn't she his mother as well as his lover, the gentle, all-embracing maternal image to whom he could confess anything, admit any terror?

I suppose she told him she would do it and he demurred. He knew Bell wouldn't have believed Cosette. Then she told him it was best to get it over. Procrastination makes things worse. Tell her and get it over. Probably she suggested taking Bell out to dinner. I am exaggerating only slightly when I say there were few things Cosette thought couldn't be ameliorated if not cured by a good dinner in an expensive restaurant.

He went upstairs, up all 106 stairs, or however many there were from the drawing room to the top. He knocked on the door, he called out to her. I don't know if she answered or if he just walked in without being invited. She was there in her room, lying on the floor with her head on the windowsill, the two windowpanes raised up to their fullest extent. A stark, nearly unfurnished room, with boxes of clothes lying about, and clothes on the bed, and Silas's paintings stacked against the walls. He went in and closed the door behind him, but he couldn't lock it. Perhaps he didn't want to lock it. He told Bell he had something to tell her.

After she had done it, some time after but before the police came, she told Elsa and me what had happened. Isn't it strange that, for all her knowledge of people, Bell had never guessed what Mark's true feelings were?

'He said he was in love with her. The fool was standing by the window, the open window, looking out. I knew he was going to marry her, that was part of the plan, that was great, fine. What did I care about the bloody house? I didn't want to live in this house. But he was in love with her? He was going away to live with her, just her, and drop me in the shit? It was him saying he was in love with her, and I knew the fool meant it, that was what did it. He said, "I know what we planned, Bell, I can't forget it, I wish I could; it makes me feel sick now to remember. I'm in love with Cosette, I love her like I never loved anyone. I have to tell you I just want her and only her for the rest of our lives." And he turned his stupid face and looked at the sky like it was full of angels singing.

'She came in then. She tapped on the door and came in saying she thought she too ought to explain. So I did it. I wanted to do it in front of her. You know what I did. I jumped up and ran at him and pushed him out. I wanted to do it, it was great – until I'd done it, and then I wanted to pull him back out of the air, undo it. Did you hear him scream, Lizzie, did you hear him scream?'

It is something I should like to forget. If someone fell from a height I'd supposed they fell in silence, that the shock stunned them, the empty air. But Mark screamed as he fell, a cry, a roar of terror that split open the still and heavy summer evening. That sound, though, that expulsion of the ultimate expression of fear, was as nothing to the sound his body made as it struck the stone paving of the grey garden, a sound I am unable even now to describe, to convey anything approaching the dreadfulness of both its solidity and its liquidness, the noise of a human being bursting bonds that are its own flesh and bones.

We were inside the house by then, Luis and I, inside the french doors, walking across the dining room. You don't speak or reflect or even pause in these circumstances. You run. Away from or towards. We both ran back into the garden and saw the exploded thing spread like a stain on the grey flagstones, and we whimpered and held each other. We held each other like lovers, and rocked and moaned.

Crying, making these sounds, clutched together, as one we turned away from what lay out there. As we staggered, locked together, towards those open doors, first Elsa came walking across the dining room and then, pushing her aside, uncaring of anyone or anything that might be in her path, Cosette ran through the room and into the garden and cast herself upon Mark's body. She lay on his body until at last they took her away and I saw she was covered with blood, as if she too had been mortally injured.

I have lost track of the times of things. It might have been ten minutes or an hour afterwards that Bell came down and spoke to us. To Elsa and me, that is. Where was Luis? I find I have no idea what became of Luis. Someone phoned the police, but I don't think it was one of us. A neighbour perhaps, a passer-by. Did Mark's terrible cry ring across Notting Hill to summon the little crowd that gathered outside our gate? I heard sirens long before the police came and found out later this wailing came from fire engines rushing to a fire in Westbourne Grove.

It was a police doctor who gently lifted Cosette from Mark's body. Her face was terrible, smeared with blood, distorted into a ferocious ugliness by naked pain. They laid her on the settee downstairs in the television room where Auntie's body had lain the night she died. The doctor gave her a sedative injection, but if she slept it wasn't a deep enough sleep to prevent her going with Leonard when he came for her late in the evening.

I never saw her again.

I heard that she gave evidence at Bell's trial. I didn't, nor did Elsa. Bell told everyone what she had done, the police, the doctor; she seemed proud of it, and I am sure she would have told the Central Criminal Court if her counsel hadn't advised her not to give evidence. There is only one penalty for murder in English law and that is life imprisonment. 'Lifers' usually come out after about ten years unless there is a recommendation from judge or jury that the convicted person serve much longer than that. This happened in Bell's case for, after sentence had been pronounced and it was possible to reveal previous offences to the court, it was revealed that, when she was twelve years old, the middle child of three, the eldest being a boy of fifteen, Bell had killed her infant sister.

Those years of mystery, sometimes hinted at, usually glossed over, had been passed by her in a section of a women's open prison, set aside to receive her and only her. She had had lessons, seldom if ever been entirely alone, and yet her loneliness while there had been intense. When she was sixteen – it was obvious they didn't know what to do with her – she was removed to a children's home and placed in the care of the local authority. Many people, over the years, have told me they tried to kill a younger sibling, the baby brother or sister who, in their eyes, had stolen all the tender exclusive love previously lavished on the potential killer by a parent. Cosette once told me how she tried to kill Oliver by stuffing his mouth and nose with zinc-and-castor-oil cream, but her mother came in in time. Most of these children fail, but through ineptitude or timely discovery, not loss of nerve. Cosette failed because her mother came in. Bell succeeded. If her mother had come into the room two minutes sooner, Bell's strangling of the two-year-old Susan would have been no more than a failed act of violence on the part of a child maddened by jealousy.

But it taught her something none of us should ever learn: that killing, once done, may be done again: *c'est le premier pas qui coute.*

Bell said to me reflectively, 'Cosette must be fantastically rich now. I mean from what you say the old man's got a lot too and he's bound to go first.'

She doesn't mind what she says, so why should I? 'Would you have killed Cosette?'

One of her sidelong glances. A pursing of the mouth. She looks well and strong, vigorous, her eye on the future. 'I thought she was going to die, didn't I? I wouldn't have had to if she'd got a fatal disease, which I thought she had.' It was a strange look she gave me, speculative, considering, utterly calm. And then, on a different note, 'Seriously, why don't you try and see her?'

'I suppose because I feel it would never be the same. The quarrel, her accusation and my inability to refute it, the silent years – all that would always hang between us.' I knew quite suddenly I wouldn't be able to make Bell understand. The nuances of human intercourse, the subtleties of affection, these are unknown to her. She knows nothing of treading softly, nothing of the kind of innocence Cosette and I had in our long mother-child friendship, which seemed strong but was fragile enough to be destroyed by a single external blow. 'Don't think I fail to appreciate your selfless attempt to secure me a legacy,' I said, 'but don't you think your own presence in my life might be a stumbling block?'

'Not when we've got a big house divided into two,' she said. 'She wouldn't have to see me. Besides' – O, Bell, unchanging, unchangeable, direct, relentless and incorrigibly selfish – 'I've got as much against her as she has against me. She stole my lover, you forget that.'

As if the years had never been. As if Mark had never died or Bell herself passed fourteen years in prison. Cosette had said she would like to steal other women's men, speaking of it as an impossible dream, but she had done it, she had stolen another woman's man, she had succeeded.

'You never told me how you met him,' I said, to deflect Bell from Cosette. 'You never said how long you knew him before you brought him to the House of Stairs.'

She gave me a strange look, sidelong, speculative, as if wondering how I shall take what she has to say – wondering, but not caring too much. 'I met him at that Global Experience.'

'No, that was where I first saw him. Don't you remember? He'd been sitting at a table with you and I said, Is that your brother?'

'You put the idea into my head.' Her smile was so wry, such a sophisticated smile. 'You've been a genius at putting ideas into my head, Lizzie.' Another cigarette, her eyes screwing up as the plume of smoke rises. 'I've got a real brother, you know that, I haven't seen him for a thousand years. When you asked that about Mark it gave me a shock, just a bit of a shock. I thought: It's Alan, but how can it be? I looked and I saw it wasn't. But I said yes when you asked. Alan, my real brother, he's so ugly and stupid, or he was, I expect he still is, but Mark was beautiful, wasn't he? I thought, I'll say he's my brother and then maybe I'll get to know him. Funny, wasn't it? I'd never seen him before, never set eyes on him before.'

I knew she told lies for pure pleasure. My voice sounded in my own ears stone-like, profoundly heavy. 'I don't believe it. It can't be. He'd been at your table.'

'It wasn't my table. I was just there. There weren't enough tables to go round. Those others sitting there, God knows who they were. When he came back – he was on his own, too – I said to him there'd been someone talking to me who asked if he was my brother because we looked alike. Did he think we looked alike? I asked him that. And that was it, Lizzie, that was the beginning of it. That was how it started. We had a drink and then we went back to his place together. He said he was glad he wasn't my brother.

'But it was useful later on. It wouldn't have worked out, him trying to marry Cosette, and her knowing he'd been my lover. It was much better that way. Using both your ideas was really good – and they'd have worked if he hadn't been such a fool!'

So I have been responsible for it all, it all happened because of what I did and what I said, and Cosette has been right to blame me. Perhaps it is the pain in my head that makes it all unreal and any action, any positive step, seem impossible. I have written nothing for weeks, and if the headache is intermittent, the depression is constant. There is something else too, something I have never heard of anyone else having. I go to bed at night and fall asleep but within moments I am awake again and in such a panic of horror, such an indescribable fear of life itself, of reality, of my black-dark surroundings, that my body jerks and twists with it and my eyes, stretched wide open, stare in terror into the empty darkness. It passes, in ten minutes or so it passes, and I return to my customary placid and resigned depression, and eventually to sleep. But what is it? And why does it come?

I told Bell. Telling Bell things like that is useless, but I told her just the same. Put the light on, she said, drink something. Keep a glass of wine there and drink that. I tried it. But the bulb had gone in the bedside lamp, so nothing happened when I pressed the switch, and though I thought I had grasped the wineglass, I succeeded only in knocking it on to the floor. I knocked it to the floor and the other things with it, my watch and the aspirins and the bloodstone ring. So I wear the ring all the time now, I never take it off.

Before we went to see the solicitor, I asked Bell a question. I asked her what she understood love to be. She thought for a while but not for long.

'Being first with someone. It's when you're the most important person in someone's life.'

'What about you?' I said. 'What about when it's you doing the loving?'

She had never thought of that. Love, to her, is something you receive – or don't receive. 'My mother and father, I was first with them till Susan came along. I thought I was first with Mark. No one was first with Silas except maybe Silas.' I could tell she didn't mind talking about it, Bell never minded talking about people, including herself. 'I'll tell you what,' she said, 'it's got to be the person you want wanting you, the rest don't count.'

It seemed safer not to pursue this. And yet do I care at all for her now? Does she care even a little for me? There is another passion in Bell's life which we never talk about and which has never yet been gratified. Isn't that the very heart and essence of frustration? To pursue always through unimaginable suffering yet never to attain? I say we never talk of it, yet in a way it was what our visit to the solicitor was all about.

Bell wouldn't come in, though she came with me as far as the offices, which are in Knightsbridge. The next hour she said she would spend in Harrods where she hadn't been for fourteen years. Among the antiques, the jewellery, the dress materials. The bit of Harrods I like best is the zoo, but Bell looked uncomprehendingly at me when I suggested this.

I went to make my will. It was Bell's suggestion, because I am really quite rich now and if I die intestate, who will it all go to, the two houses and my father's savings? The state? There is literally no one. Cousin Lily is dead now, they are all dead, or for obvious reasons have never been born. I have left everything to Bell, everything except £1,000 to Elsa for being my executor.

'Mrs Sanger is older than you,' the solicitor said.

'Yes, I know.' I didn't say any more and he didn't ask. It hurts my head if I start arguing.

When he has drawn up the will he will send it to me for me to sign in the presence of two witnesses, each to sign in the presence of the other. He said he would get it in the post on Friday, so it should be here by tomorrow. The people next door will be my witnesses. They used to feed the cats while I was away and before Bell came. Occasionally we go in there for a drink with them or they come in here. Their interest in us and the looks they exchange tell me they take us for a lesbian couple and this they find exciting.

I haven't told Bell what else I have done, that I have written to Cosette. I was determined not to do this, but Bell's telling me of her first meeting with Mark has changed my mind. Showing me my guilt, though my involvement was unconscious, has changed things for me. I know how much Cosette has to forgive and I know she will forgive me. Since I talked of her to Bell, I keep seeing her in her old habitat but translated to Maurice Bailey's house, I imagine her planting lilies in the garden. How do I know she is once more a significant presence in the Wellgarth Society, an officer in the Townswomen's Guild, a school governor, a voluntary hospital visitor? I just know. I know she has her grey worsted suits made for her by Maurice Bailey's tailor. I know she has a Volvo and he a Jaguar. Perpetua comes to clean and Jimmy to do the garden and Dawn Castle comes round and tells Cosette what a trouble her grandchildren are but she wouldn't be without them. I dream of Cosette and of these things, I dream of her coming here to rescue me, but from what? From what? After fourteen years I have written to her and now, each time the phone rings, I start and I tremble.

Bell watches me when I tremble. She watches me as if she is weighing things up, calculating her chances. She has been out house-hunting and is full of some house in Notting Dale she wants me to buy and which is so expensive I would have to take out a mortgage and, for safety's sake, cover it with an insurance policy in her favour. I may just do it, to avoid argument. I shall probably give in, though now as I in turn watch her, dressed in silvery-grey and wearing my cats as if they too were part of her clothing, taking and lighting another cigarette, her youth returned to her as when she was happy it returned to Cosette, I think how infinitely I should prefer to do what Cosette herself had in mind and buy her a home of her own.

I have my fantasies about the bloodstone. Some would call them delusions. Sometimes I see it as the bearer of love, as if love were contained inside it, in the pinpoints of jasper perhaps that are embedded in the dark green chalcedony and gleam in its depths. When Bell gave it to me I see her as giving me back Cosette's love, so long suspended. And sometimes it seems to be a carrier of affliction, resting on the fingers of those genetically prone to the disease so many of its wearers died of, passing the others by. It was loose on Bell's finger, it's tight on mine, and I pretend to her it won't come off, that unless it is cut off it must stay there for ever.

The phone is ringing. I start, of course I do, and in the seconds that separate its rings, wonder if I can in fact have a happy ending, wonder who will get to me first, Bell, who may be my fate, or Cosette, who would certainly be my salvation. Or will it be that third possibility on which Bell pins her faith . . .

I put out my hand to stop her getting up and I cross the room to answer the phone.